BELISARIUS III:
The Flames of Sunset

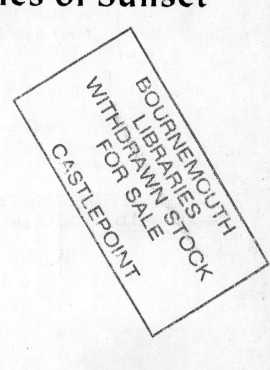

BELISARIUS III:
The Flames of Sunset

ERIC FLINT
DAVID DRAKE

BELISARIUS III: THE FLAMES OF SUNSET

A Baen Book

Baen Publishing Enterprises
P.O. Box 1403
Riverdale, NY 10471
www.baen.com

ISBN 13: 978-1-4391-3302-6

Cover art by Kurt Miller

First Baen printing, August 2009

Distributed by Simon & Schuster
1230 Avenue of the Americas
New York, NY 10020

Library of Congress Cataloging-in-Publication Data

Flint, Eric.
  Belisarius III : the flames of sunset / Eric Flint, David Drake.
    p. cm.
  ISBN 978-1-4391-3280-7—ISBN 978-1-4391-3302-6 (pbk.)
  I. Drake, David. II. Title. III. Title: Belisarius 3. IV. Title: Flames of sunset.
  PS3556.L548B455 2009
  813'.54—dc22

2009016982

Printed in the United States of America

10 9 8 7 6 5 4 3 2 1

CONTENTS

Introduction

IS THAT REALLY TRUE?

Recently I heard a presentation by a self-published novelist whose book involved a massive rise in sea levels, creating havoc. He explained that the scenario was completely true, but that it wouldn't come as a result of global warming as we might think. He had chosen to cloak his prediction in the form of a novel because, " . . . since the publication of *The Da Vinci Code*, people prefer to get their information from fiction."

I cringed. Well, actually, I cringed a number of times during the presentation. (The speaker and I appear to live in different worlds, for which I at least am thankful.) However I have a sneaking suspicion he was correct that many people believe that fiction is more likely to be true than factual writing.

It's certainly true that factual writing may be wrong. Even if the writer is completely honest and scrupulously careful, he may be wrong. If he's working in the sciences, he almost certainly will be wrong: the next generation or the generation after that one will have gathered additional information, will have improved techniques, will have new insights.

A friend of mine is a world expert on marine nematodes (roundworms a few millimeters long which live in the muck of sea bottoms). Using cutting edge DNA matching techniques, his team examined nematodes from the Atlantic and Pacific regions to determine whether the assigned species were really identical. They were not surprised to learn that the Atlantic and Pacific species were not identical.

They weren't even surprised to learn that both 'species' were actually groups of several genetically different nematodes. The best information that scientists could get from high-resolution microscopes had been inadequate—and it was the same scientists who proved that they'd been wrong previously. Very likely in a decade or a generation, the new truths unveiled by molecular bar-coding will themselves be superseded.

What's true in science is true in spades in history, though historians generally don't have as much hard data to begin with. There are problems even when you have an excellent first-hand account of events. Polybius, who is certainly in the running if you're picking the best of the ancient historians, was an Achaean aristocrat who quite obviously loathed the Aetolians and their confederacy. Does that mean he lies when he discusses events in Greece which he himself witnessed? No, I honestly don't think he does. But neither do I assume that his undoubted bias doesn't affect his description of what went on.

More to the present point, Procopius of Caesarea is an excellent writer and, as secretary to Count Belisarius, was ideally placed to write a history of his own time. He does so with admirable clarity. Much of the background around which Eric and I wove our series is based on Procopius. But—

We used what Procopius titled *The Histories of the Wars*. He also wrote the so-called *Secret History*, in which he describes the Emperor Justinian as (literally) a demon capable of being in two places at the same time. Belisarius and the wives of both men, Theodora and Antonina, are treated in similarly negative fashion, though without the supernatural element.

Later still, Procopius wrote *The Buildings*, an account of Justinian's construction projects. To describe the work's tone as fawning is to overpraise its objectivity.

I won't attempt to psychoanalyze a man who's been dead almost 1,500 years, but it's obvious that Procopius had conflicting feelings about Justinian and his associates. He had to have been lying in either *The Secret History* or *The Offices* . . . and in fact, we can be pretty sure that he was lying in both. Which means to me that he was probably lying in *The Histories* as well. Maybe not as often, maybe not so blatantly—but I still have a tinge of doubt about anything Procopius says unless it can be cross-checked, which most of it cannot be.

That's for Greece. India is a different problem: there are *no* authoritative histories for the period. And there's much less information than we would have liked on any of the other nations involved in our stories.

But that's the point: these are stories. Eric and I have been as accurate as we could (and believe me, our research is a heck of a lot better than what I've seen put into television documentaries), but we're still writing fiction. Don't take anything we tell you for The Truth—it isn't.

And *The Da Vinci Code* isn't The Truth either. But if the 1990 view of marine nematode species wasn't The Truth, it was a step toward what science now believes to be true—and a step also toward the next generation's truth. If you take the Belisarius series as a spur to further reading on the various subjects we've touched on, Eric and I will be happy.

And if you're entertained while reading it, we will have succeeded in our primary objective.

Dave Drake
david-drake.com

The Tide of Victory

To Dick and Dolores

Acknowledgements

As this series has progressed, a number of people have provided us with assistance in one manner or another. It's time to thank them:

Conrad Chu
Judith Lasker
Joe Nefflen
Pam "Pogo" Poggiani
Richard Roach
Mike Spehar
Ralph and Marilyn Tacoma
Detlef Zander

. . . and probably several others I've forgotten to mention, for which my apologies in advance.

I'd also like to take the opportunity to thank Janet Dailey for the many ways in which she's helped me out over the past year or so. I can't remember if that assistance involved my work on the Belisarius series, but it probably did—and even if it didn't, she's way overdue for my public appreciation anyway.

Eric Flint
January, 2001

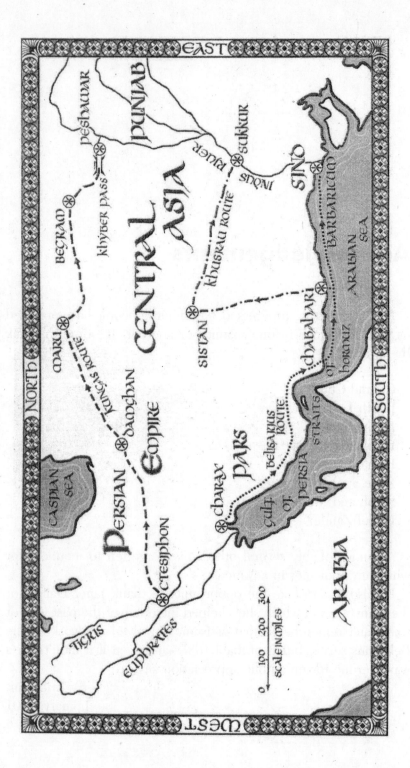

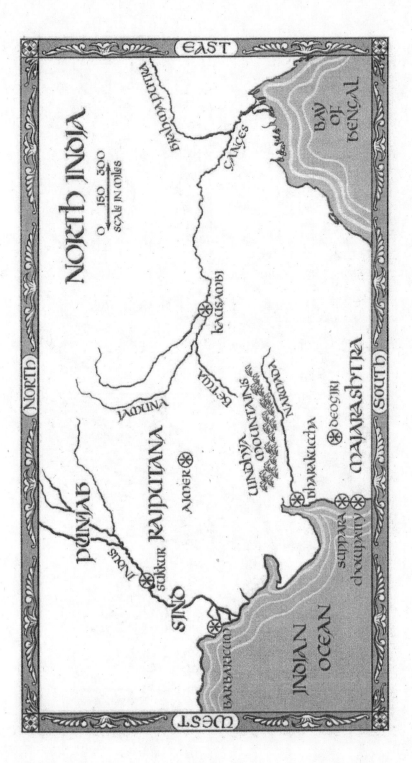

NORTH
THE INDUS
KHYBER PASS
PESHAWAR
JHELUM
PUNJAB
SULAIMAN RANGE
INDUS RIVER
CHENAB
MULTAN
QUETTA
SUTLEJ
WEST
EAST
UCH
KACCHI DESERT
IRON TRIANGLE
SUKKUR
ROHRI
KIRTHAR RANGE
KOT DIJI HILLS
THAR DESERT
SIND
BARBARICUM
0
100
SCALE IN MILES
SOUTH

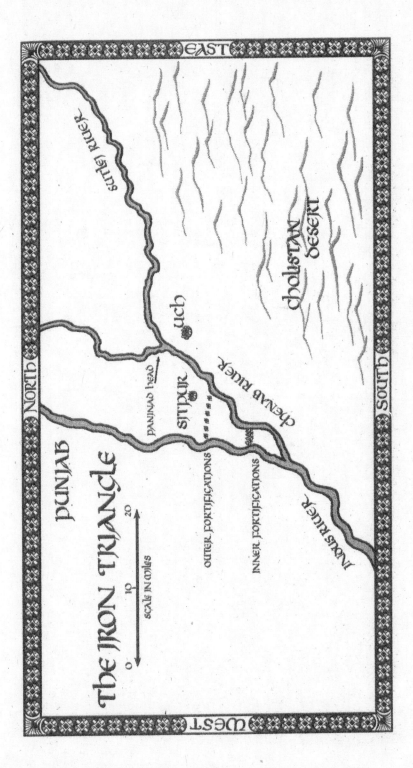

Prologue

Knowing what to expect, the two sisters had already disrobed by the time their new owner returned to his tent. The older sister's infant was asleep on the pallet. The sisters were a bit concerned that the ensuing activities would awaken him—the pallet was small and thin, oddly so for such an obviously wealthy man—but not much. The baby was accustomed to the noise, after all, having spent the first year of his life in a brothel crib.

Unless, of course, their new owner was given to bizarre tastes and habits . . .

That was the real source of the sisters' anxiety. For all its foulness, the brothel had at least been fairly predictable. Now, for the first time since their enslavement, they faced an entirely new situation. New—and unsettling. Their new owner had said nothing to them, other than commanding them into his tent after his caravan stopped for the night.

But, as they waited, they took solace in the fact that they were still together. Against all odds, they had managed to keep from being separated during the long years of their captivity. Apparently, it tickled their new owner's fancy to have sisters for his concubines. They would see to it that he was satisfied with the result. In that manner, they might preserve the remaining fragment of their family.

So it was, when their new owner pushed back the flap and entered the tent, that he found the sisters reclining nude on the pallet. The fact that they were holding hands was the only indication that any uneasiness lurked beneath their sensual poses.

Standing still and straight a few feet from the pallet, he studied them for a moment. The sisters found the scrutiny unsettling. They could detect nothing of lust in that gaze. For all the natural warmth of the man's dark brown eyes, there seemed to be little if any warmth in the eyes themselves. And not a trace of animal heat.

That was odd. Odder, even, than the austerity of the pallet and the tent's furnishings. Their new owner was obviously as healthy as he was rich. He was not especially tall, but his broad shoulders and lean hips were those of a physically active man. And there was something almost feline about the way he moved. Very poised, very balanced, very quick.

"Stand up," he commanded abruptly.

The sisters obeyed instantly. They were accustomed to inspection by prospective customers. As soon as they were on their feet, both of them assumed familiar poses. Languid, sensual, inviting. But they were still holding hands.

"Not like that," he said softly. "Just stand straight. And turn around slowly." His thin lips curved into a smile. "I'm afraid you'll have to stop holding hands for a bit."

Flushing slightly, the sisters obeyed.

"Slower," he commanded. "And lift up your arms so I can see your entire bodies."

This was *not* customary. The uneasiness of the sisters mounted. The last characteristic that slave prostitutes wanted to see in a new customer was *different*. But, of course, they obeyed.

In the long minutes which followed, the sisters found it increasingly difficult to keep the worry out of their faces. Their new owner seemed to be subjecting every inch of their bodies to a detailed and exhaustive scrutiny. As if he were trying to commit them to memory.

"Which of these scars are from your childhood?" he asked. His voice was soft and low-pitched. But the sisters took no comfort in that mild tone. This was a man, clearly enough, who had no need to raise his voice for the simple reason that command came easily to him. He would not be denied, whatever he wanted. Which, again, was not a characteristic which slave prostitutes treasured in their customers. Especially new and unknown ones.

They were so startled by the unexpected question that they did not respond immediately. Instead, they exchanged a quick and half-frightened glance.

Seeing the glance, their new owner's face broke into another smile. But this one was not thin at all, and seemed to have some actual humor in it.

"Be at ease. I have no intention of adding any new scars to the collection. It is simply information which I must have."

The smile disappeared and the question was asked again. This time, with firm command. "Which scars?"

Hesitantly, the younger sister lifted her left leg and pointed to a scar on her knee. "I got this one falling out of a tree. My father was furious with me."

Their owner nodded. "He would know of it, then? Good. Are there any other such? Did he beat you afterward? And, if so, are there any marks?"

The sisters looked at each other. Then, back at their owner.

"He never beat us," whispered the older. "Not once."

"Our mother did," added the younger sister. She was beginning to relax a bit. Enough that she managed a little chuckle. "Very often. But not very hard. I can't remember even being bruised."

The man shook his head. "What kind of silly way is that to raise children? Especially girls?" But the question was obviously rhetorical. The smile was back on his face, and for the first time the sisters detected the whimsical humor which seemed to reside somewhere inside the soul of their new owner.

He stepped up to the older sister and touched her cheek with his forefinger. "That is the worst scar. It almost disfigures your face. How did you get it?"

"From the brothel-keeper."

The man's eyes widened slightly. "Stupid," he mused. "Bad for business."

"He was very angry with me. I—" She shuddered, remembering. "The new customer had—unusual demands. I refused—"

"Ah." With a light finger, he traced the scar from the ear to the corner of her mouth.

"I think he forgot he was wearing that huge ring when he slapped me."

"Ah. Yes, I remember the ring. Probably the same one he was wearing when we conducted our transaction. A large ruby, set in silver?"

She nodded.

"Excellent," he said. "Easy for you to remember, then."

He turned to the younger sister. Placing one hand on her shoulder, he rotated her partway around. With the forefinger of his other hand, he traced the faint lines across her back.

"These are your worst. How?"

She explained. It was a similar story, except the individual involved had been the chief pimp instead of the brothel-keeper, and the instrument had been a whip rather than a ring.

"Ah. Yes, I believe I met him also. Rather short, squat. The little finger of his left hand is missing?"

The two sisters nodded. He returned the nods with a curt one of his own. "Excellent, also."

He stepped back a pace or two. "Can either of you write?"

The sisters were now utterly confused. This man was the *weirdest* customer they had ever encountered. But—

So far, at least, he did not seem dangerous. The younger sister spoke first. "Not very well."

"Our father taught us a bit," added the older sister. "But it's been a long time. Several years."

Both of the sisters, for the first time, found it almost impossible to maintain their poise. Memories of their father were flooding back. Their eyes were moist.

The man averted his gaze, for a moment. The sisters took advantage of the opportunity to quickly pinch the tears away. It would not do to offend their new owner.

They heard him snort softly. "Taught his daughters! Scandalous, what it is." Another soft snort. Again, the sisters thought to detect that strange whimsical humor. "But what else would you expect from—"

He broke off abruptly and looked back at them.

"In a few days, you will write a letter. As best you can." Seeing the uncertainty in their faces, he waved his hand idly. "I am not concerned if the handwriting is poor. All the better, in fact."

His eyes moved to the pallet, and then to the baby asleep to one side. "It will be crowded, with the four of us." Again, the thin smile. "But there's no help for it, I'm afraid. Appearances must be maintained."

Moving with that unsettling ease and speed, he glided past them and reclined on the pallet. He was lying on the opposite side from the infant. He patted the middle of the pallet with his hand.

"Come, girls. Sleep. It has been a long day, and tomorrow will be longer. And the days after, as well. We have a considerable distance to travel."

Quickly, the sisters did as they were told. After the confusion of the preceding minutes, they almost found comfort in this familiar process. Not quite.

The younger sister lay next to him. The gesture of protection for the older came automatically to her. The two of them had protected each other for years, as best they could. If she exhausted him, he might be satisfied. Her sister's infant would not be disturbed.

Their new owner was still fully clothed. She began to stroke his chest, her fingers working at the laces.

Her hand was immobilized by his own. The man's grip was gentle enough, but she could sense the iron muscles and sinews in his hand.

"No," he said softly. "That is all finished. Just sleep." He moved her hand away.

Uncertainly, she obeyed. She stared at his profile. He was not a handsome man, not in the least. His face was lean and tightly drawn. High cheekbones, a sharply curved nose, thin lips below a thin mustache, clean-shaven cheeks so taut they seemed more like leather than flesh. Except for the mustache, he reminded her more of a bird of prey than a man.

But she found herself relaxing, despite his fearsome appearance. His voice was soft, after all. And she had never been abused by a bird.

His eyes were closed. "Finished," he repeated. "There will be no more scars."

Two days later, at daybreak, he arose from the pallet with his usual energy. The sisters had become accustomed to his way of moving. They no longer even found it frightening.

"Enough time has elapsed," he announced. "I will be gone for a few days. Three, perhaps four."

His words brought instant fear. The younger sister's eyes moved immediately to the tent flap. The older sister, suckling her infant at her breast, did not look up. But her sudden indrawn breath was quite audible.

Their new owner shook his head. "Have no fear. The soldiers in my escort will not molest you. I have given them clear instructions."

He turned away and began to push back the flap of the tent. "They will obey those instructions. You can be quite certain of it."

Then, he was gone. The sisters stared at each other. After a few seconds, their tension eased. They still did not know their new owner's name, since he had not provided it. But they were coming to know him. Well enough, at least.

Yes. *His* instructions would be obeyed. Even by soldiers.

He returned at midmorning, three days later. When he entered the tent, he was carrying a leather sack in one hand and a roll of leather in the other. Once flattened on the floor of the tent, the leather roll measured perhaps eighteen inches square.

"Should be big enough to prevent a mess," he murmured. He jerked his head, motioning the sisters toward him, while he untied the sack.

When they were squatting next to him, their new owner spilled the sack's contents onto the piece of flat leather.

He had gauged correctly, and grunted his satisfaction. Even with the addition of the fluid pooled at the bottom of the sack, the two objects did not leak blood onto the floor.

Both hands had been severed at the wrist, as if by a razor. Or—

The sisters glanced at the dagger scabbarded to their owner's waist. They had seen him shave with it, every day. He shaved with the quick and sure motions with which he did everything—except honing the blade. That, he seemed to enjoy lingering over.

One hand was plump. The middle finger sported a large silver ring, with a great ruby set at its center. The other hand was thick and stubby. The little finger was missing.

He rose and moved to one of the chests against the side of the tent. Opening it, he withdrew a small piece of vellum and writing equipment.

"And now, the letter."

Long before the sisters had finished, they were sobbing fiercely. Their new owner did not chide them for it. Indeed, he seemed obscurely satisfied. As if the tears staining the words and causing the letters to run added something valuable to the message.

When they were done, he began to roll up the vellum. But the younger sister stopped him.

"Wait. There is something we can put in it." She hurried to the far side of the pallet and began plucking apart the threads along the seam. Her older sister opened her mouth, as if to protest. But whatever protest she might have made went unspoken. Indeed, by the time her sister had extracted the object hidden within the pallet, she was smiling. "Yes," she whispered. "*Yes.*"

The younger sister came back to their owner and, shyly, extended her hand. Nestled in the palm was a bright golden coin.

"It's all we have," she said. "He won't recognize it, of course, because we got it after—" She fell silent, fighting back further tears. "But still—"

The man plucked the coin out of her hand and held it up for inspection. Within seconds, he was chuckling softly.

"Freshly minted Malwa imperial coin. I wonder—"

Smiling, he tucked the coin into the vellum and rolled it up. Then, quickly folding it further, he began tying it up with cord. As he worked, he spoke softly, as if to himself.

"I wonder . . . Ha! Probably not, of course. But wouldn't that be a delicious irony?"

The work done, he transferred the smile to the sisters. They had no difficulty, any longer, recognizing the humor in it. "I'm a man who appreciates such things, you know."

They nodded, smiling themselves.

His own smile faded. "I am not your friend, girls. Never think so. But, perhaps, I am not your enemy either."

He lifted the package and hefted it slightly. "We will discover which, one of these days."

The older sister sighed. "It's not finished, then?"

Their owner's smile returned, this time with more of bright cheer than whimsy. "Finished? I think not!"

He was actually laughing, now. For the first time since they had entered his possession.

"I think not! The game has just begun!"

In the days, weeks and months to come, that package—and the ones which went with it—would cause consternation, three times over. And glee, once.

◇   ◇   ◇

The consternation came in ascending degrees. The least concerned were the soldiers who investigated the murder and mutilation of a brothel-keeper and his chief pimp.

"Who cares who did it?" yawned the officer in charge of the
squad. "Plenty more where they came from."

He turned away from the bed where the brothel-keeper's body
had been found. The linen was still soaked with blood from a
throat slit to the bone. "Maybe a competitor. Or it could have
been a pissed-off customer." It was apparent, from the bored tone
of his voice, that he had no intention of pursuing the matter
further.

The pimp who had succeeded to the brothel's uncertain ownership sighed. "No problem, then?" He fought very hard to keep
satisfaction out of his own voice. He was quite innocent of the
murders, as it happened, but as the obvious suspect . . .

"Not that I can see," stated the officer firmly. Just as firmly, he
stared at the new brothel-keeper.

"On the house!" that worthy announced promptly. "You and all
your men! For a full day!"

The officer grinned. "Case closed."

There was more consternation, a few days later, when the mur-
derer reported to his master.

"You idiot," growled Narses. "Why in the name of God did you
kill them? We don't need any attention being drawn. A simple
slave purchase, all it was. Happens every day."

"So do brothel killings," came the retort. Ajatasutra shrugged.
"Three reasons. First, I thought the hands would lend a nice touch
to the package. Proof of good intentions, so to speak."

Narses snorted. "God help us. You're pretending to *think*." He
displayed his inimitable sneer. "His daughters have been hopelessly polluted. What difference does it make—you're Indian yourself, you know how it works—that a couple of the polluters are
dead? How many hundreds are still alive?"

"You might be surprised. Purity is one thing, the satisfaction of
vengeance is another. Even we heathen Hindus are not immune
to that. *Even* a philosopher like him will feel a twitch, as much
harm as he knows that will do to his karma."

Ajatasutra leaned forward in his chair, stretching his arms and arching his back. He seemed to take as much pleasure in the supple movements as a cat. "Secondly, I've gotten out of practice." Half-growling: "Your methods are too damned subtle to keep an assassin's skills properly honed."

Again, Narses snorted. *"Pimps."*

Ajatasutra's lips twisted into a wry grin. "Best I could find." The grin faded. When it was completely gone, his still and expressionless face seemed more like that of a hawk on a limb than a man in a chair.

"And, finally. I felt like it."

Narses said nothing. He neither snorted nor sneered.

Weeks later, the package caused immense consternation. It struck the palace at Deogiri like a tornado, leaving a peshwa and his wife weeping tears of joy, an empress confused and uncertain, her advisers divided and torn.

"It's a trap!" insisted the imperial consort. Raghunath Rao sprang to his feet and practically pounced his way over to the open window in the imperial audience chamber. There, planting his hands on the wide ledge, he glared fiercely to the north. The broken hill country of Majarashtra stretched to the horizon. Beyond, invisible in the distance, lay the Narmada river and the Vindhya mountains. And, beyond that, the great Gangetic plain where the Malwa beast straddled the Indian subcontinent.

"A trap," he repeated.

Empress Shakuntala moved her uncertain gaze to the commander of her personal bodyguard. Former commander, rather. As of the previous day, Kungas was no longer her *mahadandanayaka;* no longer her *bhatasvapati.* Officially, the man once known as "great commandant" and "lord of army and cavalry" had no title at all in the empire of Andhra. He had been relieved of all responsibilities, since he and his own consort were soon to be founding their own empire.

Officially.

Kungas' shoulders made the little twitch which served him for a shrug. "Probably so." His gaze moved to the other woman in the room. Shakuntala's eyes followed.

Irene cleared her throat. "Actually, Your Majesty"—she gave an apologetic glance at the figure in the window—"I find myself in a rare moment of disagreement with Rao."

Rao barked a laugh. He turned back into the room. " 'Rare moment!' Such a diplomat."

Irene smiled. "But disagree I must. This maneuver has to be Narses' work. A simple trap is not his style."

Everyone in the room eyed her skeptically. Irene's shrug was as expressive as her future husband's had been terse. "I'm sorry. I realize that must sound hopelessly vague. Even naive. But—"

Her own frown was simply one of concentration. "But I'm really quite sure that I'm right. I can detect Narses' mind at work here. He's up to something, be sure of it. Something—" Her hands groped a bit. "Something *complex*. Something *convoluted*."

She glanced at Kungas and Rao. Her frown was instantly replaced by a wicked smile. "The problem with these two, Your Majesty, is that they think like *men*. You know—crude. Simple."

Shakuntala's laugh filled the large chamber like a bell. She and Irene exchanged a grin. Rao scowled. Kungas' face, as usual, had no expression at all.

"You must remember, Empress," continued Irene, "that Narses is a eunuch. He thinks more like a woman than a man. Subtle, tricky. *Shrewd*."

Grin. Grin. Scowl. Nothing.

"Not a trap," she insisted. "Or, at least, not the obvious trap. What would he have to gain, beyond inflicting a minor wound on Belisarius?"

"And a major one on our peshwa," growled Rao. He jerked his head angrily at the door. "Dadaji should be here, to give us his wisdom in counsel. He is absent simply because he is too overcome with—with—"

"Joy?" suggested Irene. "Relief?"

"For the moment. But what of later? If it *is* a trap, once it is sprung? When he realizes that his daughters are lost forever."

Kungas spoke. "That's foolish, Rao. And you know it. Dadaji would not be incapacitated for long. He would do the rites—just as he did months ago when the news of his son's death in battle came—and continue onward. More fiercely than ever, now that Malwa added a new wound to his soul."

Rao took a deep breath. He nodded abruptly, indicating his acceptance of Kungas' point. But, still, he was scowling. "I don't *trust* this thing!"

"Trust?" exclaimed Irene. "What has that got to do with it?" Her own laugh had none of the young empress' pealing quality. It was more like the caw of a crow.

"I don't trust *Narses*, Rao. What I trust is simply his *craftsmanship*."

She pointed a stiff finger at the opened parcel on the low table near the door. The shriveled hands and the message for the empress lay exposed. The shakily written message for Holkar, and the coin, were absent. Dadaji and his wife had those in their own chambers, clutching them as fiercely as they did each other. Adding their own tears of joy to the long-dried ones which had smeared the ink.

"He's *up* to something, I tell you!"

The empress ended the discussion, in her usual decisive manner. She clapped her hands, once. "Enough! It is not for us to decide, in any event. We are simply the conduit. If there is a trap, it is aimed at Belisarius. He must make the decision."

She pointed her own imperious finger at the parcel. "Take it with you tomorrow, Irene. Kungas. Take it with you on your journey to Persia, and put it into Belisarius' hands. Let him decide."

Mention of that journey, even more than the empress' command, ended the discussion. With not much less in the way of sorrow than Shakuntala, Rao gazed at the two people who would, within a day, be gone from their company. Probably forever. Two people who had done as much as any in the world to bring one empire back from the grave, where Malwa had thought Andhra safely planted. And now proposed to do the same yet again, in Malwa's very heartland.

"God be with you," he murmured. His usual wry smile emerged. "He is rumored to have good vision, you know. Even in the Hindu Kush, I am certain he will notice you."

The glee came as Irene and Kungas were walking through the halls of the palace, back toward their own chambers.

"I hope you're right," muttered Kungas.

Irene's eyes widened. "Are you *kidding*? Of course I'm right! He's *up* to something. And since—I know I've told you this—he's probably the only spymaster in the world as good as me, that means—"

She seized Kungas' muscular arm in both hands and began spinning her lover around her, whirling down the corridor like a top. "Oh, Kungas! We're going to have so much *fun!*"

Chapter 1

CTESIPHON

Spring, 533 A.D.

Are you sure of this? asked Aide. The crystalline thought in Belisarius' mind shivered with uncertainty. **They have protected you for so long.**

Belisarius made the mental equivalent of a shrug. *This coming campaign is different, Aide. I will be commanding—*

He broke off for a moment, scanning the imperial audience chamber. The crooked smile that came so naturally to him made its reappearance. There was enough of royalty, nobility, officers and advisers crowded about to fill even that huge and splendiferous room. The costumes and uniforms worn by that mob were as varied as the mob itself. Roman, Persian, Ethiopian, Arab—only the Kushans were absent, for reasons of secrecy.

No one in the West has assembled such a gigantic force since the days of Xerxes and Darius and Alexander the Great. I will be leading well over a hundred thousand men into India, Aide. So there's no way I'll be at the forefront of any more cavalry charges.

The crystal being from the future flashed an image in Belisarius' mind. For just an instant, the Roman general saw a Homeric figure storming a rampart, sword in hand.

Aide's voice came sour, sour. **Alexander the Great did.**

Belisarius snorted. *Alexander was a lunatic as well as a genius. Thought he was Achilles come back to life. I have no such pretensions, myself. And if I ever did—*

He winced, remembering the way Rana Sanga, Rajputana's greatest king as well as champion, had hammered Belisarius into a bleeding pulp on a battlefield in the Zagros mountains. Would have killed him, in fact, if Valentinian hadn't come to his rescue.

You should not send Valentinian away! Especially not when you're sending Anastasius also!

Belisarius ignored Aide's last remark, for the moment. The raging argument between Sittas and Kurush which had filled the audience chamber for several minutes seemed to be coming to a head, and he thought it was about time that he intervened. It wouldn't do to allow two of his top commanders to come to actual blows, after all.

Loudly, he cleared his throat. Both Sittas and Kurush stopped bellowing, although they did not leave off their ferocious mutual glares.

"Kurush will command the left," pronounced Belisarius. Sittas made a choking sound and transferred his glare from his Persian equivalent to the top commander of the joint expedition. Beneath the indignation and outrage in his expression lurked something of the small boy—*betrayed!*—by his trusted older brother.

Belisarius shook his head. "Don't be stupid, Sittas. The left wing will be responsible for protecting the entire expedition against Malwa cavalry raids. Rajputs and Pathans, most like. The Aryans are far more experienced cavalrymen than Roman cataphracts in that kind of mountainous terrain."

The words did not seem to mollify Sittas at all. To the contrary—Belisarius' huge friend was giving him the enraged boar's glare that was one of Sittas' trademarks.

Belisarius found it hard not to smile. On one level, of course, he could hardly blame Sittas. The official justification which Belisarius had just given for allowing the Persian dehgans to take the prestigious position on the expedition's left flank was absurd. By the time Belisarius' huge army was nearing the Indus valley, the Malwa would certainly have detected the northern expedition of Kungas and his Kushans. Any Rajput or Pathan raiders available to the Malwa after their crushing defeat the previous year at Charax would be busy trying to protect the Hindu Kush. They certainly wouldn't be wasting their time in futile cavalry raids against Belisarius' army far to the south in Baluchistan.

But—

The Kushan expedition was still a secret, so Sittas—choking with indignation all the while—could not argue the point. He was forced, grudgingly and angrily, to cede the argument and resume his seat. Kurush did likewise. Fortunately, the young Persian general had enough tact to keep his face expressionless rather than indulge in open gloating.

Good enough, thought Belisarius. He would make it a point to discuss the matter with Sittas privately after the council meeting. In truth, he should have discussed it with him prior to the meeting. But in the press of his responsibilities, he simply hadn't thought of it. Belisarius had been away from the imperial court at Constantinople for so long that he'd forgotten the touchy pride of the capital city's elite cataphracts. He should have realized that Sittas would find a point of honor in the issue of whether the left flank was under the command of Persians or Romans.

Stupid, he thought sourly. Sittas should have the sense to understand that I must keep the Persians satisfied. And their pride is even touchier!

His eyes met those of Agathius. Belisarius' chief of staff was sitting at a large table across the room, with the campaign maps and logistics records spread out in front of him. Seeing the easy manner in which Agathius handled that mass of written material, no one would have guessed that he had been effectively illiterate until a year ago. Beneath Agathius' brawler's appearance, the chief of staff was as intelligent and capable as any man Belisarius had ever met.

There seemed to be a little twinkle in Agathius' eyes. Belisarius gave him the faint hint of a smile, as a man does when he is sharing a subtle unspoken secret with another.

Stupid noblemen . . .

Until the injuries which had crippled him at the Battle of the Nehar Malka, Agathius had been a cataphract himself—and a great one. But the lowborn baker's son had never approached war with any attitude beyond plebeian practicality.

Agathius now cleared his own throat. "If we can move on to the logistics . . . "

Belisarius nodded his assent. As Agathius began running through the state of the logistical preparations for the coming campaign, Belisarius let his thoughts go inward again.

It is too important an opportunity to pass up, Aide. If Irene is right—

She's guessing! Nobody knows what that cryptic message means!

Belisarius made the mental equivalent of a shrug. *She's a very good guesser, you know. And I think she's right. The thing has all the earmarks of a Narses maneuver.*

He's a traitor.

No, Aide. He was a traitor. Now he is in the service of another. And, unless I miss my own guess, I suspect that he is serving Damodara very faithfully indeed. Not—there came a momentary silent chuckle—*that I think Damodara has any idea what his chief of espionage is doing.*

Aide said nothing for a moment, though his uneasiness was still evident. Then: **But why Valentinian and Anastasius?** He complained. **They aren't spies and intriguers. They—**

—Are the deadliest soldiers in my army, Belisarius completed the thought. *And they both speak the language—well enough, at least—and they are both familiar with India. I don't think Narses wants spies, Aide. He has plenty of his own. I think—*

You're guessing!

Belisarius sighed. *Yes, I am. And I am also a good guesser. And can I finish my thought without interruptions?*

He could sense the "jewel" sulking. But Aide kept his peace.

As I was saying, Belisarius continued, *I suspect that what Narses needs are people who can get someone out of India in a very big hurry. Or protect them. And who better for that than Valentinian and Anastasius and Kujulo?*

Aide was silent, but Belisarius could sense the unspoken disagreement.

Oh, stop sulking! Say what you were going to say.

The thoughts came in a rush. **And that's another thing—those three are well known to the Malwa! They will be spotted!**

By whom? The only ones who would recognize them are Shandragupta's imperial entourage—which there's no chance at all of encountering, as tightly sequestered as Skandagupta keeps himself—and—

The Rajputs! Rana Sanga fought Valentinian in single combat for hours! You think—

Belisarius drove over the protest. *And Damodara's Rajputs—who, by all accounts, have been stationed in Bihar and Bengal since they returned to India. Half a continent away from where Valentinian and—*

Things change, pouted Aide. **You say that yourself, all the time.**

Again, Belisarius made that mental shrug. *Yes, they do—and probably will again. Judging from what Irene told us of the Maratha rebellion's progress, I imagine that Damodara and Rana Sanga will soon be ordered into the Great Country. Which—*

He could sense Aide's growing surly *pout*, and had to fight down another smile. *Which is* also *half a continent away.*

Belisarius broke off the exchange. In his usual terse and efficient manner, Agathius was completing his logistics report. Belisarius braced himself for another round of bellowing and bickering.

Kurush was already on his feet. "What is this nonsense?" he roared. "Not more than *four* servants—even for Aryan nobility? Absurd! Impossible!"

Belisarius gave Sittas a quick, sharp glance. The Roman general's returning glare faded instantly into a look of suppressed glee and cunning.

Sittas shoved his great powerful form out of his chair. "Nonsense," he rumbled. "Any Roman cataphract can make do with two servants, easily. But if the noble sahrdaran thinks maintaining a lean baggage train is a problem, perhaps we could reconsider the assignment—"

Bellow, roar, rumble. Sound and fury.

Ah, the joy of command, thought Belisarius sourly.

You will keep Isaac and Priscus? came Aide's timid, fearful thought.

Yes. No point in sending them into the Malwa maw. He began to add some jocular remark, but then, sensing the genuine anguish lurking in Aide's mind, he shifted immediately.

They are almost as good as Valentinian and Anastasius, Aide. I will be safe enough.

There came a crystalline equivalent of a sigh. Then: **It is just—I love you dearly.**

◊   ◊   ◊

The roar and bellow of outraged and bickering dehgans and cataphracts continued to fill the chamber, as a gigantic army continued to take form and shape. But the commander of that army himself was oblivious to it all, for a time, as he communed with the strangest form and shape which had ever come into the world. And if others might have found something strange in the love and affection which passed between man and crystal, neither the man himself nor the crystal gave it a moment's thought.

They had been together for years now, since the monk and prophet Michael of Macedonia had brought Aide and his warning of a terrible future to Belisarius' door. Over the course of those years of battle and campaign, they had come to know each other as well as father and son, or brother and brother. What they thought—hoped—was the final campaign of the long war against Malwa was now upon them. They would survive, or not, as fate decreed. But they would go into that furnace united in heart and soul. And that, more than anything—so *they* thought, at least—was the surest guarantee of future triumph.

A sharp sound echoing in the audience chamber brought Belisarius' mind back to the present. A brisk handclap, he realized. Belisarius saw Khusrau Anushirvan rising from his throne perched at the opposite side of the chamber.

"Enough!" The Persian emperor clapped his hands again. Beneath the thick, square-cut beard, his youthful face was stern. "Enough, I say. At least for the moment. It is past noon, and we have an imperial wedding to attend."

He turned his head to Belisarius. The sternness of his expression seemed to ease a bit. "A wedding which, I'm sure the illustrious Roman general will agree, is more important than the details of marching order and logistics."

Belisarius nodded and rose to his own feet. "Indeed so, Emperor. Far more."

Chapter 2

When Tahmina's father brought her dowry down the central thoroughfare in Ctesiphon, the huge crowd of Persian onlookers began murmuring with excitement. Excitement—and deep approval. Even the street urchins knew that the dowry for an imperial wedding was the product of endless negotiations. The dowry which Baresmanas was bringing to the palace was so bizarre that it could only have resulted from the suggestion of the Romans themselves.

The approval of the crowd was profound. Many began chanting the name of the Roman emperor Photius, to whom Tahmina was about to be wed. Here and there, even a few haughty dehgan knights were seen to join in the plaudits.

They had been expecting a caravan, laden with treasure. Enough in the way of gold and silver and gems and jewelry and precious linens to bankrupt the Persian empire. A bitter price to pay for the security of a Roman alliance against the Malwa, but a price that could not be avoided. Not much more than a year before, the Malwa who had devastated Mesopotamia had only been driven off by the efforts and cunning of the Roman general Belisarius. Today, that same Belisarius would demand Persia's fortune in payment.

Instead—

Baresmanas of the Suren, the greatest of the seven great sahrdaran families who constituted Persia's highest nobility, was walking slowly down the thoroughfare. Dressed in his finest regalia, he was simply leading a horse.

27

Not any horse, of course. Even the street urchins realized that the magnificent black steed which pranced behind its master was the finest in all of Persia—a land which was renowned for its horses. But not even such a horse would bankrupt their empire.

The horse bore three things only.

The first was a saddle. No ceremonial saddle, this, glittering with gems and gold inlay. Instead, it was a heavy lancer's saddle, equipped with the new stirrups which the Romans had recently introduced into cavalry warfare. The finest such saddle imaginable, of course. No village dehgan could have afforded it. But, again, nothing to cause their emperor to raise the taxes.

The second was a bow, held in the small hand of the horse's rider. The finest that Persia's greatest bowyer could construct, of course. But, still, just a bow—to anyone but Persians.

The crowd's approval swelled and swelled, as the meaning of that horse and bow penetrated. *Photius! Photius!* By the time Baresmanas neared the great aivan in the center of the imperial palace where the wedding was to be held, the great throng was positively roaring. Precious few Persian emperors, in the long history of the land of the Aryans, had ever received such public acclaim.

A lowborn mongrel, the Roman emperor was said to be. So the crowd had heard. A bastard at birth, it was even whispered. But now, seeing the horse and the bow, they understood the truth.

Photius! Photius!

At the entrance to the aivan, Baresmanas assisted the third of the horse's burdens in her descent. The task was a bit difficult, not because his daughter Tahmina was a weakling, but simply because her wedding costume was heavy and cumbersome.

When she was securely planted on her feet, Baresmanas leaned over and whispered. "So. Who was right? I, or your mother?"

Tahmina's smile was faintly discernable through the veil. "I never doubted you, father. Even before I read the book you gave me."

Baresmanas started slightly. "Already? All of it? *Herodotus?*"

As Baresmanas handed the reins of the horse to one of his chief dehgans, Tahmina straightened. "All of it," she insisted. "My Greek has become almost perfect."

A moment's hesitation, before the girl's innate honesty surfaced. "Well . . . For reading, anyway. I think my accent's still pretty horrible."

Side by side, father and daughter walked slowly toward the aivan. The entrance to the aivan was lined with soldiers. Persian dehgans on the left, Roman cataphracts on the right.

"Then you understand," said Baresmanas. He did not have to gesture at the chanting crowd to make his meaning clear.

"Yes, father."

Baresmanas nodded solemnly. "Learn from this, daughter. Whatever prejudices you may still have about Romans, abandon them now. You will be their empress, before the day is done, and they are a great people worthy of you. Never doubt that for a moment. Greater than us, in many ways."

He studied the soldiers standing at their posts of honor alongside the aivan's entrance. To the Persians, he gave merely a glance. Baresmanas' dehgans were led by Merena, the most honorable of their number.

But it was the leader of the Roman contingent which was the focus of the sahrdaran's attention. An odd-looking soldier, in truth. Unable to even stand without the aid of crutches. The man's name was Agathius, and he had lost his legs at the battle of the Nehar Malka where Belisarius destroyed a Malwa army.

Agathius was a lowborn man, even by Roman standards. But he was counted a duke, now, by Persians and Romans alike. Merena's own daughter had become his spouse.

"A *thousand years ago*," Baresmanas said harshly, "a time that we ourselves have half-forgotten, daughter, but they have not. A thousand years ago, one of their finest historians explained to his people the Aryan way of raising a manchild."

"*Teach him horsemanship, and archery,*" murmured Tahmina. "*And teach him to despise all lies.*"

"That is the Emperor of Rome's pledge to you, daughter, and to all of the Aryans," said Baresmanas. "A boy not yet eleven years old. Do you understand?"

His daughter nodded. She turned her head slightly, studying the cheering crowd. *Photius! Photius!* "I am so astonished," she whispered.

Baresmanas chuckled. "Why? That a half-Greek, half-Egyptian bastard whoreson would understand us so well?"

She shook her head, rippling the veil.

"No, father. I am just surprised—"

Photius! Photius! They were entering the blessed coolness of the aivan, the huge open-air entrance hall so distinctive of Persian architecture. The soldiers began closing in behind them.

A whisper:

"It had never occurred to me before this moment. Not once. That I might be able to love my husband."

Inside the huge aivan, the Roman empress regent was scowling. Of course, there was nothing new about that. Theodora had been scowling since she arrived in Persia. For any number of reasons.

One. She hated to travel.

Two. She *especially* hated to travel in the desert.

Three. She didn't much like Persians. (A minor point, this. Theodora, as a rule, didn't much like anybody.)

Four. She had now been standing in her heavy official robes for well over an hour. Hadn't these stupid Persians ever heard of *chairs*? Idiots! Even the Aryan Emperor Khusrau was standing.

Five . . .

"I *hate* being proved wrong," she hissed.

"Shhh," hissed Antonina in return. "This is supposed to be a solemn occasion. And your scowl is showing, even through the veil."

"And that's another thing," grumbled Theodora. "How is a woman supposed to breathe with this monstrous thing covering her face? Especially in the heat of late afternoon?"

The veil rippled slightly as she turned her head. "At least they have enough sense to hold public ceremonies in this—this—what's it called, anyway?"

Belisarius, standing on Theodora's other side, leaned over and whispered. "It's known as an *aivan*. Clever, isn't it? Of course, it'd never work in our climate. Not in the winter, anyway."

For all its majestic size—the aivan was a hundred and forty feet long and eighty feet wide; at its highest, the arching vault was a hundred feet above the floor—the structure was open to the elements. The entrance through which Baresmanas and Tahmina were proceeding served as an enormous doorway. The style of architecture was unique to the Persians, and produced a chamber which was much cooler than either the outdoors or an enclosed room.

Theodora was now scowling at Belisarius. "Oh, all right. Go ahead and say it. You were right and I was wrong."

Belisarius said nothing. He knew better than to gloat at Theodora's expense. Not even the insects perched on the walls were *that* stupid.

His diplomacy did not seem to assuage the empress regent's temper. "I *hate* being wrong," she repeated sourly. "And I still would have preferred taking the treasure. I can *see* gold. Can even count it with my own fingers."

Belisarius decided that a response would not qualify, precisely, as "gloating." True, Theodora wasn't fond of disagreement, either. But the woman was more than shrewd enough to have learned—long since—to accept contrary advice without punishing the adviser. Listen to it, at least.

"We'd have wound up losing the treasure anyway, soon enough," he murmured. "Bankrupt Persia, and then what? The Persians go looking for treasure to replace it. The nearest of which is in Roman territory."

He paused, listening to the chants of the huge crowd outside the palace. *Photius! Photius!* Then: "Better this way."

Theodora made no reply, beyond the inevitable refrain. "I *hate* being proved wrong."

Photius was standing alone at the center of the aivan, as befitted his manly status. And that he *was* a man, no one could deny, even if he was only ten years old. He was getting married, wasn't he?

The Emperor of Rome was not pleased at that new found status. He had been perfectly content being a mere boy.

Well . . .

His eyes moved to the cluster of Roman scholars standing amidst the small mob of Persian priests packed against the far wall of the aivan. His tutors, those. Even at the distance, Photius thought their expressions could curdle milk. Greek philosophers, grammarians, rhetoricians and pedants did not appreciate being forced to mingle with Persian *mobads* and *herbads*. Bunch of heathen witch doctors. Traffickers in superstition and magic. Peddlers of—

The emperor's eyes moved away. The first trace of a smile came to his face since he'd awakened that morning. As an official "man," maybe he wouldn't have to put up with *quite* as much nattering from his tutors.

When his eyes fell on the small group of his bodyguards, the smile widened a bit. Then, seeing the vulgar grin on the face of Julian, the chief of his bodyguards, Photius found himself struggling not to grin himself.

He would have preferred it, of course, if his long-time nanny Hypatia could have been present also. Damn the implied questioning of his manly state!

Sigh. But the only women which the stiff Aryans would allow at such a public gathering were the bride and her immediate female relatives. Darkly, Photius suspected the Aryans would have dispensed with them also, if it weren't for the simple fact that—push come to shove—females were sadly necessary for the rite of marriage.

Now, catching the first hint of motion at the aivan entrance, Photius' eyes were drawn thither. His about-to-be-bride was finally entering.

Tahmina's mother, he knew, would not be coming. Her presence was customary at such events, but the woman claimed to have contracted some mysterious and incapacitating disease. Baresmanas had made fulsome apologies for her absence in advance, which the Roman delegation had accepted graciously. Even though not one of those Romans—nor, for that matter, any member of the Persian nobility—doubted for an instant the real nature of the disease. Incapacitating, yes; mysterious, no. Such is the nature of the ancient illness called bigotry.

Her daughter? Of the *Suren*, the purest blood of the Aryans short of the emperor himself! Married to—to—

The mongrel Roman whoreson bastard sighed. *Great. Just great. My wife will hold her nose whenever I'm in the same room with her.*

Tahmina was much nearer, now. Despite himself, Photius was fascinated to see her move. Even under the heavy Persian robes, he could sense the lithe and athletic figure. Tahmina was fifteen years old. Just old enough—quite unlike Photius himself—that she was beginning to bring her body under control. There was no gawkiness at all in that easy, gliding progress.

Maurice, his father's cataphract, had seen the girl before. Maurice had told him that she was extraordinarily beautiful. For a moment, Photius was cheered by the thought.

Only for a moment. Great. *Just great. I'll have the most beautiful wife in the world. And she'll still be holding her nose whenever I'm around.*

Then, finally, his eyes met those of his approaching bride. Between the heavy veil and the headdress, Tahmina's dark eyes and the bridge of her nose were all that Photius could see of her face.

The Emperor of Rome froze.

Tahmina's own eyes were fixed upon him. They never moved once, in the time it took for her to finally take her place next to him.

Beautiful eyes, of course. As clear and bright as moonshine, for all their darkness. Brown eyes, technically, but of such a deep hue they almost seemed black. So much, Photius had expected. But he had not expected the warmth he saw in them. Like embers, glowing.

And he *certainly* hadn't expected to hear the whisper, just as the ceremony finally began. In heavily accented but perfect Greek.

"Relax, husband. You will like me. I promise."

And he did relax, even if the ceremony itself was long, and tedious, and required him to follow a labyrinth of carefully rehearsed gestures and words. Photius, too, had read Herodotus. And so he knew the creed of the Aryans.

Teach them horsemanship, and archery.

And teach them to despise all lies.

Hours later, in the midst of the great festivities which were spilling all through the public areas of the palace—all through the entire city, in fact—Emperor Khusrau Anushirvan sidled up to Belisarius.

"That went supremely well, I thought."

Belisarius nodded. For once, his smile was not crooked at all. It was every bit as wide and open as the emperor's own.

"I thought so, too." They were still standing in the aivan. Through the great opening, the last colors of sunset could be seen. Belisarius glanced at the small door which led to the private quarters of the imperial entourage. Photius and Tahmina had been provided with a suite in those quarters, for their use until the imperial Roman delegation returned to Constantinople some days hence. The new husband and bride had just passed through that door, not more than ten minutes earlier.

Belisarius' smile now assumed its more familiar, crooked shape. "Of course, I'm not sure Photius is still of that opinion. He seemed cheerful enough earlier. But now—" The Roman general chuckled. "He looked for all the world like a man being led to his own execution."

Khusrau grinned. "Nonsense. I raised the girl, you know, as much as Baresmanas did. She is every bit as intelligent as she is comely. I assure you that your stepson will soon be at ease."

The Emperor of Iran and non-Iran paused. "Well . . . Not at *ease*, precisely."

Belisarius' eyes widened a bit. "He's only ten years old, Your Majesty."

Khusrau's face bore an expression of supreme smugness. "Romans. Such a primitive folk."

After his servants dressed him in his bedclothes, Photius nervously entered the sleeping chamber and found Tahmina already waiting for him. She was lazing on the bed, wearing her own nightgown. As soon as Photius entered, she smiled and patted the bed next to her. "Come, husband," she said softly.

"I'm only ten years old," Photius managed to choke out.

"Relax, I say," murmured his wife. She arose and led him gently to the bed. "Lie down."

Photius did as he was commanded. He could not imagine doing otherwise. For all of Tahmina's poise and demure demeanor—*how does she manage that, wearing nothing but a silk gown?*—her hands upon him were strong and firm. She was bigger than he was, true. But it was more the certainty of her intentions, and the sheer beauty of her person—Maurice had been right, been right, been right—that drove him to obey.

It seemed but an instant before she had him stretched out on the bed, herself alongside, and was gently caressing his little body. Slowly, Photius felt the rigidity leaving his muscles.

"I'm only ten years old," he repeated. This time, more by way of an apology than an expression of terror.

"Of course you are," murmured Tahmina. Gently, she kissed his forehead. "Relax, husband." She raised her head and smiled serenely down upon him, while her hands continued their caresses.

"You will age. Soon enough, be sure of it. And when the time comes, you will not be anxious at all. You will know everything. About me. About you. It will be so easy."

Photius thought she had the most beautiful voice he had ever heard. He felt like he was drowning in the darkness of her eyes.

The rest of the night, until they fell asleep, was a time of wonder for him. Wonder of the body, partly. Ten years old is not too young for everything, after all, and Tahmina was as sensuous as she was beautiful. Her caresses felt more wonderful than anything Photius could imagine.

But, mostly, it was wonder of the mind. He had never imagined it. Not once. That he might come to love his wife.

Within an hour after awakening the next morning, wonder turned to certainty. Ten years old was not, after all, too young for a man to understand that pleasures of the mind outweigh pleasures of the body.

His wife turned out to be a genius, too. Such, at least, was Photius' firm conviction. Who else would know so many ways to thwart officious tutors?

"And another thing," she explained, nestling his head into her shoulder. "When they start nattering about your grammar—"

For the first time, Photius assumed the proper mantle of husbandly authority.

"Hush, wife!" he commanded. He lifted his head, summoned his courage—Emperor of Rome!—and planted a kiss on his wife's cheek. After the evening and night, all those *hours*, it came almost easily to him.

Tahmina laughed. "See? Not long!"

Some time later, again, Tahmina was gazing down upon him serenely.

"You will have concubines," she said softly, "but I intend to see to it that you do not spend much time with them."

Photius cleared his throat. "Uh, actually, concubines are not permitted under Christian law." A bit guiltily: "Not supposed to be, anyway."

Tahmina's eyes grew very round. *"Really?* How odd!"

The beautiful eyes narrowed a bit. "I will be converting, of course, since a Christian empire must have a Christian empress." Narrowed further. "I foresee myself a devoted convert." Slits. "A religious fanatic, in fact."

Photius gurgled like a babe. "S'okay with me!"

"It better be," growled his wife. A moment later, she was giving him a foretaste of the punishment which awaited Christian sinners.

And so the servants found them. The servants, and Julian.

The prim and proper servants frowned, needless to say. *Such unseemly conduct for royalty!* But Julian, scarred veteran of many battlefields, was immensely pleased. A Persian empress tickling a Roman emperor, he thought, boded well for the future. Perhaps Belisarius was right, and the thousand year war was finally over.

That still left the Malwa, of course. But that thought brought nothing but a sneer to the cataphract's face. *Anything* was child's play, compared to Persian dehgans on the field of battle.

Chapter 3

That same morning, while Photius and Tahmina began laying the foundation for their marriage, another wedding took place. This wedding was private, not public. Indeed, not to put too fine a point on it, it was a state secret—unauthorized knowledge of which would earn the headsman's sword.

Another foundation was being laid with this wedding. A new empire was being forged, destined to rise up out of the ruins of Malwa. Or rather, destined to play a great part in Malwa's ruination.

The ceremony was Christian, as was the bride, and as simple a rite as that faith allowed. The bride herself had so stipulated, in defiance of all natural law—had insisted, in fact. She had claimed she wanted a brief and unembellished ceremony purely in the interests of security and secrecy. Given that the bride was acknowledged to be a supreme mistress in the arts of espionage and intrigue, the claim was accepted readily enough. Most people probably even believed it.

But Antonina, watching her best friend Irene kneeling at the altar, was a bit hard-pressed to restrain a smile. She knew the truth.

First thing that scheming woman's going to do, after she gets to Peshawar, is hold the biggest and most splendiferous Buddhist wedding in the history of the world. Last for a month, I bet.

Her eyes moved to the man kneeling next to Irene. Kungas was droning his way through the phrases required of a Christian groom with perfect ease and aplomb.

Any Christian objects, of course, she'll claim her husband made her do it.

Kungas was destined to be the new ruler of a new Kushan empire. The Kushans, in their great majority, adhered to the Buddhist faith. In secret, for the most part, since their Malwa overlords had decreed their grotesque Mahaveda version of Hinduism the established religion and forbade all others. But the secrecy, and the frequent martyrdoms which went with it, had simply welded the Kushans that much more closely to their creed.

Naturally, their new ruler would insist that his wife the empress espouse that faith herself. Naturally. He was a strong-willed man, everyone knew it.

Ha!

Belisarius glanced at down at her, and Antonina fiercely stifled her giggle.

Ha! It was her idea, the schemer! Never would have occurred to Kungas.

Kungas was the closest thing Antonina had ever met to a fabled atheist. Agnostic, for a certainty. He was prepared to accept—as a tentative hypothesis—the existence of a "soul." Tentatively, he was even willing to accept the logic that a "soul" required a "soul-maker." *Grudgingly*, he would allow that such a "soul-maker" of necessity possessed superhuman powers.

That he—or she—or it—was a *god*, however . . .

The God?

"Rampant speculation," Kungas called it. In private, of course, and in the company of close friends. Kungas was literate, now, in both Greek and Kushan. But he was no intellectual and never would be. "Rampant speculation" was his lover Irene's serene way of translating his grunted opinion. "Pure guesswork!" was the way Antonina had heard it.

But if Kungas was no intellectual, there was nothing at all wrong with his mind. That mind had been shaped since childhood in the cauldron of battle and destruction. And if, against all logic, the man who had emerged from that fiery furnace was in his own way a rather gentle man—using the term "gentle" very loosely—he had a mind as bright and hard as a diamond.

His people were Buddhists, whatever Kungas thought. So would he be, then. And his empress, too, now that she mentioned it to him.

Ha! Pity the poor Malwa!

◇   ◇   ◇

In the brief reception which followed the wedding, the Emperor
of Iran and non-Iran advanced to present his congratulations along
with his wife. So did Theodora, the Empress Regent of Rome. So
too did Eon, the *negusa nagast* of Ethiopia and Arabia, accompanied by his own wife Rukaiya. The man and woman destined to
be the rulers of a realm which still existed only in the imagination
were being given the official nod of recognition by three of the
four most powerful empires in the world.

The most powerful empire, of course, was absent. Which was
hardly surprising, since even if that empire had known of this
wedding it would hardly have approved. The new realm would be
torn from Malwa's own bleeding flank.

Belisarius and Antonina saw no need to join the crowd pressing
around Kungas and Irene. Neither did Ousanas.

"Silly business," muttered Ethiopia's *aqabe tsentsen*—vizier, in
effect, although the title actually translated as "keeper of the fly-
whisks." The quaint and modest title was in keeping with Ethiopian
political custom.

"Silly," he repeated. He glanced at Antonina. "Don't lie, woman.
You know as well as I do that she'll be a Buddhist soon enough."
He snorted. "And God knows what else. All those mountains are
full of pagans. She'll be getting remarried every week, swearing
eternal devotion to whatever prancing goat-god happens to be the
local fancy."

Antonina maintained an aloof smile. "I think that's absolute nonsense. I can't believe you could be so cynical." She bestowed the
serene expression upon Belisarius. He responded with his own
smile, more crooked than ever, but said nothing.

Antonina's smile now went to the small group of soldiers standing just behind her husband. All three of the top Kushan commanders of Belisarius' army—former commanders, as of this
moment—were gathered there. Vasudeva was in the center,
flanked by Vima and Huvishka.

"Surely you don't agree with him," stated Antonina.

Vasudeva's smile, as always, was a thin and economic affair.
"Wouldn't surprise me," he said. "Not a bad idea, in fact. Pagans
are a silly superstitious lot, of course, but they're not the least bit
inclined toward exclusivity." He stroked his wispy goatee.
"Maybe."

"*Et tu, Brute?*" muttered Antonina.

Vasudeva's smile widened. "Antonina, be serious." He nodded toward the wedding couple and the small crowd gathered about them. "Have I not myself—me and my officers—been the subject of just such a premeditated marital display this very morning?"

Antonina was a bit disconcerted by the Kushan general's perspicacity. Belisarius had told her, but she was not very familiar with the man herself.

Shrewd indeed!

All three of the Kushan generals were now smiling. "And quite well done it was, too," murmured Vima approvingly. "What ambitious general, daydreaming of his own possible lineage, would risk bringing the wrath of such empires down on his head? Wouldn't do at all to overthrow the *established* dynasty, in the face of such universal approval."

Belisarius was studying the faces of the three men. For once, there was no smile at all on his face.

"It's been done, and often enough," he said softly. His gaze came to rest on Vasudeva. Vasudeva's smile was still in place.

"Not here," said the Kushan. He glanced at Kungas. "All of us have spent time with him, Belisarius, since he arrived. We are satisfied. He will make a good emperor." His two subordinates grunted their agreement. Vima added: "And where else could you find such a scheming empress?"

Vima studied Irene. "I suppose you could marry the widow, over the body of her dead husband. But—"

Huvishka shuddered. "Talk about sleeping with both eyes open!"

A little laugh swept the group. Belisarius nodded. In truth, he was not surprised at the easy way in which the Kushan generals had accepted Kungas as their new monarch-to-be. Belisarius had come to know all three Kushan soldiers well, in the past two years. They approached life with hard-headed practicality, and were not given in the least to idle fancies.

Still—

Kungas and Irene had brought fewer than three thousand Kushan soldiers with them from Majarashtra. There were over ten thousand serving under Vasudeva's command in Belisarius' army. Two thousand of those had been with Vasudeva when Belisarius defeated them at the battle of Anatha. The rest had come over after the Malwa disaster at Charax. When the Malwa commanders started their defeated army marching back to India, their Kushan troops had mutinied. The march would be a death march, and they knew it. And knew, as well, that Kushans would do a disproportionate share of the dying. The Ye-tai, not they, would receive what little extra rations could be smuggled off boats along the coast.

It was an awkward situation, thus. All of the Kushans serving under Belisarius had been released for service in their own cause. On the one hand, that gave Kungas a small but by no means laughable army. On the other, it meant Kungas and Irene would be marching across the Persian plateau in order to rebuild the shattered empire of the Kushans accompanied by an army most of whose soldiers owed them no allegiance at all. Everything would depend on the attitude of the officers those soldiers did know and trust. First and foremost, Vasudeva and Vima and Huvishka.

Just as Vasudeva had shrewdly surmised, the main purpose of the wedding which had just been held was to make the attitude of Rome and Persia and Ethiopia as clear as crystal. *This man—and this woman—have our official seal of approval. So don't get any wild ideas.*

"Good enough," murmured Belisarius. "Good enough."

Later that morning, Irene and Kungas went to the Roman emperor's chambers to receive his own official seal of approval. Which they got, needless to say, with considerably less reserve than from his elders and nominal subordinates. Irene was eventually forced to pry him loose.

Photius was struggling with unmanly tears. "I'll miss you," he whispered.

Irene chucked him under the chin. "So come and visit. And we'll do the same."

Photius managed a smile. "I'd like that! Theodora hates to travel, but I think it's exciting." He hesitated; a trace of apprehension came to his face, as he glanced quickly at the taller girl standing next to him.

Tahmina had his little arm firmly held in her hands. "Whatever my lord and husband desires," she crooned.

Irene grinned. "Well said! My own philosophy exactly."

Kungas grunted. Irene ignored the uncouth sound. A very stern expression came to her face, and now she was wagging her finger in front of Photius' nose.

"And remember! Every new book that comes out! I'll expect it sent to me immediately! Or there'll be war!"

Photius nodded. "Every one, as soon as it comes out. I'll get the very first copy and sent it to you right off, by fast courier." He stood straight. "I can do that, you know. I'm the Emperor of Rome."

"Quite so," crooned Tahmina.

That evening, in the suite of the imperial palace which had been set aside for the use of Kungas and Irene, a different ceremony took place. At sundown, Antonina bustled into the room. Behind her came a servant, carrying a large and heavy crate.

Antonina planted her hands on hips and gave the men sitting on the various divans scattered about the large salon a ferocious glare. The glare spared no one—not her husband, not his chief commanders Maurice and Sittas and Agathius, not Ousanas and Ezana, not Kungas nor his chief officers, not the Persian general Kurush. If they were male, they were dead meat.

"*Out!*" She hooked her thumb at the door. "All of you, at once! Take this military folderol somewhere else. This room is hereby dedicated to a solemn ritual."

Maurice was the first to rise. "Got to respect hallowed tradition," he agreed solemnly. "Let's go, gentlemen. We're pretty much done with everything except"—he sighed heavily—"the logistics. And Agathius and I can do that with Belisarius in his own chambers." He gave Antonina a grin. "It'll take us hours, of course, but so what? This one won't be coming back tonight."

As he moved toward the door: "Not on her own two feet, anyway."

Antonina growled. Maurice hastened his pace. Antonina's growl deepened. A small tigress, displeased. The rest of the men followed Maurice with considerable alacrity.

When they were gone, Antonina ordered the servant to place the crate on a nearby table. He did so, and then departed at once. With a regal gesture, Antonina swept the lid off the crate. More regally still, she withdrew the first bottle of wine.

"Soldiers," she sneered. "What do they know about massacre and mayhem?"

Irene was already bringing the goblets. "Nothing." She extended them both. "Start the slaughter."

Chapter 4

"I wish you'd stop doing this," grumbled Agathius. "It's embarrassing." The powerful hands draped on the arms of the wheelchair twitched, as if Agathius were about to seize the wheel rims and propel himself forward. Then he had to hastily snatch the maps and logistics records before they slid off his lap onto the tiled floor.

Seeing the motion, Maurice snorted. "Are you crazy?" The grizzled veteran, striding alongside the wheelchair, glanced back at the young general pushing it. "It's good for him, doing some honest work for a change instead of plotting and scheming."

Belisarius grinned. "Certainly is! Besides, Justinian insisted on a full and detailed report—from me personally. How can I do that without operating the gadget myself?"

Agathius grumbled inarticulately. The wheelchair and its accompanying companions swept into one of the vaulted and frescoed chambers of the imperial palace. A cluster of Persian officers and courtiers scrambled aside. By now, many days into the ongoing strategy sessions at Ctesiphon, they had all learned not to gawk in place. Belisarius did *not* maneuver a wheelchair with the same cunning with which he maneuvered armies in the field. *Charge!*

When they reached the stairs at the opposite side of the chamber, leading to the residential quarters above, Belisarius and Maurice positioned themselves on either side of the wheelchair. As Agathius continued his grumbling, Belisarius and Maurice seized the handles which Justinian had designed for the purpose and began hauling Agathius and his wheelchair up the stairs by main force, grunting with the effort. Even with his withered half-legs, Agathius was still a muscular and heavy burden.

Below, the knot of Persian notables watched the operation with slack jaws and open eyes. They had seen it done before, of course—many times—but still . . .

Unseemly! Servants' work! The top commander of the greatest army since Darius should not—

At the first landing, Belisarius and Maurice set the contraption down and took a few deep breaths. Agathius looked from one to the other, scowling fiercely. "I *can* climb stairs myself, you know. I do it at home all the time."

Belisarius managed a grin. "*Justinian,* remember? You think the Roman Empire's Grand Justiciar—not to mention Theodora's husband—is going to settle for a secondhand account?"

"He's way off in Adulis," protested Agathius. "And he's completely preoccupied with getting his beloved new steam-powered warships ready." But it was weak, weak.

Belisarius shrugged. "Yes—and he's blind, to boot. So what? You think he doesn't have spies?"

Maurice snorted sarcastically. "And besides, Agathius, you know how much Justinian loves designing his gadgets. So just shut up and resign yourself to the inevitable." Sourly: "At least *you* don't have to lift this blasted thing. With an overgrown, over-muscled ex-cataphract in it."

They'd rested enough. With a heave and a grunt, Belisarius and Maurice lifted Agathius and the wheelchair and staggered their way upward. When they reached the top of the stairs and were in the corridor leading to Agathius' private chambers, they set the wheelchair down.

"All . . . right," puffed Belisarius. "You're on your own again. Justinian wants to know how the hand grips work also."

"They work just fine," snapped Agathius. To prove the point, he set off down the corridor at a pace which had Belisarius and Maurice hurrying to catch up—puffing all the while. Agathius seemed to take a malicious glee in the sound.

At the entrance to his chambers, Agathius paused. He glanced up at Belisarius, wincing a bit and clearing his throat.

"Uh—"

"I'll speak to her," assured Belisarius. "I'm sure she'll listen to reason once—"

The door was suddenly jerked open. Agathius' young wife Sudaba was standing there, glaring.

"*What is this insane business?*" she demanded furiously. "*I insist on accompanying my husband!*" An instant later, she was planted in front of Belisarius, shaking her little fist under his nose. "*Roman tyrant! Monstrous despot!*"

Hastily, Maurice seized the wheelchair and maneuvered Agathius into the room, leaving Belisarius—Rome's *magister militum per orientem*, Great Commander of the Allied Army, honorary *vurzurgan* in the land of Aryans—to deal alone with Agathius' infuriated teenage wife.

"A command responsibility if I ever saw one," Maurice muttered.

Agathius nodded eagerly. "Just so!" Piously: "After all, it was *his* decision to keep the baggage train and camp followers to a minimum. It's not as if *we* insisted that the top officers had to set a personal example."

"*Autocrat! Beast! Despoiler! I won't stand for it!*"

"Must be nice," mused Maurice, "to have one of those meek and timid Persian girls for a wife."

But Agathius did not hear the remark. His two-year-old son had arrived, toddling proudly on his own feet, and had been swept up into his father's arms.

"Daddy go bye-bye?" the boy asked uncertainly.

"Yes," replied Agathius. "But I'll be back. I promise."

The boy gurgled happily as Agathius started tickling him. "Daddy beat the Malwa!" he proclaimed proudly.

"Beat 'em flat!" his father agreed. His eyes moved to the great open window, staring toward the east. The Zagros mountains were there; and then, the Persian plateau; and then—the Indus valley, where the final accounts would be settled.

"They'll give me my legs back," he growled. "The price of them, at least. Which I figure is Emperor Skandagupta's blood in the dust."

Maurice clucked. "Such an intemperate man you are, Agathius. I'd think a baker's son would settle for a mere satrap."

"Skandagupta, and nothing less," came the firm reply. "I'll see his empty eyes staring at the sky. I swear I will."

◊   ◊   ◊

When Belisarius rejoined them, some time later, the Roman general's expression was a bit peculiar. Bemused, perhaps—like a stunned ox. Quite unlike his usual imperturbable self.

Agathius cleared his throat. "It's not as if I didn't give you fair warning."

Belisarius shook his head. The ox, trying to shake away the confusion.

"How in the name of God did she get me to agree?" he wondered. Then, sighing: "And *now* I'll have Antonina to deal with! She'll break my head when I tell her she's got another problem to handle on shipboard."

Maurice grinned. "I imagine Ousanas will have a few choice words, too. Sarcasm, you may recall, is not entirely foreign to his nature. And he *is* the military commander of the naval expedition. Will be, at least, once the Ethiopians finish putting their fleet together."

Belisarius winced. His eyes moved to the huge table at the center of the chamber. Agathius had already spread out the map and the logistics papers which he had brought with him to the conference. They seemed a mere outcrop in the mountain of maps, scrolls, codices and loose sheets of vellum which practically spilled from every side of the table.

"That's the whole business?" he asked.

Agathius nodded. "Yes—and it's just as much of a mess as it looks. Pure chaos!" He glowered at the gigantic pile. "Who was that philosopher who claimed everything originated from atoms? Have to ask Anastasius. Whoever it was, he was a simpleminded optimist, let me tell you. If he'd ever tried to organize the logistics for a combined land and sea campaign that involved a hundred and twenty thousand men—and that's just the soldiers!—he would've realized that everything turns *into* atoms also."

"Thank God," muttered Belisarius, eyeing the mess with pleasure. "Something simple and straightforward to deal with!"

In the event, Antonina was not furious. She dismissed the entire matter with an insouciant shrug, as she poured herself a new goblet of pomegranate-flavored water. Belisarius had introduced her to the Persian beverage, and Antonina found it a blessed relief from the ever-present wine of the Roman liquid diet. Especially when she was suffering from a hangover.

The goblet full, she took it in hand and leaned back into her divan. "Sudaba and I get along. It'll be a bit crowded, of course, with her sharing my cabin along with Koutina." For a moment, suspicion came into her eyes. "You *didn't* agree to letting her bring the boy?"

Belisarius straightened proudly. "There I held the line!"

Aide flashed an image into his mind. *Hector on the walls of Troy.* Belisarius found himself half-choking from amusement combined with chagrin.

Antonina eyed her husband quizzically. Belisarius waved a weak hand. "Nothing. Just Aide. He's being sarcastic and impertinent again."

"Blessed jewel!" exclaimed a voice. Sitting on another divan in his favored lotus position, Ousanas cast baleful eyes on Belisarius. "I shudder to think what would become of us," he growled, "without the Talisman of God to keep you sane."

Antonina sniffed. "My husband does *not* suffer from delusions of grandeur."

"Certainly not!" agreed Ousanas. "How could he, with a mysterious creature from the future always present in his mind? Ready—blessed jewel!—to puncture inflated notions at a moment's notice."

Ousanas took a sip from his own goblet. Good red wine, this—no silly child's drink for him. "Not that he has any reason for such grandiosity, of course, when you think about it. What has Belisarius actually accomplished, these past few years?"

The aqabe tsentsen of the kingdom of Axum—empire, now, since the Ethiopians had incorporated southern Arabia into their realm—waved his own hand. But there was nothing weak about that gesture. It combined the certainty of the sage with the authority of the despot.

"Not much," he answered his own question. "The odd Malwa army defeated here and there, entirely through the use of low-minded stratagems. The occasional rebellion incited within the Malwa empire itself." His sniff was more flamboyant than Antonina's, nostrils fleering in contempt. "A treasure stolen from Malwa and then given away to Maratha rebels—a foolish gesture, that!—and a princess smuggled out of captivity. Bah! There's hardly a village headman in my native land between the great lakes who could not claim as much."

Antonina grinned. As a rule, disrespect toward her husband was guaranteed to bring a hot response. But from Ousanas—

Axum's aqabe tsentsen was not Ethiopian himself. Ousanas had been born and bred in the heartland of Africa far to the south of the highlands. But he had spent years as the dawazz to Prince Eon, a post whose principal duty was to nip royal self-aggrandizement in the bud. Eon was now the *negusa nagast* of Axum, the "King of Kings," and Ousanas had become the most powerful official in his realm. But the former hunter and former slave still had his old habits.

And, besides, they were close friends. So close, in fact, that Ousanas was the most frequently cited "lover" of the huge male harem which Antonina was reputed to maintain. By now, of course—after Antonina had played a central role in crushing the Malwa-instigated Nika rebellion in Constantinople, reestablished imperial authority in Egypt and the Levant, and led the naval expedition which had rescued Belisarius and his army after their destruction of the Malwa logistics base at Charax—not even the scandal-mongering Greek aristocracy gave more than token respect to the slanders. The Malwa espionage service had long since realized that the rumors had been fostered by Antonina herself, in order to divert their attention from her key role in her husband's strategy.

So, knowing Ousanas, Antonina responded in kind. "Yes, surely. But what Bantu headman can claim to have put his stepson on the throne of the Roman Empire?"

Ousanas snorted. "Rome? Bah!" He leaned forward, gesticulating eagerly. "A realm of peddlers and peasants! No, no, Antonina—for true grandeur you must visit the great and mysterious empires in central Africa! The cities are paved with silver and jade, the palaces cut from pure crystals. The emperors—every one of them a former headman from my native region, you understand— are borne to the gold-inlaid toilets on elephants draped with—"

"And the elephants shit diamonds themselves," interrupted Ezana. The Axumite naval commander—he *was* a native-born Ethiopian—gave Ousanas a sour glance. "It's odd how these marvelous African empires of his keep moving further south as we Axumites extend our rule." Another sniff was added. "So far, though, all we seem to encounter are illiterate heathen savages scrabbling in the dirt."

Ousanas began some retort, but Ezana drove over it. "The Persian girl does not concern me, Belisarius. Not by herself. As young as she is, Sudaba is not a stranger to campaigns. She was with Agathius at the Nehar Malka, after all. Any Persian noblewoman who could manage on board one of those miserable river barges"—the inevitable Axumite pride in their naval expertise surfaced—"can *surely* manage aboard one of our craft."

That contented thought gave way to a scowl: "But if this starts a mudslide of women demanding to accompany their men—" Ezana swiveled his head and brought another occupant of the salon under his cold scrutiny. "My own half-sister, soon enough!"

Under that hard gaze, the pale face of young Menander turned pink with embarrassment. The Roman officer knew that Ezana was aware of his intimate relationship with Deborah, but he still found the casual manner in which Ethiopians handled such things unsettling. Menander was too close enough to the Thracian village of his upbringing not to be a bit edgy. In *his* village, the half-brother of a seduced sister would have blood in his eye. And no Thracian villager was half as skilled and experienced in mayhem and slaughter as Ezana!

"I've already spoken to her about it," he muttered. "She agreed to stay behind." Guiltily: "Well . . . in Charax, anyway."

"Marvelous," grunted Ezana. "Our precious naval base is about to become as populous as Bharakuccha. The women will be bad enough." His next words caused Menander to turn beet red. "The inevitable squalling brats which follow will practically carpet the city. Our stevedores will be tripping all over them trying to load our warships. Our soldiers will have to fight their way to the docks."

Belisarius sighed and spread his hands. "Yes, Ezana—I know. But I can't accomplish miracles. As it is, we'll still manage to keep the camp followers to a bare minimum." He tried to rally his pride. "In proportion, we'll have the smallest baggage train since Xenophon's march to the sea."

"Marvelous," grunted Ousanas. "Perhaps we should follow his lead then. Strand ourselves in the middle of the Malwa empire and try to fight our way *out*."

Menander recovered his aplomb. Young and sometimes bashful he might be, but no one had ever accused him of cowardice. "We already did that," he pointed out cheerfully. "Only a handful of us, of course, not Xenophon's fabled ten thousand. I much prefer the current prospect. Marching *into* Malwa, with over a hundred thousand!"

"*You* won't be in that number," retorted Ezana. "No, boy. You're for the cut and thrust of boarding parties."

"Me?" Menander's eyes widened in mock astonishment. "Nonsense. *I'm* the gunnery specialist. *I* am required to stay back while Axumite marines storm across the decks. *My* duties—"

The last occupant of the salon now spoke. "Bullshit, boy!" John of Rhodes rose from his divan and planted his arms akimbo. "The *real* gunnery specialist is Eusebius—who's too nearsighted to storm a latrine, anyway. And since *I'm* the commander of the gunship fleet, that leaves you as the top Roman officer in the armada to show these haughty black fellows"—he and the two Africans exchanged grins—"how to wield hand weapons properly in the close quarters of a desperate boarding operation."

"That's nonsense, also," said Antonina. She drained the rest of her goblet. "If all goes as planned, there won't *be* any boarding operations. Just the dazzling maneuvers of warships firing cannons at long range, destroying the Malwa with precision and style."

And that, of course, brought a storm of criticism and outrage.

Idiot! Have you learned nothing?

The First Law of Battle!

Every battle plan in history—

"—gets fucked up as soon as the enemy arrives," she finished. "Men. Such slobs. Everything always has to be messy and untidy." Serenely: "Fortunately, *this* expedition will have a woman's hand on the rudder."

Five pairs of male eyes, ranging in color from bright blue to deepest brown, joined in condemnation of such folly.

Antonina poured herself another goblet. "Trust me," she said, still with absolute serenity. "You'll see."

Belisarius' final meeting of the day took place late that night, in the back room of a small tavern to which he had come cloaked in secrecy.

"There's nothing more I can tell you," he concluded. "If we hear anything further, of course, I'll let you know. But since you'll be off as soon as Ezana can finish assembling his small fleet, I don't imagine there'll be anything else."

Anastasius grunted. "Not if you're right, and Narses is behind it all." He shrugged his massive shoulders. "Speaking for myself, I hope he is. Information's valuable, but I'd rather trust my life to Narses' fine and subtle hand."

Valentinian glared at him. Clearly enough, the weasel-thin cataphract did not share his giant companion's equanimity.

"Speak for yourself," he snarled. "I'd rather trust a scorpion than Narses." The glare shifted to Belisarius. "And *don't* repeat Irene's fancy phrases to me. Fine for her to talk about trusting Narses' so-called 'craftsmanship.' *She'll* be on the other side of the Hindu Kush from the bastard, with thirteen thousand Kushan bodyguards."

The last occupant of the room spoke up. "Ah, but you forget. She'll be without *me*. And since I'll be coming with *you*, I think that fairly evens the odds."

Valentinian was now glaring at Kujulo. But, even for Valentinian, the glare was hard to maintain. After Belisarius' rescue of then-princess Shakuntala from her captivity at Venandakatra's palace in Gwalior, Valentinian had fought his way out of India with Kushans at his side—Kujulo among them. He had then spent two years fighting against Kushans and, after Vasudeva and his men took service with Belisarius, with them at his side. There were perhaps no soldiers in the world, beyond the general's own Thracian bucellarii to whom Valentinian belonged, that he respected and trusted more than he did Kushans. And, of them, more than Kujulo himself.

Still—

"I'm not complaining," he complained. He took his own quaff of wine, and then squinted bitterly at the Persian vintage as if all the sourness of the universe were contained therein. "If it can be done, we'll get the girls out. Although I *still* don't understand why Narses would go to all this trouble—not to mention huge risks for himself—just to get Dadaji's daughters back to their father."

Belisarius shrugged. "That part doesn't make sense to any of us, Valentinian. Irene no more than me. But—"

His crooked smile made its appearance. "That's all the more reason to investigate. There's *got* to be more involved."

"What do you think?" asked Anastasius.

Belisarius scratched his chin. "I have no idea." He glanced at Valentinian. "But I can't help remembering the last words Lord Damodara said to you, before he released you from captivity."

Valentinian scowled. "That silly business about you having a proper respect for grammar?"

Belisarius nodded. "Yes, that." His chin-scratching went into high gear. "I can't help but wondering if what we're seeing here isn't a master grammarian at work. Parsing a very long sentence, so to speak."

Valentinian threw up his hands with exasperation. "I still say it's silly!" He planted his hands firmly on the table and leaned forward.

"We'll do it, General. If it can be done at all. But I'm giving you fair warning—"

He pushed himself back and took a deep breath. "If we run into Rana Sanga, I'm surrendering right off! No way in hell am I going to fight *that* monster again!"

Chapter 5

BIHAR

Spring, 533 A.D.

The knuckles on Rana Sanga's right hand, gripping the tent pole, were as white as bone. For a moment, Lord Damodara wondered if the pole would snap. The thought was only half-whimsical. The Malwa commander had once seen the leader of his Rajput troops cut an armored man in half—*Vertically*. Sanga's sword had come down through the shoulder, split the sternum and the ribs, and only come to a halt when the sword broke against the baldric's buckle.

True, his opponent had been a lightly armored rebel, and as small as Bengalis usually were. Still—

"I'm glad I'm using bamboo to hold up my tent," he remarked casually.

Startled, Rana Sanga's eyes came to his master. Then, moved to his hand. Slowly, with an obvious effort, the tall Rajput king released his grip.

The hand became a fist and the fist slammed into his left palm. Damodara winced at the noise. That punch would have broken the hands of most men. Sanga didn't even seem to notice. There were times when Damodara wondered if the Rajput was entirely human. For all Sanga's courtesy and stiff honor, there was something about the Rajput king—something that went beyond his towering stature and tigerish frame—that made the Malwa general

54

think of the asuras of the ancient chronicles and legends. Demons . . .

Lord Damodara shook the thought away, as he had so often before. The asuras had been evil creatures. However ferocious in combat, Rana Sanga could not be accused of the same. Not by any sane man, at least; and whatever else Damodara was, he was most certainly sane.

The Malwa general heaved a very faint, very controlled sigh. *And that is perhaps all I am. Sane.* He turned away from the sight of his silent, seething, enraged subordinate and studied the new maps which had been brought to the command tent. Damodara's keen mind found comfort in those maps. The lines drawn upon them were clean and precise. Quite unlike the human territory which they so glibly claimed to represent.

Honor. Morality. Those are for others. For me, there is only sanity.

"There is no leeway in the orders, Rana Sanga," he said harshly. "None whatsoever."

Sanga was now glaring at an idol perched on a small pedestal next to the tent's entrance. The very expensive ivory carving was a miniature statue of the four-armed, three-headed and three-eyed god called Virabhadra. In each of his hands, the god bore a bow, an arrow, a shield and a sword. The weapons were all made of pure gold. A necklace of sapphire skulls adorned his bare chest, and each cyclops eye was a ruby. The scarlet color of the gems seemed to reflect Sanga's rage with blithe indifference.

Virabhadra had once been a minor god, one of Siva's variations. But the Mahaveda cult which dominated the Malwa empire's new version of Hinduism had elevated him to much higher status. Damodara rather loathed the statue, himself, despite its value. But it helped to keep the ever-suspicious priests of Malwa from prying too closely into his affairs.

"I have already come under criticism for my methods of suppressing rebellion here in eastern India," he added softly. He gestured at one of the scrolls on his large desk. "I received that from Nanda Lal just two days ago. The emperor's spymaster is wondering why we have made such infrequent use of impalement."

Sanga tore his eyes away from the statue. "That idiot," he snarled, utterly oblivious to the fact that he was insulting one of the emperor's close kinsmen in front of another. For some reason—or, rather, a reason he chose not to examine closely—Damodara found that unthinking trust something of a small treasure in its own right.

Sanga began pacing back and forth in the command tent. His steps, as always, were as light and powerful as a tiger's. And his voice carried the rumbling undertones of the same predator of the forest.

"We have spilled a river of blood across this land," he growled. "Here, and in half of Bengal also. Stacked heads in small piles at the center of a hundred villages. And then burned the villages. And for what?"

He paused, for a moment, and glared at the closed flap of the tent as if he could see the ravaged countryside beyond. "To be sure, the rebellion is suppressed. But it will flare up again, soon enough, once we are gone. Does that—that—" Teeth clenched: "—*spymaster* really think that impaling a rebel instead of decapitating him will serve us for magic?"

Damodara shrugged. "In a word: *yes*. Nanda Lal has always been a firm believer in the value of terror. As much as Venandakatra, the truth be told, even if he does not take Venandakatra's personal pleasure in the doing."

Mention of Venandakatra's name, inevitably, stoked the Rajput's rage. But Damodara did not regret the doing of it. Rana Sanga, in the privacy of Damodara's tent, could afford to rage. Lord Damodara had no such luxury himself. There was no superior in front of whom *he* could pace like a tiger, snarling his fury at bestial cruelty. Damodara had no superiors, beyond Nanda Lal and the emperor himself. And the being from the future called Link which ruled them in turn. Nanda Lal and Emperor Skandagupta would—at best—immediately remove Damodara from command were he to express such sentiments to them. The *thing* would almost certainly do worse.

"My family is in Kausambi now, you know," he said softly. "All of them. I just got a letter from my wife yesterday. She is not pleased with the climate in the capital—it's particularly hard on my parents—but she says the emperor has provided them with a very fine mansion. Plenty of room, even with three children."

The quiet words seemed to drain Sanga's anger away, as quickly as water pouring out of a broken basin.

"So soon?" he murmured.

Damodara shrugged and spread his hands widely. The lithe gesture brought a peculiar little pleasure to him. After the past two years of arduous campaigning—first in Persia, and then in eastern India—the formerly rotund little Malwa general was almost as fit as any of his Rajput soldiers.

"Did you expect anything else, King of Rajputana?" Damodara chuckled harshly. "*Of course* the emperor insists on taking my family hostage, in all but name. Except for his Ye-tai bodyguard troops—arrogant bastards—everybody admits that we possess his empire's finest army."

"Small army," grunted Sanga.

Again, Damodara shrugged. "Only by Malwa standards. Anywhere else in the world, forty thousand men—half of them Rajputs, and all the rest adopting Rajput ways—would be considered a mighty host. And our numbers are growing."

He turned back to the table with its clean and simple maps. When he spoke again, his voice was as harsh as Sanga's. "But—yes, by Malwa standards, a small army. So let us put all else aside and concentrate on what we must do. *Must*—do."

He waited until Sanga was at his side. Then, tracing the line of the Ganges with a finger: "Venandakatra can squawk all he wants about immediate reinforcement in the Deccan. Nanda Lal, at least, understands logistics. We will have to follow the Ganges to the Jamuna; then, upstream to the Chambal."

The two men had spent years fighting and leading side by side. Sanga immediately grasped the logic. "Yes. Then—" His own long finger touched the map. "We make our portage here and come south into the Gulf of Khambat following the Mahi river."

Damodara nodded. "It's a roundabout way. But, in the end, we will approach Bharakuccha from the north, shielded from Rao's—ah, I believe the term Lord Venandakatra prefers is 'brigands'—by the Vindhya mountains."

"Not much of a shield," murmured Sanga. "Not from Rao and his—" The Rajput's lips pursed, as if tasting a lemon. "Brigands."

"Enough, I think. Until we reach Bharakuccha and can get reliable local intelligence, I *don't* want to be blundering about in the Great Country. Not with the Panther roaming loose."

The two men stared at the map in silence for a bit longer. Then, heaving a sigh, Rana Sanga spoke almost in a whisper.

"I used to dream, sometimes—long ago, when I was still young and foolish—of meeting him again in single combat on the field of honor."

Damodara tried to salvage something out of the ruins. "And so you shall!"

Heavily, Sanga shook his head. "No, Lord. As you say, the orders carried no leeway. Once we cross the Narmada, we will be under Lord Venandakatra's command. Politically, at least, since he is the Goptri of the Deccan. You know as well as I do that he is not called the Vile One for no reason."

Again, the heavy sigh. "There will be no honor for us in the Great Country, Lord Damodara. Not a shred."

Damodara said nothing. There was nothing to say.

Shortly thereafter, Rana Sanga left the tent and returned to his own. There, for two hours, he paced back and forth in silence. His Rajput officers stayed well clear of the tent. Sanga spoke not a word, but black anger emanated from him like an asura in captive fury.

Even the guards standing outside the entrance moved as far away from it as possible. Their presence at the tent was a formality, in any event. Rana Sanga was universally—by friend and foe alike—considered the greatest living Rajput warrior as well as Rajputana's finest general. "Guarding" him was a bit on the order of setting cubs to guard a tiger.

Late in the afternoon, a Ye-tai appeared before the tent and requested permission to pass. Toramana, that was, an officer whom Damodara had recently promoted to the status of general. Of the thousands of Ye-tai soldiers in Damodara's army, Toramana was now ranked the highest.

The Rajput guards eyed him uncertainly.

They did so, in part, because Toramana was the kind of man who, armed and armored as he was, would cause any soldier to pause. Toramana was himself considered a mighty warrior, as well as a canny general. He was big, even for a Ye-tai, and not yet thirty years old. His taut and well-muscled body was evidence of the rigorous regimen he had maintained since boyhood—a boyhood which had itself been spent in the harsh environment of the Hindu Kush. His face, bony and angular in the Ye-tai way, was quite unreadable—which was not common in that breed of men.

For the most part, however, the Rajput guards hesitated because they knew the purpose of Toramana's visit. He had come to receive the answer to a question, a question which all the Rajputs in Damodara's army had been discussing and debating privately for days. And, for most, had settled on the same answer as the two guards standing in front of Rana Sanga's tent.

"It is not a good time, General Toramana," said one of the guards quietly. "Rana Sanga is in a rage. Best you return tomorrow, when the answer is more likely to be the one you desire."

The big Ye-tai officer studied the guard, for a moment. Then, shrugging: "If the answer is the one I desire, then I will have to deal with Rana Sanga for years to come. Do you think this is the last day Rajputana's greatest king will have cause for fury? Best I get the answer in his worst moment. That alone will be a promise greater than any words."

The guards returned his calm gaze by looking away. The truth of the statement could not, after all, be denied.

"Enter then, General," said one.

"Our wishes go with you," murmured the other.

Toramana nodded. "My thanks. Things will be as they will be." He pushed aside the tent flap and entered.

Hearing someone come into his pavilion, Sanga ceased his restless pacing and spun around. His hand did not fly to the sword belted at his waist, but his mouth opened, ready to hurl words of angry dismissal. Then, seeing who it was, he froze.

For a moment, the two big men stared at each other. The light shed by the lamps in the tent caused both of their faces to be highlighted, making them seem ever harder than usual. Warrior faces, as if cast in bronze. Sanga was taller than Toramana—the Rajput king was taller than almost anyone—and even broader in the shoulders. But the smaller Ye-tai did not seem in the least intimidated.

Which was one of the things Sanga liked about him, when all was said and done. That . . . and much else. It was odd, really. Sanga had never been fond of Ye-tai, as a rule. Rather the contrary.

"I forgot," he said quietly, his rage beginning to ebb. Sanga gestured at a nearby table. The simple piece of furniture was set very low, with cushions on either side resting on the carpets. "Please sit."

When they were seated, Sanga did not pause for more than a moment before speaking.

"First, a question of my own. Why did you protect Holkar's woman and child?" Before Toramana could answer, Sanga added: "And do not tell me it was because of any strategic acumen. You had no way of knowing, in the chaos of the final assault, that the man you had cut down was the son of Dadaji Holkar. We did not discover that until the following day."

Toramana began to speak, but Sanga pressed on over the words.

"Nor do I wish to hear that you intended to keep the woman for your own concubine. You have two already, both of them more attractive than that woman. And neither one of them came with child, though the Bengali has now borne one of your own. So—why? According to reports, you even had to threaten several of your own soldiers who sought to use the woman."

"It did not take much of a threat," said Toramana. He chuckled softly. "They were subdued with a scowl and a few words. It was more in the way of old habit on their part, than any real urgency. The army, after all, has plenty of camp followers. I think they were simply feeling an urge to break free of Rajput discipline. The men who overran the rebel camp were all Ye-tai, after all."

He shrugged. "The woman was wailing, clutching her man's dead body. The baby, cast aside, was wailing louder still. What man not ridden by a demon can feel lust in such circumstances? There were only two courses of action. Kill them both, or keep them safe from harm."

Silence. The two men matched gazes. The younger Ye-tai was the first to look away. "We do what we must, Rana Sanga. Such is the nature of the world. But there is no reason to do more. A man ends at the limit of his duty. The beast continues beyond. I am a man, not a beast."

The answer seemed to satisfy the Rajput. He planted his large hands on the table and rose to his feet in a single easy movement. Then, began pacing again. This time, however, the pacing was that of a man engrossed in thoughtful consideration, not one working off a rage.

"I have a half-sister named Indira," he said quietly. "You suggested a cousin, but if we are to do this it would be best to do it properly." Teeth flashed in his beard, as much of a snarl as a smile. "If nothing else, it will bring the full weight of Malwa down upon us—you more than me—and if a man is to take on a challenge he may as well do it in the spirit of legend. I find the thought of Malwa's outrage soothing, at the moment."

Toramana's eyes were wide open, now. His body was no longer relaxed in the least. Very stiff, he was. Clearly, he had not been expecting to hear *this*—not from Rana Sanga!

The Rajput's teeth flashed again, but there was more of real humor in the expression now. "Did you really believe all the tales? *The ultimate Rajput?*" Sanga snorted. "I have given much thought, over the years, to the relation of truth to illusion. It is a simple fact—deny it who will—that the Rajputs themselves are not so many generations removed from barbarism. And came, I am quite certain, from the same mountains that produced you."

He resumed his pacing, very slowly now. "Besides, Indira is a vigorous girl. Very prone to bending custom and tradition in her own right, much to the displeasure of my family. But I am fond of her, despite the difference in our ages. I was more of an uncle to her than a brother, in years past. I can think of no cousin who would be as suitable. Most of them would wail in horror at the very thought. Indira, on the other hand—"

He paused, then chuckled. "Knowing her, she is likely to find the thing a challenge and an adventure."

The pausing stopped abruptly. All traces of humor vanished. The Rajput king stood straight and tall. Without looking at Toramana, he murmured: "Very fond of her, I say. If I discovered she has been abused, I will challenge you and kill you. Do not doubt it for a moment. Neither the challenge nor the killing."

He swiveled his head and brought the Ye-tai under his stony gaze. Then, to his satisfaction, discovered that the young warrior was not bridling at the threat. For all Toramana's own great skill at war, he was more than intelligent enough, despite his relative youth, to understand that he was no match for Sanga.

"I am not abusive to women," said Toramana. Quietly, but perhaps a bit . . . not angrily, no, but sternly for all that.

"Yes, I know." Sanga's lips tightened, as if he were tasting something a bit sour. "I asked Lord Damodara to have Narses spy upon you." His eyes moved away. "My apologies. But I needed to know. Narses says that both your concubines seem in good health, and satisfied with their position. The Bengali even dotes on you, he says, now that you have produced a child."

"I will not disown the boy," said Toramana, the words coming curt and abrupt.

Sanga made a small, dismissive gesture with his hand. "That will not be required. Nor, for that matter, that you put aside the concubines. You are a warrior, after all, bringing your blood to that of a warrior race. Let the old women chatter as they will."

Suddenly, a grin appeared on Sanga's face. His earlier rage seemed to have vanished completely.

"Ha! Let the Malwa priests and spies scurry like insects. Let Nanda Lal squirm in *his* soul, for a change."

Moving with the speed and grace which was his trademark, Sanga resumed his seat at the table. Then, leaning over, he bestowed his grin on Toramana.

"Besides, Indira is very comely. And, as I said, a spirited girl. I do not think there is much danger that you will be overly distracted by concubines."

He gestured to a bowl containing fruit and pastries. "Let us eat, Toramana. I will have my servants bring tea, as well. After the campaign in the Deccan—or as soon as there seems to be an opportunity—it will be done. Perhaps in Rajputana, which would be my preference so long as I can attend. If not, I will send for Indira and you will be wed within the bosom of the army.

"Which," he continued, reaching for an apricot, "would perhaps be best in any event. The marriage, after all, was created in the army. Only that forge was hot enough to do such difficult work."

That night, long after Sanga had departed, Lord Damodara's spymaster entered the command tent. The Malwa commander, engrossed in his study of the maps, gave the old Roman eunuch no more than a glance. Then, using his head as a pointer, he nodded toward a small package resting on his nearby field cot.

"There," he said. "Make sure my wife receives it. Send it off tonight, if possible."

"You are not planning to visit her yourself?" asked Narses. "The army will be passing Kausambi on our way to the Deccan."

Damodara's headshake was curt and abrupt. "I cannot. Nanda Lal's instructions on that matter were as clear and precise as all the rest. I am not to leave the army under any circumstances."

"Ah." Narses nodded. "I understand."

The eunuch moved over to the cot and picked up the package. By the weight and feel of it, there was nothing inside the silk wrapping beyond a few message scrolls and some trinkets for Damodara's three children. Narses began to leave the tent. Then, at the flap, he paused as if an idle thought had come to him.

"I've obtained some more slaves for your wife's household," he said. "They came cheaply. Two whores a bit too well-used to turn a profit any longer. But the brothel-keeper said they were obedient creatures, and capable enough in the kitchen."

Damodara shrugged, as a bull might twitch off annoying and meaningless insects. His finger was busy tracing a route for his Pathan trackers through the Vindhyas, where they might serve to give advance warning of any Maratha ambush.

"As you command, my lord." A moment later the eunuch was gone. Damodara was only vaguely aware of his departure.

As soon as he entered his own tent, Narses gave Ajatasutra the "thumbs up" and extended the package. The assassin rose with his usual lazy grace and took it in hand.

"I *still* say that's an obscene gesture," he murmured. But he was through the tent flap before Narses could do more than begin his baleful glare.

Outside, Ajatasutra paced through the darkness enshrouding the army's camp with quick and sure feet. The flames of the various campfires provided little in the way of illumination, but that bothered him not in the least. Ajatasutra was quite fond of darkness, the truth be told.

The soldiers clustered about the campfire in one of the more distant groves never saw him coming until he was standing in their midst. Startled, the six men rose to their feet. All of them were experienced mercenaries. Two of them were Biharis, but the others were Ye-tai. In their cups, those four would have boasted that no man could catch them unawares.

They were not in their cups now, however. Ajatasutra had left clear instructions on that matter also. They stood still, awaiting their orders.

"Tonight," said Ajatasutra. "Immediately." He handed the package to one of the Bihari soldiers. "See to it—personally—that Lady Damodara receives this."

As the mercenaries hurriedly began making ready for departure, Ajatasutra stepped over to the small tent pitched nearby. He swept back the flap and peered inside.

The two sisters were wide awake, staring at him with apprehension. The light shed by a small oil lamp made their faces seem especially taut and hollow. The older sister was clutching the baby to her chest.

"No trouble?" he asked. The two girls shook their heads.

"Get ready," he said softly. "You're leaving tonight. For your new owner. The journey will be long, I'm afraid."

"Are you coming?" asked the younger.

Ajatasutra shook his head. "Can't. I have duties elsewhere." Then, seeing the sisters' apprehension turn to outright fear, Ajatasutra chuckled dryly. "Your new owner is reputed to be quite a nice *lady*."

His slight emphasis on the last word seemed to relieve their tension a bit. But only for a moment. Now, the sisters were staring past his figure, at the dimly seen shapes of the soldiers gearing up for travel.

Ajatasutra chuckled again. "There'll be no problem on the trip, other than days of heat and dust. I will leave clear instructions."

The stiffness in the sisters' posture eased. The older cleared her throat. "Will we see you again?"

Ajatasutra tossed his head in an abrupt, almost minute gesture. "Who knows? The world's a fickle place, and God is prone to whimsy."

He dropped the tent flap and turned away. In the minutes which followed, he simply stood in place at the center of the grove, watching the soldiers make their preparations. The Ye-tai were ready within minutes, their horses soon thereafter. What little delay occurred came from the two Bihari mercenaries and the small elephant in their care. Both men were experienced in the work. They would alternate as mahout and guard riding in the howdah.

But Ajatasutra's attention was not on the Biharis. He was not concerned about them. His careful study was given, first, to the howdah itself. Then, when he was satisfied that his instructions had been followed—the cloths serving as the howdah's curtains were cheap and utilitarian, but did an adequate job of shielding the occupants from external view—he turned his scrutiny upon the Ye-tai who would serve as the howdah's escort.

As was usually the case with Ye-tai, the semi-barbarians were big men. Big, and obviously fit. They were standing just a few feet away, their mounts not far behind them. If the heavy armor and weapons draped upon their muscular bodies caused them any discomfort, there was no sign of it.

Ajatasutra drifted toward them. At that moment, out of the corner of his eye, he saw the tent flap move aside. The sisters emerged and began walking slowly and timidly toward the elephant, the older one still clutching her infant. Ajatasutra had long since provided the sisters with more modest saris than the costumes they had worn as prostitutes. But, even in the poor lighting provided by the dying campfires, their young and lithesome figures were quite evident.

The eyes of the Ye-tai followed their progress, as did Ajatasutra's.

"Pretty little bitches, aren't they?" he mused. His voice, as usual, carried an undertone of whimsy and humor.

The Ye-tai in the center, the leader of the little group, grunted. "That they are. The older one's a bit off-putting, what with that scar on her face, but the young—"

His next grunt was not soft at all. More like an explosive breath—a man kicked by a mule. But the eruption ended almost as soon as it began. As the Ye-tai's head came down, Ajatasutra's dagger plunged into his eye. Halfway to the hilt, before a quick and practiced twist removed the blade before it could become jammed in the skull.

As the Ye-tai slumped to the ground, Ajatasutra stepped aside.

"Wrong answer," he said mildly. His eyes were on the three survivors.

For perhaps two seconds, the Ye-tai seemed frozen in place. The youngest and least experienced of them began moving his hand toward his sword, but one of his companions slapped the hand away.

"Uglier than sin, the both of them," the man rasped. "Rather fuck a crocodile, myself."

Ajatasutra's lips might have quirked a bit. It was difficult to tell, in the darkness. The same darkness, perhaps, explained the ghostly ease with which he now crowded the three mercenaries.

"I can find you anywhere in India," he murmured. "Anywhere in the world. Don't doubt it for a moment."

"A crocodile," husked the young Ye-tai.

Now, even in the darkness, Ajatasutra's smile was plain to see. "Splendid," he said agreeably. His hand—his left hand—dipped into his cloak and emerged holding a small pouch.

"A bonus," he explained. Then, nodding to the corpse: "For seeing to the quiet disposal of the body."

Feeling the weight of the pouch, the newly-promoted mercenary leader grinned. "Crocodile food. River's full of them."

"See to it." Ajatasutra gave a last glance at the elephant. The younger sister was already in the howdah and the older was handing up the baby. A moment later, the two mahouts were assisting her aboard the great creature.

The Ye-tai began to watch the procedure. Then, struck by a very recent memory, tore their eyes away and moved them back to their master.

But he was gone. Vanished into the night, like a demon from the ancient fables.

That very moment, in the far-distant Malwa capital of Kausambi, a demon from the fabled future came to its decision.

"NO CHOICE," it pronounced. "THE KUSHANS GROW MORE UNRELIABLE BY THE DAY. AND THE YE-TAI ARE NOT ENOUGH TO BOLSTER THE REGIME. WE MUST WELD THE RAJPUTS TO OUR SIDE."

The Emperor of Malwa made a last, feeble attempt to safeguard the exclusivity of his dynasty. "They are bound to us by solemn oaths as it is. You know how maniacally the Rajputs hold their honor. Surely—"

"THAT IS NOT ENOUGH. NOT WITH BELISARIUS COMING. THE PRESSURE WILL BECOME INTENSE. NOT EVEN RAJPUT HONOR CAN BE RELIED UPON TO WITHSTAND THOSE HAMMER BLOWS. THEY MUST ALSO BE WELDED BY TIES OF BLOOD. DYNASTIC TIES."

Skandagupta's corpulent little body began to swell like a toad. His mouth opened, ready to utter a final protest. But the sharp glance of Nanda Lal held him silent. That, and the frozen immobility of the four Khmer assassins standing against the nearby wall of the royal chamber. The assassins were all members of Link's special cult, as were the six enormous tulwar-bearing slaves kneeling against the opposite wall. The emperor had seen those knives and tulwars flash before, more than once. They would not hesitate for an instant to spill the life of Malwa's own ruler.

Ruler, in name only. The true power behind Malwa's throne resided in the body of the young woman who sat in the chair next to him. Lady Sati, she was called, one of Skandagupta's first cousins. But the name was as much of a shell as the body itself. Within that comely female form lurked the being called Link, the emissary and satrap of the new gods who were reshaping humanity into their own mold.

"IT WILL BE DONE," decreed the thing from the future. The slender hands draped loosely over the carved armrests made a slight gesture, as if to indicate the body within which Link dwelled. "THIS SHEATH IS PERFECTLY FUNCTIONAL. MUCH HEALTHIER THAN AVERAGE. IT WILL SERVE RANA SANGA AS WIFE AND MOTHER OF HIS CHILDREN. THE DYNASTY WILL THEN BE RAJPUT AS WELL AS MALWA. THE SWORDS AND LANCES OF RAJPUTANA WILL BE WELDED TO US WITH IRON BARS. TIES OF BLOOD."

Nanda Lal cleared his throat. "There is the matter of Sanga's existing wife. And his three existing children."

The thing inside Lady Sati swiveled her head. "A DETAIL. BY ALL ACCOUNTS, HIS WIFE IS PLAIN AND PLUMP." Again, the shapely hands made that little gesture. "THIS FORM IS BEAUTIFUL, AS MEN COUNT SUCH THINGS. AND, AS I SAID, PERFECTLY FUNCTIONAL. RAJPUTANA'S KING WILL HAVE NEW CHILDREN SOON ENOUGH. HE WILL BE RECONCILED TO THE LOSS."

The Malwa spymaster hesitated. This was dangerous ground. "Yes, of course. But my spies report that Sanga dotes on his family. He will still be upset—suspicious, even—if—"

"BY ROMAN HANDS. SEE TO IT, SPYMASTER. USE NARSES. HE WILL KNOW HOW TO MANAGE THE THING IN SUCH A WAY AS TO DIVERT SUSPICION ONTO THE ENEMY. SANGA WILL BLAME BELISARIUS FOR THE MURDER OF HIS FAMILY."

Very dangerous ground. But, whatever else he was, Nanda Lal was no coward. And, in his own cold way, as devoted to the Malwa purpose as any man alive.

"Narses cannot possibly be trusted," he growled. "He was a traitor to the Romans. He can betray us as well."

For the first time, the creature from the future seemed to hesitate. Watching, Skandagupta and Nanda Lal could only wonder at the exact thought processes which went on behind that cold, beautiful exterior. Lightning calculation, of course—that much was obvious from the years they had spent in Link's service. But not even the icy spymaster could imagine such an emptiness of all emotion. Try as he might.

"TRUE, NANDA LAL. BUT STILL NOT AN INSUPERABLE PROBLEM. BRING NARSES BEFORE ME. IN PERSON. I WILL DISCOVER THE TRUTH OF HIS LOYALTIES AND INTENTIONS."

"As you will, Lady Sati," stated Nanda Lal. He bowed his head obediently. An instant later, the Emperor of Malwa followed suit. The thing was settled, beyond any further discussion and dispute. And if neither man—especially Skandagupta—faced the prospect of a future half-Rajput dynasty with any pleasure, neither did they concern themselves over the possibility of Narses' treachery. Not with Link itself to ferret out the eunuch's soul. No man alive—no woman or child—could hide its true nature from that scrutiny. Not even their great enemy Belisarius had been able to accomplish *that*.

Chapter 6
MESOPOTAMIA
Spring, 533 A.D.

"What's the matter, large one? Are you sick?" asked Belisarius.
"You haven't complained once since we left Ctesiphon."

Sittas smiled cheerfully. Planting his feet firmly in the stirrups,
he raised himself off the saddle and heaved his huge body around
to study the army following in their tracks.

"Complain?" he demanded. "Why should I complain? God in
Heaven, would you look at the *size* of that thing!"

Belisarius copied Sittas' maneuver, albeit with considerably
more ease and grace. The army following them seemed to cover
the entire flood plain. To inexperienced eyes—such as those of
the peasants who stared at it from the relative safety of their
huts—it would have seemed like a swarm of locusts. And, for
the peasants, just about as welcome. True, Emperor Khusrau had
promised to pay for any damage done by the army in its passage.
Mesopotamian peasants, from the experience of millennia, viewed
imperial promises with a skepticism that would have shamed the
most rigorous Greek philosopher.

Belisarius had no difficulty finding the underlying order in the
seeming chaos.

Kurush's Persian dehgans, fifteen thousand strong, maintained
their position on the prestigious left flank. They had done so since

69

the moment the army's core passed through the gates of Ctesiphon and began collecting the units gathered outside the city. The gesture was a bit pointless, since there was no danger of a flank attack here in Mesopotamia. But the Persian aristocracy treasured its little points of honor.

Sittas' own units, the ten thousand heavy cataphracts from Constantinople and Anatolia, were assuming the equivalent position on the army's right wing. Whatever disgruntlement they might still be feeling at the implied slight was being exercised by their vigilance in keeping raiders from the desert at bay. Not that any Arab freebooter in his right mind would attack such an army, even if Belisarius didn't have his own Arab camel contingents riding on the flank of the cataphracts.

Belisarius smiled at the sight, but his study was soon concentrated on the army's center. The cataphracts and dehgans were familiar things. They had dominated warfare in the eastern Mediterranean for centuries. It was the units marching in the army's center which were new. *Very* new.

Sittas' own scrutiny had also reached the army's center. But, unlike Belisarius, his gaze was not one of pleasure and satisfaction.

"Silliest damned thing I've ever seen," he grumbled.

"Thank God," sighed Belisarius, apparently with great relief. "A complaint! I was beginning to wonder seriously about your health."

Sittas snorted. "I just hope you're right about this—this—what's his name?"

"Gustavus Adolphus." Belisarius turned back around and faced forward. He'd seen enough, and the position was awkward to maintain even with stirrups.

"Gustavus Adolphus," he repeated. "With an army more or less designed like this one, he defeated almost every opponent he ever faced. Most of whom had armies which, more or less, resembled the Malwa forces."

Sittas snorted again. " 'More or less, more or less,' " he echoed in a sing-song. "That does not *precisely* fill me with confidence. And didn't he get himself killed in the end?"

Belisarius shrugged. "Leading one of his insanely reckless cavalry charges in his last battle—which his army won, by the way, even with their king dead on the field."

Belisarius smiled crookedly. For a moment, he was tempted to turn around in the saddle and look at his bodyguards. He was quite certain that the faces of Isaac and Priscus, that very moment, were filled with solemn satisfaction at hearing such antics on the part of commanding generals described as "insane."

But he resisted the impulse. For all that he enjoyed teasing Sittas for his inveterate conservatism—

Damned dinosaur, came Aide's sarcastic thought.

—Belisarius also needed to have Sittas' confidence. So:

"You've already agreed, Sittas—or do we have to go through *this* argument again—that armored cavalry can't face unbroken gun-wielding infantry in the field."

"I know I did. Doesn't mean I have to like it." He raised a thick hand, as a man forestalls an unwanted lecture. "And *please* don't jabber at me again about Morgarten and Laupen and Morat and all those other heathen-sounding places where your precious Swiss pikemen of the future stood their ground against cavalry. I'm sick of hearing about it."

Sittas' voice slipped into an imitation of Belisarius' baritone. " 'As long as the gunmen are braced with solid infantry to protect them while they reload, they'll butcher any cavalry that comes against them.' Fine, fine, fine. I won't argue the point. Although I will point out"—here Sittas' tone grew considerably more enthusiastic—"that's only true as long as the infantry doesn't break and run. Which damn few infantry don't, when they see cataphracts thundering down on them."

Aide's voice came again. **Stubborn as a mule. Best give him a stroke or two. Or he'll sulk for the rest of the day.**

Belisarius had reached the same conclusion. His next words were spoken perhaps a bit hastily. "I'm certainly not arguing that cavalry isn't irreplaceable. Nothing like it for routing the enemy and completing their destruction—*after* their formations have been broken."

So did Belisarius pass the next hour or so, with Aide grousing in his mind and Sittas grumbling in his ear, extolling the virtues of cavalry under the right circumstances. By the time Maurice and Agathius arrived with a supply problem which needed Belisarius' immediate attention, Sittas seemed to be reasonably content.

Have to do it all over again tomorrow, concluded Aide sourly.

◇   ◇   ◇

Sittas rode off less than a minute after Agathius began explaining the problem. The big Greek nobleman's enthusiasm for logistics paralleled his enthusiasm for infantry tactics.

How did he ever win any campaigns, anyway? demanded Aide.

Belisarius was about to reply. But Maurice, as if he'd somehow been privy to the private mental exchange, did it for him.

The Thracian cataphract, born a peasant, gazed after the departing aristocratic general. Perhaps oddly, his face was filled with nothing more than approval. "Still trying to make him happy? Waste of time, lad, until Sittas has had a battle or two under his belt. But at least we won't have to worry about him breaking under the lesson. Not Sittas. If there's a more belligerent and ferocious general in the world, I don't know who it is. Besides, who really knows the future anyway? Maybe Sittas will lead one of his beloved cavalry charges yet."

By midafternoon, Agathius' problem was well on the way to solution. Agathius had only brought the problem to Belisarius because the difficulty was purely social, rather than technical, and he felt the commanding general needed to take charge. Some of the Persian dehgans were becoming vociferously indignant. Their mules, laden with burdens which were far too heavy for them, were becoming indignant themselves. Mules, unlike horses, cannot be driven beyond a certain point. The Persian mules reached that point as soon as the sun reached the zenith, and had promptly gone on what a future world would have called a *general strike*. And done so, moreover, with a solidarity which would have won the unadulterated approval of the most doctrinaire anarcho-syndicalist.

Even Persian dehgans knew that beating mules was pointless. So, turning upon less redoubtable opponents, they were demanding that room be made for their necessities in the supply barges which were streaming down the Tigris. The Mesopotamian and Greek sailors who manned those craft—no fools, they—steadfastly ignored the shouted demands of the dehgans on the banks and kept their barges a safe distance from the shore. So—

"They've been hollering at me for two hours, now," grumbled Agathius. "I'm getting tired of it."

Dehgans! grumbled Aide. **Only thing in the world that can make Greek noble cataphracts seem like sentient creatures.**

Belisarius turned to one of his couriers. For a moment, he hesitated. In campaigns past, Belisarius had always used veteran professionals for his dispatch riders. But on this campaign, he had felt it necessary to use young Greek nobles. Partly, to mollify the sentiments of the Roman empire's aristocracy, which was slowly becoming reconciled to the Justinian dynasty. But, mostly, to mollify the Persian aristocracy, which would take umbrage at orders transmitted to them by a commoner.

This particular dispatch rider was named Calopodius. He was no older than seventeen, and came from one of the Roman empire's most notable families. Belisarius had, tentatively, formed a good opinion of the boy's wits and tact. Both of which would be needed here.

Calopodius immediately confirmed the assessment. The boy's face showed no expression at all beyond calm alertness. But his words carried a certain dry humor, under the aristocratic drawl.

"I received excellent marks from both my rhetorician and grammarian, sir."

Belisarius grinned. "Splendid! In that case, you should have no difficulty whatsoever telling Kurush to get down to the river *immediately* and put a stop to this nonsense."

Calopodius nodded solemnly. "I don't see any difficulty, sir. Be much like the time my mother sent me to instruct my father's sister to quit pestering the stable boys." A moment later, he was gone, spurring his horse into a canter.

"I wonder if Alexander the Great had to put up with this kind of crap," mused Maurice.

"Of course not!" derided Belisarius. "The man was Achilles reborn. Who's going to give Achilles an argument?"

But the retort failed of its purpose. Lowborn or not, Maurice and Agathius were every bit as familiar with the Greek epics as any senator.

"Agamemnon," they chorused in unison.

Chapter 7

Antonina viewed the gadget with some disfavor. Ousanas, with considerably more.

"Romans are madmen," he growled. "Lunatics, pure and simple." He swiveled his head, bringing Ezana under his gaze.

"You are the admiral, Ezana. A seaman, where I am a simple hunter. Explain to this supposedly nautical-minded Roman"—here a fierce glare at John of Rhodes—"the simple truths which even a simpleminded hunter can understand." He flipped his hand toward the gadget, peremptorily, the way a man dismisses an annoying servant. "Like trying to use a lioness for a hunting dog. More likely to bite the master than the prey."

Ezana, like Ousanas, was scowling. But the Ethiopian naval commander's scowl was simply one of thoughtfulness.

"Stick to hunting and statesmanship, aqabe tsentsen," he grumbled. "You're supreme at the first and not an outright embarrassment at the second." He studied the gadget for another few seconds. "Hunting lioness . . . " he murmured. "Not a bad comparison, actually."

Ezana's scowl was suddenly replaced by a cheerful grin. "Not bad! But tell me, Ousanas—what if the lioness were genuinely tame? Or, at least, not quite feral?"

Presented with this outrageous possibility—*a tame lioness?*—Ousanas practically gurgled with outrage. His usual insouciant wit seemed to have completely deserted him.

"Never seen the man in such a state," commented Antonina slyly. She cocked her head at her companion. "You, Menander?"

But Menander was not about to enter *this* fray. The expression on his face was that of a man invited to enter a den of lions and argue the fine points of dining etiquette with its denizens. Clearly enough, the young Roman naval officer intended to champion the only safe and logical course. *Silence.*

Antonina smiled. Sweetly, at Menander; jeeringly, at Ousanas.

"Tame lioness! Not bad!" she exclaimed.

John of Rhodes, the designer of the gadget in question, finally entered the fray himself. His preceding silence, while one of his beloved contraptions was subjected to ridicule, was quite unlike the man. John of Rhodes had once been Rome's most acclaimed naval officer. Forced out of the navy because of his inveterate womanizing—which, alas, included seducing wives of several of his superior officers and visiting senatorial delegates—John had been plucked out of premature retirement by Belisarius and Antonina and put to work designing the new weapons which Aide had brought from the future. Then, as he showed as much energy and ability in that work as he had in his former career, John had found himself once again elevated to high naval rank. Higher, in substance if not in form, than any rank he had previously held. Officially, he was still a captain; in reality, he was the admiral of the Roman Empire's new fleet of gunpowder-armed warships. Its smallest fleet, true, but the only one which was growing by leaps and bounds.

Throughout the course of his checkered career, however, two things about John of Rhodes had remained constant. He was still a womanizer, although—under Antonina's blood-curdling threats—he had managed to keep his attentions away from the wives of Roman officers and Persian notables. And he was perhaps the most dyspeptic man Antonina had ever encountered. His preceding silence, while Ousanas scowled and sneered, was the surest indication that even John of Rhodes was a bit leery of his new invention.

Finally, however, he rallied. "The thing is perfectly safe!" he bellowed. John began stumping about the deck of the warship, gesticulating madly. "I got the idea from Belisarius himself! And none other than *Aide* gave *him* the design!" Stump; stump. "For your information, O great hunter from Africa"—here, he and

Ousanas matched magnificent sneers—"this device insured the supremacy of Rome at sea for centuries in—in—"

His right hand groped, trying to point to that unknown and unseen future which would have been, if the "new gods" of the future had not intervened in human history. The gesture was vague and uncertain. John had tried to seduce Irene Macrembolitissa on several occasions. The attempts had been quite futile, of course. Irene was not in the least susceptible to the charms of seducers. But, in her own lioness way, she had enjoyed toying with a would-be predator. So, on one occasion, she had fended off John's advances by a learned explanation of the logical complexities involved in changing the past by intervening from the future. Notions like the "river of time" had mingled freely with "paradox" and "conundrum." By the time she was done, John was exhausted, utterly confused, and resigned to a night of celibacy.

"—in that other history," he concluded lamely.

He rallied again, pointing with a stiff finger to the gadget. " '*Greek fire*' they'll call it! The scourge of Rome's enemies at sea."

Ousanas' thundering rejoinder was cut short by Ezana. "Why don't we try the thing out," he suggested mildly. "After all, what's the harm?"

The Ethiopian admiral's eyes scanned the Roman ship in whose bow the "gadget" was positioned. Christened the *Theodora Victrix*—whatever else he was, John of Rhodes was no fool—she was the latest warship to join the Roman fleet in the Erythrean Sea. And, though the ship had been built in Adulis by Ethiopian shipwrights, she was not an Axumite vessel. So—

"Worst that happens," Ezana concluded serenely, "is that the ship burns up."

John glared at him, but remained silent.

"That's it, then," decided Antonina. She headed for the gangway connecting the ship to the dock. She fluttered her hand toward Ousanas. "No doubt the aqabe tsentsen will wish to remain on board during the trial, scrutinizing every step of the operation with his keen hunter's eye."

Ousanas refrained from trampling Antonina in his hurry to get off the ship. But he only did so by the simple expedient of picking her up and carrying her off in his arms.

Ezana, oddly enough, decided to remain. Afterward, of course, he would claim he did so to maintain the reputation of Axum's

seamen. Bold, valiant—fearless as lions. But, in truth, the Ethiopian naval officer was simply curious. And he was not enough of
a hunter himself to understand the absurdity of a tame lioness.

In the end, the trial was a roaring success. Quite literally. Once
the *Theodora Victrix* and her two accompanying ships were completely out of sight of land, the cargo vessel being towed by the
Axumite galley on which Antonina and Ousanas were safely
perched was cut loose. Wallowing in the gentle waves of the Persian Gulf, while John made his final approach, the hulk seemed
like a witless calf at the mercy of a lioness.

As soon as the *Theodora Victrix* was within range, John ordered
his chief gunner Eusebius to activate the Greek fire cannon. This
took a bit of work, since the "cannon" was more in the nature of
a primitive pump than anything else. The gadget was temperamental as well as dangerous. But, soon enough, a satisfying gush of
roaring flames spouted from the barrel and fell upon the target
vessel.

Within seconds, the cargo hulk was a raging inferno. John of
Rhodes began capering about on the deck of the *Victrix*, making
gleeful—and, from the distance, suspiciously obscene-loo-
king—gestures at Ousanas on the observer ship. Within minutes,
he was helping Eusebius and the other gunners to pour amphorae
full of sand on those portions of the warship's bow which had been
set aflame by the last dribbles of the Greek fire cannon.

"We'll call it a roaring success," Antonina pronounced. She
pursed her lips, studying the frantic activities of the men on the
Victrix's bow. Then, cocking her head at Menander, added: "But
make sure that we put in another requisition for amphorae. And
you'd better tell John to start experimenting with different kinds
of sand."

Menander sighed. "Telling John" anything was akin to giving
orders to a temperamental predator. Best done from a distance—
best of all, by somebody else.

Ousanas snorted. "Tame lioness!"

But Menander's qualms proved unfounded. By the time the two
ships arrived back at the docks in Charax, John of Rhodes was in
splendid spirits. The minor mishap at the end, clearly enough, was

beneath contempt. Indeed, he even pranced off the ship proclaiming himself the need to find *slightly* more suitable chemicals for extinguishing fires at sea than simple desert sand.

"Chalk, maybe," he opined cheerfully. Standing on the docks, arms akimbo, John surveyed the landscape surrounding Charax with great serenity. "Got to be some, out there. For that matter, sea salt might do the trick. Plenty of that. And who knows? Maybe dried camel dung. *Plenty* of that stuff!"

Antonina left the matter to him. She was already surrounded by a small horde of Roman officers and Persian officials, each of whom was clamoring for her attention on some other matter of pressing concern. Throughout, Antonina maintained her composure, and issued the necessary orders. By now, she was an accomplished general in her own right, and had long since learned one of the basic axioms of war. *Amateurs study tactics; professionals study logistics.*

By sundown, she was able to relax in the comfort of the small villa she had obtained in Charax's best quarter. More or less.

"Do we *have* to settle the question of the camel provender?" she demanded crossly, pausing in the act of pouring herself a goblet of wine. *"Tonight?"*

A sheepish expression came upon Menander's face. "Well . . . No, actually. It can wait. Not as if there's any shortage of Arabs eager and willing to provide it for us." Perched on a chair across from the divan where Antonina lounged, Menander scowled. "It's just— Damned hagglers! Always got to allow extra time dickering with Arabs."

The Thracian villager surfaced: "Bad as Greeks!"

Antonina smiled. Then, after savoring the first sip of wine and cocking an eye at Ezana and Ousanas—also lounging on nearby divans; no alert chair-perching for *them*—she murmured: "Don't you have another pressing engagement yourself tonight, Menander?"

The Roman officer flushed. His eyes were riveted on Antonina, as if by sheer force of will he would keep them from flitting to the fearsome figure of his paramour's half-brother.

Thankfully, Ezana was in a good mood. So he eased Menander over the hurdle.

"Best run, boy. Keep my eager sister waiting and she'll likely take up with some passing stray Arab." Smugly: "Who will *not*—given the way Deborah looks—waste any time at all in *haggling*."

Seeing the look of sudden alarm which now flitted across Menander's face, Antonina could not stop herself from giggling. "Go!" she choked, waving her hand. A moment later, Menander did as he was commanded.

When he was gone, Antonina looked at Ezana. "She wouldn't really, would she?"

Ezana shrugged. "Probably not. The silly girl's quite infatuated with the lad."

Antonina's head now swiveled to bring Ousanas under her gaze. The humor left her eyes entirely.

"Speaking of infatuation."

Glaring at Ousanas, in the scale of "waste of effort," ranked somewhere in the vicinity of the labors of Sisyphus. Ethiopia's aqabe tsentsen responded with the same grin with which the former slave dawazz had greeted similar scowls from Axumite royalty.

"I fail to see the problem," he said. "True, the girl was a virgin. But—"

He waved his own hand. Ousanas, like Belisarius' cataphract Anastasius, was a devotee of Greek philosophy. The gesture carried all the certainty of Plato pronouncing on a small problem of ontology. "That is by the nature of things a temporary state of affairs. Certainly with a girl as lively and pretty as Koutina. Who better than me to have assisted her through that necessary passage?"

Antonina maintained the glare, even in the face of that peerless grin.

"Besides, Antonina, you know perfectly well that having the secure loyalty of your personal maid is essential to the success of our enterprise. Koutina will be at the top of the list for every enterprising Malwa spy here in Charax. Of which there are probably several hundred by now, at least half of which are superb seducers—and just as good once they get the girl in bed as they were getting her there in the first place."

Again, Ousanas made that philosophical gesture. "So I view my activities as a necessary concomitant of my diplomatic duties. So to speak. Foiling the machinations of the wicked enemy with my own incomparable stroke of statecraft. So to speak."

Antonina hissed: "If she gets pregnant—"

Finally, the grin faded. For once, there was nothing of the brazen jester in Ousanas' expression. "I have already asked her to become my concubine, Antonina," he said softly. "Once the war is over. And she has agreed."

He did not add any further promise. There was no need. Of many things, people might wonder about the strange man named Ousanas. Of his honesty, no one had any doubt at all.

Certainly not Antonina. Indeed, she was quite taken aback by the aqabe tsentsen's statement. She had simply intended to obtain a promise from Ousanas to see to it that her maid was taken care of properly, once the dalliance was over. She had never expected—

"Concubine," in Axum's elite, was a prestigious position. The position of wife, of course, was reserved for diplomatic and political necessities. But an officially recognized concubine was assured a life of security and comfort—even wealth and power, in the case of the aqabe tsentsen's concubine.

Koutina was a peasant girl from the Fayum, born into the great mass of Egypt's poor. Her own children would now enter directly into the world of status, with not even the slight blemish which Roman society attached to such offspring.

Ousanas' grin made its triumphant reentry. "So? Are there any other concerns you wish to raise?"

Antonina cleared her throat. From long experience, she knew it was *essential* to rally in the face of Ousanas' grin.

"Yes!" she piped. Sternly: "We must see to the final preparations for the landing at Barbaricum. Belisarius, you know, *insists* on accompanying Valentinian and the others up to the very moment when they are set ashore in India. Even—so he told me in his last message—if he has to leave his army before they finish the march to Charax."

Ezana groaned. "Antonina, that's *already* the best-planned and best-prepared military expedition in the history of the world." Scowling: "The only uncertainty—you said so yourself, just this morning!—was the reliability of the Greek fire weapon. Which we just tested this very day!"

Rally. "There are still some minor logistical matters to be settled!" Antonina insisted.

Ezana groaned again. Ousanas clapped his hands.

"Ridiculous!" he stated. "Petty stuff which can be well enough handled by your host of underlings." The aqabe tsentsen drained his goblet and placed it on the small side table nearby.

"We have *much* more important matters to discuss. I got into an argument with Irene, just the day before she and Kungas set off on that harebrained expedition of theirs. Can you believe that the crazed woman has been studying these idiot Buddhist philosophers lately? Mark my words! Give it a year and she'll be babbling the same nonsense as that Raghunath Rao fellow. *Maya*, the so-called 'veil of illusion.' All that rot!"

Ousanas leaned forward on his divan, hands planted firmly on knees. "Our duty is clear. We must arm ourselves in advance—*re-arm* ourselves, I should say—with the principles of Greek philosophy. I propose to begin with a survey of the dialectic, beginning with Socrates."

Antonina and Ezana stared at each other. Even the black Ethiopian's face seemed pale.

"Logistics," choked Ezana. "Critical to any successful military enterprise." Hastily he rose and began pacing about. "Can't afford to overlook even the slightest detail. The matter of the brass fittings for the stays is particularly critical. Can't ever have enough! And the metalsmiths here in Charax are already overworked."

He slammed hard fist into firm palm. "So! I propose the following—"

Chapter 8

BARBARICUM
Spring, 533 A.D.

The first rocket was a flare, one of the newly designed ones with a small parachute. After it burst over the ramparts at Barbaricum, it drifted down slowly, lighting the area with an eerie glow. Within seconds, several other flares came to add their own demonic illumination.

"Open fire!" roared John of Rhodes.

Immediately, the small fleet of Roman warships under John's command began firing their cannons into the shipping anchored in the harbor. Under cover of night, John had sailed his flotilla into gunnery range without being spotted by the sentries on the walls of the city. The larger fleet of Ethiopian warships following in his wake began adding their own gunfire to the brew.

John's ships, pure sailing craft, would be limited to one pass at the Malwa shipping. The Axumite vessels, with their oared capability, would wind up doing most of the damage even though none of those galleys carried the same weight of cannon. Without the necessity of tacking back upwind in order to escape—*not* something John wanted to do once the huge siege cannons on Barbaricum's walls began firing—the Ethiopians would be able to take the time to launch the fireships.

For that reason, John was all the more determined to wreak as much havoc as he could in the short time available. In particular, he was determined to strike at the Malwa warships—which, unfortunately, were moored behind a screening row of merchant vessels. Now that the flares were burning brightly, he could see those war galleys moored against the piers.

"Closer!" he bellowed, leaving it to his sailing master to translate the command into nautical terms.

Standing on the deck at John's side, Eusebius winced. Through his thick spectacles—another of the many new inventions which Aide's counsel had brought into the Roman world—the gunnery officer could see the mouths of the siege cannons overlooking the harbor, illuminated by the cannon fire and the flares. Once they came into action, those guns would be firing stone balls weighing more than two hundred pounds. True, the siege cannons were as awkward to load and fire as they were gigantic, and the weapons were wildly inaccurate. Unlike smaller cannons, whose bores could be hand-worked into relative uniformity and for which marble or iron cannon balls could be polished to a close fit, the giant siege guns and their stone missiles were the essence of crudity. But if one of those balls *did* hit a ship . . .

Eusebius winced again.

"Closer, damn you!" bellowed John.

A few miles further south along the Indus delta, Belisarius had a dazzling view of the battle which was taking shape in Barbaricum's harbor. At the distance, of course, he couldn't see any of the details. Not even with his telescope. But the visual and auditory display was truly magnificent. Which, when all was said and done, was the whole point of the exercise. Whatever damage John and the Ethiopians succeeded in inflicting on the Malwa at Barbaricum, the true purpose of that bombardment was to divert attention from Belisarius' doings.

"All right, General," growled Valentinian. "You can stop smiling so damned crookedly. I admit that you were right and I was wrong." Sourly: "Again."

In the darkness, there was no way Valentinian could have spotted that smile on Belisarius' face, not even standing next to him. Still, the general removed the smile. He reflected, a bit ruefully,

that Valentinian knew him more than well enough to know Belisarius' characteristics.

So did Aide, for that matter. **Damned stupid crooked smile,**
came his own surly thought.

There was no moon that night. There was not even a starblaze.
India's monsoon season had begun, and the sky was heavily overcast. Except for the distant glare of the flares and cannon fire, the
nearby coast was shrouded in darkness.

In that same darkness, Valentinian and Anastasius and Kujulo
began lowering themselves into the river barge which had pulled
alongside their vessel. The barge had been towed all the way from
Charax. It was one of the Indian vessels which had been captured
after the Malwa invasion of Persia was defeated the year before.
Belisarius had chosen it because it would be indistinguishable from
the other barges plying their trade along the Indus river.

Lowering themselves slowly and carefully—falling into the sea
laden with armor and weapons was the fastest way to drown that
the human race had ever discovered—the three leaders of the
expedition eventually found the security of the barge's deck. As
their accompanying party of Kushan soldiers followed, Anastasius'
voice came up out of the darkness.

"Any last instructions?" the giant Thracian cataphract asked.

"No. Just be careful."

That statement was met by the sound of muttering. Valentinian's
last words, Belisarius was quite certain, consisted of pure profanity.

Don't blame him, said Aide. The thought was almost a mutter
itself. Aide had reconciled himself to Belisarius losing his best
bodyguards, but he was still not happy with the situation.

Belisarius made no reply to either voice. In truth, he was not
feeling any of the usual surety which accompanied his decisions.
This expedition—everything about it—was dictated by the logic of
spycraft, not warcraft. That was not a realm of human endeavor
in which the Roman general felt completely at ease. He was relying
heavily on Irene's advice, coupled with his own estimate of an old
eunuch. A traitor, to boot.

The lines holding the barge to the warship were cast off. Belisarius could hear the barge's oars begin to dip into the water, moving
the craft toward the unseen mouth of one of the delta's outlets.

"I hope you know what you're doing, Narses," he whispered.

The uneasy thought of Narses' former treason brought a sudden whimsy to his mind. For a moment, he hesitated, gauging the noise. Then, satisfied that the roar of the distant battle would disguise any sound, he shouted a few words toward the receding barge.

"Anastasius! You're a philosopher! What do you think of the veil of illusion?"

Anastasius' rumbling voice came back out of the darkness. "You mean that Hindu business about 'Maya?' Bunch of silly heathen rot. No, General—things are what they are. Sure, Plato says they're only a shadow of their own reality, but that's not the same—"

The rest was lost in gunroar and distance. But Belisarius' crooked smile was back.

"This'll work," he said confidently.

Mutter mutter mutter, was Aide's only comment.

"I think maybe we should—"

Eusebius fell silent. Even after his years of close association with John, Eusebius knew better than to prod the Rhodian. Right at the top of John's multitude of character traits, admirable or otherwise, *stubbornness* took pride of place.

But even John, it seemed, was satisfied at the destruction which his flotilla had inflicted on the Malwa vessels anchored in the harbor. His cannonade, combined with the guns of the Ethiopians, had pounded much of the shipping into mastless and unmaneuverable wrecks. True, he hadn't been able to strike very hard at the war galleys moored to the piers. The merchant vessels—just as the Malwa no doubt intended—had served as a protective screen.

The issue was moot. John had no doubt at all that every seaman on those merchant ships had long since abandoned their vessels and fled to the safety of the shore on whatever lifeboats had been available. There would be no one left to prevent—

"That's the first one," said Eusebius with satisfaction.

John looked to the north. The Axumites had lit the first of the fireships and were pushing it off. Within seconds, John could see the other three fireships burst into sudden flames.

He moved his cold eyes back to the harbor. "That's so much kindling, now," he grunted with satisfaction. With the prevailing winds as they were, the fireships would inexorably drift into the tangled mass of battered merchant shipping. Given the speed with which fire spread across wooden ships, all of the vessels in Barbaricum's harbor would be destroyed soon enough.

"Time to go," he stated. He turned and issued the orders to the sailing master.

No sooner was he done than a huge roar filled the harbor. The ramparts of the city were suddenly illuminated by their own cannon fire. The huge siege guns had finally gone into action.

Eusebius flinched, a little, under the sound. John grinned like a wolf.

"Relax, boy. A first salvo—fired in the darkness? They'll be lucky if they even manage to hit the ocean."

Realizing the truth of the Rhodian's words, Eusebius relaxed. His shoulders, tense from the past minutes of action, began to slump.

A moment later, not knowing how he got there, Eusebius was lying on the deck of the ship. The entire vessel was rolling, as if it had collided with something.

There are no reefs in this harbor, he thought dazedly. Every shipmaster we talked to swore as much.

The area of the ship where he had been standing was half-illuminated by the flames of the fireships drifting into Barbaricum's harbor. Eusebius could see that a section of the rail had vanished, along with a piece of the deck itself. In front of him, lying on the shattered wooden planks, was an object which Eusebius thought he recognized. By the time he crawled over and picked it up, the helmsman was shouting at him.

Still half-dazed, Eusebius realized the man was demanding instructions. The sailing master had apparently also vanished.

There was no need, really, for the steersman to be given orders. Their course was obvious enough, after all. *Get the hell out of here.* The steersman was simply seeking reassurance that leadership still existed.

Shakily, Eusebius rose to his feet and shouted something back at the steersman. Anything. He didn't even think of the words themselves. He simply imitated, as best he could, the assured authority with which John of Rhodes issued all his commands.

Apparently the tone was enough. Broken planks falling into the sea from the splintered deck and rail, the ship sailed out of Barbaricum's harbor. On what remained of that portion of the deck, Eusebius studied the object in his hands, as if it were a talisman.

◇   ◇   ◇

An hour later, the barge on which Valentinian and his expedition was making its way up the Indus was part of a small fleet of river craft, all of them fleeing from the battle at Barbaricum.

"Worked like a charm," grunted Kujulo. The Kushan gazed at the small horde of vessels with satisfaction. The vessels were easy to spot, fortunately. All of them—just as was true of their own barge—had a lookout in the bow holding a lamp aloft. For all the urgency with which the river craft were making their escape from the holocaust in Barbaricum, the oarsmen were maintaining a slow and steady stroke. Except for the meager illumination thrown out by the lamps, the night was pitch dark. No merchant—and these were all merchant vessels—wanted to escape ruin in a besieged harbor only to find it by running his ship aground.

"Worked like a charm," Kujulo repeated. "Nobody will ever notice us in this mob. Just another batch of worthless traders scurrying for cover."

As usual, Valentinian looked on the dark side of things. "They'll turn into so many pirates in a heartbeat, they learn what cargo we're carrying."

Kujulo's grin was wolfish. "Two chests full of Red Sea coral? A small fortune, true enough. I tremble to think of our fate, should these brave river men discover the truth."

Anastasius snorted sarcastically. After a moment's glower, Valentinian's own grin appeared. Very weaselish, it was.

"Probably not the worst of our problems, is it?" he mused, fingering the hilt of his sword. But it was only a momentary lightening of his gloom. Soon enough, he was back to muttering.

"Oh, will you stop it?" demanded Anastasius crossly. "Things *could* be worse, you know."

"Sure they could," hissed Valentinian. "We could be floating down the Nile, bound hand and foot, fighting crocodiles with our teeth. We could be hanging upside down by our heels in the Pit, fending off archdevils with spit. We could—"

Mutter, mutter, mutter.

By the time Belisarius and his ship made the rendezvous with the Roman/Ethiopian fleet which had savaged Barbaricum, the sun was rising. So, as he climbed the rope ladder onto John of

Rhodes' flagship, he got a good view of the damage done to it amidships. One of the huge stone cannon balls, clearly enough, had made a lucky hit in the darkness. Fortunately, the ship was still intact below the water line, and the masts had remained unscathed.

Eusebius met him at the railing.

"Where's John?" demanded Belisarius.

The nearsighted gunnery officer made a face. Silently, he led Belisarius over to a folded, blood-stained piece of canvas lying on the center of the deck. Then, squatting, he flipped back the canvas covering and exposed the object contained within.

Belisarius hissed. The canvas contained a human arm, which appeared to have been ripped off at the shoulder as if by a giant. Then, spotting the ring on the square, strong-fingered hand, he sighed.

Antonina had given John that ring, years ago, as part of the subterfuge by which she had convinced Malwa's spies that the Rhodian was one of her many lovers. Once the subterfuge had served its purpose, John had offered to return it. But he had immediately added his wish to keep the thing, with her permission. His "lucky ring," he called it, which had kept him intact through the many disastrous early experiments with gunpowder.

"May God have mercy on his soul," Belisarius murmured.

Next to him, a voice spoke. The bitterness in the tone went poorly with its youthful timber.

"Stupid," growled Menander. "Pure blind fucking bad luck. A first salvo, fired at night? They should have been lucky to even hit the damned ocean."

Belisarius straightened, and sighed again. "That's the way war works. It's worth reminding ourselves, now and again, so we don't get too enamored of our own cleverness. There's a lot of just pure luck in this trade."

The general planted a hand on Menander's shoulder. "When did you come aboard?" Menander, he knew, had been in command of one of the other ships in the flotilla.

"Just a few minutes ago. As soon as there was enough light to see what had happened, I—" The young officer fell silent, cursing under his breath.

Belisarius now squeezed the shoulder. "You realize that you've succeeded to the command of John's fleet?"

Menander nodded. There was no satisfaction at all in that gesture. But neither, Belisarius was pleased to see, was there any hesitation.

"So it is," stated the general. "That will include those two new steam-powered ships Justinian's building, once they get here from Adulis. You're more familiar with them than anyone except Justinian anyway, as much time as you've spent with the old emperor since he got to Adulis."

Menander smiled wryly. When Justinian had been Emperor of Rome, before his blinding by Malwa traitors had disqualified him under Roman law and custom, he had been an enthusiastic gadget-maker. Since he relinquished the throne in favor of his adopted son Photius, Justinian's hobby had become practically an obsession. Along with John of Rhodes, Justinian had become the chief new weapons designer for the Roman empire. And he loved nothing so much as the steam engines he had designed with Aide's advice and whose construction he had personally overseen. Even to the extent of accompanying the engines to the Ethiopian capital of Adulis and supervising their installation in ships specially designed for the purpose.

Throughout that work, Menander had been the officer assigned to work with Justinian. The experience had been . . . "Contradictory," was Menander's diplomatic way of putting it. On the one hand, he had been able to spend a lot of time with Deborah also. On the other hand . . .

He sighed. "I could usually manage an entire day in Justinian's company without losing my temper. Barely. John of Rhodes couldn't last ten minutes." He stared down at the severed arm. "Damn, I'll miss him. So will Justinian, don't think he won't."

Belisarius stooped and flipped the covering back over its grisly contents. "We'll send this to Constantinople. I'll include instructions—'recommendations,' I suppose I should say—to my son. Photius will see to it that John of Rhodes gets a solemn state funeral, by God. With all the pomp and splendor."

Even in the sorrow of the moment, that statement caused a little chuckle to emerge from the crowd of Roman officers standing nearby.

"I'd love to be there," murmured one of them. "Be worth it just to see the sour faces on all those senators John cuckolded."

Belisarius smiled, very crookedly. "John will answer to God for his failings." The smile vanished, and the next words rang like iron hammered on an anvil. "But there will be no man to say that he failed in his duty to the Empire. *None.*"

Chapter 9
INDIA
Spring, 533 A.D.

"I've had enough," snarled Raghunath Rao. "Enough!"

He spent another few seconds glaring at the corpses impaled in the village square, before turning away and moving toward the horses. Some of the Maratha cavalrymen in Rao's company began removing the bodies from the stakes and preparing a funeral pyre.

Around them, scurrying to gather up their few possessions, the villagers made ready to join Rao's men in their march back to Deogiri. None would be foolish enough to remain behind, not after the Wind of the Great Country had scoured another Malwa garrison from the face of the earth. Malwa repercussions would be sure to follow. Lord Venandakatra, the Goptri of the Deccan, had long ago pronounced a simple policy. Any villagers found anywhere in the area where the Maratha rebellion struck a blow would pay the penalty. The Vile One's penalties *began* with impalement. "Ringleaders" would be taken to Bharakuccha for more severe measures.

Other soldiers in Rao's company had already finished executing the survivors of the little Malwa garrison they had overrun. Unlike the villagers who had been impaled—"rebels," by Malwa decree; and many of them were—Rao's men had satisfied themselves with quick decapitations. Some of the cavalrymen were piling the heads in a small mound at the center of the village. There would be no honorable funeral pyre for *that* carrion. Others were readying the horses for the march.

"Enough, Maloji," Rao murmured to his lieutenant. For all the softness of his tone, the sound of it was a panther's growl. "The time has come. Lord Venandakatra has outlived his welcome in this turn of the wheel."

Maloji eyed him skeptically. "The empress is already unhappy enough with you for participating in these raids. Do you seriously expect—"

"I am her husband!" barked Rao. But, a moment later, the stiffness in his face dissolved. Rao was too much the philosopher to place much credence in customary notions of a wife's proper place in the world. Any wife, much less *his*. Trying to browbeat the empress Shakuntala—wifely status be damned; age difference be damned—was as futile a project as he could imagine.

"I made her a promise," he said softly. "But once that promise is fulfilled, I am free. To *that*, she agreed. Soon, now."

Maloji was still skeptical. Or, perhaps, simply stoic. "It's a first pregnancy, old friend. There are often complications."

Finally, Rao's usual good humor came back. "With *her*? Be serious!" He gathered up the reins of his horse with one hand while making an imperious gesture with the other. "She will simply decree the thing: *Child, be born—and don't give me any crap about it.*"

In her palace at Deogiri, Shakuntala was filled with quite a different sentiment. Staring down at her swollen belly, her face was full of apprehension.

"It will hurt, some," said Gautami. Dadaji Holkar's wife smiled reassuringly and placed a gentle hand on the empress' shoulder. "But even as small as you are, your hips are well-shaped. I really don't think—"

Shakuntala brushed the matter aside. "I'm not worried about that. It's these ugly stretch marks. Will they go away?"

Abruptly, with a heavy sigh, Shakuntala folded the robe back around herself. Gautami studied her carefully. She did not think the empress was really concerned about the matter of the stretch marks. If nothing else, Shakuntala was too supremely self-confident to worry much over such simple female vanities. And she *certainly* wasn't concerned about losing Rao's affections.

That left—

Shakuntala confirmed the suspicion. "Soon," she whispered, stroking her belly. "Soon the child will be born, and the dynasty assured. And Rao will demand his release. As I promised."

Gautami hesitated. Her husband was the peshwa of the empire of Andhra, reborn out of the ashes which Malwa had thought to leave it. As such, Gautami was privy to almost every imperial secret. But, still, she was the same woman who had been born and raised in a humble town in Majarashtra. She did not feel comfortable in these waters.

Shakuntala perhaps sensed her unease. The empress turned her head and smiled. "Nothing you can do, Gautami. Or say. I simply want your companionship, for the moment." She sighed again. "I will need it, I fear, in the future. There will be no keeping Rao. Not once the child is born."

Gautami said nothing. Her unease aside, there was nothing to say.

Once the dynasty was assured, the Panther of Majarashtra would slip his leash. As surely as the sun rises, or the moon sets. No more to be stopped than the tide. Or the wind.

Yet, while Gautami understood and sympathized with her empress' unhappiness, she did not share it herself. When all was said and done, Gautami *was* of humble birth. One of the great mass of the Maratha poor, who had suffered for so long—and so horribly—under the lash of the Vile One.

Her eyes moved to the great window in the north wall of the empress' bedchamber. As always, in the hot and dry climate of the Deccan, the window was open to the breeze. From high atop the hill which was the center of Andhra's new capital city of Deogiri—the *permanent* capital, so Shakuntala had already decreed; in this, as in her marriage, she had welded Andhra to the Marathas—Gautami could see the rocky stretches of the Great Country.

Beyond that, she could not see. But, in her mind's eye, Gautami could picture the great seaport of Bharakuccha. She had been there, twice. Once, as a young wife, visiting the fabled metropolis in the company of her educated husband. The second time, as a slave captured in Malwa's conquest of the Deccan. She could still remember those squalid slave pens; still remember the terrified faces of her young daughters as they were hauled off by the brothel-keeper who had purchased them.

And, too, she could remember the sight of the great palace which loomed above the slave pens. The same palace where, for three years now, Lord Venandakatra had made his residence and headquarters.

"Soon," she murmured.

Near the headwaters of the Chambal, Lord Venandakatra's lieutenant was haranguing Lord Damodara and Rana Sanga. Chandasena, his name was, and he was much impressed by his august status in the Malwa scheme of things.

It was a very short harangue. Though Chandasena was of noble Malwa brahmin stock—a Mahaveda priest, in fact—Lord Damodara was a member of the *anvaya-prapta sachivya*, as the Malwa called the hereditary caste who dominated their empire. Blood kin to Emperor Skandagupta himself.

Perhaps more to the point, Rana Sanga was Rajputana's greatest king.

Fortunately, Sanga was no more than moderately annoyed. So the backhanded cuff which sent Chandasena sprawling in the dirt did no worse than split his lip and leave him stunned and confused. When he recovered his wits sufficiently to understand human speech, Lord Damodara furthered his education.

"My army has marched to Mesopotamia and back again, and across half of India in the bargain, and defeated every foe which came against us. Including even Belisarius himself. And Lord Venandakatra—*and you*—presume to instruct me on the proper pace of a march?"

The short Malwa lord paused, staring at the hills about him with hands placed on hips. The hips, like the lord's belly, no longer retained the regal fat which had once adorned them. But his little hands were still as plump as ever.

"Venandakatra?" he mused softly. "Who has not marched out of his palace since Rao penned him in Bharakuccha? Whose concept of logistics is to whip his slaves when they fail to feed him appropriate viands for his delicate palate?"

Damodara brought his eyes down to the figure sprawled on the ground. Normally mild-mannered, Malwa's finest military commander was clearly fighting to restrain his temper.

"*You?*" he demanded. The hands on hips tightened. "Rana Sanga!" he barked. "Do me the favor of instructing this dog again on the subject of military travel."

"My pleasure, Lord." Rajputana's mightiest hand reached down, seized the Vile One's envoy by his finery, and hauled him to his feet as easily as he might pluck a fruit.

"In order to get from one place to another," Sanga said softly, "an army must get from one place to another. Much like"—a large finger poked the envoy's nose—"this face gets to the dirt of the road." And so saying, he illustrated the point with another cuff.

Sometime later, a less-assured envoy listened in silence as Lord Damodara gave him the reply to Lord Venandakatra.

"Tell the Vile—*him*—that I will arrive in the Deccan as soon as possible. Of which I will be the judge, not he. And tell him that the next insolent envoy he sends will be instructed with a sword, not a hand."

After Chandasena had made his precipitous departure, Rana Sanga sighed. "Venandakatra *is* the emperor's first cousin," he pointed out. And we *will* be under his authority once we enter the Deccan."

Lord Damodara did not seem notably abashed. "True, and true," he replied. Again, he surveyed the scene around him, with hands on hips. But his stance was relaxed, now, and his eyes were no longer on the hills.

His round face broke into a cheery smile. "Authority, Rana Sanga, is a much more elusive concept than people realize. On the one hand, there is consanguinity to royal blood and official post and status. On the other—"

A stubby forefinger pointed to the mass of soldiers streaming by. "On the other, there is the *reality* of twenty thousand Rajputs, and ten thousand Ye-tai and kshatriyas who have been welded to them through battles, sieges and victories. And, now, some ten thousand new Bihari and Bengali recruits who are quickly learning their place."

Sanga followed the finger. His experienced eye picked out at once what Damodara was indicating. In every other Malwa army but this one, the component forces formed separate detachments. The Ye-tai served as security battalions; the Malwa kshatriyas as privileged artillery troops. Rajputs, of course, were elite cavalry. And the great mass of infantrymen enrolled in the army—peasants from one or another of the many subject nations of the Gangetic plain—formed huge but poorly-equipped and trained levies.

Not here. Damodara's army was a Rajput army, at its core, though the Rajputs no longer formed a majority of the troops. But the Ye-tai—whose courage was admired and respected, if not their semi-barbarous character—were intermingled with the Rajputs. As were the kshatriyas, and, increasingly—and quite to their surprise—the new Bengali and Bihari recruits.

"The veil of illusion," mused Sanga. "Philosophers speak of it."

"So they do," concurred Damodara. His air seemed one of detachment and serenity. "The *best* philosophers."

That night, in Lord Damodara's headquarters tent, philosophical detachment and serenity were entirely absent.

For all that he was an old man, and a eunuch, Narses was as courageous as any man alive. But now, reading again the summons from the Grand Palace, he had to fight to keep his hands from trembling.

"It arrived today?" he asked. For the second time, which was enough in itself to indicate how shaken he was.

Damodara nodded somberly. He made a vague gesture with his hand toward the entrance flap of the tent. "You would have passed by the courier on your way in. I told him to wait outside until I had spoken to you."

Narses' eyes flitted around the interior of the large tent. Clearly enough, Damodara had instructed *everyone* to wait outside. None of his officers were present, not even Rana Sanga. And there were no servants in the tent. That, in its own way, indicated just how uneasily Damodara himself was taking the news.

Narses brought himself under control, with the iron habit of a lifetime spent as an intriguer and spymaster. He gave Lord Damodara a quick, shrewd glance.

First things first. Reassure my employer.

"Of course," he said harshly, "I will report to Great Lady Sati that you have never given me permission to do anything other than my officially specified duties. Which is the plain and simple truth, as it happens."

Lord Damodara's tension seemed to ease a bit. "Of course," he murmured. He studied his spymaster carefully.

"You have met Great Lady Sati, I believe?"

Narses shook his head. "Not exactly. She was present, yes, when I had my one interview with Great Lady Holi. After my defection from Rome, and before Great Lady Holi departed for Mesopotamia. Where she met her death at Belisarius' hands."

He left unspoken the remainder: *and was—replaced?—by Great Lady Sati.*

"But Lady Sati—she was not Great Lady, then—said nothing in the interview."

Damodara nodded and began pacing slowly back and forth. His hands were pressed together as if in prayer, which was the lord's habit when he was engaged in deep thought.

Abruptly, he stopped his pacing and turned to face Narses squarely.

"How much do you *know*, Roman?"

Narses understood the meaning. "Malwa is ruled by a hidden—something. A *being*, let us call it. I do not know its true name. Once, it inhabited the body of Great Lady Holi. Today, it resides in Great Lady Sati. Whatever it is, the being has supernatural powers. It is not of this earth. I believe, judging from what I have learned, that it claims to come from the future."

After a moment's hesitation, he added: "A divine being, Malwa believes it to be."

Damodara smiled thinly. "And you?"

Narses spread his hands. "What is divinity, Lord? For Hindus, the word *deva* refers to a divine creature. For Zoroastrians, it is the word assigned to demons. What, in the end, is really the difference—to the men who stand under its power?"

"What, indeed?" mused Damodara. He resumed his pacing. Again, his hands were pressed together. "Whatever the being may be, Narses—divine or not, from the future or not—have no doubt of one thing. It is truly superhuman."

He stopped and, again, turned to face the eunuch. "One thing in particular you must understand. A human being *cannot* lie to Li—the being—and keep the lie from being detected."

Narses' eyes did not widen in the least. The spymaster had already deduced as much, from his own investigations.

"It *cannot* be done," the Malwa lord reiterated forcefully. "Do not even imagine the possibility."

Narses reached up and stroked his jaw. "The truth only, you say?" Then, seeing Damodara's nod, he asked: "But tell me this, Lord. Can this being truly read a man's thoughts?"

Damodara hesitated. For a moment, he seemed about to resume his pacing, but instead he simply slumped a bit.

"I am not certain, Narses."

"Your *estimate*, then." The words were spoken in the tone of command. But the lord gave no sign of umbrage at this unwarranted change of relationship. At the moment, his own life hung by as slender a thread as the eunuch's.

Whatever his doubts and uncertainties, Damodara was an experienced as well as a brilliant military commander. Decisiveness came naturally to him, and that nature had been honed by his life.

"No," he said firmly. "In the end, I do not believe so. I think it is simply that the being is—is—" He groped for the words.

Narses' little exhalation of breath seemed filled with satisfaction. "A superhuman spymaster. Which can study the same things any spymaster learns to examine—posture, tone of voice, the look in the eyes—to gauge whether a man speaks true or false."

Damodara's head nod was more in the way of a jerk. "Yes. So I believe."

For the first time since he read the message summoning him to the Grand Palace, Narses smiled. It was a very, very thin smile. But a smile nonetheless.

"The truth only, then. That should be no problem."

Damodara studied him for a moment. But he could read nothing whatever in the old eunuch's face. Nothing in his eyes, his tone of voice, his posture. Nothing but—a lifetime of intrigue and subterfuge.

"Go, then," he commanded.

Narses bowed, but did not make to leave.

Damodara cocked his head. "There is something you wish, before you go?"

"Yes," murmured Narses. "The fastest courier in the army. I need to send new instructions to Ajatasutra."

"Certainly. I shall have him report to your tent immediately." He cleared his throat. "Where is Ajatasutra, by the way? I haven't noticed him about lately."

Narses stared at him coldly. Damodara broke into sudden, subdued laughter.

"Never mind! Sometimes, it's best not to know the truth."

Narses met the laughter with a chuckle. "So, I am told, say the very best philosophers."

Ajatasutra himself might not have agreed with that sentiment. But there was no question at all that he was being philosophical about his own situation.

He had not much choice, after all. His needs required that he stay at one of the worst and poorest hostels in Ajmer, the greatest city of Rajputana. And, so far as Ajatasutra was concerned—he who had lived in Constantinople as well as Kausambi—the *best* hostel in that hot and dusty city was barely fit for cattle.

He slew another insect on his pallet, with the same sure stroke with which he slew anything.

"I am *not* a Jain," he growled at the tiny corpse. His cold eyes surveyed the horde of other insects taking formation in his squalid little room. "So don't any of you think you'll get any tenderhearted philosophy from *me*."

If the insects were abashed by that grisly threat, they gave no sign of it. Another legion, having dressed its lines, advanced fearlessly to the fray.

"This won't be so bad," said the older sister. "The lady even says she'll give me a crib for the baby."

The younger sister surveyed their room in the great mansion where Lord Damodara's family resided in the capital. The room was small and unadorned, but it was spotlessly clean.

True, the kitchen-master was a foul-mouthed and ill-tempered man, as men who hold such thankless posts generally are. And his wife was even worse. But her own foul mouth and ill temper seemed focused, for the most part, on seeing to it that her husband did not take advantage of his position to molest the kitchen slaves.

In her humble manner, the sister had become quite a philosopher in her own right. "Are you kidding? This is *great*."

Below them, in the depths of the mansion's great cellar, others were also being philosophical.

"Start digging," commanded the mercenary leader. "You've got a long way to go."

The small group of Bihari miners did not even think to argue the matter. Indeed, they set to work with a will. An odd attitude, perhaps, in slaves. But they too had seen the way Ajatasutra gave *instructions*. And, like the two sisters whom they did not know, had reached an identical conclusion. The assassin was deadly, deadly. But, in his own way, a man who could be trusted. Do the work, he had told them, and you will be manumitted—and given gold besides.

There was no logic to it, of course. For whatever purpose they had been brought here, to dig a mysterious tunnel to an unknown destination, the purpose had been kept secret for a reason. The slaves knew, as well as any man, that the best way to keep a secret is to kill those who know it. But, somehow, they did not fear for their lives.

"Oddest damned assassin I've ever seen," muttered one of the mercenaries.

"For what he's paying us," said the leader, "he can sprout feathers like a chicken for all I care." Seeing that the tunnel work was well underway, he turned to face his two subordinates. His finger pointed stiffly at the casks of wine against one of the stone walls of the cellar.

"Do I have to repeat *his* instructions?"

The other Ye-tai shook their heads vigorously. Their eyes shied away from the wine.

"Good," he grunted. "Just do as we're told, that's it. And we'll walk away from this as rich men."

One of the mercenaries cleared his throat, and pointed his own finger up at the stone ceiling. "Won't anyone wonder? There'll be a bit of noise. And, after a while, we'll have to start hauling the dirt out."

Again, the captain shrugged. "He told me he left *instructions* up there also. We stay down here, and food and water will be brought to us. By the majordomo and a few others. They'll see to the disposal of the dirt."

"Shouldn't be hard," grunted one of the other mercenaries. His head jerked toward the far wall. "The Ganges is just the other side of the mansion. I saw as we arrived. Who's going to notice if *that* river gets a bit muddier?"

A little laugh greeted the remark. If the Ye-tai mercenaries retained much of their respect for Malwa's splendor, they had lost their awe for Malwa's power and destiny. All of them were veterans of the Persian campaign, and had seen—fortunately, from a distance—the hand of Belisarius at work.

None of them, in any event, had ever had much use for the fine points of Hindu ritual.

"Fuck the Ganges," muttered another. "Bunch of stupid peasants bathing in elephant piss. Best place I can think of for the dirt that's going to make us rich men."

And so, another philosopher.

Chapter 10

THE PERSIAN GULF
Summer, 533 A.D.

"So how many, Dryopus?" asked Antonina. Wearily, she wiped her face with a cloth that was already damp with sweat. "For certain."

Her secretary hesitated. Other than being personally honest, Dryopus was typical of high officials in the Roman Empire's vast and elaborate hierarchy. For all his relative youth—he was still shy of forty—and his apparent physical vigor, he was the sort of man who personified the term: *bureaucrat*. His natural response to any direct question was: first, cover your ass; second, hedge; third, cover your ass again.

But Antonina didn't even have to glare at him. By now, months after arriving in Persia to take up his new duties, Dryopus had learned that "covering your ass" with Antonina meant giving her straight and direct answers. He was the fourth official who had served her in this post, and the only one who had not been shipped back to Constantinople within a week.

"I can't tell you, for certain. At least ninety ships. Probably be closer to a hundred, when all the dust settles."

Seeing the gathering frown on Antonina's face, Dryopus hurriedly added: "I'm only counting those in the true seagoing class, mind. There'll be plenty of river barges that can be pressed into coastline service."

THE TIDE OF VICTORY   103

Antonina rose from her desk and walked over to the window, shaking her head. "The river barges won't be any use, Dryopus. Not once the army's marched past the Persian Gulf ports. No way they could survive the monsoon, once they get out of sheltered waters. Not the heart of it, at least. By the tail end of the season, we could probably use them—but who really knows where Belisarius will be then?"

At the window, she planted her hands on the wide ledge and leaned her face into the breeze. The window in the villa which doubled as Antonina's headquarters faced to the south, overlooking Charax's great harbor. The slight breeze coming in from the sea helped alleviate the blistering summer heat of southern Mesopotamia.

But the respite was brief. Within seconds, she turned back to Dryopus.

"Who's the most obstreperous of the hold-outs?" she demanded.

"Those two brothers who own the *Circe*." This time, Dryopus' answer came with no hesitation at all. "Aco and Numenius."

As Antonina moved back to her desk, her frown returned in full force. "Egyptians, aren't they? Normally operate out of Myos Hormos?"

"Yes. That's one of the things they're squealing about. They claim they can't take on military provisions until they've unloaded their cargo in Myos Hormos, or they'll go bankrupt." Dryopus scowled. "They say they're carrying specialty items which are in exclusive demand in Egypt. Can't sell them here in Mesopotamia."

"Oh—that's nonsense!" Antonina plumped down in her chair and almost slapped the desk with her hands. "They're bringing cargo from Bharakuccha, right?" With a snarl: "That means spices and cosmetics. Mostly pepper. Stuff that'll sell just as well in Persia as anywhere."

Dryopus, sitting on his own chair across from her, spread his hands in a little gesture of agreement. "They're just making excuses to try to avoid being pressed into service as part of the supply fleet for the army. By all accounts, those two brothers are among the worst chiselers in the trade—which is saying something, given the standards of merchant seamen. There's even been accusations that they burned one of their own ships a few years ago, to collect the insurance on the cargo."

He shrugged. "I don't really understand why they're being so resistant. It's true that the profit margin they'll make from military shipping is lower. But, on the other hand, they're guaranteed steady work for at least a year—which they're certainly not in the regular India trade!—and the risk is minimal. Lower, really, than the risk in trading with India. In fact, the reason the *Circe* came into port later than any of the other ships from Bharakuccha— according to Aco and Numenius, at least—is that they were detained in the harbor for a month by Malwa officials trying to shake them down."

Antonina nodded. It was the custom of the day for trade between belligerent realms to continue unchecked during wartime. Roman merchant vessels, of course, were not allowed to sail directly into Bharakuccha's harbor—any more than the Persians allowed Malwa shipping into their own ports. But the ships themselves were usually not molested. They simply had to add the extra expense of unloading their cargo with lighters.

Still . . . It was a perilous enough business. Custom be damned, there were plenty of instances where greedy officials and military officers extorted merchant vessels from enemy nations. Sometimes, even, plundered them outright. The Malwa were especially notorious for the practice.

"Nonsense," repeated Antonina. "It's a *lot* safer. They'll be under the protection of Axumite warships the whole time. And nobody has ever accused the Ethiopians of illegally sequestering cargoes." A rueful little smile came to her face. "Of course, the Axumites don't need to, after all. They take an automatic cut of anything which passes through the Red Sea."

She straightened her back, having come to a decision.

"Enough! I've got to get this thing settled, so we can firm up our numbers. If we crack down on Aco and Numenius, that'll send a clear message to the other malingerers. I want a team of inspectors crawling all over the *Circe* by the end of the day, Dryopus. They're to inspect the cargo and report back. If it's nothing but the usual stuff, we unload that ship tomorrow—by force if necessary—and start stocking it with military supplies."

Dryopus jotted a quick note, nodding. "Done."

"What's next?"

Again, Dryopus hesitated. But the hesitation, this time, was not that of a bureaucrat. In his own distant manner, Dryopus had become something of a friend for Antonina over the past months of joint work, as well as simply a subordinate. The next item of business . . .

Antonina sighed. "John?"

Dryopus nodded. "Yes. We've got to make provisions for trans- porting his—what remains of his body—back to Constantinople."

A flicker of pain crossed Antonina's face, but only briefly. Belisa- rius had brought the news back over a week ago, and she had already finished most of her grieving.

"What are the alternatives?" she asked.

"Well . . . we could dispatch one of the smaller cargo vessels—"

"No. The war comes first."

Dryopus shrugged. "In that case, I'd suggest hiring one of the Arab caravans. We could use the barge traffic on the Euphrates, of course, but the Arabs have been complaining that they're not getting their fair share of the war trade."

Antonina nodded. "Yes. They'll take it as an honor, too. But make sure you hire one of the Beni Ghassan caravans. They've been Rome's allies for centuries. They'll be offended if the job is given to anyone else. Especially the Lakhmids."

Dryopus made a note. "Done."

"What's next?"

"There's the matter of the livestock provisions. Camels, specifi- cally."

"Again?" groaned Antonina. She wiped her face with the cloth. Again. In that heat, of course, the cloth was already dry. Still . . .

She stared down at it, scowling. "I should go into business for myself," she said glumly. "Selling salt."

She fluttered the scrap of linen. "There's enough right here—" Then, seeing the look on Dryopus' face, she choked off the words.

"What?" she demanded, half-wailing. "We're running low on salt? *Again?*"

Chapter 11

Under the best of conditions, giant armies on the march throw up enormous clouds of dust. And these were not the best of conditions.

Belisarius was leading a hundred and twenty thousand men into India against the Malwa, along with as many horses, camels and mules. His army had now left the flood plains of Khuzistan province, and had entered the narrow strip of lowlands bordering the Persian Gulf.

Technically, they were marching through Pars province, the historic homeland of the ancient Achaemenid dynasty as well as the Sassanids. But this was not the Pars province that most people thought of, with its ancient cities of Persepolis and Shiraz and the irrigated regions around them.

Partly, Belisarius had chosen the southern route to avoid the inevitable destruction of farmland which a marching army produces, even if the army is under discipline. But, mostly, he had done so because of overriding logistical concerns. There was no way that an army that size could be provisioned by farmers along their route. Until they reached the Indus valley, Belisarius and his army would be entirely dependent on seaborne supplies. So, whatever other problems that route created, they would be forced to hug the coast of the Persian Gulf and the Arabian Sea.

A coast which, sad to say, was one of the bleakest coasts in the world: as arid as a desert, with little in the way of vegetation beyond an occasional palm grove.

◇   ◇   ◇

Kurush reined in his horse next to Belisarius. The Roman general was sitting on his own mount atop a small rise, observing the army marching past. Sittas was alongside him; his bodyguards, Isaac and Priscus, were a few yards away.

"Did I mention the roses and nightingales of Shiraz?" asked Kurush. "And the marvelous vineyards?"

Sittas scowled. Belisarius simply smiled.

"Several times," he replied. "Each day of our march."

The Persian general grimaced. "Can't help it, I'm afraid." He reached up a hand and wiped dust from his face, leaving little streaks behind in the veil of sweat. Then, scowling himself: "Wouldn't be quite as bad if we weren't doing this in summertime."

Belisarius shrugged. "We've got no choice, Kurush. Without the monsoon blowing to the east this time of year, this whole expedition would be impossible."

The statement was about as pointless as Kurush's remark about roses and nightingales. The Persian general was just as familiar with the logistical facts of life as Belisarius.

"So I've heard you say," muttered Kurush sourly. "Several times, in fact—each day of our march."

Belisarius' lips quirked, but he made no response. He was busy studying the marching order, trying to determine if there was any possible improvement to be made.

"Forget it," said Sittas, as if he'd read Belisarius' mind. He waved a large and thick-fingered hand at the troops. "Sure you could tidy it up—theoretically. But it'd take you three days to do it, with the army standing still. And then within another three days it'd be a mess all over again."

Belisarius sighed. He had already reached the same conclusion. The army marching past him was far larger than any army he had ever led in the past. Than *any* Roman general had led in centuries, in fact. It had not taken Belisarius long to realize that, at a certain point, quantity doesn't transform into quality. The kind of tight and precise marching order he had always managed to maintain in the past was simply an impossibility here.

"Given, at least," he murmured, "that we're under such a tight time schedule."

Kurush and Sittas said nothing. Again, the statement was point-less. They, along with all the other top commanders of the allied army, had planned this expedition for months. They knew just as well as Belisarius that the march to the Indus valley *had* to be completed before the monsoon season ended in November. Or the army would die of thirst and starvation.

It might die anyway, even if they kept to the schedule. The Indus valley was fertile, true, but Belisarius was quite certain that Link would order a scorched earth campaign in the valley once the Romans and Persians arrived at Barbaricum and began their march upriver to the Malwa heartland.

That is what he would do, after all. The Malwa had no real chance of holding Barbaricum and the coast, once Belisarius arrived at the Indus delta. The shocking and unexpected destruc-tion of their great army in Mesopotamia the year before had forced the Malwa to concentrate on fortifying their own homeland, and to shelve—at least for a time—any plans for conquest.

But fortifications strong enough to withstand the forces Belisa-rius was bringing to India simply could not be erected quickly, not even with the manpower available to the Malwa. So, according to Belisarius' spies, Link had done exactly what he would do: concen-trate on fortifying the upper Indus valley, the region called the Punjab. So long as the Malwa controlled the Punjab, they con-trolled the entrances to the Ganges. Losing the lower valley would be painful, but not fatal.

All the more so because of the geography of the region. The Indus "valley" was really two valleys, which—at least from a mili-tary point of view—were shaped somewhat like an hourglass. The lower valley, the Sind, was broad at the coast and the Indus delta but narrowed as it extended north toward the city of Sukkur and the gorge beyond. Past the Sukkur gorge, the upper valley widened again. The name "Punjab" itself meant "land of five rivers." The upper valley was shaped much like a fan, with the Indus and its main tributaries forming the blades.

If Belisarius could break into the Punjab, where he would have room to maneuver again . . .

That would truly press the Malwa against the wall. So, just as Belisarius would have done, Link would fortify the Punjab and the Sukkur "bottleneck"—but leave the Sind to its own devices. The monster would station soldiers there, to be sure. But their main task would be not to prevent Belisarius from taking the lower valley, but to delay him long enough to allow Link to transform the Punjab and Sukkur into an impregnable stronghold. Those Malwa forces would retreat slowly northward, burning and destroying everything in the valley as they went. "Scorched earth" tactics with a vengeance.

Conceivably, if the Malwa could wrest control of the sea from the Romans and the Ethiopians, they could even turn the Sind into a death trap. Do to Belisarius' great army the same thing he had done to them at Charax.

Belisarius knew that unless he could break Link's plans before they came to fruition, he was faced with years of fighting a brutal, slogging campaign which had more in the nature of siege warfare than battles in the open field. A war of attrition, not maneuver, which would charge Rome with a price in blood and treasure which it could probably not afford. He had bloodied Malwa badly, over the past two years, and the Maratha rebellion in the Deccan which he had helped set into motion was bleeding it further still. But the fact remained that the Malwa empire could still draw on greater resources than Rome and Persia and Ethiopia combined. A long war of attrition was far more likely to work in favor of the Malwa than Belisarius.

Link would certainly do its best to make it so. The cybernetic organism was just as familiar with human history as Aide. The Malwa empire was now on the defensive, and they would adopt the methods and tactics which would be used in a future world by the Dutch rebels against the Spanish.

And those tactics worked for almost a century, came Aide's voice. **Until the Spanish finally gave up.**

Belisarius made the mental equivalent of a shrug. *True. But the Spanish were never able to outflank the Dutch defenses, because the Dutch backs were protected by the sea. Malwa is not. I know Link's plans. I also believe I can foil them, when the time comes. Don't ask me how, because I don't know yet. But war is a thing of chaos, not order, and I think my understanding of that is far superior to Link's. "Superhuman intelligence" be damned. War is not a chess game. It is, in the end, more a thing of the soul than the mind. And that thing has no soul. It will try to control the chaos, where I will revel in it.*

Belisarius could sense the hesitation in Aide's mind. But the only thoughts which finally came were simply: **I trust your judgement.**

Belisarius chuckled. Hearing the soft sound, Sittas cocked an inquisitive eye at him.

"Aide was just expressing his confidence in my judgement," murmured Belisarius. "I wish I felt as much."

He expected to hear Sittas make one of his usual quips—at Belisarius' expense—but his large friend simply chuckled himself. "As it happens, I agree with the cute little fellow. I think your strategy for this campaign is damned near brilliant. Hell, not even 'damned near,' when I think about it."

Belisarius scowled. "It's too complicated. Too intricate by half. Too much step one, step two, step three. Maurice hasn't stopped nattering at me about it for a single day. And I don't disagree with him, either. It's going to start coming apart at the seams, soon enough, and I'll be back to making strategic decisions on a saddle." The scowl faded, replaced by a slight, crooked smile. "Which, I admit, seems to be something I have a certain aptitude for. More than Link does, I'm willing to bet. *Am* betting."

Sittas lifted his great bulk up on the stirrups for a moment, his eyes scanning the huge army. "Where is the old grouch, anyway?"

After a moment, he eased back in the saddle. The task of spotting a single man in that great horde of soldiers and moving equipment, even a top officer with his banners and entourage, was essentially hopeless.

"Of course he's grumbling," grumbled Sittas. "What would life be for the morose old bastard, without the pleasure of grousing to fill it up? But the fact is—this time—he's just plain wrong."

Almost angrily, Sittas gestured at the arid landscape ahead of them. "That's what it's going to be like, Belisarius, from here on. I'm not even sure the Malwa will bother to contest the delta, when we finally arrive at Barbaricum. Just cede it and let us get well established. Then, when the monsoon shifts, watch us starve beneath the walls of their fortifications upstream. By the time we get there, you know they'll have stripped the delta clean."

"Easier said than done."

Sittas shrugged. "Sure, I know." He barked a little laugh. "Easy for historians to say: 'they ravaged the countryside.' Never catch one of those languid fellows trying to destroy croplands. Hard work, that is—harder than growing stuff, that's for sure. Wouldn't wish it on a peasant."

Belisarius smiled. He doubted if Sittas had actually ever read any of those historians he was denouncing. But Belisarius knew that Sittas had once gotten embroiled in a loud argument with three historians at an imperial feast. In the end, Theodora had sent her personal guards to quell the large and outraged general.

Belisarius *had* read many of those historians, on the other hand. And while he felt none of Sittas' sputtering fury at the stupidities of over-educated and over-sheltered intellectuals, he understood it perfectly well. Aristocratic scribblers suffered from the inevitable habit of turning prosaic and complex reality into simple metaphors. Almost poetry, really, which they blithely assumed was an accurate representation of reality.

Destroy the countryside. Ravage the land.

As it happened, Belisarius had given those very orders himself over the years. Especially in his earliest years as an officer, campaigning against barbarians in the trans-Danube and Persians in the Mesopotamian borderlands. But both he and his men had understood the prose between the poetry, the unspoken qualifiers attached to the muscular verbs and nouns:

As best you can—in the time allowed. To the extent possible—given the number of men available. Whatever you can do—with military equipment instead of agricultural implements, and teams of mules instead of oxen.

He could remember hearing his men cursing bitterly, wrestling with the endless and exhausting work of trying to destroy the tough vines and wood of grape fields and olive groves. Or the backbreaking work of cutting and assembling grain in piles suitable for burning. Not to mention the well-nigh hopeless task of finding all the food caches hidden away, by peasants who were far more experienced than soldiers at hiding such things—and had a far greater incentive to do the job properly.

It could almost never be done really successfully. Time after time, throughout the future history which Aide had shown him, Belisarius recognized the same pattern. An army marching through a region, "devastating the land," and then—not a year later— everything was back again. Half of it, at least. "Mother Nature," especially when assisted by poor and industrious peasants, was far tougher than any army of soldiers.

In truth, the most successful method was the most ruthless. The method the Mongols would use in Central Asia: *kill everyone.* Don't just destroy the irrigation works and the infrastructure, but kill all the people living there as well. Eliminate the labor force which could rebuild what was destroyed.

Those were methods Belisarius would never use. Precious few armies in history ever had. But he had no doubt at all the Malwa would use them in the delta of the Indus. The last order Link would give, after its soldiery destroyed everything they could, was to kill all the peasants living there. The multitude of that poor and humble folk, whose calloused hands were so much better at rebuilding than the sinewy hands of soldiers ever were at destroying. And then heap their corpses atop their own ravaged land, so that their putrefaction could finish the work of destruction.

Malwa's *own* peasants. Who would not even be given the one mercy which peasants throughout time had usually been able to expect from their rulers, no matter how tyrannical: to be left alive, that they might be exploited further.

He found his own eyes searching the passing horde, looking for Maurice. A humble fellow himself, Maurice, in his own way. Born into the Thracian peasantry, and, despite his now exalted rank, not given to pretensions. The thought filled Belisarius with a strange, grim satisfaction. The first of the many blows he intended to rain on Malwa would be to send *that* man to rescue the enemy's own people.

He had thought Maurice would grumble at the order. Not because of its content, but because of the intricacy of the maneuvers involved. But, for once, the old veteran had not complained. Had not, even, ritually intoned his precious "First Law of Battle."

"Makes sense," he had grunted. "We'll need them for a labor force." The smile which followed had been almost seraphic. "War's a stupid, silly business, anyway. So why not turn it completely upside down?"

Oddly enough, Belisarius *did* spot Maurice in the horde. And did so in the oddest place.

"Look!" he barked, pointing an accusing finger. "He's finally going soft on us!"

Sittas' eyes followed Belisarius' finger. When he spotted Maurice himself, he burst into laughter. So did Kurush.

"He'll claim he had to work over some logistics with Agathius," chortled the Persian general. "You watch! Swear, he will, that only dire necessity forced him into it."

When Maurice finally came alongside the little rise where Belisarius and Sittas and Kurush were positioned, he glared up at them. Almost down at them, actually, perched as he was in the spacious comfort of Agathius' howdah atop a great war elephant.

"Had some logistical problems to sort out," he claimed loudly.

Agathius looked up from the papers he was studying and spotted Belisarius and the others. Then, heaving his crippled but still powerful body erect with a muscular arm on the edge of the open howdah, he grinned. "He's lying through his teeth," he shouted. "We've spent the whole morning playing with artillery positions, against these different sketches."

Even without being able to see into the howdah, Belisarius understood what Agathius was talking about. Among the many tasks he had set himself, in the months spent in Ctesiphon planning the Indus expedition, was overseeing the work of a dozen artists-become-draftsmen. Transcribing, onto parchment, Aide's descriptions of the fortifications of a future world. The designs of fortresses created in Renaissance Italy and Holland, as engineers and architects of the future grappled with the challenge of gunpowder artillery used in sieges.

Engineers and architects—and artists. Michelangelo, who would become famous to later generations as a painter and sculptor, had been famous in his own day as well; primarily, however, as one of Renaissance Italy's best military architects. He had been the city of Florence's Commissary General of Fortifications. He had lavished, over many months, as much care and attention on the critical hill of San Miniato as he would the Sistine Chapel, diverting the Mugnone and guiding the stream into a moat, as he would guide a brush; and bestowing San Miniato with as many intricate details—bastions and fascines—as he would a fresco depicting creation.

Then, having given Agathius the wherewithal to study the siege methods of the future, Belisarius had set him to work on designing, with the vast knowledge Agathius had gained from his long work as Belisarius' chief of logistics, the best methods to counter those fortresses.

Belisarius had no doubt at all that Link would distill the wisdom of Europe's best military architects in the first centuries of gunpowder warfare as it created Malwa's fortresses in the Indus valley. Of course, Belisarius would counter that with his own knowledge of history, given to him by Aide. Most of all, though, he would counter it with the keen brain of Agathius. As canny and meticulous a man as Belisarius had ever met in his life. And one whose own origins were as humble as Maurice's. Which, for Belisarius at least, added a certain zest to the whole affair.

"And how does that work go, then?" he demanded.

Agathius fluttered his hand vaguely. "Well enough. Given, at least, that Maurice picks holes in all my finest schemes. Pessimistic grouch, he is. 'If anything can go wrong, it will.' The usual."

Maurice was still half glaring at Belisarius. "Hate riding in this thing, myself. Give me a horse any day."

Kurush and Sittas immediately responded to that disclaimer with a variety of scoffing jests. Belisarius smiled, but said nothing.

As it happened, he didn't really doubt Maurice's claim. But even Maurice, as conservative as he was, had bowed to the inevitable.

The Roman army, throughout the centuries, had never favored the war elephants which so many of their opponents had treasured. True, the monsters could be ferocious in battle. But they could often wreak as much havoc in their own army as in the enemy's. Still, Belisarius had brought a number of the great beasts with him on this expedition. He had no intention of actually using them in combat. But the elephants could bear officers in howdahs, after all, along with the maps and charts and documents needed for the huge army's staff. Why waste the mind of a man like Agathius by perching him on a saddle for weeks? When the same man, even though crippled, could spend those weeks of marching engaged in the same crucial work he had overseen for months?

So, Belisarius did not join in the badinage. After a few seconds, he blocked it out of his mind entirely and returned to his study of the army passing before him.

What a hodge-podge! he thought, half-ruefully and half-cheerfully. *War elephants from ancient armies, plodding alongside men armed with our version of the Sharps rifle of the American Civil War. And look over there, Aide—a mitrailleuse in a chariot! I swear they found that relic in some Sumerian vault.*

It'll work, came the serene thought in reply. **You'll make it work.**

Chapter 12
AJMER
Summer, 533 A.D.

"Be careful," murmured Kujulo. "This city has changed."

Valentinian and Anastasius swept the streets of Ajmer with their eyes, shielded under lowered helmets. Neither of them had ever been in the largest city in Rajputana, so they had no basis for comparison.

"What's different?" asked Valentinian softly. He reached up his hand and scratched the back of his neck idly. The casual gesture exuded the weariness of a caravan guard finally reaching his destination after a long and arduous trek. Meanwhile, not casually at all, his eyes kept scouring the vicinity.

"This is not a Rajput city any longer," replied Kujulo. "Not really. Look there, for instance—down the street, to the left."

Without moving their heads, Valentinian and Anastasius looked in that direction. Valentinian couldn't really see much, since he was riding at the head of the caravan to Kujulo's right. But Anastasius, riding to the Kushan's left, had a clear view into the street in question—which was really more in the way of an alley.

"Mangy pack of dogs," he muttered. "But a big pack, too." A moment later, yawning, he added: "And you're right about that much. If any of those sorry bastards are Rajputs, I'd be astonished. I don't think I've ever seen a Rajput with as much filth all over

115

him—not even after a battle—as any of that lot have on their feet alone."

The slowly moving caravan was now passing the mouth of the alley, and Valentinian was finally able to get a good look.

" 'Dogs' is an insult to dogs. But—" He paused, until the alley was behind them. "They're hungry-looking, I give you that."

Anastasius and Valentinian now both looked to Kujulo. The "leadership structure" of their peculiar expedition was a fluid thing. Sometimes one, then another, of the three men in command had taken the lead over the weeks since they landed in the delta and made their slow way into Rajputana. Usually either Valentinian or Anastasius. But now that they had arrived at Ajmer, both of the Roman cataphracts were clearly willing to let Kujulo guide them.

This unfamiliar and exotic city was *terra incognita* to them. So too, of course, had been the Thar desert and the Aravalli mountains. But rough terrain, whatever its specific features, is much the same in many places—and both Anastasius and Valentinian were veterans of marches across such. Usually as part of an army, true, rather than a merchant caravan. But the experience had not been especially foreign. Neither, certainly, had been the two brief skirmishes with bandits.

Ajmer, however, was a different matter. Here, the "terrain" was not so much geographic as human. And neither of them knew anything about the customs and habits which characterized the city.

Kujulo immediately made clear that he was something of a novice, also. Or, it might be better to say, a man who returns to a place he had known years earlier, and finds it has been completely transformed.

"In the old days," he growled, "no gang like that would have dared lounge openly in the streets of Ajmer. Rajput women would have driven them off, sent them scampering back into their hovels."

"I'm pretty sure there's another pack in that alley up ahead," murmured Valentinian. "A more lively bunch, seems like. At least judging from the way their lookout ducked back into the alley when I spotted him."

The only sign of Kujulo's tension was a slight shift in the way he rode his saddle. The Kushan seemed slightly discomfited by the fact that he had no stirrups.

They all were, in truth. By now, of course, stirrups had become adopted by almost all Malwa cavalry units. But the devices were still rare in civilian use, and they had decided from the beginning that they couldn't afford to risk drawing attention to themselves. To all outward appearances, the two Roman cataphracts and the seventeen Kushans who accompanied them were nothing more than the guards and drivers of a merchant caravan. A relatively small one, at that.

"There's no order in this city any more," continued Kujulo. "All the Rajput soldiers, by now, must have been drawn into the Malwa army. Probably have a small unit of common soldiers policing the city, with maybe a handful of Ye-tai to stiffen them up. But their idea of 'policing' will be either lounging in the barracks or—more likely—doing their own extortions."

There was a little stir in the alley still some distance away, coming up on their right. Three men were leaning out of it, studying the oncoming caravan like so many predators in ambush. Small and mangy predators, to be sure, but . . .

As Valentinian had rightly said, *hungry-looking*.

"Hell and damn," rumbled Anastasius. Moving slowly, casually, he loosened the mace belted to his thick waist. As he did so, moving his head with the same casual ease, he glanced back over his shoulder. "Hell and damn," he repeated. "That first bunch is peeking at us from behind."

Facing forward again, his basso rumble deepened. "It's an ambush, sure. In broad daylight on a busy street."

"Let's take it to 'em, then," said Valentinian. His narrow weasel face showed not a trace of emotion. His hand loosened his own weapon, the spatha he favored, and his left leg began to rise.

Kujulo eyed him sharply. Valentinian could dismount from a horse faster than any man he had ever seen. Just as he could do anything faster than any man he had ever seen. Within seconds, he knew, the lightly armored cataphract would be plunging his whipcord body into that alley up ahead.

Of the outcome, Kujulo had no doubt at all. Even had he been faced with real soldiers, Valentinian would transform that narrow alley into a creek of blood. Dealing with dacoits, the alley would erupt like a burst dam, spilling blood and limbs and heads and intestines everywhere.

"*No*," he hissed. "The city is full of spies."

Valentinian's leg froze. His shoulder twitched irritation. "So? A caravan defending itself."

They were not more than fifteen yards from the mouth of the alley. Kujulo hissed again. "No caravan defends itself the way you will. Or Anastasius." The grunt that followed combined grim humor with exasperation. "Or me, for that matter, or my Kushans."

Ten yards, now. "What else do you suggest?" snarled Valentinian softly. "Let them kill half of us, to show Malwa spies we are nothing but merchant sheep?"

His shoulders twitched irritation again. The leg began to rise. "Damn that. Let's take it to them."

Suddenly, a little chorus of shrieks erupted from the mouth of the alley. An instant later, spewing forth like so many pieces of a bad fig from a man's mouth, six dacoits burst into the street. Two were shrieking, one was staggering. The other three, silent, simply raced off.

Raced off *away* from the caravan, not toward it. Followed, within a second or two, by the shriekers. The last dacoit staggered another step or two, then sprawled on his face and lay still. Blood was beginning to stain his filthy clothing.

Kujulo raised his hand, as any caravan leader would when faced with similar circumstances. *"Halt!"*

The caravan stopped. All the Kushans further back drew their weapons, as did Kujulo and the Roman cataphracts. The street was suddenly empty of all life, except for the group of dacoits who had begun emerging from the alley behind. But they too, seeing the new circumstances, hastily scampered out of sight.

Kujulo studied the alley. He held his own sword a bit awkwardly. Not too demonstratively, just enough to make him seem like a caravan master instead of an experienced soldier. From the corner of his eye, he saw that Valentinian's grip was expert—just as, out of that same corner, he had seen the blinding speed with which the cataphract had drawn the blade.

"Can you just *try* not to seem like the perfect killer," he muttered sourly.

Valentinian ignored him. His dark eyes were riveted on the alley mouth.

Again, motion. A dacoit emerged, slowly, clutching his throat. His eyes were gaping wide and his face was pale. Blood was pouring through his fingers. He took two steps into the street before his knees collapsed and he toppled onto his face.

Another dacoit came, this one like a limp rag being slapped against the mudbrick wall of the nearest building which formed the alley's corner. The front of his clothing was a red blotch and his head was sagging. He was being held by the scruff of the neck by another man.

"*Rob me, will you?*" snarled the man who held him. A knife flashed into the dacoit's back, flashed again. Then, contemptuously, the man tossed the would-be robber's body onto that of his fellow.

Valentinian studied him carefully. The man was average in height, but very wide-shouldered. His hawk face was sharp and angry. He strode into the street, stooped like a raptor, and wiped the gore off his dagger on the clothing of his last victim.

Then, straightening and sheathing the weapon, he glared at Kujulo and the Romans.

"And you?" he demanded.

Kujulo sheathed his sword and raised his other hand in a placating gesture. "We are merchants, lord. No more."

The man's glare did not fade in the least. His clothing, though clean, was utilitarian and plain. "No lord, I!" he barked. Then, sneering: "But neither am I one to be troubled by dacoits. Nor any man."

Despite his belligerence, the man stepped aside and waved his hand.

"Pass by, pass by!"

Kujulo set the caravan back into motion. As they drew alongside the alley, the glaring man snorted contemptuously. "A caravan, is it? Hauling what—sheep dung?"

He shook his head sarcastically. "You'll be lucky if any stable will put up as sorry a lot as you. But I suppose the low-caste inn two streets up might do so." And with that, he was gone, vanishing back into the alley like a wraith. Neither Valentinian nor Kujulo could hear his footsteps.

"Well," mused Anastasius, "that's one way to arrange a meeting. I don't remember Antonina describing him as being quite so broad-shouldered, though. You, Valentinian?"

Valentinian seemed lost in thought. He said nothing for a few seconds. Then, softly: "I don't remember her saying he could move that quickly, either." The words seemed filled more with interest than concern. One raptor gauging another.

"Splendid," growled Kujulo. "You *will* remember that we didn't come all this way to fight a duel on a mountainside?"

Valentinian's narrow smile made an appearance. "No danger of that. I don't believe he's any more taken by dramatic public duels than I am."

The words did not seem to bring much reassurance. The sour expression was still on Kujulo's face when the caravan pulled up before the inn. Nor was his displeasure primarily caused by the obvious dilapidation of the establishment.

One raptor gauging another.

"Splendid," he growled.

Chapter 13

MARV

Summer, 533 A.D.

"How are you feeling?" asked Kungas, smiling down at Irene. The expression was broader than the usual faint crack in the mask which normally did Kungas for a smile. Suspicious souls, in fact, might even take it for a . . .

"Stop grinning at me," grumbled Irene. Painfully, she levered herself up from the pallet where she had been resting. "I ache all over, that's how I'm feeling."

Now sitting up, she studied Kungas' face. Seeing that the smile showed no sign of vanishing—might even be widening, in fact!—she scowled ferociously.

"Feeling superior, are we? Enjoying the sight of the too-clever-by-half female puddled in exhaustion and fatigue? Undone by the frailty of her flesh?"

Still smiling, Kungas squatted next to her and stroked Irene's cheek. "Such a suspicious woman! Actually, no. All things considered, you are doing extremely well. The army thinks so, too."

He chuckled. "In fact, the bets are being settled right now. Most of the soldiers were wagering that you wouldn't make it as far as Damghan—much less all the way to Marv. And the ones who thought you might weren't willing to place much of a stake on it."

Irene cocked her head and listened to the gleeful sounds coming through the walls of the small tent. She had wondered—a bit, not much; as preoccupied as she had been with her own misery—why so many people seemed full of good cheer. Kushans were addicted to gambling. Those were the sounds of a *major* bet being settled, at long odds and with a big payoff.

"So who's collecting, then?" she demanded crossly.

"The camp followers, who else? The women are getting rich."

That news lightened Irene's mood immensely. She had discovered, in the long and arduous weeks of their trek across all of Persia, that she got along very well with the Kushan women. Much to her surprise, in fact. She had assumed from the outset, without really thinking about it, that the mostly illiterate and tough women who had become the camp followers of the none-too-literate and *very* tough army of Kungas would have nothing in common with her.

In many ways, of course, they didn't. Irene was sophisticated and cosmopolitan in a way that those women never would be, any more than the soldiers to whom they were attached. But women in Kushan society enjoyed far greater freedom than Irene would have expected in a society forged in the mountains and deserts of central Asia.

Perhaps that was because of the practical needs of the Kushan dispersal after the Ye-tai conquest of their homeland, and the later policies of their Malwa overlords. But Irene liked to think it was the legacy of the Sarmatians who had once, in the days of Alexander, ruled the area that would eventually become the Kushan empire. The Scythians whom the Sarmatians displaced had kept women in a strictly subordinate position. But every Sarmatian girl, according to ancient accounts, was taught to ride a horse. And—so legend had it, at least—was expected to fight alongside the men, armed and armored, and was even forbidden to marry until she had slain an enemy in battle.

Perhaps that was all idle fancy. The Kushan women, for all their undoubted toughness, were not expected to fight except under extreme circumstances. But, for whatever reason, Irene had found that the Kushan women took a certain sly pleasure in her own ability to discomfit, time after time, the self-confident men who marched under Kungas' banner.

Even the banner itself was Irene's, after all. None of the Kushans, not even Kungas, had given much thought to a symbol. They had simply assumed they would, as was custom, use some sort of simple device—a colored strip of cloth, perhaps, wound about their helmets.

Irene, guided by her own intelligence and many hours spent in discussion with Belisarius and Aide, had decreed otherwise. And so, as the Kushan army made its trek across Asia, its progress was marked by the great fluttering banners which Irene had designed. She had stolen her designs from the ancient Sarmatians and the Mongols of what would have been the future: a bronze dragon's head with a wind sock trailing behind, and the horsetail banners below it. Very flashy and dramatic, it was.

"If you are able to move," said Kungas softly, "I could use your help. Things are coming to a head."

Irene winced. At the moment, *moving* was the last thing she wanted to do. Accustomed all her life to the soft existence of a wealthy Greek noblewoman, the grueling trek had taxed her severely. Her brain understood well enough that exercising her aching muscles was the best remedy for what ailed her. But her body practically shrieked in protest.

Still, she understood immediately the nature of Kungas' problem. And knew, as well, that she was the best person to solve it. Partly because of her skill at diplomacy. And partly—

She sniffed disdainfully. "And once again! Allow stubborn men to compromise because all of them can blame their soft-headedness on a feeble and fearful woman. There's no justice in the world, Kungas."

Her husband's smile had faded back into the familiar crack-in-the-casting. "True enough," he murmured. "But it's such an *effective* tactic."

"Help me up," she hissed. "And you'll probably have to carry me."

In the event, Irene managed the task on her own two feet. Mincing through the marketplace in Marv, she even had the energy to stop along the way and banter with the Kushan women who had set up their impromptu stalls everywhere. She ignored resolutely all of Kungas' little signs of impatience and unease. First, she needed the periodic rest. Second—and more important—the attitude of the women would influence the army. Having found that secret weapon, she intended to use it to maximum advantage.

Eventually, she and Kungas made their way into the small palace which had served the former commander of the Malwa garrison for his headquarters. It was an ancient edifice. The Kushans had built it originally, centuries earlier, as a regional palace. Before the Malwa came, it had served the same purpose for the Sassanids after they conquered the western half of the Kushan empire. The Persian conquerors had decreed the former Kushan land to be one of their *shahrs*—the equivalent of a royal province—and, most significantly, had included it within the land of Iran proper.

Which was the source of the current controversy, of course. Now that Kungas had retaken Marv, with the help of Baresmanas and some two thousand Persian dehgans assigned by Emperor Khusrau to accompany the Kushan expedition (that far, and no farther), the question which had once been abstract was posed in the concrete.

Who was to be the new ruler of the region?

The Kushans, naturally enough, inclined to the opinion that Marv, originally theirs to begin with, should be theirs again. The more so since they had done the actual work of driving the Malwa garrison out of the walled city. The Persians had done nothing more than pursue and harry already broken troops trying to flee through the oasis which surrounded Marv.

The Persians, on the other hand . . .

As Irene passed through the entrance, she heaved a small sigh. Relief from the sun's heat, to some extent; mostly, exasperation at the typical haughtiness of Persians. Even Baresmanas was being stiff over the matter. Although Irene suspected that was due more to stiff instructions from Khusrau than his own sentiments.

Moving slowly and painfully, Kungas at her side ready to lend a hand if need be, Irene made her way through the narrow corridors of the palace. The walls of the palace were thick, due as much to the need for insulation from summer's heat and winter's cold as the crude nature of the original design. Narrow corridors made for a gloomy walk, and Irene took the time to steel herself for the coming fray. She let the darkness of the corridor feed her soul, swelling the stark message that she bore with her to the people who had adopted her as their queen.

By the time she and Kungas reached the chamber where the quarrel was raging, Macrembolitissa the spymaster had vanished. Queen Irene of the Kushans was the woman who made her entrance.

"*Silence,*" she decreed. Then, gratefully easing herself into a chair immediately presented by one of the Kushan officers, she nodded at Baresmanas and the three Persian officers standing by him.

"I agree with you, Baresmanas, and will see it done. Now please leave. We Kushans must discuss this matter in private."

Baresmanas bowed and complied immediately. Within seconds, he and the other Persians had left the room. Immediately, the stunned silence into which Irene's pronouncement had cast the half dozen Kushans in the room—not Kungas; he was silent but not stunned in the least—began to erupt in a quickly-growing murmur of protest.

"*Silence!*" she decreed again. Then, after sweeping them with a cold gaze, she snorted sarcastically. "Boys! Stupid boys! Quarreling over toys and trinkets because you cannot see an adult horizon."

She leaned forward in the chair—not allowing any trace of the spike of pain that movement caused to show in her face—and pointed an imperious finger to the narrow window which looked to the northeast. "In *that* direction lies our destiny, not this miserable region of dust and heat."

Kungas smiled, very faintly. Knowing Irene's purpose, and supporting it, he still felt it necessary to maintain his own dignity. He *was* the king, after all, not she. He *was* what Romans would have called the man of the house, after all, not she.

"It is one of the most fertile oases in central Asia, wife. A fertility only made possible by our own irrigation works. Which we—not Persians nor Ye-tai nor Malwa—constructed long ago."

Irene shrugged. "True. And so what? The center of Kushan strength will lie, as it always did, in our control of the great mountains to the east. The Hindu Kush—that must be the heart of our new realm. That, and the Pamirs."

The last sentence brought a stillness to the room. The Pamirs were even harsher mountains than the Hindu Kush. No one had ever really tried to rule them, in anything but name.

Irene smiled. The expression was serene, self-confident; erasing all traces of her former sarcasm and derision.

"You are thinking too small," she said quietly. "Much too small. Thinking only of the immediate task of reconquering our ancient homeland, and holding it from the Malwa. But what of our future? What of the *centuries* which will come thereafter?"

Vasudeva, who had become the military commander of Kungas' army, began tugging gently at the point of his goatee. Now that his initial outrage was fading, the canny general was remembering the fundamental reason that all of the Kushans had greeted Kungas' marriage with enthusiasm.

The damned Greek woman was *smart*.

"Explain." Then, remembering protocol: "If you would be so kind, Your Majesty."

Irene grinned, and with that cheerful expression came a sudden relaxation spreading through the room. The hard-bitten Kushan soldiers, for all that Irene's ways often puzzled and bemused them, had also come to feel a genuine fondness for the woman as well as respect for her intelligence. Irene, grinning, was a thing they both liked and trusted. They too, when all was said and done, had a sense of humor.

"We are too small to hold Marv, Vasudeva. That is the simple truth. Today, yes—with the Persians forced into an alliance with us. If we drive the issue, Baresmanas will accede. But what of the time *after* Malwa has fallen, when the Persians will seek to lick their wounds by new triumphs, new additions to their realm?"

The Kushans stared at her. Then, slowly, one by one, they pulled up chairs and took their seats. It did not occur to any of them, at the time, to ask permission of their king and queen to do so. And, remembering the omission later, they would be pleased at the fact that neither of their monarchs—for this *was* a dual monarchy, in all but name—took the least umbrage at their casual informality.

It did not even occur to Irene to do so, actually. She was at heart a thinker, and had always enjoyed thoughtful conversation. Seated on a proper chair—not a damned saddle.

"Think, for once," she continued, after all were seated. "Think of the *future,* not the past. What we can control militarily—can hold against anyone, once we have built the needed fortifications— are the mountains. But those mountains cannot provide the wealth we need for a prosperous kingdom. That, in a nutshell, is the problem we face."

She paused. Quickly, all the Kushans nodded their heads. Once she was sure they were following her logic, she went on.

"Only two avenues are open to us, to overcome that quandary. The first is to seize fertile areas in the lowlands, such as Marv . . . " She waited, just a moment, before adding: "And the Punjab, which I know many of you are assuming we will."

Again, the Kushans began to stiffen. And, again, Irene's lips twisted into an expression of scorn.

"Spare me! I know Peshawar is in the Punjab—just at the edge of it, at least. And one of the holiest cities of the Buddhist faith." She pressed herself back into the chair, using her hands on the armrests as a brace. The motion brought some relief to the ache in her lower spine. "The Vale of Peshawar we can claim, easily enough. So long as we make no claims to the Punjab itself."

She hesitated, thinking. "I am fairly certain that we can claim Mardan and its plain as well, with the Buddhist holy sites at Takht-i-Bahi and Jamal Garhi. Unless I am badly mistaken, Belisarius will allow the Persians to take the Sind. Once Malwa has fallen, therefore, it will be the Rajputs and—I suspect, at least—the Persians who will be our principal competitors for the wealth of the Punjab. *Let them have it*—so long as we control Peshawar and Mardan."

"And the Kohat pass!" chimed in Kungas. Very energetically, the way a proper husband corrects a minor lapse on the part of his wife.

Irene nodded. Very demurely, the way a proper wife accepts her husband's correction. "And the pass." Then, with a sniff: "Let others squabble over the town of Kohat itself. A Pathan town! More grief than anything else."

Vima, another of the top officers of the Kushan army, now spoke up. "In essence, what you propose is that we take just enough of the Punjab to protect the Khyber pass. Base our claim to Peshawar and Mardan on religious grounds, but make clear that we will not contest the Punjab itself. While, at the same time, locking our grip on the Hindu Kush."

"Yes."

Vima shook his head. "From a military point of view, Your Majesty, the logic is impeccable. But that small portion of the Punjab cannot possibly provide enough food for our kingdom. Not unless we are prepared to live like semi-barbarians, which I for one am not. A *civilized* nation needs agricultural area, and lots of it." Semi-apologetically: "Such as the oasis of Marv would provide us."

Irene sniffed. "Have no fear, Vima! I can assure you that I am even less inclined than you to live like a semi-barbarian." She shuddered. "God, can you imagine it! *Me?* Spending half my life in a saddle?"

The Kushans all laughed. But Irene was pleased to see that the laughter contained not a trace of derision. She *had* made her way to Marv in a saddle, after all. Resolutely spurning each and every suggestion that she ride in a palanquin, or even one of the carts which the camp followers used.

A warrior nation, the more so when it was striking a lightning blow at their hated enemy, needed a warrior queen who would not delay them with her frailties. Her illustrious Roman pedigree had pleased the Kushans, for it brought a certain glamor and aura of legitimacy to their cause. But they did not need the reality of the weak flesh it came in. So, using her intelligence and iron will to stifle that flesh, Irene had submitted to the pain. And for all that they might jest about it, the Kushan soldiers understood and respected her for it.

Once the humor of the moment had settled in, Irene shook her head. "I said there were *two* alternatives, Vima. You have over-looked the other. A kingdom—a rich kingdom—can also base itself on trade. And, over time, the expansion which trade brings in its wake."

Again, she pointed to the northeast, in a gesture which was even more imperious. Then, regally, swept it slowly to the west—until half the northland had been encompassed by her finger.

"*The north.* From the Tien Shan mountains to the Aral Sea. We will not dispute the Punjab with the Rajputs, nor the oases and badlands of Khorasan with the Persians. Let *them* toil in the fields. Let *them* maintain the dikes and canals. We will control all the passes which connect the land of the Aryans to India, and both of them to distant China. We—with our military power rooted in the Hindu Kush and the Pamirs—will reap the benefits from those ancient trade routes. Which, with Malwa gone and ourselves to maintain order, will spring back like giant trees."

Kungas chimed in again. This time, not as a husband correcting his wife, but as a king allied with his queen. "Yes. And under our rule, all of Transoxiana will flourish anew. Bukhara, Samakhand,

Tashkent—*our* cities, they will be, reborn from the ashes. And great metropolises they will become, to rival Constantinople or Ctesiphon or Kausambi."

All the Kushan generals, as was their custom, were now tugging the tips of their goatees. Vima and Huvishka were even fondling their topknots, the sure sign of a Kushan warrior lost deep in thought.

"Difficult," murmured Vasudeva. "Difficult." His goatee-tugging became vigorous. "Beyond Transoxiana lie the great steppes. Time after time, fierce tribes have come sweeping down from that vastness, burning and pillaging all in their wake. No one has ever managed to stymie them, for more than a century or two. We ourselves came from that place, and were in turn overrun by the Ye-tai after civilization made us soft. Why would it not happen again?"

Irene laughed. With delight, not sarcasm. As was true of any enthusiast trained in the dialectic of Socrates, nothing pleased her more than a well-posed question. Like a fat lamb it was, stretched bleating on the altar.

"Guns, Vasudeva! Guns! Those steppe nomads have never been numerous. You know as well as I that the accounts of 'hordes' are preposterous. It was always their mounted mobility combined with archery which made them so formidable. But firearms are superior to bows, and no primitive nomads can make the things. Once civilization became armed with guns, the threat from the steppes vanished soon enough."

She leaned forward. This time, her enthusiasm was so great that she barely noticed the pain that movement caused her. "I spent many hours, with Belisarius, speaking with the Talisman of God. Let me now pass on to you what the Talisman told me of the future. Of a great nation that would someday have been called Russia, and how it conquered the steppes."

And so, until long after nightfall, Irene told her Kushans of the great realm they would create. The realm that she called by the odd name of *Siberia*. A realm which would be created slowly, not overnight. More by traders and explorers and missionaries than armies of conquest—though armies would also come, when needed, from the secure fastnesses of the great mountains which bred them. Slowly, but surely for all that.

Let the Kushans avoid entanglements with Indians and Persians, and there was no power to stymie their purpose in Siberia. The distant Chinese, as ever, were preoccupied with their own affairs. The other power that might contest the area, the nation that would have been called Russia in a different future, was still centuries from birth. Whether it would be born in this new future was not something which Irene could foresee. But, even if it were, it would remain forever on the far side of the Urals. Siberia, with all the great wealth in its vast expanse, would be *Kushan*.

And so, while the Kushans built the foundation of their own future, they would also shield the rest of civilization from the ravages of barbarism. Having no cause for quarrel over territory, the Romans and the Persians and the Indians would acquiesce in the Kushan control of the great trade routes through central Asia. Might even, when called upon, send money to defray the costs of holding back the barbarians.

In the end, the queen's soldiers were satisfied. The queen's plan appealed to their military caution in the present as much as to their political ambitions for the future. They were small and weak, still. By planting their roots in the protected mountains, not exposing them to the peril of the oases and the plains of the Indus, they would lay the basis for the great Buddhist empire which would eventually spread throughout half of Asia. *To the north!*

As they made their way back to their tent, Irene still mincing her steps, Kungas allowed the smile to spread across his face. In the darkness, illuminated only by the cookfires and the few lanterns in the market, there was no one to see that unusually open expression on the king's face.

"That went marvelously well. Tomorrow, of course, you will twist the screw on Baresmanas."

Irene grimaced. Not at the thought of the next day's negotiations, but simply because her back now seemed like a sea of fire. "He'll shriek with agony," she predicted. "But he'll still give me the guns."

As it happened, Baresmanas did *not* squeal with pain, because he put up no more than a token resistance.

"Please! Please! I can't bear the thought of spending so many hours locked in combat." For a moment, his patrician Aryan face took on a severity which the most rigid Roman paterfamilias would have envied. "Not for myself, of course! Perish the thought. But you are a frail woman, in much pain because of the rigors of the journey. So my chivalrous instincts seem to have overwhelmed me. The guns are yours, Irene. The cannons, at any rate. Khusrau insisted that I hang onto the hand-held firearms."

"I want half of *them* as well," snapped Irene. The pain was making her grouchy. "And three-fourths of the powder and bullets. Your damned dehgans can't use the things properly anyway—and you know it as well as I do!"

Baresmanas shifted uncomfortably in his chair. "I foresaw this. Even warned the emperor!" He sighed again, and shook his head ruefully. "Ah, well. We Aryans have always been noted for our chivalry. I am a pawn in your hands."

Irene eased herself back into her own chair, again using the pressure of her hands on the armrests to stifle the pain in her spine. Then, smiled cheerfully. "Oh, don't be so gloomy. Khusrau can hardly punish you very severely, after all. Not with your own daughter being the new Empress of Rome! That might start a new war."

Three days later, the entire Kushan army departed Marv, leaving Baresmanas and his Persians in sole possession of the fertile oasis. With them went all of the Kushan artisans whom Lord Damodara had resettled in Marv the year before, in the course of his own campaign in the Persian plateau. The Kushan artisans wanted no part of Aryan rule. The Persians were notorious for their haughty ways.

But, still more, they were fired with enthusiasm for the Kushan cause. Most of them, after all, had come from Begram in the first place. And that city—the largest Kushan city in the world, and the center of Kushan industry and craftsmanship—was where Kungas proposed to march next. March upon it—and take it.

So, as Irene minced her way toward her horse, the Kushan camp followers and the new artisan families which had joined them cheered her on her way. Even more loudly than the Kushan soldiers, who were themselves cheering.

Before she reached the horse, several Kushan soldiers trotted up bearing a palanquin. They urged her to avail herself of the device—even offered, against all custom, to bear it themselves instead of putting slaves to the purpose.

Irene simply shook her head and minced past them. Behind her back, she could hear the gleeful sounds of the wagers being settled.

"The next time I see Antonina," she muttered bitterly, under her breath, "I'm going to have some harsh words to say to *her* on the subject of staring at a horse."

Three hours into the march, a party of Kushan women trotted their horses up to ride alongside her. Five of them, there were, all quite young. The oldest was no more than twenty, the youngest perhaps fifteen.

Irene was surprised. Not by the sight of Kushan women on horseback, which was uncommon but by no means considered outlandish. But by the fact that all five of them had swords belted to their waists, had bows and quivers attached to their saddles, and held lances in their hands.

"We're your new bodyguard," announced the oldest proudly. "Don't let anyone tell you otherwise!"

"The king said it was suitable," said the youngest. Very stiffly, as if she expected contradiction and argument.

The oldest, apparently fearing the same, rushed further words to the fore. "We checked with the oldsters. Every one of us—every one!—has Sarmatian ancestors." A bit uncertainly: "Some ancestors, anyway. All Kushans do, after all."

Irene grinned. "Splendid! I couldn't have asked for a better bodyguard. I feel better already."

The queen's sarcastic wit had already become famous among her Kushan subjects. So, still uncertain, the young women stared at her anxiously.

Irene erased whatever trace of humor might have been on her face. "I'm quite serious," she said serenely. "I'm sure you'll do well enough, if I'm ever attacked. But what's even more important is that you'll guard me against the *real* enemy."

The oldest girl laughed. "Boredom! Men never know what to talk about, on a march. Except their stupid wagers."

At the mention of wagers, all the girls looked smug. Irene was quite certain that every one of them had just gained a significant increase in their wealth.

"Do any of you know how to read?" she asked.

Seeing the five girls shake their heads, Irene's sarcasm returned in full force.

"Typical! Well, there'll be none of that, my fine young ladies. If you expect to be *my* bodyguard, you'll damned well learn how to read! I can teach you from saddleback—you watch and see if I can't."

Serene calm returned. "That way we'll *really* have some fine conversations, in the weeks and months ahead. Not even women, when you get right down to it, are superhuman. Ha! I sometimes wonder what those stupid illiterate goddesses talked about, other than sewing and seduction."

Chapter 14

CHARAX

Summer, 533 A.D.

Antonina surveyed the large crowd piled into the reception chamber of Emperor Khusrau's palace. *Whatever else changes,* she thought ruefully, *Persians will always insist on their pomp and ceremony.*

The palace had once belonged to the imperial official in charge of overseeing Charax. After they seized the city, the Malwa had made the building their military headquarters. Then, once Belisarius had retaken the city, the palace had been returned to the Persians. But since Khusrau had decided to plant himself in Charax for the duration of the war, the building had assumed full imperial trappings. True, the Persians had not insisted on reconstructing the entire edifice. Not with the dynamic and practical Khusrau as their emperor. But they had patched up the war damage, repainted every surface, hauled every conceivable manner of statuary and decoration from the imperial capital of Ctesiphon. And, most of all—or so it seemed to Antonina, scanning the scene—packed it with every grandee in the far-flung Persian empire.

God, will you look at that crowd! Like sardines in an amphora.

She spotted Ousanas and a handful of Axumite officers in a nearby alcove off the main audience chamber. The Ethiopians had brought some of their beloved stools, and were ensconced upon them circling a small table piled high with goblets and wine jugs. The table was obviously Persian in design, and Antonina wondered idly how the Axumites had managed to obtain the thing. There was not a single table to be seen anywhere else in the jam-packed audience hall, or any of the other alcoves she could see.

Probably by threatening mayhem on the majordomo. She emitted a faint chuckle. *Which also explains the relative population scarcity in that alcove. Even Persian grandees get nervous around testy Axumites.*

The Axumites, like the Romans, were now allies of the Persian empire. But the Ethiopians had very little of the Roman patience with imperial protocol and the elaborate social finery which went with it. There had been any number of minor clashes between the Axumites and the Persians. None of those clashes had been violent, other than a handful of brawls in the dock area between sailors, but the Persian grandees generally avoided the company of Ethiopians except when it was absolutely necessary. An attitude which the Axumites reciprocated in full.

Ousanas spotted her and waved a hand, inviting her to join them. Antonina smiled, shook her head, and wiggled her fingers. Understanding the meaning of the gesture, Ousanas grinned at her and went back to his carousing.

Antonina sighed. "*Somebody,*" she grumbled under her breath, "has to maintain diplomatic appearances."

Glumly, she eyed the mob between her and the emperor. Khusrau, perched on a throne atop a dais at the far end of the audience hall, was the only person sitting in the entire chamber. Antonina estimated that it would take her ten minutes to squeeze her way up to Khusrau's august presence in order to tender her official Roman diplomatic regards.

And twice that long to squeeze my way out, battling against the flow. I'll be mashed like a grape by the time it's over.

She had forgotten about her bodyguards.

"Allow us," murmured Matthew's voice, coming from behind her. Behind her, and well *above* her, for Matthew was practically a giant.

A moment later, Matthew and Leo were plowing a path for Antonina through the crowd. Following in their wake, she was almost amazed at the speed they were making. The more so, since the two bodyguards were actually being quite gentle in their meth-ods. Neither Matthew nor Leo was carrying any weapons, for such were forbidden in the presence of the emperor. They didn't even use their hands, just the inexorable forward movement of their immense bodies. But the combination of their size, stolidity—and Leo's truly hideous-ugly features—worked like a charm. Within two minutes, Antonina had arrived at the foot of the emperor's throne.

Seeing her, Khusrau smiled and leaned over.

"You really don't have to do this," he murmured. "It's all a pure formality, since I'll be seeing you tomorrow at our usual planning session."

"Yes, I do," hissed Antonina in reply. "Or else half your grandees will be whispering in your ear by the end of the night, predicting imminent Roman treachery. And you and I would have to waste all our time tomorrow figuring out ways to counteract the rumors instead of planning the campaign."

Khusrau chuckled. "And as many of your own officials, I'll wager."

Antonina shook her head firmly. "Only a third of them. Romans aren't as touchy as Aryans, Emperor." She scowled. "Which, I admit, probably comes to the same fraction of *active* officials. Since about one-third of my officials are so corrupt they don't pay atten-tion to anything except counting their bribes."

Khusrau laughed aloud, this time. Hearing the sound, practically everyone in the great chamber froze for an instant. A hush fell over the room. Hundreds of eyes were riveted on the sight of the emperor laughing at a jest made by the wife of Belisarius.

In some completely indefinable manner, a certain tension seemed to ease from the room. A moment later, everyone was back to their jabbering conversation.

"And another successful maneuver," said Khusrau quietly. "Begone, Antonina. It looks far more comfortable in that alcove with those disrespectful black savages. And if I know Ousanas, the wine's even better than what my servants are dispensing."

A vague look of longing came over the emperor's face, as if he felt a certain envy at the prospect. Khusrau was an energetic and active man, and Antonina had no doubt at all he would have much preferred to squat on a stool around a convivial table of Axumite officers himself than spend hours on a massive throne in an audience chamber.

But the moment was brief, and the emperor's expression resumed its normal air of serenity. Khusrau Anushirvan was the Emperor of Iran and non-Iran, after all. And, truth to tell, he much enjoyed that status, despite its occasional drawbacks.

Antonina nodded and turned away. Three minutes later, following easily in the path cleared for her by Matthew and Leo, she was perched on a stool at the table in the alcove. Reaching, with no little eagerness, for the goblet full of wine handed to her by Ousanas.

Alas. She had barely managed to sip from the goblet when she heard someone clearing his throat behind her. Another official of some kind, demanding some small decision from her.

She was in a shorter temper than usual. "Can't this wait—" she began to snarl, turning her head. Then, seeing that it was Dryopus standing behind her, she fell silent. One of the many things she liked about Dryopus was that he did not, unlike most Roman officials, insist on passing along to his superior every petty decision to be made.

Dryopus was frowning slightly. "My apologies for disturbing you, Antonina. But I am a little concerned by the situation with the *Circe*. More than a little, actually."

"Why? What did the inspectors report?"

"They *haven't* reported, Antonina. I've not seen or heard from them since we sent them off this morning to inspect the ship."

Antonina stiffened and set the goblet down on the table. "That was hours ago!"

The cheerful conviviality had left the faces of the Axumites also. "What is wrong, Antonina?" asked Ousanas.

Quickly, Antonina sketched the situation. The stubborn reluctance—odd, under the circumstances—of the brothers Aco and Numenius to allow their ship to be used for hauling military supplies; her decision to send inspectors this morning.

"Malwa," stated Ousanas firmly. "The *Circe* is loaded with gunpowder, and packed with Malwa soldiery. That's a fireship, aimed at the shipping in the harbor."

His quick conclusion summed up the worst of Antonina's fears. She rose abruptly and began heading toward the entrance to the palace. Behind her, she heard the scrape of stools as the Axumites followed suit.

"That ship *has* been kept out of the harbor itself, hasn't it?" she asked Dryopus, who was scurrying next to her.

"Oh, yes," he assured Antonina. "Until they've been inspected, no ship is allowed past the screen of galleys into the harbor. Those were your orders from the very beginning, and I've seen to it they've been scrupulously adhered to."

Ousanas had drawn alongside her and heard Dryopus' last words.

"Won't matter," he said curtly. "The Malwa are canny, and their spies are excellent. By now, those procedures of yours have become routine. The Malwa waited until enough time had elapsed for everyone to become lackadaisical."

"The procedures *have* been followed," insisted Dryopus stubbornly. "Not a single ship has ever entered the actual harbor without being inspected. Not one!"

Antonina felt compelled to defend her subordinate. "He's right, Ousanas. And while I have no doubt many ships have come in carrying contraband, that's not the same thing as sabotage. No inspector, no matter how corrupt, is crazy enough to accept a bribe from a Malwa ship loaded with soldiers and weapons."

Ousanas shook his head. "The problem is not with the inspectors. It's with the galleys. By now, those soldiers and sailors are so bored with guard duty they won't be paying attention to anything."

They had reached the palace's aivan, which was doubling for the evening as a weapons repository for the nobility enjoying Khusrau's hospitality. The Axumite weaponry was as distinctive as the Ethiopians themselves, so by the time Antonina and Ousanas came up the Persian soldiers guarding the weapons had sorted them from the rest.

Ousanas himself had brought nothing but his great spear. He waited impatiently while the other Axumite officers donned their armor and attached the baldrics holding their swords. That done, the officers took up their own spears and the entire party began hurrying through the aivan.

Antonina had brought no weapons of any kind herself, and was now regretting the loss. But when she murmured something to that effect, Ousanas smiled grimly.

"Not to worry," he said. "Your maidservant was smart and efficient even before she obtained me for a paramour."

At that moment, they passed through the entrance vault of the aivan and debouched onto the street beyond. Antonina immediately spotted Koutina, squatting among a small horde of servants waiting for their masters and mistresses to emerge from the imperial soiree.

Actually, Koutina was the only one of the servants who was *not* squatting. She was perched comfortably on a piece of luggage standing on end. The handcrafted leather-and-brass valise was something which Koutina was in the habit of carrying with her every time she and Antonina went anywhere beyond the immediate vicinity of the small mansion Antonina had appropriated for her activities. Weeks earlier, she had requested enough money from Antonina to pay for the rather expensive item. Which Antonina had given her readily enough, of course. She had long since come to have complete confidence in Koutina's ability to manage all of Antonina's household affairs.

Antonina *had* wondered about that valise. The thing was rather large, and heavy enough that Koutina had had straps attached to it by which she could hoist the thing onto her shoulders. But the one time Antonina had inquired, Koutina had simply smiled and said it contained the odd necessities which might be required by some unlikely eventuality.

Koutina had spotted them even more quickly than Antonina had spotted her, and was already hurrying toward them. Koutina had clearly realized something was wrong, judging by the frown on her face. And instead of hoisting the valise onto her shoulders, she was beginning to undo the buckles holding the valise shut.

A sudden suspicion came to Antonina. "Has that thing got—?"

Ousanas snorted. "A smart and efficient woman, I said." Scowling, he eyed the western horizon and, then, the harbor area to the south. "The sun has already set. And it will be dark tonight, with a new moon. The Malwa planned this well."

Antonina was still not quite as certain of the situation as Ousanas, but she was relieved to see the contents of the valise, once Koutina opened it up and set it before her. Inside the case was Antonina's gun and her cleaver, along with the cleaver's scabbard.

"I tried to figure out a way to carry your cuirass," said Koutina apologetically, "but the leather-maker said it would require something almost the size of a trunk. And be very heavy to carry."

"Tell me about it," grumbled Antonina, buckling on the scabbard. Then, more cheerfully: "It doesn't matter, Koutina. That damned cuirass is more of a hazard than a help at sea, anyway. Which is where I'm sure we're headed. I'm just glad you were foresighted enough to bring my weapons. Thank you for that."

Koutina reacted to the praise with a simultaneous smile and frown. Smiling: "You're welcome." Frowning: "You shouldn't be using them at all!" Koutina pointed an accusing finger at Matthew and Leo: "That's what they're here for!"

Matthew looked embarrassed. Leo might have scowled, but it was hard to tell. Leo *always* looked like he was scowling.

For a moment, Antonina considered summoning a palanquin. But she dismissed the idea immediately. It would take at least three palanquins to carry her bodyguards and the Axumites, along with herself. By the time they were assembled, they could have walked halfway to the harbor. The imperial palace was less than a mile from the docks.

The Axumites had already reached the same conclusion and were starting into a dogtrot. Antonina hurried to keep up with them. That pace was one which Ethiopian soldiers could keep up for hours. Antonina couldn't, but she was sure she could maintain it long enough to reach the harbor.

"I have no intention of mixing myself into the fray." The effort of trotting made the words come out very firmly indeed.

"You always say that," came Koutina's equally firm rejoinder. "And look what happens! At the battle with the Arabs! And you joined the assault on Lady Holi's ship!"

"Not ladylike," insisted Antonina. She was beginning to pant a little.

So was Koutina, but the maidservant wasn't about to let the issue slide. "Promises!" She gazed ahead at the darkness looming over the gulf beyond the harbor. "Are you sure we're going to have to go out on boats?" Gloomily: "I don't swim very well."

"You can stay on the docks."

"Where you go, I go. But are you sure?"

Antonina was about to reply that she wasn't really sure of anything. But, at that moment, the darkness over the waters of the gulf was suddenly streaked by flashes. A bit like horizontal lightning, perhaps.

"I'm sure," she said. "That's Malwa rocket fire. The attack has started."

Chapter 15

They reached the docks just a few minutes later. By the time they got there, Roman officers had already organized at least eight galleys to set out into the harbor. The first of the galleys, in fact, was just beginning to cast off.

"Impressive," stated Ousanas. "The galleys guarding the harbor may have been caught napping, but the rest of your naval forces were alert."

One of the other Axumite officers laughed harshly. "It helps to have a battle erupt, to wake up dozing seamen." He studied the gulf beyond the harbor—what could be seen of it, in the darkness, which was not much—and pronounced: "The three galleys on guard have been badly hammered, I think. I haven't seen a rocket flare in over a minute, and that was only the one."

"Out of action now," agreed Ousanas. "Let's hope the survivors can row their ships ashore. But it doesn't matter." He pointed to the galleys getting ready to leave the docks. "They won't be caught by surprise. That Malwa ship will never make it into the harbor."

Antonina studied the galleys. Each one held upward of two hundred and fifty men, between the rowers and the marines. Like any war galley setting into battle, each ship was crammed with as many men as could possibly fit into it. And, except for the ram bracing at the bow, each galley was built like a cockleshell. With war galleys, almost everything was sacrificed for speed.

Then, her gaze moved further down the docks and came to rest on the *Theodora Victrix*. That ship, a small sailing vessel built primarily to use its fire cannon, used only a small crew. And it was very sturdily built, with a well-designed rocket shield over the bow. The principal "maneuver" of the *Theodora Victrix* in battle was simply to sail directly at the enemy, shrugging off missiles, until it got close enough to bathe them in a gout of hellfire.

The *Victrix* was also ready to cast off. Even though harbor defense was not one of its normal duties, the officers and sailors of the ship had also responded to the emergency. Antonina could see Eusebius standing on the dock next to the ship, staring out to sea. The dock area was very well lit, even at night, and Antonina could recognize him easily.

"No," she said decisively. "We'll keep the galleys back, as a last defense, and use the *Victrix*."

She was already starting to hurry toward the *Victrix,* issuing orders as she went to the various naval officers on the docks. Fortunately, the commander of the harbor patrol came up to her at that moment, and she was able to delegate the task of holding back the galleys to him.

"And what about the cannons?" he asked. He pointed at the darkness which was all that could be seen of the gulf beyond the immediate harbor area. "I've had them holding their fire, because there's nothing to see and I was afraid they'd hit our own galleys."

Antonina glanced up at the fortifications above the harbor area. The snouts of a dozen huge cannons glimmered in the lantern-light.

"Keep them loaded and ready," she commanded. "When the time comes for them to start firing, I'll send up a signal rocket. Green flare."

"What'll they shoot at?" asked the commander.

Antonina grinned. "They won't have any trouble spotting the target. Trust me."

The commander nodded and left. Antonina's brief exchange with him had enabled Ousanas and the other Axumites to catch up with her. "Are you mad?" demanded Ousanas. "Why use the *Victrix*? The galleys can handle the matter. Quite easily, I can assure you." One of the other Ethiopians grunted his agreement.

Stubbornly, Antonina shook her head. "I don't doubt it, Ousanas. And then what?"

Seeing the look of incomprehension on his face, she sighed with exasperation. "*Think*, Ousanas." She jerked her head toward the still-unseen Malwa ship. "That ship—this is your own theory, man!—is packed with explosives. Enough to rupture the whole harbor. It's got to be crewed by Mahaveda. Fanatic priests. No one else could be trusted for such a suicidal mission."

Ousanas jerked a little, startled into a sudden understanding of her point. "Once the Mahaveda see they've no chance of reaching the harbor—"

"They'll wait until the galleys are surrounding them and blow the ship," Antonina finished, grimly. Again, she started hurrying toward the *Victrix*. "I doubt if even one of those galleys would stay afloat. Two thousand men—more than that!—would be spilled into the sea at least a mile from shore. Half of them would be dead before they hit the water. Of the rest, we'd lose half in the darkness before they could be rescued."

"At least half," muttered Ousanas, keeping pace with her. Sourly: "Why is it that Roman sailors refuse to learn how to swim? No Axumite soldier is allowed aboard a ship until he can prove—"

His comparison of the relative merits of Roman and Ethiopian sailors was broken off by Eusebius' shout of recognition.

"We're heading out!" Antonina shouted back. Under her breath: "Or whatever the proper damned nautical expression is."

"Don't sneer at proper nautical terms, woman," chuckled Ousanas. "They're all that's going to make this crazy scheme of yours work. Or hadn't you noticed that we'll be sailing before the wind?"

Guiltily, Antonina realized that she hadn't given any thought at all to the matter. She must have made a little start of surprise herself, because Ousanas immediately laughed.

"I thought not!"

They were almost at the *Victrix*. By now, Antonina was starting to pant with the exertion of their race from the palace. But she managed to gasp out: "Will we be able to do it?"

Ousanas grimaced. "The wind's right. And the current will be with us. So we'll be able to sail down on them quickly, while they're struggling to row up into the harbor. But once the contact's made—"

They were at the *Victrix* now. Antonina answered Eusebius' babbled questions by simply grabbing him and marching him ahead of her across the gangplank. By the time she and Ousanas were aboard, Eusebius was clear on his duties and was beginning to issue the needed commands.

Antonina hurried forward and entered the enclosed section of the bow. Inside the heavy and well-built rocket shield, the light cast by the lanterns on the docks and the few on the ship was blocked completely. She groped her way to the vision slits and stared into the distance. Everything in the gulf was pitch-black now. Belatedly, she realized she hadn't given any thought at all to the most basic problem: *how will we spot the enemy?*

Fortunately, Ousanas had thought about it. She heard him entering the shield a few seconds later. "I just checked with Eusebius, Antonina. The *Victrix* carries twenty rockets equipped with flares, for night operations. In addition to the usual signal rockets. We should be able to spot the Malwa ship once we get out of the harbor."

The *Victrix* was getting underway. Antonina could feel the motion of the ship, as well as hear the sounds of the sailors hurrying about their tasks. Eusebius' shrill voice periodically rose above everything else.

Some part of her was saddened to recognize John of Rhodes' training in the confidence with which Eusebius issued his commands. Antonina remembered the first time she met Eusebius, years before, at her estate in Daras. John had employed him to assist in the work of designing the new gunpowder weapons. For all his brilliance as an artificer, young Eusebius had been as shy and socially awkward a man as she had ever met in her life.

No longer. Eusebius would never have more than a portion of John's casual ease of command, true, but he had come very far from where he started. That was only one of the many legacies which John of Rhodes had left behind him, and Antonina took a moment again to grieve his loss.

Only a moment, however. There was a battle to be fought and won.

She turned away from the view-slit and began groping in the darkness. "Help me find the igniters, Ousanas, so we can light the lanterns. They should be in a cabinet around here somewh— never mind."

She'd found the cabinet, and quickly pried it open. Feeling her way, she found one of the ignition devices she was seeking. A few seconds later, the first of the lanterns located inside the shelter was lit, and she was finally able to see something.

The first thing she saw was Koutina, squeezed into the shelter alongside Matthew and Leo.

"What are you doing here?" she demanded.

Koutina smiled shyly, and held up the valise. "You didn't take your gun. Only the cleaver. So I thought I should bring it along. Just in case."

Antonina sighed, half with exasperation and half with affection. "You shouldn't be here at all. But it's too late to do anything about it now. So leave the valise here and get below decks." She looked to Matthew. "See to it, please."

Koutina started to squawk some kind of protest, but Matthew had her ushered out of the shelter before she could finish the first sentence.

The next thing Antonina saw, in the lantern-light, was Ousanas' big grin.

"And what are *you* doing here?" he demanded. "You've got no more business here than she does."

Antonina shook her head irritably. "I could ask the same of you, Ousanas! This is a Roman ship, not an Axumite one."

"I've gotten accustomed to watching out for you," he replied, as he finished lighting the rest of the lanterns. He placed the igniter back in the cabinet and shrugged.

"But I told my officers to stay back on the docks. There's no good reason to risk them on this expedition." He eyed the large, complicated-looking gadget which filled the center of the shelter. "What they know about using Greek fire cannons would fill the world's smallest book."

That comment drew Antonina's own eyes to the fire cannon. With the lanterns lit, the true nature of the "bow shelter" was apparent. She was reminded, forcefully, that the shelter could more accurately be called a "turret." An unmoving one, true. But a turret nonetheless.

For the first time since the crisis started, she felt a trace of hesitation and unease. In truth, although she understood the basic workings of the device, Antonina had no real idea how to operate it under combat conditions. Under any conditions, actually.

At that moment, Eusebius came into the bow shelter. The relaxed and casual glance he gave the fire cannon reassured Antonina. However awkward Eusebius might still be in social situations, he was as adept an artificer and mechanic as any in the world.

"You'll have to operate the cannon," she pronounced.

Eusebius' eyes widened. *Who else?* was the obvious thought behind that startled expression. Antonina found herself forcing down a giggle.

"Good," she pronounced. "That's settled. What do you want me and Ousanas to do?"

Eusebius looked back and forth from each to the other. "You, I mostly just want to stay out of the way, Antonina. Except for telling me what you want done." He eyed Ousanas' spear. "Him, I'd just as soon keep around. Never know. The *Victrix* isn't designed for boarding operations. But—you never know."

"We're *not* going to be doing any boarding, Eusebius. In fact, I want to stay as far away from that oncoming Malwa ship as possible. It's bound to be crammed with gunpowder and every incendiary device known to man."

Eusebius nodded. He'd obviously figured that much out himself. "You just want to torch it, and get as far away as possible before it blows. But the Malwa may have their own plans, and so I can't say I'm sorry to see Ousanas and that spear of his in the area. We only have a handful of marines to fend *off* any boarding attempt."

He came forward, edging his way around Antonina—the fire cannon in the center made the turret a cramped place—and peered through the viewing slit. "Can't see a damn thing. I've got the crew ready to start sending up flares. Probably ought to send up the first one very soon. We've got no idea how close that enemy ship has gotten by now."

"Go ahead and fire it off, then. But not the green one; that's my signal to the battery," said Antonina.

Eusebius worked his way past her again. Just as he reached the open space at the rear of the turret, leading to the deck beyond, a sudden thought came to Antonina.

"Eusebius! I'm puzzled by something. If *we* have flare rockets, why doesn't the battery guarding the harbor? I'd think they could handle bigger ones, in fact."

Again, Eusebius' eyes widened. If anything, he seemed more startled than before. "They could, actually. Much bigger ones. Big enough to reach several miles out to sea and light up the whole area enough for the battery to have a target even at night."

He cleared his throat. "As to why—? Well, the basic reason is that nobody ever thought of it." He ducked his head and scuttled out of the turret.

Ousanas chuckled. "War is too serious a business to leave in the hands of men, Antonina."

"My thoughts exactly!" She turned back to the viewing slit and peered into the darkness. "Mind you, they're handy to have around. When the crude muscular stuff actually happens."

Chapter 16

A few minutes later, the first flare went off. Her face pressed against one of the viewing slits in the shield, Antonina scanned the dark sea looking for any sign of the approaching Malwa suicide ship.

She didn't have very long to spot anything. When the flare erupted, about three hundred feet above the sea, it cast a very satisfactory light over a large area. But the parachute failed to deploy, and the spent rocket plunged into the water after providing only a short moment of illumination.

"Damn the thing!" She turned her head and glared at Eusebius. "What went wrong?"

Eusebius didn't seem greatly perturbed. "What usually happens." He straightened up from his own viewing slit and shrugged. "Those flare rockets are pretty crude, Antonina. Not much more sophisticated, except for the venturi, than the simplest Malwa rockets. Well over half the time, the propellant fires too unevenly—or too hot, or both—and burns through the parachute rigging before the flare goes off."

"Why don't we fix the problem?" she grumbled.

"Not worth it. That'd make for very expensive rockets. The way it is, we can carry plenty of them." He turned his head and bellowed—shrilled, more precisely—an order for another flare to the seamen waiting at the rocket trough just behind the bow shield.

They were obviously expecting the order, and the next flare went up seconds later.

"The trick," said Eusebius softly, as he pressed his eyes back to the slit, "is not to try to scan the whole area. I always assume the rocket is going to malfunction, so I always start by scanning the area just ahead. Then, for the next one, the area to my left. Then—"

He broke off. The second flare erupted—and, again, plunged almost immediately into the sea.

Antonina slapped the side of the shield in frustration. "Couldn't see anything!"

Eusebius was already shrilling another order. Then, turned back again to the viewslit. "Nothing in front of us or to the left. Now we'll see what it looks like to starboard."

Antonina held her breath. Then, erupted in more cursing. Louder, this time. The parachute for the third flare had deployed satisfactorily. But the flare itself failed to ignite, and the only light shed was the faint glow of a still-smoldering rocket fuselage as it drifted gently down to the waves.

"*Another!*" shrilled Eusebius.

But that flare became almost a moot point. Just before Eusebius issued the command, Antonina suddenly saw the enemy vessel. It was well illuminated by the back flash of a rocket volley sent their way by the Malwa. Clearly enough, the three rockets sent up by the Romans had provided the enemy with a target.

"Stupid," muttered Eusebius. "They're still three hundred yards off. They should have waited."

Antonina held her breath. But Eusebius' confidence proved justified. Five of the six rockets fired by the Malwa missed the Roman vessel by a good fifty-yard margin—one of them even exploding in midair almost as soon as it left the enemy ship. The Malwa too, clearly enough, were plagued with malfunctioning missiles.

The last missile caromed off the sea surface and skipped past the *Victrix*, missing the stern by not more than ten feet.

Antonina turned her head and saw Ousanas pressing himself into the entrance of the bow shield. There wasn't much room, with the three-man crew staffing the fire cannon. The Ethiopian aqabe tsentsen grinned at her.

"Getting hot now," he said. "Much cooler in here, behind these splendid shields."

Ironically, the fourth Roman flare went off perfectly. Looking back through her viewslit, Antonina could see that the Malwa ship was now perfectly illuminated.

"You should get back now also, Antonina," muttered Eusebius. His tone was half-apologetic, but firm for all that. "There's really nothing more for you to do. Everything's clear enough from here on. They're struggling against the wind and the current, and we're sailing right for them. Everything works for us now. They have to use oars, which means they can't fire too many more broadsides without losing way completely. And pretty soon we'll be coming at them bow-on anyway. I doubt they'll be able to fire more than two rockets at a time."

Reluctantly, Antonina backed away from the viewslit and began edging her way to the rear. Between the cramped space and her own voluptuous figure, getting past the two fire-cannon handlers on her side was a bit of a chore.

"Good thing you aren't wearing that obscene breastplate of yours," said Ousanas. "Or those men are crippled. Instead of enflamed with passion."

Antonina burst out laughing. The two cannon men tried to restrain their own laughter, but not with any great success. One of them shook his head ruefully, as he made a last minute adjustment to the complicated machinery of the flamethrower.

Some cool, calculating part of Antonina's mind recognized that their easy humor was a subtle indication of the respect and affection in which she was held by the soldiers and sailors under her command. Whatever resentment they might once have felt, being led by a woman—even if she was the wife of Belisarius—seemed to have vanished over the course of the two years since she had set sail from Constantinople.

And the same part of her mind, as she finally reached the rear of the shelter and squatted next to Ousanas, also finally understood something about her husband. She had often heard Maurice and Belisarius' bodyguards grumble at the general's stubborn insistence on exposing himself to danger. A characteristic which she, also, had always considered nothing more than childishness—even stupidity. But now, examining her own reluctance to leave the viewslit for the relative safety of the rear of the shield, she finally understood. Over the last two years, she too had internalized her own position of power and authority. And found the same profound distaste for ordering other people into danger if she was not prepared to share it herself.

Ousanas seemed to read her thoughts. "It's still stupid," he murmured. "Eusebius is perfectly correct—there's nothing further you can do now."

She stared up at him. Even squatting as they both were, the tall African hunter towered above her.

"You are a truly magnificent man, Ousanas of the lakes," she said softly. "I don't think I've ever told you that. If I weren't in love with Belisarius, I would set my sights on you."

He stared back at her. In another man, the dark eyes would have had a speculative gleam in them. Wondering if her words were a subtle invitation. But Antonina would not have spoken those words to another man. And so the eyes of Ousanas contained nothing but a soft glow of warmth and affection.

"I dare say you'd succeed, too," he chuckled. "You are quite magnificent yourself."

He shook his head, slightly. "But it probably wouldn't work, anyway. I fear with my new-found august status that my eventual marriage will be a thing of state. And I can't really see you as a concubine. A wife or a courtesan, but never a concubine."

"True," she nodded. For a moment, she paused, gauging the sounds of another oncoming Malwa volley. But her now-experienced ear recognized another miss, even before the sailor who had taken her place at the viewslit exclaimed: "Stupid bastards! They're still two hundred yards off. Waste of rockets."

"True," she repeated. Her curiosity was now aroused, and she found a welcome relief in it from the tension of simply waiting for battle to erupt. She cocked her head, smiling.

"But why wouldn't you select a high-placed Roman wife?" she asked. "Not me, of course, but someone else. It would seem a natural choice, given the new realities. I would think—certainly hope—that Axum intends to retain its alliance with Rome even after the Malwa are broken. And I'm quite sure Theodora would be delighted to round up three dozen senators' daughters for you to select from."

She spread her hands, palms up, as if weighing two things in the balance. "Granted that empires and kingdoms are fickle creatures, and not given much to sentiment. But I still can't see where the future holds any serious reason for conflict between Rome and

Ethiopia. We'd gotten along well for two centuries, after all, even before the Malwa drove us into close alliance."

"I agree," said Ousanas. The abrupt forcefulness of the statement, Antonina suspected, was a reflection of Ousanas' own tension at being forced to remain idle while others prepared to fight. "But that's part of the reason why I won't. The truth is, Antonina, there's no real reason for closer ties between Rome and Axum. The same distance that keeps us from being enemies, also makes close friendship unnecessary."

Ousanas paused for a moment, staring at the fire cannon in front of him. Something in the deadly shape of the device seemed to concentrate his thoughts. His expression became sternly thoughtful.

"Eon and I have discussed this at length, many times now. And twice—I'm not sure you even know about this—I spent hours with Belisarius, questioning Aide through him."

Antonina *hadn't* known of those sessions, as it happened, but she wasn't particularly surprised. Ousanas was one of the few people in the world, beyond Belisarius himself, who had "communed" directly with Aide. And so he understood, in a way that almost no one else would, just how encyclopedic was the crystal's knowledge of human history—including the vast centuries and millennia that would have unfolded, had the "new gods" not brought Malwa into existence. Antonina realized that Ousanas, canny as always, would have taken advantage of that opportunity to provide himself with the knowledge he would need as the aqabe tsentsen of Axum.

Translated literally, the term meant "keeper of the fly whisks." But the position was the highest in the Axumite realm, second only to that of the negusa nagast himself. His responsibility, in essence, was to guide the Ethiopian King of Kings in shaping the destiny of his people.

"Africa is the future of Ethiopia, Antonina. Not Rome, or any other realm of the Mediterranean or Asia."

He spread his own hands, palms down, as if cupping the head of a child. "A vast continent, full of riches. Populated only—except for Ethiopia and the Mediterranean coast—with tribes of hunters and farmers. Many of whom, however, are also skilled ironworkers and miners. Organized and shaped by Ethiopian statecraft, there's a great empire there to be built."

Antonina's eyes widened. "I've never pictured you—or Eon—as conquerors. Neither of you seems to have the, ah, temperament—"

"Not bloodthirsty enough?" he demanded, grinning. Then, with a chuckle: "*Statecraft*, I said."

He shrugged. "I'm quite sure we will have our share of battles with barbarian tribes. But not all that many, truth to tell, and more in the nature of short wars and skirmishes than great campaigns of conquest and slaughter. Keep in mind, Antonina—I am Bantu myself—that Africa is not heavily populated. And there is no great Asian hinterland producing Huns and such to drive the other tribes forward. We expect most of the task to be one for missionaries and traders, not soldiers. Peaceful work, in the main."

He broke off. Another Malwa volley was coming—and would strike home or come close, judging from the sound.

"Two rockets!" shouted the sailor at the viewslit. "One of them—"

An instant later, the shield shook under the impact of a missile. Antonina was a bit startled. Unconsciously, she had been expecting the same deep *booming* sound which she remembered from her experience in the battle outside Charax's harbor the year before. But the *Victrix*'s bow shield was no primitive, jury-rigged thing of leather stretched over poles. This warship was not a hastily converted galley. The *Victrix* had been designed from the keel up for this kind of battle, and the shield was a solid thing of timber clad with metal sheathing. It shrugged off the rocket as easily as a warrior's shield might shrug off a pebble thrown by a child.

"Ha!" shrilled Eusebius. "John was right! They need cannons—big ones, too, not piddly field guns—to break through this thing. And they don't have any!"

The sailor at the viewslit next to him shook his head. Antonina couldn't actually see the grin splitting his face, but she had no doubt it was there. "Not on this miserable priest-ship, anyway. Probably be a different story when we come up against the Malwa main fleet."

He turned his head toward Eusebius, showing his profile to Antonina. He *was* grinning. "But that's for a later day."

The sailor's grin faded. "Captain, I can handle this from here on. We're only a hundred yards off. Better see to the cannon. You're still the only one who can really use it very well."

Eusebius nodded. Watching, Antonina was struck by the little exchange. A different commander might have taken umbrage at such a semi-order coming from a subordinate. But although Eusebius had, more or less, become comfortable in his new role as a ship captain, he still had the basic habits and instincts of an artisan accustomed to working with others.

She didn't think John would have approved, really. But John was gone, and Antonina herself was not much concerned over the matter. She suspected that Eusebius' methods would probably work just as well.

And it was not her business, anyway. She forced her eyes away from Eusebius and looked at Ousanas. "Continue," she said. She spoke the word so forcefully that she was reminded, again, of her own tension.

"Not much else to say, Antonina. Axum has slowly been extending its rule to the south anyway, over the past two centuries. But heretofore the process was basically unplanned and uncoordinated. Most of our attention was focused on the Red Sea and southern Arabia. We will retain those, of course. But we will seek no further expansion in that direction. The Arab farmers and townsmen and merchants of Yemen and the Hijaz are content enough with our rule. But if we press further, we would simply embroil ourselves in endless conflicts with the bedouin of the interior—not to mention the certainty of an eventual clash with Persia. No point to any of it!"

He broke off. Another rocket volley. Both rockets, this time, struck the shield. And both were deflected just as easily and harmlessly.

"So after the war with Malwa," Ousanas resumed, "we will concentrate on the African interior—and do it properly. We will start by sending an expedition, led by myself, to incorporate the land between the great lakes which is my own homeland. That is the first step—along with seizing and settling the east African coast. At least as far south as the Pangani river. We will also seize the island of Zanzibar and build a fortress there. And we will found a new city on the coast, which will be destined to become a great seaport."

He smiled whimsically. "There are definite advantages, you understand, to Aide's knowledge of the future. Eon has even decreed that we will give that city the name it would have had, centuries from now. Mombasa."

He paused for a moment, his eyes becoming slightly unfocused. "The thing is, Eon and I are also thinking far into the future. We will not live to see it, of course—neither us nor our great-grandchildren—but we think our plans will eventually produce a very different Africa than the one which existed in the old future. In that future, Axum became isolated very soon by the Moslem conquests. And so, instead of being the conduit into Africa for that Mediterranean civilization of which we are becoming a part, Ethiopia retreated into the highlands. And there it remained, century after century, still more or less intact—but playing no further role in the history of the world or even Africa."

He cocked his head, gauging the sounds of the next Malwa volley. They were very close now, and both rockets missed entirely. Clearly enough, the priests manning the rocket troughs were getting rattled.

Eusebius and one of the sailors were now wrestling with the fire cannon's barrel, swiveling it to starboard. Unlike the rigid, single-piece construction of a normal cannon, the flamethrower was designed in such a way that the barrel could be positioned in any one of five locations, covering an arc of ninety degrees, without moving the main body of the device. One of the other sailors was removing the shield covering the rearmost firing slit on the starboard side. Eusebius, following Antonina's earlier terse instructions, intended to sail the *Victrix* right down the length of the Malwa galley, bathing it in hellfire as it passed. Hopefully, by the time the ship exploded, the *Victrix* would have sailed past far enough to avoid any catastrophic damage. Unless—

Again, Ousanas seemed to read Antonina's thoughts. "Let's hope one of those damned priests doesn't decide to blow the ship while we're alongside," he muttered. Then, a bit more brightly: "But probably not, since we're only one ship—and they'll have no way of knowing you are aboard."

"Or you," she retorted. "You *are* Axum's aqabe tsentsen. A Mahaveda might decide that was a satisfactory prize to take to hell with him."

Ousanas chuckled. "In the dark of night? Just another heathen black savage, that's all." He took Antonina's hand in his own and squeezed it. Then, gently, turned her wrist over and opened his palm. Her small hand, dusky-Egyptian though it was, was pale across the breadth of his own hand, black with African color.

"It means little to us, in our day," he mused, staring down at the contrast. "But a day will come—would have, at least—when that will not be so. A day when milk-white north Europeans, barbarians no longer but in some ways even more barbarous, will enslave Africans and claim that the difference in race is justification enough. A claim which they will be able to make because, for over a millennium, Africa remained isolated from world civilization."

He shook his head, smiling slightly. "Isolation is a bad thing, for a people as much as a person. So Eon and I, as best we can, will see to it that it never happens. Ethiopia's new destiny is to mother a different Africa. And I—"

His smile spread into a grin. "I am destined, I fear, to marry some half-savage creature who is even now squatting by the edge of one of the great lakes. But whose father can claim to be the 'great chief' of the land." He sighed. "Hopefully, I will be able to convince the creature to learn how to read. Or, at least, not to use my books for kindling."

"*Get ready!*" shrilled Eusebius. One of the sailors began frenziedly working the lever which filled the fire cannon's chamber. From beyond the shield, Antonina could hear the indistinct shrieks of Mahaveda priests shouting their own orders. She thought—she hoped—to detect confusion in those sounds.

But, for the moment, she blocked all of that from her mind. She would give that moment to the man named Ousanas, for whom, over the years, she had come to feel a great loving friendship.

"You will do well," she whispered. "And I have no doubt the girl will find you just as magnificent as I do."

He grinned, gave her hand a last little squeeze, and rose to his feet. Then, reaching over and grasping the great spear which he had left propped securely against the wall of the shield, he turned toward the entrance facing aft.

"First, we must survive this battle. And I suspect the Malwa priests will be pouring over the side onto our decks." His lip curled. "Screaming refugees, pretending to be fierce boarders."

Antonina said nothing. She just basked, for a few seconds, in her enjoyment at watching Ousanas move. Antonina had always had a purely sensuous side, which reveled in the sight of handsome and athletic men. And, in the case of her husband, who was one himself, the feel of such a male body.

But no man, in her life, had ever displayed such pure masculine grace and power as Ousanas. Watching him move reminded her of nothing so much as the Greek legends of Achilles and Ajax. So, for those few seconds, Antonina was able to forget all her tension in the simple pleasure of admiration.

"*Now!*" shrilled Eusebius. The sailor pumping the lever ceased; another turned a valve; Eusebius himself—this was the most dangerous task—ignited the deathspew gouting from the barrel.

"Just as I said," Antonina murmured to herself, "they're so handy to have around when the crude stuff starts happening."

Chapter 17

The interior of the bow shield, despite its small apertures, was suddenly filled with the reflected light of the fire cannon's effects. Antonina realized, even before she heard Eusebius' shout of triumph, that the very first blast must have struck the target perfectly.

"Like painting with fire!" shrieked Eusebius gleefully. "Look at it burn!"

Before his last words were even spoken, the sound of screams came through the shield, piercing Antonina's ears.

Mahaveda priests who had been positioned at the bow, she realized. Suddenly turned into so many human torches.

For all the horror in the thought, Antonina felt not even a twinge of remorse. Truth be told, with a few exceptions such as Bishop Anthony Cassian—Patriarch Anthony, he was now—Antonina had never been fond of any kind of priest, even Christian ones. She had been denounced by such too many times, in her reprobate youth.

Mahaveda priests had all the vices of any clerics, and none of their virtues. Their cult was a bastard and barbaric offshoot of Hinduism, more savage than that of any pagan tribe, and with the added evil which the sophistication of civilized India provided.

Burn in hell, then. As far as Antonina was concerned, the Mahaveda priests were finding their just reward.

During the few seconds which had elapsed, Eusebius and his cannon crew had been working feverishly. The cannon's fire-chamber was refilled; the sailor pumping the lever ceased abruptly; the valve was reopened by his mate. In those few seconds, Antonina realized, the *Victrix* must have carried alongside the *Circe*'s beam.

"Again!" cried Eusebius. *Ignition.*

Another flare filled the interior of the bow shield, brighter this time. Antonina knew in the instant that the hideous weapon had struck true yet again. More screaming filtered through the shield. Less distant.

She heard Ousanas mutter: "They'll be coming now. No choice." The aqabe tsentsen, still standing in the rear entrance of the shield, hefted his great spear.

Antonina's gaze was torn away from Eusebius and his men working at the cannon. For the first time, through the opening in the rear, she was able to see the destruction wreaked by the fire cannon. The *Circe* slid into view. The bow of the Greek merchant vessel seized by the Malwa was wreathed in flames. Even as she watched, a Mahaveda priest—she assumed it was a priest; hard to tell, from the way he was burning—stumbled on the railing and plunged into the sea.

"Again!" *Ignition.* Another flare. Most of the starboard side of the enemy vessel, Antonina realized, was now a raging inferno. More of the *Circe* slid into her view.

She hissed. Whether through deliberate effort or simply accident, the two ships were almost touching. Not more than five or six feet separated them—close enough to pose the danger of fire spreading.

A slight motion caught her eye. Antonina saw that Ousanas was shifting his stance. Clearly enough, the African was getting ready to fight.

For a moment, Antonina was puzzled. Granted, the deck of the *Circe* was level with that of the *Victrix*. Granted, also, the two ships were close enough for boarders to leap across. But—

What enemy could possibly hurl their bodies through that inferno?

The answer came almost as soon as the question.

Mahaveda priests.

Fanatics. This was a suicide mission in the first place.

Antonina scrambled to her knees and began opening the valise. Before she even managed to lay hands on her gun, she caught sight in the corner of her eye of the first priest leaping onto the *Victrix*.

The sight froze her, for an instant. The Mahaveda was like a demon—screaming and waving a sword—burning from head to foot. His garments were afire, and his face was already blackened and peeling away. She realized he must have been almost blind by now.

The priest managed to land on his feet. He stood for perhaps a second, before Ousanas leapt forward and decapitated him with a great sweep of his spear. The aqabe tsentsen was such a powerful man that he was quite capable of using that spear like a Goth barbarian would use a two-handed sword. The more so since the blade of the spear was a huge leaf, fully eighteen inches in length and as sharp as a razor.

Antonina started to rise, the gun in her hands, but Matthew shoved her back down with a hand on her shoulder.

"Stay here," he hissed. Then, as if realizing the pointlessness of that advice, the cataphract shook his head and added: "Just stay behind us, will you? Back us up if it's needed—but stay *behind* us."

That said, Matthew surged out of the bow shield. Leo had already charged onto the deck and was swinging his mace at another priest hurling himself through the flames. The heavy weapon, driven by Leo's great strength, swatted the priest back against the hull of the *Circe*. The Mahaveda seemed to stick there for a moment, before his body dropped into the small gap between the ships. Antonina could hear the simultaneous sound of a splash and a hiss. That priest's clothing had also been afire.

By the time Antonina got to her feet and came out of the bow shield, holding her double-barreled firearm, the battle on the deck was in full fury. What seemed like a horde of priests was pouring over the side, matched only by Ousanas and her two bodyguards.

Only . . .

Antonina almost burst into laughter. *Only . . .*

Three giants, great warriors one and all, matched against a tribe of troglodytes—all of whose experience at "combat" had been practiced in a torture chamber.

For a few seconds, she was mesmerized by the sight. Ousanas was in the middle, flanked by Leo and Matthew. His weapon flicked and stabbed like lightning, spearing one priest after another—half of them while still in midair. The aqabe tsentsen's skill was as great as his strength, too. Somehow he managed to land each strike without jamming the blade in bone or flesh. Most of the spear thrusts took the enemy in their throats, upending them into the sea while it spilled their lifeblood.

Matthew, with his spatha, and Leo, with his mace, made no attempt to match that precision. Nor had they any need to do so. Matthew's blade hacked bodies into pieces and Leo's warclub smashed them aside entirely.

Several of the *Victrix*'s sailors were now rushing up, swords in hand, prepared to support the three men fending off the boarders. Antonina shouted—"*Stay back! Stay back!*"—and fiercely waved them away. The sailors would be more of a hindrance than a help, she knew. In those close quarters, they would simply be an obstruction to the fighting room needed by Ousanas and Leo and Matthew.

The urgency of that task brought home to Antonina that she, also, was not thinking clearly. The three men fighting off the boarders did not need her help so much as they needed her to take charge of the situation.

Quickly, she scanned the scene. The Malwa ship was now engulfed in flames. Clearly enough, the few priests she could see frantically trying to quell the fires would not succeed. The *Circe* was doomed. No chance that the Malwa could reach the harbor and blow it up.

The danger which *did* remain was that the flames would reach the powderkegs which Antonina was certain filled every inch of the Malwa ship's hold. Unless the *Victrix* was well away by that time, she and everyone on her would join the Malwa in the ensuing destruction.

True, that would take some time. Most of the now-roaring inferno came from burning sails and rigging, not the *Circe*'s hull. By the time the fire burned through enough of the hull to reach the powderkegs, the *Victrix* could be a mile off.

Unless some priest realizes . . .

A vivid image flashed through her mind of a Mahaveda fanatic in the hold, bringing a torch to the powder. *Fanatics. And it was a suicide mission, anyway.*

She turned her head. Eusebius was no longer working at the fire cannon, but was staring at her. His face was as pale as Antonina suspected her own to be.

"Get us out of here!" she shouted.

Eusebius' face seemed to pale still further. He spread his hands in a helpless gesture.

Antonina cursed herself silently. She had forgotten that, taking charge of the fire cannon, Eusebius was no longer in control of the ship.

She turned back, facing the stern, her eyes seeking the helmsman. By now, the stern had drawn even with that of the *Circe*. Ousanas and the two cataphracts had kept moving aft down the side of the *Victrix*, fighting off the boarders doing the same on their own as the two ships passed each other. She saw two last boarders jump from stern to stern at the same instant that she spotted the helmsman of the *Victrix*.

The two priests went for the helmsman, but Ousanas intercepted them. A sweep and a thrust, and both Mahaveda were down. One dying on the deck, the other in the sea.

Antonina took no comfort at all from the sight. The fact that the priests had tried to kill the helmsman, while ignoring the onrushing Ousanas, suggested that the Mahaveda had already come to the same conclusion she had. No hope of accomplishing their original mission remained. That left . . . simply taking as many enemies with them as possible.

She started shouting at the helmsman, but broke off before uttering more than a few words. Clearly enough, the man understood the danger as well as she did. Nor, for that matter, was there much he could do that he wasn't doing already. The *Victrix* had been running before the wind as it was. No point in changing directions now.

She stared at the receding enemy ship. The *Circe* was no longer anything but a floating bonfire. There was not a chance that any man on her deck would still be alive within a minute or two. Nor, she thought—hoped—was there much chance that any of them would be able to fight their way across the deck to the hatchways leading to the hold.

That still left the possibility that at least one priest had stayed in the hold throughout the short battle, ready to ignite the powder if necessary.

Possibility?

Antonina winced. She was absolutely *certain* that a priest had been stationed there. Several of them, in fact—each one charged to make sure his fellows would not flinch at the very end when the time came to commit suicide. That had been the Mahaveda plan all along, after all. The only thing that had changed was that Antonina's intervention had prevented the *Circe* from reaching the harbor before they did so.

Ousanas trotted up to her, his spear trailing blood across the deck. "Only thing we can hope for is that they're still confused down there." Clearly enough, he had reached the same conclusion she had.

"One of the few times I've ever been glad those Mahaveda bastards are such fanatics," he said, grimly. "They'll be reluctant to blow it, not having reached their target. So until they're certain . . ."

She stared at him. Then, in a half-whisper: "They're *bound* to know that by now."

Ousanas shook his head. "Don't be too sure of that, Antonina. I got a better look at the conditions on the *Circe* than you did." He glanced at Eusebius, who had emerged from the bow shield and was charging back to the stern. The glance was very approving.

"That devil cannon of his must have hit them like a flood of fury. A tidal wave of fire and destruction. As confusing as it was horrible. I doubt the Malwa command structure survived more than a few seconds."

Again, he shook his head. "So . . . who knows? The priests in the hold may have been isolated from the beginning. And *still* don't know what's happening—and have no way of getting on deck to find out for themselves. Even Mahaveda fanatics will hesitate to kill themselves, when they're not sure what they'd be accomplishing by doing so."

Eusebius was shouting shrill orders. Some of the *Victrix*'s sailors started dousing the stern of the ship with water kept in barrels. Others began dousing the rigging. That *should* have been done before the battle even started, Antonina realized. But everything had happened too quickly.

It was getting harder to see anything. The *Circe* was now two hundred yards away, and the fierce light cast by the burning ship was no longer enough to do more than vaguely illuminate the deck of her own ship. But there was still enough light for her to see that several of the sailors, apparently at Eusebius' command, were standing ready with hatchets and axes to cut away the *Victrix*'s rigging.

"What are they doing?" she demanded. "The *last* thing we want is to lose our own sails."

Ousanas did not share her opinion. Instead, he growled satisfaction. "Smart man, Eusebius. He's figured out already that most of the explosives on board the *Circe* will be incendiaries." For a moment, he studied the ever more distant enemy ship. "We're far enough away, by now, that we can probably survive the actual shock of the explosion. But we'll soon be engulfed in fire ourselves. If we can cut away the rigging fast enough—that's what'll burn the worst—we might be able to keep the *Victrix* afloat. Maybe."

Something of Antonina's confusion must have shown in her face. Ousanas chuckled.

"Strange, really. You're normally so intelligent. *Think, Antonina.*"

He pointed back at the *Circe*. The Malwa ship was no more than a bonfire in the distance, now. "Their plan was to blow it up in the harbor, right? In order to do what?"

She was still confused. Ousanas chuckled again.

"Think, woman! The Malwa aren't crazy, after all. Insanely fanatic, yes, but that's not the same thing as actual lunacy. The harbor *itself*—even the buildings surrounding it—is built far too solidly to be destroyed by any amount of gunpowder which could be stowed on a single ship. Which means that their real target was not the harbor but the ships in it. And the best way to destroy shipping is with flame."

Finally understanding his point, she heaved a small sigh of relief. She had been imagining the Malwa ship as a giant powderkeg, which, when it exploded, would produce a large enough concussion to shatter everything within half a mile at least. But if most of the explosives were designed as incendiaries . . .

Matthew and Leo came up, looming above her in the darkness. Ousanas placed his hands on Antonina's shoulders, turned her around—gently, but she could no more have resisted him than she could have a titan—and propelled her back into the bow shield.

"So *you*," he murmured cheerfully, "will ride out the coming firestorm in the safest place available."

Once they were inside the shelter, with Matthew and Leo crowding behind, he added even more cheerfully: "Me, too. The thought of losing Africa's future because of a damned Malwa plot is unbearable, don't you think?"

Antonina put her gun back in the valise and closed it. Then, still kneeling, she looked up at the aqabe tsentsen. As she expected, Ousanas was grinning from ear to ear.

She started to make some quip in response. Then Ousanas' figure was backlit by what seemed to be the end of the universe. Armageddon's fire and fury.

Fortunately, Ousanas was quick-thinking enough to kneel next to her and shelter her in his arms before the shock wave arrived. Matthew was quick-witted enough to start to do the same.

Leo, alas, had never been accused of quick-wittedness of any kind, save his animal reflexes in battle. So the concussion caught him standing, and sent him sprawling atop Ousanas and Matthew, with Antonina at the bottom of the pile.

But perhaps it was just as well. Antonina was too busy trying not to suffocate under the weight of three enormous men to feel any of the terror caused by the firestorm which followed.

The next morning, at daybreak, Roman galleys found the *Victrix*. The vessel was still afloat, but drifting helplessly in the sea. It had proved necessary to cut away all the rigging before the fire was finally brought under control. Most of the sailors had suffered bad burns—which two of them might not survive—but were otherwise unharmed.

The ship itself . . .

"It'll take us weeks to refit her," complained Eusebius, as he watched his sailors attach the tow rope thrown from one of the galleys.

"You don't have 'weeks,' " snarled Antonina. "Two weeks, the most."

Eusebius' eyes widened with surprise. "Two weeks? But our campaign's not supposed to start until—"

"Change of plans," snarled Antonina. She glared to the east. The direction of the Malwa enemy, of course. Also, the direction in which Belisarius' army was to be found, marching slowly toward the Indus.

"Assuming my husband listens to the voice of sweet wifely reason," she added. Still snarling.

Chapter 18
THE JAMUNA
Summer, 533 A.D.

Link awaited Narses on Great Lady Sati's luxury barge, moored just downstream from the fork of the Jamuna and Betwa rivers. The fact that the monster from the future had traveled to meet *him* made the already anxious eunuch more anxious still. Link rarely left the imperial capital of Kausambi. To the best of Narses' knowledge, it had never done so since it had become—resident, lodged, whatever grotesque term might be applied—within the body of the young woman who had once been Lady Sati.

As he was escorted up the ramp leading to the barge's interior by two of Link's special assassins, Narses forced himself to settle down. If he was to survive the coming hour, his nerves would have to be as cold as ice. Fortunately, a long lifetime of palace intrigue and maneuver had trained him in the methods of calmness.

So he paid little attention to his surroundings as the black-clad, silently pacing assassins guided him through the interior of the barge. A general impression of opulence, almost oppressive in its luxurious weight, was all that registered. His mind and soul were preoccupied entirely with settling themselves within his heart.

A small, scarred, stony heart that was. With room in it for a single thought and purpose, no other.

The truth only. Narses is what I care about. Nothing more.

He entered a large chamber within the barge, somewhere deep in its bowels. At the far end, on a slightly elevated platform, sat Great Lady Sati. She was resting on an ornately carved chair made entirely of ivory. Her slender, aristocratic hands were draped loosely over the armrests. The veil was drawn back from her face, exposing the cold beauty of the young flesh.

In front of her, kneeling, were four immense men. They were naked from the waist up, holding equally naked swords in their huge hands. Great tulwars, those were. Two other such men were standing in the corners of the chamber, behind Great Lady Sati. Like the two assassins—and two others who were positioned in the corners of the room behind Narses himself—the giants were of Khmer stock. Nothing of India's flesh resided in those men.

But Narses paid them almost no attention at all. As soon as he entered the room, his eyes were drawn to the man sitting on a slightly less majestic chair directly to Great Lady Sati's right. Nanda Lal, that was. One of Emperor Skandagupta's first cousins, and the chief spymaster of the Malwa Empire.

The sight of Nanda Lal caused Narses' already-frigid soul to freeze completely. The sensation of relief was almost over-whelming.

Familiar ground, then. So be it.

A small stool was placed in the center of the floor, atop the rich carpet, perhaps ten feet from the elevated platform. Just close enough to Great Lady Sati and Nanda Lal to enable easy conversa-tion, but allowing the giant bodyguards the space needed to main-tain a shield before Link's human sheath.

Narses did not wait for an invitation. He simply moved to the stool and took a seat. Then, hands placed on knees, waited in silence.

The silence went on for perhaps a minute, as Link and Nanda Lal scrutinized him. Then Great Lady Sati spoke.

"Are you loyal to Malwa, Narses?"

The eunuch found it interesting that Sati's voice had none of the eerie quality which his spies had reported to him, from indirect reports. It was simply the voice of a young woman. Pleasant, if chilly and aloof.

"No." He thought to elaborate and expand, but discarded the notion. *The truth only!* Elaboration—expansion even more so—always carried the risk of wandering into falsehood.

"Not at all?"

"Not in the least."

"Are you loyal only to yourself?"

"Of course." A trace of bitterness crept into his voice. "Why would it be otherwise?"

"We have treated you well," interjected Nanda Lal, a bit angrily. "Showered you with wealth and honors."

Narses shrugged. "You have made me the spymaster for your finest general, and sent me off into a life of hardship and danger. Traipsing across half of Asia—at my age!—with enemies on all sides. The wealth sits idle in small coffers, locked within the emperor's vaults, while I live in a tent."

Nanda Lal shifted his weight in the chair, clutching the arm rests. He was a heavy man, and muscular. The chair creaked slightly in protest.

"I'm sure you've managed to fill your own coffers with bribes and stolen treasure!" he snapped.

Narses rasped a harsh chuckle. "Of course. Quite a bit, too, if I say so myself."

Nanda Lal's dark face flushed with open anger at the sneering disrespect which lurked just beneath the eunuch's words. His heavy lips began to peel back from his teeth in a snarl. But before he could utter a word, Great Lady Sati spoke. And, this time, in *the voice.*

All thoughts of derision and banter fled from Narses, hearing that voice. It was sepulchral beyond any human grave or tomb. The words were still spoken with the tone produced by a young woman's throat and mouth; but the sound of them was somehow as vast and cavernous as eternity. This, Narses knew, was the true voice of the *thing* called Link.

"DESIST, NANDA LAL. YOUR ANGER IS POINTLESS AND STUPID."

Link's young-woman-shell kept its eyes on Narses, giving the Malwa spymaster not so much as a glance. The eyes, too, seemed as empty as a moonless, cloudcast night.

"YOUR SOLE LOYALTY IS TO YOURSELF, NARSES. YOUR HEART CANNOT BE WON BY ANY CAUSE, YOUR DEVOTION BY ANY HONOR OR SENTIMENT, YOUR MIND BY ANY TREASURE. YOU SEEK, NOW AS AT ALL TIMES, SIMPLY YOUR OWN ADVANTAGE."

There didn't seem to be anything to say in response. So Narses said nothing. Link studied him in silence for quite some time. Narses had never in his life felt so closely scrutinized.

"NO. I MISJUDGED. THERE IS SOMETHING MORE. SOMETHING YOU ARE HIDING."

Narses' hands did not so much as twitch, resting on his knees. He simply leaned forward slightly and replied:

"Yes. I enjoy the game itself. Perhaps even more, I sometimes think, than the advantage it brings me. I hide that from sight, because it gives me yet another advantage. People assume me to be driven by ambition. Which is true enough, of course. But ambition is ultimately nothing more than a tool itself."

Silence reigned, for a few seconds. Then:

"YES. YOU REVEL IN THAT SENSE OF SUPREMACY. AN EMPTY MAN—NO MAN AT ALL, BY HUMAN RECKONING—WHO FILLS HIMSELF WITH HIS ABILITY TO SURPASS ALL OTHERS."

Narses bowed his head slightly.

"WE CANNOT THEREFORE TRUST YOU IN THE LEAST. NO MORE THAN WE COULD A SWORD WHOSE HILT WAS SMEARED WITH GREASE."

"Even less," snorted Narses. "A sword has neither a brain nor a will. It will twist in your hand only from mishap or accident, or carelessness. I can be counted on to do it from my own volition."

"YES. TREASON WHICH REVELS IN TREASON. NOT BECAUSE IT IS TREASON BUT BECAUSE IT IS THE GREATEST GAMBIT IN THE ULTIMATE GAME."

Again, Narses made that little bow of the head. A master acknowledging another, and one perhaps greater than he.

"SO BE IT. YOU THINK YOURSELF IMPERVIOUS, BECAUSE NOTHING CAN THREATEN YOU EXCEPT PAIN AND DEATH. BUT I WILL HAVE A HOSTAGE, NARSES."

Nothing in Narses' face or body—he would have sworn it!—registered so much as a twitch. Though somewhere through his icy, barren soul ran a sudden hot spike of terror. *Ajatasutra. My son!*

"THERE IS SOMEONE CLOSE TO YOU, THEN? YOU ARE NOT QUITE SO DETACHED FROM HUMANKIND AS YOU PRETEND."

Narses tried to speak, but found the words frozen in his throat. He could think of no truth, nor lie, which could shield him against that inhuman perception.

Nanda Lal spoke again. "We will find out who it is," he said, through tight teeth. "Then—rest assured—"

"BE SILENT. I WILL NOT SAY IT AGAIN. DO NOT SPEAK WITHOUT MY PERMISSION."

Nanda Lal's dark face seemed to pale. He pressed his heavy body back into the chair.

As before, the eyes of the shell called Great Lady Sati had never left Narses' face, even while uttering that apparently deadly threat. She spoke again, her words moving directly from the threat to Nanda Lal to the promise to Narses.

"SUCH A HOSTAGE WOULD BE MEANINGLESS. NARSES WAS CLOSE TO EMPRESS THEODORA ALSO. YET HE BETRAYED HER SOON ENOUGH. NO. I WILL HAVE THE ONLY HOSTAGE WHICH MEANS ANYTHING TO THIS MAN."

Her left hand lifted from the armrest and made a slight gesture. Narses could sense one of the assassins behind him coming forward, though he could not actually hear any footsteps on the heavy carpet.

A hand seized his neck. Not harshly, not with the intent to manhandle, simply to hold him still. A moment later, sharp pain lanced in the back of his head. A blade of some kind, he realized, had penetrated his flesh and cut out a small portion. He could feel blood slowly trickling down his back.

The assassin retreated. Narses stared at Link.

"HAVE YOU EVER HEARD OF A 'CLONE,' NARSES? NO? IT IS A HUMAN BEING MADE ENTIRELY FROM ANOTHER. A PERFECT COPY. A MAN GROWN LIKE A BUD. YOU, A EUNUCH WHO CAN HAVE NO CHILDREN, CAN STILL SIRE YOURSELF. WITH NO WOMB OR WOMAN NEEDED FOR THE PURPOSE."

The *thing's* eyes left Narses for a moment, looking behind her.

"TAKE THE FLESH AND DEPOSIT IT IN THE ICE CHEST. THEN RETURN." The young-woman/empty-void eyes returned to Narses. "I WILL HAVE IT GROWN, NARSES. WHILE YOU GO ABOUT MY WORK, I WILL RAISE THE HOSTAGE YOU HAVE GIVEN ME. BETRAY MALWA, AND YOU WILL LOSE YOURSELF. YOU WILL BE, IN THE END, AS EMPTY AS YOU HAVE ALWAYS THOUGHT YOURSELF

TO BE. CONSIDER THAT, EUNUCH OF ROME. I—ONLY I—CAN GIVE YOU ETERNITY."

Narses did not bow his head, this time, so much as lower it. A gesture not of respect so much as defeat.

"WE UNDERSTAND EACH OTHER, THEN. AND NOW, I HAVE A TASK FOR YOU."

The voice changed, in that instant, back to the voice of Great Lady Sati. And in that voice it remained, for the following minutes, as it explained to Narses the nature of his new assignment.

After Great Lady Sati finished, Narses immediately shook his head.

"It is a bad plan. Unworkable. Rana Sanga will not believe it for a moment."

Nanda Lal began to speak, then glanced apprehensively at Sati. She raised her hand in a stilling gesture. But the motion conveyed no threat. Simply an admonition to listen, before advancing an argument.

"Continue, Narses," she commanded.

"He has met Belisarius in person, Great Lady Sati. Indeed, he has spent many hours in his company. No matter what evidence I leave, he will not believe for an instant that the Roman general ordered the death of his family. Instead, his suspicion will rest upon the Malwa dynasty. And become confirmed, the moment you advance the proposal of marriage. Trust me in this, if nothing else. The plan—*as conceived*—is unworkable."

Silence. Then:

"You have an alternative, I see. What is it?"

Narses shrugged. "For your purpose, there is no need to make Sanga suspect Belisarius directly. Simply to arouse his anger and rage at the chaos which the war has brought. India is in turmoil now, nowhere more so than the western borderlands. Summon Rana Sanga's family to Kausambi, at the emperor's command. Hostages themselves, to assure Sanga's loyalty along with Damodara's. Send a small force from the emperor's Ye-tai bodyguard battalions to escort them. Perhaps a dozen men. Then, along the route—while they are still in Rajputana—"

"Yes!" exclaimed Nanda Lal. His earlier anger at Narses vanished, in the excitement of the scheme. "Yes. That will be perfect. The caravan is attacked by brigands."

"Better, I think." Narses cocked his head, thinking. "*Kushan* brigands. As the loyalty of the Kushans unravels, due as much as anything to Belisarius' cunning, many of them have turned to banditry. And Kushan deserters make ferocious bandits. Far more believable that they would attack such a caravan than any common dacoits. Not to mention *succeed* in the attack. The treasure looted, Sanga's wife hideously abused, herself and the children slain afterward. Their bodies left for carrion eaters, mingled with the butchered corpses of their Ye-tai guards."

Narses shrugged. It was a small, modest gesture. "I imagine I can probably even find one or two deserters from the Roman army to include in the bandit force. Just enough—there will be eyewitnesses to the attack, of course—to weight Sanga's anger even further."

"He will be angry at us as well," opined Nanda Lal, pursing his lips. "After all, had *we* not summoned his family out of the safety of his palace . . ."

"That is meaningless," stated Great Lady Sati. "Sanga's resentment we can tolerate. So long as his rage remains unfocused, it will channel itself into the war and his oath. When the time comes, he will accept the marriage."

The slim young-woman's hands made a small curling gesture, indicating the entire body to which they belonged. "He will feel no sentiment toward this sheath. But we do not need his sentiment. The sheath is well-shaped, and has been well trained. It will arouse his lust, when the time comes. And when the children arrive, soon enough thereafter, his sentiment will have another place to become attached. That is sufficient for the purpose."

Great Lady Sati stared at Narses for a moment. Then: "Do it, traitor. And remember my hostage."

Narses arose and bowed deeply from the waist. After straightening, he looked at Nanda Lal.

"The Ye-tai general Toramana, as I'm sure you know, is the commander of the troop which escorted me here. I saw to that. I suggest this would be a good time for you to interview him. There are . . . excellent possibilities there, I think."

Nanda Lal nodded. Narses' lips twisted into a bitter little smile.

"You'll have spies on me also, of course. So let's save some time. I need to pay a visit on Lady Damodara in any event, to give her a parcel from her husband. Beyond that—"

He transferred his eyes to Great Lady Sati. "It would be best, in any event, if I set up my headquarters in Lady Damodara's palace. In order to organize this maneuver, I will need to see any number of people. Better to have such folk coming in and out of *her* palace than any other. Even if Sanga stumbles across any knowledge of my doings, he will simply assume I was acting on behalf of Damodara himself. And he will never suspect Damodara of such a cruel deed."

Great Lady Sati did not even pause. "I agree. Do it."

Nanda Lal chuckled. "It hardly matters, Narses. I don't have to bother to have you followed. You think I don't have spies inside Lady Damodara's palace?"

Narses regarded him calmly. "I'm sure you do. I am also sure that within three days of my arrival, those spies will be expelled from the house. Those who are not dead."

Nanda Lal froze, his eyes widening. Narses snorted—very faintly—and bowed to Malwa's overlord.

"I'm sure you understand the logic, Great Lady Sati."

"It is obvious. There must be *no* suspicion. Your loyalty to Damodara must be unquestioned. Do not hesitate to kill all of Nanda Lal's spies, Narses. But do it shrewdly."

In the end, Narses did not kill all the spies. He saw no reason to kill the two cooks. Expulsion would serve as well, theft being the excuse—as it happened, a valid one. They *were* thieves.

He did not even bother to expel the two maids. He simply saw to it that their duties were restricted to the laundry, in a different wing of the palace than that where Lady Damodara and the children had their bedrooms. It was a large palace. There was no way the maids could find their way unobserved to the only other place in the palace which Narses needed to keep secret. The cellar deep below where a tunnel was being slowly extended.

He did have the two guards in Nanda Lal's employ assassinated, along with one of the majordomo's assistants. The guards simply had their throats slit while they slept, the night Ajatasutra arrived at the palace. The assistant, on the other hand, had been a retainer of Damodara's family since boyhood. So, before his own demise, Narses thought it was fitting to show the traitor the greatest of the secrets he had been trying—and failing—to ferret out for Nanda Lal. The secret he had never even suspected.

The assistant's body then vanished in the bowels of the earth, folded into a small niche which the Bihari miners dug in one side of the tunnel and then covered over. They did not even mind the additional work. Men of their class were not fond of majordomos and their assistants.

Although they did find a certain charm in the way the major-domo had pronounced many curses on his assistant's body as it was enfolded into its secret tomb. Quite inventive, those curses. And who would have thought such a stiff and proper old man would know so many?

If Lady Damodara noticed the disappearance of the guards and the assistant, or the reassignment of the maids, she gave no sign of it. Which, of course, was not surprising. The running of the household was entirely in the old majordomo's hands. Being also a man who had been a retainer of the family since boyhood—and one who was extraordinarily efficient—he was trusted to manage the household's affairs with little interference.

The daughters of Dadaji Holkar noticed, of course. They could hardly help notice, since they were assigned to replace the two maids—an assignment which they greeted with much trepidation.

"We don't know anything about how to take care of a great lady," protested the younger. "She'll have us beaten."

The majordomo shook his head. "Have no fear, child. The lady is not hot-tempered. A very kind lady, in fact. I have explained to her already that you are new to the task, and will need some time to learn your duties. She will be quite patient, I assure you."

Still hesitant, the girls looked at each other. Then the older spoke. "My infant will cry at night. The great lady will be disturbed in her sleep. She will be angry."

The old servant chuckled. "She has borne three children of her own. You think she has never heard such noises before?" He shook his head. "Be at ease, I tell you."

The girls were still hesitant. With most majordomos, they would not have dared to press the matter further. But this old man . . . he had been kind to them, oddly enough.

"Why?" asked the younger sister, almost in a whisper. "A great lady should have experienced maids, not . . . not kitchen drudges."

Kindly the old man might be, but the look he gave them now was not kind in the least. A hard gaze, it was. As if he were ponder-ing the same question himself.

Whatever answer he might have given went unspoken. For a new voice echoed in the girls' little sleeping chamber.

"Because I say so."

The girls spun around. Behind them, standing in the doorway, was the man who had rescued them from the slave brothel so many months earlier.

They were so delighted to see him that they almost squealed with pleasure. The youngest even began to move toward him, as if she were almost bold enough to clasp him in an embrace.

The man shook his head, although he was smiling. The headshake turned into a small gesture aimed at the majordomo. Making neither argument nor protest, the august head servant immediately left the room.

After he was gone, the man bestowed upon the girls that calm, hooded gaze which they remembered so well.

"Ask no questions," he said softly. "Just do as you are told. And say nothing to anyone. Do you understand?"

Both girls nodded instantly.

"Good," he murmured. "And now I must leave. I simply wanted to make sure all is well with you. It is, I trust?"

Both girls nodded again. The man began to turn away. The older sister had enough boldness left in her to ask a last question.

"Will we ever see our father again?"

The man paused in the doorway, his head turned to one side. He was not quite looking at them.

"Who is to say? God is prone to whimsy."

A little sob seemed to come from the younger sister's throat; almost instantly squelched. The man's broad shoulders seemed to slump a bit.

"I will do my best, children. More than that . . . " Whatever slump might have been in the shoulders vanished. They stood as square and rigid as ever.

"God is prone to whimsy," he repeated, and was gone.

"This is an unholy mess," grumbled Ajatasutra. "By the time I get back to Ajmer, Valentinian and Anastasius and the Kushans will have been festering for weeks in that miserable inn. When they hear about *this* little curlicue to your schemes, they will erupt in fury."

"All the better," snapped Narses. "Imperial Ye-tai troops aren't chosen for their timid ways, you know. And I can't have a smaller escort than ten—a dozen would be better—or the whole affair will ring completely false."

"Make it a dozen," chuckled Ajatasutra harshly. "Imperial Ye-tai be damned. Against *those* two Romans? Not to mention Kujulo and that pack of cutthroats he brought with him."

The assassin ran fingers through his beard. Then, smiled grimly. "You know what would be perfect? Have the escort led by some high Malwa mucky-muck. Nothing less than a member of the dynastic clan itself, *anvaya-prapta sachivya*. Some distant cousin of the emperor's. A young snot, arrogant as the sunrise and as sure as a rooster. He'll fuck up the assignment—probably insist on having himself and all the Ye-tai at the head of the convoy, leaving Rana Sanga's wife and kids to trail behind in the dust. Easy to separate them out and—"

As he spoke, Narses' eyes had widened and widened. "Why didn't *I* think of that?" he choked. "Of course!"

He eyed Ajatasutra oddly. "This is a little scary. I'm not sure I like the idea of you outthinking me."

Ajatasutra shrugged. "Don't get carried away with enthusiasm. Nanda Lal will have a fit, when you raise the idea."

"Not worried about that," retorted Narses, waving a casual hand. "If he gives me any argument, I'll just go right over his head. Great Lady Sati and I have an understanding."

Now it was Ajatasutra's turn to give Narses an odd look.

"S'true," insisted the old eunuch. "A very fine lady, she is, and an extraordinarily capable schemer." He paused. "For an amateur."

Chapter 19

CHARAX
Summer, 533 A.D.

By the time Belisarius got back to Charax, racing there in a swift war galley as soon as he got the news of the Malwa sabotage attempt, Antonina had her arguments marshaled and ready. And not just her arguments, either—in the few days which had elapsed, she had been working like a fiend to organize the "change of plans."

By the time the argument between them was just starting to heat up—

It's too early, Antonina! The army isn't ready! Neither is the Ethiopian fleet!

Get them ready, then! We can't wait any longer here!

Idiot woman! We have no way of knowing if Kungas has created a diversion yet!

I'll create one, you dimwit! A way, way bigger one than something happening in far-off Bactria! With or without the Ethiopians!

And that's another thing! I don't want you taking those kinds of chances!

Chances? Chances!? What do you think I'm facing here? There's no way to stop Malwa plots here in Charax! The place is a menagerie! Chaos incarnate!

—the argument got cut short by royal intervention.

Two royal interventions, in fact.

The first, by Khusrau Anushirvan. The Emperor of Iran and non-Iran had known of Antonina's new plans, of course. He had excellent spies. And he knew of Belisarius' opposition within an hour after the argument between them erupted on the general's return to Charax.

But it took him those few days, waiting for Belisarius' return, to ponder his own course of action. For all Khusrau's youth and energy, he was already a canny monarch, one for whom statecraft and long-term thinking was second nature. So he, unlike Antonina herself, immediately saw all the possible implications of her new proposal. And, for a variety of reasons—not the least being the opposition he expected to arouse among his Roman allies—he needed to take some time to examine all aspects of the problem.

A few days, no more. By midafternoon of the same day that Belisarius returned in the morning and began his raging quarrel with Antonina, Khusrau intervened. Understanding the delicate nature of the business, he even restrained his normal "Persian Emperor reflexes" and came to the Roman headquarters accompanied by no advisers and only a handful of Immortals for a bodyguard.

When he was ushered into the chamber where the dispute was taking place, Belisarius and Antonina broke off immediately. Neither one of them was surprised to see Khusrau appear, although they hadn't thought he would show up this soon. For the moment, the argument was still largely an internal Roman affair.

Belisarius' face eased a bit. Antonina's jaws set more tightly still. Clearly enough, both of them expected Khusrau would be introducing yet another voice of masculine reason. Doing his best to aid Belisarius in calming down a somewhat hysterical female.

The emperor disabused both of them immediately. He saw no reason to dance around the issue. Nor, of course, was there any need to disguise the fact that he had spies in the Roman camp. That much was taken for granted—just as was the existence of Roman spies in Khusrau's own entourage.

"I agree with Antonina, Belisarius," Khusrau stated abruptly. With well-honed imperial reflexes, he headed for the largest and most luxurious chair in the chamber and eased into it.

Belisarius and Antonina were both staring at him, speechless. Neither of them, clearly enough, had expected to hear *those* words coming from the Emperor of Iran and non-Iran.

Khusrau wriggled his fingers. "My reasons are rather different from hers, however." He gave Antonina a very stern look. "Personally, I think her fears for the security of Charax are overstated. Certainly they are not sufficient to justify such a radical and ill-prepared change in the campaign."

That last statement, perhaps oddly, caused Belisarius' jaws to tighten—and almost brought a smile to Antonina's face. Both of them were experienced negotiators in their own right, and immediately recognized Khusrau's ploy for what it was. The emperor would side with Belisarius' *logic*, thus providing the Roman general with a face-saving gesture of male solidarity, while agreeing with the *substance* of Antonina's proposal.

Since Belisarius didn't require much, if anything, in the way of face-saving or male solidarity, and Antonina cared not a fig *why* her proposal was adopted . . .

Antonina, exuding feminine modesty and poise, eased herself into her own chair. Belisarius remained standing in the center of the chamber. "Get to it, Khusrau," he growled. Normally, the Roman general would not speak so abruptly to a Persian emperor, but his mood was getting fouler by the moment.

"Yes, do," murmured Antonina. The sound was practically a coo.

Khusrau's teeth flashed briefly through his beard. The smile, for all its brevity, was heartfelt and not a gesture. If there was anything the Emperor of Iran and non-Iran appreciated, it was negotiating partners who were smart enough not to require him to waste endless time in diplomatic folderol.

"Have either of you given much thought to the future?" he asked. "I am speaking of the more immediate political future after our triumph." He paused for a moment. "Not of the philosophical profundities regarding human destiny which are raised by the existence of the Talisman of God in our midst."

Again he paused, allowing Belisarius and Antonina time to absorb the fact that Khusrau was well aware of Aide's existence. He did not expect that either of them would be much surprised by that, but Aide's existence had only been revealed to a single Persian. And that one—

"Baresmanas said nothing to me," he added, "until I made clear to him that I already knew the secret. You may rest assured of that, Belisarius."

The Roman general nodded. "No, he wouldn't." Belisarius sighed and abruptly sat down on a chair next to him. "But there was no way to keep the Talisman a secret anyway. Nor, really, much reason to do so at this point."

None at all, agreed Aide.

Belisarius touched the pouch which lay on his chest under the tunic. The pouch where, as always, Aide lay nestled. "Would you like to see him?"

Khusrau's eyes widened slightly. " 'Him'?" he asked. "A mystical jewel has a sex?" Under the thick, short, square-cut beard, the Persian emperor's teeth gleamed again. "Or is it simply—familiarity and ease? If so, I am a bit relieved."

He shook his head. "Not now, Belisarius. Later—yes, very much. But we have this to deal with first."

He waited. After a moment, Belisarius shrugged.

"You'll have to be more precise, Emperor. I have given quite a bit of thought to the political future after the fall of Malwa. But I suspect you have something very specific in mind."

Khusrau nodded. "At all costs, I wish to avoid a resumption of the ancient war between Rome and Persia. A war which, as things now stand, is almost certain to resume within a decade after Malwa is finished."

This time, both Belisarius and Antonina were genuinely startled. Over the past two years, since Rome had answered Persia's desperate plea for an alliance against the Malwa invaders, the relations between the two empires—for all that they had been frequently locked in warfare over a period measured in centuries—had been quite good.

Khusrau lifted his shoulders and spread his hands. "The problem lies with Iran, not Rome. Consider—which I think neither of you really has done—what the world will look like to the Aryans after this war is over. Especially to Iran's nobility."

He gave both of them a long, measured stare. "Rome emerges splendid and triumphant. Its lands untouched by the war, its populace unravaged, its military power and commercial might enlarged, its future bright and certain." After a brief pause: "And Iran? A land half-ruined by the Malwa. And a land, moreover"—here his voice hardened—"whose emperor is bound and determined to transform its ancient customs. Specifically, is bound and determined to bridle the rambunctious Aryan nobility which is both the source of Iran's traditional military power and, always, the shackle to its forward progress."

He's right, said Aide unhappily. **I've been thinking about it myself, now and then. I didn't want to raise it with you, because you have enough to worry about. But . . . he's right. Persia will be a powderkeg after the war.**

"You fear rebellion," stated Belisarius. Seeing Khusrau's impassive face, the Roman general's lips quirked in a crooked smile. "No, not really. Not Khusrau Anushirvan. If it comes to it, you will lead that nobility into war against Rome in order to keep their allegiance."

"If need be. But there is a way to avoid the entire problem. Simply give my nobles a different field of conquest. Or, it might be better to say, a vast new realm in which to exercise their energies and ambitions." Khusrau shrugged. "Not even the Aryan *azadan*"—the term meant *men of noble birth*, and referred to the class of armored knights who formed the backbone of Persia's military strength—"are enamored of war for its own sake, after all. Give them new lands, new wealth, new areas in which to exercise their authority and their talents . . . "

He let the thought trail off, certain that the two other people in the room would see the point.

Antonina, for one, did not. She saw not a trailing thought, but a vast leap of logic.

"You can't be serious, Emperor! If you march into Central Asia, you will clash with the Kushans. Who, comes to it"—her jaws set—"are ultimately a more important ally for Rome than Persia. At least in the long run. And the same if you march into the Deccan against our Maratha allies. That leaves only the Ganges plain, and that would embroil you in an endless war with the Malwa successor state. In a land teeming with a multitude of people who have no reason—none!—to welcome another wave of conquerors from the west. The whole idea—"

"That's not what he's talking about, Antonina," interrupted Belisarius. The Roman general *had* followed the trailing thought to its logical end point. "He's talking about the Indus valley."

Belisarius scratched his chin. "Whose political future, now that the subject is raised, we have never really decided. I assumed some sort of military occupation, in the interim, followed by—"

"Lengthy negotiations!" barked Khusrau. "With me bidding against Shakuntala and Kungas, and Rome acting as an 'honest broker'!" He snorted. "And probably against someone else, too. As Antonina says, the Ganges will not remain unruled for long after Malwa's fall. Even leaving aside those damned Rajputs perched on the border."

He swept his hand in a firm gesture. "So let us forestall the whole process. The Indus will go to the Aryans. The delta, at the very least, and the valley itself to the edge of the Thar desert and as far north as the fork with the Chenab."

"Sukkur and the gorge," countered Antonina immediately. "Further north than that, you'll simply have endless trouble with the Rajputs and the Kushans." She smiled sweetly. "Let them bicker over control of the Punjab. You'll have the whole of the Sind, which is more than enough to keep the azadan busy. Besides—"

"Enough!" snapped Belisarius. He glared at Antonina, and then transferred the glare to Khusrau.

"We are *not* going to get into this. Neither Antonina nor I have the authority to negotiate such things for the Roman Empire. And you can be quite certain that Theodora is going to have a tighter fist than"—another glare—"my idiot wife. Whose only purpose in agreeing with you—"

"Is because it makes her proposal workable," concluded Khusrau forcefully. "It means your thrust into the central valley can be done by *me*, leading an army of dehgans, instead of requiring you to split your own forces. It simplifies your logistics enormously, and makes possible moving up the assault on Barbaricum and the seizure of the delta."

Belisarius' eyes almost bulged. "By *you*? That's impossible, Khusrau! You're needed here in Persia to—"

He broke off, choking a little.

Khusrau's teeth were gleaming in his beard, now. "To keep the Empire of Iran and non-Iran stable? To keep the always restive azadan from their endless plots and schemes? So that Mesopotamia can continue to serve as the stable entrepot for the campaign in the Indus?"

Antonina was unable to suppress a giggle. "That's one way to keep the azadan from being, ah, 'restive.' Take them off on a great plundering expedition. Like the Achaemenids of old!" Without rising from her chair, she gave Khusrau an exaggerated bow. "Hail, Cyrus reborn!"

Khusrau chuckled, and returned the bow with a nod. "Darius, at the very least." He moved his eyes back to Belisarius. "You *do* have wide-ranging authority on anything that concerns military affairs. You can always present the thing to Empress Theodora— excuse me, Empress *Regent* Theodora—as a necessity for the success of the campaign against the Malwa."

He bestowed another nod on Antonina. "In light of the new circumstances uncovered by Antonina, Theodora's best and most trusted friend."

Belisarius started to snarl a reply, but forced it down. Then, growling: "I agree that it might work. With the emperor *personally* leading a campaign into the central valley . . . "

He fell silent, for a moment, his acute military mind working feverishly almost despite himself. " . . . staging itself in the little known fertile basin of the Sistân, as we'd already planned . . . "

There was a large campaign map lying on a nearby table. By the time Belisarius finished half-mumbling those last words he was leaning over it. Antonina and Khusrau both rose and came to his side.

The Roman general's finger traced the route. "It'd be a monster of a trek. Even if . . . assemble an army of dehgans in the Sistân—from where?"

"I'd start in Chabahar," stated Khusrau, pointing to a port on the coast of the Gulf of Oman. "Exactly as you were planning to do, anyway, with Maurice's expedition. Most of the dehgans are here in lower Mesopotamia already, so it would be easy to ship them to Chabahar. And from there—just as you've been planning—the expedition would march north to the Sistân. Shielded from any enemy view by the mountains to the east. Take—let us say—a week to refit and recuperate, and we'd begin the invasion of the middle Indus valley. Just as you were planning all along."

Belisarius' scowl was now ferocious. "*That* route? An entire army of Persian dehgans? Impossible, Khusrau! You'd have two deserts and a mountain range to cross, before you reach the Indus at Sukkur."

"Just below the Sukkur gorge, which separates the Sind from the Punjab," said Antonina brightly. "The natural northern frontier of the new Aryan province of Industan."

Both men glared at her. Then, glared at each other.

"Impossible!" repeated Belisarius. "I was only planning to send a small expedition. Six thousand men, most of them light Arab cavalry. Just enough to surprise the Malwa and drive the population south while we established a beachhead in the delta. How in creation do you expect to get a large army of *dehgans*—heavily armored horsemen—through that kind of terrain?"

Khusrau smiled beatifically. "You forget two things, Belisarius. First, you forget that village dehgans from the plateau and the northeast provinces—thousands upon thousands of whom are gathered here in lower Mesopotamia, grumbling about the absence of any prospect for glorious battle—are far more accustomed to traveling in arid terrain than you, ah, perhaps more civilized Romans."

He understood the sarcastic raise of the Roman general's eyebrow, and shook his head in response. "You are not really familiar with that breed, Belisarius. Most of your contact has been with the higher nobility of the Aryans. Most of whom, I admit, could be accused of loving their creature comforts. But the dehgans from the east . . .

"A crude lot!" he barked, half laughing. "But, for this campaign, the cruder the better."

Belisarius scratched his chin. He understood Khusrau's point, and was remembering various jests which high Persian noblemen like Kurush had made to him in the past concerning the rough, frontier nature of the eastern dehgans.

"And the other thing?"

Khusrau looked smug. "You forget, I think, that the Sistân is the home of the legendary Rustam. National hero of the Aryans."

Belisarius groped, for a moment, at the significance of this last statement. But Aide understood it at once. The crystal's excited thoughts burst into Belisarius' mind.

He's right. He's right! The Sistân is just today's name for ancient Drangia. The Sistân—its population, I mean—will be awash in mythology. A sleepy, isolated province—but it's

still fertile and densely inhabited, because Tamerlane hasn't wrecked it yet—won't ever, now, actually, because we've already changed history—

Aide was practically babbling with excitement.

Don't you see? How they'll react—when *the Emperor of Iran and non-Iran himself* comes? And demands their assistance in a great new feat of glory for the Aryans?

Belisarius' eyes widened.

It's perfect! It's perfect! The whole population will turn out! Men, women and children—oldsters!—cripples! You couldn't ask for a better logistics train! Not that those rubes would understand the word "logistics," of course. For them it'll just be a crusade. The one and only chance they've had in centuries to rekindle the old legends and bring them back to life.

Widened. Aide babbled on.

Perfect, I tell you! Everyone of them—most of the men, anyway—will be expert camel drivers. There's already food, and plenty of water. Before Tamerlane destroyed the area—in the future that would have been, I mean, and we need a new tense for that because that's such a stupid way of saying it—the Sistân was famous for its irrigation works—well, not exactly "famous," but it had them even if almost nobody knew about them—dams and qanats, everything!

Then, perhaps a bit aggrieved: **I already told you that, which is why you came up with your original plan. You must have forgotten the specifics, though, or you'd understand right off why Khusrau's scheme is so much better.**

Belisarius made a wry smile. *Et tu, Aide?*

There came the image of a crystalline snort, as impossible as such a thing was to describe in words. Belisarius was reminded of a mirror, splintering in pieces and reforming in an instant.

Don't be petty. It's beneath your dignity. It *is* a better plan. All you hoped to do was drive some of the population south. Khusrau, with—with—

"How many dehgans, Emperor?" asked Belisarius, on behalf of Aide.

"I am confident I can marshal twenty thousand heavy cavalry. Not all of them dehgan lancers, of course. A third, perhaps—but the rest will be armored archers, and you of all people know how ferocious—"

Belisarius waved his hand. "Please! An army of twenty thousand Persian lancers and archers, with another ten thousand infantry, is heavy enough to punch through any Malwa force that will be available in the mid-Indus. Especially—"

More than enough! For a moment, Aide's enthusiasm waned a bit. **Of course, the Persians won't be able to besiege any real citadels or fortifications . . .**

"Don't need to," said Belisarius aloud, forgetting in the excitement of the moment that neither Khusrau nor Antonina could have followed his mental exchange with Aide. Then, remembering, he began to explain—but Khusrau interrupted him.

"No need to," he concurred. "With twenty thousand heavy cavalry I can break any Malwa force in the field. So what if they retreat into their fortresses along the river? I can quickly establish military rule and bring almost the entire population under my control. Keep them working in the fields, providing us with food and billeting while we protect them against Malwa sallies."

"You'll wind up saving the lives of a lot more peasants this way," added Antonina quietly. She understood fully, even if Khusrau did not, how heavily the thought of those peasants slaughtered at Malwa hands had weighed upon her husband. Belisarius had hoped to save perhaps a few tens of thousands with his light cavalry expedition. No more than that.

But now—with such a powerful force in the mid-valley . . .

"We could save almost all of them," he murmured. Then, giving Khusrau a somewhat stony eye: "Not that their lives will be all that splendid, under Aryan martial law."

"Better than being butchered," retorted Khusrau. "As for the rest . . . " He shrugged. "I can keep the dehgans from committing any real atrocities. The first few days will be rough, of course. No way to keep such soldiers from pilfering what little treasure there might be and pestering the local women."

" 'Pestering'!" snorted Antonina.

Again, Khusrau shrugged. "And so a number of Indian peasants find themselves with bastards soon thereafter. Not even many of those, truth to tell, because my dehgans will be looking for concubines anyway. So they will formalize the relationships, more often than not, and see to the well-being of their new offspring."

"The peasant men won't like that much," pointed out Belisarius. He cut off Khusrau's rebuttal with his own. "But that's neither here nor there. They've doubtless been suffering worse under the Malwa as it is. They'll adjust, soon enough. Especially since Indian peasants are even less inclined than most of the world's peasantry to care two figs who happens to rule their area. As long as their new masters don't tax them dry—you *will* extend your new tax system to the Indus, yes?—"

Khusrau nodded. "I'll do more than that. I'll use the Indus as the testing ground. Along with much else." The emperor began pacing about slowly. "I'm sure, by now, you have deduced my plans for transforming Aryan society. I've had enough of these damned squabbling noblemen. As much as possible, I intend to duplicate Rome's more efficient and intelligent system. Advancement by merit, not birth, with the *new* aristocracy tied with ropes to the imperial dynasty."

Belisarius said nothing. He had not, in fact, "deduced" any such thing. He had not needed to. Aide, with his encyclopedic knowledge of human history, had long since acquainted the Roman general with the sweeping changes which Khusrau the Just—as future history would have called him—would make in Persian culture and society. Replacing a feudal system with an imperial one, and instituting a tax system so efficient and fairly spread that even the later Moslem conquerors would adopt it for their own.

"The Indus will be the perfect place to plant that shoot," mused Khusrau. "My army will be made up almost entirely of modest dehgans from the impoverished eastern borderlands. Not rich and haughty grandees from Mesopotamia. They'll be willing enough, in exchange for land and wealth, to accept new terms of imperial service."

He clenched his fist. "And with *them* to back me, I can deal with any fractious Mesopotamian sahrdaran as roughly as I need to." He quirked a smile. "Who knows? Perhaps, upon my eventual death, my designated successor can take the throne without having to wage the usual civil war."

Belisarius leaned over the map, planting both his hands, and studied the terrain depicted there. "All right," he said softly. "I can see where the land campaign has a good chance for success. A *very* good chance, actually, since the one thing not even the superhuman mind of Link will be expecting is to see twenty thousand Persian heavy cavalry come charging into the Indus valley out of the Kacchi Desert."

Chuckling: "The whole idea's insane, after all. And if there's one thing that damned monster is not, it's given to illogical planning."

It will never understand the power of such myths as Rustam, came Aide's soft thought. **I would never have understood either, had I not spent so many years now living in your mind. And your heart.**

True, said Belisarius in reply. *In the end, Link and the "new gods" who sent it here will fail, as much as anything, because they tried to shape humanity's future without ever understanding its soul.*

He straightened from the table. "But that still leaves the naval problem," he said forcefully. "The fact is that none of this can possibly succeed without a total mobilization of the entire fleet for the logistical effort. That, and—of course—the actual assault on Barbaricum."

His next words sounded harsh even to himself, but they needed saying. "And that, in turn, is impossible so long as the Malwa have that great fleet of theirs in Bharakuccha. At harbor today, yes, but only because of the monsoon. By the time we can take the delta, no matter how fast we move, summer will be over and we will be into autumn. Come November, the change in winds will be upon us. At which point, the Malwa fleet will be able to ravage our own shipping. And because of the inevitable disruption in our careful planning which Antonina's scheme will create, our navy will be ill prepared to fend them off. The only way to get the whole army into the delta ahead of schedule is to transport them by sea instead of having them march. Which will completely tie up all of our shipping, military as well as civilian. Whether we like it or not, the fact is that until the Ethiopians finish expanding their navy—which won't be for months—we haven't got the additional maritime power to make this work. It's as simple as that."

He gave both of them a stony look. "Without complete command of the sea—which depends on the Ethiopian fleet—we could easily wind up in exactly the same position we left the Malwa last year—with a huge army stranded, and dying of starvation. We can't possibly weather through the first few months in the Indus simply on the food which the valley's peasants might provide us. Their own situation will have been completely disrupted also. We *need* our own stable logistics train for that first winter, no matter what else may happen."

Neither Khusrau nor Antonina responded. They were both bridling at the logic, but neither of them could *quite* figure out how to gainsay it.

Still, they intended to try, clear enough. Belisarius braced himself for renewed quarrel.

Whereupon came the second royal intervention.

The doors opened, and Agathius limped in, shouldering his way through the ornate and heavy portals with rough abandon, even knocking one aside with a crutch. He seemed excited—excited enough, at least, that he began speaking in the presence of royalty without so much as a polite cough of apology.

"You won't believe this, but a whole slew of ships just showed up on the horizon. Biggest damn fleet I've ever seen. Axumites, no doubt about it. And if we're interpreting those newfangled flag signals of yours correctly, King Eon himself is leading them."

Belisarius stared at Khusrau. Then at Antonina.

"You planned this," he accused.

"Nonsense!" retorted Khusrau. "How could she?"

"Indeed," concurred Antonina with demure reproof. "Just feminine intuition, that's all. As reliable as ever."

Chapter 20

THE JAMUNA
Summer, 533 A.D.

The first thing Nanda Lal saw, after Toramana ushered him into his small pavilion, was the statue resting on a small table in a corner. The statue was a representation of Virabhadra, the chief deity in the Mahaveda cult which had become the central axis of the Malwa version of Hinduism.

The Mahaveda priest who accompanied Nanda Lal wandered over and gazed upon the statue with . . . not reverence, so much as satisfaction. After a few seconds, he turned away and fixed Toramana with a stern gaze.

"And do you practice the rites?"

Toramana nodded. "Three times, every day. Have done so, since I was a child. My father was a devout man."

The priest grunted. "Good. And how is your father now?"

Toramana's face remained impassive. The big Ye-tai officer's shoulders simply shifted, in what might be interpreted as a shrug. "He's dead. Killed at Ranapur, when the rebels set off the detonation. My brother was killed there also."

Nanda Lal's jaws tightened a bit. He hadn't been given that information by his spies, before he left Kausambi. It was an oversight which several of them would regret.

But he said nothing. Nanda Lal had already made clear to the priest that he wanted him to do most of the talking. The priest had not forgotten. After a brief, quickly suppressed start of surprise, the Mahaveda cleared his throat. "I'm sorry, I didn't know. My condolences."

"It was quick. All men die. The rebels were punished."

The Ye-tai officer seemed to find those curt sentences adequate. Watching him carefully, Nanda Lal decided the man was stolid by nature. Intelligent enough, clearly—Damodara was not in the habit of promoting dullards, certainly not to general rank—but not given to excessive flights of imagination.

"My name is Vishwanathan," announced the priest. "As you perhaps already know, I was sent here specifically on the instructions of the emperor."

"So Narses informed me." Toramana extended his hand, inviting the priest to sit on the cushions before a lowset table. In some indefinable way, the hand gesture also included Nanda Lal without giving him the precedence which the chief spymaster for the entire Malwa Empire—and, like Venandakatra, a first cousin of the emperor—would normally enjoy.

Nanda Lal was impressed. He would not have expected such subtlety from a Ye-tai, not even a general officer. In a very short time, he realized, Toramana had already deduced that Nanda Lal intended to use the priest as his unofficial "envoy."

"Something to eat?" asked the Ye-tai. "Drink?"

The priest shook his head, but accepted the offer to sit. Nanda Lal remained standing, a few feet back from the table.

"I wish no servants to be present," said the priest, after settling himself comfortably on the cushions. As Toramana took a seat across from him at the table, the priest's eyes ranged through the pavilion.

The Ye-tai officer interpreted the movement of his eyes correctly. "There are no servants present, anywhere in the pavilion. If we need them, they wait outside. I assumed you wanted a private audience."

Not a dullard at all, thought Nanda Lal. *Which, in itself, is good. So long as—*

Toramana's next words surprised the spymaster. And caused him to revise upward his estimate of the Ye-tai general's intelligence.

"You wish to determine my loyalty. You are concerned over the implications of my future marriage into the Chauhar dynasty."

Vishwanathan nodded. "Exactly. There was much discussion in the Imperial Council, once the news arrived. I was present myself, at some of those discussions."

In the brief silence which followed, Nanda Lal gauged Toramana's reaction to the news that his affairs had been subjected to careful imperial scrutiny. Most Ye-tai officers—most officers of any kind in the Malwa army—would have been both surprised and apprehensive.

Toramana's reaction was—

Nothing. Might as well have told a tree it was made of wood. Or a stone that it was solid.

Before Nanda Lal's own apprehensiveness could do more than stir, Toramana surprised him again.

"I expected it would be," said the Ye-tai. "For obvious reasons, a marital alliance between Ye-tai and Rajput would be cause for imperial concern."

The priest, startled by the Ye-tai's frankness, cast a quick glance at Nanda Lal. The spymaster returned the glance with a stony gaze. The priest looked away hastily. Then, after a pause, lifted an eyebrow at the Ye-tai general, inviting further elaboration.

"Obvious," repeated Toramana. "The power of the Malwa dynasty, beyond its control of the Deva weapons, rests primarily on the pillars of the Ye-tai and the Rajputs. A tripod, as it were." Again, Toramana made that little shoulder-shifting gesture. "And the Kushans also, once—to a degree. But that leg is now cracked, and may splinter."

For the first time since he entered the pavilion, Nanda Lal spoke. "Three legs will still support a stool, even if the fourth breaks."

Toramana nodded, without looking at the spymaster. He kept his eyes on the face of the priest.

"Yes. The more so when that fourth leg was never much trusted at any time. Provided that the remaining three legs remain stationed at very different angles. Let two of them merge into one, and you no longer have a stool. You have a two-legged spill waiting to happen. Which, of course, is why the emperor is concerned about my marital plans."

The Ye-tai fell silent. After a few seconds, Nanda Lal realized that he would speak no further without another invitation. And realized, as well, that in so doing Toramana was making an invitation of his own.

The spymaster relaxed still further. He was an experienced bargainer, and could recognize a bargain in the making when he saw one.

That recognition brought another. The priest was now out of his depth, and Nanda Lal would have to abandon completely his pose of disinterested observer. The decision made, Nanda Lal stepped forward and took his own seat at the table.

"Tell me, then," he commanded, "why the emperor should permit the marriage."

Toramana's barrel chest rose in a slow, deep breath. Obviously enough, he was taking the time to marshal his arguments.

"One. The strength a stool needs depends on the weight to be placed upon it. With Belisarius threatening the Indus and Rao the Narmada, that weight has grown three—or four-fold.

"Two. A three-legged stool, more than a four-legged one, requires thick and sturdy legs. In human terms, that means loyal ones. Even devoted ones.

"Three. The weakness lies with the Rajputs. To the moment, they are bound to the Malwa by oaths alone. Not by much in the way of blood, and still less by way of confidence. Vows—even Rajput vows—are brittle things.

"Four. The surest way to bind the Rajputs tighter is to bind them with blood. Encourage high-ranking Rajputs, as you have Ye-tai, to marry into the Malwa clan."

Toramana broke off and gave Nanda Lal a long and steady gaze. "I am telling you nothing that you do not already understand. Let us suppose, for a moment, that Rana Sanga were to become a widower. Perhaps by disease, or accident—or even some unfortunate incidence of random banditry. I am certain that the dynasty would offer him a high-rank marriage into the Malwa clan. A very high-rank marriage, in fact. For the first time ever, a Rajput king—and he the greatest of them all—will be tied to the Malwa by blood, not simply by vows."

Nanda Lal could feel himself stiffening, for all his attempts to conceal his emotions. He couldn't help it. He was almost paralyzed with shock. Never—*never!*—had he imagined that this brutish-looking half-barbarian could have deduced so much, from so little. And how much else had he deduced? "By unfortunate incidence of random banditry" had been his *words*, true enough. But what thoughts—what guesses—lay beneath those words?

For a moment, Nanda Lal almost raised his voice, calling on the five assassins who waited outside the tent to come in and kill Toramana on the spot. But he managed to restrain himself. Barely.

Barely—and for two reasons. Only the second being that he was also intrigued by the possibilities which Toramana's unexpected acuity opened up.

The first reason for his restraint was even simpler. In addition to Nanda Lal's five assassins, there were dozens of soldiers within a few steps of the tent's entrance. Ye-tai, in the main, but with no small sprinkling of Rajputs among them. All of whom—so much had already become obvious to Nanda Lal—were as tightly bound to their commander Toramana as any of the soldiers of the splendid army from which they were temporarily detached were bound to Lord Damodara and Rana Sanga.

In short, this was the only army of the Malwa Empire where the work of assassins would surely be repaid, within a minute, by the work of enraged soldiers. Nanda Lal's assassins could kill Toramana, of that the spymaster had no doubt at all, even if the impressive-looking young warrior-general took two or three of them with him into the afterlife. But only if Nanda Lal was prepared to have his own hacked-apart body lying next to Toramana's a few seconds later.

And that, in a nutshell, is the entire problem. The empire cannot afford to lose this magnificent army. But can we afford to have them at all? If this razor-sharp sword ever turns in our grasp . . .

Long seconds of silence had gone by. Throughout, Toramana's eyes had never left those of Nanda Lal. Now, still without showing a trace of anxiety—emotion of any kind—the young Ye-tai general once again made that economical shrug.

"You are worrying too much, I think. Were his beloved wife to die, for whatever reason short of Malwa involvement, Rana Sanga would have all the more reason to weld himself to the dynasty." In some subtle way, the next words came with a slight emphasis. "For all his martial prowess, you know, he is not given to subtlety."

Translation: I might have my doubts about "unfortunate circum-stances," but Sanga would not.

Nanda Lal reviewed in his mind all he knew about the Rajput king, and decided the Ye-tai's assessment was accurate. That still left Damodara . . .

As if he were a mind-reader, Toramana spoke again.

"As for Lord Damodara, his gratitude at the emperor's generos-ity in providing his own family with a palace in the capital—safe from Roman assassins, and almost on the emperor's own doorstep—has also welded him completely to the dynasty. Not, in my opinion, that there was any reason to doubt his loyalty at all."

Nanda Lal discounted the last sentence immediately. Pure diplomacy, that was. The operative sentence was the first. *Transla-tion: so long as Damodara's family is held hostage by the emperor, Damodara will remain obedient.*

Again, Nanda Lal reviewed the assessment; and, again, decided the Ye-tai was correct. For all his brilliance, Damodara had never once shown any inclination toward boundless ambition. Some ambition, of course—but enough to cast a death sentence on his wife and children? And parents?

No. I have seen him playing with his children myself, in days past when his family visited the capital. He is a doting father and, by all my spies' accounts, a loving husband as well as a devoted son.

"Good enough," stated the spymaster. The two words were abrupt, almost harsh. But not as harsh as the next: "That leaves you."

For the first time since he'd invited Nanda Lal and the priest into the pavilion, Toramana's face showed an expression. Humor, in the main, alloyed with a touch of irony.

"Me?" The word was almost a bark. "Do you know my clan status within the Ye-tai, Lord?"

Nanda Lal nodded; then, extended his thick hand and waggled it a bit. "Middling. Not high; not low."

"More low than high, I think," countered Toramana. The Ye-tai general cocked his head a little and gave Nanda Lal an inquisi-tive look. "A question, Lord. What is the chance that I would ever be offered a marriage with a lady of the Malwa clan?"

Nanda Lal hesitated. In the silence, Toramana elaborated the question. "Assume, for a moment, that I returned from the Roman war covered with glory. The victor on a hundred battlefields."

"Possible," grunted Nanda Lal. "Not likely."

Toramana's inquisitive look became almost inquisitorial. Nanda Lal sighed, and—again—revised upward his estimate of the man's intelligence.

"No real chance at all."

The Ye-tai nodded. "Purity of blood has always lain at the center of Malwa rule." He gave the priest a little nod. "As well as at the center of Mahaveda creed."

The statement did not seem to be accompanied by any anger or chagrin. In fact, the Ye-tai chuckled. "So be it. I am an ambitious man, Lord, but not a foolish one. The world has limits. So it is, so has it always been, so will it always be. I simply wish to reach my own, and nothing less."

All humor left the hard face—half-Asiatic; half-occidental, as was the usual Ye-tai visage—to be replaced by stolidity. "Now, perhaps, you understand."

Silence, once again, filled the pavilion. For quite a long period, this time. Perhaps five minutes in all. Five minutes during which a Ye-tai general and a Malwa spymaster stared at each other; and a Mahaveda priest, knowing he was well out of his depth, tried to make himself as inconspicuous as possible.

"Good," stated Nanda Lal, at the end of that silence. "Not even 'good enough.' Simply: *good.* We understand each other, I believe."

The Ye-tai general's nod was more in the way of a bow of fealty. "Yes, Lord, we do. Allow me to advance as far as I may, in this world that is, and you need have no fear at all of the consequence."

Nanda Lal spoke his last reservation. "The day might come—with Rana Sanga as your brother-in-law—when, perhaps . . ."

"If that day comes, Lord, which would surprise me greatly—rest assured that I will do what needs to be done. True, blood flows thick. Ambition flows thicker still. Like a glacier out of the mountains."

"And even a poet!" exclaimed Nanda Lal. Smiling cheerfully, he rose to his feet. For all his thickness of body, and decades of life, Nanda Lal was a vigorous and muscular man. He was on his feet before the priest had even started to rise.

"I look forward to long and mutually satisfactory relations, General. And I will make it a point to attend your wedding personally, whenever it might happen. And come what may."

Toramana, now also standing, bowed deeply at the waist. "I am honored, Lord." When his head came back up, there seemed to be a slightly mischievous twist to his lips. "But I give you fair warning—I will hold you to that promise. Come what may."

Nanda Lal waved Vishwanathan out of the pavilion ahead of him. After the priest had left, the spymaster paused at the tent flap and gave the statue in the corner a hard and scrutinizing gaze.

"Ugly damn thing," he murmured.

Toramana was standing a few feet away. The Ye-tai glanced at the statue, then made that little shrug.

"Ugly indeed. Much like me. And, like me, serves its purpose."

Nanda Lal chuckled and left, revising his estimate of Toramana's intelligence yet again. Upwards.

The thought—now—filled him with good cheer. Not so good, of course, that he didn't instruct one of his spies to keep an eye on the general at all times.

The spy, unfortunately, did not really share his master's estimate of Toramana's brains. So, late that night, the Ye-tai general had no difficulty eluding him in the darkness. Had no difficulty, even, in keeping the spy completely unaware that he had done so.

And, since Narses was equally adept at evading the spies which had been set upon him, the two men made the rendezvous which had been agreed upon earlier that evening, in the course of an exchange of a pound of tea for an equal value of incense made by two of their servants in the informal "market" which the soldiers and local villagers had set up on the banks of the Jamuna.

The exchange was also, needless to say, unobserved by Nanda Lal's spies. Both Toramana and Narses knew how to select servants.

They met in a small tent, set aside for some of the troops' more perishable goods. Narses was already there, perched on a sack. As soon as Toramana entered, he spoke.

"Tell me everything that was said. Word for word."

In the minutes which followed, Toramana may not have actually repeated the entire conversation, word for word. But he came very close. Nanda Lal, had he been present, would have revised his estimate upward once again. The Ye-tai's memory was as phenomenal as his intelligence.

When he was done, Narses issued a harsh, dry little laugh. "'Allow me to advance as far as I may, in this world that is, and you need have no fear at all of the consequence.' That's a beautifully parsed sentence."

Toramana's shrug, as always, was a slight thing. "I know nothing about grammar. As anyone can see, I am a crude Ye-tai—not much more than a barbarian. But even as a child playing in the mud, I knew that the best way to lie is to tell the truth. Simply let he who hears the truth set his own boundaries to it. The boundaries, not the words themselves, are what make them a lie."

Narses nodded, smiling in his humorless and reptilian way. "And that, also, is a beautifully crafted sentence." The smile faded. His next words were spoken impassively.

"If the time comes—*when* the time comes—you will have to—"

Toramana cut him off with a quick, impatient wave of the hand. "Move quickly, decisively, and so forth." He rose to his feet, with even greater agility than Nanda Lal had shown in his own tent. "Have no fear, Narses. You and I understand each other perfectly well."

"'Ambition flows thicker still,'" the old eunuch quoted softly. "'Like a glacier out of the mountains.'"

Again, Toramana made that quick, impatient gesture. "Poetry," he snorted. "There is no poetry in ice grinding against mountains. I know. I have seen it. I was born in the Hindu Kush, Narses. And learned, while still a boy, that ice is the way of the world."

He turned, stooped through the tent flap, and was gone. As silently as he had come.

Chapter 21
CHARAX
Summer, 533 A.D.

"We thought we'd find you here," said Eon.

"Where else?" snorted Ousanas.

Startled, Antonina tore her eyes away from the mare she was staring at, and turned her head toward the stable entrance. Eon and Ousanas were standing just inside the open doors, backlit by the late morning sunshine.

Antonina began to flush. Then, dropping her eyes, she began brushing pieces of hay off her gown. When she'd entered the stable earlier that morning, after Belisarius left to rejoin his army, she'd been paying little attention to fastidiousness. Even now, the effort stemmed more from habit than any real care for her appearance.

"Am I so predictable?" she murmured.

Ousanas grinned. "Every time Belisarius goes haring off on one of his expeditions, you spend half the next day staring at a horse. Practically a thing of legend, by now."

Eon strode over to a nearby pile of hay and plumped himself down upon it. Clearly enough, the negusa nagast of Ethiopia was no more concerned with appearances than Antonina herself. He even spent a few seconds luxuriating in the sensation, for all the world like a carefree boy instead of the ruler of one of the world's most powerful kingdoms.

"Been a long time," he said cheerfully. Then, waving a hand: "Come, Ousanas! Why are you standing on dignity?"

Ousanas' grin became a bit sardonic. "Horse food! No thank you." He glared at the mare in the nearby stall. The inoffensive animal met his gaze placidly.

"Treacherous creatures," proclaimed Ousanas. "As are they all. 'Dumb beasts'—ha! I'm a hunter. Was, at least. So I know what wickedness lurks in the hearts of wild animals."

He stalked over to another nearby stall—an empty one—and leaned his shoulder against a wooden upright. "And they are all wild, don't think otherwise for a moment." He bestowed the same sardonic grin on the pile of hay Antonina was sitting on. "I'd rather feed on the horse than use its own feed for a chair. More civilized."

Antonina did not raise to the bait. She simply grinned back. For all that Ousanas often claimed to fear and loathe animals, she knew full well the man was an expert horseman as well as elephant mahout. And a superb camel driver as well, she suspected, although she had never seem him get close to one of the surly brutes.

Eon snorted his own skepticism. Then, his young face became serious. "We need to talk, Antonina. I am sorry to bother you now—I know you'd rather spend the day, ah . . . "

"Pining over a departed husband whom you've known for years, as if you were a silly lovestruck girl," concluded Ousanas unkindly.

"I *am* a silly lovestruck girl," protested Antonina. Not with any heat, however. Indeed, the ridiculous phrase brought her some comfort. Odd, perhaps. But her harsh childhood in the streets of Alexandria, followed by a long period in which she had been a courtesan—a time which had been, in some ways, even harsher—made her treasure the new life she had begun after Belisarius married her. She was catching up on things she had missed, the way she looked at it.

But—

She *was* married to Belisarius, after all. *Belisarius*, not some obscure small merchant or petty official. And, for all that she treasured the marriage, it did bring great responsibilities in its train.

She started to sigh, but suppressed it. "You want to plan the coming naval campaign. Immediately."

Eon nodded. "The change in Belisarius' tactics and timing makes it even more essential that our own expedition set forth as soon as possible. And since that expedition will now *require*"—the emphasis on that last word was perhaps a bit harsh, as if Eon expected an argument—"the involvement of the Roman fleet, we have no time to lose. Coordination between allies can be sometimes difficult. We need to, ah, establish clearly, ah—"

Eon trailed off into stumbling silence. Ousanas curled his lip, in a sneer which was as magnificent as his grin. "What the fool boy is fumbling at—supposed to be the King of Kings!—is who is going to command the thing. He or some Roman."

Antonina couldn't help bursting into laughter. "You're no longer his dawazz, you know!" she exclaimed. "And he's no longer a mere prince! Can't slap him on the head any longer!"

It was Eon's turn to grin, now. Ousanas scowled.

"Can't help it," he grumbled. "Being dawazz was easier than this silly fly whisk business. Polite! Respectful! Not my strength."

Antonina waved her hand. "It's not a problem. You will be in command, naturally. The only Roman ships which can be detached for the expedition are the half dozen new gunships which John designed. 'Carvels,' as he called them. Belisarius took the older ships with him for the assault on Barbaricum. You brought one hundred and eight war galleys. Each of them carries over two hundred men—approximately twenty thousand, all told, a far larger force than we Romans will provide. And since you refitted them all with cannons, you are even bringing a greater weight of guns to the expedition."

She broke off, distracted by a side thought. "I'm *still* amazed you managed to assemble such a fleet so quickly. How did you do it?"

Eon looked smug. "You can thank my wife Rukaiya for that. If there's anyone left in Ethiopia or Arabia who thinks a seventeen-year-old queen is still almost a child—*that* one, for sure—you could count them on your fingers."

"The fingers of *one* hand," amended Ousanas. "Huh," he grunted. "A will of iron, that girl has. As any number of quarrelsome shipbuilders discovered, not to mention supply merchants."

"And she's *smart,* too," continued Eon, not done with boasting about his wife. "It was Rukaiya's idea to refit our existing galleys for cannons, rather than trying to build gunships like you Romans have. 'Carvels,' you're calling them now?"

His expression grew somewhat apologetic. "We can build ships quickly, following the modifications which Rukaiya suggested, as long as we stick to our old methods. It would have taken us much longer to match John's design. We just don't have the same manufacturing base, especially not with metalworking."

"Couldn't have fitted carvels with the right guns, anyway," said Ousanas. "Even your Roman armorers in Alexandria can barely produce enough of those for your own ships. But Rukaiya's design only needs small guns—four-pounders—and only four to a ship, which Alexandria could make readily enough."

Antonina nodded. And, silently, congratulated herself for having chosen Rukaiya as Eon's queen in the first place.

But the self-satisfaction was not long-lasting. She could see, from the somewhat stiff expression on the Axumites' faces, that they were still concerned over the issue of command.

"What's the problem now?" she asked bluntly, seeing no reason to be diplomatic with these two men.

Ousanas shook his head. "Antonina, I believe your assessment is based more on abstractions than concrete reality. What Irene would call 'book learning.' " He began to speak further, but Eon interrupted.

"Our ships are still basically *galleys*, Antonina." A bit of pride rallied: "Axumite galleys, of course! Which are quite capable of sailing across open sea. But . . . "

He shrugged. "But can't carry much in the way of supplies. Not with a full complement of soldiers and sailors. No more than a few days' worth. And not even Ethiopians, in a few days, can make that great voyage across the Erythrean Sea which the expedition requires for success."

"We'd run out of food and water," elaborated Ousanas. "Not to mention gunpowder and shot, after a single major engagement."

Understanding dawned on Antonina. And, with it, the source of the Axumites' concern. The Ethiopians could provide the striking force—most of it, at least—but only if the Romans provided the supply ships.

She couldn't help herself. Much as she tried to stifle the impulse, she broke into a fit of giggling.

"What's so funny?" demanded Eon, half-crossly and half-uncertainly. The king mixed with the boy.

Antonina forced down the giggles, with a hand over her mouth. Then: "Sorry. I was just thinking of a gaggle of Roman merchant ships, taking orders from Ethiopians. Like trying to herd cats."

Ousanas spread his hands. "The problem, exactly. That breed is insubordinate under the best of circumstances. There is not a chance we could maintain control over them, without threatening physical violence every leg of the voyage. Every day, most like. Which would eventually defeat its own purpose."

Antonina frowned. *Another damn problem in logistics!* But then, seeing the expectant faces of Ousanas and Eon, she realized their own solution to the quandary. One which they were apparently afraid to broach, because they feared her reaction. And probably knew, as well, that before he left Belisarius had extracted from his wife a promise to stay out of combat.

That knowledge produced, not a fit of giggling, but a gale of laughter.

"You have no idea!" she exclaimed. "I would *love* to sail across an ocean instead of staying here in this miserable city managing a pack of surly merchants and traders. And even my fussing husband agreed that I could not refrain from doing anything which was—I quote—'*necessary for the success of the campaign.*' "

Grinning: "Done!"

Ousanas grinned back. "Yes. With *you* on the expedition, I dare say no merchant will argue the fine points of command."

Antonina sniffed. "I dare say not."

Less than an hour later, Antonina gave the first order which set the new plan in motion. To Dryopus, her efficient and trustworthy secretary.

"You're promoted. I'll send a message to Photius and Theodora telling them to give you a fancy new title. Something grand. Maybe a seat in the Senate. Certainly an estate somewhere to maintain you in the style you'll need."

She swept out of the chamber where she had *formerly* made her headquarters, leaving a befuddled former secretary in her wake.

Dealing with the twenty merchant captains who would provide the expedition with its supply ships took more time.

Not much.

"Let me make this perfectly clear," Antonina said firmly, after listening to their protests for perhaps an hour while standing on the docks. She pointed her finger to the Roman carvels anchored in Charax's harbor. The red light of the setting sun gave the vessels a rather sinister appearance.

"Those warships will sink any one of you who so much as gives me a peep of protest once we set sail. Which we will do the day after tomorrow."

She allowed them some time to ponder her words.

Not much.

"And you *will* be ready to set sail the day after tomorrow." Again, the finger of doom. "Or those warships will sink whichever one of your ships hasn't cast off within an hour of the remainder of the fleet. The city's poor folk have been complaining about a lack of driftwood, anyway, so it won't be a total loss."

Dealing with Menander and Eusebius, on the other hand, took most of the evening. Their protests could not be brushed aside.

The ones which didn't involve them personally, at least. The young officers' insistence on accompanying Antonina on the expedition, she gave short shrift.

"Don't be stupid. I'll have twenty thousand men—most of them Axumite marines—to keep me out of harm's way. I'm not *leading* this expedition, you understand—certainly not in combat! I'm simply going along to make sure that the Roman supply effort which is critical for success doesn't slack off."

Menander and Eusebius stared at her stubbornly. Antonina clapped her hands. "Enough! Belisarius will need you far more than me. Since I'm taking all the carvels and their experienced captains, he'll be relying on the two of you to fend off Malwa attacks on his supply route up the Indus. You *do* remember that he's a leading a much larger expedition, no?"

At the mention of Belisarius and his needs, Menander flushed. Eusebius, darker complected, did not. But he did look aside. No longer meeting her hard gaze, he managed a last little protest.

"You'll need the *Victrix*, Antonina. To make sure the Malwa shipping at Chowpatty and Bharakuccha is completely destroyed. And I'm really the only one who can still handle the fire cannon. Well enough under combat conditions, anyway."

Antonina hesitated. They were now moving into an area which was beyond her expertise.

Fortunately, Ezana made good the lack. The Dakuen commander had come with Eon and Ousanas to Antonina's villa, where the final arrangements for the division of Roman naval forces were being made. Before Eusebius had even stopped talking, Ezana was already shaking his head.

"Not true, Eusebius. In fact, having the *Victrix* along would be more of a problem than a help. You've been training with that odd weapon, we haven't. Trying to mix it in with Ethiopian forces and tactics—especially at the last minute—would cause nothing but grief. Like as not, by accident, you'd wind up burning more Axumite ships than Malwa."

Hurriedly, seeing the young Greek's gathering protest: "Not because of *your* error, but because some eager Ethiopian captain would sail right into the spout. Trust me. It'll happen."

Eusebius took a deep breath, then let it out slowly. Watching, Antonina was certain that the young officer was remembering similar veteran wisdom expounded in times past by John of Rhodes. And, again, felt grief at his loss. A small grief, now, softened by time. But grief nonetheless.

"All right," said Eusebius. "But if you don't want the *Victrix* along on your expedition, Antonina, I'm not quite sure what role you *do* see for the ship." Shrugging: "The fire cannon itself would be ideal for destroying Malwa ships in the confines of the Indus. But the *Victrix* is a sailing ship, not a galley. Once the monsoon ends, it'll be well-nigh impossible to move her up the Indus—not against that current—unless we hauled her with oxen. And what kind of a warship can go into battle being drawn by livestock?"

Again, Antonina felt herself floundering out of her depth. But she could tell from the expressions on the faces of the experienced naval men around her that they all understood and agreed with Eusebius' point.

"Difficult—at best—to convert a sailing ship to a galley," muttered Ezana. "Have to rebuild her almost completely."

"We could just transfer the fire cannon to an existing galley," offered Eon. But the look on his face didn't evidence any great enthusiasm. "True, you'd lose the advantage of height. Be a bit dangerous, that, in close quarters. Which"—his enthusiasm was fading fast—"is of course how the weapon can be used best."

Ousanas started to say something, but Menander interrupted.

"Go the other way," he said forcefully. He jerked a thumb toward the southern wall of the room, pointing to an invisible harbor. "You all know the new steam-powered warship the old emperor designed arrived here three days ago. What you may not know is that the *Justinian* brought an extra steam engine with her, in case of major mechanical problems. But I can't really use the thing anyway. Can't possibly fit it in the *Justinian* as a spare engine. We could use it to refit the *Victrix* as a paddle wheeler." He paused, looking at Eusebius. "I think."

As ever, having a technical problem posed immediately engrossed Eusebius. The naval officer was still an artisan at heart. He ran fingers through his hair, staring at the tile floor through thick spectacles.

"Could be done. Easier to make her a stern-wheeler, but a side-wheeler would have a lot of advantages in a river like the Indus. Slow and muddy as it is, bound to be hidden sandbars all over the place. With a side-wheeler you can sometimes walk your way over them. That's what Aide says, anyway."

"Can't armor a side-wheeler," countered Menander immediately. Although he was not exactly an artisan himself, the young cataphract had quickly picked up the new technological methods which Aide had introduced. He was comfortable in that mechanical world in a way in which older cataphracts were not.

Eusebius lifted his head, his eyes opening wide. "Why are we messing with paddle wheels, anyway? The *Justinian* and her sister ship were designed for screws. It wouldn't be that much harder to redesign the *Victrix* for screw propulsion."

Menander got a stubborn, mulish look on his face. Seeing it, Eusebius sighed. "Forgot. You've only got one spare screw, don't you? And as many problems as the *Justinian* has already—typical prototype stuff—you don't want to find yourself stranded somewhere on the Indus without an extra propeller."

By now, Antonina and the Ethiopians were completely lost. Seeing the blank expressions on their faces, Eusebius explained.

"You can't just slap together a propeller. Tricky damn things. In the letter he sent with the *Justinian*, the emperor—I mean, the Grand Justiciar—told us he had to fiddle for months—his artisans, I mean—until they got it right. No way we could make one here, without the facilities he's got at Adulis."

Their faces were still blank. Menander sighed.

"You *do* know what a propeller is?"

Blank.

Menander and Eusebius looked at each other. Then, sighed as one man.

"Never mind, Antonina," said Menander. "Eusebius and I will take care of it. You just go and have yourself a nice ocean cruise."

Chapter 22
BARBARICUM
Autumn, 533 A.D.

The pilot in the bow of Belisarius' ship proved to be just as good as his boasts. Half an hour before dawn, just as he had promised, the heavily laden ship slid up onto the bank of the river. The bank, as could be expected from one of the many outlets of the Indus, was muddy. But even a landsman like Belisarius could tell, from the sudden, half-lurching way in which the ship came to a halt, that the ground was firm enough to bear the weight of men and horses.

For two weeks, once it had become clear that monsoon season was drawing to a close, Belisarius had been sending small parties to scout the Indus delta. Landing in small boats under cover of night, the scouts had probed the firmness of the ground along the many mouths of the river. Every year during the monsoon season, the great flow of the Indus deposited untold tons of silt in the delta. Until that new soil was dry enough, the project of landing thousands of men, horses and equipment was impossible.

"Nice to have accurate scouting," said Maurice, standing next to the general.

"It'll still be a challenge, but the ground should be firm enough. Barely, but enough."

Belisarius turned his head. In the faint light shed by a crescent moon, he could make out the shape of the next ship sliding alongside his own onto the bank. Other such ships, he knew, were

208

coming to rest beyond that one—and many more still along two other nearby outlets of the river. Over the course of the next three days, Belisarius intended to land a large part of his entire army. Thirty thousand men, in all. Aide claimed it was the largest amphibious assault in all of human history to that day.

The general's eyes now moved to the bustling activity on his own ship. Already, the first combat engineers—a new military specialty which Belisarius had created over the past year—were clambering over the side of the ship. Those men were completely unarmored and bore no weapons of any kind beyond knives. Their task, for the moment at least, was not to fight. Their task was to make it possible for others to do so.

No sooner had the first engineers alit on the bank than others began handing them reed mats. Moving quickly, the engineers began laying the mats over the soft soil, creating a narrow pathway away from the still-soggy ground immediately by the riverbed.

"They're moving faster than I expected," grunted Maurice. "With as little training and preparation as we'd been able to give them . . . "

Belisarius chuckled. Maurice was *still* a bit disgruntled over the change of plans which had been made the past summer, after the sabotage attempt at Charax.

He's just grumbling, grumbled Aide. **That man is *never* satisfied. How much training does it take to lay down some simple reed mats, anyway?**

It's not all that simple, replied Belisarius. *Moving in the dark, in unfamiliar territory, with the fear of enemy attack in the back of their minds—and them with neither weapons nor armor? Not to mention that probably half of them are still seasick.*

He glanced at the sky. Still no sign of dawn, but the moon gave out just enough light to see that the sky was cloudless.

Pray this clear weather holds up, he continued. *The three days we spent at sea waiting for it took a toll on most of the men. They're not sailors, you know.*

Aide accepted the implied reproof without protest. For all that the crystal being had come to understand the nature of what he called his "protoplasmic brethren," Aide knew he was still prone to overlook the crude facts of protoplasmic existence. On the other hand . . . *he* couldn't have laid down those simple mats at all.

There was a new clattering noise. The Arab scouts were bringing their mounts out of the hold and beginning to walk them off the gangplank onto the reed-matted soil of the river. The horses had suffered from rough weather at sea at least as much as the men. But they were so eager to get their feet on terra firma that they made no effort to fight their handlers. The biggest problem the Arab scouts faced, in fact, was keeping the beasts from stampeding madly off the deck of the ship.

Abbu rolled over to Belisarius. The old Arab scout leader was practically swaggering.

"One day, General, no more." Abbu's pronouncement came with the certainty of a prophet. "One day from now, all opposition will be cleared to the walls of Barbaricum."

The old man's cheerful assurance transformed instantly into doom and gloom. He and Maurice exchanged a mutually satisfactory glower. Two natural-born pessimists agreeing on the sorry state of the universe.

"Thereafter, of course, disaster will follow." Abbu's thick beard jounced with satisfaction. "Disaster and ruin. The cannons will not arrive in time. The seaward assault will fail miserably, most of your newfangled gunships adrift or sunk outright. Your army will starve outside the walls of the city."

"Barbaricum doesn't have any walls," commented Belisarius mildly. "The cannons we're offloading are mostly to stop any relief ships bringing reinforcements from upriver. If there are any, that is. Khusrau should be starting his own attack out of the Kacchi desert any day now. Who knows? He may have begun already."

Abbu was not mollified. "Persians! Attacking through a desert? By now, half of them are bones bleaching in the sun. Mark my words, General of Rome. We are destined for an early grave."

Belisarius had to fight to keep from grinning. Abbu's high spirits were infectious. From years of working with the old bandit-in-all-but-name, Belisarius knew full well that Abbu's confidence stood in direct—and inverse—proportion to his grousing. A gloomy and morose Abbu was a man filled with high morale. A cheerful Abbu, dismissing all danger lightly, was a man with his back to the wall and expecting imminent demise.

"Be off, Abbu," Belisarius chuckled. "Clear any and all Malwa from my path."

"That!" The Arab scout began to turn away, heading for his horse. "That! The only thing which will go as planned!"

Within a minute or so, Abbu was over the side and organizing the Arab outriders. Within ten minutes, hundreds of lightly armed Arabs—from many ships—were disappearing into the darkness. Moving as swiftly as any light cavalry on earth, they would fall on any Malwa troops outside Barbaricum's shelter and either kill them or drive them into the port.

When the last Arab had vanished into the purple gloom of a barely breaking day, Belisarius turned to Maurice.

"So? Where are *your* predictions of catastrophe?"

Maurice grunted. "Abbu said it all. Nothing to add."

A heavier clattering began. The first of the Roman warhorses were being brought onto the deck, and the heavily armored cataphracts were clumping around to lead them off the ship.

Maurice's face seemed to lighten a bit. Or, perhaps, it was simply that daylight was beginning to spread. "Might not be so bad, though. Abbu always was a pessimist. We might be able to fight our way back through the mountains, after the disaster, with maybe a tenth of the army still alive."

By the time Belisarius caught sight of Barbaricum, the city was already burning. Burning fiercely, in fact—far more than any city made primarily from mudbrick should have been.

"No way the ships' guns caused that," said Maurice.

Belisarius shook his head. He halted his horse atop a slight rise in the landscape—more like a little mound of dry mud than a "rise"—and cocked an ear. He couldn't see the Roman fleet beyond the port, but he could hear the sound of its cannonade.

"Sounds good, though," he said quietly. "I don't think the fleet has suffered much damage."

He listened for perhaps five minutes longer. Only once, in that time, did he hear the deeper roar of one of the Malwa siege guns positioned to protect the harbor. And even that one sounded odd. Slightly muted, as if—

"They're using light powder loads," said Gregory. The commander of the artillery force which was off-loading onto the delta—miles behind them, now—had accompanied Belisarius and Maurice. "Looks like you were right, General. They're saving it for something else."

Belisarius left off listening to the cannon fire and studied Barbaricum. Much of the city was invisible, shrouded in smoke. But, here and there, he could see portions of the mudbrick buildings which made up most of the city's outlying areas.

Barbaricum was an unwalled city. But its residential areas were so tightly packed, one building abutting another, that at a superficial glance they appeared to form a defensive wall. The more so since, so far as he could see, there were no windows in any of the exterior walls of the buildings. That might be due to conscious planning, but Belisarius suspected it was simply a matter of cost. The population of Barbaricum, as the name itself implied, was polyglot and largely transient. The simplest and cheapest construction would be the norm.

He reached down into a saddlebag and pulled out his telescope. Then, looking for gaps in the smoke, he began studying the few alleyways which opened into the city's interior. Still, he could see hardly anything. The alleyways were narrow and crooked, providing only short lines of sight. Needless to say, they were filled with refuse. Only one of the alleys—the one Belisarius focused his attention upon—provided a glimpse of more than a few yards into Barbaricum.

A sudden lull in the cannon fire, perhaps combined with a slight shift in the wind, allowed him for the first time to hear sounds coming from the city itself. Sounds of screaming.

"You were right," repeated Gregory. The words were almost hissed.

Belisarius tightened his jaws. As soon as Gregory began to speak, he had caught sight through the telescope of the first signs of movement in the city. Four people, dressed in rags—two women and two children, he thought—were running down one of the alleyways. Trying to get out of the city.

As he watched, one of the women stumbled and fell. For a moment, Belisarius thought she had tripped over some of the refuse in the alley. Twisted an ankle or broken a bone, judging from the way she was writhing on the ground. Her face was distorted by a grimace. Belisarius could hear nothing, but he was quite sure she was screaming.

Then he spotted the arrow sticking out of the back of the woman's leg. An instant later, another arrow took her in the ribs. Now he *could* hear her screams.

When the woman fell, one of the children had stopped and hesitated. Began to turn back, until the other woman grabbed the child and resumed the race to get out of the city.

Too late. Three soldiers came into sight, racing down the alley. A second or two later, a Mahaveda priest became visible also. The priest was shouting something. When the soldiers reached the wounded woman lying in the alley, one of them paused just long enough to slash her neck with a sword. Arterial blood spurted against the grimy walls of the nearest building.

The other two soldiers kept up their pursuit of the surviving woman and the two children. The refugees were now almost out of the city.

Behind him, Belisarius heard one of his bodyguards snarling a curse. Priscus, that was—his eyesight was superb, and he had no need of a telescope to follow what was happening.

"We could maybe reach—" said the cataphract, uncertainly.

Before Belisarius could shake his head, Aide's voice was ringing in his mind.

No! *No!* That city is a death-trap!

Belisarius sighed. He lowered the telescope and turned his head.

"I'm sorry, Priscus. We can't risk it. The Malwa started those fires, not our cannons. That was deliberate. They always knew they couldn't hold Barbaricum against a serious assault. Not so long as we control the sea. So they're starting the scorched earth policy right here. And, as I feared—and expected—that will include slaughtering the populace."

He turned back, forcing himself to watch the last moments, though he saw no reason to use the telescope. The two soldiers had overtaken the fleeing woman and children just outside the city. Blades flashed in the distance. Then, moving more slowly, the two soldiers jogged back to their fellow and the priest, who were standing at the mouth of the alley. Once the small party was reunited, they began prowling back into the city's interior. They reminded Belisarius of scavengers, searching rubbage for scraps of food.

"Fucking animals," snarled Priscus. "But wait till they try to leave themselves."

The cataphract's eyes ranged the landscape behind the small command party. The sight seemed to fill his hard face with satisfaction.

Already, columns of Roman troops could be seen marching through the flat terrain. Some of those soldiers were following the path left by Belisarius and his party. Most of them, however, were ranging inland. Within a few hours, Barbaricum would be surrounded by the Roman army. The city was already surrounded by a cavalry screen.

"No prisoners," Priscus growled. He gave Belisarius a hard, almost angry stare. The Roman commander's policy of not allowing atrocities had, over the past two years, become firmly established throughout his army. With, as always, his personal household troops—*bucellarii*, as the Romans called them—ready to enforce the policy. Priscus was one of those bucellarii himself, and normally had no quarrel with the policy. Today, clearly enough, discipline was straining at the leash.

Belisarius returned the stare with one that was just as hard, if not angry. "Don't be stupid, Priscus," he said calmly. "Most of those soldiers are just following orders. And after they finish butchering the civilians, we're going to need *them* for a labor force."

His lips quirked for a moment, before he offered the consolation prize. "Mahaveda priests, on the other hand, are unaccustomed to hard labor. So I don't believe there's any need to keep *them* alive. Or any officers, for that matter."

Priscus scowled, as did Isaac and the rest of Belisarius' small squad of bodyguards. But none of them made any further argument or protest.

"Cheer up, lads," said Maurice. The words were accompanied by a burbling laugh so harsh it sounded like stones clashing in a torrent. "Nobody said anything about making their life easy."

The chiliarch—the term meant, literally, "ruler of a thousand," though Maurice commanded far more than a thousand men—turned in his saddle and grinned at Priscus and the other cataphracts. The teeth, shining in his rough-hewn, high-cheeked, gray-bearded face, gave the man more than a passing resemblance to an old wolf.

"We may not work the bastards to death," he continued cheerily. "Not *quite*. But they'll be wishing we had, be sure of it."

His words, beginning with "bastards to death," were punctuated by a ripple of sharp, cracking explosions.

"They're destroying the big guns at the harbor," pronounced Gregory.

No sooner were those words out, than a sudden roar erupted from the city. The sound of a gigantic explosion billowed across the countryside. A large part of Barbaricum—the port area, it seemed—vanished under a huge cloud of smoke and debris.

"They're blowing the whole harbor area itself, now." Gregory grimaced. "I'd have thought they'd wait a bit. Most of the men destroying the guns must have been caught . . . " His words trailed off, as he shook his head.

Belisarius was a bit surprised himself. Malwa artillery was staffed exclusively by Malwa kshatriyas, the warrior caste. As a rule, the Malwa tended to coddle that elite class. He had expected the Malwa commander of Barbaricum to try to include the kshatriya in the break-out.

There won't be a break-out, said Aide suddenly. **No way to be sure, but . . .**

As with Gregory, faced with such incredible ruthlessness, Aide's thoughts trailed into silence. Belisarius could almost picture the crystalline equivalent of a headshake.

Belisarius completed the thought, speaking aloud for the benefit of the men around him.

"At a guess, I'd say the Mahaveda have usurped command in Barbaricum. Probably had the actual military commander summarily executed. For incompetence, or dereliction of duty— whatever. The priests will be running the show entirely, from now on."

Clearly enough, from the look of satisfaction which came over the faces of Maurice, Gregory, and his bodyguards, that thought caused them no great discomfort. None at all, truth be told.

"Good riddance," muttered Isaac. "Let the bastards all burn in hell."

Priscus rumbled a laugh, of sorts. "Nice. We can just sit out here and watch them fry."

Gregory's face was now creased with a frown. "Maybe not. If there are any Kushans in Barbaricum, I'd be surprised if they didn't mutiny. Once they finally understood what the priests have in store for them."

Belisarius began to speak, but fell silent once he saw Maurice shake his head. Unlike Gregory, who had been preoccupied with off-loading his troops' equipment, Maurice had been present two nights before when Belisarius heard the report of the spies returned from Barbaricum.

"There aren't any Kushans here," announced Maurice. "In fact, according to our spies, the Malwa are pulling them out of the Indus entirely." Again, he grinned like a wolf. "I'm willing to bet Kungas has been chewing his way through central Asia, and the word is spreading. Apparently, several thousand Kushans stationed in the upper valley mutinied. Last anyone saw, they were heading up the Jhelum, with the heads of Mahaveda priests and Malwa kshatriyas—and not a few Ye-tai—perched on their pikes."

Geography was not Gregory's best subject. "What's the Jhelum?"

"One of the tributaries of the Indus," replied Belisarius. "It provides the easy access—relatively easy, that is—to the Hindu Kush. And Peshawar, where Kungas plans to rebuild the Kushan capital."

"Oh."

Priscus laughed. "Oh! The fucking Malwa empire is starting to come apart at the seams."

Belisarius saw no reason to correct the cataphract's overly optimistic assessment. In reality, he knew, the great Malwa empire—still the world's most powerful—could hardly be described as "coming apart at the seams."

True, the northwest Deccan was lost entirely, except for Bharakuccha and the lowlands along the Narmada river. But the Malwa conquest of the Andhra empire was only a few years in the past, and the region had never really been incorporated by the Malwa. Even the southern and eastern portions of conquered Andhra had been sullen and restive. The northwest—Majarashtra, the heartland of the Marathas—had never stopped fighting openly, even before Shakuntala escaped captivity and provided the rebels with a rallying point.

As for the Kushans . . .

They never fit very well into the Malwa scheme of things, said Aide. **Not pampered and privileged like the Ye-tai, not locked in by custom and tradition like the Rajputs—a square peg in a round hole. Always were, at the best of times. They were bound to break away, given any chance at all.**

After a moment's silence, Aide continued his thoughts:

You can't say the Malwa empire is "coming apart at the seams" until the heartland erupts in rebellion. The Ganges valley where the tens of millions of Malwa subjects are concentrated. And not just rebels in the forests of Bihar and Bengal, either. Peasants in the plain, and townsmen in the great cities. That's what it will take. And they won't risk rebellion—not after the massacre of Ranapur—unless they see a real chance of winning. Of which there is none, so long as the Malwa dynasty stays intact and commands the allegiance of the Ye-tai and Rajputs.

Again, a moment's silence. Then, in a thought filled with satisfaction: **Still . . . I think it's fair to say that cracks are showing. Big ones.**

Belisarius said nothing in response. In the minutes that followed, as one great explosion after another announced the rolling destruction of Barbaricum, he never even bothered to watch. He was turned in the saddle, staring to the northeast. There, somewhere beyond the horizon, lay Rajputana. That harsh and arid hill country was the forge in which the Rajputs had been created.

And if they begin to crack . . .

The Malwa will still have the Ye-tai, cautioned Aide. **The Ye-tai have nowhere else to go. Especially if Kungas succeeds in reconquering the lands of the former Kushan empire, where the Ye-tai once had their stronghold. Before they accepted the Malwa offer to become the most privileged class in India after the Malwa themselves.**

Belisarius smiled crookedly. *"Nowhere else to go?" Don't be too sure of that, Aide. Enterprising men—especially ones who can see the handwriting on the wall—can find avenues of escape in many places. What was it that fellow said? The one you told me about in the future that would have been, who made so many fine quips.*

Dr. Samuel Johnson. "Depend upon it, sir, when a man knows he is to be hanged in a fortnight, it concentrates his mind wonderfully."

Chapter 23

THE DECCAN
Autumn, 533 A.D.

Rana Sanga kept his eyes firmly fixed on the ivory half-throne which supported the flaccid body of Lord Venandakatra. Not on the Goptri of the Deccan himself. Much like Venandakatra's face—with which Sanga had become all too familiar in the weeks since Damodara's army had arrived in the Deccan—the chair was carved into a multitude of complex and ornate folds and crevices.

But the Rajput king found it far easier to look at the chair than at the Malwa lord who sat in it. The piece of furniture, after all, had been shaped by the simple hand of a craftsman, not the vices and self-indulgences which had shaped Venandakatra's fat toad-lizard parody of a human face.

The Rajput king dwelled on that comparison, for a moment. He found it helped to restrain his fury. The more so since, whenever the rage threatened to overwhelm him, he could deflect it into a harmless fantasy of hacking the chair into splinters instead of . . .

Lord Venandakatra finally ceased his vituperative attack on the Rajput troops which formed the heart of Damodara's army. Lord Damodara began speaking. The sound of his commander's calm and even-tempered voice broke through the red-tinged anger which clouded Sanga's brain.

Sanga lifted his eyes and turned them to Damodara. The commander of the Malwa forces newly arrived in the Deccan was leaning back comfortably in his own chair, apparently relaxed and at ease.

"—are more than welcome to transmit your displeasure to the emperor and Nanda Lal," Damodara was saying. His tone was mild, almost serene. "Please, Lord Venandakatra! Do me the favor! Perhaps the emperor might heed your words—unlikely though that is—and send me and my army elsewhere. To fight a war instead of attempting to indulge a spoiled child."

Venandakatra hissed at the insult. He began gobbling incoherent outrage and indignation, but Damodara's still-calm voice slid through it like a knife.

"A stupid child, as well as a spoiled one. I told you from the beginning that not even Rajputs with Pathan trackers could hope to match Rao's Maratha hillfighters on their own terrain. The Panther has hillforts scattered throughout the Great Country. If we match him in the hills and valleys, he retreats to the hilltops. If we besiege the forts—which is easier said than done, Venandakatra—he fades down the slopes. Not without, each time, bleeding us further."

Gobble, gobble, gobble.

Damodara heaved a little half-snort, half-sigh. Derision mingled with exasperation. "From the day I arrived, I told you to cease your terror campaign. Butchering and torturing Maratha villagers does nothing beyond swell the ranks of Rao's army. By now, that army is at least as large as my own. Half again the size, I estimate."

The gobbling began producing coherent half-phrases. *Have you impaled yourself . . . I am the emperor's first cousin . . . you only distantly related . . . insubordination and mutiny and treason . . . on a short stake . . .*

"Be silent!" snarled Damodara. For once, the Malwa military commander's normal placidity was frayed. "Just exactly *how* do you propose to have me impaled, you foul creature?"

Damodara's round face twisted into a sneer. He waved a hand at Venandakatra's bodyguards. The five Ye-tai were standing against the rear of the audience chamber. They seemed a bit nervous.

"With them?" demanded Damodara, his sneer turning into a savage grin. Sitting next to him, Sanga casually placed a powerful hand on the hilt of his sword. That sword had been a minor legend throughout India even before the war began. Today, the legend was no longer minor.

The five Ye-tai bodyguards were definitely nervous.

Behind Sanga and Damodara, where they squatted on cushions, Sanga could sense the slight manner in which his two Rajput and one Ye-tai officers shifted their own stances. Without having to look, Sanga knew that all three men were now ready to leap to their feet in an instant, weapons in hand.

The Ye-tai bodyguards were *very* nervous. For all the outwardly respectful manner of their unmoving stance, the five men against the wall practically exuded fear and apprehension. Their eyes were no longer on their master, Venandakatra. They were riveted on the men sitting behind Sanga, even more than on Sanga himself.

One of those men, rather. Sanga knew—and suddenly had to fight down a cheerful laugh—that it was the Ye-tai officer squatting behind him who most thoroughly intimidated the bodyguards. Not so much because Toramana was a fearsome warrior, but simply because he was Ye-tai himself.

Ye-tai, yes—just like the bodyguards. But it was already known by all the Malwa forces in the Deccan that Rana Sanga, the greatest king of Rajputana, had promised one of his own half-sisters to Toramana as a wife. And had done so, because Toramana had requested marriage into the Chauhar dynasty.

The implications of that liaison had not escaped anyone. *Certainly not Venandakatra . . .*

The Goptri of the Deccan was now glaring past Sanga's shoulder. Past his hip, rather, where the face of Toramana would be visible to him. For all his fury and his self-indulgence, Venandakatra had not missed the subtleties of the matter at hand.

"This—this absurd marriage has *not* been agreed to by the emperor! All Ye-tai are still—"

He choked off whatever might have been the last words. As the pressure of the Roman-Persian campaign led by Belisarius mounted on the Malwa empire, the Malwa were being forced to relax the long-standing principles of their rigid system of caste, status and hierarchy. Venandakatra knew full well that Nanda Lal had already given his approval to the marriage. The emperor's approval was bound to follow.

In times past, of course, they would not have done so. Would, in all likelihood, have punished any Rajput or Ye-tai who even proposed it. High-ranking and meritorious Ye-tai, and occasionally Rajputs, had been allowed to marry into the Malwa clan as a means of cementing their allegiance to the ruling dynasty. But never had the two principal pillars of Malwa rule been allowed to marry each other. The threat of such liaisons was obvious.

In times past . . .

Damodara chuckled harshly. "Times past are times past, Venandakatra. In times past, Belisarius was not at our borders."

The Malwa army commander thrust himself abruptly to his feet. "There's no point in this," he said, again speaking calmly and evenly. "If you wish to do so, you may complain to the emperor. But, after all your complaints and failures over the past three years, I doubt he will give you an ear."

For a moment, Damodara studied his nominal superior. Then, still as calmly as ever:

"You are a military cretin as well a pustule, Venandakatra. 'Vile One' you are called, and never was a man more justly named. I will no longer subject my soldiers to casualties because of your asinine demands. Henceforth, my army will patrol the approaches to Bharakuccha and the line of the Narmada river. Let Rao have the hills and the rest of the Great Country."

He clasped his hands behind his back and stared down at Venandakatra. The Goptri of the Deccan returned the stare with a pale face, and eyes which seemed as wide as lilypads. *People did not speak to the emperor's first cousin in such a manner!*

"So long as Bharakuccha remains firmly in our grasp," continued Damodara, "we have our hands on the throat of Majarashtra. When the time comes, and we have once again the strength to do so, we shall squeeze that throat. But in the meantime—"

Again, he sneered. "*Cretin,* I named you, and named you well. Tomorrow is tomorrow, and today is today. *Today* the task at hand is beating down Belisarius. For that we need Bharakuccha intact—intact, along with the great fleet in its harbor."

Finally, Venandakatra found his voice. "I want you out of Bharakuccha!" he screeched. "Out—do you hear? Out! *Out!* You and every one of your stinking Rajputs!" For an instant, the Goptri glared at Toramana. "Every one of your soldiers! Out of the city! Live in camps along the river!"

The Goptri was shaking with rage. He began beating the arm-rests of his chair with his thin-boned, pudgy hands. "Out! Out! Out! This minute!"

Damodara shrugged. "So be it. Although you'd be wiser to keep at least a third of my army in the city itself. But"—another shrug—"I've long since given up any hope of teaching you wisdom."

Damodara's gaze moved to Sanga and, then, to the three officers squatting behind him. "Come," he commanded. "I want the army out of this city by tomorrow night."

"At once!" screamed Venandakatra. "Not tomorrow night! Now! *Now!*"

Damodara's ensuing laugh was one of genuine amusement. " 'Cretin,' didn't I say?" The next words were spoken as if to a child. A badly spoiled brat.

"You do not move an army of forty thousand men—*and* their horses, *and* their equipment, *and* their supplies—in the blink of an eye. Vile One."

He turned away and began walking toward the entry to the chamber. "As it is, I think we'll be working a miracle. By tomorrow night."

Shakuntala, Empress of Andhra, spent four hours searching her palace at Deogiri before she finally accepted the truth. It had been a waste of time, and she knew it. Not by accident, the search ended with her standing in her baby's room. She took the boy from his nurse's arms and cradled him in her own.

"He's gone, Namadev," she whispered, fighting back the tears. Then, slumping into a chair, she caressed the little head. "Once he knew his son was healthy . . . "

The baby smiled happily at his mother's face, and gurgled pleasure. Namadev was a cheerful boy. Cheerful and healthy. As good an assurance that the ancient Satavahana dynasty would continue as anyone could ask for.

Which, therefore, freed the father for a long-postponed task. Once again, the Wind of the Great Country was free to roam, and wreak its havoc.

Chapter 24
THE INDUS
Autumn, 533 A.D.

As soon as Belisarius emerged at daybreak from his small cabin on the cargo vessel which was slowly moving up the Indus, he began scanning the area on both sides of the river with his telescope.

He was relieved by what he saw. The monsoon season, by all reports as well as his own experience escaping from India three years before, ended earlier in the Indus valley than it did in the subcontinent itself. The view through the telescope seemed to confirm that. Everywhere he looked, the fertile grasslands which constituted the alluvial plains of the Indus seemed dry and solid. Except for the canals and small tributaries which divided the landscape into wedges—*doabs*, as the natives called them—he could not spot any indications of the wet terrain which would be a serious obstacle to his campaign plans.

For a moment, basking in the knowledge and the bright, dry, early morning sunshine, he spent a few idle seconds following the flight of a kingfisher up the riverbank. Then, his eyes arrested by the sight of a white heron perched on the back of a water buffalo, he burst into laughter.

Maurice had arisen still earlier, and was standing at his side. The chiliarch, when he saw what Belisarius was laughing at, issued a chuckle himself. For once, it seemed, even Maurice was in a good mood.

Belisarius lowered the telescope. "Wheat and barley, everywhere you look. Some rice, too. And I saw a number of water buffaloes. Say whatever else you will about the Malwa, at least they maintained the irrigation canals. Extended and developed them, it looks like."

Maurice's inevitable scowl returned. "We still don't have a labor force. There aren't any *people* anywhere. At least, I haven't seen any except a small fishing craft at sundown yesterday. And they beached the boat and scuttled into the grasslands as soon as we came near."

"Do you blame them?" Belisarius turned his head and looked back down the river. As far as his eye could see, moving up the Indus behind his own ship, the great Roman fleet was bringing as many of his troops as could be fit into their hulls into the interior of the river valley. The bulk of his army, including most of the infantry, was marching up the river under the command of Bouzes and Coutzes. Belisarius and his waterborne troops were now almost entirely out of the coastal province called Thatta, and entering the heartland of the Sind.

After the seizure of Barbaricum—the rubble that had been Barbaricum, it might be better to say—Belisarius had immediately begun building a new port. The work would go slower than he had originally planned, because his decision to accept Antonina's change of schedule meant that the preparations for that port had lagged behind. But his combat engineers assured him they could get the harbor itself operational within days.

Fortunately, Belisarius' attack seemed to have caught the Mahaveda in the middle of their own preparations as well. The fanatic priests had succeeded in destroying the city, along with most of its population and garrison, but they had been able to do little damage to the breakwater. The biggest problem the engineers faced was erecting enough shelter for the huge army that was beginning to offload behind the initial wave which had taken Barbaricum.

There too, the change in timing had worked to Belisarius' advantage. Even along the coast, the monsoon season was ending. They were now entering India's best time of year, the cool and dry season Indians called *rabi*. That season would last about four months, until well into February, before the heat of *garam* arrived. But *garam,* for all its blistering heat and the discomfort of dust, was a dry season also. Not until next May, when the monsoon returned, would Belisarius have to deal with the inevitable epidemics which always accompanied large armies on campaign. Until then there would be some disease, of course, but not the kind of plagues which had crippled or destroyed armies so many times in history.

Movement would be easy, too. And even though Belisarius knew full well that the kind of fluid, maneuver warfare which he preferred would be impossible soon enough—fighting his way through the Malwa fortifications in the gorge above Sukkur would be slogging siege warfare—he intended to take full advantage of the perfect campaign conditions while he still could.

That thought brought the telescope back to his eye. This time, however, he was not scanning the entire countryside. His attention was riveted to the north. There, if all had gone according to plan—or even close to it—the Persian army of Emperor Khusrau would be hammering into the mid-valley out of the Kacchi desert. Between Belisarius coming from the south, and Khusrau from the northwest, the Roman general hoped to trap and crush whatever Malwa forces hadn't yet been able to seek shelter in the fortifications along the river.

He hoped to do more than that, in truth. He hoped that the Malwa army stationed in the lower valley would still be confused and disorganized by the unexpectedly early Roman assault—and the completely unexpected heavy Persian force coming out of the western desert. Disorganized enough that he might be able to shatter them completely and actually take the fortifications all along the lower Indus. According to his spies, none of those river fortifications except for the city of Sukkur had been completed yet. He might be able to drive the Malwa out of the lower valley altogether. They would have to regroup at Sukkur and the upper valley north of the Sukkur gorge.

If Belisarius could accomplish *that*—and provided his army and Khusrau's could salvage enough of a labor force from the Malwa massacre—he would have a position from which the Malwa could not hope to dislodge him. Not, at least, so long as Rome and its Axumite allies retained naval superiority. The entire lower valley of the Indus would be securely in Roman and Persian hands. An area sizeable enough and rich enough to provide them with far more than a mere "beachhead." The theater of war would have been irrevocably shifted entirely into Indian territory.

"All of the Sind . . ." he murmured.

Maurice, as was usually true except when Belisarius' crooked mind was working through some peculiar stratagem, was following his commander's thoughts. "Remind me to compliment Antonina on her feminine intuition," he said, with a little smile.

"Isn't that the truth!" laughed Belisarius. His own smile was not little at all—nor even in the least bit crooked.

The experience of the past few days had driven home to him quite forcefully how much Antonina's insistence on moving up the invasion schedule had ultimately worked to his advantage. Impulsive and narrowly focused that insistence might have been, but in the end it had proven wiser than the sagacity of experienced soldiers. From everything Belisarius could determine, the Malwa had been caught by surprise. As much surprise, at least, as an opponent could be when faced by an inevitable invasion route.

He chuckled harshly. "I suspect Nanda Lal's excellent spy service worked against him, too. He *knew* we wouldn't attack this soon. He had hundreds of spies feeding him information on every stage of our preparations and planning. Down to every amphora full of grain, I don't doubt. Of course, once we changed plans and started scrambling, he would have heard of that as well. But—"

"Too late," finished Maurice. "That's the problem with having such a gigantic and powerful empire. It's just too big to react quickly."

Like a stegosaurus, chimed in Aide, flashing an image of a bizarre giant reptile into Belisarius' brain. **By the time the nerve impulse gets to the brain . . . True, that brain is Link's, not a stupid reptile's. But Link can't be everywhere. The monster has no magic powers. It's not clairvoyant. It relies on information provided by others.**

Aide's words reminded Belisarius of a phrase the crystal had used occasionally, when Aide lapsed into the language of a future accustomed to artificial intelligence. The expression had never *quite* made sense to Belisarius, until this moment.

Again, he smiled. Garbage in, garbage out. GIGO.

Belisarius' good cheer was not entirely shared by Maurice. "They'll recover from the surprise soon enough. Not quick enough, maybe, to keep us from taking the Sind up to Sukkur and the gorge. But that won't do us much good if we don't get a labor force to bring in the food. Not to mention maintaining the irrigation works. Not to mention keeping the towns and cities working."

The gray-bearded chiliarch glared at the carpet of doabs which stretched to the horizon. The multitude of canals and riverlets winkled in the sun, holding the dry patches of land in place like lead holding stained glass. "Picture soldiers doing that, will you? Even if most of them were peasants not too long ago. It'd take us half the army to keep the other half working."

The telescope was back at Belisarius' eye. "Unless I miss my guess, Maurice, those grasslands are practically crawling with peasants and their families. Laying low, out of sight. By now, the Malwa must have begun their butchery, and word travels fast.

"Besides," he added, sweeping his telescope around to the north, "they can't be too thrilled to see us coming, either."

Maurice didn't argue the point. He knew from his own experience, both as a peasant and a cataphract, how astute a rural population could be when it came to keeping out of sight of a passing army. And knew, as well, that they usually had good reason to do so.

As it happened, they had little to fear from Belisarius' army. That army, in fact, was all that would save their lives. But Maurice knew perfectly well that the Romans had as much chance of "convincing" the Indus peasantry of that as a cat would have convincing mice it was a vegetarian. Especially a peasantry which had been yoked by Malwa for half a century now. First they would have to force the peasantry out of hiding. Only then, as experience unfolded, could they hope to gain their allegiance. Or, at the least, their acquiescence in the new regime. And it would all have to be done fairly quickly, or the Roman army pouring into the Sind would begin starving.

He began to say something to that effect. But then, seeing the sudden tension in the way Belisarius pressed the telescope to his eye, Maurice fell silent. Something was happening.

"I think—" Belisarius muttered. "I think—"

An instant later he removed the telescope and nodded his satisfaction. "Sure of it. That's Abbu in the prow of that oncoming galley. And those oars are beating to double time."

He folded up the telescope with a vigorous motion. The cleverly designed eyepiece collapsed with not much more than a slight clap. The superb workmanship involved reminded Maurice of John of Rhodes, who had built the thing, and a little wave of sadness rolled over him.

Just a little wave, however, and not for long. Maurice had been a soldier for decades. Men died in war; it was the nature of the beast. Often enough, as with John, from pure and simple bad luck.

"Finally!" exclaimed Belisarius. "We'll get some real news. Abbu wouldn't be returning—not in a war galley beating double-time, for sure—unless he had something to report."

Maurice grunted his own satisfaction. Like Belisarius—like any soldier worthy of the name—he *hated* being forced to maneuver blindly. And since the capture of Barbaricum, and a few initial clashes with Malwa detachments down in the delta, the Romans had lost contact with their enemy. Someone in Malwa command had moved quickly, so much was clear enough, and ordered a withdrawal.

But where had they withdrawn? How many? To what end? Those questions and a hundred others remained unanswered.

Abbu provided some of the answers as soon as he clambered aboard Belisarius' little "flagship." The old Arab was grinning, and practically danced across the deck.

"Khusrau hit them like a sledge!" he barked. Then, slapping one hand into the other: "Broke the Malwa outside Sukkur when the fools sallied, thinking they faced only light cavalry—ha! Persian dehgans! They must have voided their bowels when they realized—and then—" The scout leader paused for dramatic effect and, again, slammed one hand into the other. "Then he took the city itself!"

Belisarius and Maurice were frozen, for an instant.

"He *took* Sukkur?" demanded Belisarius. "But—that city was supposed to be walled. I even got descriptions of the walls from two of my spies!"

"He had no siege guns," protested Maurice.

Abbu grinned. "It *is* a walled city, General. Very great walls, too—I have seen them myself." The grin widened. "Great enough to withstand even the great Malwa army which is now besieging it themselves."

Maurice was still groping with the puzzle. Belisarius' quick mind leapt immediately to the only possible solution.

"The populace rebelled. The moment word arrived that Khusrau had broken the Malwa in the field, the populace rose up against the garrison."

Abbu nodded vigorously. "Butchered plenty of the bastards, too, before Khusrau arrived. Of course, they couldn't have subdued the garrison once it rallied. They would have been massacred. But they drove them off a section of the walls long enough to open the gates. And once the Persians were into the city, the Malwa were so much carrion."

Belisarius' thoughts were still ranging far. His eyes were fixed on the northern horizon, as if by force of will he could study everything that was transpiring there. Then, slowly, he scanned the surrounding countryside.

"I was wrong," he murmured. "I saw only their fears." His tone was half-bemused—and half-sad. "I have been a soldier too long."

Aide understood, if no one else did.

Malwa has terrorized them for two generations. And now the fabled Emperor of Persia arrives, in his splendor and his glory, thundering out of the desert and surrounded by the might of his iron dehgans. The thoughts came soft and warm. **Even peasants in the Sind will have heard tales of Rustam and his great bull-headed mace. Dim legends, and those of another people to boot. But for all their scarred memories, they will want to *believe* those legends. Especially now, with Malwa sharpening the ax.**

"Yes," said Belisarius. "Yes. It's become a war of liberation. In *name* as well as in deed. And with Khusrau here himself, there is an immediate pole around which confused and frightened—and angry—people can rally. Khusrau will bring a *legitimacy* to the thing, which a purely military invasion force could not. A foreign ruler, true enough—but so what? The Sind has been ruled by foreigners for centuries. Now, at least, they will have one who is splendid as well as mighty. *Just*, as well as fearsome."

He turned to Maurice. "Pass the word. Make sure everyone understands it. Brand it into their foreheads if you have to—or I will brand it into their corpses. Any Roman soldier who commits any crime in this valley will be summarily executed. *Any* crime, Maurice, be it so much as pilfering a goat."

The general's brown eyes were glaring hot, something which was almost as rare as a solar eclipse. Maurice turned his own head and gazed at the three couriers who accompanied him at all times.

"You heard the general," he said curtly. "Do it. Now. Use as many men as you need to pass the word."

His eyes fell on Leo. Antonina had insisted that Belisarius add Leo to his personal bodyguard, retaining only Matthew for herself. The ugliest and most savage-looking of Belisarius' small squad of bodyguards—and they were all enormous, savage-looking men—was standing well within earshot.

"You heard?" Leo nodded heavily.

"You understand?" Leo nodded heavily.

Maurice glanced at Belisarius. The general smiled crookedly. "I shouldn't imagine I'll need Leo for a bit," he murmured.

Maurice turned back to Leo. "Would you like a break from your normal duties?"

Leo nodded heavily.

For a moment, Maurice hesitated. Outside of battle, where his strength and trained reflexes were quite sufficient, Leo was so dull-witted he was often mistaken for a deafmute.

"You sure you understand what—"

Leo interrupted. "Not hard to understand. Do what the general says or I will hit you."

Leo hefted the huge mace which was his favored weapon. True, the thing was simply-made; no fancy bull-headed carving here. But perhaps not even the Rustam of Aryan legend could have hefted it so lightly.

"Hit you very hard. Two, three, maybe ten times. General burns his name into what's left. Not much."

Everyone standing on the deck of the ship who was close enough to hear burst into laughter. Even Abbu laughed heartily, despite the fact that maintaining discipline over his own scouts during the days to come would tax him greatly. For the most part those scouts were bedouin, who considered pillaging a conquered village an act as natural as eating. Nothing outrageous, of course, unless the village had done something to aggravate them. But—*goats*?

Before Leo and the couriers had even begun lowering themselves over the rail into the galley tied up alongside, Belisarius was issuing new orders. For one of the few times in his life, Belisarius' normally relaxed and calm demeanor had vanished. He was pacing back and forth on the deck like a tiger in a cage.

"This breaks it wide open!" he exclaimed. He slapped both hands together like a gunshot. Once, twice, thrice. Then, come to

a decision, he abruptly halted his pacing and spun around to face
his officers.

"Separate the army, Maurice. I want the sharpshooters and the
engineers in the galleys. As many field guns as you can manage
also, along with their crews, as long as you leave room for Felix's
musketeers to defend the counter-siege. The galleys can get there
faster than the sailing ships, with this damn erratic wind."

Belisarius now turned to Ashot, the Armenian cataphract whom
Belisarius considered the best independent commander among his
subordinates, save Maurice himself. "You're in charge of pinning
the Malwa at Sukkur, from the south. You'll have to hold them,
Ashot. It won't be easy. You'll be heavily outnumbered. But unless
I miss my guess, the Malwa are still fumbling at the new situation.
They'll be so preoccupied with trying to storm into Sukkur that if
they're building lines of circumvallation at all they'll be doing so
only fitfully. Probably haven't even started yet."

Ashot nodded, immediately grasping the implication of the general's words. "Lines of circumvallation" meant the fortifications
which a besieging army built to protect itself from other armies
while, using their "lines of countervallation," they tried to reduce
the fortress or city. The terms came from a future history, but did
not confuse him in the least. Over the past year, as they prepared
for this campaign, Belisarius had spent countless hours training
his top subordinates in the complex methods of siege warfare he
expected to witness in the Indus. Aide had taught Belisarius those
methods, from the experience of future wars. The Roman general
had no doubt at all that Link had done as much for its own Malwa
subordinates.

"Without good lines of circumvallation," Ashot elaborated, "the
sudden appearance of Roman soldiers relieving the siege—
seeming to, anyway—will pose an immediate threat. They'll *have*
to attack us. No choice."

He cocked his head. "Which, I assume, is exactly what you want.
We're not really a relief column. We're a decoy."

"Exactly," replied Belisarius. He paced back and forth again,
just for a few steps. Stopped, jabbed a finger to the north, then
swept it to the east. "If we can get you planted just south of the
Malwa besieging Khusrau in Sukkur—"

He broke off and looked to Abbu. "Two questions: Are all of
the Persians forted up in Sukkur? And *is* there any suitable terrain
to the south where Ashot can set his lines?"

"Not all the Persians, General. After he broke the Malwa in the open field—maybe thirty miles northwest of Sukkur—and then heard the city had risen in rebellion, Khusrau sent a good part of his army back to Quetta. Almost all his infantry, except the gunners."

For a moment, Belisarius' face registered confusion. Then: "Of course. He was thinking ahead. His dehgans could hold the walls of Sukkur, with the populace in support. The biggest danger would be starvation, so the fewer soldiers the better. And his infantry can stabilize the supply lines back to Quetta—and Quetta itself, for that matter, which controls the pass into Persia."

For the first time since he got the news of Khusrau's seizure of Sukkur, Belisarius seemed to relax. He scratched his chin, chuckling softly. "Bold move, though. And he's counting on me a lot. Because if we don't relieve that siege . . . "

"And relieve it pretty soon!" barked Maurice. "Fewer soldiers be damned. He's still got thousands of dehgans in that city, and dehgans mean warhorses. Each one of those great brutes will eat six to seven times as much as a man."

Belisarius nodded, and cocked an eye at Abbu. "And the other question?"

The old Arab glowered. "Am I a be-damned gun-man?" The last term was almost spit out. Abbu was a ferocious traditionalist. He transferred the glare to Gregory. "Who knows what those new-fangled devices need in the way of terrain?"

Gregory laughed. "Nothing special, Abbu. Something flat, with soft soil my gun crews and the engineers can mound up into berms." He glanced at Felix Chalcenterus. The Syrian officer was the youngest member of the staff of superb officers which Belisarius had forged around him since the war began. Although Felix was primarily a commander of musketeers, both Belisarius and Gregory thought his knowledge of artillery tactics was good enough for this purpose. Which Felix immediately proved by chiming in confidently:

"Trees would be useful, for bracing. Beyond that, anything which allows the guns to control the approaches, at least a bit. And lets me station musketeers and pikemen to protect the guns from Malwa sallies. Rivers would be ideal, or canals. Marshes will do."

"Bad for horses," muttered Abbu, who was reputed to sleep with his own.

"That's more or less the idea," retorted Gregory. "The *Malwa* will have the cavalry, not Ashot. The more they have to slog to get at him—in the face of Felix's guns—the better."

Abbu ran fingers through his thick beard. "Yes. I will leave you the men who went with me to Sukkur, and many of my other scouts. They can find you such ground. There is a great bend in the Indus, just below Sukkur. Little creeks and rivers and loops—like Mesopotamia. Somewhere in there will be a place where your be-damned *guns* can strike at Malwa. While they—"

Good cheer returned. "While they feed themselves against your gunfire. Nowhere wide enough to extend their lines. No way to flank you without boats. Many boats."

The fingers stroking the beard turned into a fist, tugging it. "Malwa don't have so many boats." Now he was practically beard-ing himself. "My Arabs—true bedouin!—will burn those boats they have. You watch."

He turned to Belisarius and gave the general a little bow. "Your plan will work, General. So long as you get there in time." Abbu's eyes ranged the northeast like a hawk's. Beyond those grasslands lay the edge of the great Thar desert. "It will be a difficult march. But if you can circle to the east—especially if you keep the Malwa from seeing you—"

Belisarius shrugged. "We'll get spotted, sooner or later. But by then—if all goes well—it will be too late for the Malwa to extricate themselves from their entanglement with Ashot and Felix. Thou-sands of their soldiers will be mired in flood river terrain. They simply can't maneuver them quickly. And they also can't release too many of their troops from the lines around Sukkur. Not with Khusrau and his dehgans inside, ready to sally. They'll be trapped between Ashot to the south and Khusrau to the north—and me hitting them from the east. With every cataphract Sittas can bring along. And once Bouzes and Coutzes get the mass of our infantry up to Sukkur, the Malwa there will be finished. They'll have to retreat back to the Punjab, with all the losses that kind of forced march always brings."

As always, Abbu was unmoved by the subtlety of a Belisarius maneuver. "Fancy, fancy. Maybe. But it will work. Provided you get there in time."

Chapter 25

Belisarius began his march to outflank the Malwa besieging Emperor Khusrau once the flotilla of small cargo vessels and river barges carrying his cavalry and field artillery was well past the great bend of the Indus. In straight line distance he was less than a hundred miles from the besieged city.

But Belisarius had no intention of approaching Sukkur either from the river or even directly from the south. He intended, once his troops off-loaded, to move almost due east. He would cross the Khairpur canal, skirt the hills directly south of Sukkur where the ancient fortress city of Kot Diji was perched, and find the channel of the Nara. Then, following the Nara just east of the Kot Diji hills, he would eventually reach the Indus again at Rohri.

Rohri, of course, was on the wrong side of the river for any army which proposed to relieve a siege of Sukkur—and Maurice had poured sarcasm and derision all over Belisarius' plan the moment the general started explaining it.

Sittas, on the other hand, was enthusiastic.

"Oh, be quiet, you old grouch," he said, half-scowling. (Half-laughing, too, for Maurice's witticisms had been genuinely amusing. If grossly uncouth and disrespectful of an acknowledged military genius.)

"He's an acknowledged military genius, you know," continued Sittas, with a sly glance at Belisarius. The Roman commander

234

returned the glance with a glare. "I'll bet all the history books will say so in the future."

Then, more seriously, tracing the route of the Indus on the map with a thick finger: "You should know his methods by now. Our young genius likes to force his enemies to attack *him*, not the other way around. 'Strategic offensive, tactical defensive,' he likes to call it, when he's in a philosophical mood."

Sittas' finger slid past Sukkur and Rohri and moved up the line of the Indus until it reached the juncture of the Chenab, the first major fork in the Punjab. "Right here. That's where we'll really hit them. If we can bypass Sukkur and that damned gorge north of it, we'll have a powerful force of cataphracts and field artillery in the Punjab, where the flood plain opens up again."

"'Punjab' means 'land of five rivers,'" chimed in Belisarius. "That gives you an idea of how much maneuvering room we'll have when we resume the offensive next year. We'll be in a vastly better position than trying to fight our way out of the lower valley. *If* we can keep pushing Malwa off balance and prevent them from stabilizing the front further south at Sukkur."

Maurice did not seem mollified. "You've already divided your forces into three separate detachments, as risky as that is." He began counting off on his fingers. "You left Bouzes and Coutzes behind to bring up the infantry, who are still far to the south marching up the Indus. You're peeling off Ashot to continue straight up the river and take up positions against the Malwa with your big guns and Felix's musketeers. And now, you're proposing a forced march of heavy cavalry and field artillery across hundreds of miles—"

"Three hundred, by my estimate."

Maurice plowed on. "—Through unknown terrain—poorly known, at best—with a fragile supply route and a pitched battle at the end where you'll have cavalry trying to fight on the defensive." Stubbornly: "It's too big a gamble. You should stick to the original plan."

Belisarius gazed at his most trusted subordinate. His expression was attentive and solemn, not sarcastic. No one but a fool would dismiss Maurice's advice when it came to war.

But, when he spoke, his tone was as firm as ever. "What 'original' plan, Maurice? The original plan to attack Barbaricum weeks after we did? We've already scrapped that plan, and—you know it as well as I do—I'm improvising as I go along. I was planning to concentrate on Sukkur, but now . . . the more I think about it, I've come to the same conclusion Sittas obviously has. We'll hit them at Sukkur, leave enough of a force to make them *think* we're stopping there, but keep going up the Indus. By now, Malwa communications have *got* to be tattered. They have *got* to be confused. Their command structure has *got* to be rattled, maybe even cracking. And don't forget that Link is still in Kausambi, not in the Punjab where it might rally them quickly."

Belisarius leaned over the map and began making fierce little jabs with his finger. "If I didn't have an army and officers I trusted, I wouldn't dream of trying this. But . . . " Jab, jab, jab. "While Bouzes and Coutzes bring up the main forces, I want to move as fast as possible, hitting the Malwa again and again. Pin them in one place, force them to attack the forces I leave behind in good defensive positions, while I keep outflanking them by moving east by north."

The jabbing turned into a more thoughtful drumming of the fingers. Belisarius' eyes seemed slightly out of focus, as if he were trying to visualize enemy armies like a clairvoyant. "They'll be doing the same thing I am, right now, except I'm willing to bet they're less organized and not moving as quickly. And don't have commanders as good as Bouzes and Coutzes. They'll be bringing big forces down the river from the Punjab, just as I'm bringing them up from the lower valley. A race to see who gets to Sukkur first."

The drumming ended in an sharp, emphatic slap of his hand on the map. "But I'm not going to play their game. I'll let them get drawn into Sukkur while I move around them to the northeast. Then, if we can reach the fork of the Chenab and set up our own field fortifications, we'll have broken into the Punjab."

Maurice tugged at his beard fiercely, reluctance and eagerness obviously contesting within him. The grizzled veteran understood exactly what Belisarius was counting on. *The chaos and fog of war.* If the Romans could ride that chaos while the Malwa floundered in it . . .

"If we can end this campaign with a foothold in the Punjab," said Belisarius, "we can avoid entirely the problem of fighting our way out of the Sind through that damn bottleneck at Sukkur. And you know what a bloodbath that would be! We'll need some time to refit and recuperate after that, of course, but once we're ready to resume the offensive we'll be in a far better position to do it. We'll be attacking the Malwa in the Punjab, which spreads out before us with five rivers to serve as supply lines and invasion routes. As good a terrain as you could ask for, even given that the Malwa will have the Punjab covered with fortresses and lines of fortification. And—*and*—by then Kungas might be threatening them from the northwest, which will force them to fight on two fronts.

"I know it's a gamble, Maurice," concluded Belisarius quietly. "But I think it's not as risky as you do, and the payoff would be gigantic."

A crooked little smile replaced the solemn expression. "I can also remember a veteran telling me, years ago when I was a sprat of an officer, that the stupidest thing you can do in war is let the enemy regain his balance once you've staggered him. 'Knock 'em off their feet entirely, and kick 'em when they're down,' as I recall his words. And I recall them perfectly, because he repeated them, oh, maybe a thousand times."

Maurice scowled. Belisarius continued.

"Moving up the assault on Barbaricum surprised the Malwa. Khusrau's strike out of the Kacchi caught them completely off guard. Now they're staggering, off balance, trying to restabilize the front lines. That's why they'll be so completely preoccupied with crushing Khusrau at Sukkur. If we can hammer them hard enough at Sukkur to keep them pinned, then make a lightning strike into the upper valley and establish a stronghold at the fork of the Chenab, we'll force the Malwa—*force them*, Maurice, they won't have any choice—to lift the siege at Sukkur and try to bring their entire southern army back into the Punjab. An army which will be caught between us and Khusrau, and forced to march along the Indus where *we* can control the river with our river fleet." Shrugging: "They might be able to escape the pocket, but they'll suffer big losses in the doing."

Belisarius' eyes ranged over the map. "Of course, we'll probably encounter other Malwa armies on the way. But I'm willing to bet the Malwa forces converging from everywhere their commanders can scrape them up on short notice will be coming in ragged and disorganized. We've got a powerful and concentrated field army here, with a cohesive leadership. We can probably defeat them in detail and complete the march to the fork of the Chenab with enough of our army intact to hold it."

"And then what? You're sliding over the fact that we will *also* be caught between two armies," countered Maurice. He set his feet like a wrestler beginning a match. "You can be certain that the Malwa will bring every soldier they've got in the upper valley to hit us at the Chenab—keep *us* pinned down—while they bring that army up from Sukkur to crush us. And they've got a huge army in the Punjab, all the spies say so. Leaving aside the fact that by the time we get to the Chenab our logistics train won't be 'fragile.' It'll be in complete tatters. They don't even have to crush us. They can starve us out."

As if they were one man, the eyes of Maurice, Belisarius and Sittas came to rest on the figure of Menander. Menander had left Eusebius behind in newly conquered Barbaricum and followed Belisarius' flotilla up the Indus on the steam-powered warship named after its designer. He and the *Justinian* had caught up with Belisarius' army in time for Menander to participate in this staff meeting. The young officer had been standing a few paces back from the table in Belisarius' command tent where the argument between the general and his top staff had been occurring.

Belisarius was a bit amused—and very pleased—to see that the young Thracian managed to speak without any of the flushed embarrassment which had often characterized Menander in times past when he was called upon to give his opinion. The inexperienced cataphract who had accompanied Belisarius on his scouting expedition into the Malwa heartland had been transformed, during the four years which followed, into a self-confident officer. A commander in his own right. Uncertainty-covered-by-braggadocio had been replaced by relaxed assurance.

"I can do it, Maurice," he said firmly. "*Provided* we move at once. We're still catching the tail end of the monsoon winds. For a few more days—although it'll be hit-or-miss any given day—we can use the wind to move the ships upriver and the current to bring us back down. But once rabi settles in—"

Without a second thought, Menander used the Indian term for the cool, dry season where the winds came out of the Himalayas. India was no longer an exotic and foreign place to him.

"—It'll be a different story," he continued. "After that, moving supplies upriver will be a matter of pure sweat. The sailing ships will be almost useless, unless we can tow them with oxen. Eusebius is already starting up the river with the *Victrix,* but that hurried reconversion he did to turn her into a steam-powered paddle wheeler isn't . . . all you could ask for. So I doubt he'll be able to tow more than one barge behind him. That means we'll have to use galleys, for the most part, which aren't anywhere near as good for supply ships because so much space has to be taken up by the rowers."

"There's always your ship," said Belisarius. His smile was now more crooked than ever. "The *Justinian.*"

Menander was startled. Then, running fingers through his straw-colored hair: "Yes, I suppose. Wouldn't even really require much in the way of refitting to enable it to tow several barges. And a courier vessel just brought word from Queen Rukaiya that the *Justinian's* sister ship has left the shipyards at Adulis. So the *Photius* ought to be available to us also, before too long. Between the two of them—"

The young officer winced. "Jesus, when Justinian finds out . . . "

A little burst of laughter erupted in the tent. The new steam-powered warships were Justinian's pride and joy. The former emperor had spent years overseeing a large team of artisans to build those engines and design the ships which they would drive.

Drive into *combat,* not—not—

"Glorified tug boats!" barked Maurice, grinning. "Justinian will have apoplexy, if he finds out. Probably demand that Theodora have Menander flayed alive."

Menander did not seem to find that last particularly amusing. Neither Justinian nor Theodora was famous for their sweet temper.

"Have to keep it a secret . . . " he muttered, grimacing with anxiety.

"Don't worry about it!" boomed Sittas, taking two steps and buffeting Menander with a hearty backslap. The young officer staggered a bit under the blow. Sittas was built like a boar; his idea of a "hearty backslap" was on the excessive side. "You won't even have to lie about it. If those supply ships being towed upstream by your fancy new boats aren't forced to fight their way through every time, it'll be a miracle. Guns blazing the whole way. According to our spies, there's even a big new Malwa fortress in the Sukkur gorge they'll have to run if they try to get into the Punjab."

The fact that Menander so obviously found the prospect of desperate river battles a great relief brought another round of laughter to the tent.

Maurice, still smiling faintly, went back on the offensive. "All right, but that still leaves the critical moment up in the air." His stubby finger jabbed at the map. "You know as well as I do, General, that this 'lightning strike' of yours is most likely to come apart at the seams right at the start. In order for it to work, we've got to get the expedition through open terrain. Six thousand Arab and Syrian light cavalry can probably do it easily enough. But fifteen thousand cataphracts and two thousand artillerymen and combat engineers? And don't forget we'll be *crossing* rivers and canals, not using them for supply routes."

Scowling again, all trace of humor gone: "That's a recipe for disaster, young man. They always said Julian was a military genius too, when he was hacking his way into Persia. Until the damn fool burnt his ships and tried to march overland through Mesopotamia."

Belisarius shrugged. "Julian had four or five times as many soldiers as I'm taking. And—if I say so myself—my logistical methods are better than his were."

He paused for an instant, giving Maurice a level gaze. The chiliarch tightened his lips and looked away. Years earlier, when Maurice had been training a brilliant but inexperienced Thracian officer, he had convinced the youth to adopt the logistical methods of the great Philip of Macedon. Use mules as much as possible for his supply train, instead of the cumbersome wagons preferred by other Roman armies. The methods had proved themselves in action since, over the course of many campaigns.

"Still . . . " he grumbled, staring at that portion of the map which showed the terrain in question. "We don't know how good the foraging will be. Mules can only carry so much, and you *have* to use some wagons for the artillery supplies. And if that territory is all that fertile, you can be sure the Malwa will have plenty of troops stationed there."

Belisarius scratched his chin. "I doubt it, Maurice. Not now. The Malwa commanders have probably pulled most of their soldiers back to the river. They'll be expecting us to use the Indus as our marching route, not the Nara. The more so since—"

He fell silent, groping for a way to explain. Over the years, fighting Link, Belisarius had come to have a certain sense for how the monster's mind worked. The same superhuman intelligence imparted to Link by those "new gods" of the future was also, often enough, a gap in its armor.

Aide understood. **It always knows so much, but the knowing comes from recorded history. Not experience. And it doesn't *listen*, really. It hears, but it does not pay attention. Because it "knows" already. History—the records Link will have, which are the same as I do—will tell it that the Indus valley is largely arid. But that's because of the environmental degradation caused by the later centuries of human habitation. Its subordinates may have told it otherwise, but . . .**

The thought trailed off for a moment, then came back as firm as ever. **It will not really think about it. I have been surprised myself, many times, by how much more life there is in lands which my "knowledge" told me was half-barren. But I am not Link. I do not think the way it does. So I have learned to listen, not just hear.**

Belisarius nodded. To his subordinates, the gesture carried that certain solid air about it which they had come to recognize and respect deeply even if they were not privy to its origin. *Aide agrees with me.*

"I doubt they stationed a large force there to begin with," he stated firmly. His officers, recognizing the weight of Aide's opinion which nestled inside that confident statement, nodded their acceptance. Even Maurice.

The chiliarch sighed. "All right, then. But we should take all the mitrailleuse with us. And all the sharpshooters." He gave Mark of Edessa, standing well back in the tent, a glance of approval. "They've been trained as dragoons, so they'll be able to keep up."

Belisarius eyed him skeptically. Maurice snorted. "*All* of them, dammit. Ashot will be counter-besieging the Malwa at Sukkur, with a supply route as wide as the Indus—literally—and a fortified position guarded by our entire infantry once Bouzes and Coutzes arrive."

Another look of approval came to Maurice's face, as he thought of the twin brothers who, in the course of the Mesopotamian and Zagros campaigns, had hammered Belisarius' infantry into shape. If there was one thing in the world that Maurice treasured, it was *veteran* troops. True, most of the soldiers in the gigantic Roman army which was now taking the war to the Malwa were recent recruits, pouring into military service in hopes of sharing the spoils which smaller armies of the famous Belisarius had gleaned from earlier campaigns. But every branch of that army had been built around a core of veterans, experienced against the Malwa.

Bouzes and Coutzes' Syrian infantry and cavalry, Gregory's artillerymen, Felix's musketeers and pikemen, Mark of Edessa's new force of sharpshooters, Belisarius' own Thracian bucellarii directly commanded by Maurice himself—and, not least, the magnificent Greek cataphracts who had broken the Malwa at Anatha and the Dam, and held off Rana Sanga's ferocious cavalry charges at the Battle of the Pass.

For a moment, Maurice exchanged glances with Cyril, the man who had succeeded to command of the Greek cataphracts after Agathius was crippled at the Battle of the Dam. The glance was full of mutual approval.

Sittas suddenly laughed. "And will you look at those two? As if I don't know what they're thinking!"

He bestowed another "hearty backslap," this time on the shoulder of Cyril. The Greek cataphract, more sturdily built than Menander, did no more than flinch.

"Don't worry, my lowborn comrade. I'll see to it that my haughty noble cataphracts follow your lead." Sittas frowned. "Even if I can't say I'm too thrilled myself at the idea of fighting dismounted behind fortifications."

His face lightened. "But—who knows? There's bound to be the need for an occasional sally, now and then. History may still record that the last great charge of heavy lancers was led by Sittas the Stupendous."

Again, laughter filled the tent. This time, not so much with humor as simple satisfaction. Whether Belisarius' daring maneuver would lead to victory or defeat, no one could say. But all hesitation and doubt would now be set aside. If the plan *could* work, these men would see to it.

Chapter 26
INDIA
Autumn, 533 A.D.

Kungas studied Irene carefully. The sly humor which was normally to be found lurking somewhere in his eyes was totally absent.

"You are certain?" he demanded.

She nodded. Quite serenely, she thought. Such, at least, was her hope. "What is there to fear, Kungas? The fact that the Malwa put up only a token fight to hold Begram tells us that Belisarius must be hammering them in the south. They are apparently withdrawing all their troops into the Punjab."

Kungas said nothing in response. Instead, he stepped over to the edge of the roof garden and planted his hands on the wide ledge which served it for a railing. From there, atop the palace that his men had seized to serve as the residence for the reborn Kushan monarchy, he gazed onto the streets of Begram. He swiveled his head slightly, studying the scene below. Listening to it, for the most part.

The city was awash in sound and moving color, almost rioting with celebration. After the Ye-tai had destroyed Peshawar long years before, Begram had become the major city of the Kushans. Four fifths of the population, approximately, was either Kushan or part-Kushan by descent. And the Pathans who formed most of the remaining population had no great allegiance to Malwa. None at

243

all, truth be told. So if the Pathans were not exactly joining the Kushan festivities, they were not huddling in fear from it either. And there was certainly no indication that they were planning any sort of countermoves.

No expression at all could be read on his face. It was a pure mask. But Irene, now long experienced in what she jokingly called "Kungas interpretation," could tell that her husband was not happy with the situation.

On a purely personal level, she found that knowledge warming. More than warming, really—she felt a little spike of passion race through her body. But she suppressed that spike even more firmly than the warmth. Not so much from the old habits of a spymaster but from the new habits of a woman who had come to think like a queen. Thoughts which were, in truth, even more cold-blooded.

Although she did feel a moment's regret that there would be no time to satisfy her passion. Time was of the essence, now.

"Stop this, Kungas," she said firmly. "You know as well as I do—more than I do, for you are a general and I am not—that you *must* march on the Khyber pass immediately. *Now.* Today!"

Kungas did not look at her. The only sign that he had heard her words was that his fingers began tapping the ledge on which his hands were planted.

"Move fast," he mused. "Yes, I should. All signs point to a Malwa empire in panic. Their troops are racing out of the Hindu Kush, not making an orderly withdrawal." He snorted wryly. "They certainly aren't doing so in fear of my small army. They are not being *forced* out of the mountains—they are being *sucked* out. As if, somewhere in the Indus valley, a great whirlpool has erupted into existence. A greater monster than Charybdis has arrived. Belisarius, at his work."

Sensing the shift in Kungas' mood, Irene pressed home the advantage. "If you move now—instantly—you can catch them at the Khyber before they have time to stabilize a defensive position. It will still be hard fighting, though—which is why you need to take the *entire* army—but if you move fast we can end this campaign with *us* in control of the Khyber. Which would mean that the gateway to our new kingdom is in *our* hands, not Malwa's."

He said nothing. The fact that his finger-tapping had become a little drumbeat was, again, the only sign that he was paying attention to her.

"You are only hesitating because of me!" Irene protested. Then, chuckling: "If I weren't a bedraggled bag of bones—almost dead from exhaustion—you'd probably insist on hauling me along."

Finally, the mask cracked. Kungas' trace of a smile emerged. "Hardly that," he said cheerfully. "At least, you didn't seem to be dying from exhaustion last night. Nor do I recall that you felt like a bag of bones. Quite the opposite, in fact."

He turned his eyes and gave Irene's figure a quick and warm appraisal. "The trek has been good for you, I'd say, for all the aches and pains."

Irene grinned. As it happened, she agreed with Kungas' assessment. Her figure was still as slim as ever, but the somewhat flaccid flesh of a Greek noblewoman was now long gone. The change, of course, would not have met with approval from high society in Constantinople. Pale skin and soft flesh was the female ideal in that aristocratic society. But her bronzed skin and firm muscle tone fit her new kingdom far better.

"Exhausted," she insisted. "On the edge of the grave."

Then, more seriously: "Kungas, I couldn't possibly keep up with the march you must now undertake, and we both know it. I may not be a whimpering Greek noblewoman any longer, but I'm hardly in the same condition as your soldiers. In truth, I doubt if even the camp followers will be able to keep up."

He stopped the little finger-drumming and slapped the ledge firmly. "Won't even try! I'm leaving them all behind."

The decision finally made, Kungas, as was his way, cast all hesitation aside. "This will be a march out of legend. My whole army will put the memory of that pitiful Athenian runner from Marathon into the shade. Twenty-six miles, pah. A trifle. And then—drop dead at the end? Not likely. Not Kushans."

He began pacing slowly along the ledge, running his hand across the smooth surface as if he were caressing the stone. Remembering the feel of that hand on her body the night before, Irene felt a moment's regret that Kungas was accepting her advice. But if she rued the coming absence of fleshly pleasure, she took a greater pleasure in Kungas' words. Not because of his decision, but because of the classical allusions. It had been she who told Kungas of Charybdis, and Marathon. And, as always, her husband had forgotten nothing of what she said to him.

"I will be safe," she said softly.

Kungas stopped his pacing and turned to face her. The little crack of a smile vanished without a trace.

"You will be in deadly peril, and we both know it. With the entire army gone from Begram—except for the handful of soldiers I will leave you for a bodyguard—you will be at the mercy of any sizeable force in the area. Doesn't even have to be Malwa. Any Pathan tribe in the region could swoop down and take the city."

Irene began to brush back her hair, from old habit, but halted the gesture midway. The long, flowing chestnut tresses she had once possessed had vanished along with the rest of the Greek noblewoman she had once been. The hair was still there—still chestnut and still long, in fact—but it was bound up tightly in the female equivalent of the Kushan topknot. What the Kushan women called a "horse tail."

"You let me worry about the Pathans. There won't be any danger from them immediately, no matter what. Begram is not a village, after all. It is a sizeable city, with walls, and a large population to guard it. An *enthusiastic* population, to boot."

She inclined her head, indicating the riotous celebration going on in the streets below. "Any Pathan chief will know full well that, while he might take Begram, he will pay a hard price for it. And if the price is too hard—which it is likely to be; the populace is Kushan, after all—his tribe will be at the mercy of your army when you return."

"*If* we return."

"'If' you return," Irene allowed. "But the Pathans will wait to see what happens at the Khyber, Kungas. Not even the most hot-headed tribesman will make any attempt on Begram until they are certain your army is not something to be feared. And besides—"

Old habit triumphed. She reached back, drew the horse-tail over her shoulder, and began stroking it. "And besides," she said softly, almost crooning with anticipation, "I will not be spending those weeks idly. Diplomacy, after all, can often accomplish greater wonders than feats of arms."

"You must be joking," hissed Valentinian. He stared at the implements in Ajatasutra's hands as if they were so many cobras. In the moonlight, his narrow face and close-set features made him look not so much like a weasel as a demon.

And a greatly offended demon, at that.

Ajatasutra shrugged. "There is another alternative, if you prefer."

Lifting his left hand, still holding one of the digging tools, he indicated Ajmer at the bottom of the slope which served the city for a cemetery. "I can purchase a suitable woman and three children in the slave market. A quick bit of blade work—much less effort than all this digging—and we'll have what we need."

He lowered the digging tool and gave Valentinian a hard-eyed stare. "Of course, *you* will have to do the work. Not me."

Valentinian stared down at the city below, his face even sharper than usual. Clearly enough, he was considering the alternative . . .

Anastasius heaved up a sound which was as much of a sigh as a humorless chuckle. "Not even you, Valentinian. And you know it. So there's no point postponing the inevitable."

The giant cataphract stepped forward and took one of the tools from Ajatasutra. "You *do* know which graves we want, I hope. Or are we digging at random?"

Ajatasutra's chuckle was quite full of humor. "Please! I am no fonder of labor than either of you. I did not spend my weeks here idly, I assure you." Handing one of the tools he still had in his hands to Valentinian, he began working at the soil with the other. "One grave will do. This one. A big family, it was, although we will need only four of the bodies. One woman and three children. Two boys and a girl, of approximately the right age."

Although he began sharing in the work, Valentinian was still sour. "Died of the plague? Wonderful. We're digging up disease too."

"No disease. Just an impoverished family—one of many, now—huddling in a shack on the outskirts of the city. Easy pickings for a street gang. So the bodies will even show suitable injuries."

Some time later, after the four bodies had been extracted, Valentinian's sourness was still as strong as ever.

" 'Suitable injuries,' " he mimicked. "Who could possibly tell?" He scowled down at what was left of four corpses, still wrapped in what was left of rags. Which was not much, in either case.

Ajatasutra shrugged. "There will be enough signs to satisfy anyone who investigates. We will burn the caravan after the attack, so there wouldn't be much left anyway."

Anastasius, unlike Valentinian, was devoted to the study of philosophy. So he had already walked through the steps of the logic. And, having done so, heaved another great sigh.

"It gets worse," he rumbled. "The corpses will be suitable. But those rags have got to go."

Valentinian's eyes began widening with new indignation. Indignation which became outrage, when he saw what Ajatasutra was hauling out of a sack he had brought with them.

"Indeed," said the assassin cheerfully, as he began tossing items of clothing to the two Romans. "These cost me a small fortune, too. Narses, at least. The garments of Rajput royalty are enough to bankrupt a man."

That same night, in Kausambi, Lady Damodara entered the chamber where her new maids slept. It was the first time she had ever done so.

The two sisters drew back a little, on the bed where they were both sitting. For all the subtlety of the movement, it exuded fear and apprehension.

"I'm sorry, great lady," said the older hastily. She bounced the little boy in her arms, trying to quiet the squalling infant. "He isn't usually so bad."

Lady Damodara swept forward to the bed and leaned over, studying the child. She was a short woman. But, though she was as plump as her husband had been in times past, there was a certain solidity to her form which made her stature seem much greater than it was. The fact that she was wearing the expensive garments of a member of the Malwa royal clan, of course, added a great deal to the impression.

"He's sick," she pronounced. "You should have told me. Come."

She straightened and swept out of the chamber. Confused and fearful, the two sisters followed her.

In the course of the next few hours, their fear abated. Almost vanished, in fact. But their confusion grew. It was unheard of, after all, for a great Malwa lady to serve as a physician for a slave servant's infant. Using her own chamber for the purpose! Feeding him potions with her own hands!

As they began to leave, the infant having finally fallen asleep, Lady Damodara's voice stopped them in the doorway.

"You remember, I trust, what Ajatasutra told you?"

The sisters, more confused than ever, turned around and stared at her.

Lady Damodara sighed. "Spymasters, assassins," she muttered. "He did not even tell you his name?"

After a moment or two, the meaning of her words finally registered on them. Both sisters' eyes widened.

"What did he tell you?" demanded Lady Damodara. "The most *important* thing?"

"Ask no questions," the younger sister whispered. "Do as you are told. Say nothing to anyone."

Lady Damodara stared at them. Short she might have been, and plump besides, but in that moment she resembled a great hawk. Or an owl, which is also a predator.

The moment lasted not more than seconds, however. "Oh, pah!" she suddenly exclaimed. "Spymasters are too smart for their own good. If any part of the thing is discovered, we are all dead anyway. Better you should know, so that when the time comes you are not overwhelmed with confusion."

She moved over to her own great regal bed and sat down on the edge. "Come here, girls," she commanded, patting the bedding. "Sit, and I will tell you who you are."

The sisters—now completely confused, and again fearful—moved toward the bed. On the way, the youngest clutched to the only certainty which their universe had possessed for years. "We are the daughters of Dadaji Holkar."

Lady Damodara laughed. Softly, with gentle humor. "Indeed so!"

And then, in the minutes which followed, she told them who their father was. Told them that the humble small town scribe from whom they had been torn had since become the peshwa of mighty Andhra. An Andhra growing mightier by the day.

By the time she finished, both girls were weeping. From joy, because they knew their father—and mother, too—were still alive. From grief, hearing of the death of their brother.

But, mostly, from fear and heartbreak.

"You are holding us hostage, then," whispered the youngest.

"Our father will never want us back, anyway," sobbed the older, clutching her child to her breast. "Not now. Not so great a man, with such polluted daughters."

Lady Damodara studied them for a moment. Then, rose and went to the window of her bedchamber. Once at the window, she stared out over great Kausambi.

"Hostages?" The question seemed posed as much to herself as anyone. "Yes. It is true. On the other hand . . . "

She studied the sleeping city. It reminded her of a giant beast, washing on the waves of a deep and black ocean.

"Let us rather think of it as a pledge. Malwa has much to answer for. Many fathers struck childless, and children orphaned." She turned her head away from the window and gazed on the sisters. "So perhaps the day may come when a family reunited will serve as an offering. And so a father grown powerful might be moved to hold his hand from vengeance, and counsel others to do the same. Because the sight of his living children might remind him of the cost of more dead ones."

The sisters stared at her, their eyes still wet with tears. "We will mean nothing to him now," repeated the oldest. "No longer. Not after everything which has passed."

Lady Damodara issued another soft, gentle laugh. "Oh, I think not." She turned her face back to the window, this time studying not the city so much as the land it sat upon. As if she were pondering the nature of the great, dark ocean through which the beast swam.

"Whatever happens," she said quietly, "India will never be the same. So I would not be so sure, children, that your father will think as he might have once. A man does not go from such obscurity to such power, you know, if he is incapable of handling new truths. And besides—"

Again, the laugh. "He is said to be a philosopher. Let us all hope it is true!"

When she turned back from the window this time, the movement had an air of finality. She came to stand before the two sisters on her bed, and planted her hands on her hips.

"And now, I think, it is time for us to start anew as well. You will continue in your duties, of course, for that is necessary. Ask no questions. Say nothing to anyone. But, for the rest . . . what are your *names*?"

That simple question seemed to steady the girls, and bring them back from the precipice of fear and sorrow.

"I am called Lata," said the youngest, smiling a bit timidly. "My sister is named Dhruva."

"And my little boy is Baji," concluded her sister. "Who is as dear to me as the sunrise, regardless of whence he came."

Lady Damodara nodded. "A good start. Especially that last. We will all need your wisdom, child, before this is through."

No one took any notice of the beggar squatting outside Venandakatra's palace. He was simply one among many beggars. The old man had been plying his trade there for several weeks, and had long since become a familiar part of the landscape. Few people paid any attention to him at all, in truth—and certainly not the arrogant Ye-tai who guarded the Goptri.

Some of the other denizens of the city's slums noticed him, of course. For all the old man's apparent poverty, his garments were a bit unusual. Not in their finery—they were rags, and filthy at that—but simply in their extent. Most beggars wore nothing more than a loincloth. This old man's entire body was shrouded, as if by a winding sheet.

There was a reason for that, which was discovered by a small band of street toughs when they assaulted the old beggar. The attack occurred a few days after he first began plying his trade, in the crooked alley where the old beggar slept at night. The toughs had noticed that the beggar's bowl had been particularly well-endowed that day, and saw no reason such a miserable creature should enjoy that largesse.

The first thug who seized the old beggar by the arm was almost paralyzed with shock. Beneath the filthy garment, that arm was not the withered limb he had been expecting to feel. It was thick, and muscled so powerfully that the thug thought for a moment that he had seized a bar of iron.

The impression was reinforced an instant later—very briefly—when the elbow attached to the arm swept back and crushed the thug's throat. And that first attacker's new wisdom was shared, within a matter of a few seconds, by his three comrades. A very brief enlightenment, it was.

A few days later, another gang of toughs made the same discovery. Thereafter, the old beggar was left alone. The word spread, as it always did in such crowded and fetid slums, that the new beggar who lived in that alley was guarded by a demon. How else explain the mangled and battered corpses which had appeared of a morning—twice, now—in the mouth of that alley? While the beggar himself emerged unharmed, at the break of day, to resume plying his pathetic trade.

No word of this, of course, ever came to the ears of the authorities. Nor, if it had, would they have paid any attention. The slums of any city—especially a great metropolis like Bharakuccha—are full of superstition and rumor.

And so, day after day, the old beggar plied his trade against the wall of the palace. And so, day after day, the Ye-tai who guarded the entrance gave him no more than a casual glance.

Venandakatra himself did not give the beggar so much as a glance, in his own comings and goings. Such creatures were simply beneath the Goptri's notice. So he was completely oblivious to the way in which, without seeming to, the beggar's eyes followed his every movement while the beggar's head remained slumped in abject misery. Showing, in their hidden depths, a gleam which would have seemed odd in such a man. Almost yellow eyes, they were, like those of a watchful predator.

Chapter 27
THE SIND
Autumn, 533 A.D.

Belisarius and his army encountered the first Malwa force shortly
after rounding the southern slopes of the Kot Diji hills and crossing
the Nara. Fortunately, the Romans had received forewarning that
enemy troops were in the vicinity—not from any spies or scouts,
but from the stream of refugees coming south from the Indus.

Abbu and his scouts captured a small group of the refugees,
what appeared to be an entire extended family. Not knowing their
language, he brought the group to the general. Belisarius' fluency
in foreign tongues was a byword among his troops. The Talisman
of God allowed him to understand any language—even, some said,
the speech of animals.

The truth, of course, fell far short of that legend. Aide did provide Belisarius with a great facility for *learning* foreign languages.
But it was not magic, and did not allow Belisarius to understand
and speak a language in an instant.

So the group of peasants huddling on the ground before him,
with their few belongings strapped to their backs and their one
precious cow "guarded" in the center, were unable to communicate with him. In truth, the people were so terrified that Belisarius
doubted they would have been able to speak in any event. The
eyes of the men and women were downcast. They stared at the

soil before them as if, by ignoring the armed and armored men who surrounded them, they could change reality itself.

The children were less bashful. Or, at least, less ready to believe that reality was susceptible to such easy manipulation. They ogled the Roman soldiers around them, wide-eyed and fearful. One young girl—perhaps six or seven—was sobbing wildly, ignoring the way her mother was trying to shake her into silence. Because of the mother's own terror, the shaking was a subdued sort of thing, not the kind of ferocious effort which could hope to subdue such sheer hysteria.

Belisarius winced and looked away. His eyes met those of a boy about the same age. Perhaps the girl's brother; perhaps a cousin. Between the dirt and grime which covered the peasants, and the distortion which fear produced in their faces, it was hard to detect family resemblance. More accurately, family resemblance was buried under the generic similarity which makes all desperate people look well-nigh identical.

The boy was not sobbing. He was simply staring at the general with eyes so open they seemed to protrude entirely from his face. Belisarius gave him a smile. The boy's only reaction was to—somehow—widen his eyes further.

There was nothing of childlike curiosity in those wide eyes. Just a terror so deep that the lad was like a paralyzed rodent, facing a cobra.

"Oh, Christ," muttered Maurice.

Belisarius sighed. He dismissed any thought of trying to interrogate the peasants. They would tell him nothing, in any event. *Could* tell him nothing, even if he spoke their language. The war had smote the peasants as war always does—like a thunderstorm cast down by distant and uncaring deities, sweeping them aside like debris in a river raging in flood. They would understand nothing of it, beyond chaos and confusion. Troop movements, maneuvers, terrain as a military feature rather than just a path of panic-stricken flight—these were beyond their ken and reckoning.

"Let them go," he ordered. "Make sure you have our own Thracians escort them to the rear. I don't expect there'd be any trouble with other soldiers, but . . ."

"There's no reason to risk the temptation," finished Maurice, scowling a bit. "Not that these have anything worth stealing, but some of the Greeks—the new ones, not Cyril's men—are starting to complain about the lack of booty."

He eyed one of the peasant girls. Older, she was—perhaps sixteen or seventeen. "They might take out their frustration with other pleasures. And then—" He grated a harsh little laugh. "You'd give the army another demonstration of Belisarius discipline, and we'd look a bit silly charging into battle dragging executed cataphracts behind us."

Belisarius nodded. "The fact these people are here at all tells me what I need to know. The Malwa have started their massacre."

He gathered up the reins of his horse. His brown eyes, usually as warm as old wood, glinted like hard shells in a receding tide. "Which means they'll be spread out and disorganized. So it's time for another demonstration." The next words were almost hissed. *"I will put the fear of God in those men. Old Testament fear."*

He fell on the Malwa less than two hours later. Early afternoon it was, by then. The Arab scouts had begun bringing in further reports, this time based on direct observation of the enemy. As Belisarius had expected, the Malwa soldiers were spread out across miles of terrain.

"Some burning, not much," summarized Abbu. The old desert chief's face was tight with anger. "Probably they plan to do the burning later. Now it is just the killing."

That too, Belisarius had also deduced. As they marched forward, the Roman army had encountered other refugees since the first group. The trickle had become a stream, until the entire countryside seemed to have little rivulets of frantic people pouring through it. The Malwa were butchering everyone in the area they could catch. A scorched earth campaign Tamerlane would have been proud to call his own. Tear out the ultimate roots of the land by destroying the work force itself, not simply the products of its labor.

"Is there a depression in the land we can drive them toward?" he asked.

Abbu pointed east by north. "Yes, General. That way, not far—maybe five miles. A little riverbed, almost dry. Runs northwest by southeast."

The scout leader's face tightened still further. The anger was still there, but it was now overlaid with anticipation. He understood immediately Belisarius' purpose.

"Good killing ground," he snarled. "The opposite bank will channel them downriver. Not high, but sharp and steep."

He pointed again, this time more east than north. "There. A small rise slopes down toward our bank of the river, which is shallow."

Belisarius nodded. Then:

"Sittas, take all your cataphracts and flank them on the west. Take Cyril's, too. Roll the bastards up. Don't try to smash them, just herd them toward Abbu's river. As disorganized as they are, they'll run, not fight."

He gave the big Greek general a hard stare. "Run, not fight. As long as you don't corner them."

Sittas returned the stare with a grin. "Stop fussing at me. I do know how to do something other than charge, you know." He began turning his horse. "Besides, I like this plan. We'll show these swine how to run a *real* slaughter."

Before Sittas had finished, Belisarius was issuing new orders. "Gregory, set up the artillery on that rise. But *don't* use the mitrailleuse or the mortars unless I give the command. In fact, keep them covered with tarpaulins. I want to keep those weapons a secret as long as possible, and they require special ammunition anyway. Which we need to use sparingly, this early in the campaign. Abbu, guide them there—or have one of your men do it."

As Gregory and Abbu peeled off to set their troops into new motion, Belisarius continued to issue orders. They were obeyed instantly, with one exception.

"No, Mark," said Belisarius forcefully. "I know you want to give your sharpshooters their first real taste of battle, but this is not the time and place. We can't replenish your ammunition from the general stock, and we'll need it later."

He eased any sting out of the rebuke with a slight smile. "You'll have plenty of combat, soon enough. At Sukkur and elsewhere. For today, I just need you to guard the guns. They'll do the killing."

Mark, as always, was stubborn. It was a trait Belisarius had managed to wear down some, over the years. But not much, because in truth he had never really made much of an effort to do so. If there was any single word which captured the spirit of Mark of Edessa, it was *pugnacious*—a characteristic which Belisarius prized in his officers.

At the Battle of the Pass, that pugnacity had broken a Ye-tai charge like so much kindling. That it would do so again, and again—or die in the trying—was one of the lynchpins of Belisarius' entire campaign.

"The damn artillery doesn't have much ammunition either," grumbled Mark. "And they chew it up like a wolf chews meat."

"They can also chew up enemy troops like a wolf," pointed out Belisarius. "Especially at close range, with canister. And I can keep them restocked from any kind of gunpowder. Even that cruddy Malwa stuff, if I have to. I can't replace your special cartridges easily."

Mark of Edessa knew he had pushed the general as far as he could. Stubborn he was, yes, but not insubordinate. So, still scowling, he trotted off on his horse, venting his resentment by barking his commands to the sharpshooters. He sounded like a wolf himself.

"God help the Malwa if they try to overrun the batteries," said Maurice, smiling grimly. "Mark's been wanting to test the bayonets, too. And don't think he won't, if he gets half a chance."

Maurice too, it seemed, had caught the general bloodlust. "Not that I wouldn't enjoy watching it, mind you. But, you're right—this is not the time and place." He sighed with happy satisfaction. "This is just a time and place for butcher's work."

By the time the real butchery began, the Malwa were already badly blooded. Sittas, if he had not violated the letter of his orders, had obviously stretched the spirit of them as far as he could. Watching the Malwa soldiers pouring down the river bed in complete disorder, Belisarius knew that Sittas and his Greek cataphracts had "rolled them up" the way a blacksmith rolls a gun barrel—with hammer and flame.

Belisarius had chosen to take his own position with the artillery and the sharpshooters. These were his least experienced troops—in the use of these weapons, at any rate—and he wanted to observe them in action.

The slant of the terrain gave him a view of at least half a mile of the riverbed. The first Malwa units had almost reached the slight bend where he intended to hold them. Behind, moving more like fluid water than solid men, came enough enemy soldiers to fill the riverbed from bank to bank.

"How many, do you think?"

Maurice shook his head. "Hard to say, exactly, with a mob like that. At a guess, we'll wind up facing maybe twelve thousand."

That was a little higher than Belisarius' own estimate, but not by much. He nodded, continuing to study the oncoming enemy. Some of the Malwa soldiers, perhaps instinctively sensing a trap, were trying to clamber out of the riverbed over the shallow southwestern bank. But Sittas—who, for all the fury with which he could drive home a charge, was as shrewd as any cataphract commander in the Roman army—had foreseen that likelihood. So he had peeled off Cyril's men to flank the enemy yet again. The Greek cataphracts were already on the southwestern bank, ready and eager to drive the Malwa back with lance and saber.

A few Malwa tried to clamber over the opposite bank. But, as Abbu had said, that far bank was steep if not especially high. Close to vertical, in many places; and, nowhere that Belisarius could see, shallow enough to allow a man to scamper rather than climb.

The opposite bank ranged in height from eight to twelve feet. Not much of a climb, perhaps—except for a man laden with armor and weapons, being driven in a packed crowd of confused and frightened soldiers. Not many of the Malwa even attempted to make that climb, and most of them were swept off the bank by their fellows pouring past in a rout. And for the few who made it, the ground beyond proved no refuge in any event. Abbu and his Arabs had crossed the riverbed and taken up positions on the opposite bank half an hour earlier. Their lances and sabers were just as eager as those of the cataphracts.

"It's working," said Maurice. "Damned if it's not."

Belisarius nodded. His tactics for this battle were proving themselves in action. Sittas and the main body of cataphracts had caught the Malwa infantry spread out, in the open. And the forces were evenly matched—twelve thousand against twelve thousand. The heavily armed and armored cavalry might be "obsolete" in this new age of gunpowder weapons, but obsolescence does not happen overnight.

A cataphract charge struck like a mailed fist. Well-organized and prepared troops could withstand such a charge, even bloody and break it, with pikemen shielding musketeers and volleys coming like clockwork thunder. But an army caught off-guard, driven off balance and never allowed to regain it, was like grain in a thresher.

Routed soldiers, like water, will follow the path of least resistance. Especially with Sittas and his cataphracts pouring into the riverbed themselves and driving the Malwa before them. With Cyril and his men guarding the shallow bank and Abbu guarding the other, almost the entire Malwa army was being herded toward the guns. Penned into a perfect killing ground.

The rise where Gregory had stationed the field guns had a clear line of fire into the river bed, and at enough of an angle to enfilade the coming troops. There remained only to place the "stopper" in the bottle.

"Now, I think," said Maurice.

Belisarius nodded. The chiliarch made a motion and the cornicenes began blowing. The Thracian bucellarii, awaiting the signal, trotted across the riverbed some two hundred yards down and took up positions. As the lead elements of the Malwa spotted them, they began slowing their pell-mell race. Several of them stopped entirely. Behind them, the Malwa soldiers started piling up in a muddle. They formed a perfect target for cannon fire, not more than four hundred yards away—almost too close, for round shot.

Belisarius leaned toward Gregory, who was sitting a horse to his left. "You're loaded with round shot, or canister?"

"Round shot," came the immediate and confident reply. "On that ground—most of the near bank is shale and loose rock—the ricochets will work as well as canister. And I've got more round shot than anything else."

Belisarius wasn't quite sure Gregory was right, but he wasn't about to second-guess him and order the guns reloaded. In truth, the artillery commander was more experienced at this than he was, at least in training and theory. This would be the first time ever in the Malwa war that either side used field guns as the major element in a battle. And since the range was at the outer limits of canister effectiveness, anyway . . .

"Go ahead, then. Fire whenever you're—"

"*Fire!*" bellowed Gregory, waving his arm. The cornicenes, waiting for the cue, began blowing the call. But the sound of the horns was almost instantly drowned under the roar of the guns. Gregory's entire battery—thirty-six three-pounders—had fired at once.

That volley . . . did much less than Belisarius expected. True, a number of Malwa soldiers went down—ripped in half, often enough. But instead of cutting entire swaths, the volley had simply punched narrow holes in the packed mass of soldiers.

He rose up in his stirrups, now tense. His whole battle plan *depended* on those field guns. And he didn't want to be forced to use the mitrailleuse and the mortars this early in the campaign. He turned to Gregory, about to order a switch to canister.

But Gregory was no longer there. The artillery commander had sent his horse trotting behind the guns. Gregory was up in his own stirrups, bellowing like a bull.

"Down, you sorry bastards! Lower the elevation! I want grazing shots, damn you!"

The artillerymen were working feverishly. In each gun crew, two men were levering up the barrels while the gun captain sighted by eye. On his command, a fourth man slid the quoin further up between the barrel and the transom, lowering the elevation of the gun and shortening the trajectory of the fire. That done, they raced to reload the weapons. Again, with the cast iron balls of simple round shot.

Belisarius hesitated, then lowered himself down to his saddle. He still wasn't sure Gregory was right, but . . .

Good officers need the confidence of their superiors. Best way for a general to ruin an army is to meddle.

While the guns were reloading, the Greek cataphracts who were now massing on the southwestern slope began firing their own volleys of arrows into the packed mass of Malwa troops in the riverbed. As Belisarius had insisted—he wanted to keep his own casualties to a minimum—Sittas and Cyril were keeping the armored horse archers at a distance. But, even across two hundred yards, cataphract arrows struck with enough force to punch through the light armor worn by Malwa infantrymen.

Belisarius could see a knot of Malwa begin to form up and dress their ranks. Somewhere in that shrieking and struggling pile of soldiers, apparently, some officers were still functioning and maintaining order. Good ones, too, from the evidence—within the few minutes it took for the Roman guns to reload, they managed to put together a semblance of a mass of pikemen, flanked by musketeers. Within a minute or so, Belisarius estimated, they would begin a charge.

He glanced at his own artillerymen. They were getting ready to fire again, waiting for Gregory to give the order. Belisarius moved his eyes back to the enemy. He wanted to study the effect of this next volley. "Grazing shots," Gregory had demanded. Belisarius understood what he meant, but he was uncertain how effective they'd be.

"*Fire!*" The cannons belched smoke and fury. Then—

"*Sweet Mary*," whispered Belisarius.

Gregory got his wish. Almost all of the cannonballs struck the ground anywhere from twenty to fifty yards in front of the Malwa soldiery. Three-pound cast-iron balls came screaming in at a low trajectory, hit the ground, and caromed back up into the enemy at knee to shoulder level. Where the first volley had plunged into the middle and rear of the Malwa soldiery, killing and maiming a relative few, this volley cut into them from front to back.

Far worse than the balls themselves, however, was the effect of the ricochets. The ground which those cannonballs struck was loose rock and shale. The impact sent stones and pieces of stone flying everywhere. For all practical purposes, solid shot had struck with the impact and effect of explosive shells. For each Malwa torn by the balls, four or five others were shredded by stones.

Most of those ricochet wounds, of course, were not as severe as those caused by the cannonballs themselves. But they were severe enough to kill many soldiers outright, cripple as many more, and wound almost anyone not sheltered from the blow.

That single volley also put paid to the charge the Malwa were trying to organize. Whether by accident or design, the worst effects of the cannon fire were felt by the semi-organized men in the middle.

The riverbed was a shrieking, blood-soaked little valley now. The cataphracts continued their own missile fire while the guns reloaded again.

"*Fire!*"

Another round of perfect grazing shots. Belisarius was beginning to sicken a little. Through his telescope, he could see Malwa soldiers trying to stand up, slip and slide on bloody intestines and every other form of shredded human tissue, fall, stagger to their feet again . . .

He lowered the telescope and waved at Sittas. But then, seeing that the big Greek general was preoccupied with keeping his men from moving too close and therefore hadn't seen his wave, Belisarius turned in his saddle and shouted at the cornicenes. For a moment, the buglers just stared at him.

Cease fire was the last order they had been expecting to blow. But, seeing Belisarius' glare, they obeyed with alacrity.

Startled, Gregory and his artillerymen lifted their heads. Belisarius swore under his breath.

"Not you, Gregory! You keep firing! I want the *cataphracts* to hold their fire!"

Gregory nodded and went back to his work. Sittas, meanwhile, started trotting—then cantering—his horse toward Belisarius. Seeing him come, Belisarius didn't know whether to scowl or smile. He had no doubt at all that Sittas was going to protest the order.

But, to his surprise, when Sittas pulled up his horse the big man was smiling broadly.

"I was going to chew your head off—respectfully, of course—until I figured it out." He hefted himself up in the stirrups and studied the Malwa. Another volley of cannon fire ripped them again.

"You've got no intention of finishing them off, do you?" The question was obviously rhetorical. "Which means we wouldn't be able to recover our arrows. No small problem, with our light supply train, if we use up too many this early in the campaign."

It had been a long time since Belisarius had actually been on campaign with his barrel-chested friend. Sittas looked so much like a boar—and acted the part, often enough—that Belisarius had half-forgotten how intelligent the man was underneath that brawler's appearance.

"No, I'm not. At close quarters, we'll suffer casualties, no matter how badly they're battered. There's no purpose to that, not with almost the whole campaign still ahead of us." For a moment, he studied the enemy. "That army's finished, Sittas. By the end of the day, what's left of that mass of men will be of no military value to the Malwa for weeks. Or months. That's good enough."

Sittas nodded. "Pity not to finish 'em off. But, you're right. Cripple 'em and be done with it. We've got other fish to fry and"—he glanced up at the sun—"at this rate we can still manage to make another few miles before making camp."

He gave the bleeding Malwa his own scrutiny. Then, with a grimace: "No way we want to camp anywhere near this place. Be like sleeping next to an abattoir."

For the next half an hour, Belisarius forced himself to watch the butchery. Eight more volleys were fired in that time. That rate of fire could not be maintained indefinitely, since firing such cannons more than ten shots per hour over an extended period ran the risk of having them become deformed or even burst from overheating. But against such a compact and massed target, eight volleys was enough. More than enough.

For Belisarius, too, this was the first time he had been able to see with his own eyes the incredible effectiveness of field artillery under the right conditions. He had planned for it—he wouldn't have made the gamble this whole campaign represented without that presumption—but, still . . .

Gustavus Adolphus' guns broke the imperialists at Breitenfeld, said Aide softly. **And those men in that riverbed are neither as tough nor as well led as Tilly's were.**

Belisarius nodded. Then sighed. But said nothing.

I know. There are times you wish you could have been a blacksmith.

Belisarius nodded; sighed; said nothing.

By the end of that half-hour, Belisarius decided to break off the battle. There was no point in further butchery, and the Malwa soldiers were finally beginning to escape from the trap in any event. By now, corpses had piled so high in the riverbed that men were able to clamber over them and find refuge on the steep, opposite bank. Abbu and his Arabs were no longer there to drive them back. Belisarius had pulled them back, fearing that some of the light cavalry might be accidentally hit by misaimed Roman cannons—as he and Agathius' cataphracts had been at the battle of Anatha, by Maurice's rocket fire.

Most of the killing was done by the big guns, but not all of it. Twice, early on, bold and energetic Malwa officers succeeded in organizing sallies. One sally charged down the riverbed toward the Thracian bucellarii, the other upstream against Sittas' Greeks. Both were driven back easily, with relatively few casualties for the armored horsemen.

Thereafter, Belisarius gave the Malwa no further opportunities for such sallies. To his delight, Mark of Edessa was finally able to give his sharpshooters their first test in battle. Whenever it seemed another group of officers was beginning to bring cohesion back to some portion of the Malwa army bleeding to death in the riverbed, Belisarius would give the order and concentrated fire from the sharpshooters would cut them down. Mark's men, shooting weapons which were modeled after the Sharps rifle, were still indifferent marksmen by the standards of the nineteenth-century America which would produce those guns. But they were good enough, for this purpose.

By the time Belisarius broke off the engagement, the enemy forces had suffered casualties in excess of fifty percent. Far more than was needed to break almost any army in history. The more so because the casualty rate was even higher among officers, and higher still among those who were brave and capable. For all practical purposes, a Malwa army had been erased from the face of the earth.

Even Maurice pronounced himself satisfied with the result. Of course, Maurice being Maurice, he immediately moved on to another problem. Maurice fondled worries the way another man might fondle a wife.

"None of this'll mean shit, you understand, if the Ethiopians can't give us supremacy at sea." The comfort with which he settled back into morose pessimism was almost palpable. "Something will go wrong, mark my words."

"I can't see a damned thing," complained Antonina, peering through the relatively narrow gap between the foredeck's roof and the bulwarks which shield the cannons in the bow.

"You're not supposed to," retorted Ousanas, standing just behind her. "The sun is down. Only an idiot would make an attack like this in broad daylight on a clear day."

Scowling, Antonina kept peering. She wasn't sure what annoyed her the most—the total darkness, or the endless hammering of rain on the roof.

"What if we go aground?" she muttered. Then, hearing Ousanas' heavy sigh, she restrained herself.

"Sorry, sorry," she grumbled sarcastically. "I forget that Ethiopian seamen all sprang full-blown from the brow of Neptune. Can see in the dark, smell a lee shore—"

"They *can*, as a matter of fact," said Ousanas. "Smell the shore, at least."

"Easiest thing in the world," chimed in Eon. The negusa nagast of Axum was standing right next to Ousanas, leaning on one of the four cannons in the bow. In the covered foredeck of the large

Ethiopian flagship, there was far more room than there had been in the relatively tiny bow shield of the *Victrix*.

"People call it the 'smell of the sea,' " he added. "But it's actually the smell of the seacoast. Rotting vegetation, all that. The open sea barely smells at all." He gestured toward the lookout, perched on the very bow of the ship. "That's what he's doing, you know, along with using the lead. Sniffing."

"How can anyone smell *anything* in this wretched downpour?" Antonina studied the lookout. The man's position was well forward of the roof which sheltered the foredeck. She thought he looked like a drowned rat.

At that very moment, the lookout turned his head and whistled. Then whistled again, and twice again.

Antonina knew enough of the Axumite signals to interpret the whistles. *Land is near. Still no bottom.*

For a moment, she was flooded with relief. But only for a moment.

"We're probably somewhere on the Malabar coast," she said gloomily. "Six hundred miles—or more!—from Chowpatty."

Suddenly she squealed and began dancing around. Eon was tickling her!

"Stop that!" she gasped, desperately spinning around to bring her sensitive ribs away from his fingers.

Eon was laughing outright. Ousanas, along with the half dozen Axumite officers positioned in the foredeck, was grinning widely.

"Only if you stop making like Cassandra!" boomed Eon. Who, at the moment, looked more like a very large boy than the Ethiopian King of Kings. A scamp and a rascal—royal regalia and vestments be damned. The phakhiolin, as Ethiopians called their version of an imperial tiara, was half-askew on Eon's head.

With a last laugh, Eon stopped the tickling. "*Will* you relax, woman? Ethiopian sailors have been running the Malwa blockade of Suppara for almost two years now. Every ship in this fleet has half a dozen of those sailors aboard as pilots. They know the entire Maratha coastline like the back of their hand—good weather or bad, rain or shine, day or night."

He went back to lounging against the cannon, and patted the heavy flank of the great engine of war with a thick and powerful hand. "Soon enough—soon enough—we will finally break that blockade. Break it into pieces."

Antonina sighed. Abstractly, she knew that Eon was right. Right, at least, about the dangers of the voyage itself.

A long voyage that had been, and in the teeth of the monsoon's last days. The entire Axumite warfleet had sailed directly across the Erythrean Sea, depending entirely on their own seamanship—and the new Roman compasses which Belisarius had provided them—to make landfall. A voyage which would, in itself, become a thing of Ethiopian legend. Had the negusa nagast not led the expedition personally, many of the Ethiopian sailors might well have balked at the idea.

But, just as Eon and his top officers had confidently predicted weeks before, the voyage had been made successfully and safely. That still left . . .

A voyage, no matter how epic, is one thing. Fighting a successful battle at the end of it, quite another.

Antonina went back to fretting. Again, her eyes were affixed to the view through the foredeck.

"Silly woman!" exclaimed Eon. "We are still hours away. That Malwa fleet at Chowpatty is so much driftwood. Be sure of it!"

Again, for a moment, her fears lightened. Eon's self-confidence was infectious.

To break the Malwa blockade . . . Break it into pieces!

Such a feat, regardless of what happened with Belisarius' assault on the Sind, would lame the Malwa beast. The Maratha rebellion had already entangled the enemy's best army. With Suppara no longer blockaded, the Romans would be able to pour supplies into Majarashtra. Not only would Damodara and Rana Sanga be tied down completely—unable to provide any help to the larger Malwa army in the Indus—but they might very well require reinforcements themselves. Especially if, after destroying the Malwa fleet at Chowpatty which maintained the blockade of Suppara, the Ethiopian fleet could continue on and . . .

That "and" brought a new flood of worries. "It'll never work," Antonina hissed. "I was an idiot to agree to it!"

"It was your idea in the first place," snorted Ousanas.

"Silly woman!" she barked. "What possessed sane and sensible men to be swayed by such a twaddling creature?"

The Roman army made camp that night eight miles further north of the "battle" ground. North and, thankfully, upwind.

Just before they did so, they came upon the ruins of a peasant village. Bodies were scattered here and there among the half-wrecked huts and hovels.

There was a survivor in the ruins. An old man, seated on the ground, leaning against a mudbrick wall, staring at nothing and holding the body of an old woman in his arms. The woman's garments were stiff with dried blood.

When Belisarius rode up and brought his horse to a halt, the old man looked up at him. Something about the Roman's appearance must have registered because, to Belisarius' surprise, he spoke in Greek. Rather fluent Greek, in fact, if heavily accented. The general guessed that the man had been a trader once, many years back.

"I was in the fields when it happened," the old man said softly. "Far off, and my legs are stiff now. By the time I returned, it was all over."

His hand, moving almost idly, stroked the gray hair of the woman in his arms. His eyes moved back to her still face.

Belisarius tried to think of something to say, but could not. At his side, Maurice cleared his throat.

"What is the name of this village?" he asked.

The old peasant shrugged. "What village? There is no village here." But, after a moment: "It was once called Kulachi."

Maurice pointed over his shoulder with a thumb. "Today, we destroyed the army which did this. And now, as is Roman custom, we seek a name for the victory."

Belisarius nodded. "Quite right," he announced loudly. "The Battle of Kulachi, it was."

Around him, the Roman soldiers who heard growled their satisfaction. The peasant studied them, for a moment, as if he were puzzled.

Then, he shrugged again. "The name is yours, Roman. It means nothing to me anymore." He stroked the woman's hair, again, again. "I remember the day I married her. And I remember each of the days she bore me a child. The children who now lie dead in this place."

He stared to the south, where a guilty army was bleeding its punishment. "But this day? It means nothing to me. So, yes, you may have the name. I no longer need it."

On the way out of the village, several soldiers left some food with the old man. He seemed to pay no attention. He just remained there, stroking a memory's hair.

Aide did not speak for some time thereafter. Then, almost like an apology:

If you had been a blacksmith, this would have happened also. Ten times over, and ten times worse.

Belisarius shrugged. *I know that, Aide. And tomorrow the knowledge will mean something to me. But today? Today it means nothing. I just wish I could have been a blacksmith.*

Chapter 28
CHOWPATTY
Autumn, 533 A.D.

Just after daybreak, the first Malwa ship at Chowpatty was sunk by ramming. Unfortunately, the maneuver was completely unplanned and badly damaged an Ethiopian warship in the process. Coming through the pouring rain into the bay where the Malwa kept their fleet during the monsoon season, the lead Ethiopian warship simply ran over the small Malwa craft stationed on picket duty.

The Malwa themselves never saw it coming. The crew—exhausted by the ordeal of keeping a small ship at sea during bad weather—had been preoccupied with that task. They had no lookouts stationed. The thought that enemy warships might be in the area didn't even occur to them.

As it was, they considered their own commander a lunatic, and had cursed him since they left the docks. Nobody, in those days, tried to actually "maintain a blockade" during the stormy season. The era when English warships would maintain year-round standing blockades of French ports was in the far distant future.

In times past, once the monsoon came, the Malwa fleet blockading Suppara had simply retired to the fishing town of Chowpatty further south along the coast, which the Malwa had seized and turned into their naval base. There, for months, the sailors would enjoy the relative peace and pleasures of the grimy town which had emerged on the ruins of the fishing village. The fishermen were long gone, fled or impressed into labor. Those of their women who had not managed to escape had been forced into the military brothels, if young enough, or served as cooks and laundresses.

But this monsoon season had been different. The Malwa ruler of southern India—Lord Venandakatra, Goptri of the Deccan—had always been a foul-tempered man. As the strength of the Maratha rebellion had grown, he had become downright savage. Not all of that savagery was rained down upon the rebels. His own subordinates came in for a fair portion of it.

So . . . the Malwa commander of the Suppara blockade had taken no chances. As preposterous and pointless as it might be, he would keep one ship stationed at sea at all times. Lest some spy of Venandakatra report to the Goptri that the blockade was being managed in a lackadaisical manner—and the commander find himself impaled as several other high-ranked officers had been in the past. Their flayed skins hung from the ceiling of the audience chamber of the Goptri's palace in Bharakuccha.

The Ethiopian ship did have a lookout posted in the bow. But he, too, had not been expecting to encounter enemy ships at sea. He had been concentrating his attention—with his ears more than his eyes—on spotting the first signs of approaching landfall. So he didn't see the Malwa vessel until it was too late to do anything but shout a last-minute warning.

Seconds later, the Ethiopian seaman died. When the prow of the Axumite craft struck the Malwa vessel amidships, he was flung from his roost into the enemy ship and broke his neck against the mast. His body then flopped onto two Malwa sailors huddling next to the mast, seeking shelter from the rain. Panic-stricken, the sailors heaved his corpse aside.

They had good reason to panic. The Ethiopian ship was not only heavier and larger, its bow was designed to serve as a platform for cannons. The hull structure was braced to support weight and withstand recoil. The small Malwa craft, on the other hand, was nothing more than a small fishing boat refitted as a warship. Even that "refitting" amounted to nothing more than mounting a few rocket troughs along the side.

The Ethiopian ship, running with the wind, caved in the hull of the Malwa vessel and almost ran over it completely before falling away. Within half a minute of the collision, half the Malwa sailors were in the water and the other half would be within another minute.

Cursing, the captain of the Ethiopian ship raced below deck to check the extent of the damage. His lieutenant, in the meantime, hastily ordered the signal rockets fired which would alert the rest of the Axumite fleet that they had reached their target.

Those signal rockets, of course, would also alert the Malwa defenders of the port. But Eon and his top advisers had already decided that it was too risky to attempt a complete surprise attack in bad weather. The Axumite ships might very well destroy or strand themselves by running ashore. Besides, Eon and his officers were confident that prepared and ready Axumite marines could overwhelm any Malwa garrison caught off guard during monsoon season. Half of those garrison sailors and soldiers—at least half—would be carousing or sleeping or foraging. And the ones on duty would be concentrated primarily on the inward walls of the town, guarding against attacks from Rao's guerrillas.

The negusa nagast even took the time, as his ship loomed out of the rain-drenched sea, to pull alongside the crippled Ethiopian warship. By then, the captain had returned from below, scowling more fiercely than ever.

"What's the damage?" hailed Eon.

The captain shook his head. "Taking water badly!" he shouted back. "She'll sink soon enough if we don't beach her for repairs!"

On his flagship, Eon didn't hesitate for more than a few seconds. Nor did he bother to consult with Ousanas or Ezana or Antonina, all of whom had gathered by the rail next to him.

"Forget repairs!" the Ethiopian king shouted. "Beach her in the middle of the Malwa fleet and do what damage you can! We'll salvage what we can after we take the port!"

Before he had even finished, the captain was shouting new orders. The fact that he had just been sent on what seemed to be a suicide mission did not faze him in the least.

Nor did it faze Ousanas and Eon, although Antonina's face registered a bit of shock.

"Good plan," grunted Ezana. Seeing the distress on the Roman woman's face, he chuckled harshly and shook his head. "Have no fear, Antonina. Those men will hold off the Malwa until we get there. Axumite marines!"

And so it was that the Ethiopian assault on the Malwa fleet at Chowpatty was led by a crippled ship limping into the harbor. The few sailing ships possessed by the Malwa—again, refitted sailing craft—were sheltered behind a small breakwater. The war galleys which constituted the heart of the fleet had simply been drawn up on the beach itself. That great beach had been the main reason the Malwa had chosen Chowpatty for their monsoon naval base.

The Ethiopian captain ignored the sailing ships in their little marina. His target was the galleys. So, when his ship grounded, it grounded on the beach right in the middle of the Malwa warships.

Near them, rather. By now the Ethiopian ship had taken so much water that it grounded while still twenty yards offshore. The captain issued a string of bitter curses, until he saw that his gunnery officer was practically dancing with joy as he ordered the two guns in the stern of the ship levered around to face forward as much as possible. The crews of the two guns in the bow were already getting ready to fire.

The curses trailed off. The captain of the ship had been thinking in terms of the Axumite traditions he grew up with. War at sea, to him, was a matter of boarding. His gunnery officer, trained by Antonina's Theodoran cohort, understood the realities of gunpowder combat better than he did. A ship grounded offshore provided a reasonably level firing platform. Had they actually reached the beach, the ship would almost certainly have canted so far over that none of the cannons could be brought to bear.

In effect, the crippled Ethiopian ship was now a small fortress planted in the midst of the enemy. Once he realized that, the scowl which had been fixed on the captain's face since the collision vanished instantly.

"Sarwen to the side!" he bellowed. "Prepare to repel boarders!"

The Ethiopian marines who had been pulling on the oars left the benches and began taking positions in the bow and alongside the rails. Any Malwa who tried to silence those guns would be met by spears and the heavy cutting swords favored by Ethiopian soldiers.

That still left—

The captain squinted into the rain, trying to spot the Malwa fortress which guarded the harbor. The fortress, perched on a hill overlooking the bay, held at least eight large siege guns, any one of which could destroy his vessel with a single well-placed shot.

Especially if they had time to use the heated shot which all fortresses—allied or enemy alike—had adopted over the past year of the war. Fortunately, five of the eight field guns in the fortress were positioned to protect Chowpatty on its landward side from Maratha rebels.

The Ethiopians knew of that fortress. They had been in regular contact with the Marathas for two years, and Shakuntala's spies had given them a good description of Chowpatty's defenses. But they did not possess any of the detailed battle maps which would be taken almost for granted by armies of the future. Warfare was still, for the most part, a matter of words and muscle.

The rain seemed to be lightening, and the captain estimated that they were already into the afternoon. But visibility was still too poor to see more than perhaps fifty or sixty yards. He couldn't spot the fortress at all.

"Good," grunted his lieutenant, standing next to him. "If we can't see them, they can't see us."

The words echoed the captain's own thoughts. He now turned his gaze to the breakwater, barely visible through the rain. Already, two Ethiopian warships had come alongside the pier and were offloading marines, and two more were not far behind.

There was—had been, rather—a wooden structure perched on the very end of the breakwater where the Malwa kept a small squad of soldiers on guard at all times. The thing had been a glorified shack, really. Now it was half-collapsed—not by gunfire but simply by the spears and swords of the first marine contingent. The captain could see no corpses anywhere, although some enemies might have been buried beneath the shattered planking. But he suspected the handful of Malwa soldiers stationed there had run away before the marines landed.

"They're coming now," said his lieutenant. "Finally! What a sorry lot of bastards."

The captain followed the pointing finger. Sure enough, Malwa soldiers were beginning to appear at the land end of the breakwater and, here and there, streaming onto the beach where the galleys rested.

Small streams. More like hesitant and uncertain trickles. Most of the Malwa soldiers were still buckling or strapping on their gear. The way they held their weapons did not, even at the distance, seem to indicate any great confidence and enthusiasm to the captain.

"Garritroopers," he muttered. "What do you expect?"

The Malwa getting organized at the end of the breakwater must have had a fairly efficient officer, however. By the time the first Ethiopian marines reached them, the Malwa had managed to set up an actual shield wall of sorts, bristling with spears. A handful of musketeers, positioned in the rear, sent a ragged little volley at the Axumites.

It did them about as much good as a picket fence against charging bulls. Ethiopian boarding tactics leaned very heavily on shock. The Axumite marines were trained and conditioned to expect an initial round of severe casualties. Over the decades, obtaining a "boarding scar" was a matter of pride and honor.

These marines didn't bother with an initial volley of javelins, or even use their stabbing spears. They just raced forward and hammered into the line; deflecting spears as best as possible with their small light shields and getting into the enemy's midst with those horrid, heavy swords which were basically big meat cleavers. Strength and fury did the rest. Wolverine tactics, developed by an African nation which had never heard of the beasts.

The lieutenant had better eyesight than the captain. Suddenly he emitted a sharp, wordless cry full of distress.

"What's wrong?" demanded the captain, squinting at the distant melee. So far as he could tell, the Ethiopian marines were shredding the Malwa line.

"The negusa nagast is leading the charge!" came the hissing response. "Damned idiot!"

The captain's jaws tightened. So did his squint, as he tried to force slightly nearsighted vision to his will.

"Idiot," he echoed. Then, with a small sigh: "Always the danger, with a young king. Especially one who never fought enough battles while still a prince."

Yet, for all the condemnation in the words, the tone in which they were spoken—as had been true of the lieutenant's—echoed a dim but profound contentment. A mighty empire, Axum had become over the centuries. Its King of Kings might rule over half of Arabia and have a navy whose power could stretch across an ocean. But at the heart of that power still lay the fierce highland warriors whose sarwen, as Axumites called their regiments, were the spine and sinew of Ethiopian might.

Today's negusa nagast might carry, as had all those before him, a long list of grandiose and splendid titles. "He who brings the dawn" being not the least of them. But he had begun his life simply as Eon bisi Dakuen—*Eon, man of the Dakuen regiment.*

That was his most important name, the one that captured his true soul. Today, did any man doubt it, he would prove it true. Even without good eyesight, the captain knew full well that the first Axumite marine who had hurled his lightly armored body onto that shield wall had been the king who commanded his loyalty.

And so, despite the disapproval of his brain, the man's heart erupted. And, like every Ethiopian soldier in that fleet now pouring its strength against the Malwa bastion at Chowpatty, he spent the remaining time in that battle—even while he oversaw the cannonade which began shredding Malwa galleys on the beach and turning them into kindling for the torching squads—shouting the name of his emperor.

The *name*, not the titles. *Eon bisi Dakuen!*

From beginning to end, the battle lasted slightly longer than three hours. Throughout, the captain kept shouting that name.

The battle was ferocious enough, once the Malwa commander was able to organize the resistance. "Garritroopers," the Ethiopian captain had called his men, but the term was quite unfair. Most of the Malwa stationed at the port had been seamen, accustomed to the hardships of naval life and no stranger to savage boarding actions. Nor were they strangers to Axumite tactics, for they had clashed many times over the past year with Ethiopian ships running the blockade. And the soldiers, because Chowpatty was an isolated bastion surrounded by the Maratha rebellion, were no strangers to bitter fighting.

Still, the contest was uneven. The Ethiopians had been prepared, ready, on edge. The Malwa caught off guard, even if their commander rallied them before they were completely routed. Most of all, the difference in leadership was simply too great to withstand.

Not military leadership, as such. The Malwa commander was a capable and courageous officer, experienced in both land and naval combat. As an infantry officer, one of the Malwa kshatriyas who fought with grenades in the front lines, not cannons in the rear, he had been one of the first to pour through the breach of Amaravati's walls which brought down the Andhran empire ruled by Shakuntala's father. Later, transferred into the navy, he had shown the same aptitude with maritime warfare. Promotions had come quickly enough, and not one of those promotions had come from bribes or favoritism.

If truth be told, he was not only more experienced than the king who led his enemies, but a more capable commander as well. In that battle, the negusa nagast could hardly have been said to "command" at all. He simply *led*, cutting his way through the Malwa defenders like any one of the marines at his side. Like Alexander the Great before him—though with little if any of Alexander's strategic and tactical genius—Eon bisi Dakuen would lead a battle in the front ranks, wielding a sword himself.

Indeed, in the course of that battle, Eon even managed to restage one of Alexander's most famous exploits. The negusa nagast was among the first marines who reached the walls of the fortress and began erecting their siege ladders. And then—despite the vehement protests of the soldiers surrounding him—insisted on being the first to scale the wall.

Stupid, really—even idiotic. Eon's great strength carried him to the parapet and cleared it quickly enough of the handful of Malwa soldiers who guarded his section. Just as Alexander's strength had carried him to the parapet at one of the cities he conquered from the Mallians. And then, just as happened to Alexander, he was isolated atop the parapet when the defenders pushed aside the scaling ladders.

Finding himself now the target of every Malwa bowman within range, and with nowhere to take shelter from the arrows on the *inside* of the parapet, Eon was forced to emulate Alexander again. He leapt into the interior of the fortress itself—alone, but at least no longer as vulnerable to missiles. There he took his stand next to a small tree, just as the Macedonian had done—although this was not a fig tree as in the Alexandrian legend—and began fiercely defending himself against a small mob of Malwa attackers.

The Malwa commander died not long afterward. By the time the sarwen poured over the walls of the fortress, taking no prisoners in their fury, the commander had managed to organize a rear guard action which enabled him to lead a small column of soldiers down to the beach. There, in a brief but savage melee, he tried to stop the Axumite marines who were putting the Malwa ships to the torch.

Tried, and failed, and died himself in the doing. In his case, died in the actual combat, not in the slaughter which followed as the sarwen pursued the routed Malwa soldiers for miles inland until the fall of night gave the few Malwa survivors blessed sanctuary.

There would be no mercy for Malwa that day. Although, the next day, the sarwen retrieved the body of the Malwa commander from the piled corpses on the beach and gave him a solemn burial. That was done at the command of Ezana, the leader of the Dakuen sarwe, who also commanded the erection of a small, simple gravestone over the commander's grave.

Another nation's warriors might have mutilated that body. But the Dakuen soldiers, like their commander, came from a different tradition. One whose origins in tribal custom was not so far removed. Beneath the civilized names of regiments, lurked the not-so-dim faces of old totems. And it was that tradition which gave honor to the commander.

A hunting people will kill a tiger, but they will not dishonor it. Not even—especially not even—when the tiger, in its death throes, manages to slay the leader of the hunting party.

Eon bisi Dakuen had gained his treasured boarding scar. The wound, rather. The scar itself would never form, because the negusa nagast of Ethiopia would die from it before it could.

His soldiers had known, from the moment, still fighting their way over the rampart, they saw the spear thrust which took Eon in the belly as he fought alone inside the fortress. The knowing fueled the rage which destroyed the Malwa fleet and slaughtered Malwa's men.

Eon himself had known, and the knowing had fueled his own fury as he beat down his last assailants before collapsing unconscious to the packed-earth floor.

Ousanas had known, from the moment he reached the body and examined the wound. The young king he had reared in the way of kingship since he was a boy would be gone from this earth within a time measured by, at most, a few days. And for the first time in years, the man named Ousanas had no philosophical insights and no quip to make and no sarcasm to utter and no grin to present to the universe. He fell to his knees and simply wept, and wept, and wept.

And Antonina had known, from the moment she saw the first Ethiopian warship pull away from the breakwater and begin rowing toward the flagship on which she had remained throughout the battle. Slow, solemn oarstrokes, accompanied by a rhythmic drum beat which was not so much a time-keeper as a lament.

In truth, deep inside, she had known from the moment she saw the blazing fury with which Axum's marines cut down the Malwa sailors attempting to protect the ships along the strand. Ethiopian sarwen were always ferocious in battle, to be sure, but this went beyond ferocity. This was pure slaughter, animal rage tearing at flesh, the bloodlust of maddened wolverines.

When Eon's body was brought aboard the flagship and carried into the negusa nagast's cabin, Antonina had accompanied it. Had done what she could, with the aid of an Axumite healer, to minimize the damage of the horrible wound. But, long before Ousanas came into the cabin, his face drawn and haggard, Antonina had faced the truth. The negusa nagast would live, for a time. Might even, if she and the healer used every method at their disposal, regain consciousness and speak. But he would not live to see another month go by. Probably not more than two weeks. Not with that wound. The spear had cut great slices of his intestines; damage that would inevitably bring fatal disease in its train.

In her heartbreak and despair, Antonina thought of summoning Belisarius and Aide—somehow, someway—but gave up that thought soon enough. Aide would know of some method of the future which could save Eon—*did* know, for her husband had ordered experiments begun to create the medications of the future. But there had been no time—*no time*—for that, along with everything else. And now, time had run out. Even if—somehow, someway—she could summon Aide, the crystal being from the future would be able to do no more than Antonina herself.

Weep, and weep, and weep. And, as she wept, nestled in Ousanas' arm while he joined her in the weeping, Antonina wondered, now and then, how a crystal might weep as well.

Not whether. Simply how.

Chapter 29
SUKKUR
Autumn, 533 A.D.

When Belisarius first heard the guns roaring at Sukkur, he felt a great sense of relief. Granted, Abbu's scouts had already reported that the Roman and Persian forces at Sukkur were holding back the Malwa besieging the city. Still, there was nothing quite as comforting as hearing the sound of those Roman cannons himself.

Even at a distance—Sukkur and the Indus were still a mile away—he could tell the difference in the sound between the Roman and the Malwa guns. The difference, ironically, was not in the guns themselves. Most of the siege guns which Belisarius had brought with him to the Indus—and all of the forty-eight-pounders —were Malwa in origin. Belisarius and the Persians had captured them in Mesopotamia the year before. But the Roman powder was uniformly "corned" powder, whereas the Malwa often used the older "serpentine" powder.

Here, as in many areas, the Malwa were handicapped by their sluggish economy—a handicap which was inevitable, given their insistence on maintaining rigid caste distinctions. The enemy *had* corned powder, but not enough of it to keep all their units supplied through a long battle or siege. Just as they were perfectly capable of making horseshoes and the new harnesses for draft animals—but, making them without replacing caste handicraft methods by the

279

"industrial" system the Romans had adopted, they weren't able to supply enough for their entire army. Where every single one of Belisarius' cavalryman rode a shod horse, and all of his supply train animals used the new harnesses instead of the old collars, at least half of the Malwa army was not so equipped.

With large, small-number items like cannons or even muskets, the Malwa could compensate for their more primitive methods by substituting a mass of production. Even workers using older methods, remaining within caste boundaries, could produce a lot of such items—given that enough of them were put to work on the projects. Where the Malwa's reactionary fanaticism tended to really show up was in their inability to mass produce small and cheap items like horseshoes and large quantities of corned powder.

What pleased Belisarius the most, listening, was the comparative rate of fire. The Malwa were firing volleys, where Ashot's guns were firing individually. Under some circumstances, that would have concerned Belisarius. A volley was more effective in breaking a charge than uncoordinated fire. But Ashot knew that as well as anyone, and the fact that he was allowing his gun crews to set their own pace meant that he was not repelling any assaults. He was simply engaged in an artillery duel.

"Good," grunted Maurice, who had reached the same conclusion. The chiliarch leaned back in his saddle. "We're still in time, then."

He scanned the surrounding area, his gray beard bristling. "Which is a good thing, since *this* little part of your plan came all to pieces. Greedy damn Greeks!"

Belisarius' jaws tightened a little. He shared Maurice's anger at the indiscipline of the Greek cataphracts, and had every intention of chewing on Sittas' ear about it. But . . .

He sighed heavily. "I suppose it couldn't have been avoided." His eyes moved to the right, where what was left of Rohri was being plundered by Sittas' Constantinople cataphracts. Then, with considerably greater satisfaction, moved on to examine the ordered ranks of his Thracian bucellarii and the Greeks who were under the command of Cyril.

The "old Greeks," as they were called by the rest of Belisarius' troops, were the cataphracts who had served with Belisarius in Mesopotamia. Along with the Thracians and the field artillery, they were almost back in formation after the assault which took Rohri.

Belisarius would be able to resume his advance with *them* within the hour.

The others . . .

"Leave them to it," he growled. "I'll have words with Sittas later. Not fair to him, really, since he's been doing his best to rein them in. But he'll take out his anger at getting reprimanded on his own troops. All the better. Sittas will gore them worse than I would, with his temper up."

Maurice nodded, stroking his beard. "Then, after Sittas rages at them, you can give them a calm little speech about the need for discipline—*if* we're to win this campaign and get ten times more in the way of booty than this piddly little river town provides."

"Bound to happen, I suppose," repeated Belisarius. "They've been complaining for weeks about the lack of booty. As if our men last year just walked into a treasure room without fighting for months!"

"Well, look on the bright side. The Greeks paid for it, well enough."

Maurice's words didn't bring Belisarius much in the way of satisfaction. True, the enthusiastic assault of Sittas' cataphracts had overwhelmed the Malwa garrison in Rohri, far quicker than Belisarius could have done with the siegecraft he had been planning to use. And, true also, had thereby gained him more precious days in which to continue outmaneuvering the enemy.

But the cost had been steep. At a rough estimate, he had lost a thousand cataphracts in that pell-mell—and completely impromptu—charge. And he knew he would lose as many afterward to wounds suffered in the course of taking the city. As always, war had been an unpredictable mistress. Gain something, lose something, then shift plans accordingly.

There was no point dwelling on it. And there was this much to be said: at least the "Greek fury" was not producing the atrocities against native civilians which usually accompanied the uncontrolled sacking of a city. Not because the Greeks were restraining themselves—they had already put the entire Malwa garrison to the sword, refusing any and all attempts at surrender—but simply because there were no civilians left in Rohri. The Malwa garrison had already massacred them.

"It's insane," snarled Belisarius. "The Malwa are still carrying out their orders long after the situation which called for those orders has changed. No point in a scorched earth policy in the Sind *now*. We're already at the gates of the Punjab. They ought to be corralling the populace in order to use them for a labor force themselves."

Half-gloomily, half with philosophical satisfaction, he studied the ruins of Rohri's outer fortifications. The only reason the first charge of the Greek cataphracts had broken through, for all its headlong vigor, was that the fortifications had not been completed before the Roman army arrived unexpectedly from the south. The civilians who could have finished the work were dead before it got well underway.

"Insane," he repeated. Then, shaking his head, looked away and studied the terrain ahead. What was done was done.

"Send a courier to Sittas and tell him to follow us whenever he can get those maniacs back under control. If we wait here for them, we'll lose the initiative. I think, judging from Abbu's report and the sound of those guns, that if we move now we can take the good ground on the south bank."

Maurice nodded, summoned a courier, and gave him the necessary commands. By the time that was done, Belisarius had already set his army into motion.

What was left of it, at least, with the Greek cataphracts now out of action for a time. So, the army which finally reached the bank of the Indus across from Sukkur was the smallest Belisarius had led in years. Three thousand of his own bucellarii, two thousand of Cyril's men, several thousand Arab and Syrian light cavalry, two thousand artillerymen—and, fortunately, Felix's five hundred sharpshooter dragoons.

Which rump of a rump army was what made the difference, in the end. Because by the time Belisarius and his army reached the south bank, the Malwa commander of the great army besieging Sukkur across the river had already sent thousands of his men across the Indus to relieve the garrison under attack in Rohri.

But . . . that flotilla of barges and river boats hadn't *quite* reached the bank, when Belisarius arrived. Quickly, Gregory began bringing up the field guns to repel the looming amphibious assault. In the meantime, moving much more quickly, Felix had his sharpshooters—firing under discipline, at coordinated targets—begin taking out the helmsmen and sailors controlling those ships.

It was a close thing. But Felix managed to throw the oncoming flotilla into enough confusion to give Gregory the time he needed to position the field guns. Thereafter, volleys of cannon-fire added their much heavier weight to the battle between land and water. By then it was already sunset. And if three-pounders were far too small to make much of a dent in good fortifications, they were more than enough to hammer river boats into pieces. Enough of them, at least, for the Malwa to call off the assault and retreat back to the opposite bank.

Not for long, of course. Early the next morning, just after dawn, the Malwa boats came again. This time, spreading out to minimize the damage of the cannon and sharpshooter fire. The Malwa suffered considerable casualties in that crossing, but they did manage to land a total of ten thousand men in three separate places along the south bank by midmorning. In numbers, at least, they now had almost as many men as Belisarius on his side of the Indus.

It did them no good at all. By then, Sittas had restored order among his cataphracts and pulled them out of Rohri. The Malwa had barely gotten their feet on dry land when yet another furious cataphract charge, sallying from the Roman lines, crushed them like an avalanche. Eight thousand armored horsemen, using bows and lances and sabers, throwing their weight atop the forces Belisarius already had hammering the Malwa in their three enclaves, were more than enough to destroy yet another Malwa army.

Although, this time, Belisarius was able to save the Malwa soldiery trying to surrender. The Greeks had sated their bloodlust in Rohri the day before. Even they, belatedly, had come to understand that a captured soldier was someone *else* to do the scut work of erecting fieldworks. And even they, belatedly, were beginning to realize that real war was a lot more complicated than simply a series of charges.

Three battles and three victories, thus, were added to the luster of Belisarius' name by the time he finally reestablished contact with Ashot and Emperor Khusrau.

Kulachi. Rohri. The Battle of the Crossing.

None of those battles was exactly a "major" battle, of course, measured in any objective sense. Two small armies destroyed, and a town taken. But it mattered little, if at all. The importance of the names lay in the names themselves, not the truth beneath them. Belisarius had a blooded army, now, whose new troops—which was most of them—had the satisfaction of adding themselves into that long roll call of triumph against Malwa which began at Anatha.

Eight times, now, since the war began, Belisarius and his army had met the Malwa on the battlefield or in savage siege. Anatha, and the Dam; The Battle of the Pass and Charax and Barbaricum— and now these new victories. Except for the Battle of the Pass against Damodara and Sanga, each clash had ended in a Roman victory. Even the defeat at the Pass had been a close thing, tactically—and had set up, strategically, the annihilation of the giant Malwa army at Charax.

Such a string of victories gives confidence to an army. A kind of confidence which doubles and triples their strength in war. Real war, which, unlike the maneuvers drawn by pen on paper, is as much a thing of the spirit as the flesh.

Confidence alone, of course, is not enough. As important is an army's sense of cohesion and solidarity. Achieving *that* was a bit more difficult. The indiscipline and selfish greed of the Greeks at Rohri had infuriated the rest of the army—the more so when they found themselves forced to fend off a Malwa assault immediately afterward, unaided by their supposed "comrades" for a full day.

For their part, the Greeks were outraged to discover that the rest of the army expected them to *share* the loot they had obtained by their own furious energy (and loss of blood) in the assault which took Rohri. Abstractly, they knew of that traditional policy of Belisarius' army. But . . . but . . . applied to *them*? *Here and now*?

Belisarius let the troops sort the matter out in their own manner. He was busy enough, as it was, preparing for his coming council of war with Ashot and Khusrau. Even if he hadn't been, he probably would have stayed out of it. Some things are best handled informally, when all is said and done.

He *did* grow a little concerned when Gregory's artillerymen began training their field guns on the Greek encampment, true. And he kept an eye cocked on the maneuvers of the Thracian cataphracts to the south and Cyril's men to the east, blocking the Greek line of retreat. Not to mention the enthusiasm with which Felix's sharpshooters began making wagers on how big a hole their magnificent rifles could punch through a Greek nobleman's finest armor.

But . . . it all sorted itself out after a single tense day. Soon enough, the Greeks decided that largesse and generosity on the morrow of victory and triumph was a fine and splendid thing. And, for their part, the Thracians and others allowed that the Greek charges at Rohri and the south bank had been conducted with panache and flair well worthy of any man who ever marched with Belisarius.

In the end, the worst problem left to Belisarius was trying to make himself heard in the command tent while discussing stratagems and tactics with Ashot and Khusrau. The din of the great victory celebration was well nigh overwhelming: Greek cataphract shouting his praise of Thracian, artilleryman lifting his voice in chorus with sharpshooter—*a capella* which sent every frog nearby into shock—and Arab ululation adding its own special flavor to the acoustic stew.

"What *is* that incredible racket?" demanded Khusrau, as soon as he entered the command tent.

"Music to my ears," replied Belisarius.

"We can withstand them," said Khusrau confidently. "It was a tight thing, for a time. Once, they even breached a small section of the walls before we drove them back. But since Ashot arrived and took positions to the south, the Malwa have become more cautious."

The Persian emperor gave the Armenian cataphract a look full of approval. "Most clever, he's been!" he stated cheerfully. "His positions are so well designed and camouflaged that the Malwa have no real idea how few soldiers he has."

"They made two major assaults early on," chimed in Ashot. "The second one came close to over-running our positions. But—"

He bestowed his own look of approval on Abbu. "The Arabs found us splendid ground for a defensive stance. Both times the Malwa charged, the terrain bunched them in front of our guns. Their casualties were horrendous, and I don't think their commanders even realize how close they came to success in the second assault. I don't believe they'll try that again."

Belisarius scratched his chin. "So now, in effect, everything has bogged down into a long siege and continual counter-battery fire.

We're tying up a very large Malwa army with much smaller forces of our own."

Both Khusrau and Ashot nodded.

"What is your stock of powder?" Belisarius asked the Armenian.

"Good enough for a bit," replied Ashot, shrugging. "Although if Menander doesn't get us some supplies within a few days, that will change."

The Armenian officer frowned. "It's those big guns that really keep them at bay, General. The truth is that with as few troops as I have, the Malwa *could* overrun our position. Not without taking great losses, of course. But Malwa is always willing to shed the blood of its soldiers. And if their commanders ever realize how much our defenses rely on the big guns, they'll pay the price."

"Which means you can't afford to slack off your fire," interjected Maurice, "in order to conserve ammunition. That would give away your weakness."

All the men in the tent turned their heads, looking to the south, as if they could see the river through leather walls.

"I hope this Menander of yours is a capable officer," mused Khusrau. "He seems very young."

"He'll do the job, if it can be done," said Belisarius firmly. "The problem isn't him, in any case. It's whether those steam engines of Justinian's work properly. Which, unfortunately, we'll have no way of knowing until Menander gets here. Or Bouzes and Coutzes arrive with the main army."

Maurice heaved a sigh. "Even that last won't do it, by itself. With the twins' infantry added into the mix, of course, the Malwa will not have a chance of breaking Ashot's position. In fact, they'll have to retreat back to the Punjab. But those soldiers will need food and supplies themselves, especially if we hope to pursue. Unless Menander can get the logistics train working—which means using the river; no way to haul that much by land—we're hanging on here by our fingernails."

For the first time since the conference began, Gregory spoke. "True. But at least once Bouzes and Coutzes arrive, we'll be back in touch with all of our forces strung out along the river—all the way back to Barbaricum. They're laying telegraph wire as they come."

He gave a sly little glance at Abbu. As always whenever "newfangled ways" were brought up, the old Arab traditionalist was glowering fiercely.

"My scouts can maintain communications down the river!" he snapped. Then, reluctantly: "If need be."

Belisarius shook his head. "I've got a lot better use for your men than being couriers." He decided to toss Abbu a bone—and a rather large one at that. "This newfangled system is fine for staying in touch with the rear. Only *men* can scout the front."

Abbu's chest swelled. The more so, after Belisarius' next words: "Which is precisely where I propose to go. Back to the front. I want to keep pushing Malwa off balance."

Leaning over the map, Belisarius gave the Persian emperor a concise summary of his plans. To his relief, Khusrau immediately nodded agreement. Belisarius was not under the command of Khusrau, of course, but maintaining good and close relations with the Persians was essential for everything.

"Yes," stated the emperor forcefully. "That is the way to go. The Aryan way!"

The last, boastfully barked statement was perhaps unfortunate. The last time the Roman officers in that tent had seen an Aryan army attacking in "the Aryan way" was when they charged Belisarius at Mindouos. And lost an army in the doing, in one of the worst defeats in Persia's long history.

Obviously sensing the little awkwardness in the room, Khusrau smiled. "Not, of course, as stupidly as has sometimes been done in the past."

Maurice—of all people—played the diplomat. "You broke Malwa yourself, Emperor, not so long ago. When you led the charge in the Aryan way which cleared the road to Sukkur."

Khusrau's smile turned into a grin. "I? Nonsense, Maurice." The emperor slapped the shoulder of the young Persian officer standing at his side. "*Kurush* led that magnificent display of Aryan martial prowess. I assure you I stayed quite some distance behind. Arrayed in my finest armor, of course, and waving my sword about like the great Cyrus of ancient memory."

A little laugh swept the room. For all the historic animosity between Rome and Persia, every Roman officer in Belisarius' army had long since fallen under the sway of Khusrau's magnetic personality. That little witty remark of his being a good part of the reason. Of Khusrau Anushirvan's personal courage, no man in the tent had any doubt. But it was refreshing, for once, to see a Persian monarch—any ruler, for that matter—who did not fear to speak the truth as well.

"God save us from reckless leaders," murmured Maurice. "Especially those who try to assume the mantle of Alexander the Maniac. Nothing but grief and ruin down that road."

Belisarius straightened. "Mention of your sagacity outside Sukkur, Emperor of the Aryans, leads me to the next point I wanted to raise." He hesitated. Then, seeing no way to blunt the thing:

"Now that you have smuggled your way out of Sukkur, you should not return. If Sukkur falls, that is just a setback. If you fall with it, a disaster."

Sagacious or not, Khusrau's back was stiffening. Before he could utter words which might irrevocably commit him to any course of action, Belisarius hurried on.

"But that is only one reason you should not return. The other—the more important—is that your people need you in the Sind."

As Belisarius had expected, and counted on, the last words broke through Khusrau's gathering storm of outrage. The Persian emperor's eyes widened.

"*My* people?" he asked, confused. "In the *Sind*?"

Belisarius nodded sagely. "Exactly so, Emperor. The Sind—as we agreed—is now Persian territory. And it is filled with terrified and desperate people, fleeing from the Malwa savagery. *Your* subjects, now, Khusrau of the Immortal Soul. Who have nowhere to turn for aid and succor but to you. Which they cannot do if you are locked away behind a Malwa siege at Sukkur."

Sittas—would wonders never cease?—took his turn as diplomat. "The Malwa were not able to do that much damage to the Sind itself, Emperor, before they were driven out. Burn some crops, destroy some orchards, ravage some towns and break open a part of the irrigation network. It is not irreparable damage, and much of the land remains intact. The problem is that the people who work that land are scattered to the winds. Still alive, most of them, but too confused and terrified to be of any use."

Belisarius picked up the thread smoothly. "That is where you are truly needed now, Emperor. Kurush can hold Sukkur, if any man can. You are needed in the south. Touring the countryside, visible to all, reassuring them that their new ruler has their interests at heart and will protect them from further Malwa outrages.

And, as you go, organizing them to return to their villages and fields."

Khusrau swiveled his head and looked at Kurush. The young Persian officer straightened and squared his shoulders. "I agree, Emperor. No one can replace you in *that* work. I can—and will—hold Sukkur for you, while you forge a new province for our empire."

Khusrau took a deep breath, then another. Then, as was his way, came to quick decision.

"So be it." He paused for a moment, thinking, before turning back to Belisarius. "I do not wish to drain any significant number of the men in Sukkur. Kurush will need them more than I."

The emperor jerked his head, pointing toward the entrance of the tent. "Twenty Immortals accompanied me here. I will keep those, as an immediate bodyguard. But I will need some of your Roman troops. Cavalrymen. Perhaps a thousand, in all."

Belisarius did not hesitate for an instant. He turned toward the small group of officers standing toward the rear of the tent. His eyes found the one he was seeking.

Jovius. He's steady and capable, but slow on maneuvers. An asset to Khusrau, and a bit of a headache to me.

"Take five hundred men, Jovius. All from the Thracian bucellarii. The emperor will want to start by going down the Indus"—he gave Khusrau a glance; the emperor nodded—"so you should encounter the Syrian cavalry coming north soon enough. When you do, tell Bouzes and Coutzes to provide you with another five hundred men. Or whatever number the emperor feels he might need. I'll write the orders to that effect later tonight."

Jovius nodded. Belisarius now gave Maurice a glance, to see if the commander of the bucellarii had any objection.

Maurice shrugged stolidly. "Five hundred Thracians won't make a difference, to us. Not where we're going. Your fancy plans will either work or they won't. And if they don't, five *thousand* Thracians couldn't save us from disaster."

Another little laugh arose in the tent. "Besides," continued Maurice, listening for a moment to the revelry still going on outside, "from the sound of things we won't be having too many discipline problems in the future. And those Greeks—I'll say it, just this once—are probably as good as Thracians on an actual battlefield."

"Done, then," said Khusrau. He cocked his head quizzically at Belisarius. "And is there anything else? Any other subtle Roman stratagem, which needs to be finagled past a dimwitted Aryan emperor?"

The laugh which swept the tent this time was neither small nor brief. And, by its end, had given the alliance between Rome and Persia yet another link of steel.

Odd, really, came Aide's soft thoughts in Belisarius' mind. **That humor can be the strongest chain of all, binding human destiny.**

Belisarius began some philosophical response, but Aide drove over it blithely. **It's because you protoplasmic types are such dimwits, is what it is. Logic being beyond your capability, you substitute this silly fractured stuff you call "jokes."**

Whether or not Belisarius' face got a pained expression at those words was impossible for him to determine. Because it certainly did as Aide continued.

Speaking of which, did I tell you the one about the crystal and the farmer's daughter? One evening, it seems, the daughter was in the field—

Chapter 30

Trying not to wince, Belisarius studied the young—the *very* young—officer standing in front of him. As always, Calopodius' smooth face showed no expression at all. Although Belisarius thought—perhaps—to detect a slight trace of humor lurking somewhere in the back of his eyes.

I hope so, he thought, rather grimly. *He'll need a sense of humor for this assignment.*

Aide tried to reassure him. **It worked for Magruder on the peninsula.**

Belisarius managed his own version of a mental snort. *Magruder was facing McClellan, Aide. McClellan! You think that vaudeville trickery would have worked against Grant or Sherman? Or Sheridan?*

He swiveled his head, looking through the open flap of his command tent toward the Malwa across the river. He couldn't see much in the way of detail, of course. Between the width of the Indus and the inevitable confusion of a large army erecting fieldworks, it was impossible to gauge the precise size and positions of the Malwa forces besieging Sukkur.

But Belisarius wasn't trying to assess the physical characteristics of his enemy. He was trying, as best he could, to gauge the mentality of the unknown Malwa officer or officers who commanded that great force of men. And, so far at least, was not finding any comfort in the doing.

True, the enemy commander—whoever he was—seemed to be somewhat sluggish and clumsy in the way he handled his troops. Although, as Belisarius well knew, handling large forces in siege warfare was a sluggish and clumsy task by its very nature. "Swift and supple maneuvers" and "trench warfare" fit together about as well as an elephant fits into a small boat.

But the enemy commander didn't *have* to be particularly talented to make Belisarius' scheme come apart at the seams. He simply had to be . . . determined, stubborn, and willing to wrack up a butcher's bill. If anything, in fact, lack of imagination would work in his favor. If McClellan hadn't been such an intelligent man, he wouldn't have been spooked by shadows and mirages.

It's not the same thing, said Aide, still trying to reassure. **If Magruder hadn't kept McClellan pinned in the peninsula with his theatrics, Richmond might have fallen. The worst that happens if Calopodius can't manage the same—**

For a moment, the crystal's faceted mind shivered, as if Aide were trying to find a term suitably majestic. Or, at least, not outright . . . But he failed.

All right, I admit it's a stunt. But if it doesn't work, all that happens is that Calopodius and his men retreat to the south. There's no disaster involved, since you're not depending on him to protect your supply lines.

Another pause, like a shivering kaleidoscope, as Aide tried to find another circumlocution. Belisarius almost laughed.

Because I won't have any supply lines, he finished. Because I'm going to be trying a stunt of my own. Marching through two hundred miles of enemy territory, living off the land as I go.

Aide seemed determined to reassure, no matter what. **It worked for—**

I know it worked for Grant in the Vicksburg campaign, interrupted Belisarius, a bit impatiently. *I should, after all, since this whole campaign of mine is patterned after that one—except that I propose to take Atlanta in the bargain. Well . . . Chattanooga, at least.*

This time he did laugh aloud, albeit softly. *Even Grant and Sherman would have called me a lunatic. Even Sheridan!*

Apparently realizing the futility of reassurance, Aide got into the mood of the moment. Brightly, cheerily: **Custer would have approved.**

Belisarius' soft laugh threatened to turn into a guffaw, but he managed to suppress it. The face of young Calopodius was now definitely showing an expression. A quizzical one, in the main, leavened by—

I'd better explain, lest he conclude his commander has lost his mind.

Quickly, pushing his doubts and fears aside, Belisarius sketched for Calopodius the basic outlines of his plan—and the role assigned for the young Greek nobleman. Before he was halfway into it, as Belisarius had hoped—and feared—Calopodius' eyes were alight with enthusiasm and eagerness.

"It'll work, General!" exclaimed the lad, almost before Belisarius completed his last sentence. "Except—"

Calopodius hesitated, obviously a bit abashed at the thought of contradicting his august commander. But the hesitation—as Belisarius had hoped, and feared—didn't last for more than a second.

Almost pulling Belisarius by the arm, Calopodius led the way out of the tent onto the sandy soil beyond. There, still as eager and enthusiastic as ever, he began pointing out his proposed positions and elaborating on his subterfuges.

"—so that's how I'd do it," he concluded. "With logs disguised to look like cannons, and the few you're leaving me to give some teeth to the illusion, I can make this island look like a real bastion. That'll put us right in the face of the Malwa, intimidate the bastards. They'll never imagine we'd do it unless we had big forces in reserve at Rohri. And I'll keep the walking wounded on the mainland marching around to seem like a host."

Belisarius sighed inwardly. *Smart lad. Exactly how I'd do it.*

He directed his thoughts toward Aide: *Which is what I was really worried about. If Calopodius loses the gamble, it won't be a disaster for me. True enough. But he and well over a thousand men will be doomed. No way they could retreat off this island in the middle of the Indus if the Malwa launch a major assault on them, and press it home.*

Aide said nothing. Belisarius scowled. *It's a damned "forlorn hope," is what it is. Something of which I do not generally approve.*

Seeing his commander's scowl, and misinterpreting it, Calopodius began expanding on his proposal. And if his tone was somewhat apologetic, the words themselves were full of confidence.

Belisarius let him finish without interruption. Partly to gauge Calopodius' tactical acumen—which was surprisingly good for such a young officer, especially a noble cataphract asked to fight defensively, on foot—but mostly to allow his own nerves to settle. Throughout his career, Belisarius had tried to avoid inflicting heavy casualties on his own troops. But, there were times . . .

And this was one of them. "Forlorn hope" or not, if Calopodius could succeed in this tactical military gamble, the odds in favor of Belisarius' own great gamble would be much improved.

Belisarius scanned the island, following the eager finger of Calopodius as the teenage officer pointed out his proposed field emplacements. As he did so, Belisarius continued his own ruminations on the larger strategy of which this was a part.

In order for his campaign to break out of the Sind to work, Belisarius needed to effectively disappear from his enemy's sight. For at least two weeks, more likely three, as he took his army away from the Indus—and thus out of sight of the Malwa troops who would be marching and sailing down the river to reinforce the siege of Sukkur. He would lure them into a trap at Sukkur, while he marched around them to lock the door shut in their rear.

Belisarius would take his main army directly east and then, skirting the edges of the Cholistan desert, sweep to the northeast. He would be marching parallel to the Indus, but keeping a distance of some thirty miles between his forces and the river. Enough, with a screen of Arab scouts, to keep his movements mysterious to the Malwa.

Even if Abbu's men encountered some Malwa detachments, the enemy would most likely assume they were simply a scouting or foraging party. Never imagining that, behind the screen of light cavalry, a powerful striking force of Roman heavy cavalry and artillery was approaching the Chenab fork—two hundred miles away from the pitched siege warfare raging around Sukkur.

The plan relied on its own boldness to succeed. That—and the willingness of Calopodius and fewer than two thousand cataphracts left behind to die, if necessary, on a island across from the huge Malwa army besieging Sukkur. Again, the very boldness of the gambit was the only thing that gave it a chance to succeed. Belisarius estimated—and Calopodius obviously agreed—that the Malwa commander would assume that the forces on the island were simply a detachment of Belisarius' main force. Which, he would assume—insanity to think otherwise!—were still positioned in Rohri.

Positioned, refitted—and ready to take advantage of a failed Malwa assault on the outlying detachment on the island to push across the Indus and link up with the Persians forted up in Sukkur and Ashot's Roman forces south of the city.

Aide chimed in, back to his mode of reassurance: **By now, after Anatha and the Dam and Charax, the Malwa will be terrified of another "Belisarius trap." Their commander at Sukkur will stare at that island and wonder. And wonder. What trap lies hidden there? He will study that island, and conclude that Calopodius is simply bait. And—wise man!—he will conclude that bait is best left unswallowed.**

Belisarius nodded, responding simultaneously to Aide and the young and eager officer standing in front of him.

"It'll work," he said firmly, his tone exuding a confidence he did not really possess. But . . .

Belisarius had made up his mind, now. As much as anything, because listening to Calopodius' enthusiastic words had convinced him of the key thing. If this scheme had any chance of success, it would be because of the boldness and courage of the officer who led it. And while some part of Belisarius' soul was dark and grim—almost bitter—at the thought of asking a seventeen-year-old boy to stand and die, the cold-blooded general's mind knew the truth. For some odd reason buried deep within the human spirit, such "boys," throughout history, had proven their willingness to do so.

Time and time again they had, in places beyond counting. It was a characteristic which recognized neither border, breed, nor birth. Such "boys" had done so in the Warsaw Ghetto, and at Isandhlwana, and in the sunken road at Shiloh. As if, on the threshold of manhood, they felt compelled to prove themselves worthy of a status that no one, really, had ever challenged—except themselves, in the shadowy and fearful crevices of their own souls.

He sighed. *So be it. I was once seventeen years old myself.* Coldly, his eyes moved over the landscape of the island, remembering. *And would have—eagerly—done the same.*

There remained, only, to sharpen the sacrificial blade. Belisarius steeled himself, and spoke.

"Remember, Calopodius. *Bleed them.* If they come, spill their guts before you die." His tone was as hard as the words. "I'm hoping they don't, of course. I'm hoping the fake guns and the constant movement of a few troops will convince the Malwa my main force is still here. The few guns and troops I'm leaving you will be enough to repel any probes. And once Menander gets here with the *Justinian*, any Malwa attack across the river will get savaged. But—"

"If they come across in force before Menander gets here, they'll mangle us," concluded Calopodius. "But it won't be all that easy for them, if we stand our ground. Don't forget that we captured or destroyed most of their river boats in the Battle of the Crossing. So they can't just swamp me with a single mass attack. They'll have to work at it."

He shrugged. "It's a war, General. And you can't live forever, anyway. But if they come, I'll bleed them. Me and the Constantinople cataphracts you're leaving behind." His young voice rang with conviction. "We maybe can't break them—not a large enough assault—but we will gore them badly. Badly enough to give you that extra few days you need. That much I can promise."

Belisarius hesitated, trying to think of something to add. Before he could shape the words, a small sound caused him to turn his head.

Maurice had arrived. The chiliarch looked at him, then at Calopodius. His eyes were as gray as his beard.

"You agreed, boy?" he demanded. Seeing the young officer's eager nod, Maurice snorted.

"Damn fool." But the words glowed with inner fire. Maurice, too, had once been seventeen years old. He stepped over and placed a hand on Calopodius' shoulder. Then, squeezing it:

"It's a 'forlorn hope,' you know. But every man should do it at least once in a lifetime, I imagine. And—if by some odd chance, you survive—you'll have the bragging rights for the rest of your life."

Calopodius grinned. "Who knows? Maybe even my aunt will stop calling me 'that worthless brat.' "

Belisarius chuckled. Maurice leered. "That might not be the blessing you imagine. She might start pestering you instead of the stable boys."

Calopodius winced, but rallied quickly. "Not a problem!" he proclaimed. "I received excellent marks in both rhetoric and grammar. I'm sure I could fend off the ploys of an incestuous seductress."

But a certain look of alarm remained on his face; and it was that, in the end, which reconciled Belisarius to the grim reality of his scheme. There was something strangely satisfying in the sight of a seventeen-year-old boy being more worried about the prospect of a distant social awkwardness than the far more immediate prospect of his own death.

You're a peculiar form of life, observed Aide. **I sometimes wonder if the term "intelligence" isn't the ultimate oxymoron.**

Belisarius added his own firm shoulder-squeeze to Maurice's, and strode away to begin the preparations for the march. As he began issuing new orders, part of his mind examined Aide's quip. And concluded that, as was so often true, humor was but the shell of reason.

True enough. An intelligent animal understands the certainty of his own eventual death. So it stands to reason his thought processes will be a bit—what's the word?

Weird, came the prompt reply.

Two days later, Belisarius and his army moved out of their fieldworks on the banks of the Indus near Rohri. They left behind, stationed on the island in the new fieldworks which had been hastily erected, three field guns and their crews and a thousand of Sittas' cataphracts. Also left behind, in Rohri itself, were all of the wounded. Many of those men would die from their injuries in the next few days and weeks. But most of them—perhaps six or seven hundred men—were healthy enough to provide Calopodius with the troops he needed to maintain the pretense that Rohri was still occupied by Belisarius' entire army.

They pulled out shortly after midnight, using the moonlight to find their way. Belisarius knew that his soldiers would have to move slowly in order not to make enough noise to alert the Malwa positioned across the river that a large troop movement was underway. And he wanted—needed—to be completely out of sight by the break of dawn.

Under the best of circumstances, of course, heavy cavalry and field artillery make noise when they move. And doing so at night hardly constituted "the best of circumstances." Still, Belisarius thought he could manage it. The cavalry moved out first, with Gregory's field artillery stationed on the banks of the Indus near Rohri adding their own fire to that of Calopodius' guns on the island. At Belisarius' command, the guns were firing staggered shots rather than volleys. The continuous sound of the cannons, he thought, should serve to disguise the noise made by the cavalry as they left the river.

Then, as the night wore on, Gregory would start pulling his guns away from the river. Taking them out one at a time, following the now-departed cavalry, leaving the rest to continue firing until those leaving were all gone. As if Belisarius was slowly realizing that an artillery barrage at night was really a poor way to bombard an unseen and distant enemy entrenched within fieldworks. By the end, only Calopodius' three guns would remain, firing until a courier crossing to the island on one of the few small boats left behind would tell Calopodius that his commander had succeeded in the first step of his great maneuver.

That barrage, of course, would cost Belisarius still more of his precious gunpowder. But he had managed to save all of the special ammunition used by the mitrailleuse and the mortars, and most of the sharpshooters' cartridges. And he was sure he would have enough gunpowder to keep the field guns in operation against whatever enemy he encountered on the march to the Chenab. Whether there would be enough ammunition left thereafter, to fend off the inevitable Malwa counterattack once he set up his fortifications at the fork of the Chenab . . .

Worry about that when the time comes, he thought to himself. Yet, despite that firm self-admonition, he could not help but turn around in his saddle and stare back into the darkness over the Indus.

He was staring to the southwest now, not toward the guns firing on the river. Trying, as futile as the effort might be, to find Menander somewhere in that black distance. In the end, the success of Belisarius' campaign would depend on yet another of the young officers whom he had elevated to command in the course of this war. Just as he was relying on the courage and ingenuity of Calopodius to cover his break from enemy contact, he was depending on the energy and competence of Menander to bring him the supplies he would need to make this bold maneuver something more than a reckless gamble.

Perhaps oddly, he found some comfort in that knowledge. If Belisarius was willing to condemn one young man to possible destruction, he could balance that cold-blooded deed with his willingness to place his own fate in the hands of yet another. Throughout his military career, Belisarius had been firmly convinced that the success of a general ultimately rested on his ability to forge a leadership team around him. Now that he was taking what was perhaps the boldest gamble in that career, he took no little satisfaction in the fact that he was willing, himself, to stake his life on his own methods of leadership.

In for a penny, in for a pound. You stick with the ones who got you here. Put your money where your mouth is.

On and on, as he guided his horse through a moonlight-dim landscape, Belisarius recited proverb after proverb to himself. Some of which he had long known, others of which Aide had taught him from future saws and sayings.

Aide remained silent, throughout. But Belisarius thought to detect a faint trace of satisfaction coming from the crystal being. As if Aide, also, found a philosophical comfort in matching actions to words.

Far to the southwest, at one of the many bends in the Indus, Menander was in the hold of the *Justinian*, cursing fate and fortune and—especially!—the never-to-be-sufficiently-damned gadgetry of a far-distant one-time emperor.

"Justinian and his damn contraptions!" he snarled, glaring at the steam engine and the Greek artisans feverishly working on it. His own arms were covered with grease up to the elbows, however, and the curse was more in the way of a ritual formality than anything truly heartfelt. This was not the first time the *damned gadget* had broken down, after all. And, judging from past experience . . .

"That's it," said one of the artisans, straightening up. "She should be all right again. Just that same miserable stupid fucking—"

Menander didn't hear the rest of the ritual denunciation. Before the artisan was well into the practiced litany, he had clambered onto the deck and was beginning to issue orders to resume the voyage upriver.

Ten minutes later, studying the river barges being towed behind the *Justinian* and the *Victrix*, Menander's mood was much improved. Even in the moonlight, he could see that the flotilla was making good headway. Far better—far, far better—than any galleys could have done, sweeping oars against the current of the great river. And the four cargo vessels, needing only skeleton crews, were carrying far more in the way of supplies—far, far more—than five times their number of galleys could have done.

His eyes lifted, looking into the darkness to the south. Somewhere back there, many miles behind, a much larger flotilla of sailing ships was moving up the river also, carrying men and supplies to reinforce Ashot at Sukkur. But the monsoon winds were but a fickle remnant now. The sailing craft were not making much faster headway than were Bouzes and Coutzes, who were marching the main forces of the Roman army along the riverbanks.

Still, they were not dawdling. They were moving as fast as any huge army made up primarily of infantry could hope to do. Fifteen miles a day, Menander estimated. And Bouzes and Coutzes, when he left them, had been confident they could maintain that pace throughout the march.

"Three weeks," Menander muttered to himself. "In three weeks they'll be at Sukkur." He growled satisfaction, almost like a tiger. "And once they get to Sukkur, the Malwa there are done for. If Khusrau and Ashot can hold out that long, Bouzes and Coutzes will be the hammer to the anvil. The Malwa will have no choice but to retreat back to the Punjab."

He pictured that retreat in his mind. Practically purring, now.

Two hundred miles they'll have to retreat. With our main forces coming after them, Belisarius blocking their way—the possibility that Belisarius might fail in his attempt to reach the Chenab never crossed Menander's mind—*and me and Eusebius to hammer them from the river with the* Justinian *and* Victrix. *And the* Photius, *coming later.*

Fondly, Menander patted the thick wooden hull of the newfangled steam-powered warship. According to the last message received by Bouzes and Coutzes over the telegraph line they had been laying behind them, the *Justinian*'s sister ship had reached

Barbaricum and was starting up the Indus herself. Towing yet another flotilla of precious supplies to the front.

"Fine ships!" he exclaimed, to a distant and uncaring moon.

Not long after daybreak, the next morning, Menander was snarling at the rising sun. But, this time, simply at the vagaries of fate rather than the madness of a far-distant one-time emperor besotted with gadgetry.

For the fifth time since the voyage began, the *Justinian* had run aground on an unseen sandbar in the muddy river. While the ship's navigator dutifully recorded the existence of that sandbar on the charts which the expedition was creating for those who would come after them, Eusebius towed the *Justinian* off the sandbar with the *Victrix*, its paddle wheels churning at full throttle. Once the *Victrix* succeeded in breaking Menander's ship loose, the *Justinian*'s own engine did the rest.

A few minutes later, having cleared the obstruction and carefully towing the cargo vessels away from it, Menander's mood became sunny once again.

So was that of his chief pilot. "Good thing the old emperor"—such was the affectionate term which had become the custom in Menander's river navy, to describe a blind emperor-become-craftsman—"designed this thing to go in reverse. Odd, really, since he never planned it for river work."

Menander curled his lip. "Who says he never planned it for river work?" he demanded. Then, shaking his head firmly: "Don't underestimate the old emperor. A wise man, he is—ask anyone who's ever been up for judgement in his court."

The pilot nodded sagely. "True, true. No bribing the old emperor to make a favorable ruling for some rich crony. Worth your head to even try."

Affectionately, the pilot patted the flank of the ship and cast an approving glance at one of the heavy guns nearby. "She'll put the fear of God into the Malwa. You watch."

Menander began to add his own placid words of wisdom to that sage opinion, but a shrieking whistle cut him short.

"Again!" he bellowed, racing for the hatch leading to the engine room below. "Justinian and his damned contraptions!"

The same rising sun cast its light on Belisarius' army, now well into its march away from the Indus.

"We've broken contact, clear enough," said Maurice with satisfaction. "The men will be getting tired, though, after marching half the night. Do you want to make camp early today?"

Belisarius shook his head. "No rest, Maurice. Not until nightfall. I know they'll be exhausted by then, but they'll get over it soon enough."

He did not even bother to look behind him, where he had left two young men to bear a load far heavier than their years warranted.

"Drive them, Maurice," he growled. "By the time we reach the Chenab, I want every man in this army to be cursing me day and night."

Maurice smiled. "Think they'll take it out on the Malwa, do you?" The smile became a grin. "I imagine you're right, at that."

Chapter 31
THE GULF OF KHAMBAT
Autumn, 533 A.D.

"Tomorrow you will strike the Malwa at Bharakuccha," whispered Eon. The voice of the dying king, for all its weakness, did not tremble or waver in the least. Nor did any of the people assembled in the royal cabin of the flagship, which consisted of all the top commanders of the Axumite navy, have any difficulty making out the words. If they leaned forward on their stools, bracing hands against knees, it was not because they strained to hear. It was simply from deep respect.

Antonina, watching from her own position standing toward the rear of the cabin, found herself fighting back tears. Now, at the end of his short life, all traces of Eon the rambunctious young prince were gone. What remained was the *dignitas* of the negusa nagast of Axum.

Eon reminded her of his father, in that moment, the Kaleb who had gone before him—and had also been slain by Malwa. And not simply because his face, drawn by pain and exhaustion, made him look much older than he was. Kaleb had possessed little of his younger son's intellect, but the man had exuded the aura of royal authority. So too did Eon, now that he was on the eve of losing authority and life together.

303

"You will destroy their fleet completely. The merchant vessels as well as the warships." The words issued by Eon's dry and husky voice blurred together a bit. The blurring did not detract from their weight. They simply made the words come like molten iron, pouring into molds. Not to be denied, but only received. The sarwen commanders nodded solemnly.

"You will destroy the docks. Destroy the shipyards. Burn and ravage the entire harbor." Again, came the solemn nods.

Eon shifted slightly, where he lay reclined against his cushions. No sign of pain came to his face with the movement, however. For all intents and purposes, it seemed like a face carved in monumental stone.

And would be, Antonina knew, soon enough. As they had done with Wahsi the year before, the Axumite sarwen were transforming a stupid battle death into a thing of legend and myth. Before a year had passed, she had no doubt at all, Eon's face would be carved into monuments throughout the Ethiopian highlands. And woven into the tapestries of Yemen and the Hijaz.

"This I command," said Eon. "Let the navy of Axum be destroyed in the doing—*this I command*."

He took a long and shuddering breath before continuing. "Our people can build new ships, raise new sarwen. But only if Belisarius is given the time to break Malwa. Time only we can give him, by penning Malwa to the land." Slowly, laboriously: "Let them, even once, get loose on the sea, and the great Roman's back will be exposed."

The heads of the sarwen did not so much nod as bow in obedience. Eon watched them for a moment, as if to assure himself of their fealty, before he concluded.

"Bharakuccha is the key. It is the only great port left to Malwa on its western coast. Destroy that great fleet, destroy that harbor"—finally, a little hiss came—"and by the time they can recover their naval strength, Belisarius will have his sword to Malwa's neck. Ethiopia's future will be assured, even if no man in this fleet lives to see it."

Ezana cleared his throat. The other sarwen commanders turned their heads to gaze upon him. Formally, Ezana was simply one of many sarawit commanders, no greater than they. But, over the past two years, he had become the "first among equals." He and the great hero Wahsi had been Eon's personal bodyguards, had they not? Eon's son had been named after Wahsi, and Ezana was the commander of the royal regiment to which Eon himself belonged. As would young Wahsi himself, once his father was dead.

"It will be done, negusa nagast. Though this navy die in the doing."

The words were echoed by all the regimental commanders. *"Though this navy die in the doing."*

"Indeed so," added Ousanas. The aqabe tsentsen, as always, had been sitting in lotus position on the floor rather than on a stool. Now he unfolded and rose with his inimitable grace. Then, stooping a little, he placed a hand on Eon's brow.

"It will be done, negusa nagast. Have no doubt of it. And now you must rest."

"Not yet, old friend," whispered Eon. "There is still another task to be done." His dark eyes moved to the only woman in the cabin. "Step forward, Antonina."

Antonina felt herself grow tense. Dread piled upon heartbreak. Eon had said little to her, since he regained consciousness after the battle of Chowpatty. But she was certain of the subject he would now broach.

Not this, Eon! You cannot ask me—your mother in all but name—to do this! Anything else, but not this!

Eon's eyes had never left her. Slowly, trying not to let her reluctance show, Antonina moved toward the bed where Ethiopia's king lay dying.

Once she was standing alongside Ousanas, however, Eon's thoughts seemed to go elsewhere. Antonina felt a moment's relief. The negusa nagast's eyes moved to Ezana.

"At the end, I am a man of the Dakuen. So I will be in that battle myself, Ezana. As my commander as well as my subject, I demand that right."

Ezana's eyes widened a bit. A veteran of many battles, the sarwen knew full well that Eon would probably be dead before the coming battle even started. He certainly would be incapable of even standing, much less wielding a weapon.

But then, as if some mysterious signal had passed between them, Ezana nodded his head gravely. "Be certain of it, negusa negast. Eon bisi Dakuen will lead us to victory at Bharakuccha, as surely as he led us at Chowpatty."

Antonina remained confused by that exchange, but she had no time to puzzle over it. Eon's eyes were now resting on her. The moment she dreaded was here.

"With my death," husked Eon, "the dynasty will be in danger."

Antonina forced herself not to hiss. Behind her, she could sense the commanders of the sarawit stiffening. Eon had now, for the first time, exposed to the light the great shadow which had hung over everyone since his mortal injury.

To her astonishment, Eon managed a chuckle. The effort seemed to wrack his body with pain, though the amusement did not leave his face.

"Look at them," he half-gasped. "Like saints accused of sin."

He broke off, coughing a bit. Then, very firmly: "It is true, and all here know it. My son is but a babe, his mother an Arab. A queen from Mecca, to rule over Ethiopians? With every Axumite suspicious of her family's ambitions? And every sarwe eyeing the rest with equal suspicion?"

For a moment, he bestowed a stony haze on the regimental commanders. None of them but Ezana could meet that gaze for long. Within seconds, they were staring at the deck of the cabin.

"True!" stated Eon. "I know it. You know it. All know it."

He paused, drawing in a slow and painful breath. "I will not have it. First, because Rukaiya is my wife and Wahsi is my son, and they are dear to me. I will not have my wife and child suffer the fate of Alexander's. Second, because Axum is poised on the threshold of grandeur, and I will not see my empire brought down by my own rash folly."

Again, he coughed; and, again, fought for breath.

"Let the dynasty survive—survive and prosper—and my folly will become transformed into a glorious legend." He managed a faint smile. "As, I suspect, has usually been true with legends. Let it fall . . . "

He could no longer prevent the pain from distorting his features. "It will all have been for nothing," he whispered. "The Diadochi reborn in Axum, and Ethiopia's empire—like Alexander's—torn into shreds."

The king's strength was fading visibly, now. Ezana cleared his throat. "Tell us your wish, negusa nagast." For an instant, his hard eyes ranged right and left. "We—I, for one—will see it done."

For a moment, Antonina felt a rush of hope. She held her breath. But then, seeing Eon's little shake of the head, she felt herself almost trembling.

No! Not this!

"I am too weak," whispered Eon. "Too—not confused, no. But not able to think well enough. The thing is too difficult, too complex. And—"

Again, he broke off coughing. "And, to be truthful, cannot think beyond my own love for Rukaiya and Wahsi. Only the sharpest mind can find the way forward in this fog. And only one whose impartiality and wisdom is accepted by all."

Understanding, finally, the eyes of the all the regimental commanders moved to Antonina. An instant later, seeing their nods—nods of agreement; even relief—Antonina knew that protest was impossible.

She stared at Eon. There was nothing of majesty left in those dark eyes. Simply the pleading of a small boy, looking to his mother—once again, and for the last time—for salvation and hope.

She cleared her own throat. Then, to her surprise, managed to speak with a voice filled with nothing but serenity.

"I will do it, Eon. I will see to the safety of your wife and child, and the dynasty. I will ensure that your death was not in vain. There will be no Diadochi seizing power in Axum and Adulis. Your heritage will not be destroyed by ambitious generals and scheming advisers."

Her eyes moved from the dying king to the regimental commanders. Serenity, cool serenity, hardened into diamond. "You may be sure of it."

"*Sure of it,*" echoed Ousanas. His great powerful arms were crossed over a chest no less powerful. He made no effort to shroud his own glare at the sarawit commanders with anything which even vaguely resembled serenity. Unless it be the serenity of a lion studying his prey.

"Sure of it," repeated Ezana, his voice ringing as harshly as that of the aqabe tsentsen. Ezana did not even look at his fellow commanders. He kept his eyes fixed on those of his king. Eon, clearly enough, was about to lapse back into unconsciousness. Ezana almost rushed to speak the next words.

"The negusa nagast has appointed the Roman woman Antonina to oversee the transition of authority in Axum. I bear witness. Does any man challenge me?"

Silence. Ezana allowed the silence to stretch unbroken, second after second.

"*Any man? Any commander of any sarwe?*"

Silence. Stretching unbroken.

"So be it. It will be done."

The negusa nagast seemed to nod, perhaps. Then his eyes closed and his labored breathing seemed to ease.

"The king needs rest," pronounced Ousanas. "The audience is over."

When all had gone except Antonina and Ousanas, she leaned weakly against the wall of the cabin. Slow tears leaked down her cheeks.

Through blurred vision, she met the sorrowing eyes of Ousanas.

"I married him, Ousanas. Found him his wife and gave him his son. How can I—?"

Almost angrily, Ousanas pinched away his own tears with thumb and forefinger.

"I would not have wished it on you, Antonina," he said softly. "But Eon is right. The dynasty could shatter into pieces—*will* shatter, if there is not a strong mind and hand to lead us through. And no one but you can provide that mind and hand. All the rest of us—Ethiopian and Arab alike—are too close to the thing. The Ethiopians, fearful that Rukaiya's relatives will grow too mighty, will seek to humble the Arabs. And then, in the humbling, squabble among themselves over which regiment and which clan will be paramount. The Arabs, newly hopeful of a better place, will fear reduction to vassalage and begin to plot rebellion."

"You are neither Arab nor Ethiopian," retorted Antonina. "You could—"

Ousanas' old grin almost seemed to make an appearance. "Me? A savage from the lakes?"

"Stop it!" snapped Antonina. "No one thinks that—has not for years—not even you! And you know it!"

Ousanas shook his head. "No, not really. But it hardly matters, Antonina. If anything, my sophistication will make everyone all the more suspicious. What does that odd man really want? He reads philosophy, even!"

Now, the grin did appear, even if for only an instant. "Would *you* trust someone who could parse sophisms with Alcibiades?"

Antonina shrugged wearily. "You are not Alcibiades. Nor does anyone believe so." She managed a semblance of a grin herself. "Assuming that hardheaded and practical sarwen knew who Alcibiades was in the first place. But if the name is unfamiliar, the breed is not. I do not believe there is one man or woman in all of Axum or Arabia who believes that Ousanas is a scheming, duplicitous adventurer seeking only his own gain."

Ousanas shrugged. "That, no. I believe I am well enough trusted. But trust is not really the issue, Antonina. The problem is not one of treachery, to begin with. It is simply—confusion, uncertainty. In which fog every man begins to wonder about his own fate, and worry, and then—" He took a breath. "And then begin scheming, and lying, and seeking their own gain. Pressing to their own advantage. Not from treason, simply from fear."

Antonina tried to protest, but could not. Ousanas was right, and she knew it.

"Only you, Antonina, are far enough away from the thing. Have no ties at all to any part of Axum, except the ties of loyalty and wisdom. They might trust me, but they would never trust my *judgement*. Not in this. Whereas they will trust the judgement—the ruling—made by you. Just as they did before."

She slumped. Ousanas came over and embraced her. Antonina's tears now trickled down his chest.

"I know," he whispered. "I understand. You will feel like a spider, weaving a web out of your own son's burial shroud."

And now, all of it said, she began sobbing. Ousanas stroked her hair. "Ah, woman, you were never a hunter. Many hours I spent, waiting in the thickets for my prey, whiling away the time in a study of spiderwebs. There is, in truth, nothing so beautiful in all the world. Gossamer delicate yet strong; and does it really matter how it came to be? All of creation, in the end, came from the humblest of substance. Yet is there, now, and it is glorious."

The battle of Bharakuccha began early the next morning, when the Axumite galleys came into the harbor, followed by the handful of Roman warships. The Malwa defenders were waiting, alert. There was no surprise here. Except, perhaps, the lack of surprise itself. The Ethiopian fleet came forward, not like a lioness springing from ambush, but with an elephant's almost stately rush of fury.

Certain in its might, imponderable in its wrath, unheeding of all resistance. On the deck of each galley, the drummers pounded a rhythm of destruction. The sarwen at the oars kept time with their own chants of vengeance. The commanders in the bow, standing atop the brace of four-pounders, held their spears aloft and clashed the great blades with promise.

And, on the great flagship at the center of the fleet, the Malwa commanders peering through their telescopes could see the leader of the fleet. An emperor himself, of that they were instantly certain. Who else would come to a battle ensconced on a throne and garbed in royal finery? The sun gleaming off the iron blade of his pearl-encrusted, gold-sheathed spear was almost blinding.

The commanders, uncertainly, looked to their own leader. Venandakatra the Vile, Goptri of the Deccan, was on the ramparts of the harbor himself, glaring at the oncoming enemy fleet through his reptilian eyes. His thin-boned, flabby hand patted the great siege gun next to which he was standing.

"Fire on them as soon as they are in range," he commanded. "Soon enough, that fleet will be so much flotsam. The fools!"

The commanders glanced at each other. Then the most senior, almost wincing, cleared his throat and said: "Goptri, I believe you should summon Lord Damodara. We will be needing his Rajputs, soon enough, and it will take them hours to return to the city. Even if you summon them immediately."

Venandakatra almost spit. "Rajputs? *Rajputs*?" He pointing a finger, quivering with outrage and indignation. "That's just a fleet, you idiot! Of what use would Rajput cavalry be?" Again, he patted the cannon; almost slapped it. "Sink them—that is enough!"

The senior commander hesitated. Incurring the Vile One's wrath was dangerous. But—

His eyes returned to the enemy warship. But the commander had fought Axumites, before, and . . . he could *sense* the fury under those drums, and he could *sense* what the strange sight of that royal figure on the flagship held in store.

"They will not stop, Goptri. That is not a raiding fleet. That is an army bent on destruction. They will accept the casualties to get into the harbor. And then—"

Venandakatra spluttered fury, but the commander pressed on. He was a kshatriya, after all, bred to courage even in Malwa lands.

The commander squared his shoulders. "I have fought Axumite marines. We will need the Rajputs."

When the first Malwa gun was fired, it did not signal the start of a volley. It was a single shot, and the missile fell far short of the Ethiopians. Pieces of flesh have poor aerodynamic properties, after all, and Venandakatra the Vile had chosen to start the battle of Bharakuccha by blowing his top commander out of the barrel of a siege gun.

The sound of a cannon shot startled Antonina. She lifted her head from the book in her lap and stared at the still-distant ramparts which protected the fleet sheltered in Bharakuccha's harbor.

"Why have they—"

Standing on the other side of Eon's throne, Ousanas shrugged. "Nerves, I suppose. No way that shot could reach us." He chuckled savagely. "God help the commander of that battery. Venandakatra will punish him, be sure of it."

The sound also seemed to stir Eon. His drooping head lifted, bringing the tiara and phakhiolin which was the symbol of Axumite royalty against the headrest of the great throne which his sailors had erected on the deck of his flagship. For a moment, his eyes opened again.

The wasted, pain-wracked body which was all that a mortal wound had left of his once-Herculean physique, was invisible now. The full robes and imperial regalia which Eon had not worn since the weddings at Ctesiphon shrouded him completely. He was strapped to the throne, lest he slip aside; and the spear held proudly in his hand, the same. Even his fist was bound to the spear with cloths. Come what may, Eon would sail through this battle.

"What—?" he murmured.

"Nothing, negusa nagast," pronounced Ousanas. "The Malwa squall in fear. Nothing more."

Eon nodded heavily. Then, his eyes closing, he whispered: "Keep reading, Antonina."

Antonina's eyes went back to the book. A moment later, finding the place, she continued her recitation of the feats of ancient warriors beneath the walls of Troy. Eon had always loved the *Iliad*.

He did not hear the end of it. Perhaps an hour later, when the battle was in full fury, Eon stirred to wakefulness and spoke again.

"No more, Antonina," he whispered. "There is no time. I am done with battles forever. Read from the other."

Clenching her jaws to keep from sobbing openly, Antonina lowered the *Iliad* to the deck. Then, picked up the book which lay next to it. She spent a few seconds brushing aside the splinters of wood which covered it. A Malwa cannonball, minutes before, had struck the rail of the flagship. Eight Axumite marines had been killed or badly injured. Many others, including Antonina herself, had suffered minor wounds from the splinters sent flying everywhere.

It had been a lucky shot. Eon would have risked himself, but not Antonina or Ousanas. So he had ordered the flagship to stay out of the battle once it began, just beyond cannon range. But Venandakatra, either because he recognized what a blow sinking the flagship would have struck at Ethiopian morale or simply because he was beside himself with rage, had ordered a volley with overloaded powder charges. One of the cannonballs had struck the flagship. Four had missed widely. The last shot had barely cleared the rampart—the gun had exploded, killing most of its crew.

The effort of lifting the heavy tome opened the gash in her hand. Blood seeped anew through the cloth bandage, staining the pages of the book as she opened it. That was a shame, really. It was a beautiful book. But Antonina thought it was perhaps appropriate.

She began reading from the New Testament. The Gospel According to Mark was Eon's favorite, and so that was the one she selected. She read slowly, carefully, enunciating every word. Throughout, until she came to the end, she never lifted her eyes from the book, never so much as glanced at the king beside her.

Eon bisi Dakuen died somewhere in those pages, as Antonina had known he would. But she never knew when or where, exactly. And, to the day of her own death, would thank the gentle shepherd for allowing her that blessed ignorance.

Chapter 32

Venandakatra squalled, scrambling from the masonry collapsing not more than three yards away. He tripped and fell, knocking the wind out of himself. As he gasped for breath, he stared spellbound at the cannonball that had shattered that portion of Bharakuccha's defenses. The ugly iron thing, almost all its energy lost in the impact with the wall, rolled slowly toward him. Then, following some unseen little imperfection in the stone platform, veered away until it dropped out of sight over the edge. A second or two later, dimly, Venandakatra heard the thing come to its final rest. From the sound, the horrid missile had taken yet another life in the doing, falling on one of the Malwa soldiers cowering in the supposed shelter below.

Silently, still fighting for breath, Venandakatra cursed that soldier and savored his destruction. Just as he cursed all the soldiers who cowered beside him, and all the others who had failed to drive back the Axumite assaults and the Roman cannonade.

Almost glazed, his eyes now stared at the hole that the cannonball had made in the ramparts. Venandakatra was astonished by the power of the gun that had fired it. He had not expected that.

He should have—and would have, had he paid any attention to his military advisers or Damodara. But Venandakatra, whose last personal experience with naval warfare had been years before, had not really grasped the rapid advances that both the Malwa and their enemies had made in gunpowder weaponry since the war began. His memory had been of war galleys armed with rockets, not cannons. And his logic had told him that galleys, by their nature, could never carry many guns in any event.

On that, of course, he was correct. Like all war galleys armed with cannon, the Axumite vessels carried only as many guns as could be fit in the bow and stern. Firing a "broadside" was impossible because of the rowers' benches. And the Ethiopian ships, for all that they were designed to cross the open sea under sail, were still essentially oared galleys in time of battle.

So, yes, they had few guns on each ship—four only, on most of them, two in the bow and two in the stern. Nor were the guns particularly powerful. But the Ethiopians had many ships—and still had, even after running through Venandakatra's volleys. And the Roman ships coming behind them *were* designed to fire broadsides, and *did* carry powerful guns. Venandakatra was not certain, but he thought every Roman vessel was firing what his own gunners called "elephant feet." The Romans, if he remembered correctly, called them thirty-two-pounder carronades. For the most part, the Romans were firing grapeshot, designed to kill the men manning the huge Malwa guns. But they fired solid shot at regular intervals also, and those heavy balls had proven more than powerful enough to begin shattering the ramparts which protected Malwa's batteries. The ramparts were old stonework, erected long ago in an era of medieval warfare, not the newer style of fortifications designed to withstand cannon fire. The Malwa had simply never expected to be defending Bharakuccha against such an attack—at least, Venandakatra hadn't—so the Goptri had not ordered new construction to replace the ancient walls.

The battle had now been raging for hours. The Ethiopians had lost many ships to gunfire, true. But even those losses had been turned to their purpose, as often as not, by the sheer fury of the Ethiopian assault. Unless a ship was destroyed completely, sunk in the harbor, the Axumite sailors had driven their crippled ships into the midst of the anchored Malwa fleet. Then, after pouring over the side in that now all-too-familiar and terrifying way of boarding, had turned their own ships into floating firebombs. Between the gunfire of their galleys and the torchwork of their marines, the Ethiopians completed the destruction of the Malwa navy and began doing the same to the merchant fleet.

With any chance of being intercepted by Malwa galleys now eliminated, the Romans had sailed their warships directly before the Malwa fortifications guarding the harbor and begun firing broadsides at a range which was no more than two hundred yards. So close, ironically, that the Malwa could no longer depress the huge siege guns enough to strike back.

At which point, to Venandakatra's shock, *all* of the surviving Axumite galleys had offloaded their marines onto the piers of Bharakuccha itself.

Insane! Are they maddened bulls? This was a raid! They cannot hope to take one of Malwa's greatest cities!

Then, as their marines rampaged through the harbor area of the city, putting everything to the torch—the shipyards, the warehouses, everything—the galleys had pulled away from the docks. Again, Venandakatra had been shocked. Manned by skeleton crews, the Ethiopian warships had turned their guns on the fortifications. With the Ethiopians now firing the grapeshot which kept the ramparts clear of troops, the Romans had been freed to hammer the fortifications themselves with those terrifying great iron balls.

Why? Why? Not even those guns are great enough to collapse these walls!

Which, indeed, they weren't. But, again, Venandakatra had misgauged the fury of Axum. Collapse the walls, no—but splinter them, and break them in pieces here and there, yes. As he had just discovered himself. And, as he was discovering himself, do enough damage to suppress Venandakatra's own guns and send his artillerymen rushing to shelter.

While the marines in the harbor below, finished with their work of destruction, began storming . . .

Venandakatra finally realized the truth. The Ethiopians could not take Bharakuccha, true enough. But, driven by that near-suicidal fury which still bewildered the Goptri, they could ruin the city completely as a working port and naval base. They would not stop until they had stormed the fortifications guarding the harbor, spiked all the siege guns and blown up the magazines. Even if half their marines died in the assault.

Frantic with fear, now, Venandakatra levered himself painfully erect. Still gasping for breath, he staggered toward the steps which led to the city below. The Axumite marines would be coming soon, he knew—and knew as well that his pitiful artillerymen had no more chance of repelling those insensate madmen than children could repel rogue elephants.

Damodara! And his Rajputs! Only they—!

Venandakatra was flooded with relief to see that his squad of chaise-bearers had remained faithful to their post. Despite the fear so obvious in their faces, they had not left the conveyance and run away, seeking shelter from the fury deep in the city's bowels.

He repaid them with curses, lashing the leader with a quirt as he clambered aboard.

"To the palace!" he shrieked. *"Any slave who stumbles will be impaled!"*

One of them *did* stumble, as it happens. Inevitably, some of the Roman guns had badly over-ranged their targets, sending iron cannonballs hurtling into the streets and tenements of Bharakuccha beyond the harbor. One such ball, striking a tenement wall—by accident, but at a perfect angle—had collapsed the front of the mudbrick edifice into the street. The chaise-carriers were forced to clamber over the rubble bearing their awkward burden, and one of them lost his feet entirely.

Fortunately, although Venandakatra was tumbled about in the chaise, he barely noticed. Partly because his own terror made him oblivious to the sudden terror of his slave. Mostly, however, because he was preoccupied with cursing all the modern technology and devices which Malwa had adopted so eagerly over the years.

There had been a time, once, when he would have had mounted couriers with him at all times. Ready to carry the Goptri's messages everywhere, to all his subordinates—and Damodara *was* still his subordinate in name, even if Venandakatra's authority was threadbare in reality.

But Damodara would have come, in answer to a courier-borne summons. Of that, Venandakatra had no doubt at all. For all that the Vile One hated the little military commander, he did not doubt either his courage or his competence.

Damodara *would* come, in fact, once Venandakatra *did* summon him. The only way Venandakatra now had available to do so, unfortunately, was with the telegraph which connected his palace with

Damodara's field camp miles upstream on the Narmada. The marvelous, almost magical, device which Link had brought to Malwa from the future.

As his chaise-bearers lumbered toward the palace, panting with exhaustion and effort, Venandakatra kept up his silent cursing of all *technology*. Belatedly, he was realizing that the very splendor of the gadgetry disguised its inner weakness. Men were cheap and plentiful; technology was not. In the old days, he would have had many couriers. Today, he had only a few telegraph lines.

Only two, really—the line which connected Bharakuccha and Damodara's army camp, and the line which went over the Vindhyas to the imperial capital city of Kausambi. Early on, Rao's bandits had realized the importance of those new wires stretching across Majarashtra. So, wherever they roamed—and they roamed everywhere in the badlands which they called "the Great Country"— they cut the wires.

No, did more than cut them! Copper was valuable, and the polluted Marathas were born thieves. So, until Venandakatra stopped even trying to maintain the telegraph lines anywhere except where Damodara's tough Rajputs could patrol them, the filthy Maratha rebels simply stole the lines and filled the coffers of the bandit Rao—he and his whore Shakuntala—with Malwa's precious magic.

For a few satisfying moments, Venandakatra broke off his cursing of technology to bestow various curses on Rao and Shakuntala. But that entertainment paled, soon enough, and he went back to damning the never-to-be-sufficiently-damned *telegraph*.

Because the problem, at bottom, was that humanity itself was a foul and despicable creature. Except for those favored few who were beginning—just beginning—to forge a new and purer breed, all men were cast in that despised Maratha mold. *All* men were thieves, if the truth be spoken plainly.

Venandakatra, understanding that truth, had naturally taken steps to protect the valuable telegraph. The precious device was guarded at all times, and only one such device had he permitted being installed in the city—the one adjoining his own personal chambers in the palace. Lest the grandeur of his dynasty be polluted by still more thievery.

They were almost at the palace, now. The roar and fury and the flames and the smoke of the battle in the harbor was a faded thing, two miles behind him. Venandakatra leaned forward in his chaise and began lashing the bearers with his quirt.

Faster! Faster! I'll impale the slave who stumbles!

At the end, just as they drew up before the palace entrance, the slaves did stumble—and not just one alone, but three of the four. Venandakatra had driven them at an impossible pace, and they were utterly exhausted. The sudden end of their exertions simply overcame them.

It would have been better, in truth, if the fourth man had collapsed as well. Then, falling all at once, the slaves might have lowered Venandakatra more or less gently to the ground. Instead, one man standing erect with the pole on his shoulder—too dazed and weary to realize what was happening—the sudden tipping of the chaise dumped Venandakatra onto the flagstones like a flabby fruit from an upended basket.

Shrieking with rage, he lashed the sole standing slave with the quirt. But the lash was feeble. Barely landed at all, in fact, because the Vile One had bruised his shoulder when he fell. The pain of lashing caused him to hiss and clutch the shoulder.

Then, turning away, he half-stumbled and half-lunged through the palace doors. Fortunately, the doors were already open, as they always were during daylight to allow the edifice to ventilate. As soon as he passed into the shadows of the vestibule, Venandakatra pointed with his quirt to the slaves and snarled at the guards.

"Impale them! All of them!"

Then . . .

Snarled again. There *were* no guards. The three men who were stationed at all times inside the palace entrance were absent. Gone.

Gone. Not there.

For a moment, Venandakatra simply gaped. Then, a new fury piling onto existing fury—he felt like he might burst from sheer rage—he hurried toward the staircase which led to his chambers above.

"I will have them impaled also!"

Some remote part of his mind tried to caution himself that, in the middle of a raging battle, soldiers might have gotten involved in the fighting. But Venandakatra ignored it. Duty was duty, and there's an end to it—especially the duty of servants to their master. Those guards were *supposed* to be there. At all times!

At the top of the stairs, he snarled again. Then, so great was his rage, uttered a wordless shriek.

And where were these guards? Two of them—at all times!

The almost-animal shriek seemed to steady his nerves. He managed to control himself enough to march, not stagger or stumble, to the doors which led to his own chambers.

He was not surprised to discover that the soldier who was supposed to remain on guard just inside his personal quarters—at all times!—was also gone.

Not there. No one.

Venandakatra realized, then, what had happened. He had been too lenient with his men. Had allowed them to soften with garrison duty, while the Rajputs and Ye-tai of Damodara and Rana Sanga campaigned in the hills against the Maratha bandits. The sudden and furious battle had panicked them all. They had fled— abandoned their lord!

He stalked toward the door which led to the telegraph chamber. On the way, he made himself a vow.

Two vows. First, every member of his personal bodyguard— whether stationed on duty that day or not—would be impaled on the morrow. Second, despite his hatred for Damodara, he would accept the military commander's proposal to rotate the garrison soldiers into the field along with the Rajputs.

Venandakatra did not stride through the door to the telegraph chamber so much as burst through it. He noticed, but ignored—*why should he be different?*—the absence of the guard who was normally to be found inside the chamber. At all times.

He *was* surprised, however, to see that the telegraph operator had remained faithful to his duty. The man was there, as he was supposed to be, sitting on a chair in front of the telegraph apparatus.

"Someone!" he barked. Then, striding forward, he grabbed the man's shoulder.

"Send an immediate tele—"

He stopped in mid-word. The telegraph operator's head lolled back. Too stunned to think—though that remote part of his mind was shrilling and shrilling and shrilling—Venandakatra simply stared at the man's neck.

It took him a few seconds to understand what he was seeing. The device which had strangled the operator was almost invisible. So mighty had been the hands which had driven that silk cord that it was almost buried in the flesh.

A soft voice spoke from behind him.

"I have bad news, Venandakatra."

Slowly, the Vile One turned his head, looking to the corner of the room behind him and to his left. He could barely discern a figure in the shadows.

"My son, as you may well know, was born recently. And now the priests who attend him say he is healthy. Has every chance of reaching his manhood."

The shrilling voice in Venandakatra's mind began to shape a name. But he was too paralyzed to really hear.

The shadows moved. The figure stepped forward into the light.

Prowled forward, it might be better to say. He moved more like a predator than a man. Then, as he began slipping an iron-clawed gauntlet over his right hand, assumed the form of a predator completely.

"So now it is time for our unfinished business. Let us dance, Vile One. The dance of death you would have once given my beloved, I now give to you."

Finally, Venandakatra broke through the paralysis. He opened his mouth to scream.

But it never came. It was not so much the powerful left hand clamped on his throat which stifled that scream, as the pure shock of the iron claws on the right hand which drove into his groin and emasculated him.

The agony went beyond agony. The paralysis was total, complete. Venandakatra could not think at all, really. Simply listen to, and observe, the monster who had ruined him.

So strange, really, that a panther could talk.

"I trained her, you know, in the assassin's creed when slaying the foul. To leave the victim paralyzed, but conscious, so that despair of the mind might multiply agony of the body."

The iron-clawed gauntlet flashed again, here and there.

When Venandakatra's mind returned, breaking over the pain like surf over a reef, he saw that he was still standing. But only because that incredible left hand still held him by the throat. Under his own power, Venandakatra would have collapsed.

Collapsed and never walked again. Nor fed himself again. His knees and elbows were . . . no longer really there.

"Enough, I think. I find, as I age, that I become more philosophical."

The monster, still using only the one hand, hefted Venandakatra's body like a man hefts a sack full of manure and drew him toward the corner where it had waited in ambush. On the way, that remote part of Venandakatra's mind was puzzled to see the gray hair in the monster's beard. He had never imagined a panther with a beard of any kind. Certainly not a grizzled one.

Now in the corner, the monster swept aside the heavy curtain over the window. Tore it aside, rather, sweeping the iron claws like an animal. Sudden light poured into the chamber.

When Venandakatra saw the chair now exposed, he suddenly realized how the monster had whiled away the time he spent lurking in ambush. The chair had been redesigned. Augmented, it might be better to say. The remote part of his brain even appreciated the cunning of the design and the sturdiness of the workmanship.

The rest of his mind screamed in despair, and his ruined body tried to obey. But the monster's left hand shifted a bit, the iron claws worked again, and the scream died with the shredded throat which carried it.

"You may bleed to death from that wound, but I doubt it. It certainly won't kill you before the other."

The claws worked again, again, again.

"Not that it probably matters. There are no guards left in this palace to hear you. It seems a great wind has scoured it clean."

Venandakatra now stood naked, his expensive clothing lying tattered about the chamber. The iron claws raked his ribs, the iron left hand turned him. He was now facing away from the chair. His throat and joints leaked blood and ruin.

Despair of the mind, to multiply agony of the body. That was Venandakatra's last, fully conscious thought, except for the final words of his executioner.

"I thought you would appreciate it, Vile One. You always did favor a short stake."

Chapter 33

THE INDUS
Autumn, 533 A.D.

Abbu leaned over the map and studied it. His face was tense, tight; half-apprehensive and half-angry. The lighting shed by the lamps hanging in Belisarius' command tent brought out all the shadows in the old man's hawk face. Brow and nose were highlighted; thick beard framed a mouth and cheeks in shadows; the eyes were pools of darkness. He looked, for all the world, like a sorcerer on the verge of summoning a demon. Or, perhaps, about to sup with the devil—and wishing he had a longer spoon.

Belisarius glanced quickly around the table. Judging from their stiff expressions, he thought Maurice and Sittas and Gregory were fighting the same battle he was—to keep from laughing outright at the scout chief's reluctance to have anything to do with the *cursed new-fangled device*. The detested, despised—*map*.

Maps were toys for children! *At best*. Real men—father teaching son, generation after generation!—relied on their own eyes to see; their memory to recall; the verbal acuity of a poetic race to describe and explain!

Too bad he doesn't mutter, except in his own mind, mused Aide. **I'm sure he could give even Valentinian an education in the art.**

322

Belisarius' lips tightened still further. If so much as a single chuckle emerged . . .

"Here," rasped Abbu, pointing with a finger at a bend in the Chenab. The mark on the map was recent. So recent the ink had barely dried. Which was not surprising, since Belisarius had just drawn that stretch of the Chenab himself, following Abbu's stiff directions.

"A bit far to the north," rumbled Sittas. Now that real business was being conducted, the big general was no longer having any trouble containing his amusement. His heavy brows were lowered over half-closed eyes, and his lips were pursed as if he'd just eaten a lemon.

Abbu flashed him a dark glance. "Here!" he repeated. "The ships at Uch are big. Both of them. The whole army could be transferred across the river in a single day. And there are good landings at three places on the opposite bank."

He leaned over the map again, his earlier reluctance now lost in the eagerness of a prospective triumph.

"Here. Here. Here." Each word was accompanied by a jab of the finger at a different place on the map, indicating a spot on the opposite bank of the Chenab. "I would use the second landing. Almost no risk there of grounding the ships."

For a moment, Abbu hesitated, reluctant again. But the reluctance, this time, stemmed from simple tradition rather than outrage at newfangled ways. Like any master scout, Abbu hated to allow any imprecision into his description of terrain.

But . . . Abbu was the best scout Belisarius had ever had because the man was scrupulously honest as well as infernally capable. "I can't be certain. We did not cross the river ourselves, because there is no ford. But the river looks to run deep at that second landing, with no hidden sandbars. Not even a beach. So the fishing village built a small pier over the water. Too small for these ships, of course, but the simple fact it is there at all means that we could unload the big ships without running aground."

Sittas was still scowling. "Too far to the north," he grumbled again. "Both the town and the landing across the river. A good twenty or thirty miles past the fork of the Chenab and the Indus. Hell of a gamble." He straightened up and looked at Belisarius. "Maybe we should stick to the original plan. Seize *this* side of the Indus and set up our lines right at the fork itself."

Belisarius did not reply immediately. He understood Sittas' reluctance, but . . .

What a coup if we could pull it off!

You'd have no line of retreat at all, said Aide.

"No line of retreat," echoed Maurice. The chiliarch had no way of hearing Aide's voice, of course, but the situation was so obvious that Belisarius was not surprised their thoughts had run in tandem. "If it goes sour, we'll be trapped in the triangle, bottled up by the Malwa. The Chenab to our right and the Indus to our left."

Sittas shook his head. "I can't say I'm much concerned about *that*. Once we make the thrust into the Punjab—wherever we strike, and wherever we set up our fieldworks—'lines of retreat' are pretty much a delusion anyway."

He gestured toward the army camped just outside the tent, unseen behind its leather walls. "You know as well as I do, Maurice, that we'll have no way to retreat across the country we just passed through. Even if we *could* break contact with the Malwa after the fighting starts. Which isn't too likely, given how badly we'll be outnumbered."

"We've already foraged the area clean," said Belisarius, agreeing with Sittas. "As it was, the thing was tight. If the peasants hadn't been panicked by reports of Malwa massacres in the Sind and fled, we might not have had enough to get this far."

Maurice winced a little, but didn't argue the point. The stretch of territory which Belisarius' army had marched through, with the Indus to one side and the Cholistan desert to the other, had been—just as Aide suspected—far less barren than future history would record. But it had still not been anything which could be called "fertile." If the fleeing peasantry hadn't left a good deal of already collected food behind them, the Roman army would have been forced to move very slowly due to the need for constant foraging.

As it was, they had been able to make the trek in sixteen days—better than Belisarius or his top subordinates had expected. But, in doing so, they had stripped the land clean of all easily collectable food. Trying to retreat through that territory, with much larger forces in pursuit, would be a nightmare. Most of the Roman soldiers would never make it back alive. And it was quite possible that the entire army would be forced to surrender.

"Surrender," into Malwa hands, meant a rather short stint in labor battalions. The Malwa had the charming practice of working their prisoners to death.

"Do or die," said Sittas calmly. "That's just the way it is, regardless of where we hit the enemy in the Punjab."

He leaned over the map, placing both large hands on the table it rested upon. "But I still think it's too much of a risk to go for the inside of the big fork. The problem's not retreat—it's getting supplies from downriver."

Belisarius understood full well the point Sittas was making. In order to reach a Roman army forted up in the fork itself, Roman supply vessels would have to run a gauntlet of enemy fire from the west bank of the Indus. Whereas if the Romans set up their fortifications on the opposite bank of the Indus just below the Chenab fork, the supply ships would be able to hug the eastern shore.

Still—

He scratched his chin. "The ships will *still* have to run the supplies in under fire, Sittas. Not as heavy, I grant you, but heavy enough. The Malwa have already built a major fortress on the west bank of the Indus, still further south, and you can be certain they've positioned big siege guns in it. The river's a lot wider south of the Chenab fork, true enough, but not so wide that those big guns won't be able to carry entirely across. So, no matter where we set up, the supply ships will be under fire trying to reach us."

Maurice started to say something, but his commander cut him off. Belisarius had relied on boldness throughout this campaign. His instincts told him to stay the course.

"I've made up my mind. We'll follow Abbu's proposal. Take Uch in a lightning strike, smash that small Malwa army there, and then use the ships to ferry our army into the triangle. We'll set up our lines across the triangle, as far down into the tip as we need to be to have enough of a troop concentration. Then—"

He straightened. "Thereafter, we'll be relying on the courage of our cataphracts to hold off the Malwa counterattack. And the courage of Menander to bring the supplies we need to hold out. Simple as that."

He scanned the faces of the men at the table, almost challenging them to say anything.

Maurice chuckled. "I'm not worried about their *courage*, general. Just . . . These damn newfangled contraptions of Justinian's better work. That's all I've got to say."

Sittas, like Maurice, was not given to challenging Belisarius once a decision had been made. So, like the excellent officer he was, he moved directly to implementation.

"Leaving the logistics out of it, the position in the fork is the best possible from a defensive point of view. We can design our fieldworks to provide us with continual lines of retreat. The more they press us, the more narrow the front will become as we retreat south into the tip of the triangle. As long as we can provide the men with enough to eat . . . "

Suddenly, he burst into laughter. "And they'll demand plenty, don't think they won't! Ha! Greek cataphracts—half of them aristocrats, to boot—aren't accustomed to digging trenches. They'll whine and grouse, all through the day and half the night. But as long as we keep them fed, they'll do the job."

"They won't have much choice," snorted Abbu. "Even Greek noblemen aren't that stupid. *Dig or die.* Once we cross the Chenab, those are the alternatives."

"I just hope they don't argue with me about the details," grumbled Gregory. "Those hide-bound bastards of Sittas'—on the rare occasions when they think about fieldworks at all—still have their brains soaked in legends about Caesar. The first time I use the words 'bastion' and 'retired flank' and 'ravelin' they're going to look at me like I was a lunatic."

Sittas grinned. "No they won't." He gestured with a thick thumb at Belisarius' chest. "Just tell them the Talisman of God gave you the words. That's as good as saints' bones, far as they're concerned."

Gregory still looked skeptical, but Belisarius was inclined to agree with Sittas. Even the notorious conservatism of Greek noble cataphracts could be dented, on occasion. And all of them, by now, were steeped in the Roman army's tradition of awe and respect for the mysterious mind of Aide.

"If I need to," he chuckled, "I'll give them a look. Aide can put on a dazzling show, when he wants to."

Great, muttered Aide. **I travel across the vastness of time in order to become a circus sideshow freak.**

Belisarius was back to scratching his chin. And his crooked smile was making an appearance.

"I like it," he said firmly. "Let's not get *too* preoccupied with logistics. There's also the actual fighting to consider. And I can't imagine better defensive terrain than the triangle."

"Neither can I," chimed in Gregory.

All the men in the tent turned their attention toward him. Other than Agathius—who was far to the south in Barbaricum, organizing the logistics for the entire Roman army marching north into the Sind—no one understood the modern methods of siege warfare better than Gregory.

The young artillery officer began ticking off on his fingers.

"First—although I won't be sure until we get there—I'm willing to bet the water table is high. Flat terrain with a high water table—those are exactly the conditions which shaped the Dutch fortifications against the Spanish. Whom they held off—the most powerful army in the world—for almost a century."

The names of future nations were only vaguely familiar to the other men in the tent, except Belisarius himself, but those veteran officers could immediately understand the point Gregory was making.

"Earthen ramparts and wet ditches," he continued. "The hardest things for artillery to break or assaulting infantry to cross. Especially when there's no high ground anywhere in the area on which the Malwa could set up counterbatteries."

He stroked his beard, frowning. "We can crisscross that whole area with ditches and fill them with water. Biggest problem we'll have is keeping our own trenches dry. Raised ramparts—using the same dirt from the ditches—will do for that. The Dutch used 'storm poles'—horizontal palisades, basically—to protect the ramparts from escalade. I doubt we'll have enough good wood for that, but we can probably use shrubbery to make old-style Roman hedges."

The mention of old methods seemed to bring a certain cheer to Sittas. He even went so far as to praise modern gadgetry. "The field guns and the sharpshooters will love it. A slow-moving, massed enemy, stumbling across ditches . . . What about cavalry?"

"Forget about cavalry altogether," said Gregory, almost snapping the response. He gave Sittas a cold eye. "The truth is—like it or not—we'll probably wind up eating our horses rather than riding them."

Both Sittas and Abbu—especially the latter—looked pained. Maurice barked a laugh.

"And will you look at them?" he snorted. "A horse is a horse. More where they came from—*if* we survive."

"A good warhorse—" began Sittas.

"Is worth its weight in silver," completed Belisarius. "And how much is your life worth?"

He stared at Sittas, then Abbu. After a moment, they avoided his gaze.

"Right. If we have to, we'll eat them. And there's this much to be said for good warhorses—they're big animals. Lots of meat on them."

Sittas sighed. "Well. As you say, it's better than dying." He cast a glance to the south. "But I sure hope Menander gets here before we have to make *that* decision."

The *Justinian* and the *Victrix* encountered the first Malwa opposition barely ten miles from Sukkur. Menander could hear, even if dimly, the guns firing in the north.

It was nothing more than a small cavalry force, however. A reconnaissance unit, clearly enough. The Malwa, perched on their horses by the riverbank, stared at the bizarre sight of steam-powered warships chugging upriver, towing four barges behind them. Menander, perched in the armored shell atop the bridge which held one of the *Justinian*'s anti-boarding Puckle guns, stared back.

For a moment, he was tempted to order a volley of cannon fire, loaded with canister. The Malwa were close enough that he could inflict some casualties on them. But—

He discarded the thought. The cavalry patrol was no danger to his flotilla, except insofar as they brought word of his approach back to the Malwa forces besieging Sukkur. And since there was no possibility of killing all of them, there was no point in wasting ammunition.

Quickly, Menander did some rough calculations in his head. The result cheered him up. By the time the cavalry patrol could return and make their report, Menander's flotilla would already have reached Ashot's positions. Thereafter, freed from towing all but one or two of the barges, Menander could make better time up the Indus. The Malwa would have a telegraph line connecting their army around Sukkur with their forces in the Punjab, of course. But—assuming that Belisarius had succeeded in his drive to reach the fork of the Chenab—the Malwa were probably too confused and disorganized, too preoccupied with crushing this unexpected thrust into their most vital region, to organize a really effective counter against Menander's oncoming two-ship flotilla.

So, he simply watched as his ships steamed past the foe. A rare moment, in the midst of bitter war, when enemies met and did nothing about it. He even found himself, moved by some strange impulse, waving a cheerful hand at the Malwa cavalrymen. And three of them, moved by the same impulse, waved back.

Odd business, war.

The Malwa did make a feeble attempt to intercept his flotilla when he was less than a mile from Ashot's fortifications. Two river boats, crammed with soldiers, came down the Indus toward him. Their movement was slow, however, because the wind was fitful at best. The Malwa boats were sailing ships, not galleys, so they were forced to rely mainly on the sluggish current.

Menander gave the order to prepare for battle. He and Eusebius had planned to leave such work to the *Victrix,* but the *Victrix*'s engine—every bit as balky as the one in Menander's ship—had broken down a few miles back. By the time Eusebius could repair the problem and arrive, the battle would be over. Menander was not overly concerned.

One boat, soon enough. Ashot, ever alert to the possibility of an amphibious attack on his flank, had two field guns stationed on the river. A few well placed shots were enough to sink one of the boats.

Menander, stationed next to one of the long twenty-four-pounder bowchasers was fascinated by what happened next. So fascinated, in fact, that he paid little attention for a time to the enemy ship still approaching him.

The Malwa commander was quite clearly doing his best to steer the vessel to the bank before it foundered completely. Right into the waiting arms of the Roman forces. He almost made it before his men were forced into the water. But the swim was short—many of them were actually able to wade ashore. And, sure enough, Roman troops were there to accept their surrender.

There was no fighting, no resistance of any kind. The wet and bedraggled Malwa troops seemed quite resigned to their new condition.

Menander looked away. The surviving enemy warship was almost within range of his forward guns, and soon he would give the order to fire. But he took the time, before concentrating all his attention on the coming little battle, to ponder over his great commander's methods of war. Methods which were sometimes derided—but never by those who had witnessed them.

Mercy can have its own sharp point. Keener than any lance or blade; and even deadlier to the foe.

"Will you look at the sorry bastards scramble!" laughed one of the gunners. "Like ducklings wading to mama!"

Menander met the gunner's jeering face. Then, softly: "And who do you think has been doing all of Ashot's digging for him? You can be damned sure that *Ashot's* men haven't been worn out by it. Fresh for the fighting, they've been. Day after day, while Malwa prisoners work under conditions not much worse than they faced in their own ranks. Which makes them always ready enough to surrender."

The amusement faded from the gunner's face, as he grappled with a new concept. Seeing his confusion, Menander was hard-pressed not to laugh himself.

Mind you, I think Ashot will be ecstatic when we arrive. I'll bet his supply problems have been even worse than he expected, with all those extra mouths to feed.

A few minutes later, the battle began. A few minutes after that, it was over. The two big guns in the bow of the *Justinian* simply shredded the Malwa river boat. The two shots the Malwa managed to fire from their own little bowchaser missed the *Justinian* by a wide margin.

Again, Malwa soldiers and sailors spilled into the water. But, this time, they were too far from shore for many of them to have a chance of reaching it.

Menander hesitated, for an instant. Then, remembering a friendly wave and his revered commander's subtleties, he made his decision.

"Steer right through them!" he barked. "And slow down. Any Malwa who can grab a line we'll tow ashore with us."

He turned and moved toward the rear of the ship, issuing orders to his soldiers as he went. By the time the desperate Malwa in the river had managed to seize one of the tow lines tossed by the Romans, Menander had soldiers ready to repel any possible boarding attempt. And he had both Puckle guns manned, loaded and ready to fire.

Long before they reached the docks that Ashot's men had erected in anticipation of their arrival, however, Menander was no longer worried about boarders. It was clear as day that the Malwa being towed to safety had no more intention of turning on their rescuers than ducklings would attack their mama. On those faces which were close enough for Menander to read any expression, he could see nothing beyond relief.

For those men, obviously, the war was over. And glad enough they were, to see the end of it come. Most of them were peasants, after all. Hard labor on too little food was no stranger to them. Nothing to enjoy, of course. But also—nothing to fear.

Ashot himself met Menander at the dock, shouting his praise and glee, and clapping the young officer on the shoulder.

"Knew you'd make it! Good thing, too—we're running low on everything."

Ashot's merry eyes moved to the Malwa surrendering as they came ashore. "And another fine catch, I see. I tell you, Menander, there have been times over the past weeks when I've felt more like a fisherman than a soldier."

Chapter 34
THE HINDU KUSH
Autumn, 533 A.D.

"How many Pathans, do you figure?" asked Kungas.

As Vasudeva pondered the question, Kungas kept studying the Malwa positions through the telescope which Belisarius had given him when he left Charax. His position, standing atop the ruins of a centuries-old Buddhist stupa destroyed by the Ye-tai when they conquered the Kushans, gave him a good view of the fortress which blocked the Khyber Pass at its narrowest point.

"Hard to say," muttered his army commander. "They're scouts and skirmishers, only, so they move around too much to get a good count."

"Not more than a few hundred?"

"If that many. With Sanga and the Rajputs a thousand miles away, the Pathan 'allegiance' to the Malwa is threadbare at best. At a guess, the only Pathans the Malwa have under their command down there are maybe two hundred tribal outcasts. The tribes themselves seem to be pulling back to their fortified villages and assuming a neutral stance."

"Let's hope Irene can keep them there," murmured Kungas. He lowered the telescope. "Which will depend, more than anything, on whether we can take that fortress and drive the Malwa out of the Khyber Pass entirely."

332

He began clambering down from the ruins. "With that few Pathans on the other side, we can seize the high ground. Use grenades to clear the outlying fortifications and then set up mortars and the field guns to start bombarding the big fortress across the narrows. Stupid bastards! They haven't fought in mountain country for too many years."

Now that they were on level ground, Vasudeva was able to concentrate on Kungas' plan. The way he was tugging the tip of his goatee and the furrows in his face indicated some doubts.

"Mortars, yes. Easy enough to haul up those rocks. But field artillery too? We could get them up there, sure enough. Not easily, mind you, but it can be done. But what's the point? All we have in the way of field guns are three-pounders. They're too light to break down the walls and—firing round shot, which is all we have—they won't produce many casualties."

Kungas shook his head. "I got a better look at that fortress than you did, Vasudeva, using the telescope. The outer walls are thick enough, to be sure, but everything—including all the interior walls and pits—is typical sangar construction. Nothing more than piled up fieldstone. They weren't expecting to be defending the Khyber Pass—of all places!—so that fortress was built in a hurry. Probably didn't even finish it until a few weeks ago, judging from what I could see of the outlying forts. Half of those forts are unfinished still."

Vasudeva was still frowning. Although he actually had more experience than Kungas using gunpowder weaponry, his mind was slower to adjust to the new reality than was that of his king.

Kungas helped him along. "Think what will happen when a solid ball of iron hits that loose fieldstone."

Vasudeva's face cleared, and he left off tugging the goatee. "Of course! As good as shrapnel!"

The army commander looked down at the soil between his feet and gave it a little stamp. "Solid rock, for all it matters. No way to dig rifle pits *here*." His eyes lifted, and he studied the distant fortress. "There neither. All their men will be above ground, using elevated sangar instead of holes in the ground. May as well have surrounded themselves with shells."

All hesitation gone, Vasudeva became as energetic and decisive as ever. "It will be done, King! We will take the high ground—clear the Malwa from every outlying hillfort with grenade and

sword—bring up the mortars and artillery . . . and then! Place half
the army further down the pass to stymie any Malwa relief column.
It'll be a siege, with us holding them in a grip of iron."

Kungas smiled, in a manner of speaking. "I give them two weeks.
Maybe three. And they can't even try to retreat back to the Vale
of Peshawar, once we've blocked their route. We outnumber them
three to one. We'd cut them to pieces on open ground, and they
know it. They'll have no choice but to surrender."

He planted his hands on his hips and surveyed the mountains
surrounding the Khyber Pass with approval. "After which—using
them to do the scut work—we can fortify this pass the way it
should be done. And we'll have plenty of time to do it, with the
Malwa preoccupied with Belisarius in the plains. Before Malwa
can counterattack, the Hindu Kush will be secure. The Pathans
will bow to our rule—and why not, since it will be lighter than
Malwa's—and next year . . . "

But he was speaking to himself, now. Vasudeva, being no more
prone than his king to worry about formality, was already hurrying
away to send the Kushan army back into motion.

Kungas remained in the ruins of the stupa for the rest of that
day, and all the days which followed. He thought it was fitting
that the founder of the new Kushan kingdom should make his
headquarters in a holy place desecrated by those who had
destroyed the old one. By the morning of the third day, Kushan
shock troops had taken the outlying hillforts in two solid days of
savage hand-to-hand combat, using both their traditional swords
and spears as well as the Roman grenades for which all Kushan
soldiers had developed a great affection. The Malwa troops were
good—much better than usual—but they were not Rajputs. Nor
did they have more than a few hundred Ye-tai to stiffen them.

So began, on the morning of the fourth day, the bombardment
of the Malwa fortress which was the key to control of the Khyber
pass. The Kushan troops were able to place many mortars within
a thousand yards of the fortress. The devices were crude, true.
They had been patterned after what Belisarius called a "coehorn
mortar," nothing more complicated than a brass tube mounted at
a fixed forty-five-degree angle on a base. The only way to adjust
the weapon's range was by adjusting the powder charge. But the
four-inch shells they fired, with a fuse ignited by the powder, could

still wreak havoc within the fortress even if they could not shatter the walls.

And, two days later, once the Kushans had wrestled the field guns into the hillforts they had taken, the mortar fire was augmented by solid shot. Which, in the days which followed, began slowly pulverizing the inner fortifications and—more slowly still—crumbling the outer. Fieldstone being returned to fieldstone, with blood and flesh lubricating the way.

And each morning, as he arose, Kungas completed the thought. Speaking aloud, to the mountains which would shelter a kingdom being reborn.

"Next year—*Peshawar!*"

The oldest and most prestigious of the Pathan chiefs stroked his beard, frowning fiercely. Part of the frown was due to his ruminations. Most of it was because, being the grand patriarch of a patriarchal folk, he did not approve of the woman sitting on the chair across from him. Outrageous, really, for this self-proclaimed new king to have left his *wife* in charge of his capital!

Still—

Different folk, different customs. So long as the Kushans did not meddle with his own—which the scandalous woman had assured him they would not—the chief did not much care, in the end, what silly and effeminate customs the dwellers of the towns maintained.

Too, there was this: effeminate they might be, in some ways, but there was no doubt at all that the Kushans were not to be taken lightly on the battlefield. And the fact that—judging from reports which Pathan scouts had brought from the siege in the Khyber Pass—they seemed as much at home fighting in the mountains as in the plains, was added reason for caution.

As a rule, the Pathans did not much fear the armies of civilization. *Plains armies.* Dangerous enough on flat ground, but ill-prepared to challenge the Pathans in their own mountains. But the chief had not lived to such an age, nor risen to such prominence, by being an arrogant fool. Civilized kingdoms, with their wealth and rich soils, could field much larger armies than the Pathans. And whenever those armies proved capable of adapting to mountain warfare . . .

It had happened once before, after all. The old chief barely managed to repress a shudder, remembering the savage punitive expeditions of the Rajputs.

"Done," he said firmly, bowing his head—slightly, and a bit reluctantly—to the woman seated before him. Then, rising from his own chair, he cast an imperious gaze over the eight other Pathan chiefs seated alongside him. As he expected, none of them seemed prepared to challenge his decision.

"Done," he repeated. "So long as you do not meddle with us—nor interfere with our caravans—we will respect the peace. Send annual tribute to the King of the Kushans."

Three of the other chiefs seemed to stir a bit. The oldest, snorting, added the final condition for Pathan allegiance to the new realm:

"This all presumes, you understand, that the King of the Kushans can take the Khyber. And *hold* it, once Malwa strikes the counterblow. We will not face Rana Sanga again!"

The Kushan queen nodded her head. The old chief could not tell, but he suspected that the *damned woman* was smiling at him. Impossible to tell, for sure, because of the heavy veil she was wearing. But he did *not* like the hint of humor and wit which seemed to lurk in her eyes.

Damned Kushans! He had been told that the Kushan queen had only donned the veil when the Pathans arrived. He could well believe it. She was reputed to be a sly creature, tricky and devious.

Still—

Customs were customs. And they depended, in the end, on survival. So, controlling his bile in the way such a wise old patriarch had learned how to do over the decades, he kept his face from showing his distaste.

"I am not concerned about Rana Sanga," said the woman, speaking as softly and demurely as she had since the Pathan chiefs first entered her audience chamber. "I have been led to believe, for reasons I cannot divulge, that he will remain preoccupied elsewhere. For years, probably his lifetime."

The old Pathan chief stared down at her. The idle chatter of a silly woman? Perhaps.

Still—

Perhaps not, also. The woman was reputed to be *very* cunning, and so well-informed that some were already whispering about witchcraft. That possibility, oddly enough, brought the fierce old patriarch a certain relief. Customs were customs, survival was survival. And so he allowed that it was perhaps just as well—since the effeminate Kushans seemed determined to be ruled by a woman—that they had at least had the good sense to choose a sorceress.

Chapter 35
CHOWPATTY
Autumn, 533 A.D.

Antonina stared down at the crowd gathered in the harbor of Chowpatty. The gathering, it might be better to say, crowding onto the narrow stone causeways and spilling dangerously onto the rickety wooden piers. Some of those piers were far worse than "rickety," in truth. In the time since the Ethiopians had departed Chowpatty and then returned, bearing triumph and grief in their ships, the Marathas who had poured into Chowpatty after the destruction of the Malwa garrison had begun rebuilding the city. But the work was only beginning, and had not yet extended to the harbor. Partly, because the harbor was the most ravaged portion of the town; but, for the most part, because the fishermen who would have used it had not returned.

For them, who had once been its center, Chowpatty was and would remain a name of horror. A place of ruin and rapine. They wished no part of it, now or forever more. They would use other ports, other towns, to ply their ancient trade. Not Chowpatty. Never Chowpatty.

But to the hill people who came, Chowpatty was a name of victory and hope. The place where Malwa had been broken yet again—and by the same folk who were now seen as Malwa's closest ally. Closer, even, than great Belisarius and the Romans.

338

Belisarius was a legend among them, true enough. But, except for that handful who had met him during his time in India, years before, it was a vague and distant legend. The Marathas had heard of Anatha and the Dam; and Charax. And now, Barbaricum added to that list of triumphs. (Soon, too, they would hear of Kulachi.) But none of them knew those places. Few could even say exactly in what direction they were to be found, other than somewhere to the west or, possibly, the north.

Chowpatty, they knew. Bharakuccha, they knew. So the black folk who had taken Chowpatty and shattered Bharakuccha—had done more, had dragged the Vile One himself to his impalement post—were as real as the sunrise. Not a legend, but heroes walking among them.

Oh, yes—dragged him to it they had, even if no African hand had ever touched the monster. For all Marathas knew, from the mouth of their champion himself, that without Axum's assault on Bharakuccha he could not have finally dealt the Great Country's vengeance. In the short time since his return, Rao had said so time and again. And those who heard his words directly passed them on to others, and they to others, and they to others still. For it was now the great tale of Majarashtra, and would be for generations to come.

No wind could have swept that palace clean, except that a greater wind had smote its city. Not even the Panther could have cut his way to the Vile One through the mass of soldiery who normally protected the beast. But the soldiery had been drawn aside, all save a handful, in order to fend off the wrath of Ethiopia. Into that sudden emptiness, the Wind had slipped its way. Softly, quietly, stealthily, before it struck the mighty blow.

The deed was done by the hand of the Great Country, yes—and all Marathas swelled in the knowledge. But only because a black folk had broken Bharakuccha, half breaking themselves in the doing, and lost their king besides.

So the crowd gathered—or the gathering crowded—onto those treacherous piers. Because that was where they could see the people of Africa, and touch them, and speak to them, and bring what little gifts their village or town might have scraped together.

Antonina had been standing on the battlements of the fortress above Chowpatty since the break of day. She had come there, at first, out of some obscure need to see for herself the place where

Eon had received his death wound. She had watched the sun rise over that place, gazing hollow-eyed into the fortress for perhaps an hour or so.

But then, finally, the sounds growing behind her had registered. So she had turned away from the fortress, to look down at the harbor it guarded. And, in the hours which followed, had begun to find some warmth returning to her soul. Perhaps . . .

Perhaps . . .

Ousanas' harsh voice broke into her thoughts. "Do not presume, woman."

Startled, Antonina jerked her head around. She had never heard Ousanas' steps, coming up to the battlements. Not surprising, really, given his skill as a hunter.

"What?" Her mind groped for the meaning of the words. "Presume what?"

Ousanas crossed his powerful arms over his chest. Then:

"You think you are Ethiopia's curse? The foreign woman—the Medea—who wreaked havoc upon it? Slew two kings—the father, and then the son? Spilled half a nation's blood, and broke half its ships in the bargain?"

Antonina looked away. She tried to find words, but could not.

Ousanas snorted. "Do not presume, woman."

"How many of them will return, Ousanas?" she whispered, almost choking. "How many?" She brought tear-filled eyes back to face him.

"This year? None," he replied forcefully. "Except the Dakuen sarwe, which will escort Eon's regalia home. That half of it, at least, which is still alive and not so badly injured that they can make the trip across the sea."

Her eyes widened. Ousanas snorted again.

"For the sake of God, Antonina—*think*. Think, for once, instead of wallowing in this stupid misery." He waved an arm toward the harbor. "That is a warrior nation, woman. Traders too, yes, but a nation built on the training ground of the highland regiments."

The next snort was more in the way of a laugh. "I will grant you the beauty of Helen. But it was not because of you that Axum bled. So will you *please* desist from this idiot imitation of that puerile woman, standing on the walls of Troy."

The image caused Antonina to giggle, and then laugh outright. Ousanas smiled, stepped forward, and placed an arm around her shoulders. Once Antonina had managed to stifle her laughter, he turned her to face the harbor.

"Look at them, Antonina. There is no grief in those faces. Sorrow for a young king they loved and treasured, yes. Sadness for those of their brave comrades who have died or been maimed, yes. But grief? Not a trace."

Watching Axum's sarwen below, as they moved easily among the crowd—jesting, laughing, strutting, preening, basking in the admiration of old men and young girls alike (especially the latter)—Antonina knew he spoke the truth. And that small *perhaps* in her heart seemed to grow like a shoot in spring.

"They know, Antonina. They *know*. Now, at last—they truly *know*. That which Eon promised them, if they would follow him, has truly come to pass. Ethiopia is great, now. Axum has its empire. And that empire spans the seas themselves. No obscure land tucked away in a corner of Africa, but a nation which could reach its strength across the ocean and buckle great Malwa itself."

He drew in a deep breath, gazing across the very ocean of which he spoke. "Who will doubt now? Who will question Axum's rule of the Erythrean Sea *now*? Not Malwa! Nor, in the future, Rome or Persia, or anyone else. Axum's coinage will be as good as Roman here. And don't think"—he pointed to the crowd below—"that every one of those sarwen isn't thinking about it, in at least one part of his mind."

Another snort. "That part, at least, which is not preoccupied with seduction, and wallowing in the knowledge that no great skill will be needed for that *here*. Not this night, for a certainty."

Antonina chuckled. Ousanas continued:

"No, they are already starting to think about the future. About the time *after* the war, when they will return. War heroes one and all, with the holds of their trading ships full to bursting. Bringing wealth back to their towns and villages, to add golden luster to their already glorious names."

He gave her shoulder a little shake. "So it is time—past time—for you to do the same. We do not need your guilt and misery, Antonina. Nor want it. We *do* need your shrewdness and wisdom. Athena we could use. Helen is nothing but a damned nuisance."

On the way down from the battlements, Antonina paused. "But why aren't the other regiments returning with the Dakuen?"

Ousanas gave her a stony stare.

"Oh." She giggled. "Of course. Silly of me not to have seen that."

"Praise God," he sighed. "I think the woman's wits may be returning."

After they reached the foot of the battlements, picking their way carefully through the rubble which still lay strewn about, Antonina started giggling again. "That's *such* a devious tactic, Ousanas."

The aqabe tsentsen shrugged. "Not really. Every regimental commander understands the logic perfectly. And why not? Ezana explained it to them plainly enough."

"You stay here," chuckled Antonina, "too far away to even think of meddling. Win more fame and fortune both for Axum and yourselves. While I, commander of the royal regiment to which Wahsi is sworn, will return and give the newborn negusa nagast the large fist the baby needs. Should it be needed."

She looked at Ousanas through the corner of her eyes. "And they did not balk? Not even a bit?"

"Not a bit. In truth, I think they were all secretly relieved. None of them *wants* a disruption in the dynasty, Antonina. With your hand to guide the thing, and Ezana to provide the fist, their distance relieves them of any burden at all. They are simply left with a warrior's simple task, far away in a foreign land. Win more fame, more glory, more fortune."

His famous grin made its appearance. "You noticed, I'm sure, that every sarwen in that harbor—wounded or whole—is practically staggering under his load of treasure. So careless of the Malwa, to leave their gold and silver and gems in the fabled vaults of Bharakuccha's harbor."

The grin began to fade. "So. How *do* you plan to guide the thing?"

Antonina scrutinized him, almost as if he were a sphinx posing a riddle.

"I don't know yet," she said abruptly. "I'm thinking about it."

He scrutinized her in return. Almost as if he were a man studying a riddle. Then grimaced, as a man might do when he cannot find the riddle's answer—and remembers that sphinxes have an unfortunate diet.

"Maybe you should go back up," he muttered.

"Not a chance," she replied, taking him by the arm and leading him away. "For one thing, I would be late for Shakuntala's audience. She's an empress, you know. And for another—" She broke off, studying Ousanas out of the corner of her eyes. "I'm thinking."

"I have wakened a monster." Ousanas rolled his eyes. "I can sense a demon rising."

"Nonsense. I'm just a woman, thinking."

"Same thing," he whined.

The empress shook her head. "I will not presume to override my commanders, but I think you are misreading the man completely. Rao most of all."

Shakuntala's officers stared at her in confusion. Her husband most of all. They were seated on cushions in a semicircle, facing the empress. She too sat on cushions, and those no higher than their own. Yet, despite her short stature, Shakuntala seemed to loom over them. As always, her posture was so erect that the small young woman seemed much larger than she really was.

Rao stroked his beard. "I will not deny the possibility. Still, Empress, I know something about Rajputs. And that army is entirely Rajput now, in all that matters. The name 'Malwa' applied to Lord Damodara has become a bare fiction. A tattered cloak, covering very different armor. Even the Ye-tai in his army are adopting Rajput ways and customs. The top Ye-tai commander, Toramana, is said to be marrying into the Chauhar clan itself. A half-sister of Rana Sanga's, no less."

"Others are doing the same," added Shakuntala's cavalry commander Shahji, "and not only Ye-tai. Nothing happens in Bharakuccha now that we do not learn almost within the day. We have gotten innumerable reports from Maratha merchants and vendors. Day after day, they tell us, Rajput soldiers are conducting marital negotiations with their Ye-tai and other comrades—even Malwa kshatriya—who seek to weld themselves to Rajputana."

Somehow, Shakuntala seemed to sit even more erect. "Yes, I know. And you think that means Damodara and Sanga will now wage war against us in the Rajput manner? Sally forth, finally, to meet us on a great open field of battle?"

"They will *try*," murmured Rao. "Whether we accommodate them is another manner." Perhaps sensing the sudden stiffness in the posture of the Maratha officers who sat to either side, he smiled slightly.

"Oh, do be still. It is no dishonor to say that our army is not yet a match in the open field against Damodara and his men. And will not be, for some time to come. Do not forget that army fought Belisarius—and won."

The officer Kondev stirred. "Belisarius was outnumbered at the Pass, by all accounts. Our forces are as great as Damodara's. Greater, if we bring in all the outlying units."

"And so what?" shrugged Rao. "Damodara's army has fought great battles, against Roman and Persian alike. They are experienced, sure, confident. Our forces have fought no such thing as that. A thousand skirmishes and ambushes, yes. A hundred small battles in narrow terrain, yes. Defended and taken a dozen hillforts, yes. It is not the same. In the open field, Damodara would break us like a stick."

An uncomfortable silence fell. From the sour look on their faces, it was plain to see the officers *wanted* to deny Rao's words. But . . .

Couldn't. And the fact that Majarashtra's greatest champion had been so willing to say them, calmly and openly, made denial quite impossible. Who were they to tell the Wind of the Great Country that he was mistaken in a matter of war?

Shakuntala, as it happened.

"You are wrong, Rao." She made a small, abbreviated gesture with her left hand. "Not about the correct tactics *if* Damodara comes out for battle. On that, I can say nothing." Her tone of voice, for just a moment, became demure. As demure, at least, as the empress was capable of. "I would not dream of disagreeing with my husband on such matters."

Rao grinned. But his wife the empress ignored him aloofly. "Where you are wrong is in the *politics* of the thing. Damodara, I am quite sure, knows that he could break us in battle. But not without suffering great losses himself. And *that*, I think, lies at the heart of things. He is waiting, and will continue to wait."

Rao frowned. "For what?" His eyes opened a bit. Then, for just one moment, the old Rao returned. The hill chieftain who had once trained an emperor's daughter. Long before he married her, in a time when such a marriage was unthinkable.

"Nonsense, girl! *Rajput*, I tell you. Even if Damodara himself were willing to seize the Malwa throne—and with his family hostage in Kausambi, what is the chance of that?—his soldiers would not follow him. Were he to press the matter, Rana Sanga himself would cut him down. The Rajputs swore an oath of fealty to the emperor of Malwa. And a Rajput oath—you know this well as I do—is as hard to break as iron."

Shakuntala shook her head. If the empress was displeased by her consort's sudden reversion to old and uncouth ways of addressing her, she gave no sign of it. Indeed, from the hint of a smile on her lips, one might almost think she enjoyed it.

Still, the headshake was vigorous.

"That was not my meaning—although, Rao, I think you are forgetting the lessons in philosophy you once gave an impatient and headstrong girl." Yes, she *was* smiling. "The business about truth becoming illusion, and illusion truth. The veil of Maya is not so easily penetrated as you might think."

A little chuckle swept the room. The officers seemed to relax a bit. Badinage between the empress and her consort was a familiar thing. Familiar, and immensely relaxing.

Shakuntala continued:

"It is Damodara's nature to *wait*. People miss that in him, because he is so capable in action when he moves—and moves so often, and so fast when he does. But, mostly, he is a waiting man. That is the core of his soul. He does not *know* the difference between truth and illusion, and—most important—knows that he doesn't. So . . . he waits. Allows the thing to unfold itself, until truth begins to emerge."

"What 'truth'?" asked Rao, a bit crossly.

She shrugged. "The same 'truth' we are all pondering. The 'truth' which is unfolding in the Indus, not here. We have no knowledge of what has happened with Belisarius, since he left Barbaricum and led his expedition into the interior of the Sind."

She glanced at Antonina, who, along with Ousanas and Ezana, was sitting on a stool not far to Shakuntala's left. Antonina shook her head slightly. *I don't know anything more than you do.*

Rao and the officers caught that little exchange, as Shakuntala had so obviously intended them to do. She pressed on.

"What will happen in the Indus? When Belisarius and Malwa clash head on? Who will win, who will lose—and how great will be the winning or the losing?"

She paused, defying anyone to answer. When it was obvious no answer was coming, she made that little hand wave again.

"So Damodara will wait. Wait and wait. Until the truth begins to emerge. And, in the meantime, will do nothing beyond rebuild Bharakuccha's harbor and fortifications. He will send nothing beyond patrols, up the Narmada—large enough to defeat any ambush, but not so large as to risk any great losses to himself."

Kondev stroked his beard. "It is true that all the punitive expeditions have ceased, since Damodara took command after the Vile One's death. But it was known that he had already opposed them, even while the beast was alive. So I am not sure that tells us much of anything regarding his future plans."

Antonina decided it was time for her to speak up. She cleared her throat, to gain everyone's attention. Then, as soon as Shakuntala nodded her permission, began to speak.

"I agree with the empress. Not so much with regard to Damodara's intentions"—she shrugged, waving her hand more broadly than Shakuntala had done—"although I suspect she is right there also. But who can read that man's soul? The key thing, however, is what she *proposes*. And in that, I am in full agreement with her."

Rao seemed a bit frustrated. "That means we would do nothing."

Antonina shook her head. "That is not what the empress said. She did not propose doing *nothing*, Rao. She proposes, instead, that we *prepare*."

She turned her head, looking toward the wide window which looked out over the city. Half-ruined Chowpatty was invisible, for the window was too high. But Antonina could see the ocean beyond, calm now that the monsoon season had ended.

"The Axumites will need to spend much time, in any event, recuperating from their wounds and repairing damaged ships. As soon as the eastern monsoon begins, Ousanas and I and the Dakuen sarwe will return to Ethiopia. But the rest of the Axumite army could use a long period in which to rest and rebuild their strength."

There was a little stir in the room. The officers had heard that most of Ethiopia's forces would stay in India, but this was the first time that rumor had been confirmed by an authoritative voice. They glanced at Ousanas and Ezana, and saw by their stern and solemn faces that Antonina had spoken truly. The stir grew a bit, before it settled. The news, clearly enough, filled all the Marathas with satisfaction.

Majarashtra and Axum combined. Now there might be a force which could even challenge Damodara and the Rajputs in open battle.

"Not yet," said Antonina firmly, as if gainsaying her earlier skepticism about the possibility of mind reading. "Axum needs time." More forcefully: "And so do *you*. If you intend to face Damodara and Rana Sanga in anything other than ambush, you will need to train your army. Marathas are not accustomed to such methods of warfare. You are not ready yet."

Although there was no expression on Shakuntala's face beyond respectful attentiveness, it was plain as day that Antonina's words encapsulated her own opinion. And Antonina, though she herself was not Belisarius, carried the penumbra of his reputation for strategic sagacity.

"Wait," repeated Antonina. "Train, prepare. Let the Axumites rest, and then begin training with them. Prepare."

She sat up as straight as Shakuntala. "The time will come, do not doubt it. But when it comes—when the truth has begun emerging from the mists—you will be ready for it."

Whether or not Rao agreed with her was impossible to tell. The Panther of Majarashtra, when he so desired, could be as impenetrable as any man. But, clearly enough, he was ready to bring the thing to a close. He was facing Shakuntala now, not Antonina.

"This is your desire, Empress?"

"Yes."

"So be it, then." Rao bowed his head. There was nothing of the husband in that gesture, simply the servant. "It shall be as you command."

Later, as Rao and Shakuntala and Antonina relaxed in the empress' private chambers, Rao suddenly chuckled and said: "That went quite well, I think. Even my hot-blooded Marathas are satisfied enough to settle for the rigors of training camp."

Shakuntala gave her husband a skeptical lifted eyebrow.

"Preposterous!" he exclaimed. "I was merely playing a part. Surely you don't think I—Raghunath Rao himself!—would have been so foolish as to advocate challenging Damodara on the morrow?"

"Tomorrow, no." Shakuntala sniffed. "The day after tomorrow . . ." The eyebrow lifted and lifted.

"I am wounded to the heart," groaned Rao, a hand clutching his chest. "My own wife!"

The air of injured innocence went rather poorly with the sly smile. Not to mention Rao's own cocked eyebrow, aimed at Antonina.

"And you, woman of Rome? Are you still immersed in this role of yours? What did Ousanas call it—someone named Helen?"

Antonina's sniff matched Shakuntala's own in imperial dignity. "Nonsense. I'm thinking, that's all."

Before Rao could utter a word, she scowled at him and snapped: "Don't say it! One Ousanas is bad enough."

Chapter 36
RAJPUTANA
Autumn, 533 A.D.

The Ye-tai guarding Rana Sanga's family reacted to the attack as well as Malwa imperial troops could be expected to. No sooner had Kujulo and the Kushans charged out of ambush than the Ye-tai had their weapons cleared and were moving their horses out to intercept them. But, as Ajatasutra had foreseen, the anvaya-prapta sachivya commander of the escort had placed himself and all of his men at the front of the little caravan. So, since the Kushans were attacking from the front, within seconds the ornately carved and heavily decorated wagon which carried Rana Sanga's wife and children was left isolated.

"Now!" cried Ajatasutra. A moment later, pounding out from their own hiding place in a small grove of trees which was now to the caravan's right rear, the assassin and the two cataphracts raced their horses toward the wagon and the three carts following it.

Seeing them come, five of the six men guiding the supply carts—already on the verge of bolting after seeing the Kushans spring from ambush—sprang off the carts and began running toward a nearby ravine. The sixth man, a Rajput from his clothing, snatched up a bow and began frantically groping for one of the arrows in a quiver attached to the side of the cart.

He never got as far as notching an arrow to the bowstring. Before he could do so, Valentinian's first arrow took him in the chest. The arrow, driven at less than forty yards range from a powerful cataphract bow, punched right through the man's light armor and drove him off the cart entirely. He was dead before he hit the ground.

Anastasius' first arrow and Valentinian's second did the same for the two Rajput guards riding on Lady Sanga's wagon, except that Anastasius' man was not killed outright. Anastasius had neither Valentinian's accuracy with a bow nor his speed. His arrow took the man in the shoulder. On the other hand, Anastasius used such a powerful bow that the wound was terrible. For all practical purposes, the Rajput's shoulder was destroyed. The man slumped off the wagon, unconscious from shock.

By now, the battle between the seventeen Kushans and twelve Ye-tai was in full melee. Three of the Ye-tai—the commander not being one of them—spotted the three enemy bandits attacking the wagon and tried to come to the rescue. But the Kushans, taking advantage of their sudden distraction, killed two of them within seconds. Only the third Ye-tai was able to break free from the small battle and return to the wagon. He came on, galloping his horse and waving his sword and bellowing curses.

"I'll deal with it," rumbled Anastasius. "You see to the wagon." The giant trotted his horse forward a few paces, drew the mount to a halt, and notched another arrow. When the Ye-tai was less than ten yards away, he drew and fired. At that range, not even Anastasius could miss. The arrow drove right through the Ye-tai's chest armor, his sternum, his heart, and severed the spine before it emerged. The bloody blade and eighteen inches of the shaft protruded from the man's back armor. When he fell off the horse, the arrow dug into the ground, holding the corpse up as if it were on display.

Ajatasutra and Valentinian, meanwhile, had left their horses and clambered into the small balcony at the rear of the great wagon which provided Lady Sanga and her children with a place where fresh air could be obtained, partially sheltered from the dust thrown up by their escort. The door leading to the interior was shut. Locked, too, as Ajatasutra immediately discovered when he tried the latch.

"Stand back!" he ordered. Valentinian drew off to the side, holding his spatha in one hand and a knife in the other. He had left his shield behind on the horse. Ajatasutra had not even bothered to bring his sword. He was armed only with a dagger.

The assassin stepped back the one pace the balcony allowed, lifted his knee to his chest, and kicked in the door. No sooner had the door flown open than a man charged out of the wagon's interior. His head was lowered, allowing no glimpse of his face beneath the turban. He was unarmored, wearing nothing but regular clothing, and carrying a short sword.

Valentinian's blade began the swing which would have decapitated the man, but Ajatasutra's sudden cry—*stop!*—stayed his hand. Ajatasutra avoided the awkward sword thrust easily, seized the man by his clothing, slammed him back against the wall of the wagon, and rendered him unconscious with two short, swift, merciless strikes with the dagger's pommel. As he dropped the man's body, the face was finally visible.

Valentinian bit off the curse with which he had been about to condemn Ajatasutra's recklessness. That was the face of an old man. A relative, perhaps. More likely, from the plainness of the clothing, an old and faithful retainer. Ajatasutra's quick action in sparing the man's life—maybe; those head blows had been ferocious—might save them trouble later.

A woman's voice was screaming inside the wagon. Valentinian stooped and entered, both his weapons ready for combat. Ajatasutra delayed a moment, leaning his head over the side to assess the progress of the battle between the Kushans and the Ye-tai. Then, grunting soft satisfaction, he followed Valentinian within.

"The Kushans should have it wrapped up soon," he said cheerfully. "I think we only lost four of them, too. Better than I expected."

Then, seeing Valentinian's rigid stance, Ajatasutra tensed. He couldn't really see most of the wagon's interior, because the cataphract was in the way. All Ajatasutra could spot was a young servant huddled in one far corner, shrieking with terror. The moment his eyes met hers, the servant's screaming stopped abruptly. Clearly enough, her terror had now gone beyond shrieks.

Crouched in the other corner, wearing very fine clothing, was a little girl. Sanga's daughter, he supposed. The girl's face was pale, and she was wide-eyed as only a six-year-old girl can be. But she seemed otherwise composed. At least she hadn't been screaming like the servant.

But what was in *front* of Valentinian? Ajatasutra had never seen the deadly cataphract so utterly prepared for mortal combat. As taut and alert as a mongoose facing a cobra. Apparently— Ajatasutra had not foreseen this possibility—Lady Sanga had brought one of her husband's most capable Rajput warriors along as a personal bodyguard.

"You draw him off to one side," Ajatasutra hissed, speaking in Greek. "I'll take him from the other."

Valentinian began to mutter something. Then, as he obeyed Ajatasutra's instructions, the mutter became something more in the way of a laughing exclamation.

"Good! *You* figure out how to handle this, you genius!"

With Valentinian out of the way, Ajatasutra could finally see the whole interior of the wagon. Lady Sanga, a plump, plain-faced and gray-haired woman, was sitting on the large settee at the front of the wagon. On her lap, clutched tightly, she was holding a four-year-old boy.

In front of her, standing between his mother and Valentinian, was the last of Sanga's children. A twelve-year-old boy, this one was. Ajatasutra knew that his name was Rajiv, and that the gap in age between himself and his two siblings was due to the death in infancy of two other children.

What he *hadn't* known . . .

—although he *should* have assumed it—

"Great," muttered Valentinian. "Just great. 'You draw him off and I'll take him from the other side.'"

Suddenly, the cataphract straightened and, with an abrupt—almost angry—gesture, slammed his spatha back in its scabbard. A moment later, the knife vanished somewhere in his armor.

Now empty-handed, Valentinian crossed his arms over his chest and leaned casually against the wagon's wall. Then he spoke, in clear and precise Hindi.

"I fought the kid's father once already, Ajatasutra. And once is enough to last me a lifetime. So *you* can kill the kid, if you want to. *You* can spend the rest of your life worrying that Sanga will come looking for you. *I* am not an idiot."

Ajatasutra stared at the boy. Rajiv held a sword in his hand and was poised in battle stance. Quite adeptly, in fact, given his age.

Of course, the boy's assurance was not all *that* surprising, now that Ajatasutra thought about it. He *was* the son of Rana Sanga, after all.

Ajatasutra was still trying to figure out how to disarm the boy without hurting him, when Rajiv himself solved his quandary. As soon as Valentinian finished speaking, the boy curled his lip. Quite an adult sneer it was, too.

"Had you truly fought my father, bandit, you would not be alive today." The twelve-year-old spit on the floor of the wagon. Quite a hefty glob of spittle it was, too. Ajatasutra was impressed.

"Only two men have ever faced my father in battle and lived to speak of it afterward. The first was the great Raghunath Rao, Panther of Majarashtra. The other was—"

He broke off, his eyes widening. Then, for the first time since Ajatasutra got sight of him, the boy's eyes lost that slightly vague focus of the trained swordsman who is watching everything at once, and fled to Valentinian's face.

His eyes widened further. Behind him, his mother uttered a sharp little cry. Ajatasutra couldn't tell if the wordless sound signified fear or hope. Possibly both.

"*You* are the Mongoose?" Rajiv's question was barely more than a whisper.

Valentinian grinned his narrow-faced weasel grin. Which was a bit unfortunate, thought Ajatasutra. That was *not* a very reassuring expression.

But then, moving quickly but easily, Valentinian removed the helmet from his head and dropped to one knee in front of the boy. Seeming completely oblivious to the naked blade not more than inches from his neck, he reached up a hand and parted the coarse black hair on his head.

"You can still see the scar," he said quietly. "Feel it, too, if you want to."

Rajiv lowered the sword, a bit. Then, slowly and hesitantly, reached out his other hand and ran fingers over Valentinian's scalp.

"It's a big scar," he said wonderingly. And now, in a tone of voice more appropriate to his age.

His mother finally spoke, after clearing her throat. "My husband always said the Mongoose was an honorable man. And certainly not a bandit or cutthroat."

Ajatasutra sighed with relief and sheathed his own dagger. "Nor is he, Lady Sanga. Nor am I or the men who came with us. I apologize for killing and injuring your Rajput companions. But we had no choice."

Mention of those men brought home to Ajatasutra that all noise coming from without the wagon had ceased. Clearly enough, the battle was over.

Proof came immediately. Making very little noise, Kujulo landed on the balcony and stuck his head into the interior.

"The Ye-tai are all dead. We're driving off those gutless cart-drivers now. Killed three so far. We thought to leave two, maybe three alive."

Ajatasutra nodded. "Just so long as they're driven far away. Near enough to see the caravan burn, but too far to see any details."

"What about the one guard? He'll never use that shoulder again—not for much, anyway—but he'll live if we take care of the wound. So will the old man."

Ajatasutra hesitated. There had been no room in his plans for bringing badly injured men with them. But, seeing the new stiffening in Rajiv's stance, he decided the alternative was worse. Clearly enough, Sanga's son—probably the mother, too—would put up a struggle to save their close retainers.

"Bind them up," he ordered curtly. "We can probably disguise them as diseased men. Or simply the victims of a bandit attack. Who knows? That might even help keep prying eyes away."

That done, he turned back to Lady Sanga. "We did not come to kill you, but to save you from harm. It is all very complicated. I do not have time now to explain it to you. You will just have to trust us, for the time being. We *must* move immediately or—"

"*Malwa*," hissed Lady Sanga. "Men and their stupid oaths! I told my husband they would play him for a fool." Seeing her son stiffening in front of her, she reached out a hand and swatted his head. Half-playfully, half . . . not.

"Stupid!" she repeated. "Even you, at twelve! Malwa will ruin us all."

When her eyes came back to Ajatasutra's, the assassin was almost stunned by the warmth and humor gleaming in them. For the first time, he began to understand why the great Rana Sanga had such a reputation for fidelity, despite the lack of comeliness of his wife.

◇   ◇   ◇

An hour later, as they rode away from the scene of an apparent massacre, a pillar of smoke rising behind them, Valentinian claimed to have *almost* fallen in love with her.

"Would have, actually, except not even *that* woman is worth fighting Sanga again."

"You'd do anything to get out of doing a stint of honest work," jibed Anastasius.

Valentinian sneered. "Pah! The way she arranged the bodies from the cemetery? Perfect! Didn't even flinch once. Didn't even grimace."

The cataphract turned in his saddle and bestowed a look of mighty approval on the woman who was following them not far behind on a mule, wearing the clothing of a bandit's woman and clutching a rag-wrapped bandit's child before her. Two other bandit children—wrapped in even filthier rags—rode tandem on a mule alongside hers.

"I'll bet you my retirement bonus against yours that woman can cook anything. She probably laughs while she's chopping onions."

By evening, Valentinian was feeling positively cheerful. As it turned out, Lady Sanga apparently *could* cook almost anything.

"I was getting *so* sick of that damned Kushan food," he mumbled, around a mouthful of some savory item which Lady Sanga had prepared. Out of what, exactly, no one knew. The one item Lady Sanga had insisted on salvaging from her wagon, before the thing was put to the torch with the corpses from the cemetery in it, was a small chest full of her cooking supplies.

"No one will notice its absence," she'd claimed. Ajatasutra, despite some misgivings, had not pressed the point. He'd simply insisted that she transfer the supplies—which consisted mostly of onions, packets of herbs and spices and other savories, and a small knife—into various sacks, leaving the empty chest behind to burn in the flames. He agreed with her that no one would notice the absent supplies. But the chest, though not an expensive item likely to be stolen, had solid fittings which would survive the flames. Someone—someone like Nanda Lal and his best spies, at any rate—*might* notice the absence of those fittings, and start to wonder.

"Got onions in't," Valentinian continued happily. "I love onions."

Anastasius sighed heavily. "I don't miss their cooking, but I do miss the Kushans. I felt better with Kujulo and his maniacs around."

Ajatasutra began to say something, but Anastasius waved him down. "Don't bother! I understand the logic, you damned schemer. Five men—two of them injured, and one of them elderly—a woman, and three children can make their way across the Ganges plain without being noticed much. No way a large party of armed men could. Especially not Kushans. Not when we got to Kausambi, for sure."

Valentinian had finished devouring the savory by then, and Anastasius' last words brought back his normal gloom.

"I still say this plan is insane. We could get Lady Sanga and the children out *now*." He pointed to the southwest. "Easy enough—well, after a hard trek through the Thar—to reach the general's forces. Then—"

Ajatasutra began to speak again, but, again, Anastasius waved him down. "I'll deal with the little weasel." Glowering: "Valentinian, that'd be even more insane. This whole little rescue operation was a side trip added on at the last moment. We *still* have the main thing to accomplish. If we brought out Lady Sanga now that would expose the whole scheme—no way it wouldn't come out, in the middle of a whole army—and make the rest of it impossible. The only way to keep the secret is to hide it in the belly of the beast. In Kausambi, the last place Nanda Lal would think to look."

"*Narses!*" hissed Valentinian. "Too clever by half!" But he left off arguing the point.

The supremacy of logic having been restored, Anastasius went back to his own worries. "I just miss having the Kushans around. I don't begrudge it to them, mind you, getting back to their own folk. And since they'll pass through the Sind on their way, they can probably give the general word of how we're doing. But—" He sighed, even more heavily than before. "It's going to be tricky, with just the three of us, if we get attacked by *real* bandits."

Lady Sanga and the children had eaten earlier, and she had given the two wounded Rajputs what care she could. So now she and her children were sitting around the campfire listening to the exchange. No sooner had Anastasius finished than Rajiv sprang to his feet, drawing his sword and waving it about.

"Bandits—*pah*! Against the Mongoose? And there are *four* of us!"

The twelve-year-old boy's enthusiasm did not seem to mollify Anastasius. Ajatasutra shared the giant cataphract's skepticism. Having an overconfident and rambunctious lad as an "additional warrior" struck him as more trouble than help.

And, judging from the fierce scowl on his face, Valentinian felt even more strongly about it. But Valentinian's displeasure, it became immediately apparent, had a more immediate focus.

"You hold a sword that way in a fight, boy, you're a dead man."

Rajiv lowered the blade, his face a study in contradiction. One the one hand, chagrin. On the other, injured—even outraged—pride.

"My father taught me to hold a sword!" he protested. "Rana Sanga himself!"

Valentinian shook his head, rose with his usual quick and fluid speed, and drew his own sword. "He didn't teach you *that* grip," he growled. "If he had, I wouldn't have this scar on my head and he'd be buried on a mountainside in Persia."

The cataphract stalked off a few paces onto an empty patch of ground. The sun had set over the horizon, but there was still enough light to see. He turned, and made a come-hither gesture with his sword.

"May as well start tonight, boy. If you're going to be any help against bandits, your swordwork has got to get better."

Eagerly, Rajiv trotted forward to begin his new course of instruction. Behind him, Lady Sanga shook her head, not so much ruefully as with a certain sense of detached irony.

"There's something peculiar about all this," she chuckled. "The son being trained by the father's great enemy. To fight whom in the end, I wonder?"

"God is prone to whimsy," pronounced Ajatasutra.

"Nonsense," countered Anastasius. "The logic seems impeccable to me. Especially when we consider what Aristotle had to say about—"

Chapter 37
THE PUNJAB
Autumn, 533 A.D.

Belisarius went across on the first ship, leaving Maurice to stabilize the Roman defensive lines at Uch. He had no intention of trying to hold Uch, beyond the two or three days necessary to transfer the entire army across the Chenab. But keeping an army steady while it is making a fighting withdrawal requires a very firm hand in control, a characterization which fit Maurice perfectly.

Belisarius wanted to get a sense of the land he would be holding as soon as possible, which was why he decided to take the risk of being part of the initial landing. His subordinates had protested that decision, rather vehemently, but Belisarius fit the description of "very firm" quite well himself.

Besides, he thought the risk was minimal. The small triangle of land formed by the confluence of the Chenab and the Indus was not well situated to defend *against* an invasion of the Punjab. For that purpose, it made far more sense to fortify the Indus south of the fork—which was exactly what the Malwa had done. So Belisarius expected to encounter no enemy troops beyond cavalry patrols. And against those, the cataphracts and Arab scouts crammed into the ship should suffice.

"Crammed" was the operative term, however, and Belisarius was thankful that the river crossing took not much more than an hour. By the time his own ship began offloading its soldiers, the second ship the Romans had captured when they took Uch was halfway across the river bearing its own load of troops.

Belisarius landed on the bank of the Chenab just north of Panjnad Head, which marked the confluence of the Chenab and the Sutlej. That position was much too far north for him to hold for long. The Indus was fifteen miles away, and the confluence of the Indus and the Chenab was twenty-five miles to the southwest, forming a triangle well over sixty miles in circumference—more likely eighty or ninety miles, considering all the loops and bends in the two rivers. With the twenty thousand men he still had left, he could not possibly hope to defend such a large territory for more than a few days.

But unless the Romans encountered a sizeable Malwa force in the triangle—which he didn't expect to happen—Belisarius *could* hold that position for those few days. Just enough time to begin throwing up his fortifications further south, in a much smaller triangle, while his men foraged as much food and fodder as possible. Their supplies were now running very low. They had captured a fair amount of gunpowder in Uch, but not much in the way of provisions.

Even more important, perhaps, than rounding up food would be rounding up the civilian population. The Punjab was the most fertile region of the Indus, and the population density was high. Here, the Malwa had not conducted the savage massacres of civilians which they had in the Sind—although word of those massacres had undoubtedly begun spreading. Which, from Belisarius' point of view, was all to the good. The peasants in the triangle would not have fled yet, but they would be on edge. And more likely to fear their Malwa overlords than the Roman invaders.

Once again, Belisarius intended to use mercy—defining that term very loosely—as a weapon against his enemy. His cavalry would cut across to the Indus and then, much like barbarian horsemen in a great hunt on the steppes, drive the game before them to the south, penning them into a narrower and narrower triangle. Except the "game" would be peasants, not animals. And the purpose of it would not be to eat the game, but to use them as a labor force. The kind of fortifications Belisarius intended to construct would require a *lot* of labor—far more than he had at his disposal from his own soldiers, even including the thousands of Malwa prisoners that they had captured.

How many, Aide, do you think?

Aide gave that shivering image which was his equivalent of a shrug. **Impossible to say. There are no records of such things, at this point in history. In later times, the Punjab would hold a population numbering in the millions, with a density of five hundred people to a square mile. It won't be that high today, of course, but I wouldn't be surprised if it was half that. So you may well wind up with tens of thousands of people for a work force. Many of them will be oldsters and children, of course.**

Belisarius paused to exchange a few last words with Abbu. The Arab scouts were offloading first. As always, Abbu and his men would provide Belisarius with reconnaissance. That done, he returned to his mental conversation with Aide.

So many? Better than I had hoped. With twenty thousand, I am confident I can erect the fortifications I need before the Malwa can organize a serious siege.

I cannot be positive. But—yes, I think so. With no more civilians than that, Gustavus Adolphus was able to erect the fortifications at Nürnberg in two weeks time. On the other hand . . . *those* civilians were enthusiastic partisans of the Protestant cause. These Punjabi peasants you will be rounding up could hardly be described as "partisans" of Rome.

Belisarius chuckled. *True, true. But that quip of Dr. Johnson's will apply here as well, if I'm not mistaken. I think the Malwa savagery in the Sind will come back to haunt them. If you were a Punjabi peasant conscripted to build fortifications for Roman troops fending off a Malwa siege, would you be a reluctant laborer?*

"The prospect of being hanged . . . " mused Aide. **No, I think not, especially if you maintain discipline among your own soldiers and do not allow the civilians to be abused. Beyond being forced into hard labor, at least. They will know full well that if the Malwa overrun you, they will be butchered along with the Roman troops. The Malwa will consider them "rebels," and they showed at Ranapur the penalty for rebellion.**

◇   ◇   ◇

Three days later, Maurice came across with the last of the Roman forces. By then, Belisarius had an approximate count.

"Better than twenty thousand civilians, for sure," were the first words he spoke when Maurice entered the command tent Belisarius had erected near the village of Sitpur. "Probably at least twenty-five. Maybe even thirty thousand."

Maurice grunted satisfaction. He removed his helmet and hung it on a peg attached to a nearby pole supporting the small pavilion. The helmets of Gregory and Felix and Mark of Edessa were already hanging there.

That grunt of satisfaction was the last sign of approval issued by the chiliarch. Before he had even reached the table where a new map had been spread, showing the first sketched outlines of the terrain, he was already accentuating the negative.

"You're too far north, still. If you think you can hold this much land with so few troops, you're out of your mind. What is it to the Indus from here? It must be a good ten miles!"

Gregory and Felix and Mark of Edessa burst into outright laughter. Belisarius satisfied himself with a crooked smile.

"Oh, *do* be quiet. I have no intention of building my principal lines up here, Maurice. I intended to erect them—have started to already, in fact—ten miles southwest of here." He pointed to a place on the map where lines indicating heavy fortifications had been drawn. "That far down into the tip of the triangle, the distance from the Chenab to the Indus is no more than six miles. And I'm building the outer line of fortifications here, a few miles north of that."

"We're just setting up field camps here," added Gregory. "Nothing fancy. Enough for large cataphract units to sally out and keep the first Malwa contingents held off for another few days. We have *got* to keep Sitpur in our hands as long as possible."

"Why?" demanded Maurice.

Belisarius' three other top commanders grinned. "Would you believe—talk about luck!—that Sitpur is the bakery center for the whole area?"

Maurice exhaled so forcefully it was almost as if he were spitting air. His hard gray eyes fell on Belisarius, and grew harder still.

"You don't deserve it, you really don't. This is almost as bad as the silly *Iliad*, where every time that reckless Achilles gets himself into a jam Athena swoops in and saves him."

Belisarius winced, acknowledging the hit. Then, shrugged. "I'll admit I assumed the local bread would be made by village women. Like trying to collect pebbles on a beach, that would have been. But I was prepared to do it."

"Instead," interrupted Mark, "we've had the villagers rounding up everything else—mostly lentils, and lots of them—while we keep the bakers in Sitpur working night and day. The biggest problem we're having right now is finding enough carts to haul the bread off to the south."

By this time, even Maurice was beginning to share in the excitement. Although he did make a last rally, attempting to salvage some portion of sane pessimism. But the effort was . . . feeble.

"I suppose the so-called 'bread' is that flat round stuff. Tastes awful."

"It's called *chowpatti*," chuckled Felix, "and I think it tastes pretty good, myself."

Maurice did not argue the point. Culinary preference, after all, was a small issue in the scope of things. Food was food, especially in a siege. Before it was all over—assuming things went *well*—Maurice fully expected that at least half of the Roman horses would have been eaten.

"Lentils too, eh?" he murmured, stroking his beard and staring down at the map. "And we'll be able to get fish from the rivers."

That last thought seemed to relieve him. Not because it suggested that the Roman army would be able to stave off starvation, even in a long siege, but because it brought a new problem to the fore.

"We'll have enough fishing boats for that," he growled, "but don't think the Malwa don't have plenty of boats of their own. And no little fishing vessels, either. They have enough large river craft in the Punjab, from what I can see, to start ferrying their own troops across to the triangle before we'll have the fortifications finished."

He turned and pointed back in the direction of Uch. "The whole area is starting to crawl with Malwa troops. With a lot heavier artillery than anything we have. As we were pulling out of Uch, the Malwa were starting to set up twenty-four pounders around the town. Real siege guns, those, not like these little popguns we've got."

The chiliarch was comfortably back in his favorite groove. He began stroking his beard with great vigor and satisfaction. "They must have thirty thousand men within a week's march. Three times that, within a month. And once they start transferring troops from the Ganges valley, we'll be looking at two hundred thousand." A bit lamely: "Soon enough."

"Maurice," said Belisarius patiently, "nobody can move that many troops that far very quickly. It took us months to get our army from Mesopotamia to the Indus, and we could use the sea. The Malwa cannot possibly move any large number of soldiers through Rajputana. The area is too arid. That means they'll have to march any reinforcements from the Ganges to the headwaters of the Jamuna, and then cross over to the headwaters of the Sutlej. It'll take them until well into next year, and you know it as well as I do."

He jerked his head backward, pointing to the north. "Until then, the Malwa will have to rely on whatever forces they already have in the Punjab. Which is a massive army in its own right, of course, but I'll willing to bet—I *am* betting—that by now they're scattered all over the place. Half of them are probably in or around Sukkur, hammering themselves into a pulp against Khusrau and Ashot."

Maurice did not argue the point, but he was not mollified either. "Fine. But they can still bring three or four times as many men to bear as we've got. Sure, with good fortifications across the neck of the triangle, we can mangle them before they break through. But there are enough boats in these rivers to enable them to land troops downstream."

With his finger, he traced on the map the Indus and Chenab rivers as they converged south of their own location. "Almost anywhere along here. So we have to leave enough of a striking force, centrally positioned, to stop any landing before it gets established." Gloomily: "We can manage it for a while, sure. We've still got twelve thousand cataphracts, and we can use half of them for a quick reaction force against any amphibious attack. But . . ."

Gregory finished the thought for him. "But sooner or later, they'll establish a beachhead. And when they do, the whole thing will start unraveling."

"So let's make sure it happens later than sooner," said Belisarius firmly. "Because sooner or later, Menander and Eusebius are going to get here also. There's been no indication at all that the Malwa have any real warships on these rivers. Once the *Justinian* and the *Victrix* arrive, we should be able to control the banks of the triangle well enough."

At the moment, neither Menander nor Eusebius quite shared the general's confidence. First, because they still had to run the fortress which the Malwa had built on the Indus below the Chenab fork. Secondly, because they had found themselves laden with a far greater cargo than they had expected. Instead of towing one barge behind the *Justinian*, the gunship was towing three and the fireship yet another. One of the three extra barges was loaded with all six of the twenty-four-pounders which Ashot had possessed; the second with the artillerymen and engineers needed to set them up and keep them in operation; and the third with the powder and shot to get them in operation through pitched battles.

Ashot had insisted. Rigorously.

"I don't need them anymore," he'd told them. "After Calopodius broke that Malwa assault on the island—the one they must have been *sure* would succeed—the Malwa stopped all their attacks on the Roman positions. They must be getting a little desperate now. Their food is running low, and now that you've arrived—don't think they didn't spot you—they'll know that they're most likely going to be losing their water supplies. They don't have any boats on the river which can stand up to either the *Justinian* or the *Victrix*, much less both combined."

"You'd think they would!" protested Eusebius.

Ashot shook his head. "You're thinking like an engineer instead of a military man, Eusebius. A year ago, the Malwa still thought they were conquering Mesopotamia. The last thing in their minds was building armed and armored gunships to defend the heartland of the Indus valley. And that's not the kind of thing you can do overnight, as you well know."

"You think they're going to lift the siege of Sukkur?" asked Menander.

"Who knows?" shrugged Ashot. "If they had any sense, they would. Unless they can break into Sukkur, which there's no sign they can after weeks of trying, they'll start starving before too long.

But I'm pretty sure the general was right: Link is still way off in Kausambi, not close enough to the scene to make informed decisions. So the Malwa commanders are probably operating based on the kind of 'stand at all cost' orders which seem reasonable to a commander a thousand miles away. And the Malwa high command has made crystal clear what the penalty is for disobeying orders.

"So take the twenty-four pounders," he'd concluded. "That'll still leave me the really big guns, in case of another Malwa assault. And Belisarius can use them up north. Those monsters *can* break down walls, if the Malwa start building lines of countervallation, which they will if he's managed to take the triangle. His little three-pounder field artillery can't."

On their way up the Indus, Menander and Eusebius had picked up another load as well. A small one, however—just one man. When they came ashore on a boat to the island where Calopodius had made his stand, in order to pay him their regards, Calopodius pleaded with them to take him along.

Menander and Eusebius stared down at him. The young Greek officer was lying on a pallet in his tent. Nothing of his face above the mouth could be seen. The entire upper half of his head was swathed in bandages. Calopodius' trickery had delayed a Malwa assault, but it had not prevented it. He had still managed, by his heroism and that of his men, to beat off that attack. But not without suffering a great price. His force had suffered terrible casualties, and Calopodius himself had been blinded by the shrapnel from a mortar shell.

"Please," he whispered. "I'm useless here, now. Anthony of Thessalonica has taken charge of the forces since I was injured—doing a good job of it, too—and I've got nothing to do but lie here." He managed a weak chuckle. "Practicing my rhetoric and grammar. A pastime which pales very quickly, I assure you."

The two naval officers hesitated. Neither one of them wanted to come right out and make the obvious rejoinder: *there'll be nothing for you to do up north, either, except die if Belisarius can't hold.*

The rejoinder was so obvious that Calopodius already had an answer prepared. Clearly enough, his request was not a spur-of-the-moment impulse. The young nobleman—not much more than a boy, really—must have been lying there for days hoping for an opportunity to leave the place where he had lost his eyesight. And, in the fierce manner of youth, try to return to the fray despite the loss.

"The general will be able to use me in some fashion or other," he insisted. "He'll be fighting what amounts to a siege, on the defensive. Lots of quartermaster work, and a lot of that can be done without eyes. Most of it's arguing with soldiers over what they can and can't get, after all." Again, the weak chuckle. "And I really *am* quite good in rhetoric and grammar."

Menander looked at Eusebius, then shrugged. "Why not? If he really wants it."

Eusebius had his doubts. But, within a day after leaving the island, the doubts began to recede. Much to his surprise—astonishment, rather—the noble Greek youth proved to have an aptitude for machinery. Or, at least, didn't look upon it as utterly unfathomable.

Working down in the hold with the steam engine, of course, was far too dangerous for a blind man. But, after a bit of experimentation, Eusebius discovered that a blind man who was willing to learn could manage the work of pumping the chamber of the fire cannon readily enough.

"It's kind of dangerous," he said hesitantly.

"All the better," replied Calopodius. Then, after thinking about it: "Unless I'd be putting you and the crew at risk."

Eusebius began to shake his head, until he realized the gesture would be meaningless to Calopodius. "I didn't mean it that way. I meant it'll be risky being stationed up here when we run the fortress. There'll be picket boats, sure as anything. I'll have to torch them as we go past, or they might board the cargo ships. That will give the big Malwa guns on the fortress as good a target as anyone could ask for at night. You'd really be safer on the *Justinian.*"

But he didn't press the issue. Safety, clearly enough, was not what Calopodius was seeking. There was something almost suicidal about the young officer's eagerness to return to combat. As if, by sneering at death itself, he could somehow restore his sight. That part of it, at least, with which a young man measures his own worth.

Chapter 38

Belisarius hunched, covering his head with his hands. The motion was more instinctive than reasoned, since his helmet would provide far more protection than his hands. From the sound of it, the mortar shell had landed too far away to be any danger anyway.

"Those are the worst," said Gregory. "The round shot, even from their big twenty-four-pounders, can't really make a dent in these soft-earth berms. But those damned big mortars of theirs . . . "

"Just one of them killed eight men earlier this morning," muttered Felix. He gave Belisarius a keen scrutiny. "Are you sure . . . "

Belisarius shook his head, as he rose up from his crouch. "Not yet, Felix. Don't think Sittas hasn't been hounding me about it, either." The general placed the periscope back over the rampart. The optical device was one of twenty which Belisarius had brought with him from Charax. Aide had recommended the things, and, sure enough, they had proved invaluable once the Malwa siege began biting in.

"He's champing at the bit to lead a sally, because he's positive he can get to those trenches and butcher the Malwa mortar crews without losing too many cataphracts."

Belisarius slowly scanned the enemy forces in the trenches not more than a few hundred yards away. "He's probably right, too. Unless I miss my guess, the Malwa commanders are still preoccupied with getting their forces into position. Those fieldworks are pretty badly designed. Sloppy. The kind of thing soldiers throw up in a hurry, each unit working on its own, without any real overall planning or coordination."

He heard the soft *whump* of a Roman mortar being fired, and followed the trajectory of the shell with his naked eyes. A few seconds later, the missile struck almost dead on in a Malwa trench. By now, two days since the fighting at the forward fortifications had begun, the Roman crews manning the coehorn mortars had become very accurate with the crude devices. They were using Malwa powder instead of Roman, since Belisarius had wanted to reserve the better grade for his field guns. But, with a little experimentation, the Roman mortar crews had adapted handily. This many years into the war, even Malwa gunpowder was far more uniform and standard in grade than had been the case earlier.

"I don't think those men out there are convinced yet that they've got a *real* siege on their hands," he mused. "Which, if I'm right, means that they'll be mounting a mass assault pretty soon. That's why I've kept the mitrailleuse out of sight, and have been using your sharpshooters so sparingly. I want to mangle them as badly as possible when they come in. *Then*—when they're retreating— Sittas can lead out his beloved sally. That'll turn the whole thing into a complete bloodbath."

The savage nature of the words went poorly with the soft, almost serene voice. But Belisarius had long since learned to put his personal feelings aside in the middle of a battle. A man who was warm by nature was also capable of utter ruthlessness when he needed to be. He no longer even wondered much at the dichotomy.

Neither did Aide. The crystal's thoughts were even more cold-blooded than the general's. **They won't have any real experience with modern fortifications, either. Even if they've been instructed, the instructions won't mean much. They'll come straight at the curtain wall, instead of the bastions like they should. The mitrailleuse will catch them enfilade, piled up against the wall with scaling ladders.**

Belisarius was standing in one of those bastions himself. The bastion was shaped liked an arrowhead, with the rear sides of the "blade" facing the curtain wall at a ninety-degree angle. Those sides were what was called a "retired flank," invisible to an attacking enemy because of the protecting lobes of the "arrowhead"—what were called, technically, "orillons"—and sheltered from cannon fire. The gun ports in the retired flanks were empty now. But mitrailleuse crews waiting in a bunker below would bring the weapons up once the attack began. From those gun ports, the crews would have a protected and perfect line of fire down the entire length of the curtain wall which separated this bastion from the next one, some two hundred and fifty yards away.

The fortifications, which were thick earthen ramparts rather than stone construction, were fronted by a wide ditch. There was perhaps two feet of water in the ditch, due to natural seepage from the high water table. In the more elaborate fortifications which Belisarius was having built several miles to the rear, where he planned to make his real stand, his engineers were designing the ditches to be suddenly flooded by ruptured dikes. But these simpler outer fortifications had no such elaborate designs.

They didn't need to. The purpose of the outer fortifications was twofold:

First, give Belisarius the time he needed to finish scouring the area north of his "inner line" of any and all foodstuffs. That work was now almost finished.

Second—hopefully—draw the Malwa into an ill-conceived mass assault which would enable Belisarius to bleed them badly. That remained to be done. But, from what he could detect through the periscope—and even more from his well-honed "battle sense"—it should be happening very soon.

"Tomorrow," he pronounced. "No later than the day after." His gaze, looking through the gun ports in the retired flank, ranged down the length of the curtain. He could envision already the mass of Malwa soldiers piled up against that wall, and the pitiless enfilade fire of the mitrailleuse and canister-loaded field guns which would turn a muddy ditch bright with color.

It was a cool thought, for all that the color red figured so prominently in it. Containing no more in the way of mercy than a blacksmith shows mercy to a rod of iron. As he examines the metal's own red glow, gauging the strength of his hammerstrike.

That night, Menander and Eusebius ran the fortress on the Indus. Ideally, they would have preferred to wait for another week, when they could take advantage of a new moon. But time was critical. They still had no way of knowing if Belisarius had succeeded in his plan to seize the lowest fork in the Punjab. But, if he had—and neither of them was prone to doubt on that score—the general would soon enough be in desperate need of the men and supplies they were bringing. And, perhaps even more, the control of the river which the *Justinian* and the *Victrix* would provide.

Ideally, also, they would have hugged the eastern bank of the Indus, keeping as far away as possible from the huge guns in the Malwa fortress. But the river was uncharted this far north—at least, for Romans if not Malwa—and Menander was far more concerned about the danger of running aground at night on a hidden sandbar. So he would stick to the middle of the river, where that risk was lowest.

The *Victrix* would have to take the risk, of course. In order to intercept the Malwa picket boats which were certain to be stationed on the river near the fortress, Eusebius would have to steam close to the western shore. Although it was theoretically possible to "walk" a side-wheeler across a submerged sandbar, neither Menander nor Eusebius had any desire to test the theory under enemy fire. So the *Victrix* would have to rely on speed alone. For which reason, the barge which the fireship had been towing was now attached to the *Justinian*.

"Talk about sitting ducks," muttered Menander to himself, as he watched the outlines of the fortress looming up to his left. "I'm moving as slow as a snail, and Eusebius is practically walking into the lion's den."

The faint light shed by a crescent moon didn't provide enough illumination to make it possible to discern the details of the fortress' construction. It just looked very dark, very big—and very grim. Already Menander could spot the glowing lights which indicated that the fortress had long since fired up the hearths where the shot was being heated.

There would be no surprises here. Belisarius' drive to the Punjab had shredded the enemy forces stationed to the east of the Indus, but the Malwa retained complete control of the west bank north of Sukkur. Malwa cavalrymen had been keeping pace with the small Roman flotilla since it steamed out of Rohri, reporting its whereabouts to the fortress by using the telegraph line which the Malwa had stretched from their camp besieging Sukkur all the way to their headquarters in the Punjab. And from there, Menander had no doubt at all, to the capital at Kausambi.

Still, he and Eusebius had one "secret weapon" up their sleeve. Menander turned his eyes away from the fortress and studied the fireship which was starting to pull out ahead of him. Any moment now . . .

A sudden flash of light came from a dinghy being towed behind the *Victrix*, as the small explosive charge was ignited. Within seconds, the infernal chemical concoction which Eusebius had prepared was burning fiercely and emitting a huge cloud of smoke. Less than a minute a later, the *Justinian* and its four barges began disappearing into that smoke. Until the powder burned itself out, or the boat sank from the heat of the burning, Menander would have a certain amount of protection. The Malwa would be firing blind.

The thought did not comfort him overmuch. The big Malwa siege cannons were so inaccurate that they could just as well hit from a miss, as it were. He had only to remember the fate of John of Rhodes to be reminded that perhaps the real mistress of battle was the Goddess of Luck.

The damned stuff was acrid, too. Within seconds, Menander was trying to hold his breath as much as possible. And he was already regretting the fact that just as the Malwa could no longer see him, he could no longer watch the progress of the *Victrix* as it went against the picket boats.

"Good luck, Eusebius."

Eusebius, a proper artisan, did not really believe in luck. Even his new career as a naval officer had not much shaken his faith in logic and order. So, as he positioned the barrel of the fire cannon to rake the oncoming picket boats, he did not give much thought to the possibility of being sunk by cannon fire coming from the guns on the fortress. If for no other reason, he would be sailing so close to the picket boats that they would not fire at him for fear of sinking their own craft.

A great roar announced the first volley being fired by the fortress. Not too many seconds later, Eusebius was muttering fierce curses and frantically repositioning the barrel of the fire cannon.

His intended target had disappeared. The Malwa *had* fired at the *Victrix*. They had undershot, however, and managed to sink the lead picket boat coming toward him.

◊   ◊   ◊

Whether from chagrin or simply because the Malwa commander of the fortress decided that Menander's ships made a more suitable target, the second volley was fired at the *Justinian* and the four barges it was towing. As was the third.

And Menander, cursing even more bitterly than Eusebius, was confirmed in his belief that the Goddess of Luck reigned supreme in battle. None of the ships were hit by the fortress' fire. Indeed, none of the great cannon balls landed closer than thirty yards to any of the Roman vessels. But one ball, guided by incredible good fortune, did manage to neatly sever the cable towing the last barge.

That barge, containing most of the powder and shot for the twenty-four pounders, fell away and began drifting aimlessly in the sluggish current. The handful of soldiers stationed on the barge were completely helpless. None of them were really sailors; even if they had known how to raise the sails, there was no wind to fill them; and they were far too few—nor was the barge properly designed for the task anyway—to drive it against the current using oars. All they could do was drift, awaiting their certain doom.

Menander was not even aware of the problem immediately. The change in the flotilla's speed due to the sudden lightening of the load was too minor to register. It was not until the *Justinian* and the three barges still attached to it had steamed completely out of the smoke bank that he realized what had happened.

For a moment, he was torn by indecision. He was still within range of the fortress' guns, and would remain so for several minutes. If he cast loose the three barges he was towing in order to steam back to rescue the fourth, he might lose them all. On the other hand, if he waited until he had towed them far enough upstream to be safe from cannon fire, it would take him quite some time to rescue the stray and return—assuming he wasn't hit himself. During which time, the three barges cast off might very well ground ashore or drift back into range. The Indus' current was not swift, but it was irresistible for a barge not under any form of powered control.

His eyes fell on the *Victrix*, now almost a mile away. He could see another gout of flame spurting from its bow and engulfing a Malwa picket ship. In the fireship's wake, he could see that two others were burning fiercely. As expected, river craft could not hope to match the *Victrix* in close quarter combat. A single burst of that hideous weapon was enough to turn any small vessel into an inferno.

There was only one Malwa picket boat left. The commander of that boat, no coward, was still rowing toward the *Victrix*. Menander could see a small flash in the bow of the boat, as it fired the puny little bowchaser it carried. That would be a three pounder, at best. Even at short range, the heavy timber which shielded the *Victrix*'s bow would shrug it off.

To Menander's surprise, however, the *Victrix* began to turn away. Within seconds, he realized that Eusebius had spotted the orphaned barge—which was now not more than three hundred yards away from him—and was intending to go to its rescue.

"You fucking idiot!" shouted Menander. He was so infuriated that he repeated the curse three time over, despite the utter impossibility that Eusebius could hear him.

He started pounding the rail of his ship with frustration. Already he could see the Malwa picket boat picking up the tempo of its oars. The *Victrix*'s advantage in combat lay entirely in a head-on attack, using its irresistible weapon protected within that heavy bow shield. From astern—and the clumsy jury-rigged paddle wheeler was no faster than an oared ship—the advantage would lie entirely with a vessel designed for boarding. Between the steam engine which drove it and the fire cannon in the bow, the *Victrix* was far too cramped to carry a large crew. And half of them were mechanics, not soldiers. Before the *Victrix* could reach the drifting barge and secure another cable, the Malwa picket boat would have overhauled it and overwhelmed the fireship's crew.

The only thing the *Victrix* had to fend off such an attack was the Puckle gun mounted in an armored shell atop the engine house. It was basically a large, long-barreled cap-and-ball revolver on a stand, which was operated by a two-man crew. All nine of its chambers could be fired in quick succession by a gunner turning a crank, whereupon the cylinder could be removed by the loader and replaced by another. It gave them the closest thing possible to a true machine gun, short of the heavy and unwieldy mitrailleuse assigned to the field artillery.

The Puckle gun was a handy little weapon, admittedly. But Menander had no illusions that it would be enough to drive off as many men as the Malwa had crammed into that picket boat.

The pilot of the *Justinian* came to Menander's side. Clearly enough, the man had reached the same conclusion. "What you get for trying to make a damned artisan a naval officer," he snarled. "He's just going to lose his own ship in the bargain."

Menander sighed. He took the time, before bowing to the inevitable, to regret once again that the mad rush in which Belisarius' change of strategy had thrown everything had left many projects unfinished in its wake. Among them had been the plans which he and Eusebius had begun to develop in Charax for designing an effective signaling system by which a fleet could be controlled by a single officer. Which would be *him*, not—not—*that damned artisan*!

As it happened, he and Eusebius had developed part of the system. The easy part. Signal flags hoisted in daylight. But those flags—all of them neatly arrayed in a nearby chest—would be useless in the middle of this dark night. They had never gotten as far as designing a system of lamp signals.

"Nothing for it," he growled. "If we turn back, we'll just be compounding the damage. Maintain course."

"Aye," said the pilot, nodding his approval. "Spoken like a navy man."

"Let's hope this works," muttered Eusebius. They had almost reached the stranded barge. He was standing just outside the bow shield, leaning over the rail in order to gauge the distance between the *Victrix* and the pursuing picket boat. Then, deciding the range was about right, he looked up at the fortress.

So far, the Malwa had maintained volley fire. Eusebius wasn't quite sure why they were doing so, since the undoubted advantage of volley fire on a battlefield was a moot point in this situation. He suspected that the Malwa commander was afraid that, working in the dark, crews left to their own pace might hurry the work and cause a disastrous accident.

Whatever the reason, he was glad of it. The maneuver he was about to try would leave the *Victrix* more or less stationary for a time. He was still far too close to the fortress to want to take that risk, until a volley had been fired. Thereafter, it would take the Malwa gunners long minutes to reload the huge guns. Long enough, Eusebius thought, to carry out his hastily conceived plan.

The dark outlines of the fortress were suddenly backlit by the enormous flash of the guns. The instant Eusebius saw the guns erupting, he leaned into the bow shield and shrilled at Calopodius: *"Now! Now!"* The words barely carried over the roar of the cannons.

As soon as he saw Calopodius begin pumping the lever which would fill the fire chamber, Eusebius leaned back over the rail to get a final look at the distance between the *Victrix* and her pursuer.

Started to, rather. He was almost knocked off his feet by a wave of water hammering over the rail. And then, almost pitched overboard as the *Victrix* began rolling wildly.

The Malwa volley had missed again. Just barely.

Sputtering and coughing, Eusebius began shrilling new orders. The helmsman, awaiting those orders, disengaged the gears to the left paddle wheel and then reengaged them in reverse. With the two paddle wheels now working in opposite directions, the *Victrix* shuddered to a halt and began—slowly, painfully—swinging back to face the oncoming picket boat.

The worst of it was the first half minute or so. Thereafter, the bow of the *Victrix* began turning more rapidly. As it swung around, Eusebius could see the picket boat begin frantically trying to turn itself.

"Too late, you bastards," he hissed. Then he plunged into the gloom of the bow shield and worked his way to the barrel of the fire cannon. The two-man crew in the shield had already positioned the barrel in the first slot which would come to bear on the picket ship. As Menander squeezed past Calopodius, the blind young Greek handed him the striker and said cheerfully: "Ready to go—but don't miss."

"Not likely," replied Eusebius, just as cheerfully. Looking through the slot, he could see that the picket boat had drifted inexorably within range. "Roast Malwa, coming up."

A moment later he turned the valve and lit the striker, and matched the deed to the word.

Looking back, watching the *Victrix* begin steaming upstream again with the lost barge once again secured, Menander heaved a sigh of relief.

The pilot had returned to his side. "God bless the old emperor!" he exclaimed. "If he hadn't designed these gears to work both ways . . ."

Menander nodded sagely. "There's something to be said for artisans, you know."

Shortly thereafter, Menander's superstition was confirmed. A cannon ball from the fortress' final volley, fired at extreme range, smashed into the barge's stern. Fortunately, the powder was not ignited—or the *Victrix* towing the barge would probably have been destroyed along with the barge itself. But within a minute, it became obvious that there was no hope of saving the vessel. Eusebius was just barely able to put the engines in reverse and reach the barge in time to save the crew before it sank. The cargo he had maneuvered so cleverly to salvage was a complete loss.

Chapter 39
INDIA
Autumn, 533 A.D.

As the great vessel which Eon had used for his flagship sailed out of Chowpatty's harbor, Antonina and Ousanas remained on the stern of the ship. That position gave them the best possible view of the long, steep-sided promontory which overlooked the harbor. The fortress where Eon had met his end was atop that promontory. Malabar Hill, as the natives called it. And so was his tomb.

Antonina had thought the Ethiopians would want to return Eon's body to Axum. But, leaving aside the practical difficulties of transporting a corpse across an ocean, the sarawit commanders—with Ousanas and Ezana agreeing—had decided it would be more fitting to bury him on Malabar Hill. So, like Alexander, Eon would be laid to rest in the land he had conquered rather than the land of his origins.

Conquered, yes, not simply occupied. At a great ceremony three days earlier, Empress Shakuntala had formally bestowed ownership of Chowpatty and the immediate region surrounding it onto the kingdom of Axum. That area would become a piece of Ethiopia on Indian soil, an enclave where Axumite traders and merchants and factors could establish an anchor for the Erythrean trade which everyone expected to blossom after the war.

◇   ◇   ◇

"It is only just and fitting," Shakuntala had told the crowd of Andhran and Maratha notables who had assembled in her palace for the ceremony. "Our debt to Axum is obvious. And I have a debt of my own to pay."

Then, for the first time to any Maratha except her husband, Shakuntala told the tale of how she first met the prince of Ethiopia, in the days when she was still a princess, and of the manner in which Eon had rescued her from Malwa captivity.

It was lively tale. The more so because the empress made no attempt, as she normally did in imperial audience, to restrain her own lively sense of humor. And if the tale bordered on salaciousness—Shakuntala depicted in lavish detail the episode where Eon kept her out of sight from Malwa soldiers searching his quarters by tossing the princess into his bed and pretending to mount her—himself, if not she, stark naked—none of the assembled notables reacted with anything but laughter. For all their obsession with ritual purity, Indians were not prudes. Anyone had but to walk a short distance from the palace to see a temple whose exterior carvings depicted—in even greater detail than the empress' story—copulations which were real and not simulated.

"I thought, once," she concluded, "that a day might come when I would marry Eon. For the sake of advancing Andhra's cause, of course. But the thought itself was not unpleasing to me."

Her little hand reached out and squeezed the large hand of her husband. Unusually, for such an affair, Shakuntala had insisted that Rao stand by her side throughout the audience.

"Destiny decreed otherwise, and I am glad of it. But there will always remain a part of me which is still that young princess, sheltered from harm by the noblest prince in the world. And so, I think, it is fitting that Andhra should give Axum the dowry which would have come in a different turn of the wheel. I would not be here—none of us would be here—except for Eon bisi Dakuen."

She rose and stepped down from the throne, then presented it to Saizana, the commander of the Hadefan regiment, whom Ousanas had appointed the Axumite viceroy of the new territory.

Watching the feverish work of the Axumites and the Marathas they had hired atop Malabar Hill, Antonina began to laugh softly.

Not satisfied with simply rebuilding those portions of the Malwa fortress which they had destroyed in the assault, the Ethiopians were dismantling it still further. Antonina had heard, from Ousanas himself, the plans which the Ethiopians had developed for the new great fortress they would build. A fortress within whose fastnesses the body of Eon was buried, and which they intended to serve as his monument.

"I was just remembering," she said, in response to Ousanas' quizzical expression, "the time Eon took me on a tour of the royal ruins at Axum. So sarcastic, you were, on the subject of royal aggrandizement congealed in stone."

She pointed to the fortress under construction. "And now—look! By the time you're finished, that thing will make any monument in Axum seem like a child's pile of pebbles."

Ousanas grinned. "Not the same thing at all, Antonina!" He clucked his tongue. "Women. Never practical. That *thing* is not a monument of any kind. True, it will be gigantic and grandiose and—between us, in private—rather grotesque. But it is really a *fortress,* Antonina. Living proof of Axum's real power, not"—here, he waved his hand in a regal gesture of dismissal—"some silly curio recalling a long-dead and half-forgotten petty monarch."

Antonina stared at him, her eyebrows arched in a skeptical curve.

"It is true! We Ethiopians are a practical folk, as all men know. Very economical. We saw no reason to waste all that space, and so why not use a small corner of it to serve double duty as a modest grave? Rather than require some poor grave digger to do unneeded and additional work?"

A very arched curve, those eyebrows made. "I have *seen* a sketch of that 'modest grave,' Ousanas. Saizana showed it to me, bragging fiercely all the while. He told me, furthermore, that the design originally came from none other than *you.* Some dawazz you turned out to be!"

Ousanas' grin never wavered, never flinched. "True, true. Actually, I got it from Belisarius. Long ago, during one of those evenings when he was passing along Aide's secrets of the future to me. I've forgotten how we got onto the subject. But we starting talking about great conquerors of the future that would have been and Aide wound up describing a monument which rather caught my fancy. Mainly because it was perhaps the most garish and tasteless one imaginable. And what better, I ask you, for a nation to remind all skeptics that what it did once it might still do again, if it is crossed?"

His grin was now positively serene. "Indeed, it seemed fitting." He pointed to the gigantic fortress under construction, within which a "modest grave" was being placed. As if it were the heart of the thing.

"Napoleon's Tomb, that is. A replica of it. Except"—he spread his hands wide—"I decreed that it should be much bigger."

The expression on Antonina's face was still quizzical, but all traces of sarcasm had vanished. "That's the first time I've ever heard you say that," she murmured. " 'We Ethiopians.' "

Ousanas shrugged, a bit uncomfortably. "A man cannot be a hunter and a rover forever, it seems. Not even me."

Antonina nodded, very serenely. "I had come to the same conclusion."

"You're *thinking* again," accused Ousanas, frowning worriedly. Then, when she made no attempt to deny the charge, the worry deepened.

"A demon," he muttered. "Same thing."

"Make way! Make way!" bellowed the Ye-tai officer trotting down the road which paralleled the Jamuna river. Here, in the Malwa heartland of the Ganges valley not far from the capital at Kausambi, the road was very wide and well-made. The small party of petty merchants hastily moved aside, barely managing to get the cart which held two sick men off the paved road and into the weeds before the Ye-tai soldiers who followed the officer stormed past.

The red and gold colors they were wearing, which matched those of the great banners streaming from their lances, indicated that these soldiers were part of the imperial troops which served the Malwa dynasty for an equivalent to the old Roman Praetorian Guard. And, as more and more soldiers thundered past the party of merchants—hundreds and hundreds of them—it became apparent that a very large portion of the elite unit was traveling down that road.

Mixed in with the soldiers were many Malwa officials, of one sort or another. From the pained look on most of their faces, it was obvious that those splendidly garbed men were unaccustomed to riding a horse instead of traveling in a palanquin or howdah.

There were some exceptions, however. One of them was a very large and barrel-chested man, who apparently served as some kind of herald. He had a herald's ease in the saddle, and certainly had the voice for the job.

"Make way! Make way!" he boomed. *"Prostrate yourselves before the Great Lady Sati!"*

Seeing the enormous wagon which was lurching behind the soldiers, almost careening in the train of twenty horses drawing it, the merchants hastily prostrated themselves. No grudging formality, either. It was noticeable—had any bothered to notice, which none did—that all of the men, as well as the woman and even the children, kept their faces firmly planted to the soil. Not even daring so much as a peek, lest a haughty imperial dynast be offended in her passage by the sight of polluted faces.

The wagon flashed past, its gems and gold inlay and silk accouterments gleaming in the sunlight. It was followed by still more Malwa elite bodyguards. Hundreds and hundreds of them.

When the imperial expedition had finally gone, the merchants rose to their feet and began slapping off the dust of their passage. Despite the dust and the prospect of hard labor to haul the hand-drawn cart back onto the road, one of the merchants was grinning from ear to ear. On the man's narrow visage, the expression was far more predatory than one would have expected to see on the face of such a man.

"I'd say all hell has broken loose," he announced cheerfully. "Imagine that! The Great Lady Sati herself, racing toward the Punjab. As if some disaster were taking place. Dear me, I wonder what it could be?"

"Shut up," growled his enormous companion. "And will you *please* wipe that grin off your face. You look like a weasel in a henhouse. *Merchants*, we're supposed to be, and piss-poor ones at that."

The faces of the unarmed Malwa soldiers who marched out of the fortress in the Khyber Pass were not grinning. Although a few of them, obeying ancient instinct, did attempt to smile at the Kushan troops who were accepting their surrender, in that sickly manner in which men try to appease their masters.

"Look at 'em," snorted Vima. "Like a bunch of puppies, flat on their backs and waving their little paws in the air. *Please don't hurt me.*"

"Enough of that," commanded Kungas. His mask of a face was just that—an iron mask. Even the men who surrounded him, who had come to know the man well in the months of their great march of conquest, could not detect a trace of humor lurking beneath.

He turned his head and gazed upon them, his eyes like two pieces of amber. "There will be no cruelties inflicted on those men. No disrespect, even. Such was my word, given to their commander. And that word—the word of King Kungas—must become as certain in these mountains as the stones themselves. Or the avalanche which buries the unwary. Do you understand?"

All of his commanders bowed their heads. The obedience was instant, total. Nor was it brought by any idle humor concerning a queen in Begram, weaving her cunning webs. The king himself was enough to command that allegiance. More than enough, after the months which had passed.

King Kungas he was, and did no man doubt it. Not Malwa, not Persian, not Pathan—not Kushan. The mask, which a man had once made of his face to conceal the man himself, was no longer a mask at all. Not of the king, at least, whatever warmth might remain in the man's heart.

"See to their well-being," the king of the Kushans commanded. "Set them to work building the new fortifications, but do not allow the labor to cripple or exhaust them. See that they are fed well enough. Some wine, on days they have done well."

He did not have to add the words: *obey me.* Such an addendum would have been quite pointless.

Toramana first caught sight of his bride-to-be when the girl and her entourage came into the palace where Lord Damodara made his headquarters. It was a different palace than the one which Venandakatra had inhabited. That palace had been designated as the residence of the Goptri, not the military commander of the Malwa forces in the Deccan. Lord Damodara, as all men knew, was not given to self-aggrandizement. He would not presume to inhabit the Goptri's palace without the emperor's permission.

On the morrow, as it happened, he would be moving into the palace. Nanda Lal had arrived three days before the Rajputs bringing Toramana's bride, as an official envoy from the emperor. Skandagupta had decided to bestow the title of Goptri upon Damodara, in recognition of his great services to the dynasty.

Toramana was pleased by the sight of the girl's face, as any groom would be seeing such a face on his bride. Nanda Lal, standing next to him, leaned over and whispered in his ear.

"I had heard Indira was comely. My congratulations."

Solemnly, Toramana nodded. His face, composed as faces should be at formal ceremonies, indicated nothing of his amusement at Nanda Lal's words. The spymaster had quite mistaken the source of his pleasure.

For the most part, at least. True, some portion of Toramana was delighted with the girl's face. But the real source of his pleasure lay in the simple fact that the face was exposed at all. Most Rajput women, at such an event, would have been wearing a veil. The fact that his bride-to-be did not told him two things. First, she was spirited, just as Rana Sanga had depicted his half-sister. Second, she saw no need to hide herself behind a disguise.

Which, since Toramana himself thought a disguise generally defeated its own purpose, boded well for the future. He had high hopes for the girl moving slowly through the palace, exchanging greetings with her Rajput kinsmen as she made her way toward Rana Sanga. Even more as a wife than a bride.

Indira had now reached her half-brother. From the distance where he was standing, Toramana could not hear the words which passed between them. But he had little doubt, from the anguish so evident on both faces, of the subject they were discussing.

"Such a tragedy," murmured Nanda Lal. "His entire family, you know."

Toramana cocked his head slightly. "Was it truly just a band of brigands? You conducted the investigation yourself, I understand."

Nanda Lal's thick lips tightened. "Yes, I did. A horrible scene. Fortunately, the bodies were so badly burned that I could, in good conscience, tell Rana Sanga that there had been no signs of torture or abuse. That much relief, at least, I was able to give him."

The Malwa empire's chief spymaster sighed heavily. "Just bandits, Toramana. A particularly bold and daring group, to be sure. Kushans, according to the few surviving eyewitnesses. By now, I'm sorry to say, the monsters have undoubtedly found refuge with the other Kushan brigands in the Hindu Kush."

Nanda Lal's lips were very thin, now. "Brigands, no more. Remember that, Toramana. All who oppose Malwa are but brigands. Which we will deal with soon enough, have no doubt of it."

Both men fell silent, watching the Rajput king leading his half-sister out of the audience chamber toward his own quarters in the palace. When all the Rajputs in the chamber were gone, Nanda Lal leaned over and whispered again.

"My best wishes on your marriage, Toramana. The emperor asked me to pass along his own, as well. We are quite sure, should it ever prove necessary, that you will do whatever is needed to protect Malwa from its enemies. *All* of its enemies, whomever they might be."

Again, Toramana nodded solemnly. "You may be sure of it, Lord. I am not given to subterfuge and disguise."

Late that night, Narses was summoned to the private chambers of Rana Sanga. The eunuch obeyed the summons, of course, though not with any pleasure. It was not that he objected to the lateness of the hour. Narses was usually awake through half the night. It was simply that the old intriguer hated to be surprised by anything, and he could think of no logical reason why the Rajput king would wish to see him.

Narses moved furtively through the dark corridors of the palace. That was simply old habit, more than anything else. Narses was not in the least bit worried of being overseen by Nanda Lal's spies. Here, in his own territory, Narses' webs of intrigue and espionage were far superior to those of the Malwa spymaster.

Very rarely, in times past, had Rana Sanga spoken to Narses at all, except in the presence of Lord Damodara. And those occasions had been in daytime, in military headquarters, while on campaign. To summon him for a private audience in his own chambers . . .

After Narses entered the Rajput king's quarters, a servant led him to the private audience room and then departed. Courteously, his face showing nothing of the grief and rage which must have lain beneath, Rana Sanga invited him to sit. The Rajput was even courteous enough to offer the Roman a chair, knowing that the old eunuch's bones did not adjust well to the Indian custom of sitting cross-legged on cushions.

After taking his own seat on some cushions nearby, Rana Sanga leaned over and spoke softly. "The news of my family's murder has caused me to ponder great questions of philosophy, Narses. Especially the relationship of truth to illusion. That is why I requested your presence. I thought you might be of assistance to me, in my hour of sorrow. My hour of great need."

Narses frowned. "I'm not even conversant with Greek philosophy, Rana Sanga, much less Hindu. Something to do with what you call *Maya,* the 'veil of illusion,' as I understand it. Don't see what help I could be."

The Rajput nodded. "So I understand. But I was not intending to ask your help with such profound questions, Narses. I had something much simpler in mind. The nature of onions, to be precise."

"Onions?" Narses' wrinkled face was deeply creased with puzzlement. The expression made him look even more reptilian than usual. *"Onions?"*

"Onions." Sanga leaned over and picked up a thick sheaf of documents lying next to him. He held them up before Narses and waggled them a bit. "This is the official report of the ambush and killing of my family. Nanda Lal, as you may know, oversaw the investigation himself."

The Rajput king laid the mass of documents on the carpet before him. "It is a very thorough and complete report, as you would expect from Nanda Lal and his top investigators. Exhaustive, actually. No detail was left unmentioned, except the precise nature of the wounds, insofar as they could be determined."

For a moment, his face grew pinched. "I imagine those details exist in a separate addendum, which Nanda Lal thought it would be more merciful not to include in this copy of the report. As if"—almost snarling, here—"I would not understand the inevitable fate of my wife and children in the hands of such creatures."

The Rajput straightened his back. For all that he was sitting on cushions, and Narses on a chair, he seemed to tower over the old eunuch. "But there is one small detail which puzzles me. And I have now studied this report carefully, reading it from beginning to end over and over again. It involves onions."

Seeing Narses' face—*onions?*—Rana Sanga managed a smile. "You see, included in Nanda Lal's report is a detailed—exhaustive

—list of every thing which was found. Among those items was the remains of a small chest which my wife always used to carry her cooking materials. Nothing fancy, that chest. No reason for bandits to steal the thing, so they didn't."

Narses was completely lost. A state of affairs which infuriated him. But he continued to listen to Sanga with no hint of protest, allowing no sign of his anger to show. He was no fool, was Narses. And he realized—though he had no idea from whence it was coming—that a terrible peril was looming over him. Like a tidal wave about to break over a blind man.

"Nor would bandits bother to steal anything *in* that chest, Narses. Except, perhaps, the small packets of herbs and spices. Those might be of some value to them, I suppose. But, for the most part, that chest contained onions. My wife was very fond of using onions in her cooking."

Sanga glanced at the documents. "Apparently, judging from the charred remains, the bandits looted the onions also. Nanda Lal's report was so exhaustive that they measured the ashes and charred pieces which remained. There is no mention of onions. Which would not have burned up completely, after all. And something else is missing which should not have been missing at all, for it couldn't have burned—the knife which my wife always used to cut onions."

"Bandits," husked Narses. "They'll steal anything."

Rana Sanga shook his head. "I think I know more about the bandits of mountain and desert than you do, Narses. They're not likely to steal onions, much less a simple knife. The one thing such men—and their women—do *not* lack are blades. If they did, they couldn't be bandits in the first place."

The Rajput king placed his large and powerful hand atop the documents. "It is not there, Narses. Nanda Lal and his men could not have possibly overlooked it, in the course of such a thorough report. The knife was a small and simple one, to be sure, but not that small—and very sturdy. The blade would have survived the fire, at the very least. The thing was made by a Rajput peasant as a gift to my wife on her wedding. She adored it, despite its simplicity. Refused, time after time, to allow me to replace it with a finer one." He took a deep breath, as if controlling grief. "She always said that knife—that knife alone—enabled her to laugh at onions."

Seeing the stiffness of Narses' posture—the old eunuch looked, for all the water, as if he were carved from stone—Sanga emitted a dry chuckle. "Oh, to be sure, Nanda Lal himself would never have noticed the absence of onions or the knife. How could he or his spies know anything of that? The thing was just a private joke between my wife and me. To everyone else, even our own servants, it was just one of many knives in the kitchen."

"Undoubtedly, he failed to notice its absence." Narses' words were not so much husked, as croaked. "Undoubtedly." As a frog might pray for deliverance.

"Undoubtedly," said Sanga firmly. "Nor did I see any reason to raise the matter with him, of course. What would such a great spymaster and dynast as Nanda Lal know about onions, and the knives used to cut them?"

"Nothing," croaked Narses.

"Indeed." And now, for the first time, the severe control left Rana Sanga's face. His eyes, staring at Narses, were like dark pools of sheer agony, begging for relief.

Narses rubbed his face with a hand. "I am sworn to tell nothing but the truth, king of Rajputana. Even to such as Great Lady Sati. *As you know.*"

Sanga nodded deeply. The gesture reminded Narses of a man placing his neck on a headsman's block. "Give me illusion, then," he whispered, "if you cannot give me the truth."

Abruptly, Narses rose. "I can do neither, Rana Sanga. I know nothing of philosophy. Nothing of onions or the knives needed to cut them. Send for your servant, please, to show me the way out of these chambers."

Sanga's head was still bent. "Please," he whispered. "I feel as if I am dying."

"Nothing," insisted Narses. "Nothing which cannot bear the scrutiny of the world's greatest ferret for the truth. *Great Lady Sati*, Rana Sanga."

"Please." The whisper could barely be heard.

Narses turned his head to the door, scowling. "Where *is* that servant? I can assure you, king of Rajputana, that I would not tolerate such slackness in my own. My problem, as a matter of fact, is the exact opposite. I am plagued with servants who are given to excess. Especially sentimentality. One of them, in particular. I shall have very harsh words to say to him, I can assure you, when next I see the fellow."

And with those words, Narses left the chamber. He found his way through Sanga's quarters easily enough. Indeed, it might be said he passed through them like an old antelope, fleeing a tiger.

Behind, in the chamber, Sanga slowly raised his head. Had there been anyone to see, they would have said the dark eyes were glowing. With growing relief—and fury—more than ebbing fear. As if a tiger, thinking himself caught in a cage, had discovered the trapper had been so careless as to leave it unlocked.

A state of affairs which, as all men know, does not bode well for the trapper.

Chapter 40
THE PUNJAB
Autumn, 533 A.D.

Despite the protests of his officers and bodyguards, Belisarius insisted on remaining in one of the bastions when the Malwa launched their mass assault on his fortifications. His plans for the coming siege were based very heavily on his assessment of the effectiveness of the mitrailleuse, and this would be the first time the weapons had ever been tested under combat conditions. He wanted to see them in action himself.

Blocking out of his mind the noise of mortar and artillery fire, as well as the sharper sounds of Felix's sharpshooters picking off Malwa grenadiers, Belisarius concentrated all his attention on watching the mitrailleuse crew working the weapon in the retired flank he was crouched within.

The mitrailleuse—the "Montigny mitrailleuse," to give the device its proper name—was the simplest possible form of machine gun except for the "organ gun" originally designed by Leonardo da Vinci. Like the organ gun, the mitrailleuse used fixed instead of rotating barrels. But, unlike its more primitive ancestor, the breech-loading mitrailleuse could be fired in sequence instead of in a single volley, and fire many more rounds in any given period of time.

Belisarius watched as the gun crew inserted another plate into the breech and slammed it into place with a locking lever. The plate held thirty-seven papier-mâché cartridges, which slid into the corresponding thirty-seven barrels of the weapon. A moment later, turning a crank, one of the men began triggering off the rounds while another—using the crude device of a wooden block to protect his hands from the hot jacket—tapped the barrel to traverse the Malwa soldiery piled up in the ditch below the curtain wall.

Belisarius had wanted a more advanced type of machine gun, preferably something based on the Gatling gun design which Aide had shown him and which he had detailed for John of Rhodes. But all the experiments of John's artificers with rotating barrels—much less belt-designed weapons like the Maxim gun—had foundered on a single problem.

Roman technology was good enough to make the weapons. Not many, perhaps, but enough. The problem was the ammunition. Rotating barrel and belt-fed designs all depended on uniform and sturdy brass cartridges. John's artificers could make such cartridges, but not in sufficient quantity. As had proven so often the case, designs which could be transformed into material reality in small numbers simply couldn't be done on a mass production scale.

The sixth-century Roman technical base was just too narrow. They lacked the tools to make the tools to make the tools, just as they lacked the artisans who could have used them properly even if they existed. That was a reality which could not be overcome in a few years, regardless of Aide's encyclopedic knowledge.

Since there was no point in having a "machine gun" which ran out of ammunition within minutes on a battlefield, Belisarius had opted for the Montigny design. The small number of brass cartridges which could be produced would be reserved for the special use of the Puckle guns mounted on river boats. The mitrailleuse, because it used a plate where all thirty-seven cartridges were fixed in position, did not require drawn brass for the cartridges. Rome *did* have plenty of cheap labor, especially in teeming Alexandria. The simple plate-and-papier-mâché units could be mass produced easily enough, providing the mitrailleuse with the large quantities of ammunition which were necessary for major field battles.

It was a somewhat cumbersome weapon, but, as he watched it in operation, Belisarius was satisfied that it would serve the purpose. The two mitrailleuse which were raking the Malwa along the curtain wall—one firing from each opposed retired flank of two adjacent bastions—were wreaking havoc in the closely packed and unprotected troops. Combined with the grenades being lobbed by soldiers on the curtain wall, and the grapeshot being fired by field guns positioned in the sharply raked angle of the bastions themselves, the water in the ditch where hundreds of Malwa soldiers were already lying dead or wounded had become a moat of blood.

Satisfied by that aspect of the battle, Belisarius began studying the sharpshooters at work. There were a dozen such men positioned in each bastion, whose principal responsibility was to target those Malwa soldiers carrying grenades or satchel charges. Or, possibly—although Belisarius had so far seen no indication of such a weapon in use—attempting to use a Malwa version of the flame-thrower which John of Rhodes had designed for the *Victrix*.

He didn't envy the sharpshooters their task. The crude design of the breech-loading rifles—again, a result of the severe shortage of brass cartridges, which required a rifle which could fire a linen cartridge—produced a certain amount of leakage blowing upward around the breech block. Every sharpshooter soon acquired a blackened face and a few powderburns on his forehead.

The other drawback to being a sharpshooter, naturally, was that the man was singled out by the enemy for special attention. As Belisarius watched, one of the sharpshooters on the bastion wall was suddenly slammed backward, sprawling dead on the bastion's fighting surface. His face was a pulped mass of flesh and blood, with brains leaking from a shattered skull. The horrible wounds looked to have been inflicted by several musket balls striking at once.

Felix cursed bitterly. "Those damned organ guns! I hadn't counted on those. Not so many of them, at any rate."

Ignoring the murmured protests of his bodyguards Isaac and Priscus, Belisarius crawled over to the inner side of the bastion and propped his periscope over the wall. Within seconds, he was able to spot what he was looking for.

The Malwa, sensibly enough given their numerical advantage over the Romans, had opted for organ guns rather than mitrailleuse. The organ guns were even cruder in design—about the most primitive conceivable quick-firing gunpowder weapon—but they had the great advantage of being easy to produce in quantity, using the skills and material available. The Malwa had an even narrower technical base than the Romans.

An organ gun looked like a wheelbarrow more than anything else, with a dozen barrels laid side by side in a row across the equivalent of the bucket. Except that it used two wheels instead of one, like a rickshaw Aide had shown him. They were muzzle-loaders, and so required some time to reload. But they could be easily moved into position manually, with only a two-man crew, and were surprisingly easy to aim. The recoil was small enough that an experienced organ gun handler could aim simply by using the two wooden handles—even adjust the elevation of the weapon by the simple expedient of rolling it up or down on the big wheels which held up the barrels.

And the Malwa had a *lot* of them. Just in the area Belisarius could sweep easily with his periscope, he counted no fewer than seventeen. The organ guns were positioned about a hundred yards away from the bastions, providing covering fire for the troops trying to storm the walls.

He glanced again through the gun ports in the retired flanks of the bastion. Then, satisfied that the mitrailleuse and grenades were enough to hold off the Malwa soldiers trying to scale the curtain walls, he turned to Gregory and ordered:

"Tell all the three-pounder crews to start firing on the organ guns instead of providing extra coverage for the curtain wall. With grape shot, at this close range, they ought to pulverize them soon enough. The one big disadvantage of those weapons is that they pretty much *have* to be aimed and fired by men standing in the open."

Gregory nodded. A moment later, he was clambering down the ladder which provided access to the bastion's fighting platform. Below, in a shielded bunker, a telegraph operator was waiting to transmit orders to every part of the outlying fortifications. And to the inner fortifications, for that matter, since one of the first things Belisarius had had his combat engineers do was lay telegraph wire to every key location in the triangle.

One of those locations was not more than half a mile away: the nearest of the fortified camps where Sittas and his thousands of cataphracts lay waiting for the order to sally. Belisarius had seen enough of the battle from the vantage point of the bastion. It was time he returned to his communication center. The sun was beginning to set in any event.

As he made his way to the ladder, he ignored the sighs of relief loudly—even histrionically—issued by his bodyguards. He also ignored the crystalline equivalent which Aide was rattling around in his brain. He even managed to ignore Maurice's first few words when he entered the telegraph bunker.

"Finally decided to stop playing junior scout, did we?" To Isaac and Priscus, shouldering their way behind him through the narrow entrance to the bunker: "You *did* manage to keep the damn fool from actually dancing on the wall, didn't you?"

The essentials having been taken care of, Maurice moved immediately to the necessities. "It's just about time to order Sittas out," he growled. "At daybreak, tomorrow. Every fortress is now reporting the same thing: the Malwa have been beaten off the walls, and are starting to trickle through the gaps. You could call it a 'flanking maneuver,' if you wanted. Except that I doubt any high-ranked officer ordered it."

Belisarius shook his head. "I saw the butcher's bill they've been paying at the walls, Maurice. Those soldiers have had enough. They're just trying to get out of the line of fire without actually retreating."

He stared down at the map spread across a table. The map showed the location of every one of the outlying forts, as well as the camps where Sittas and his armored cavalry were lying in wait. Like tigers, ready to spring from ambush. The outer lines had been designed for that purpose. In effect, they channeled the Malwa troops away from the fortresses into four areas which were tailor-made for cataphract tactics. The most solid ground in the area, cleared of obstructions, with nowhere to take cover.

"Give the order," he said. "Tomorrow morning, let's finish this."

The biggest problem Menander faced as they neared the fork of the Chenab was restraining himself from engaging enemy forces on shore in a series of pointless gun duels. During the daytime, Malwa dragoons were constantly peppering the Roman flotilla as it made its way upriver. Menander was keeping the *Justinian* and its barges as far from the west bank as possible, while still avoiding the danger of hidden sandbars. But even at that range, a number of the Malwa shots struck his ship. The Roman vessel, with its heavy load of barges, was moving very slowly. It was for all practical purposes a stationary target.

Granted, the shots were more in the way of a nuisance than an actual danger. Especially since, so far as Menander could determine, the Malwa were firing simple muskets instead of the equivalent of the Sharps breech-loading rifle with which Belisarius had equipped his own dragoons.

Justinian had designed his namesake to fight pitched battles at sea, with little concern for speed. Something which John of Rhodes, in times past, had criticized sourly—though not within earshot of the former emperor. Like most naval men, John had prized speed and maneuverability over all else. But, as things had turned out, Justinian's decision was working to Roman advantage. Speed and maneuverability were not as important as sheer strength of armor and firepower in the close and cramped quarters of river battles. And while the only iron armor on Menander's warship was the plating which protected the pilot house and the Puckle guns, the *Justinian* was what later ages would call a "wood-clad"—a ship whose hull was so thick that most round shot could not penetrate, much less musket fire. Moreover, it was heavy and sturdy enough to carry heavy guns which could overpower any kind of easily maneuvered land-based field artillery. So the Malwa dragoons posed no real threat at all.

Still . . . it was *annoying*!

But, he restrained himself. The dragoons made poor targets anyway, and gunpowder was too precious to waste on volleys fired out of temper rather than necessity, the more so now that the barge which carried most of the powder had been sunk.

Still . . . it was *so* annoying!

Only once did he fire a broadside. That was on an occasion where the *Justinian*'s engine had to be shut down for repairs. Eusebius and the *Victrix*—whose own engine, for whatever reason, was proving a lot more reliable than the *Justinian*'s—attached themselves to Menander's warship with a cable. The paddle wheeler was not powerful enough to tow the entire flotilla on its own, but it could keep the Roman ships from drifting downstream out of control.

The delay gave the Malwa enough time to bring up a small battery of three-pounders, five in all, which they began positioning on a small promontory within range of the Roman flotilla. Alas, the promontory was *also* within range of the *Justinian*'s much heavier guns. Eusebius had to tow the bow of Menander's warship around in order to bring the guns to bear. But, thereafter, two broadsides with Menander's thirty-two-pounder carronades were enough to destroy the little field guns and send the surviving Malwa artillerymen scampering for cover.

There had been one night engagement, when a Malwa river boat packed with marines approached from behind and tried to seize the last barge in the train. But the Romans had been alert for such a maneuver, and the men on the barge sent up a signal flare. Eusebius turned the paddle wheeler around—the *Victrix* was steaming at the head of the flotilla, as usual—and charged back downriver.

Fortunately, the Malwa boat was a sailing craft hastily refitted with oars, not an actual war galley. So its own progress upriver was slow. Not as slow as the heavy barges being towed by the *Justinian*, of course, but slow enough that Eusebius had time to come to the rescue before the enemy ship had gotten so close to the barge that the fire cannon couldn't be used.

One gout of flame from that fearsome weapon was all it took to end the engagement. Those Malwa who survived the initial holocaust dove overboard and swam for shore. The others died the peculiarly horrible death which that weapon produced.

By now, Eusebius was a hardened veteran. So he blithely ignored the screams rippling across the dark water and steamed back to his assigned position at the head of the flotilla. As he passed the *Justinian*, he spotted Menander standing on the deck and gave him a jaunty wave.

And why not? Eusebius, the former artisan, had learned enough of military strategy and tactics by now to understand a simple truth. "Simple," at least, to him—though he would have been amazed to discover how many prestigious military leaders understood it very poorly. But perhaps that was because, as an artisan, Eusebius had an instinctive grasp of the reality of *momentum* and its effects.

Mass, multiplied by *speed*. The second factor, if large enough, could offset a small mass. A bullet, after all, is not very heavy. But it can create even more damage to soft tissue than a ponderous sword.

Belisarius, by taking a relatively small force of men and striking so swiftly into the Punjab, had shattered the Malwa plans for grinding the Roman advance to a bloody stalemate in the Sind. Like a bullet piercing the soft vitals, tumbling through flesh leaving a trail of wreck and ruin, Belisarius had effectively disemboweled the enemy.

The Malwa who faced him had larger forces—and would, even after Bouzes and Coutzes arrived at Sukkur—but those forces were like so many vital organs spilled on the ground. One army here, another there, yet another stranded over there . . . none of them able to coordinate properly, and none of them with what they needed to put up an effective resistance.

As he gazed serenely over the landscape—which was perhaps a useless exercise, since on a moonless night he could see almost nothing—Eusebius basked in his invincibility. One of the many Malwa vital organs which Belisarius had spilled on the floor of the arena was their control of the Indus.

The Malwa had not expected to be contesting the Indus at all, until Belisarius destroyed their army at Charax. Then, realizing that they were now on the defensive, they had begun a belated program of shipbuilding.

But—too late, after Belisarius struck at the Punjab. Too late, in any event, to provide them this year with armored and steam-powered warships which could contest the Indus with such craft as the *Justinian* and the *Victrix*.

Next year might be different. Eusebius knew that the Malwa were creating a major shipbuilding complex near Multan, the city which the enemy had turned into their military headquarters for the Punjab. According to spies, the Malwa were starting to build their own steam-powered riverboats—and these would apparently be ironclads. Once those warships came into action, Menander's two screw-driven warships and the *Victrix* would be hard-pressed.

But—that was still many months away. And by then, Eusebius was certain, Belisarius would have figured out a way to stymie the Malwa again.

How? He had no idea. But he was serene in his confidence in his great commander. And so, as the *Victrix* paddled its slow way up the Indus, still more was added to its *momentum*. For that, too, the former artisan Eusebius had come to understand about warfare. The tide of victory was flowing with the Romans, as much because of their own confidence as the weight of men and material they brought with them.

The next morning, just after daybreak, Eusebius spotted a Malwa warship under construction tied up to a small pier along the river bank. The effort had all the earmarks of a last-minute, jury-rigged project. From what he could see of the half-completed ship, the Malwa had taken a small oar-powered river barge and were attempting to armor it with iron plate and place a handful of field guns aboard.

A pitiful thing, really, even had it been completed.

But, pitiful or not, no lion allows a jackal to contest its domain. So, after a quick exchange of signals with Menander—the flags were working quite well—Eusebius paddled over to put paid to *that* upstart nonsense.

Before he got there, the Malwa managed to wrestle around one of the field guns and fire two shots at the *Victrix*. One shot missed entirely. The second struck the heavy bow shield a glancing blow which did no worse than loosen a few bolts and scatter some chips of wood into the river.

Thereafter, the enemy gunners ceased their efforts and scampered hurriedly off the half-finished little warship. Which, within a few minutes, made a splendid bonfire to warm Roman souls as they continued chugging up the river toward Belisarius.

They were not far away now, if Menander was reading the skimpy charts correctly. (Charts which had become very far from skimpy as they made their way upriver. Future expeditions would not have to guess and grope their way through hidden sandbars.) And Eusebius had no doubt at all that the great uncertainty in the equation—had Belisarius reached the fork of the Chenab and seized it?—was no longer uncertain at all. Everything about the Malwa behavior that he could see practically shrieked panic and confusion.

Which, of course, is what you expect from a pack of jackals after a lion enters their lair.

Chapter 41

Whatever else could be said of Sittas, he was the most aggressive cavalry commander Belisarius had ever known. As soon as the order was given, not long after daybreak, the Greek nobleman led all eight thousand of his cataphracts in a charge out of the four camps in which they had been waiting. In four columns, the heavily armored horsemen smashed into twice that number of Malwa soldiers who had piled up in the areas between the fortresses during the preceding day and night.

Despite the disparity in numbers, the battle was really no contest. The Malwa were confused and disorganized. More often than not, their soldiers were no longer part of coherent and organized units. Nothing but individuals, in many cases, who had sought shelter from the bloodbath beneath the fortress walls.

Their shelter lasted no longer than the darkness of night. With dawn, the cataphracts turned it into yet another holocaust. Well-led, properly organized and coordinated volley fire—with the musketeers braced by pikemen—could stave off any cavalry assault. But a huge mass of infantrymen out of formation, even when many of them were armed with guns and grenades, could not possibly stand up to the weight of a heavy cavalry charge.

The more so when that charge was made by *cataphracts*. The Roman armored horsemen bore no resemblance at all to the sloppy hordes which a later medieval world would call "cavalry." They were highly disciplined, fought in formation, and obeyed orders.

Orders which were transmitted to them by officers—Sittas most of all—who, for all their occasional vainglory, were as cold-blooded and ruthless as any commanders in history.

Although the cataphracts emerged from the camps at a gallop, in order to cross the distance to the enemy as soon as possible, the charge never once threatened to career out of control. As soon as the cornicenes blew the order, the cataphracts reined their mounts to a halt and drew their bows. Then, firing volley after volley from serried ranks, they shredded whatever initial formations the Malwa officers had hastily improvised.

At close range—a hundred yards or less—cataphract arrows struck with as much force, and far greater accuracy, than musket balls. And even Roman cataphracts, though not such quick archers as their Persian dehgan counterparts, could easily maintain a rate of fire which was better than any musketeers of the time.

A better rate of fire, in truth, than even Roman sharpshooters could have managed, using single-shot breech-loading rifles. The drawback to the bow as a weapon of war had never been its inferiority to the gun, after all—not, at least, until firearms developed a far greater sophistication than anything available until the nineteenth century. In the hands of a skilled archer, a bow could be fired faster and more accurately than a musket, much less an arquebus. Nor, in the case of the hundred-pound-pull bows favored by cataphracts, with anything less in the way of penetrating power.

The real advantage to the gun was simply its ease of use. A competent musketeer could be trained in weeks; a skilled archer required years—a lifetime, in truth, raised in an archer's culture. Moreover, powerful bows required far more in the way of muscle power than guns. Only men conditioned to the use of the weapons for years could manage to keep firing a bow for the hours needed to win a battle. The wear which a musket placed on its user was nothing in comparison.

And so, the bow was doomed. But in the conditions which prevailed on *that* battlefield, on *that* day, the bow enjoyed one of its last great triumphs. Within minutes, whatever might have existed of a Malwa "front line" resembled nothing so much as a tattered and shredded piece of cloth.

That done, the cornicenes blew again. The cataphracts put away their bows and took up their lances. Then, cantering forward in tight formation, they simply rolled over the thousands of Malwa soldiers who were now trying to scramble out of the way.

Within a few more minutes, the scramble turned into a precipitous rout. The cornicenes blew again, and the cataphracts took up their long Persian-style sabers. And then, in the hour which followed, turned the rout into a massacre. As always, infantry fleeing in panic from cavalry were like antelopes pursued by lions—except *these* lions, seeking victory rather than food, were not satisfied with a single prey. They did not give up the pursuit until the open terrain between the fortresses was almost as red with blood as the moats which surrounded them. In their wake, thousands of enemy bodies lain strewn across the landscape.

When the cornicenes blew again, sounding the recall, the cataphracts trotted back to their camps. Full of fierce satisfaction, and arguing among themselves over what proper name to use to label yet another battlefield triumph.

In the end, although the town itself was no longer within Belisarius' line of outer fortifications, they settled on the name of *Sitpur*. Perhaps because the name was short, and had a nice little ring to it. More likely, because the cataphracts had become rather fond of the chowpatti which had been baked there, and which gave them their strength. Even Maurice was now claiming to have developed a taste for the foreign bread.

"*The Battle of Sitpur!*" roared Sittas triumphantly, as he strode into Belisarius' new command post many miles to the south. "You can add that one to your list, O mighty Belisarius!"

Belisarius smiled. Then, so infectious was Sittas' enthusiasm, grinned outright. "Has a nice sound, doesn't it?"

"Yes, it does," proclaimed Sittas. The words came out in a bit of a mumble, because the cataphract general was already stuffing himself from the pile of chowpatti on a small table just inside the bunker entrance. "Great stuff," he mumbled.

"Any problems?" asked Maurice. Like Belisarius himself, Maurice had retreated to the inner line of fortifications as soon as the charge began. Neither one of them had expected Sittas to fail, and they had the next stage of the siege to plan.

"Not much," mumbled Sittas, waving what was left of the chowpatti. An instant later, that fragment joined its fellows in his maw.

Once he finished swallowing, Sittas was able to speak more coherently.

"Only real problem was the organ guns. A few places, here and there, they managed to put together a little line of them. Firing at once, that makes for a pretty ferocious volley. Killed and injured probably more of my men than everything else put together."

Despite the grim words, Sittas was still exuding good cheer. Which became still cheerier with the next words, which were downright savage:

"Of course, that ended soon enough. Once my cataphracts made clear that there'd be no quarter given to organ gun crews, the rest of them left the damned gadgets lying where they were and scampered off with all the others. Tried to, at least."

Belisarius started to speak, but Sittas waved him silent. "Oh, do be still! Yes, we took as many prisoners as possible. We're already starting to shepherd the sorry bastards to the south. Tame as sheep, they are. You'll have plenty more men to add to your labor gangs. At least five thousand, I'd say."

Belisarius nodded. Then, resuming his study of the map which depicted the complex details of his inner line of fortifications, he said: "We'll need them. The civilians need a rest, as hard as they've been working. So do the prisoners we took earlier."

Sittas laughed. "From what I've been told, those civilians of yours will need as many guards to keep them *from* working as you need to keep the prisoners at it."

Maurice echoed the laugh. "Not far from the truth, that. Once they sized up the new situation, the Malwa civilians—"

"*Punjabis,*" interrupted Belisarius forcefully. "It's a war of liberation now, Maurice. Those people are *Punjabi*—not Malwa."

Maurice nodded cheerfully, accepting the correction without quarrel. "Punjabis, right. Anyway, once they saw what was happening, they became the fiercest Belisarius loyalists you could ask for. Their necks are on the chopping block along with ours, and they know it perfectly well—and know the Malwa ax better than we do."

"What about the prisoners?" asked Sittas. The casual way in which he reached for another chowpatti suggested he was not too concerned with the answer. "Any trouble there?"

Gregory shrugged. "Since Abbu and his scouts aren't much use in the siege warfare we're starting, the general put them to work guarding the Malwa prisoners."

Sittas choked humor, spitting pieces of chowpatti across the table. "Ha! Not much chance of any prisoner rebellion, then. Not with bedouin watching them!"

For all the cruel truth which lurked beneath those words, Belisarius couldn't help but smile. Abbu and his Arabs had made as clear as possible to the Malwa under their guard that the penalty for rebellion—even insubordination—would be swift and sure. As much as anything, Abbu had explained to their officers, because bedouin hated to do any work beyond fighting and trading.

Far easier to behead a man than to do his work for him, after all. A point which the old man had demonstrated by beheading, on the spot, the one Malwa officer who had raised a protest.

Thereafter, the Malwa prisoners had set to work with a will—and none more so than the officers who commanded them. Abbu had also explained that he was a firm believer in the chain of command. Far easier to behead a single officer, after all, than twenty men in his charge. A point which the old man had demonstrated by beheading, the next day, the Malwa officer whose unit had done a pitiful day's work.

Under other circumstances, Belisarius might have restrained Abbu's ferocious methods. But siege warfare was the grimmest and cruelest sort of war, and now that he had put the arch stone of his entire daring campaign into place, he would take no chances of seeing it slip. So long as Belisarius could hold the area within the fork of the Indus and the Chenab—the "Iron Triangle," as his men were beginning to call it—the Malwa would have no choice but to retreat from the Sind entirely. Belisarius would be in the best possible position to launch another war of maneuver once his forces recuperated and were refitted. He would have bypassed the Sukkur bottleneck entirely and opened the Punjab for the next campaign. The Punjab, the "land of five rivers," where all the advantages of terrain would lie with him and not his enemy. And he would have saved untold Roman lives in the process—even Malwa lives, when all was said and done.

If he could hold the Iron Triangle long enough to relieve the pressure on Khusrau and Ashot at Sukkur and allow a reliable supply route to become established on the Indus, using Menander's little fleet of steam-powered warships to clear the way.

One challenge to him having been beaten off, another immediately came to fore. One of the telegraphs in a corner of the large bunker began chattering. Seconds later, as he leaned over the telegraph operator's shoulder and read the message the man was jotting down, Belisarius began issuing new orders.

"The Malwa are trying to land troops in that little neck of land at the very tip of the Triangle," he announced. "Eight boats, carrying thousands of men."

Then, straightening and turning around: "We'll use the Thracians for this, Maurice. Give the Greeks a rest. See to it."

Maurice snatched his helmet from a peg and hustled toward the bunker's entrance, shouting over his shoulder at Sittas: "You Greeks won't get all the glory this day! Ha! Watch how Thracians do it, you sorry excuses for cataphracts! You'll be crying in your wine before nightfall, watch and see if . . ." The rest trailed off as the chiliarch passed through the entrance into the covered trench beyond.

Sittas smirked. "Poor bastard. I guess he doesn't know yet that the wine's all gone. My Greeks finished the last of it yesterday. Come nightfall, when they're wanting to celebrate, his precious Thracians will be drinking that homemade beer the Malwa civilians—I mean, *Punjabi* civilians—are starting to brew up." He stuck out his tongue. "I tried some. Horrible stuff."

Belisarius gave no more than one ear to Sittas' cheerful rambling. Most of his attention was concentrated on the map, gauging the other forces he could bring to bear if Maurice ran into difficulty. His principal reserve, with the Thracians thrown into action, were the two thousand cataphracts which Cyril had under his command. Those "old Greeks" hadn't participated in Sittas' charge. Belisarius trusted their discipline far more than he did those of Sittas' men, and so he had put them in charge of the small city which was being erected in the very center of the Iron Triangle. A city, not so much in the sense of construction—its "edifices" were the most primitive huts and tents imaginable—but in population. Over twenty-five thousand Punjabi civilians were huddled there, along with Cyril's men and half of Abbu's Arabs. Already, Belisarius' combat engineers were working frantically to design and oversee the construction of a crude sanitation system to forestall—hopefully—the danger of epidemic which siege warfare always entailed.

That worry led to another. *Supplies.* They were starting to get low again. Not so much in terms of food as gunpowder. Even with the Malwa gunpowder which Sittas' men would have captured in their sally this day . . .

Belisarius' train of thought was cut short by another burst of chatter from the telegraph. This time, he charged out of the bunker himself as soon as he read enough of the message to understand the drift. After Sittas read it, the big Greek nobleman came fast on his heels.

"No glory for you today!" Sittas cheerfully informed Maurice, as soon as he trotted his horse alongside the Thracian's. "Just as well, really. You would have been *so* disappointed by the libation cup."

Maurice, perhaps oddly, didn't seem discomfited in the least. "I don't think the local beer is really all *that* bad," he said. "I've tried it already. No worse than the stuff a Thracian villager grows up with, after all." The chiliarch stroked his gray beard complacently. "We Thracians are a lot tougher than you pampered Constantinople Greeks, you know. What's more to the point, we're also a lot smarter."

He pointed to the three Malwa ships drifting down the Indus, wreathed in flame and smoke. Five others could be seen frantically trying to reach the opposite bank. "Let Eusebius and his artisans do all the work, what we say. Charging into battle on a horse—all that damned armor and equipment—is too much like farm labor. Hot, sweaty, nasty business, when you get right down to it."

"That last one's not going to make it," opined Gregory. The artillery commander was perched on his own horse on Maurice's left, opposite Sittas. "Anyone want to make it a wager?"

Sittas was known to be an inveterate gambler. But, after a moment's pause while he gauged the situation, the Greek nobleman shook his head firmly. "I don't know enough about these newfangled gadgets to figure out the odds. But since Eusebius is a *Greek* artisan—best in the world!—I don't think I'll take the bet. He'll catch it, you watch."

Five minutes later, Eusebius did catch the trailing ship. Another spout of hellfire gushed from the *Victrix*, and yet another Malwa would-be landing craft became a scene of hysterical fear and frenzy, as hundreds of Malwa soldiers stripped off their armor and plunged into the river.

Those who could swim started making their way toward the west bank of the Indus. The others—perhaps half of them—floundered helplessly in the water. Most of them would drown. Those who survived did so only because they were close enough to the lines which the *Victrix*'s sailors tossed from the stern to be towed ashore into Roman captivity.

"Reminds me of fishing," mused Maurice. "A good catch, that. Maybe we'll be able to get enough latrines dug to stave off an epidemic after all."

Belisarius took no part in that exchange. He had ridden his horse directly to the pier which his combat engineers had started erecting from the first day the Iron Triangle was seized. Even the pier itself was still unfinished, much less the massive armored "sheds" which Belisarius had ordered built to provide shelter from enemy fire for the Roman warships once they arrived. But enough of it was in place to allow Menander and his barges to start offloading.

"We lost most of the gunpowder and shot," Menander confessed, as soon as he came ashore. "Their damned fortress in the gorge did for that. We'll need to take that, as soon as possible, or we'll probably lose supplies on every trip. Might even lose the *Justinian*."

The news about the gunpowder was of some concern to Belisarius, but not much. "We'll have enough gunpowder to get by, through at least two more major assaults. Maybe three. By that time, hopefully, the *Photius* will have brought more supplies. But there's no chance at all of the *Justinian* being sunk—not by that fortress, at least. You're staying here, Menander. You and Eusebius both. With the *Justinian* and the *Victrix* here, the Malwa have no chance at all of bypassing the fortified lines across the neck of the Triangle with an amphibious attack."

That cheerful thought drove all worries about gunpowder aside. "And wait till you see what those fortifications look like! Even now, before they're completely finished, those earthworks are the strongest the world's ever—"

He broke off, seeing a figure being helped onto the pier by one of Menander's sailors. Even with the bandage covering half the man's head, Belisarius immediately recognized him. All trace of gaiety vanished.

"Oh, Christ in Heaven," he murmured. "Forgive me my sins. That boy wasn't more than eighteen years old."

Chapter 42

Calopodius' first words, almost stammered, were an apology if his presence proved to be nothing but a burden for the general. But he was sure there was *something* he could do—quartermaster work, maybe, or—

"I've got plenty of clerks to do that!" snapped Belisarius. "What I *really* need is an excellent officer who can take command of this mare's nest we've got of telegraph communications." A bit hurriedly: "Blindness is no handicap for that work, lad. You have to listen to the messages anyway, and we've got plenty of clerks to transcribe them and transmit orders."

Calopodius' shoulders seemed to straighten a bit. Belisarius continued. "What I *really* need is an officer who can bring the thing under control and make it work the way it needs to. The telegraph is the key to our entire defensive plan. With instant communications— *if* the system gets regularized and properly organized—we can react instantly to any threat. It multiplies our forces without requiring a single extra man or gun, simply by eliminating confusion and wasted effort."

He took Calopodius by the shoulders and began leading him the rest of the way off the pier himself. "I can't tell you how delighted I am to see you here. I don't think there's a better man for the job."

Calopodius' lips quirked in that wry smile which Belisarius remembered. The sight lifted at least some of the weight from his heart.

"Well, there's this much," said the young officer. "I got excellent marks in grammar and rhetoric, as I believe I mentioned once. So at the very least I'm sure I can improve the quality of the messages."

By the end of the following day, Belisarius had withdrawn his entire army behind the inner lines of fortification. The final shape of the Iron Triangle—the term was now in uniform use throughout the army, and even most of the Punjabis were picking it up—was in place.

The Iron Triangle measured approximately three miles in width, across the narrow neck between the Indus and the Chenab. The other two legs of the triangle, formed by the meandering rivers, were much longer. But those legs were guarded by the two Roman warships, which made them impervious to Malwa assault by water. The *Justinian*, a faster ship than the *Victrix*, guarded the wide Indus. The *Victrix*, whose paddles made the risk of sandbars less of a menace, patrolled the narrower Chenab.

In the week that followed, the Malwa launched two mass assaults on the fortifications across the neck of the Triangle. But the assaults were driven back with heavy casualties. Belisarius had not been boasting, when he told Calopodius about the strength of those fortifications. In the world which would have been, the Dutch earthworks which Belisarius and Agathius and Gregory had used for their model would hold off the mighty Spaniards for almost a century. So long as his supplies held out, and epidemic could be averted by the rigorous sanitation regimen which the Romans were maintaining, Belisarius was certain he could withstand the Malwa as long as he needed to.

And, every night, as he gazed down on the map in his command bunker and listened to Calopodius' calm and cultured voice passing on to him the finest military intelligence any general had possessed thus far in history, the shape of that Roman-controlled portion of the map filled Belisarius with fierce satisfaction.

It was only a small part of the Punjab, true enough. And so what? An arrowhead is small, too. But, lodged in an enemy's heart, it will prove fatal nonetheless.

After the second assault, the Roman gunpowder supplies were running very low. Belisarius ordered a change in tactics. The big twenty-four pounders which Menander had brought would no longer be used. The great guns went through powder as quickly as they slaughtered attackers with canister and grapeshot. The three-pounders would only be used in case of absolute necessity.

Henceforth, the defense would rely entirely on the mitrailleuse and the old-fashioned methods of sword and ax atop the ramparts. Roman casualties would mount quickly, of course, depending so much on hand-to-hand methods. But Belisarius was sure he could fight off at least three more assaults before the decline in his numbers posed a real threat. Calopodius was doing as good a job as Belisarius had hoped. With the clear and precise intelligence Belisarius was now getting, he was able to maximize the position of his troops, using just as many as he needed exactly where they were needed.

The third mass assault never came. The Malwa began to prepare it, sure enough, but one morning Belisarius looked across the no-man's-land which had been the deathground of untold thousands of Malwa soldiers and saw that the enemy was pulling back. As the morning wore on, it became clearer and clearer that the tens of thousands of troops were being put to building their own great lines of fortification. As if they were now the besieged, instead of being the besieger.

Which, indeed, was the truth. And Belisarius knew full well who had been able to see that truth.

"The monster is here," he announced to his subordinates at their staff meeting that evening in the bunker. "In person. Link has arrived and taken direct charge. Which means that it's ending."

Gregory frowned. "What's ending? I'd think—"

Belisarius shook his head. "Ending. Our campaign, I'm talking about. *We won*—and Link knows it. So it's not going to order any more mass assaults. Not even Malwa can afford to keep paying that butcher's bill. Finally—finally!—even that monster has to start thinking about the morale of its troops. Which is piss poor and getting worse, every time they spill an ocean of blood against our walls."

His subordinates were all frowning, now. Seeing that row of faces, Belisarius was reminded of schoolboys puzzling at a problem.

A very difficult problem in rhetoric and grammar, to boot, chimed in Aide. **Awful stuff!**

The quip caused Belisarius to chuckle softly. Then, as the reality finally began pouring through him, he raised triumphant fists over his head and began laughing aloud.

"We won, I tell you! It's finished!"

In the hours that followed, as Belisarius began sketching his plans for the *next* campaign—the one which would drive Malwa out of the Punjab altogether, the following year, and clear the road for the final Roman advance into their Ganges heartland—the frowns faded from his subordinates' faces. But not, entirely, from their inner thoughts.

Maybe . . .

True enough, their great general wasn't given to underestimating an enemy, so . . . maybe . . .

But . . .

Then, just before dawn three days later, the telegraph began chattering again and Calopodius relayed the message to Belisarius' tent. The general had already awakened, so he was able to get himself to the pier—what Menander and his sailors were now calling Justinian's Palace—within half an hour.

Maurice had gotten there ahead of him. Within no more than fifteen minutes, all of the other commanders of the Roman army were gathered alongside Belisarius atop the platform which the Roman engineers had thrown up to protect the *Justinian* and the *Victrix*. A great, heavy thing that platform was—massive timbers covered with stone and soil, which could shrug off even the most powerful Malwa mortars which the enemy occasionally sent out in riverboats in an attempt to destroy the warships which gave Rome its iron grip on the Indus.

By then, Maurice had made certain of his count. The *Photius*, steaming toward them out of the dawn, was towing no fewer than three barges. If even only one of those barges was loaded with gunpowder, it no longer mattered whether Belisarius was gauging his enemy correctly. Even Maurice—even gloomy, pessimistic Maurice—was serenely confident that with enough gunpowder the Iron Triangle could withstand years of mass assaults.

"It's over," he pronounced. "We won."

Those were the very same words pronounced by Ashot, as he came ashore.

"It's over. We won." The stubby Armenian pointed back down-river. "The Malwa lifted the siege of Sukkur five days ago. God help the poor bastards, trying to retreat back through the gorge, with Khusrau and his Persians pursuing them and no supplies worth talking about. They'll lose another twenty thousand men before they get to the Punjab, unless I miss my guess, most of them from starvation or desertion."

His enthusiasm rolled all the eager questions right under. "Bouzes and Coutzes are pressing them, too! They got to Sukkur a day after the Malwa started their retreat and just kept going, with the whole army. We've got over seventy thousand men coming through the gorge, not one of them so much as scratched by enemy action, and with nothing in their way except that single miserable damn fortress along the river."

His lip curled. "If the Malwa even *try* to hold that fortress, Coutzes swears his infantry will storm it in two hours. I wouldn't be surprised if he's right. Those men of his haven't done anything for weeks except march. By now, they're spoiling for a fight."

The pent-up enthusiasm burst like a dam. Within a minute, the officers atop Justinian's Palace were babbling a hundred new plans. Most of them, initially, involved the ins-and-outs of logistics. Keep one of the screw-powered warships on station at the Triangle at all times, using the other to tow more barges—no risk from that stinking miserable fortress once Coutzes gets his hands on it!—alternate them, of course, so all the sailors can share in the glory of hammering those wretched Malwa so-called riverboats—don't want anyone to get sulky because his mates are starting to call him a barge-handler—

From there, soon enough, the officers started babbling about maneuvers and campaigns. Race up the Sutlej—nonsense, that's exactly where Link will build their heaviest forts!—better to sweep around using the Indus—hook up with Kungas in the Hindu Kush, you know he's gotten to the Khyber by now!

Long before it was over, Belisarius was gone. There would be time enough for plans, now; more than enough time, before the next campaign. *It's over. We won.* But today, in this new dawn, he first had a debt which needed paying. As best he could.

◇   ◇   ◇

Calopodius, as Belisarius had known he would be, was still at his post in the command bunker. The news of the *Photius'* arrival—and all that it signified—was already racing through the Roman forces in the Iron Triangle. The advance of the news was like a tidal bore, a surge of celebration growing as it went. When it reached the soldiers guarding the outer walls, Belisarius knew, they would react by taunting the Malwa mercilessly. To his deep satisfaction, he also knew that nowhere would the celebration be more riotous and unrestrained than among the Punjabi civilians living in the city which they had come to call, in their own tongue, a word which meant "the Anvil."

But Calopodius was taking no part in the celebration. He was sitting at the same desk where he sat every day, doing his duty, dictating orders and messages to the clerk who served as his principal secretary.

Hearing his arrival—Calopodius was already developing the uncanny ear of the blind—the Greek officer raised his head. Oddly enough, there seemed to be a trace of embarrassment in his face. He whispered something hurriedly to the secretary and the man put down the pen he had been scribbling with.

Belisarius studied the young man for a moment. It was hard to read Calopodius' expression. Partly because the youth had always possessed more than his years' worth of calm self-assurance, but mostly because of the horrible damage done to the face itself. Calopodius had removed the bandages several days earlier. With the quiet defiance which Belisarius knew was his nature, the young man would present those horribly scarred and empty eye sockets to the world, along with the mutilated brow which had not been enough to shield them.

The general, again, as he had so many times since Calopodius returned, felt a wave of grief and guilt wash over him.

It's not your fault, insisted Aide.

Of course it is, replied Belisarius. *It was I—no other man—who sent that boy into harm's way. Told him to hold a position which was key to my campaign plans, knowing full well that for such a boy that order was as good as if a god had given it. I might as well have asked him to fall on his sword, knowing he would.*

Other boys will live because of it. Thousands of them in this very place—Punjabi boys as well as Roman ones.

Belisarius sighed. *That's not the point, Aide. I know that's true, which is why I gave the order in the first place. But that order—and its consequences—remain mine to bear. No one else. Nor can I trade it against other consequences, as if ruthlessness was a commodity which can be exchanged in a village market. A sin is a sin, and there's an end to it.*

Calopodius interrupted the silent exchange. Rising to his feet, he asked: "Can I be of service, General?"

Some part of Belisarius' mind was fascinated to note that the blind youth was already able to distinguish one man's footsteps from another. But that part was pushed far down, while another part—much closer to the man's soul—came to the fore.

He strode forward and swept the boy into his embrace. Then, fighting to keep his voice even and hold back the tears, whispered: "I am sorry for your eyes, Calopodius. If I could give you back your sight with my own, I would do so. I swear I would."

Awkwardly, the boy returned the embrace. Patting the general's back as if, for all the world, he was the adult comforting the child.

"Oh, I wouldn't want you to do that, sir. Really, I wouldn't. We will need your eyes more than mine, in the time to come. This war isn't over yet. Besides—"

He hesitated, then cleared his throat. "Besides, I've been thinking a lot. And, if you'd be willing, there *is* a great favor you could do for me."

Belisarius pushed himself away and held the lad by both shoulders. "You need but ask. Anything."

Calopodius gestured toward the secretary sitting at the desk. "Well, it's this. I got to thinking that Homer was said to be blind, too. And who ever got as much fame and glory as he did? He'll be remembered as long as Achilles, after all. Maybe even longer."

Before Belisarius could respond, Calopodius was waving his hands in a little gesture of denial. "Not me, of course! I tried my hand at poetry once, but the results were awful. Still, I *am* good at rhetoric and grammar, and I think my prose is pretty good. So—"

Calopodius took a deep breath, as a boy does before announcing a grandiose ambition to a skeptical world. "So I decided to become an historian. Polybius is just as famous as the men he wrote about, really. Even if he's not as famous as Homer. And by the time it's over—even now!—your war against Malwa will be the stuff of legend."

Belisarius moved his eyes from the ruined face and looked at the sheet held limply in the secretary's hand. Now that he was closer, he could see that the writing covered the entire page—nothing like the terse messages which were transmitted to and fro on the telegraph.

"You've already started," he declared. "And you want to be able to question me about some details."

Calopodius nodded. The gesture was painfully shy.

Aide's voice came like a clear stream. **And what could make a finer—and a cleaner—irony? In the world that would have been, your life and work would be recounted by a snake named Procopius.**

Belisarius clapped Calopodius on the shoulder. "I can do much better than that, lad! You'll have to do it in your spare time, of course—I can't possibly spare you from the command bunker—but as of this moment you are my official historian."

He led Calopodius back to his chair and drew another up to the desk for himself. Then spoke in as cheerful a tone of voice as he had used in weeks. "The last historian I had—ah—proved quite unequal to the task."

Chapter 43

Khusrau arrived at the Iron Triangle a week later. He came, along with two thousand of his Immortals, in a fleet of war galleys rowing their stately way up the Indus. The fact that he came in those galleys was enough, in itself, to tell Belisarius that Coutzes had made good his boast to storm the Malwa fortress in the gorge. No Persian emperor would have risked himself against those huge guns in a cockleshell galley, not even one so bold as Khusrau.

Khusrau confirmed the fact as soon as he stepped ashore. That, and many others, as Belisarius led him to the command bunker.

The Malwa were in desperate retreat through the Sukkur gorge, trying to reach the relative safety of the Punjab before they were overtaken by Khusrau's dehgans or simply starved to death.

Thousands—at least fifteen thousand—had either been captured or surrendered on their own initiative. Khusrau estimated that as large a number were simply deserting Malwa altogether and seeking refuge in the plains or mountains.

Sukkur was secure, and the entire Roman army under Bouzes and Coutzes would reach the Iron Triangle within two weeks. No Malwa force could possibly prevent the reunion of the Roman army. Once they arrived, Belisarius would have an army numbering almost a hundred thousand under his command.

Couriers had arrived from Kungas, announcing that the Kushans had cleared the Khyber Pass and held the northwest entrance to the Punjab in their hands. The Malwa were now facing the prospect of a war on two fronts.

Also—very mysterious, this message, but Khusrau asked no questions—another small party of Kushans passed through Sukkur on their way to the Hindu Kush. They asked the Persian emperor to tell Belisarius that all was going well with a certain problem in grammatical usage. Whatever that might mean.

The emperor looked around the command bunker. "This will continue to serve well enough as a headquarters. But you'll need to plan for major encampments along the Indus south of the fork. No possible way you could fit your entire huge army in this—what did you call it?—oh, yes, the Iron Triangle. An excellent name, that."

Khusrau accepted the chair being offered to him by Gregory. Needless to say, the artillery officer had chosen the best one in the bunker, but . . . that wasn't saying much.

Khusrau did not seem disgruntled by the modesty of the chair. It was a bit hard for Belisarius to tell, however, because ever since he'd arrived the Persian's face had been stiff and severe. Quite unlike his usual self, which—certainly by the standards of Aryan royalty—was rather relaxed and expressive.

The Roman general was certain he knew the source of that stiffness. He had deduced Khusrau's purpose the moment he first realized that the Aryan emperor himself had chosen to come to the Triangle. And saw no reason to postpone the issue.

Nor, apparently, did Khusrau. After seating himself, the emperor addressed all the officers in the bunker—Roman and Persian alike—in a tone of voice which was courteous enough, but unmistakably regal.

"Belisarius and I need to speak in private," he said. "I would much appreciate it if you would all comply with my wishes."

The Persian officers left immediately. The Roman ones paused just long enough to see Belisarius' quick little nod. Calopodius, moving in the slower manner which his blindness required, was the last to exit.

As soon as everyone had left, Belisarius went straight to the issue at hand.

"You want the lower Punjab turned over to Aryan sovereignty. Including the Iron Triangle. I will agree to that on the following two conditions:

"First, Persian territory will extend no farther north than Multan—after we take it next year—and will remain on the western bank of the Sutlej. I want to *end* this war, someday, not find myself caught in a new one between the Aryans and the Rajputs. And the biggest inducement the Rajputs will have to agree to a lasting peace is possession of the Punjab and its agricultural wealth. The more so since Rajputana is an arid country."

Khusrau began to speak, but Belisarius held up his hand. "Please. Let me finish. That will still leave you in control of the outlet to the Sind, along with a fair share of Punjab's riches."

Again, Khusrau began to speak; again, Belisarius held up his hand. "The second condition. The Punjabis who have placed themselves under Roman care must be treated well, and respectfully. No parceling out of their land to greedy and hard-fisted dehgans. Do as you will in the Sind, Khusrau Anushirvan, but *here* you must agree to rule directly. These lands must be imperial domain, governed by your chosen officials. And, though I obviously cannot make this part of the conditions, I do urge you to choose those officials wisely."

Finally, Khusrau was able to get in a word. The first of which was a mere snort of amusement. Then: "Have no fear, Belisarius. I have no more desire than you to get into an endless war with Rajputana. Nor—I can assure you of this!—do I intend to allow my dehgans to aggrandize themselves at imperial expense."

The emperor's momentary levity was replaced by his former sternness. "I have already made clear to the dehgans that the conditions of rule in my new provinces will be *imperial* ones. Those of them willing to accept positions as *imperial* servants will be welcome to do so. Those who insist on retaining their ancient rights will be invited to return to the barren lands they came from."

He waved his hand majestically. "Very few of them seem inclined to argue the point. Fewer still, now that I have expanded the ranks of the Immortals to include a full third of the dehgans themselves."

He fell silent, his face as stiff as ever. Belisarius began to feel a small terror growing in his belly. He realized, suddenly, that Khusrau's unusual solemnity had nothing to do with diplomacy. Not, at least, in the sense of that term used by empires instead of . . . friends.

Perhaps Khusrau sensed that growing terror. A bit hurriedly, he drew a scroll from within his imperial robes and handed it to Belisarius.

"This is from Antonina herself, General. She is quite well, I assure you." He hesitated. "Well, not from *herself*, exactly. It is a transcription which one of your scribes made of a message she sent from Barbaricum by way of the telegraph line to Sukkur."

Belisarius took the scroll and began untying the silk ribbon which held it close. "From Barbaricum? She is not coming up the river herself? I assume—"

Khusrau cut him off. "Best you read the message, General. Antonina *cannot* come up the river. The expedition was a great success. A tremendous success, rather—the Malwa fleet at Chowpatty destroyed, and Chowpatty itself taken; the fleet at Bharakuccha destroyed likewise, and its harbor wrecked if not taken. But she could not linger at Barbaricum, much less take the time to travel upriver. She is, as you will see, needed immediately in Axum. By now, I imagine, she will be almost there."

The small terror, receding as Khusrau began to speak, surged back like a monster. If Antonina herself was well—why an immediate presence in Axum?—it could only be . . .

Finally, the stiffness left Khusrau's face, replaced by simple sadness. "There is bad news also."

Once the scroll had been read, and read again, and then again, and the tears were pouring freely down Belisarius' cheeks, the Emperor of Iran and non-Iran sighed heavily and rose. He came over to Belisarius and laid a hand on the Roman general's shoulder. "I am sorry," he said softly. "Truly I am. I did not know the young king well myself, but I know you were close. You have been a good friend, to me as well as my subjects, and it distresses me to see you in such pain."

Belisarius managed to regain enough composure to place his own hand over the imperial hand gripping his shoulder. It was a rare moment of intimacy, between two of the most powerful men in the world.

"I thank you for that, Khusrau of the Immortal Soul. And now, if you would, I would like to be alone. I need to spend some time with my own."

There he remained for the rest of the day, never moving once from his chair. Noon come and gone, his officers began defying his request to be left alone. One by one, beginning with Maurice, they came into the bunker. Not to speak with their grieving general, but simply to place that same hand of comfort on his shoulder. Each hand he covered with his own, though he said nothing in response to their murmured phrases of sympathy and regret.

The only words he spoke, until sundown, were to Aide. And those were not words so much as inner shrieks of pain and sorrow. Words which Aide returned in his own manner.

What Antonina had wondered, Belisarius came to know. Indeed, a crystal could weep, and weep, and weep. But Belisarius never spoke of it to her in the years which came after, not once, except to acknowledge the fact itself. The manner of that weeping remained his secret alone, because it was a wound he would neither reopen for himself nor inflict on his beloved wife.

After evening came, Belisarius rose from the chair and went to the entrance of the bunker. Speaking softly to the sentry standing some feet away, he passed on a request for Calopodius and his secretary.

When the young officer and his scribe entered the bunker, stepping forward somewhat timidly, they found Belisarius sitting at Calopodius' desk, in the same chair he always used when reciting his history. Only by the redness of his eyes and the hoarseness in his voice could the two men, each in his own way, discern any sign that the general had spent the day mired in sorrow.

After Calopodius and the scribe had taken their seats, Belisarius began to speak.

"Every great war, I suppose, requires its own Achilles. Perhaps that is God's way of reminding us that the glory of youth carries a price worthy of it. I like to think so, at least. It makes the loss bearable, in a way nothing else could. So I will now tell you of this war's Achilles, whence he came and how he came to be what he was."

Calopodius leaned forward, intent, enraptured. The scribe, likewise.

"We must begin with his name. His true name, not the many titles which came after. *Eon bisi Dakuen. A man of his regiment.* Record my words, historian, and record them true and well."

Epilogue
AN ARTISAN AND HIS OFFICERS

"I can't believe he's doing this. Theodora is going to have my *head.*"

Stop muttering, said Aide. **You're setting a bad example for your officers.**

Guiltily, Belisarius glanced to his right and left. Sure enough, at least half of his commanding officers looked to be muttering under their breath. Belisarius wasn't the only Roman military leader standing on the docks who, at the moment, was far less concerned with the danger from the enemy than Empress Regent Theodora's headsman's ax.

He turned his eyes back to the man being helped off the steamship which had towed the newly-arrived flotilla to the Iron Triangle. The *Justinian*, that was.

Appropriately enough.

Belisarius gritted his teeth. *I am* not *in the mood for jests.*

Who's jesting? Oh, look what they're starting to unload from the first barge!

Puzzled, Belisarius tried to figure out what Aide was getting so excited about. The cargo being offloaded by one of the simple cranes alongside the dock was a large wicker basket full of . . . *wheels?*

Wheelbarrow wheels, if I'm not mistaken. We can assemble the rest of the gadgets easily enough, with what we have

available here—*if* we have the wheels. They'll probably triple the work rate on the fortifications.

The mood lurking beneath Aide's thoughts was insufferably smug. **I *did* suggest wheelbarrows to you, you might recall. But did you pay any attention? No, no. I'm glad to see *someone* isn't blind. If you'll pardon the expression.**

By now, Menander had guided Justinian off the dock and into the protected shed where Belisarius and his officers were waiting. As soon as he sensed that he was in their presence, by whatever means a blind man senses these things, Justinian grinned from ear to ear.

Belisarius was almost stunned by the expression. When Justinian had been Emperor of Rome, Belisarius could recall precious few occasions where the man had so much as smiled. Fewer still, when Justinian became the Chief Justiciar.

"I thought you'd have forgotten about the wheelbarrows," said Justinian cheerfully. "First thing I asked Menander when he showed up at Barbaricum. He was surprised to see me. Still more surprised when I told him it was time to start transferring the shipbuilding design team to the Iron Triangle."

Justinian swiveled his head, turning eyeless sockets to Menander's apprehensive face. Then, swiveled it slowly to face all the officers in the shed.

"Oh, stop scowling," he said, more cheerfully still. "By the time Theodora finds out you let me come to the front lines, erupts in a fury, and sends off a headsman to execute the lot of you, months will have gone by. We'll either all be dead by then, anyway, or we'll be marching triumphantly on Kausambi. In which case I'll have the headsman executed for interfering with imperial military affairs. I can do that, you know. Since I'm still the Chief Justiciar—first one ever, too—I can do pretty much whatever I want."

Belisarius managed not to sigh. Barely. "Welcome to the Iron Triangle, Justinian."

"Thank you." The blind man, who had been many things in his life, but none he seemed to enjoy so much as being an artisan, cocked his head quizzically. "Tell me something, Belisarius. Are you glad to see me?"

Belisarius thought about it, for a moment. His thought processes were helped along by Aide.

Don't be a complete idiot.

"Yes," he said. "I am delighted to see you here. We're going to need you badly, I suspect, before this is all over."

AN EMPEROR AND HIS REALM

"The actual shipyard, of course, will be moved to Barbaricum," explained Justinian. He leaned back in his chair and placed the drained cup on a nearby table, moving in the slightly deliberate manner of a blind man. "Your local beer's not bad, if you ask me. No worse than what you get in Egypt or Axum."

Belisarius frowned. "To Barbaricum? Why not keep it in Adulis?" He started to make a waving motion with his hand, until he remembered the gesture wouldn't be seen. "I can understand the advantages of having it closer, but—moving all those artisans and shipbuilders, most of them Ethiopian—"

"Oh, stop fussing at me!" snapped Justinian. "By now, I do believe I know a lot more about this than you do. The disruption will only be temporary, and after that we'll save a *lot* more time by having much closer contact with the shipyard. Instantaneous contact, once the telegraph lines are laid all the way through."

The former emperor leaned forward, gesticulating with energy. "You *do* understand, don't you, that the Malwa will already have started building ironclad riverboats? Ha! Wait till they see what *I'm* planning to build to counter them!"

Belisarius was still frowning. "That's going to cause some trouble with Khusrau . . ."

"*Trouble?*" demanded Justinian. "Say better—an imperial tempest. The Ethiopians are going to demand that Barbaricum be made an Axumite enclave. Ethiopian territory, pure and simple—just like Chowpatty."

Makes sense, said Aide. **Between Barbaricum and Chowpatty—they'll probably want a piece of Gujarat, too, before this is all over—the Axumites will have—**

"Impossible!" proclaimed Belisarius.

"Oh, nonsense," replied Justinian airily. "The Axumites can certainly claim to be entitled to it, after all they've sacrificed for Persia."

Yes, they can. Greedy damned Persians! Wanting everybody to rescue them and then trying to grab everything at the same time. The *least* they can do for Axum is give them Barbaricum. Of course—

Belisarius could feel a diplomatic pit opening beneath him. The fury of the Aryan emperor—naturally, *he* would have to be the one to negotiate with Khusrau—

—I can see why Khusrau will be a mite testy. The Persians are a trading nation, unlike the Indians, and so they won't like the fact that between Chowpatty and Barbaricum—Gujarat, too, you watch—the Ethiopians will have something of a lock on trade in the Erythrean Sea.

Justinian reached into his robes—still imperial purple, whatever else might have changed—and pulled out a bound scroll. "Besides, you don't have a lot of choice. Antonina was just arriving in Adulis when I was about to leave. Once we had a chance to talk—my plans for a closer shipyard, her plans for a stable transition in Axum—she wrote this for you. Lays out everything, as neatly as you could ask for."

Normally, Belisarius would have been delighted to receive a letter from Antonina. But this one . . . He reached for it gingerly.

"She's quite firm in her opinion, needless to say."

She was, indeed. Gloomily, as he read Antonina's letter, Belisarius could foresee furious times ahead of him. Negotiations with his Persian allies which would be almost—not quite—as ferocious as his battles with the Malwa.

Somewhere in the middle of his reading, a part of his mind noticed that Menander and Eusebius had come charging into his headquarters. (Which was still a pavilion. Permanent construction was taking place all over the Iron Triangle, but it was devoted to the necessities of war, not the creature comfort of officers. Although the Persians were starting to make noise about requiring a "suitable residence" for Khusrau, when he came to visit.) But Belisarius paid no attention to their eager words, or the way they were waving around the design sketches Justinian had brought with him. Not until Aide jolted him out of his misery.

You really *might* want to pay attention to this, you know. Persians are Persians. The war goes on. And I personally think you need to squelch any idea about a submarine before it even gets started—hopeless, that is—but Justinian's ideas

about spar torpedoes strike me as having some promise. **Let the Malwa fuss around with those clumsy ironclads! We can circumvent them entirely, the way Justinian's thinking runs.** With great satisfaction: **Smart man, now that he's not burdened with all that imperial crap.**

Startled, Belisarius looked up. To his surprise, he saw that Justinian was grinning at him again.

"So, my favorite General. Are you *still* glad to see me?"

This time, Belisarius didn't even have to think about it.

"Yes, I am."

AN EMPRESS AND HER GRIEF

By the time Rukaiya was finally able to speak, Antonina felt her ribs might be on the verge of breaking. The sobbing Queen of Axum had been clutching her like a drowning kitten.

"Thank you," Rukaiya whispered, wiping away her tears. "I have been so terrified since the news came—more for Wahsi than myself—that I was not even able to grieve properly. I was afraid that if anyone saw even a sign of weakness . . . Horrible enough that Eon is dead. To have his son murdered also . . ."

Antonina stroked the girl's hair, nestling her head in her shoulder. "It won't happen, Rukaiya. I promise. Between me and Ousanas and Ezana, you have nothing to fear. Wahsi is the negusa nagast, and there's an end to it. There will be no struggle over the succession. No Ethiopian version of the Diadochi."

Again, the young queen burst into tears. "I loved him so! I can't believe he's gone."

Rukaiya said nothing further for quite a while. Antonina was glad of it, despite the additional stress on her ribcage. No widow that young should be faced with anything in such a time, other than her own grief. Just . . .

Weep, and weep, and weep.

A RULER AND HER DECREES

"As long as she needs," said Antonina firmly. "Weeks, months, whatever it takes. Grieving must be done properly."

Seated on the imperial throne elevated on its great dais, she stared down at the crowd of notables assembled in the audience chamber. The large room was packed with such men, Ethiopian and Arab alike. Officials, military leaders, merchant princes—all of Axum's elite was gathered there.

"As long as she needs," Antonina repeated. She scanned the crowd with cold eyes, daring anyone to challenge her.

The crowd was mute. Clearly enough, from their expressions, any number of the notables would have liked to utter a protest. Of some kind. *Trade will be disrupted! Decrees must be made! Legal disputes must be settled! Promotions to the officer ranks—now more than ever, with all the losses—must be made!*

"I will rule in her stead," decreed Antonina. "Until the queen is able to resume her responsibilities. Her *new* responsibilities, as the regent until the negusa nagast is old enough to rule on his own."

She stared down the crowd, *daring* them to challenge her. That they wanted to, she didn't doubt for a moment. But—

Ousanas was there, standing at her right. Ethiopia's aqabe tsent-sen. With the fly whisk of his office in one hand, as was normal during imperial sessions. Ousanas was grinning. Which, in itself, was also normal enough. But there was not a trace of humor in the thing. It was a great cat's grin, a lion's grin, contemplating its prey.

And, on her left, stood Garmat. The old half-Arab, half-Ethiopian adviser to two kings, Kaleb and Eon both, was famous throughout Axum for his sagacity and wisdom. Since Eon's death, and until Antonina's arrival, he had been keeping the kingdom from collapsing into turmoil. Providing his teenage queen, at a time when being queen was the last thing she wanted to think about, with his invaluable counsel and steady support. In its own way, Garmat's solemn forehead was as much of a caution as Ousanas' predator grin, to anyone who might harbor thoughts of contesting the succession.

It was a fearsome triumvirate, between the seated woman and the men standing on either side of her. In the end, however, whatever hesitations any of the notables still retained were dispelled by someone else. A man who, at that moment, reminded them of the ultimate nature of all power.

Ezana, standing at the rear of the chamber, slammed the iron ferrule of his spearbutt onto the stone floor. The harsh sound caused at least half of the notables to jump a bit.

"The Roman woman Antonina was appointed by Eon the Great to oversee the transition of power in Axum," he announced. His loud voice was as harsh as the spearbutt. "I was there, as he lay dying, and bear witness. *Does any man challenge me?*"

Again, the ringing spearbutt on the floor. "*Any man?*"

He allowed the silence to last for a full five minutes. Then:

"It is done. Until the queen is ready to resume her responsibilities—which will take as long as she needs—Antonina rules Axum. Do not doubt it. Any of you. Do not doubt it for an instant."

Again, the spearbutt. "My name is Ezana, and I am the commander of the Dakuen sarwe. The regiment of the negusa nagast, which will serve the baby Wahsi for his fist. Should he need it. Pray to whatever God you pray to, O ye notables, that he does not. Pray fervently."

A QUEEN AND HER WEDDINGS

"And here I thought the *Christian* ceremony took forever," whispered Kungas. "At least they managed it in one day."

"Be quiet," hissed Irene. "You're supposed to be silent for the next hour or two. Even whispering, people can see your lips move."

"You've been whispering too," he hissed back.

"Doesn't count for me," replied Irene smugly. "*I'm* wearing a veil."

In actual fact, the Buddhist wedding did not take more than a day—although it did consume that one in its entirety. But the fault lay not with the religion so much as the circumstances. Irene could have easily chosen a simpler and shorter ceremony, which Kungas would have much preferred. But she told him, in no uncertain terms, not to be an idiot.

"You want to drag half your kingdom to see the glorious stupa you're having rebuilt on the ruins of the old one? Which just—so conveniently!—happens to be within eyesight of the great new fortifications you're building in the Khyber Pass? And then keep it *short*? Not a chance."

"You'll have to wear a veil all day," whined Kungas, grasping for any hope. "You hate wearing veils."

Irene began stroking her horse-tail. By now, she had become as accustomed to that mannerism as she had ever been to brushing back her Greek-style hair. And found even more pleasure and comfort in the deed. Her old habit had been that of a spymaster; the new one, that of a queen. The horse-tail was a daily reminder that the same insignia flew under the banners of her army.

"I said I *personally* detested wearing a veil, Kungas. But I have to tell you that the day men invented the silly things was the day they sealed their own downfall." The horse-tail stroking became smug, smug. "Take it from me, as a professional intriguer. Best aide to diplomacy ever invented!"

The day after the ceremony, Irene introduced Kungas to the Pathan chiefs. The meeting went quite well, she told him afterward.

"How can you tell?" he demanded, a bit crossly. "They spent most of their time glowering at you, even though you didn't say a single word after the introductions."

Then: "And take off that damned veil! We're in our own private chambers now, and I'm handicapped as it is. Besides"—much less crossly—"I love the sight of your face."

When the veil came off, Irene was grinning. "The reason they're glowering is because I made sure they found out, beforehand, that I'm planning to bring my female bodyguard with me to the pagan wedding ceremony we're having in their hills next month."

Kungas groaned. "Wonderful. Now they'll be *certain* I am the most effeminate ruler in the history of the Hindu Kush."

Irene's grin never wavered. "Oh, stop whining. You're just grouchy at the thought of another wedding, that's all. You know perfectly well that the reason they're unhappy is because they'd *like* to think that—but can't. Not standing in the shadow of that great fortress you're building in the Khyber, watching thousands of Malwa prisoners do the work for you. Those sour old chiefs would give anything to have a set of balls like yours. 'Manly'—ha! Bunch of goat-stealers."

Irene cocked her head slightly. Kungas, by now, was well accustomed to that mannerism also. Again, he groaned. "There's something else."

"Well . . . yes," admitted Irene. "The other reason they're irked with me is because I also made sure they found out, ahead of time, that three Pathan girls recently came into Begram and volunteered for my bodyguard unit. And were cheerfully accepted."

Her horse-tail stroking almost exuded *smugness*. "It seems—who would have guessed?—that the old Sarmatians have *lots* of descendants in the region. And who am I to defy ancient customs, even newfound ones?"

Kungas scowled. For him, the expression was almost overt. The man had found, as his power grew—based in no small part on the diplomatic skills of his wife—that he no longer needed to keep the mask in place at all times. And he was finding that old habit surprisingly easy to relinquish.

The more so under Irene's constant encouragement. She was firmly convinced that people preferred their kings to be open-hearted, open-handed, and—most of all—open-faced. *Let them blame their miseries on the scheming queen and the faceless officials. No harm in it, since they won't forget that the king still has his army, and the fortresses it took for him.*

"You're going to start a feud with those damned tribesmen," he warned. "They find a point of honor in the way one of their women is looked at by a stupid goat. Pathan girls in the queen's body-guard!"

"Nonsense. I told them I wouldn't *meddle*. Which I'm not. I didn't *recruit* those girls, Kungas. They came into Begram on their own, after having—much to their surprise—discovered that they really weren't Pathan at all. Who can object if Sarmatian girls follow their ancient customs?"

Kungas tried to maintain his scowl, but found the effort too difficult. He rose from his chair and went over to the window. The "palace" they were residing in was nothing more than a partially-built portion of the great new fortress being erected in the Khyber. Atop one of the hills, not in the pass itself. Kungas had grasped the logic of modern artillery very quickly, and wanted the high ground.

He also enjoyed the view it gave him, partly for its own scenic splendor but mostly because it was a visible reminder of his own power. Let anyone think what they would, but the fact remained—Kungas, King of the Kushans, owned the Khyber Pass. And, with it, held all of the Hindu Kush in his grasp. A grasp which was open-handed, but could be easily closed into a fist should he choose to do so.

He made a fist out of his right hand and gently pounded the stone ledge of the window. "Sarmatians," he chuckled. "Well, why not? Every dynasty needs an ancient pedigree, after all."

Irene cleared her throat. Kungas, without turning around to see her face, smiled down at the Khyber Pass. "Let me guess. You've had that gaggle of Buddhist monks who follow you around every day investigate the historical records. It turns out—who would have guessed?—that Kungas, King of the Kushans, is descended from Sarmatian rulers."

"On your mother's side," Irene specified. "In your paternal ancestry—"

Again, she cleared her throat. Rather more noisily. Kungas' eyes widened. "Don't tell me!"

"What can I say? It's true, according to the historical records. Well, that's what my monks claim, anyway, and since they're the only ones who can decipher those ancient fragments who's going to argue with them?"

Kungas burst into laughter.

"It's true!" insisted Irene. "It seems that when Alexander the Great passed through the area . . . "

A PESHWA AND HIS FAMILY

In her own palace, except for public occasions, Shakuntala was not given to formality. So, even though some of her courtiers thought the practice was a bit scandalous, she was in the habit of visiting her peshwa in his own quarters rather than summoning him to hers. And, as often as not, bringing Rao along with her.

There were a variety of reasons that she chose to do so. Mainly, two.

First, she was energetic by nature. Remaining in her own quarters at all times would have driven her half-insane. Not so much because of physical inactivity—since she and Rao had married, Shakuntala had resumed training in the martial arts under his rigorous regimen—but simply because of pure boredom.

The second reason was less ethereal. Downright mundane, in fact.

"Ha!" exclaimed Rao, as they neared the entrance to Dadaji Holkar's quarters. He turned his head and cast a skeptical eye upon the baby being borne behind them by his nurse. "You dote on that child, true enough. But you haven't the patience for proper mothering."

Shakuntala swept through the wide entrance leading to her peshwa's portion of the palace. "That's what grandmothers are for," she pronounced, as imperiously as she made all her pronouncements.

And, indeed, Gautami was ready and willing to take care of Namadev. The more so since the baby was not that much younger than her own actual grandchild.

As he watched his wife and the two infants, the peshwa Dadaji Holkar—as was his habit—fell into philosophical musing.

"It's odd, really, the way these things work. I am more and more convinced, by the day, that God intends us to understand that all things of the flesh are ultimately an illusion." He pointed to the two children. "Consider, first, my grandson."

Shakuntala and Rao studied the infant in question, the older of the two boys being played with by Gautami. The boy, along with his mother, had been turned over to a unit of Rao's Maratha guerrillas by a detachment sent by Lord Damodara after his men had overrun the rebel forces led by Dadaji's son.

"That the child's lineage is mine, as a matter of flesh, cannot be doubted. At his age, my son looked just the same. But as for the spirit—it remains to be seen."

Rao frowned. "You are worried about the mother's influence? Dadaji, given the circumstances, the fact that the poor woman's wits are still a bit addled is hardly surprising. The boy seems cheerful enough."

"That's not what I meant," replied Holkar, shaking his head. "Are we really so tightly bound to the flesh at all?"

He fell silent, for a moment. Then, gave Rao a keen glance. "I'm sure you heard the report of your men. The Ye-tai officer who brought my son's wife and child told them, quite bluntly, that he had killed my son himself. Yet, with Damodara's permission, was turning the family over to our safekeeping. An odd thing to do, for a Malwa."

Rao shrugged. "Damodara is a subtle man. No doubt he thinks—"

"Not Damodara," interrupted Holkar. "It's the *Ye-tai* who interests me. It must have been him—not Damodara—who spared the mother and child after slaying my son. Why did he do so?"

"Men are not always beasts. Not even Ye-tai."

"Indeed so. But why did God choose *that* vessel to remind us, Rao? As well send a tiger into a burning hut to bring out a child to safety."

There was no answer. After a moment, Holkar spoke again. "When the war is over, certainly if my daughters are returned to me safely, I will no longer be able to function as your peshwa. I have been thinking about it a great deal, lately, and have decided I no longer accept the basic premises of our Hindu system. Not as it stands, at any rate. There is a possibility—some glimpses which I got in conversations with Belisarius, and, through him, with what the Christians call the Talisman of God but I think—"

"He is Kalkin, the tenth avatar who was promised," stated Rao firmly. "Belisarius himself said as much, in a letter he once sent me."

Holkar nodded. "So I believe also. In any event, there will be—would have been—a version of our faith called Vedanta. I intend to explore it, after the war, but the effort will make it impossible—"

"Oh, nonsense!" snapped Shakuntala. "My peshwa you are, my peshwa you will remain. Philosophize at your leisure. You'll have plenty of it, after the war. But I will hear of nothing else."

Dadaji hesitated. "My daughters—after all that has happened, they will be unsuitable for a peshwa." His kindly face hardened. "And I will not set them aside. Under no circumstances. Therefore—"

"Nonsense, I said!" The imperial voice, as always, rang with certainty. So might the Himalayas speak, if they had a tongue. "Do not concern yourself with such trifles as your daughter's status. That is merely a problem. Problems can be solved."

Still, Holkar hesitated. "There will be much talk, Empress. Vicious talk."

"And there won't be, if you become some kind of silly monk?" demanded the empress. "Talk is talk, no more than that." She waved her hand, as if brushing aside an insect. "Problems can be solved, certainly the problem of gossip. If nothing else, by my executioners."

AN EMPEROR AND HIS EXECUTIONERS

"If it happens again, I *will* have that man executed," declared Photius firmly. He sat upright at the head of the enormous imperial bed, doing his best to look imperial while in his nightclothes. "I *told* him Irene was to have the very first copy."

Tahmina, lying prone on the bed with her head propped up on her hands, giggled in a manner which did not bode well for the emperor's dignity. "You're just angry because you had a bad day with the tutors. Take it out on them, instead of some poor book dealer. Besides, Irene won't really care if she gets the second copy."

Photius' face was as stiff as any boy's can be, at his age. "Still!" he insisted.

"Oh, stop it. Do something useful. Give me a back rub."

Some time later, Tahmina sighed happily. "You're getting awfully good at this."

Photius, astraddle his wife, leaned over and kissed the back of her head. The motion was easy, relaxed. "I love touching you," he whispered. "I'm almost eleven, now."

"I know," she sighed, very happily. "Soon."

A LORD AND HIS MEN

Lord Damodara watched Rana Sanga carefully, as the Rajput king strode back and forth in the chamber which Damodara used for his military headquarters. Sanga was giving his opinion on the progress being made incorporating the garrison of Bharakuccha into the ranks of the regular army.

Damodara was not ignoring Sanga's words, exactly. But he was far more interested in what he could determine of the Rajput's mood than he was of the item actually under discussion. Sanga was given to pacing, and his pacing always reminded Damodara of a tiger's movement. But he was struck by the absence of any sense of fury. He found that absence . . . surprising. And, given what it might imply, more than a little unsettling.

Finished with his report, Sanga came to a halt. As it happened, he stopped his pacing in that corner of the room which held the most peculiar item of furniture in it.

Sanga stared down at the chair, with its gruesome modification. The old bloodstains were still visible. They were brown now, not red, and flies had long since lost any interest in it.

"Why don't you get rid of this damned thing?" he demanded.

"I find it a helpful reminder," replied Damodara. The chuckle which accompanied the words held not a trace of humor. "Of the consequences of misjudgement."

Sanga turned his head and examined his commander. Over the years, he had come to have as good an understanding of the man as Damodara had of him.

"Something is troubling you," he stated.

Damodara shrugged. "It's hard to explain. I am . . . a bit puzzled that you do not seem as enraged as I would have thought. You were devoted to your family."

The Rajput looked away, his expression stony. After a brief silence, he said: "I take comfort in philosophy, Lord. In the end, this is all the veil of illusion."

Damodara swiveled his head toward another corner and brought the other two occupants of the room under his scrutiny. Narses, as usual, was sitting in a chair. Toramana, also as usual, was standing.

"Do you also find comfort in philosophy?" he asked. The question seemed addressed at either or both of them.

"I have precious little faith in *any* philosophy," replied Narses, almost snarling. "On the other hand, I believe quite firmly in illusion. More than that, I'm not prepared to express any opinion."

The Ye-tai crossed his arms over his chest. "When I was a boy, my father and brothers taught me to ride a horse and use weapons. They neglected any instruction in philosophy. I never saw any reason since to make good the lack. It's as dangerous to think too much as too little."

This time, Damodara's chuckle did hold some humor. Very wry humor. "I suppose," he said quietly, studying the instrument of Venandakatra's execution, "delving into philosophical waters can be more dangerous than anything."

"Indeed so," agreed Narses. The old eunuch gazed upon Damodara as a statue might gaze upon its beholder. Blank, unreadable. "Especially for a lord. Best to leave such questions unasked. And therefore unanswerable, should someone ever ask you the same."

Damodara returned Narses' gaze for a moment, then looked at Sanga and Toramana. The three men who had become his principal subordinates, over the past two years. The three men who, each in their own way, held his fate in their hands.

That done, he studied the chair in the corner. And concluded, as he did each day when he examined the thing, that there were some experiences best left unknown.

A MAN AND AN INFANT

The two sisters knew of the arrival of the odd party of merchants, almost as soon as it happened. Not because they had seen them arrive, however. As always, such low caste traders and tinkers were taken in through the rear entrance of the palace, far from the wing where Lady Damodara and her maids lived. But the majordomo brought word to his mistress immediately and she, in turn, gave instructions to her maids.

The instructions were clear and simple. Once she was done, her maids were more confused than ever. And not at all happy.

"They will be staying with *us?*" asked the younger sister, Lata. "But—"

"We don't have enough room," said Dhruva, the older. Her tone was respectful, but insistent. "Our chamber is much too small."

"You will be getting new chambers," said Lady Damodara. "Several of them, connected together—and quite isolated from the rest of the palace. It's a suite of sorts, which I think was originally designed for the poor relatives of the palace's original owners. Comfortable, and spacious—I've inspected the rooms myself—though not as fancy as these quarters."

She hesitated a moment. Then: "It's down on the lowest floor. Just above the basement, to which it's connected by a staircase."

Lata grimaced. It no longer even occurred to her to disguise her emotions from Lady Damodara. Their mistress was a friendly woman, and not one she and her sister feared. With many Indian nobles—especially Malwa—such an open expression of sentiment on the part of a servant would have been dangerous.

Seeing her face, Lady Damodara laughed. "You are worried about being pestered by the men who work down there?"

The presence of a large party of workmen down in the basement was by now known to many of the palace's inhabitants. Their presence had been explained by the majordomo as being due to Lady Damodara's desire to expand the basement and, in the process, shore up the palace's foundations. The explanation was accepted by everyone, almost without any thought at all. The palace, for all its luxurious and elaborate design, was an ancient one. Over the centuries, it had suffered considerable decay.

Lata nodded. "There's no way to stop the rumors about our history. You know how men will act toward us."

Her older sister Dhruva added: "Some of them are Ye-tai, I think. They'll be the worst."

The majordomo appeared in the doorway, ready to lead the sisters to their new quarters. Lady Damodara considered him for a moment, and then shook her head.

"I think I'll guide Dhruva and Lata there myself," she announced. "They can return for their belongings later."

The first person the sisters noticed in their new quarters was the hawk-faced man. Ajatasutra, his name was, according to Lady Damodara. They were so relieved to see him that they paid almost no attention to the rest of her introductions. Although, once Lady Damodara had left and Ajatasutra informed them that he would soon be leaving the palace himself—and not returning for an indefinite time—their concerns returned.

"Oh, stop worrying," he chuckled. "I can assure you that being 'pestered' by workmen is the least of your problems."

The gray-haired woman sitting on a nearby settee—a Rajput, by her accent, somewhere in early middle age—laughed cheerfully. The laugh was a rich and warm thing, which matched the woman's face. The sisters felt at least half of their concern drain away. There was an unmistakable *confidence* in the woman's laugh; and, as always, being in the presence of an older woman sure of herself brought confidence to younger ones.

"The *least* of your worries," the Rajput woman chortled. "Trust me, girls. The least."

There were three children in the room, also. The Rajput woman's, presumably. The oldest of them, a boy approximately twelve years of age, stepped forward and bowed stiffly.

"You are under the protection of my family," he announced proudly. "I myself, being the oldest male of the family present, will see to it."

Again, the Rajput woman laughed. "The least of your worries!" She wagged a finger at her son. "Enough of this, Rajiv! You'll cause more trouble with your damned honor than anything else. The girls will be quite safe."

Then, serenely: "Our retainers will see to it." She bestowed an approving gaze upon the two men who were sitting on a settee across the room. Also Rajputs, the sisters suspected, judging from their appearance.

That same appearance, both sisters thought, was a bit at odds with the woman's confidence. One of the men was quite elderly. The other, though young, had an arm in a sling. The signs of long-suffered pain were quite evident in his drawn face, which led the sisters to suspect that his arm was essentially not functional.

Which, finally—reluctantly—brought their attention to the last two men in the room. Who, very obviously, were quite functional.

Hesitantly, the sisters stared at them. Barbarians from somewhere in the west. So much was obvious from their faces. That alone would have made them a bit frightening. The fact that one was a giant—obvious, even while the man was sitting—and the other was perhaps the most vicious looking man either sister had ever seen . . .

The tension was broken by the infant in Dhruva's arms. For whatever odd reason, something about the vicious-looking man had drawn little Baji's attention. He began gurgling happily and waving his arms.

"Look, Valentinian—he likes you!" exclaimed the Rajput woman, smiling. She transferred the cheerful smile to Dhruva and motioned with her head. "Hand the child to him. It's good for him. And he has to get accustomed to children anyway." With a deep, rich chuckle: "Given his new duties."

The man Valentinian did not seem pleased at the prospect. Nor was Dhruva pleased herself, at the idea. But there was something about the Rajput woman which exuded authority, and so she obeyed.

The man Valentinian accepted the child with even greater reluctance than Dhruva handed him over. From the awkward way he held the infant, it was obvious he had no experience with the task. Despite her misgivings, Dhruva found herself smiling. There was something comical about the combination of such a wicked-looking man and a gurgling infant.

In the course of groping as babies do, Baji seized one of Valentinian's fingers in a little fist. Oddly enough, that seemed to bring a certain relief to the man. As if he were finally being presented with a familiar challenge.

"The kid's got a good grip," he announced. Dhruva was surprised by the ease with which he spoke Hindi. A bit of an accent, but much less than she would have expected.

"I guess he's too young to hold a knife," the man mused. "But I can probably start him with something."

Dhruva was startled. "He's not kshatriya!" she protested.

Valentinian's face creased in a cold, evil-looking smile. "Neither am I, girl, neither am I. You think I give a damn about any of that Indian foolishness?"

He looked up at her. And, for the first time, Dhruva got a good look at his eyes. Very dark, they were, and very grim. But she decided they weren't actually evil, after all. Just . . .

"I don't give a damn about much of anything," he added.

The statement was callous. Oddly, Dhruva found herself relaxing. He was still the most vicious looking man she had ever seen. But Baji was gurgling happily, and tugging at the finger, and grinning in the innocent way that infants do. Perhaps her infant, she decided, had the right of it.

A man who didn't give a damn about much of anything, when she thought about it, probably wouldn't go out of his way to imagine slights and difficulties and problems, either. The statement was callous, looked at from one angle. Yet, from another, it was simply . . . relaxed.

She had known few relaxed men in her life. After all that had happened since she and her sister were led into captivity, she found that prospect rather refreshing.

"I'll bet he could hold a breadstick," the man muttered. "You got any breadsticks in India?"

A GENERAL AND AN HISTORIAN

"Let's quit for the day," said Belisarius. "Tomorrow we can start with the campaign into Mesopotamia. But I've got to get ready for the staff conference. Can't forget, after all, that I'm waging a campaign *now*. Or will be, soon enough."

Obediently, Calopodius leaned back in his chair, leaving unspoken the next question he had been about to ask. The scribe began putting away the writing equipment.

"How soon, do you think?" Technically, of course, an historian had no business asking such a question. But from their days of close association, Calopodius had become much bolder in the kind of questions he would ask his general.

"Too soon to tell," replied Belisarius, shrugging. "As always, it depends mostly on logistics. Which is complicated enough on paper, much less in the real world. At a guess? Not more than a few weeks."

He gestured with a thumb toward the north, where the sound of distant cannon fire was more or less constant, day and night. "I see no reason at all to give the Malwa any more of a breathing space than I absolutely must. Time is something which is entirely on that monster's side, not mine."

Calopodius hesitated. Then, boldly: "And what, would you say, is the factor which is most on *your* side?"

Belisarius stared at the young historian. Calopodius was so acute than Belisarius tended to forget about his blindness. But now, remembering, he let his crooked smile spread across his face in a manner so exaggerated that it would have brought down instant derision and sarcasm from Maurice and Sittas. Who, happily, were not present.

So he indulged himself in the smile. And indulged himself, as well, by speaking the plain and simple truth.

"The biggest factor in my favor is that I'm just a lot better at this than the monster is. Way better. War is an art, not a science. And for all that monster's superhuman intelligence, it's got about as much of an artistic streak as a carrot."

He rose to his feet and stretched his arms, working out the stiffness of a two hour session sitting in a chair, recounting his history.

"There are times," he said softly, "when I wish I could have been a blacksmith. But then there are other times when I'm glad I couldn't. This time and place more than any other in my life. War is also an honorable trade, after all—or can be, at least. And I suspect I'm a lot better at it than I ever would have been as a blacksmith."

He cocked his head a little, listening to the gunfire. "Soon, Calopodius. Soon I'll put paid to that monster. And teach it, and its masters, that a professional craftsman at the top of his trade can't possibly be matched by any know-it-all cocksure *dilettante*."

The Dance of Time

To Lucy

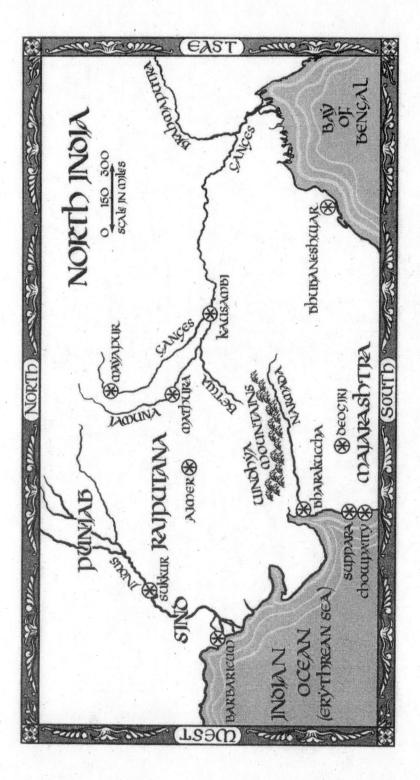

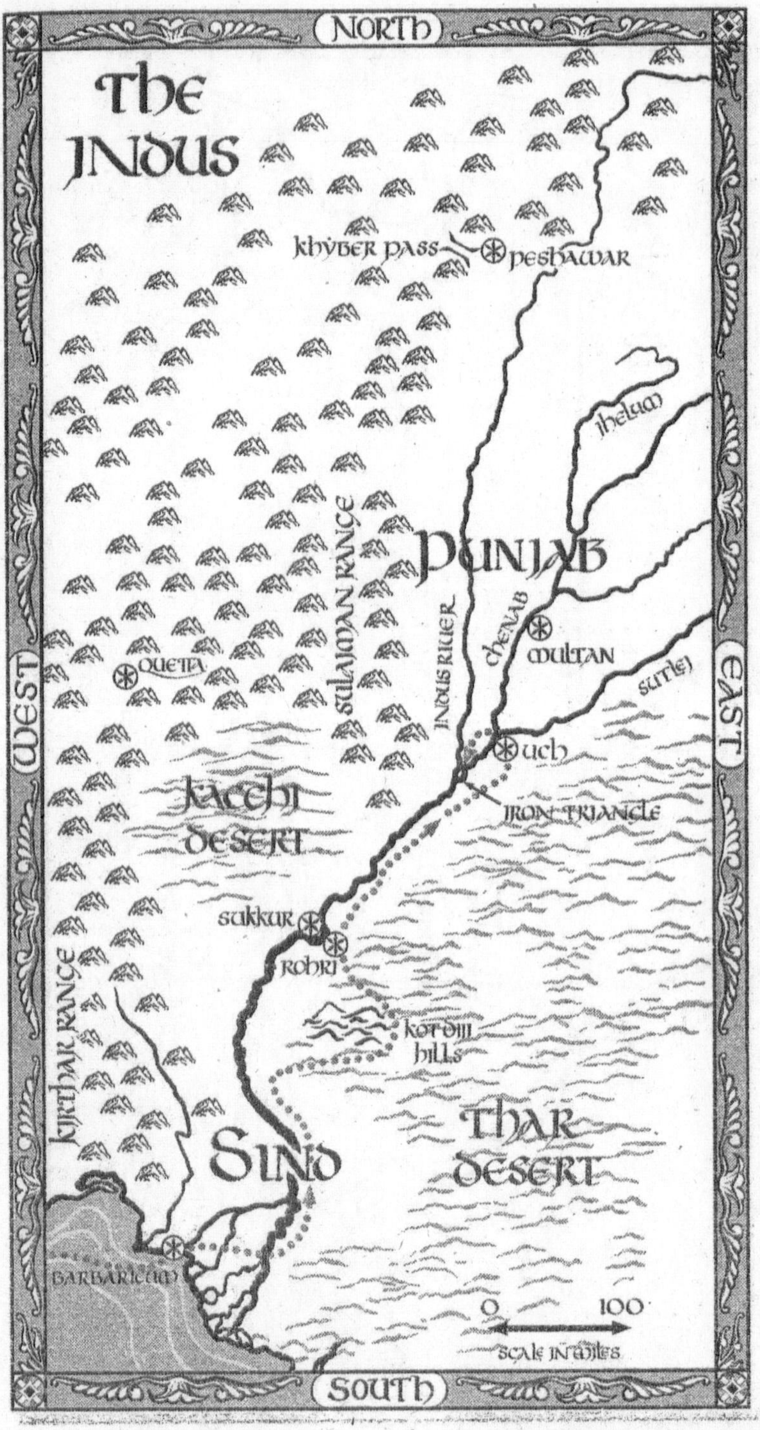

THE INDUS

NORTH

WEST

EAST

SOUTH

KHYBER PASS ✴ PESHAWAR

JHELUM

SULAIMAN RANGE

PUNJAB

QUETTA ✴

CHENAB

MULTAN ✴

SUTLEJ

INDUS RIVER

✴ UCH

KACCHI DESERT

IRON TRIANGLE

KIRTHAR RANGE

SUKKUR ✴

ROHRI ✴

KORDJI HILLS

THAR DESERT

SIND

✴ BARBARICUM

0   100

SCALE IN MILES

Prologue

The Iron Triangle

Autumn, 533 A.D.

Belisarius watched Eusebius and his crew as they carefully slipped the mine off the deck of the *Victrix*, using a ramp they'd set up in the stern for the purpose. Because of its design, it had been relatively easy to adapt the fireship to the task of becoming a mine-layer. Doing so with the *Justinian* would have required a major reconstruction of the armored gunship.

The sun still hadn't come up, but there was enough light from the approaching dawn for Belisarius to see. Quietly, almost sound-lessly, the mine slid below the surface of the water. Eusebius mea-sured off the depth of the mine's placement using the prepared lines, squinting at the marks nearsightedly.

A trio of ducks flew past swiftly, just above the level of the reeds. Their quacking sounded like the slap of bamboo canes.

You are fortunate to see them, said Aide, the crystalline being that rested in Belisarius' neck pouch. **Those are pink-headed ducks, very rare here in the Indus Basin. Indeed, they're not common even in Brahmaputra**.

When we've defeated the Malwa, Belisarius replied silently to the voice in his mind, *perhaps I'll retire to a monastery and write a treatise on natural history based on my travels. Of course, first we have to defeat the Malwa.*

We will, said Aide firmly; and *that* was not a joke.

Aide had come—been sent—to Belisarius from the far future; from one of two alternate futures, more precisely. Aide's purpose was to prevent the Malwa Empire from conquering the world as it had already conquered most of the Indian subcontinent.

The real horror of a Malwa victory would come tens of tens of thousands of years in the future, when the Earth was ruled by the so-called "new gods" that had evolved from men. In human terms, though, what a Malwa victory meant in this 533rd Year of Christ was bad enough.

Laying the mine took some time, because the crew had to lower it slowly and carefully. There wasn't really much danger of the charge going off simply due to a rough landing on the river bottom, especially as muddy as the Indus was. But, understandably, no one wanted to take any chances.

Eventually, the lines grew slack. The heavy stone weight that had dragged the mine below the surface had reached the bottom.

"About where we want it," Eusebius proclaimed, checking the marks on the lines. "She'll be sitting just the right depth to cave in any ironclads the Malwa send at us."

By now, his crew had placed so many mines in the rivers that formed two sides of the Iron Triangle that the rest was routine. The lines were hauled up, after the ends were released so they could slip easily through the mine's handles. Very easily, since the shell of the mine was nothing more than an amphora sealed to contain the charge and the air that kept it floating above the weight that anchored it to the river bottom.

All that was left was the very thin wire that would transmit the detonation signal when given. Like all the mines the Romans had placed in the Indus and the Chenab, the mines were designed to be exploded on command. It would have been possible to design contact fuses, but the things were tricky and Belisarius saw no need for them.

In fact, mines with contact fuses could conceivably become a handicap. Belisarius wasn't expecting to use the rivers for a rapid assault, but war was unpredictable. If he did find himself doing so, he didn't want to be delayed by the dangerous and finicky work of removing the mines. With command detonation mines, if need be, he could clear the rivers in less than a minute. Just blow up all the mines.

Eusebius leaned over the rail of the *Victrix* and handed the end of the signal wire to a soldier in a rowboat. Moments later, while the soldier holding the wire kept a good grip on it, the other soldiers in the boat rowed it ashore. The wire would join others in one of the many little mine bunkers that lined the banks of both rivers in the Triangle. A spotter in the bunker would already have noted the location of the mine.

Eusebius straightened. "And that's pretty much all there is to the business, General. The old emperor had the right of it."

Grinning, then: "Much as he still pisses and moans about how much he'd like to build a submarine. But the fact is that for the purpose of fending off those ironclads the Malwa are building upriver, these mines will do the trick just fine. And it's a lot less risky than spar torpedoes."

"Not to mention a submarine," Belisarius chuckled. "All right. I just wanted to get a sense of how it was going."

Had the Malwa been simply an Indian dynasty, they would not have posed a threat to the present world, let alone that of the far future. Aide had showed Belisarius visions of both past and future. Indian nations had often been rich and powerful and influential, and would be again; but never in the timeline that led to Aide and those who created him had the men and women who ruled India looked beyond their own subcontinent. Missionaries and traders from India would turn most of Southeast Asia into a cultural extension of Hindu India; and, through Buddhism, India would have a major impact on the societies of the Far East. Still, no Indian ruler in that timeline ever attempted to conquer the world in the manner that the Malwa Empire was doing—using methods of conquest that were even more savage than Genghis Khan's, with an end goal that had none of the Mongols' tolerance as actual rulers.

But the ruler of the Malwa Empire was not a man or woman, to begin with. The real ruler of the empire was not the official emperor, Skandagupta. It was Link, a machine, a *monster*, which the "new gods" had sent to change the past and bring their bleak future into existence. If the Malwa armies defeated Belisarius and his outnumbered forces here in the angle of the Indus and Chenab Rivers, the losers would not only be the citizens of the Roman Empire but also all other humans in all times.

Belisarius glanced to the side, where the *Justinian* was slowly steaming. The gunship was keeping a distance from the mine-laying activity, but it was still close enough to come to the *Victrix*'s support in the unlikely event that the Malwa tried to launch an attack on the fireship.

The very unlikely event. The *Victrix* herself had already proven to the Malwa, several times, that she could destroy any wooden riverboats sent against her. And the one time the Malwa had sent down a partially armored boat, the *Justinian* had blown it into wreckage in less than a minute. For the past several weeks, there had been no Malwa incursions on the river at all. From the reports of spies, the enemy had apparently decided to wait until their new heavy ironclads were finished.

Furthermore, if Justinian and Eusebius were right, even those wouldn't do them any good. The Malwa had no way to build completely iron ships; none, at least, that would have a shallow enough draft for these rivers. Their ironclads were just that: *clad* in iron. The underlying boats were still wooden—and even these small mines would be enough to break such hulls in half.

"To tell you the truth, General," Eusebius commented, "I don't even understand why the Malwa have kept building those ironclads. There's no way to lay these mines secretly, even working at night the way we've been doing. By now, they must know we've got both rivers saturated with them."

Belisarius had wondered about that himself. Link had just as much knowledge of future warfare as Aide did. The effectiveness of mines against warships in any constricted area of water was so well established in that future that he couldn't imagine Link having any real hope his ironclads could bull their way through a large and well-laid mine field.

Your theory's the right one, I think, Aide said. **Link is shifting to the defensive.**

Yes. I hadn't thought it would, not this quickly. I'd expected the monster to try a massive assault to drive us out of the Punjab, before we could get really settled in. But . . . it's not. And if it waits much longer, it'll be too late.

Too late, indeed. The Romans and their Persian allies were slowly but surely gaining control of the Indus and both of its banks all the way from the Sukkur gorge to the Iron Triangle, after already having conquered the Sind south of the gorge. So the spearhead that Belisarius had driven into the Punjab during the course of his campaign the previous year would soon be well supplied. The fortifications across the northern side of the Triangle were already strong enough to break any army Link could send against them within a year or two. Not even the Malwa Empire had an inexhaustible supply of men and munitions, ready to hand.

Especially men. Their morale must be close to the breaking point, I think. Link's army needs a rest, and it knows it. That's why it didn't order the assault. It can afford a stalemate, even for long period, where it can't afford another string of defeats.

The sun was coming up.

Softly, proudly: **You really hammered them, these past few years.**

Chapter 1

BUKKUR ISLAND, ON THE INDUS RIVER

He dreamed mostly of islands, oddly enough.

He was sailing, now, in one of his father's pleasure crafts. Not the luxurious barge-in-all-but-name-and-glitter which his father himself preferred for the family's outings into the Golden Horn, but in the phaselos which was suited for sailing in the open sea. Unlike his father, for whom sailing expeditions were merely excuses for political or commercial transactions, Calopodius had always loved sailing for its own sake.

Besides, it gave him and his new wife something to do besides sit together in stiff silence.

Calopodius' half-sleeping reverie was interrupted. Wakefulness came with the sound of his aide-de-camp Luke moving through the tent. The heaviness with which Luke clumped about was deliberate, designed to allow his master to recognize who had entered his domicile. Luke was quite capable of moving easily and lightly, as he had proved many times in the course of the savage fighting on Bukkur Island. But the man, in this as so many things, had proven to be far more subtle than his rough and muscular appearance might suggest.

"It's morning, young Calopodius," Luke announced. "Time to clean your wounds. And you're not eating enough."

Calopodius sighed. The process of tending the wounds would be painful, despite all of Luke's care. As for the other—

"Have new provisions arrived?"

There was a moment's silence. Then, reluctantly: "No."

Calopodius let the silence lengthen. After a few seconds, he heard Luke's own heavy sigh. "We're getting very low, truth to tell. Ashot hasn't much himself, until the supply ships arrive."

Calopodius levered himself up on his elbows. "Then I will eat my share, no more." He chuckled, perhaps a bit harshly. "And don't try to cheat, Luke. I have other sources of information, you know."

"As if my hardest job of the day won't be to keep half the army from parading through this tent," snorted Luke. Calopodius felt the weight of Luke's knees pressing into the pallet next to him, and, a moment later, winced as the bandages over his head began to be removed. "You're quite the soldiers' favorite, lad," added Luke softly. "Don't think otherwise."

In the painful time that followed, as Luke scoured and cleaned and rebandaged the sockets that had once been eyes, Calopodius tried to take refuge in that knowledge.

It helped. Some.

"Are there any signs of another Malwa attack coming?" he asked, some time later. Calopodius was now perched in one of the bastions his men had rebuilt after an enemy assault had overrun it—before, eventually, the Malwa had been driven off the island altogether. That had required bitter and ferocious fighting, however, which had inflicted many casualties upon the Roman defenders. His eyes had been among those casualties, ripped out by shrapnel from a mortar shell.

"After the bloody beating we gave 'em the last time?" chortled one of the soldiers who shared the bastion. "Not likely, sir!"

Calopodius tried to match the voice to a remembered face. As usual, the effort failed of its purpose. But he took the time to engage in small talk with the soldier, so as to fix the voice itself in his memory. Not for the first time, Calopodius reflected wryly on the way in which possession of vision seemed to dull all other human faculties. Since his blinding, he had found his memory growing more acute along with his hearing. A simple instinct for self-preservation, he imagined. A blind man *had* to remember better than a seeing man, since he no longer had vision to constantly jog his lazy memory.

After his chat with the soldier had gone on for a few minutes, the man cleared his throat and said diffidently: "You'd best leave here, sir, if you'll pardon me for saying so. The Malwa'll likely be starting another barrage soon." For a moment, fierce good cheer filled the man's voice: "They seem to have a particular grudge against this part of our line, seeing's how their own blood and guts make up a good part of it."

The remark produced a ripple of harsh chuckling from the other soldiers crouched in the fortifications. That bastion had been one of the most hotly contested areas when the Malwa launched their major attack the week before. Calopodius didn't doubt for a moment that when his soldiers repaired the damage to the earthen walls they had not been too fastidious about removing all the traces of the carnage.

He sniffed tentatively, detecting those traces. His olfactory sense, like his hearing, had grown more acute also.

"Must have stunk, right afterward," he commented.

The same soldier issued another harsh chuckle. "That it did, sir, that it did. Why God invented flies, the way I look at it."

Calopodius felt Luke's heavy hand on his shoulder. "Time to go, sir. There'll be a barrage coming, sure enough."

In times past, Calopodius would have resisted. But he no longer felt any need to prove his courage, and a part of him—a still wondering, eighteen-year-old part—understood that his safety had become something his own men cared about. Alive, somewhere in the rear but still on the island, Calopodius would be a source of strength for his soldiers in the event of another Malwa onslaught. Spiritual strength, if not physical; a symbol, if nothing else. But men—fighting men, perhaps, more than any others—live by such symbols.

So he allowed Luke to guide him out of the bastion and down the rough staircase which led to the trenches below. On the way, Calopodius gauged the steps with his feet.

"One of those logs is too big," he said, speaking firmly, but trying to keep any critical edge out of the words. "It's a waste, there. Better to use it for another fake cannon."

He heard Luke suppress a sigh. *And will you stop fussing like a hen?* was the content of that small sound. Calopodius suppressed a laugh. Luke, in truth, made a poor "servant."

"We've got enough," replied Luke curtly. "Twenty-odd. Do any more and the Malwa will get suspicious. We've only got three real ones left to keep up the pretense."

As they moved slowly through the trench, Calopodius considered the problem and decided that Luke was right. The pretense was probably threadbare by now, anyway. When the Malwa finally launched a full-scale amphibious assault on the island that was the centerpiece of Calopodius' diversion, they had overrun half of it before being beaten back. When the survivors returned to the main Malwa army besieging the city of Sukkur across the Indus, they would have reported to their own top commanders that several of the "cannons" with which the Romans had apparently festooned their fortified island were nothing but painted logs.

But how many? That question would still be unclear in the minds of the enemy.

Not all of them, for a certainty. When Belisarius took his main force to outflank the Malwa in the Punjab, leaving behind Calopodius and fewer than two thousand men to serve as a diversion, he had also left some of the field guns and mortars. Those pieces had savaged the Malwa attackers, when they finally grew suspicious enough to test the real strength of Calopodius' position.

"The truth is," said Luke gruffly, "it doesn't really matter anyway." Again, the heavy hand settled on Calopodius' slender shoulder, this time giving it a little squeeze of approval. "You've already done what the general asked you to, lad. Kept the Malwa confused, thinking Belisarius was still here, while he marched in secret to the northeast. Did it as well as he could have possibly hoped."

They had reached one of the covered portions of the trench, Calopodius sensed. He couldn't see the earth-covered logs which gave some protection from enemy fire, of course. But the quality of sound was a bit different within a shelter than in an open trench. That was just one of the many little auditory subtleties which Calopodius had begun noticing lately.

He had not noticed it in times past, before he lost his eyes. In the first days after Belisarius and the main army left Sukkur on their secret, forced march to outflank the Malwa in the Punjab, Calopodius had noticed very little, in truth. He had had neither the time nor the inclination to ponder the subtleties of sense perception. He had been far too excited by his new and unexpected command and by the challenge it posed.

Martial glory. The blind young man in the covered trench stopped for a moment, staring through sightless eyes at a wall of earth and timber bracing. Remembering, and wondering.

The martial glory Calopodius had sought, when he left a new wife in Constantinople, had certainly come to him. Of that, he had no doubt at all. His own soldiers thought so, and said so often enough—those who had survived—and Calopodius was quite certain that his praises would soon be spoken in the Senate.

Precious few of the Roman Empire's most illustrious families had achieved any notable feats of arms in the great war against the Malwa. Beginning with the top commander Belisarius himself, born into the lower Thracian nobility, it had been largely a war fought by men from low stations in life. Commoners, in the main. Agathius—the now-famous hero of Anatha and the Dam—had been born into a baker's family, about as menial a position as any short of outright slavery.

Other than Sittas, who was now leading Belisarius' cataphracts in the Punjab, almost no Greek noblemen had fought in the Malwa war. And even Sittas, before the Indus campaign, had spent the war commanding the garrison in Constantinople that overawed the hostile aristocracy and kept the dynasty on the throne.

Had it been worth it?

Reaching up and touching gently the emptiness which had once been his eyes, Calopodius was still not sure. Like many other young members of the nobility, he had been swept up with enthusiasm after the news came that Belisarius had shattered the Malwa in Mesopotamia. Let the adult members of the aristocracy whine and complain in their salons. The youth were burning to serve.

And serve they had . . . but only as couriers, in the beginning. It hadn't taken Calopodius long to realize that Belisarius intended to use him and his high-born fellows mainly for liaison with the haughty Persians, who were even more obsessed with nobility of bloodline than Greeks. The posts carried prestige—the couriers rode just behind Belisarius himself in formation—but little in the way of actual responsibility.

Standing in the bunker, the blind young man chuckled harshly. "He used us, you know. As cold-blooded as a reptile."

Silence, for a moment. Then, Calopodius heard Luke take a deep breath.

"Aye, lad. He did. The general will use anyone, if he feels it necessary."

Calopodius nodded. He felt no anger at the thought. He simply wanted it acknowledged.

He reached out his hand and felt the rough wall of the bunker with fingertips grown sensitive with blindness. Texture of soil, which he would never have noticed before, came like a flood of dark light. He wondered, for a moment, how his wife's breasts would feel to him, or her belly, or her thighs. Now.

He didn't imagine he would ever know, and dropped the hand. Calopodius did not expect to survive the war, now that he was blind. Not unless he used the blindness as a reason to return to Constantinople, and spent the rest of his life resting on his laurels.

The thought was unbearable. *I am only eighteen! My life should still be ahead of me!*

That thought brought a final decision. Given that his life was now forfeit, Calopodius intended to give it the full measure while it lasted.

"Menander should be arriving soon, with the supply ships."

"Yes," said Luke.

"When he arrives, I wish to speak with him."

"Yes," said Luke. The "servant" hesitated. Then: "What about?"

Again, Calopodius chuckled harshly. "Another forlorn hope." He began moving slowly through the bunker to the tunnel which led back to his headquarters. "Having lost my eyes on this island, it seems only right I should lose my life on another. Belisarius' island, this time—not the one he left behind to fool the enemy. The *real* island, not the false one."

"There was nothing *false* about this island, young man," growled Luke. "Never say it. Malwa was broken here, as surely as it was on any battlefield of Belisarius. There is the blood of Roman soldiers to prove it—along with your own eyes. Most of all—"

By some means he could not specify, Calopodius understood that Luke was gesturing angrily to the north. "Most of all, by the fact that we kept an entire Malwa army pinned here for two weeks—by your cunning and our sweat and blood—while Belisarius slipped unseen to the north. *Two weeks.* The time he needed to slide a lance into Malwa's unprotected flank—we gave him that time. *We did. You did.*"

He heard Luke's almost shuddering intake of breath. "So never speak of a 'false' island again, boy. Is a shield 'false,' and only a sword 'true'? Stupid. The general did what he needed to do—and so did you. Take pride in it, for there was nothing false in that doing."

Calopodius could not help lowering his head. "No," he whispered.

But was it worth the doing?

THE INDUS RIVER IN THE PUNJAB BELISARIUS' HEADQUARATERS THE IRON TRIANGLE

"I know I shouldn't have come, General, but—"

Calopodius groped for words to explain. He could not find any. It was impossible to explain to someone else the urgency he felt, since it would only sound . . . suicidal. Which, in truth, it almost was, at least in part.

But . . .

"May—maybe I could help you with supplies or—or something."

"No matter," stated Belisarius firmly, giving Calopodius' shoulder a squeeze. The general's large hand was very powerful. Calopodius was a little surprised by that. His admiration for Belisarius bordered on idolization, but he had never really given any thought to the general's physical characteristics. He had just been dazzled, first, by the man's reputation; then, after finally meeting him in Mesopotamia, by the relaxed humor and confidence with which he ran his staff meetings.

The large hand on his shoulder began gently leading Calopodius off the dock where Menander's ship had tied up.

"I can still count, even if—"

"Forget that," growled Belisarius. "I've got enough clerks." With a chuckle: "The quartermasters don't have that much to count, anyway. We're on very short rations here."

Again, the hand squeezed his shoulder; not with sympathy, this time, so much as assurance. "The truth is, lad, I'm delighted to see you. We're relying on telegraph up here, in this new little fortified half-island we've created, to concentrate our forces quickly enough when the Malwa launch another attack. But the telegraph's a new thing for everyone, and keeping the communications straight and orderly has turned into a mess. My command bunker is full of people shouting at cross-purposes. I need a good officer who can take charge and *organize* the damn thing."

Cheerfully: "That's you, lad! Being blind won't be a handicap at all for that work. Probably be a blessing."

Calopodius wasn't certain if the general's cheer was real, or simply assumed for the purpose of improving the morale of a badly maimed subordinate. Even as young as he was, Calopodius knew that the commander he admired was quite capable of being as calculating as he was cordial.

But . . .

Almost despite himself, he began feeling more cheerful.

"Well, there's this much," he said, trying to match the general's enthusiasm. "My tutors thought highly of my grammar and rhetoric, as I believe I mentioned once. If nothing else, I'm sure I can improve the quality of the messages."

The general laughed. The gaiety of the sound cheered up Calopodius even more than the general's earlier words. It was harder to feign laughter than words. Calopodius was not guessing about that. A blind man aged quickly, in some ways, and Calopodius had become an expert on the subject of false laughter, in the weeks since he lost his eyes.

This was real. This was—

Something he could *do.*

A future which had seemed empty began to fill with color again. Only the colors of his own imagination, of course. But Calopodius, remembering discussions on philosophy with learned scholars in far away and long ago Constantinople, wondered if reality was anything *but* images in the mind. If so, perhaps blindness was simply a matter of custom.

"Yes," he said, with reborn confidence. "I can do that."

For the first two days, the command bunker was a madhouse for Calopodius. But by the end of that time, he had managed to bring some semblance of order and procedure to the way in which telegraph messages were received and transmitted. Within a week, he had the system functioning smoothly and efficiently.

The general praised him for his work. So, too, in subtle little ways, did the twelve men under his command. Calopodius found the latter more reassuring than the former. He was still a bit uncertain whether Belisarius' approval was due, at least in part, to the general's obvious feeling of guilt that he was responsible for the young officer's blindness. Whereas the men who worked for him, veterans all, had seen enough mutilation in their lives not to care about yet another cripple. Had the young nobleman not been a blessing to them but rather a curse, they would not have let sympathy stand in the way of criticism. And the general, Calopodius was well aware, kept an ear open to the sentiments of his soldiers.

Throughout that first week, Calopodius paid little attention to the ferocious battle which was raging beyond the heavily timbered and fortified command bunker. He traveled nowhere, beyond the short distance between that bunker and the small one—not much more than a covered hole in the ground—where he and Luke had set up what passed for "living quarters." Even that route was sheltered by soil-covered timber, so the continual sound of cannon fire was muffled.

The only time Calopodius emerged into the open was for the needs of the toilet. As always in a Belisarius camp, the sanitation arrangements were strict and rigorous. The latrines were located some distance from the areas where the troops slept and ate, and no exceptions were made even for the blind and crippled. A man who could not reach the latrines under his own power would either be taken there, or, if too badly injured, would have his bedpan emptied for him.

For the first three days, Luke guided him to the latrines. Thereafter, he could make the journey himself. Slowly, true, but he used the time to ponder and crystallize his new ambition. It was the only time his mind was not preoccupied with the immediate demands of the command bunker.

Being blind, he had come to realize, did not mean the end of life. Although it did transform his dreams of fame and glory into much softer and more muted colors. But finding dreams in the course of dealing with the crude realities of a latrine, he decided, was perhaps appropriate. Life was a crude thing, after all. A project begun in confusion, fumbling with unfamiliar tools, the end never really certain until it came—and then, far more often than not, coming as awkwardly as a blind man attends to his toilet.

Shit is also manure, he came to understand. A man does what he can. If he was blind . . . he was also educated, and rich, and had every other advantage. The rough soldiers who helped him on his way had their own dreams, did they not? And their own glory, come to it. If he could not share in that glory directly, he could save it for the world.

When he explained it to the general—awkwardly, of course, and not at a time of his own choosing—Belisarius gave the project his blessing. That day, Calopodius began his history of the war against the Malwa. The next day, almost as an afterthought, he wrote the first of the *Dispatches to the Army* which would, centuries after his death, make him as famous as Livy or Polybius.

Chapter 2

AXUM
CAPITAL CITY OF THE ETHIOPIAN EMPIRE

Across the Erythrean Sea, Belisarius' wife Antonina woke to the rising sun, coming through the window in her chamber in the Ta'akha Maryam. By now, more than a year and a half since Malwa agents had blown up the royal palace of the Ethiopian kingdom of Axum, the Ta'akha Maryam's reconstruction was virtually complete.

Stubbornly, as was their way in such things, the Axumites had insisted on rebuilding the palace exactly as it had been. If the heavy stonework was still susceptible to well-placed demolitions, they would prevent such by the spears of their regiments, not the cleverness of their architects.

In the mornings, at least, Antonina was glad of it. At night, in the gloom of candlelight, she sometimes found the Ta'akha Maryam oppressively massive. But, in the daytime—especially at daybreak, with her east-facing chamber—the Ethiopian penchant for placing many windows even in outer walls was very pleasant.

The windows were massive too, admittedly, with their Christian crosses in every one to serve as supports for the heavy stone as well as reminders of the new Ethiopian faith. Still, the sunlight flooding through bathed her sleeping chamber in a golden glory that matched her mood.

Which it did, she suddenly realized. Sitting up in her bed, holding the coverings tight to ward off the chill, she pondered the fact. *Why?*

It wasn't the morning. Yes, the sunlight was splendid. On the other hand—this late in autumn, in the mile-high altitude of the Ethiopian highlands—it was also damnably cold.

She shivered a little. But that was solely a matter of the body. Her spirits remained higher than they'd been in . . .

Months. Since Eon died, leading the Axumites in their seizure of the Indian port of Chowpatty. Not only had Antonina lost one of her closest friends in that battle, but the unexpected death of the young ruler of Ethiopia—the *negusa nagast,* or "King of Kings"—had plunged the kingdom of Axum into a succession crisis. A crisis which Eon himself, as he lay dying, had appointed Antonina to solve.

She'd dreaded that task almost as much as she'd grieved Eon's death. Yet now, this morning, she felt light-hearted again. *Why?*

It was not an idle question. By now, a lot closer to the age of forty than thirty, Antonina had come to know herself very well. Her mind did not work the same way as her husband's. Belisarius was a calculator; a man who considered all the angles of a problem before deciding how he would handle it. Antonina, on the other hand, reached her conclusions through more mysterious, instinctive ways.

This was not the first time in her life she'd awakened in the morning, flush with the satisfaction of having come to a decision during her sleep. And if Belisarius sometimes shook his head wryly over the matter, Antonina remained serene in the knowledge that her way of handling such difficult business was *so* much easier than her husband's.

A servant entered, after politely coughing to announce her arrival. The woman didn't knock, for the simple reason that the Ta'akha Maryam had very few doors—and knocking on the thick walls of the entrance would be akin to rapping on a granite cliff.

"The *aqabe tsentsen* wishes an audience."

Antonina grinned. She really *was* in a good mood.

"I'll bet he didn't put it that way."

The servant rolled her eyes. "So rude, he is! No, Lady, he did not. He—ah . . ."

Antonina slid from under the thick coverings and scampered toward her wardrobe against the far wall. Her haste was not caused by any concern for keeping Ousanas waiting, it was simply due to the cold.

"He told you to roll the lazy Roman slut out of bed." Still grinning, Antonina removed her night clothes and began dressing for the day.

"Well. He didn't call you a slut. Lazy Roman, yes."

Ousanas was waiting impatiently in the salon of her suite.

"About time," he grumbled. He gave her figure a quick look, up and down. "How does it take so long to put on such simple garments? By now—almost mid-morning—I expected to see you bedecked in jewels and feathers."

Antonina turned her head and looked out a window. The sun had just barely cleared the rim of Mai Qoho, the great hill to the east of Ethiopia's capital.

"If this is 'mid-morning,' I'd love to see your definition of 'dawn.'" She moved to a nearby settee and sat down. "Oh, leave off, Ousanas. Whatever brought you here at this unfit hour, it can't be *that* urgent."

She pointed to a nearby chair. "Sit, will you?"

Ousanas sneered at the chair. Then, folded himself onto the carpet in a lotus position. Ever since he'd traveled to India with Belisarius, he claimed that awkward-looking posture was a great aid to thought—even if he'd have no truck with the ridiculous Indian notions concerning philosophy.

"That depends on how you define 'urgent.' Antonina, we *must* resolve the succession problem. Soon. Garmat's agents are telling him that the Arabs in the Hijaz are getting restive, especially in Mecca. And, especially, of course, the Quraysh tribe."

Antonina pursed her lips. "What about the Ethiopians themselves? Not to be crude about it, Ousanas, but so long as it's only the Arabs who are 'restive,' there's really not much they can do about it. Militarily speaking, at least."

"To be sure. The regiments of Axum can suppress any combination of Arabs, even with much of the army in India. But neither I nor Garmat is worried about an actual rebellion. What we *are* concerned with is the erosion of trade. Things had been going very well, in that regard, until the news of Eon's death arrived. Now . . . "

He shrugged. "All the Arab merchants and traders had thought the situation secure for them, with Eon married to a princess of the Quraysh and the succession running through his half-Arab son. But with a babe for a prince and a young girl for a widowed regent queen, they are fretting more and more that the dynasty will be overthrown by *Ethiopians*. Who will impose a new dynasty that will return the Arabs to their earlier servitude."

Antonina grimaced. "In other words, the Axumites are reasonably content with the situation but the Arabs don't believe it, and because they don't believe it there'll be more and more trouble, which will start making the Axumites angry."

The aqabe tsentsen nodded curtly. "Yes. We really can't postpone this matter, Antonina. The longer we wait, the worse it will get. We need to assure everyone that the dynasty is stable."

"More than 'stable,' " Antonina mused. "Those Arab merchants the Axumites, too, for that matter won't simply be worrying about attempts at rebellion. There's also a more insidious, long-term danger."

She rose and moved slowly toward another window. The glorious mood she'd awakened with was growing stronger by the minute. She was on the verge of making her decision; she could sense it. She thought the sight of the southern mountains would help. So majestic, they were. Serene, in their distance and their unmoving steadiness.

The problem was figuring out what the decision was in the first place. At was often the case, she'd made her decision while asleep—and now couldn't remember what it had been.

She smiled, thinking of how Belisarius had reacted so many times in the past to her habits. Peevish, the way men usually got when the workings of the world upset their childish notions.

How in the world can you make a decision without knowing what it is in the first place?

Antonina was moving slowly enough that she was able to finish her thought before reaching the window.

"There are really only two options, it would seem—neither of which will please anyone. The first option, and the simplest, would be for Rukaiya to remain unmarried. If not for the rest of her life, at least until the infant negusa nagast is old enough to take the throne and rule himself."

"Unmarried *and* chaste," Ousanas grunted. "We can't afford any royal bastards, either. Not produced by a widowed queen."

His tone skeptical, he added: "And I don't see much chance of that, being honest. Wahsi is only a few months old, and Rukaiya . . . "

"Has the normal urges of a young woman. Yes, I know."

She did know, in fact—and in considerable detail. She was not guessing based on generalities. In the time after their wedding, Rukaiya had confided in Antonina the great physical pleasure she took from being married to Eon.

"She's only eighteen. Expecting her to abstain from sex until she is in her late thirties is . . . not a gamble anyone will be pleased with. Rukaiya least of all, once her grief for Eon finally fades away. As it happens, I think she'd do it, if she agreed. She's a very strong-willed and self-disciplined person. But she wouldn't like it—and even if she restrained herself, the gossip would be endless."

"Endless—and savage," Ousanas agreed. "That would be true for any young widowed queen, even an ugly one. For one as beautiful as Rukaiya? Not a chance, Antonina. Long before Wahsi could reach an age to assume the throne, the ugly rumors would be believed by half the populace—and a much bigger portion of the kingdom's elite."

Antonina had reached the window, by now, but didn't look out of it yet. Instead, she turned to face Ousanas.

"Yes. That leaves the second option, which is no better. If she marries anyone prestigious enough to be an acceptable match, everyone will start worrying that her children by her second husband will become too powerful. A second and informal dynasty, as it were, growing up within the formal one. A recipe for civil war, a generation from now."

Ousanas nodded. "The Axumites would not accept an Arab husband, and the Arabs—though they'd have no choice, given the military realities—wouldn't like an Axumite one any better. For that matter, the *Axumites* wouldn't like it—except those who were part of the husband's clan."

He scowled at the floor's covering. "Ugly carpet. Ethiopians may know stone and iron work, but their weaving is wretched. You should get a Persian one."

His eyes widened, slightly, and he looked up. "Persian . . . You know, Antonina, that may be the solution. Find her a foreign husband of suitable rank. A Persian grandee or a Roman senator."

Antonina shook her head. "That won't work, either. A Persian husband is impossible, from Rukaiya's standpoint. Now that she's had the experience of being Eon's wife, just how well do you think she'd take to a Persian husband? With *their* attitudes?"

Ousanas went back to scowling at the carpet. "She'd have him poisoned, within a year. Or simply stab him herself. But a Roman . . . "

"No. I could probably find her a suitable Roman husband—suitable from *her* standpoint—but that wouldn't solve the political problem. Rome is now simply too strong, Ousanas. A Roman husband during Rukaiya's regency would make everyone fear—Arabs and Ethiopians alike—that Axum was becoming a Roman satrapy. In reality, if not in name."

"True." He gave her a sly little look. "Perhaps you should poison *your* husband, Antonina. It's his fault, you know. If Belisarius hadn't spent the past five years proving to everyone that Roman military power is supreme . . . even against the Malwa empire, the world's greatest . . . "

Antonina smiled back, sweetly. "Can't, I'm afraid. I'm here and he's in the Punjab. Damnation. One of the reasons I'd like to settle the succession problem is so that I can get back to him—at which point, I assure you, poisoning the fellow will be the last thought on my mind. I'm finding that my own urges haven't subsided any, even at my advanced and decrepit age."

Finally, she turned and looked out the window. "So. We need an impressive husband. Impressive to Rukaiya as much as her subjects, so she isn't tempted to stray and no one thinks otherwise. But—*but!*—one who has no preexisting ties that will make anyone worry about undue influences. And whose loyalties to Axum are unquestioned."

Far to the south, the snow-capped peaks of the Simien Mountains shone brightly, but the flanks were still dark. The sun hadn't risen high enough yet to bathe them in light.

Dark, massive, majestic beneath their crowns—and quite indifferent to any of those words. What did mountains care about attempts to depict them—much less the petty political frets and worries of humans? They simply *were*. And, being so, dwarfed any dynasty.

She understood her decision, then. It came to her, all at once, and in all its splendor.

"It's so *obvious*," she said happily. "I can't believe it took me this long to figure it out."

"Perhaps you will be so kind as to make clear this 'obvious' decision to me, at some point?" Ousanas said grumpily.

Antonina bestowed the sweet smile on the mountains. "Oh, yes. You can be sure of it, when the time comes."

PESHAWAR, IN THE HINDU KUSH

Kungas launched the final assault just before dawn. By sunrise, his Kushan soldiers had demonstrated to the Pathan clansmen that they were just as adept at fighting in the rocks as the rebels—and far more disciplined.

Not to mention numerous. Kungas had calculated—correctly, it was now clear—that the Malwa were too preoccupied with Belisarius in the southern Punjab at the moment to launch any serious attack on the new Kushan kingdom he was forging in the mountains to the northwest. So, he'd left a skeleton force guarding the passes while he took most of his army to suppress this first attempt by any Pathan tribesmen to rebel against his rule.

First—and hopefully last. For all his ruthlessness, when need be, Kungas took no pleasure in killing.

"Suppress" was a euphemism.

By late morning, the clansmen were routed and the Kushans had broken into their walled town nestled in the rocks of the mountains. Then, they began the massacre Kungas had ordered. No member of that Pathan clan would be allowed to survive. Not women, not children, not oldsters. All animals in the town were to be slaughtered also. Then, the town itself would be completely destroyed. Not simply gutted by fire, but blown up. Razed from existence. Kungas had enough gunpowder to afford that, now that the supply lines through Persia had been stabilized.

While his Kushans finished that business, Pathans from other clans allied to Kungas chased down and butchered the Pathan warriors who tried to flee into the shelter of the mountains.

There weren't many of those. Pathans could be as stupid as any humans alive, but they never lacked courage. All but a handful of the defeated clansmen died in the town, desperately trying to defend their kinfolk.

By mid-afternoon, it was done. The entire clan had ceased to exist.

Throughout, Kungas remained at his position high on a nearby mountain—a spur of the same range, really—watching.

Throughout, there was no expression on his face. None at all. To the Pathan chieftains who stood there with him, the leaders of the allied clans, it did not even seem like a face at all. Just an unmoving, iron mask.

Those old men had been told that, in his palace in Peshawar, the new king of the mountains was known to show an expression, now and then. Not often, and usually only in the presence of his Greek wife.

That was possible, they thought, although they had their doubts. It was hard to imagine that inhuman mask of a face ever showing an emotion.

Still . . .

Maybe. The woman was known to be a sorceress, after all.

What the clan chieftains *knew*, however, was that with a king like this and his witch of a queen, rebellion was insane.

Any form of open resistance. The destroyed clan hadn't even rebelled. They'd simply thought to use the old and well-tested method of intimidating a new would-be ruler of the mountains by assassinating one of his officials.

The official had, indeed, been assassinated.

In return, Kungas had now proved that he was, indeed, the king of the mountains. The arithmetic of the equation was clear even to those illiterate clan leaders.

Clans assassinated officials.

Kings—real ones—assassinated clans.

So be it. The old men, no strangers to brutality themselves, chose to look on the bright side. The new king did not meddle with them much, after all, as long as they obeyed him. And trade was picking up a lot. Even the clans in the far mountains were getting richer.

When Kungas returned to Peshawar, he was in a very foul mood.

"That was a filthy business," he told his wife Irene. Scowling openly, now, in the privacy of their quarters in the palace. "It's your fault. If you hadn't stirred up those idiot clansmen letting their young women claim to be Sarmatians and join your idiot so-called 'queen's guard,' it wouldn't have happened."

The accusation was grossly unfair, and on many counts, but Irene kept silent. Until Kungas' mood lightened, there was no point arguing with him.

Yes, it was true that Irene's subtle undermining of Pathan patri-archalism irritated the clan chiefs. So what? *Everything* irritated those barbaric old men. They were to "conservative thinking" what an ocean was to "wet and salty." They practically defined the term.

And, again, so what? Irene and Kungas—with Belisarius, in times past, while they'd still been with him in Persia—had discussed the matter thoroughly. No one had ever ruled these moun-tains, in the sense that "ruled" meant in the civilized lowlands. Just as no one had ever "ruled" the great steppes to the north into which she and Kungas planned to expand their kingdom.

But if a king couldn't rule the mountains and the steppes, he could *dominate* them. Dominate them as thoroughly and as com-pletely as, in a future era in another universe, the Mongol khans would dominate them.

There was one key difference, though, and Kungas understood it as well as she did. The new Kushan realm in central Asia would use the same methods as the Mongols, true enough. Methods which, in the end, amounted to the simple principle: *oppose us and we will slaughter all of you, down to the babes and dogs.*

But it did not have the same goal. In the future of that different universe, Genghis Khan and his successors had had no other pur-pose than simply to enjoy the largesse of their rule which came with the annual tribute. Kungas and Irene, on the other hand, intended to forge a real nation here in central Asia, over time. And that could not be done simply by dominating the ancient clans. The domination was itself but a means to an end—and the end was to undermine them completely, in the only way the human race had ever found it possible to do so.

"Civilization," in a word. Create a center of attraction in the new cities and towns, with their expanding wealth and trade and education and culture and opportunities for individuals from anywhere. And then just let the old clan chiefs rot away, while their clans slowly dissolved around them. Irene's "Sarmatian women's guard" that Kungas had just denounced was only one of a hundred methods that she and Kungas were using for that purpose.

It was not even the one that irritated the clan chiefs the most. That honor probably belonged to the new Buddhist monasteries that Kungas was starting to set up all over. In the end, for all their savage attitudes toward women, the old clan chiefs didn't really care what women did—as long as they did it outside their tightly controlled villages.

Why should they? From their viewpoint, beyond the sexual pleasure they provided, women were simply domestic animals and beasts of burden. No different, really, from their other livestock. As long as they had enough women to keep breeding clansmen, who cared what wild women did somewhere else?

Boys, on the other hand, *mattered*. And now—curse him!—the new king was seducing boys away from their proper and traditional allegiances to babble mystical nonsense in monasteries. Even teaching them to read, as if any Pathan tribesman ever needed such an effeminate skill.

The process would take decades, of course, even generations. But it would work, as surely as the sunrise—provided that Kungas established from the beginning that however much the clan chiefs hated him they did not dare to oppose him openly. Or try any violent tactic against him, whatsoever.

Which he had just done. More efficiently, ruthlessly, pitilessly, and savagely than any of the clan chiefs had ever imagined he would. Just as, in a different universe, the Mongols had obliterated the cult of the Hashasin which had given the world the term "assassin" to begin with—by demonstrating that they were perfectly willing to transform the definition of the word by an order of magnitude.

Yet . . .

Irene knew her husband very well, by now. Kungas enjoyed her intelligence and her sense of humor, but this was no time for rational argument, much less jests.

She fell back on an emotional appeal that was even more power-ful than horror and disgust and anger.

"There's this, if it helps. The dynasty is secured."

She looked down, stroking the silk raiment covering her belly. She was still, to all appearances, as slender as ever. "Well. Most likely. I might have a miscarriage."

His eyes were drawn to her waist, and she could sense Kungas' mood shifting. So, smiling gently, she ventured a little joke.

"Of course, you'll make that good, soon enough."

For a moment, Kungas tried to maintain his ferocious mood. "Typical! Salacious Greek women. Seductresses, every one of you. If you weren't so beautiful . . . "

In point of fact, Irene wasn't beautiful at all. Attractive, perhaps, but no more than that. Her thick and luxurious chestnut hair was not even much of an asset, any longer, tied back as she now had it in a pony tail. And she'd found, to her disgruntlement, that becoming a queen hadn't made her big nose any smaller or made her narrow, close-eyed face any fuller. Even with the ponytail, she still looked like exactly what she was—an intellectual, not a cour-tesan.

Happily, none of that mattered to Kungas. Her little joke wasn't really even that. By the end of the evening, most likely—tomorrow night, at the latest—Kungas would demonstrate that there wasn't any danger that the new dynasty would die out from lack of vigor.

Kungas sighed. "It really was a hateful business, Irene. Damn those old men! I would have preferred . . . "

He let the thought trail away. Then, gave her something in the way of an apologetic shrug.

In point of fact, it had been Irene who suggested that he restrict himself to simply executing all of the clan chiefs—and Kungas who had declined the suggestion.

"No," he'd said. "That won't be enough. However stupid and vicious, no clan chief is a coward. They'll accept their own deaths, readily enough, as stubborn as they are. The only thing that will really terrify them is the extinction of their entire clan. So I have no choice but to demonstrate that I'm quite willing to do so. Maybe if I do it once, right now, I'll never have to do it again."

He'd been right, and Irene had known it. She'd only advanced her suggestion because she knew how much Kungas detested the alternative. As hard a man as he was, and as hard a life as he'd led, not even Kungas could butcher babies to punish octogenarians without shrieking somewhere in his iron-masked soul.

Finally, she could sense the mood breaking. The surest sign came when Kungas made his own jest.

"And who's the father, by the way?"

Irene's eyes narrowed. "Don't be stupid. As often as you mount me, when would I have the time to cuckold you? Even assuming I wasn't too exhausted, you insensate brute."

Kungas was still scowling. In his own way, he could teach stubbornness to clan chiefs.

"Not that," he said curtly, waving the notion aside with an economical little gesture. "I don't doubt my cock's the only one that gets into you. But it's just a conduit. Spiritually speaking. Who's the *real* father? Have we moved up to gods, yet? Will I discover as an old man that the children I thought mine were actually sired by Zeus and who knows how many randy members of the Hindu pantheon?"

"What a heathen notion!" Irene exclaimed. "You should be ashamed of yourself!"

"I'm not a Christian," he pointed out.

"You're not really a Buddhist, either, even if you insist on the trappings. So what? It's still a barbarous notion."

She drew herself up with as much dignity as she could manage. That was . . . hard, given that she was almost laughing.

"And it's all nonsense, anyway. Of course, you're the *father*. The ancestry gets interesting, though."

His first smile came, finally. "More interesting than Alexander the Great? Whom—to my immense surprise—you have explained was one of my forefathers. Odd, really, given that he passed through this area long before we Kushans got here."

"My scholars assure me it is true, nonetheless. But now, they tell me, it seems that in addition—"

"Please! Don't tell me I'm descended from Ashoka also!"

Irene *had* considered Ashoka, in fact, and quite seriously. But, in the end, she'd decided that claiming India's most famous and revered emperor as one of her husband's forefathers would probably cause too many political problems. India's ever-suspicious rulers would assume that meant the Kushans had designs on India also.

Which, they didn't. To meddle in India's affairs—even the Punjab, much less the great and populous Gangetic plain—would be pure folly. As long as she and Kungas controlled the Khyber Pass and the Hindu Kush, they could expand to the north without stirring up animosities with either the Indians or the Persians. Animosities, at least, that would be severe enough to lead to war. Soon enough, of course, Persians and Indians—and Romans and Chinese too, for that matter—would be complaining bitterly about Kushan control of the trade routes through central Asia.

But those quarrels could be negotiated. Irene was an excellent negotiator—even without the advantage of having a husband who could terrify Pathan clan chiefs.

"Nonsense," she said firmly. "You're no relation to Ashoka at all, so far as my scholars can determine. Just as well, really, since we have no ambitions toward India. However—what a happy coincidence, given the centrality of Buddhism to our plans—would you believe that—"

Kungas choked. Irene pressed on.

"It's true!" she insisted. "Not the Buddha *himself*, of course. After he became the Buddha, that is. He was quite the ascetic sage, you know. But *before* that—when he was still just plain Siddhartha Gautama and was married to Yashodhara. It turns out that their son Rahula—"

Kungas burst into laughter, and Irene knew that she'd saved his soul again. That was always her greatest fear, that a soul which had shelled itself in iron for so long would eventually become iron itself.

The mask, the world could afford. Even needed. But if the soul beneath the mask ever became iron, in fact, she dreaded the consequences. If so, in the new universe they were helping to shape, the name "Kungas" would someday become a term like "Tamerlane" had been in another. A name that signified nothing but savagery.

No fear of that, so long as she could make Kungas laugh that way. No fear at all.

THE IRON TRIANGLE

As always, the sound of Luke's footsteps awakened Calopodius. This time, though, as he emerged from sleep, he sensed that other men were shuffling their feet in the background.

He was puzzled, a bit. Few visitors came to the bunker where he and Luke had set up their quarters. Calopodius suspected that was because men felt uncomfortable in the presence of a blind man, especially one as young as himself. It was certainly not due to lack of space. The general had provided him with a very roomy bunker, connected by a short tunnel to the great command bunker buried near the small city that had emerged over the past months toward the southern tip of the Iron Triangle. The Roman army called that city "the Anvil," taking the name from the Punjabi civilians who made up most of its inhabitants.

"Who's there, Luke?" he asked.

His aide-de-camp barked a laugh. "A bunch of boys seeking fame and glory, lad. The general sent them."

The shuffling feet came nearer. "Begging your pardon, sir, but we were wondering—as he says, the general sent us to talk to you—" The man, whoever he was, lapsed into an awkward silence.

Calopodius sat up on his pallet. "Speak up, then. And who are you?"

The man cleared his throat. "Name's Abelard, sir. Abelard of Antioch. I'm the hecatontarch in charge of the westernmost bastion at the fortress of—"

"You had hot fighting yesterday," interrupted Calopodius. "I heard about it. The general told me the Malwa probe was much fiercer than usual."

"Came at us like demons, sir," said another voice. Proudly: "But we bloodied 'em good."

Calopodius understood at once. The hecatontarch cleared his throat, but Calopodius spoke before the man was forced into embarrassment.

"I'll want to hear all the details!" he exclaimed. "Just give me a moment to get dressed and summon my scribe. We can do it all right here, at the table there. I'll make sure it goes into the next dispatch."

"Thank you, sir," said Abelard. His voice took on a slightly aggrieved tone. "T'isn't true, what Luke says. It's neither the fame nor the glory of it. It's just . . . your *Dispatches* get read to the Senate, sir. Each and every one, by the Emperor himself. And then the Emperor—by express command—has them printed and posted all over the Empire."

Calopodius was moving around, feeling for his clothing. "True enough," he said cheerfully. "Ever since the old Emperor set up the new printing press in the Great Palace, everybody—every village, anyway—can get a copy of something."

"It's our families, sir," said the other voice. "They'll see our names and know we're all right. Except for those who died in the fighting. But at least . . ."

Calopodius understood. "Their names will exist somewhere, on something other than a tombstone."

Chapter 3

THE EUPHRATES

Autumn, 533 A.D.

They had approached Elafonisos from the south, because Calopodius had thought Anna might enjoy the sight of the great ridge which overlooked the harbor, with its tower perched atop it like a hawk. And she had seemed to enjoy it well enough, although, as he was coming to recognize, she took most of her pleasure from the sea itself. As did he, for that matter.

She even smiled, once or twice.

The trip across to the island, however, was the high point of the expedition. Their overnight stay in the small tavern in the port had been . . . almost unpleasant. Anna had not objected to the dinginess of the provincial tavern, nor had she complained about the poor fare offered for their evening meal. But she had retreated into an even more distant silence—almost sullen and hostile—as soon as they set foot on land.

That night, as always since the night of their wedding, she performed her duties without resistance. But also with as much energy and enthusiasm as she might have given to reading a particularly dull piece of hagiography. Calopodius found it all quite frustrating, the more so since his wife's naked body was something which aroused him greatly. As he had suspected in the days before the marriage, his wife was quite lovely once she could be seen. And felt.

So he performed his own duty in a perfunctory manner. After-ward, in another time, he might have spent the occasion idly con-sidering the qualities he would look for in a courtesan—now that he had a wife against whose tedium he could measure the problem. But he had already decided to join Belisarius' expedition to the Indus. So, before falling asleep, his thoughts were entirely given over to matters of martial glory. And, of course, the fears and uncertainties which any man his age would feel on the eve of plunging into the maelstrom of war.

When trouble finally arrived, it was Anna's husband who saved her. The knowledge only increased her fury.

Stupid, really, and some part of her mind understood it perfectly well. But she still couldn't stop hating him.

Stupid. The men on the barge who were clambering eagerly onto the small pier where her own little river craft was tied up were making no attempt to hide their leers. Eight of them there were, their half-clad bodies sweaty from the toil of working their clumsy vessel up the Euphrates.

A little desperately, Anna looked about. She saw nothing beyond the Euphrates itself; reed marshes on the other bank, and a desert on her own. There was not a town or a village in sight. She had stopped at this little pier simply because the two sailors she had hired to carry her down to Charax had insisted they needed to take on fresh water. There was a well here, which was the only reason for the pier's existence. After taking a taste of the muddy water of the Euphrates, Anna couldn't find herself in dis-agreement.

She wished, now, that she'd insisted on continuing. Not that her insistence would have probably done much good. The sailors had been civil enough, since she'd employed them at a small town in the headwaters of the Euphrates. But they were obviously not overawed by a nineteen-year-old girl, even if she did come from the famous family of the Melisseni.

She glanced appealingly at the sailors, still working the well. They avoided her gaze, acting as if they hadn't even noticed the men climbing out of the barge. Both sailors were rather elderly, and it was clear enough they had no intention of getting into a fracas with eight rivermen much younger than themselves—all of whom were carrying knives, to boot.

The men from the barge were close to her, and beginning to spread out. One of them was fingering the knife in a scabbard attached to his waist. All of them were smiling in a manner which even a sheltered young noblewoman understood was predatory.

Now in sheer desperation, her eyes moved to the only other men on the pier. Three soldiers, judging from their weapons and gear. They had already been on the pier when Anna's boat drew up, and their presence had almost been enough to cause the sailors to pass by entirely. A rather vicious-looking trio, they were. Two Isaurians and a third one whom Anna thought was probably an Arab. Isaurians were not much better than barbarians; Arabs might or might not be, depending on where they came from. Anna suspected this one was an outright bedouin.

The soldiers were lounging in the shade of a small pavilion they had erected. For a moment, as she had when she first caught sight of them, Anna found herself wondering how they had gotten there in the first place. They had no boat, nor any horses or camels—yet they possessed too much in the way of goods in sacks to have lugged them on their own shoulders. Not through this arid country, with their armor and weapons. She decided they had probably traveled with a caravan, and then parted company for some reason.

But this was no time for idle speculation. The rivermen were very close now. The soldiers returned Anna's beseeching eyes with nothing more than indifference. It was clear enough they had no more intention of intervening than her own sailors.

Still—they *could*, in a way that two elderly sailors couldn't.

Pay them.

Moving as quickly as she could in her elaborate clothing—and cursing herself silently, again, for having been so stupid as to make this insane journey without giving a thought to her apparel—Anna walked over to them. She could only hope they understood Greek. She knew no other language.

"I need help," she hissed.

The soldier in the center of the little group, one of the Isaurians, glanced at the eight rivermen and chuckled.

"I'd say so. You'll be lucky if they don't kill you after they rob and rape you."

His Greek was fluent, if heavily accented. As he proceeded to demonstrate further. "Stupid noblewoman. Brains like a chicken.

Are you some kind of idiot, traveling alone down this part of Mesopotamia? The difference between a riverman here and a pirate—"

He turned his head and spit casually over the leg of the other
Isaurian. His brother, judging from the close resemblance.

"I'll pay you," she said.

The two brothers exchanged glances. The one on the side, who
seemed to be the younger one, shrugged. "We can use her boat
to take us out of Mesopotamia. Beats walking, and the chance
of another caravan . . . But nothing fancy," he muttered. "We're
almost home."

His older brother grunted agreement and turned his head to
look at the Arab. The Arab's shrug expressed the same tepid enthusiasm. "Nothing fancy," he echoed. "It's too hot."

The Isaurian in the middle lazed to his feet. He wasn't much
taller than Anna, but his stocky and muscular build made him
seem to loom over her.

"All right. Here's the way it is. You give us half your money
and whatever other valuables you've got." He tapped the jeweled
necklace around her throat. "The rivermen can take the rest of it.
They'll settle for that, just to avoid a brawl."

She almost wailed. Not quite. "I *can't*. I need the money to
get to—"

The soldier scowled. "Idiot! We'll keep them from taking your
boat, we'll leave you enough—just enough—to get back to your
family, and we'll escort you into Anatolia."

He glanced again at the rivermen. They were standing some
few yards away, hesitant now. "You've no business here, girl,"
he growled quietly. "Just be thankful you'll get out of this with
your life."

His brother had gotten to his feet also. He snorted sarcastically.
"Not to mention keeping your precious hymen intact. That ought
to be worth a lot, once you get back to your family."

The fury which had filled Anna for months boiled to the surface.
"I don't *have* a hymen," she snarled. "My husband did for that,
the bastard, before he went off to war."

Now the Arab was on his feet. Hearing her words, he laughed
aloud. "God save us! An abandoned little wife, no less."

The rivermen were beginning to get surly, judging from the
scowls which had replaced the previous leers. One of them barked
something in a language which Anna didn't recognize. One of the

Aramaic dialects, probably. The Isaurian who seemed to be the leader of the three soldiers gave them another glance and an idle little wave of his hand. The gesture more or less indicated: *relax, relax—you'll get a cut.*

That done, his eyes came back to Anna. "Idiot," he repeated. The word was spoken with no heat, just lazy derision. "Think you're the first woman got abandoned by a husband looking to make his fortune in war?"

"He already *has* a fortune," hissed Anna. "He went looking for fame. Found it too, damn him."

The Arab laughed again. "Fame, is it? Maybe in your circles! And what is the name of this paragon of martial virtue? Anthony the Illustrious Courier?"

The other three soldiers shared in the little laugh. For a moment, Anna was distracted by the oddity of such flowery phrases coming out of the mouth of a common soldier. She remembered, vaguely, that her husband had once told her of the poetic prowess of Arabs. But she had paid little attention, at the time, and the memory simply heightened her anger.

"He *is* famous," Anna insisted. A certain innate honesty forced her to add: "At least in Constantinople, after Belisarius' letter was read to the Senate. And his own dispatches."

The name *Belisarius* brought a sudden little stillness to the group of soldiers. The Isaurian leader's eyes narrowed.

"Belisarius? What's the general got to do with your husband?"

"And what's his name?" added the Arab.

Anna tightened her jaws. "Calopodius. Calopodius Saronites."

The stillness turned into frozen rigidity. All three soldiers' eyes were now almost slits.

The Isaurian leader drew a deep breath. "Are you trying to tell us that you are the wife of *Calopodius the Blind*?"

For a moment, a spike of anguish drove through the anger. She didn't really understand where it came from. Calopodius had always seemed blind to her, in his own way. But . . .

Her own deep breath was a shaky thing. "They say he is blind now, yes. Belisarius' letter to the Senate said so. *He* says it himself, in fact, in his letters. I—I guess it's true. I haven't seen him in many months. When he left . . ."

One of the rivermen began to say something, in a surly tone of voice. The gaze which the Isaurian now turned on him was nothing casual. It was a flat, flat gaze. As cold as a snake's and just as deadly. Even a girl as sheltered as Anna had been all her life understood the sheer physical menace in it. The rivermen all seemed to shuffle back a step or two.

He turned his eyes back to Anna. The same cold and flat gleam was in them. "If you are lying . . . "

"Why would I lie?" she demanded angrily. "And how do you expect me to prove it, anyway?"

Belatedly, a thought came to her. "Unless . . . " She glanced at the little sailing craft which had brought her here, still piled high with her belongings. "If you can *read* Greek, I have several of his letters to me."

The Arab sighed softly. "As you say, why would you lie?" His dark eyes examined her face carefully. "God help us. You really don't even understand, do you?"

She shook her head, confused. "Understand what? Do you know him yourself?"

The Isaurian leader's sigh was a more heartfelt thing. "No, lass, we didn't. We were so rich, after Charax, that we left the general's service. We—" he gestured at his brother "—I'm Illus, by the way, and he's Cottomenes—had more than enough to buy us a big farm back home. And Abdul decided to go in with us."

"I'm sick of the desert," muttered the Arab. "Sick of camels, too. Never did like the damn beasts."

The Arab was of the same height as the two Isaurian brothers—about average—but much less stocky in his frame. Still, in his light half-armor and with a spatha scabbarded to his waist, he seemed no less deadly.

"Come to think of it," he added, almost idly, "I'm sick of thieves, too."

The violence that erupted shocked Anna more than anything in her life. She collapsed in a squat, gripping her knees with shaking hands, almost moaning with fear.

There had been no sign; nothing, at least, that she had seen. The Isaurian leader simply drew his spatha—so quick, so quick!—took three peculiar little half steps and cleaved the skull of one of the rivermen before the man even had time to do more than widen his eyes. A second or two later, the same spatha tore open another's throat. In the same amount of time, his brother and the Arab gutted two other rivermen.

Then—

She closed her eyes. The four surviving rivermen were desperately trying to reach their barge. From the sounds—clear enough, even to a young woman who had never seen a man killed before—they weren't going to make it. Not even close. The sounds, wetly horrid, were those of a pack of wolves in a sheep pen.

Some time later, she heard the Isaurian's voice. "Open your eyes, girl. It's over."

She opened her eyes. Catching sight of the pool of blood soaking into the planks of the pier, she averted her gaze. Her eyes fell on the two sailors, cowering behind the well. She almost giggled, the sight was so ridiculous.

The Isaurian must have followed her gaze, because he began chuckling himself. "Silly looking, aren't they? As if they could hide behind that little well."

He raised his voice. "Don't be stupid! If nothing else, we need you to sail the boat. Besides—" He gestured at the barge. "You'll want to loot it, if there's anything in that tub worth looting. We'll burn whatever's left."

He reached down a hand. Anna took it and came shakily to her feet.

Bodies everywhere. She started to close her eyes again.

"Get used to it, girl," the Isaurian said harshly. "You'll see plenty more of that where you're going. Especially if you make it to the island."

Her head felt muzzy. "Island? What island?"

"*The* island, idiot. 'The Iron Triangle,' they call it. Where your husband is, along with the general. Right in the mouth of the Malwa."

"I didn't know it was an island," she said softly. Again, honesty surfaced. "I'm not really even sure where it is, except somewhere in India."

The Arab had come up in time to hear her last words. He was wiping his blade clean with a piece of cloth. "God save us." He half-chuckled. "It's not really an island. Not exactly. But it'll do, seeing as how the general's facing about a hundred thousand Malwa."

He studied her for a moment, while he finished wiping the blood off the sword. Then, sighed again. "Let's hope you learn *something,* by the time we get to Charax. After that, you'll be on your own again. At least—"

He gave the Isaurian an odd little look. The Isaurian shrugged. "We were just telling ourselves yesterday how stupid we'd been, missing out on the loot of Malwa itself. What the hell, we may as well take her the whole way."

His brother was now there. "Hell, yes!" he boomed. He bestowed on Anna a very cheerful grin. "I assume you'll recommend us to the general? Not that we deserted or anything, but I'd *really* prefer a better assignment this time than being on the front lines. A bit dicey, that, when the general's running the show. Not that he isn't the shrewdest bastard in the world, mind you, but he *does* insist on fighting."

The other two soldiers seemed to share in the humor. Anna didn't really understand it, but for the first time since she'd heard the name of Calopodius—spoken by her father, when he announced to her an unwanted and unforeseen marriage—she didn't find it hateful.

Rather the opposite, in fact. She didn't know much about the military—nothing, really—but she suspected . . .

"I imagine my husband needs a bodyguard," she said hesitantly. "A bigger one than whatever he has," she added hastily. "And he's certainly rich enough to pay for it."

"Done," said the Isaurian leader instantly. "Done!"

Not long afterward, as their ship sailed down the river, Anna looked back. The barge was burning fiercely now. By the time the fire burned out, there would be nothing left but a hulk carrying what was left of a not-very-valuable cargo and eight charred skeletons.

The Isaurian leader—Illus—misunderstood her frown. "Don't worry about it, girl. In this part of Mesopotamia, no one will care what happened to the bastards."

She shook her head. "I'm not worrying about *that*. It's just—"

She fell silent. There was no way to explain, and one glance at Illus' face was enough to tell her that he'd never understand.

Calopodius hadn't, after all.

"So why the frown?"

She shrugged. "Never mind. I'm not used to violence, I guess."

That seemed to satisfy him, to Anna's relief. Under the circumstances, she could hardly explain to her rescuers how much she hated her husband. Much less why, since she didn't really understand it that well herself.

Still, she wondered. Something important had happened on that pier, something unforeseen, and she was not too consumed by her own anger not to understand that much. For the first time in her life, a husband had done something other than crush her like an insect.

She studied the surrounding countryside. So bleak and dangerous, compared to the luxurious surroundings in which she had spent her entire life. She found herself wondering what Calopodius had thought when he first saw it. Wondered what he had thought, and felt, the first time he saw blood spreading like a pool. Wondered if he had been terrified, when he first went into a battle.

Wondered what he thought now, and felt, with his face a mangled ruin.

Another odd pang of anguish came to her, then. Calopodius had been a handsome boy, even if she had taken no pleasure in the fact.

The Isaurian's voice came again, interrupting her musings. "Weird world, it is. What a woman will go through to find her husband."

She felt another flare of anger. But there was no way to explain; in truth, she could not have found the words herself. So all she said was: "Yes."

The next day, as they sailed back to the mainland, he informed Anna of his decision. And for the first time since he met the girl, she came to life. All distance and ennui vanished, replaced by a cold and spiteful fury which completely astonished him. She did not say much, but what she said was as venomous as a serpent's bite.

Why? he wondered. He would have thought, coming from a family whose fame derived from ancient exploits more than modern wealth, she would have been pleased.

He tried to discover the source of her anger. But after her initial spate of hostile words, Anna fell silent and refused to answer any of his questions. Soon enough, he gave up the attempt. It was not as if, after all, he had ever really expected any intimacy in his marriage. For that, if he survived the war, he would find a courtesan.

Chapter 4

THE IRON TRIANGLE, IN THE PUNJAB
Winter, 533 A.D.

"You can describe it better than that," rasped Justinian. The former Emperor of the Roman Empire was now its Grand Justiciar, since his blinding at the hands of traitors and Malwa agents had made him ineligible for the throne under Roman law. But he'd lost very little of his peremptory habits.

No reason he should, really. Although Belisarius' son Photius was officially the new Emperor, Justinian's wife Theodora was the Empress Regent and the real power in Constantinople. Still, it was exasperating for the premier general of the Roman empire to be addressed like an errant schoolboy. Tightening his jaws a bit, Belisarius brought the telescope back to his eye.

"At an estimate—best I can do, since they haven't finished it yet—the tower will be at least three hundred feet tall. From the looks of the—"

"Never mind, never mind," interrupted Justinian. "It doesn't really matter. With a tower that tall, they're obviously planning for general AM broadcasting."

The former emperor's badly scarred eye sockets were riveted on the distant Malwa tower, as if he could still see. Or glare.

"In God's name, *why*?" he demanded. "For military purposes, directional broadcasting would make a lot more sense and require a lot less massive construction. That's what we're doing."

Justinian waved a hand toward the south, where the Roman army was erecting its own "antenna farm" almost at the very tip of the triangle of land formed by the junction of the Indus and Chenab rivers.

Only the tips of the antennas could be seen from the fortifications on the north side of the Iron Triangle. The Roman radios were designed to be directional, not broadcast, so there was no need for an enormous tower. The key for directional radio was mostly the length of the antennas, not their height.

Folding up the telescope, Belisarius shrugged. "Maybe for the same reason we're having Antonina and Ousanas build exactly such a tower in Axum. It'll give us general relaying capability we wouldn't have otherwise."

"That's nonsense," Justinian grumbled. "I could understand them building a tower like that in their capital city of Kausambi. But why build one *here,* on the front lines? We're not, after all."

Belisarius said nothing.

After an uncomfortable moment, Justinian chuckled harshly. "Fine, fine. Presumably they don't have quite our motivation. At least, I think it's safe to assume that monster from the future doesn't have a peevish wife like I do."

Belisarius smiled crookedly. Although they had never discussed it quite openly, both he and Justinian knew perfectly well—and knew each other knew—that one of the main reasons they'd tacitly agreed not to build a general AM tower in the Iron Triangle was so that the Empress Regent could not easily bombard them with instructions.

More easily bombard them, it might be better to say. As it was, just using the telegraph, Theodora averaged at least two messages a day to the Iron Triangle.

One of which, almost every day, was either a peremptory demand that Justinian stop playing soldier and get back to a position of safety far to the south in Barbaricum, or a pleading request for the same, or a threat of dire consequences if he didn't—or, often enough, all three rolled into one.

"Is there something we're overlooking?" Justinian demanded.

The question wasn't aimed at Belisarius so much as it was at the "jewel" that hung in a pouch suspended from the Roman general's muscular neck. Inside that pouch rested Aide, the crystalline being from the future who had come back into the human past to thwart—hopefully—the intervention of the so-called "new gods" of the future.

Aide's response came only into Belisarius' mind. **No,** the crystal being said, rather curtly. **We're not overlooking anything. Tell that nasty old man to stop being so paranoid. And tell him to stop being so nasty, while you're at it.**

Since Justinian couldn't see the expression, Belisarius grinned openly. Outside of himself, Justinian was the only human being who regularly communicated with Aide via direct contact with the jewel. Most people found direct contact with Aide rather unsettling. The jewel's means of communication typically involved a flood of images—many of them quite disturbing—not simply words, which could be easily sanitized in the mind of the recipient.

Justinian probably found it unsettling also. Belisarius certainly did, often enough. But if the former emperor was "nasty" and "paranoid"—terms which Belisarius would allow were fair enough, even if "old" was a bit off the mark—he was also just about as tough-minded as any human being who'd ever lived. So he seemed to tolerate the problem well enough—and, on the other hand, got the benefit of the direct contact with Aide that had enabled Justinian, in a very short time, to become the Roman Empire's master artisan.

Or designer for artisans, it might be better to say. Blind as he was, it was difficult for Justinian to do the work himself.

Although Aide tolerated that extensive contact for the sake of their mutual project, he didn't like it at all. He didn't like Justinian.

And why should he, really? Most people didn't like Justinian.

His peeve apparently satisfied by the remarks, Aide added uncertainly: **I don't really know why they're doing it. But I'm sure it's not some clever trick we're missing.**

Belisarius gave Aide the mental equivalent of a nod. Then, said to Justinian: "Aide doesn't think so, although he doesn't know why they're doing it. What I think is that—"

"Oh, it's obvious enough," interrupted Justinian, as if he hadn't been the one to demand an answer in the first place. "Morale, that's all."

Again, he waved toward the south. "That mass of wires we've got stuck all over down there is just something that annoys the soldiers. We've even had to position guards to keep the silly bastards from stumbling over them in the dark. Especially when they're drunk on the local beer. As many defeats as the Malwa have suffered these past few years, that monster Link has got to be worried about morale. A great big impressive-looking radio tower will help boost its soldiers' spirits, even if it isn't really that useful. Especially *those* soldiers. Ignorant and illiterate peasants, most of them."

Again, Belisarius grinned. "Ignorant and illiterate peasants" was a fair description of most of the Malwa army, true enough. On the other hand, it could be applied to most Roman soldiers also. Over time, the changes Aide had brought to the world would produce a rapid increase in the general level of literacy—was already doing so, in fact, among many of the Empire's youngsters. The ones living in big cities, at least. But, even five years after Aide's arrival, very little of that had penetrated the Roman soldiery. It was still true that, below the rank of hecatontarch, not more than one in ten of them could read and write. For that matter, a hefty percentage of the empire's officer corps was illiterate also, beyond—in most cases—being able to painfully write out their own name.

So be it. Wars were fought with the armies available. Whatever weaknesses and limitations the Roman army possessed, Belisarius knew it was far superior to that of the enemy. Man for man, certainly, on average. The Roman Empire, whatever its many flaws and failures, was still a society in which a determined and capable man could rise based on his own merits. The Malwa, on the other hand, with their rigid adherence to a caste system, had to rely primarily on the sheer mass of the army that northern India's teeming population could produce.

That had been, from the very beginning of the war, the basic equation Belisarius had had to deal with: using quality against quantity, in such a way as to eventually defeat the Malwa without ever giving them the chance to use their immense strength against him in a way that was effective.

It had worked, so far—but it took time. Time, and patience.

Alas, patience was not a virtue often associated with Justinian, as he proved an hour later, once they entered the sunken bunker behind the front lines that served Belisarius for his headquarters.

"So how much longer are you going to dilly-dally?" he asked, after taking a chair.

Belisarius decided to try the tactic of misunderstanding. "About the submarine?" He harrumphed very sternly, almost majestically. "*Forever*, Justinian—so you can just forget about trying to cajole me—"

He didn't think the tactic would work. Sure enough:

"Stop playing the fool. I don't even disagree with you about the submarine—as you know perfectly well. I just think it'd be an interesting experiment, that's all. I'm talking about the offensive against the Malwa that you keep postponing and postponing. I'm beginning to think you've converted to that heathen Hindu way of looking at things. All time is cyclical and moves in great yugas, so why bother doing anything for the next billion years or so? Or is it that you think the way your soldiers are copulating with the local natives, you'll have a huge population of your own within a generation or two?"

The former emperor sneered. "Idiot. The population density here is already horrible. You'll be facing starvation soon enough, you watch."

Belisarius tried to keep from scowling, but . . . couldn't, quite. Given that the Romans controlled the Indus south of the Iron Triangle and their Persian allies were rapidly bringing agricultural production in the Sind back up to normal, he wasn't really worried about running out of food. Still, rations were tight, and . . .

He sighed, audibly. There wasn't much point trying to keep anything from Justinian, as smart as he was. "It's a problem, I admit. Not the food, just the endless headaches. I'm beginning to think—"

"Forget it! I'm the Grand Justiciar of the *Roman* Empire. There's no way I'll let you wheedle me into adjudicating the endless squabbles you're having with the damn natives here. Bunch of heathens, anyway."

"Actually, they're not," said Belisarius mildly. "A good portion of them, at least. You'd be surprised how many are converting to Christianity."

Justinian's eye sockets were too badly scarred for him to manage the feat of widening them with surprise. Perhaps thankfully, since they were horrible-enough looking as it was. Justinian, naturally, refused to cover them with anything.

Calopodius did the same, but in his case that was simply a young man's determination to accept adversity squarely. In Justinian's, it was the ingrained, arrogant habit of an emperor. What did he care if people flinched from his appearance? They'd done so often enough when he'd still been sighted. More often, probably. Justinian had never been famous for his forbearance.

"It's true," Belisarius insisted. "Converting in droves. By now, the priests tell me, at least a fourth of the Punjabis in the Triangle have adopted our faith."

Justinian's head swiveled toward the bunker's entry, as if he could look out at the terrain beyond. Out and up, actually, since the bunker was buried well beneath the soil.

"Why, do you think?"

"It might be better to say, why not?" Belisarius nodded toward the entrance. "Those are all peasants out there, Justinian. Low caste and non-Malwa. It's not as if the Malwa Empire's mahaveda brand of Hinduism ever gave them anything."

Justinian was almost scowling. He didn't like being puzzled. "Yes, yes, I can see that. But I'd still think they'd be afraid . . ."

His voice trailed off.

Belisarius chuckled harshly. "Be afraid of what? That the Malwa will slaughter them if they overrun the Triangle? They will *anyway*, just as an object lesson—and those Punjabi peasants know it perfectly well. So they're apparently deciding to adhere to Rome as closely as possible."

Still looking at the heavily timbered entrance to the bunker, Belisarius added: "It's going to be a bit of a political problem, in fact, assuming we win the war."

He didn't need to elaborate. Emperor he might no longer be, but Justinian still thought like one—and he'd been perhaps the most intelligent emperor in Rome's long history.

"Ha!" he barked. "Yes, I can see that. If a fourth have already converted, then by the time"—his scowl returned briefly—"you finally launch your long-delayed offensive and we hammer the Malwa bastards—"

"I'm glad *you're* so confident of the matter."

"Don't be stupid!" Justinian snapped impatiently. "Of course you will. And when you do—as I was saying before I was interrupted—probably two-thirds of them will be Christians. So what does that leave for Khusrau, except a headache? Don't forget that you *did* promise him the lower Punjab as Persian territory."

Belisarius shrugged. "I didn't 'promise' the Emperor of Iran anything. I admit, I did indicate I'd be favorable to the idea—mostly to keep him from getting too ambitious and wanting to gobble all of the Punjab. That would just lead to an endless three-way conflict between the Persians, the Kushans and the Rajputs."

"You'd get that anyway. You want my advice?"

Naturally, Justinian didn't wait for an answer before giving it. "*Keep* the Iron Triangle. Make it a Roman enclave. It'd be a good idea, anyway, because we could serve as a buffer between the Persians, the Kushans and the Rajputs—and now we could justify it on religious grounds."

He made an attempt to infuse the last phrase with some heartfelt piety. A very slight attempt—and even that failed.

Belisarius scratched his chin. "I'd been thinking about it," he admitted. "Kungas won't care."

"*Care?* He'd be delighted! I never would have thought those barbarous Kushans would be as smart as they are. But, they are that smart. At least, they're smart enough to listen to Irene Macrembolitissa, and *she's* that smart."

In point of fact, while Belisarius knew that the king of the Kushans listened carefully to the advice of his Greek wife, Kungas made his own decisions. He was quite smart enough on his own to figure out that getting his new Kushan kingdom embroiled in endless conflicts with Persians and Rajputs over who controlled the Punjab would just weaken him. A Roman buffer state planted in the middle of the Punjab would tend to keep conflicts down—or, at least, keep the Kushans out of it.

"The Rajputs . . . "

"Who cares what they think?" demanded Justinian. "All of this is a moot point, I remind you, until and unless you finally get your much-delayed offensive underway—at which time the Rajputs will be a beaten people, and beaten people take what they can get."

That was Justinian's old thinking at work. Shrewd enough, within its limits. But if nothing else, the years Belisarius had spent with Aide's immense knowledge of human history in his mind had made him highly skeptical of imperialism. He'd been able to scan enormous vistas of human experience, not only into the future of this planet but on a multitude of other planets as well. Out of that, when it came to the subject of empires, Belisarius had distilled two simple pieces of wisdom:

First, every empire that ever existed or would exist always thought it was the end-all and be-all.

Second, none of them were. Few of them lasted more than two hundred years, and even the ones that did never went more than a couple of centuries without a civil war or other major internal conflict. The human race just naturally seemed to do better if it avoided too much in the way of political self-aggrandizement. The notion that history could be "guided"—even by someone like Belisarius, with Aide to serve as his adviser—was pure nonsense. Better to just set up something workable, that contained as few conflicts as possible, and let human potential continue to unfold within it. If the underlying society was healthy, the political structure tended to sort itself out well enough to fit whatever the circumstances were.

In short, not to his surprise, Belisarius had come to conclude that the ambitions and schemes of his great enemy Link and the "new gods" who had created the monster were simply the same old imperial folly writ large. Belisarius didn't really know exactly what *he* believed in. But he knew what he didn't—and that was good enough.

"Agreed, then," he said abruptly. "We'll plan on keeping the Triangle. Who knows? Khusrau might even be smart enough to see that it's in his benefit, too."

"Might be," grunted Justinian skeptically. "I doubt it, though. Don't forget he's an emperor. Wearing the purple automatically makes a man stupider."

The scarred, savaged face grinned. "Take my word for it. I *know*."

Their conversation was interrupted by a particularly loud ripple in the never-ceasing exchange of barrages between the Romans and the Malwa. Some of the enemy shells even landed close enough to make the bunker tremble.

Not much. But enough to bring Justinian's scowl back.

"I'm getting tired of that. When in the name of all that's holy are you going to stop lolling about and start the offensive?"

Belisarius didn't bother to answer.

When the time is right, came Aide's voice. Then, a bit plaintively: **Which is when, by the way? I'd like to know myself.**

Et tu, Aide? The answer is that I don't know. When it feels right. Which it doesn't yet. Things have to keep brewing for a while, in the Hindu Kush—and most of all, in Majarashtra.

You don't have any way to get in touch with Rao by radio, Aide pointed out. **Or Kungas, for that matter.**

Teach your grandfather to suck eggs! I know I don't. What's worse still, is that even if I did have radio contact with India, I couldn't talk to the three men who matter the most.

There was silence for a moment, as Aide tried to follow Belisarius' train of thought. For all his immense intellect, Aide had little of the Roman general's intuitive sense of strategy.

Oh, he said finally. **Narses the eunuch.**

Yes. And Rana Sanga. And, most of all, Lord Damodara.

There was a moment's silence, again. Then Aide added, somewhat timidly: **You probably better not mention to Justinian—certainly not Theodora!—that you're stalling the offensive because you're counting on a Roman traitor and the two best generals on the enemy side.**

Teach your grandfather to suck eggs!

Chapter 5

BHARAKUCCHA, ON INDIA'S WEST COAST

"It must be unnerving," Ajatasutra said chuckling.

"*What* must be unnerving?" asked Narses irritably. "And why do you keep thinking such pointless chatter will help you win?" The old eunuch moved his bishop, taking the assassin's knight. "Check. It distracts you more than it does me. That's partly why you lose, nine games out of ten. The other part is because I'm smarter than you."

Ajatasutra didn't even glance at the chess board. His thin smile was still directed at Narses. "It must be unnerving to have Rana Sanga watching you the way he does, whenever you're in sight. Reminds me of a tiger, trying to decide if you're prey."

Narses' lips tightened, slightly. "He doesn't *know* anything. He only suspects."

"Just as I said. Trying to decide whether you're prey."

That was enough to make Narses scowl, although he still didn't look up from the board. "Why? Until he's sure he knows the truth, he won't do anything. He'd be too afraid to. And once he does discover the truth, why would he . . . "

His voice trailed off. Even Narses couldn't help but wince a little.

Ajatasutra chuckled again. "I will say you love playing with danger, old man. I'd never gamble at the odds you do. Yes, there's

493

the chance that the fiercest warrior of Rajputana—not to mention its greatest king—might forgive you once he finds out that his wife and children, whom he thought murdered by bandits, are alive and well. Then again—"

Ajatasutra cleared his throat. "He might be a bit peeved at the man who had them kidnapped in the first place and faked the murders."

Narses pointed to the chessboard. "*Check,* I said."

Smiling, Ajatasutra moved up a pawn to block the bishop. "Granted, you had them hidden in a safe place afterward. Even in a comfortable place. Granted, also, that the Malwa had ordered you to have them *actually* murdered, so looking at it from one angle you saved their lives. But, then again, that brings up the next problem. What will Lord Damodara—Malwa's best general and a blood relative of the emperor—"

"*Distant* relative," Narses growled.

"Not distant at all," the assassin pointed out mildly, "if your scheme works. And stop trying to change the subject. What will Damodara think when he discovers you corralled *his* wife into the kidnapping? And thereby put *his* children in mortal danger?"

Narses took the pawn with the bishop. "Mate in four moves. I didn't *corral* the woman into providing Sanga's family with a hideaway. That was Lady Damodara's idea in the first place."

"So? When all the rocks are turned over and your machinations exposed to the light of day, the fact remains that Damodara and Rana Sanga will discover that you manipulated and cajoled their wives into the riskiest conspiracy imaginable—and, unfortunately for you, both men dote on those wives."

Casually, Ajatasutra reached out and toppled his king. "I concede. So when the wives bat their eyelashes at their husbands and look demure—like only Indian women can do!—and insist that they were pawns in your hands, which way you do you think the lightning will strike?"

Finally, Narses looked up. His eyes were half-slits; which, as wrinkled as his face was anyway, made the eunuch look more like a reptile than usual. "And why are *you* so amused? I remind you that—every step of the way—it was *you* who did the actual work."

"True. Another game?" The assassin began setting up the pieces again. "But I'm in prime physical condition, and I made sure I've got the fastest horse in Bharakuccha. You aren't, and you didn't.

That mule you favor probably couldn't outrun an ox, much less Rajput cavalry."

"I like mules." The board now set up—Narses playing the white pieces, this time—the eunuch advanced his queen's pawn. "And I've got no intention of running anyway, no matter how the lightning strikes."

The assassin cocked his head. "No? Why not?"

Narses looked aside, staring at a blank wall in the chambers he shared with Ajatasutra. All the walls in the palace suite were blank, except for those in the assassin's bedroom. The old eunuch liked it that way. He claimed that useless decorations impeded careful thought.

"Hard to explain. Call it my debt to Theodora, if you will."

Ajatasutra's eyebrows lifted. Although his gaze never left the wall, Narses sensed his puzzlement. "I betrayed her, you know, for the sake of gaining an empire."

"Yes, I was there. And?"

"And so now that I'm doing it again—"

"You're not betraying *her*."

Narses waved his hand impatiently. "I'm not betraying my current employers, either. But I'm still gambling everything on the same game. The greatest game there is. The game of thrones."

The assassin waited. Sooner or later, the explanation would come. For all the eunuch's acerbic ways, Ajatasutra had become something of a son to him.

It took perhaps three minutes, during which time Narses' eyes never left the blank wall.

"You can't cheat forever," he said finally. "I'll win or I'll lose, but I won't run again. I owe that much to Theodora."

Ajatasutra looked at the same wall. There still wasn't anything there.

"I've been with you too long. That actually almost makes sense."

Narses smiled. "Don't forget to keep feeding your horse."

KAUSAMBI, THE MALWA CAPITAL AT THE CONFLUENCE OF THE GANGES AND YAMUNA RIVERS

Less than a week after his thirteenth birthday, Rajiv knew the worst despair and the two greatest epiphanies of his short life. One coming right after the other.

Gasping for breath, he lowered himself onto a stool in one of the cellars beneath Lady Damodara's palace. He could barely keep the wooden sword in his hand, his grip was so weak.

"I'll never match my father," he whispered, despairingly.

"Don't be an idiot," came the harsh voice of his trainer, the man he called the Mongoose. "Of course, you won't. A man as powerful as Rana Sanga doesn't come to a nation or tribe more than once a century."

"*Listen* to him, Rajiv," said his mother. She had watched this training session, as she had watched all of them, from her stool in a corner. With, as always, the stool surrounded by baskets into which she placed the prepared onions. Cutting onions relaxed the woman, for reasons no one else had ever been able to determine.

The epiphany came, then.

"*You* couldn't match him, either."

The narrow, weasel face of the Mongoose twisted with humor. "Of course I couldn't! Never thought to try—except, like a damn fool, at the very end."

Casually—not a trace of weakness in *that* grip—the Mongoose leaned his own imitation sword against a wall of the cellar. Then, with the same lean right hand, reached up and parted his coarse black hair. The scar beneath was quite visible. "Got that for trying."

Rajiv was as disturbed as he was exhilarated by his new-found wisdom. "I should stop . . . "

Almost angrily, his mother snapped: "Yes! Stop trying to imitate your father!" She pointed to the Mongoose with the short knife she used to cut onions. "Learn from *him*."

She went back to cutting onions. "You're not big enough. Never will be. Not so tall, not so strong. Maybe as fast, maybe not." The onion seemed to fly apart in her hand. "So what?"

Again, the knife, pointing like a finger. "Neither is he. But the Mongoose is still a legend."

The man so named chuckled. Harshly, as he did most things. "My name is Valentinian, and I'm just a soldier of Rome. I leave legends to those who believe in them. What I *know*, boy, is this. Learn from me instead of resisting me, and you'll soon enough gain your own fame. You're very good, actually. Especially for one so young."

Valentinian took the wooden sword back in his hand. "And now, you've rested enough. Back at it. And remember, this time—*small* strokes. Stop trying to fight as if you were a king of Rajputana. Fight like a miser hoarding his coins. Fight like me."

It was difficult. But Rajiv thought he made some progress, by the end of the session. He was finally beginning to understand—really understand—what made the Mongoose so dangerous. No wasted effort, no flamboyance, nothing beyond the bare minimum needed. But *that*—done perfectly.

The session finally over, the second epiphany came.

Rajiv stared at his mother. She was almost the opposite of his father. Where Rana Sanga was tall and mighty, she was short and plump. Where the father was still black-haired and handsome—had been, at least, until the Mongoose scarred his face in their famous duel—the mother was gray-haired and plain.

But he saw her. For the first time, really. As always, the baskets were now full—those to her right, of the prepared onions; those to her left, of the discarded peelings.

"This is how you cut onions."

"My boy too," she said calmly. "Yes. This is how I cut onions. And men are easier to cut than onions. If you don't think like a fool."

"Listen to your mother," said the Mongoose.

Later, in the evening, in the chamber they all used as a central salon, Valentinian complained with the same words. "Listen to your mother, you little brat!"

Baji gaped up at him cheerfully, in the manner of infants the world over. He said something more-or-less like: "Goo." Whatever the word meant, it was clearly not an indication that the infant intended to obey his mother's instructions to stop pestering the Roman soldier. In fact, Baji was tugging even more insistently on his sleeve.

"What does he want, anyway?" Valentinian demanded.

"*Goo*," Baji explained.

Dhruva laughed. "You spoil him, Valentinian! That's why he won't pay attention to me." She rose from her stool and came over to pluck her infant son out of Valentinian's lap.

Baji started wailing instantly.

"Spoil him, I say."

Perched on his own stool in the chamber, and looking much like a rhinoceros on the small item of furniture, Anastasius started laughing. The sound came out of his huge chest like so many rumbles.

Valentinian glared at his fellow Roman cataphract. "What's so damn funny?"

"Do you really need to ask?"

Lady Damodara came into the room. After taking in the scene, she smiled.

Valentinian transferred his glare to her. "You realize we're almost certainly doomed? All of us." He pointed a stiff finger at Baji, who was still wailing. "If we're lucky, they'll cut the brat's throat first."

"Valentinian!" Dhruva exclaimed. "You'll scare him!"

"No such luck," the Roman cataphract muttered. "Might shut him up. But the brat doesn't understand a word I'm saying."

He glared at Lady Damodara again. "Doomed," he repeated.

She shrugged. "There's a good chance, yes. But it's still a better chance than my husband would have had—and me and the children—if we'd done nothing. Either you Romans would have killed him because he wasn't a good enough general, or the Emperor of Malwa would have killed him because he was. This way there's at least a chance. A pretty good one, I think."

Valentinian wasn't mollified. "Narses and his damned schemes. If I survive this, remind me to cut his throat." As piously as he could, he added: "He's under a death sentence in Rome, you know. The rotten traitor. Just be doing my duty."

Anastasius had never quite stopped rumbling little laughs. Now, the rumbles picked up their pace. "Should have thought of that sooner!"

There was no answer to that, of course. So Valentinian went back to glaring at the infant.

"And besides," Lady Damodara said, still smiling, "this way we have some entertainment. Dhruva, let your child go."

As pleasantly as the words were said, Lady Damodara was one of the great noblewomen of the Malwa empire. More closely related to the emperor, in fact, than her husband. So, whatever her misgivings, Dhruva obeyed.

Set back on the floor, Baji immediately began crawling toward Valentinian.

"Goo!" he said happily.

Still later, in the chamber they shared as a bedroom, Anastasius started rumbling again.

Not laughs, though. Worse. Philosophical musings.

"You know, Valentinian, if you'd stop being annoyed by these minor problems—"

"I kind of like the brat, actually," Valentinian admitted. He was lying on his bed, his hands clasped behind his head, staring at the ceiling.

"It'd be better to say you dote on the little creature." Anastasius chuckled. "But that's not even a minor problem. I was talking about the other things. You know—the danger of being discovered—hiding out the way we are here in their own capital city—swarmed by hordes of Ye-tai barbarians and other Malwa soldiers, flayed and impaled and God knows what else by mahami-mamsa torturers. Those problems."

Valentinian lifted his head. "You call those *minor* problems?"

"Philosophically speaking, yes."

"I *don't* want to hear—"

"Oh, stop whining." Anastasius sat up on his bed across the chamber and spread his huge hands. "If you refuse to consider the ontology of the situation, at least consider the practical aspect."

"What in God's name are you talking about?"

"It's obvious. One of two things happens. We fall prey to a minor problem, in which case we're flayed and impaled and gutted and God knows what else—but, for sure, we're dead. Follow me so far?"

Valentinian lowered his head, grunting. "An idiot can follow you so far. What's the point?"

"Or we *don't* fall prey to a minor problem. In which case, we survive the war. And *then* what? That's the real problem—the major problem—because that's the one that takes real thinking and years to solve."

Valentinian grunted again. "We retire on a pension, what else? If the general's still alive, he'll give us a good bonus, too. Enough for each of us to set up on a farm somewhere in . . . "

"In *Thrace?*" Anastasius rumbled another laugh. "Not even you, Valentinian! Much less me, half-Greek like I am and given to higher thoughts. Do you really want to spend the rest of your life raising pigs?"

Silence came from the other bed.

"What's so fascinating about that ceiling, anyway?" One of the huge hands waved about the chamber. "Look at the *rest* of it. We're in the servant quarters—the *old* servant quarters, in the rear of the palace—and it's still fancier than the house of the richest peasant in Thrace."

"So?"

"So why settle for a hut when we can retire to something like this?"

Anastasius watched Valentinian carefully, now. Saw how the eyes never left the ceiling, and the whipcord chest rose and fell with each breath.

"All right," Valentinian said finally. "All right. I've thought about it. But . . ."

"Why not? Who better than us? You know how these Hindus will look at it. The ones from a suitable class, anyway. The girls were rescued from a brothel. Nobody knows who the toddler's father is. Hopelessly polluted, both of them. The kid, too."

Valentinian scowled, at the last sentence.

More cheerfully still, seeing that scowl, Anastasius continued. "But we're just Thracian soldiers. What do we care about that crap? And—more to the point—who better for a father-in-law than the peshwa of Andhra?"

Valentinian's scowl only seemed to deepen. "What makes you think *he'd* be willing? The way they look at things, we're about as polluted as the girls."

"Exactly! That's what I meant, when I said you had to consider the ontological aspects of the matter. More to the point, consider this: who's going to insult the girls—or the kid—with him for a father and us for the husbands?"

Anastasius waited, serenely. It didn't take more than a minute or so before Valentinian's scowl faded away and, in its place, came the smile that had terrified so many men over the years. That lean, utterly murderous, weasel grin.

"Not too many. And they'll be dead. Right quick."

"You see?"

As easily and quickly as he could when he wanted to, Valentinian was sitting up straight. "All right. We'll do it."

Anastasius cocked his head a little. "Any problems with the philosophy of the matter?"

"What the hell does that—"

"The kid's a bastard and the girl's a former whore with a face scarred by a pimp. If any of that's a problem for you, I'll take her and you can have the other sister, Lata."

Valentinian hissed. "You stay the hell away from Dhruva."

"Guess not," said Anastasius placidly. "We have a deal. See how easy it is, when you apply philosophical reasoning?"

Chapter 6

THE NARMADA RIVER, IN THE NORTHERN DECCAN

Lord Damodara reined in his horse and sat a little straighter in the saddle. Then, casually, swiveled his head back and forth as if he were working out the kinks in his neck. The gesture would seem natural enough, to anyone watching. They'd been riding along the Narmada river for hours, watching carefully for any sign of a Maratha ambush.

In fact, his neck *was* stiff, and the movement was pleasant. But the real reason Damodara did it was to make sure that no one else was within hearing range.

They weren't. Not even the twenty Rajputs serving as his immediate bodyguard, who were now halting their mounts also, and certainly not the thousand or so cavalrymen who followed them. More to the point, the three Mahaveda priests whom Nanda Lal had instructed to accompany Damodara today were at least a hundred yards back. When the patrol started, the priests had ridden just behind Damodara and Sanga. But the long ride—it was now early afternoon—had wearied them. They were not Rajput cavalrymen, accustomed to spending days in the saddle.

"Tell me, Rana Sanga," he said quietly.

The Rajput king sitting on a horse next to him frowned. "Tell you what, Lord? If you refer to the possibility of a Maratha ambush, there is none. I predicted as much before we even left Bharakuccha. Rao is playing a waiting game. As I would, in his position."

The Malwa general rubbed his neck. "I'm not talking about that, and you know it. I told you this morning that I knew perfectly well this patrol was a waste of time and effort. I ordered it—as you know perfectly well—to keep Nanda Lal from pestering me. Again."

Sanga smiled, thinly. "Nice to be away from him, isn't it?" He reached down and stroked his mount. As long as his arm was, that was an easy gesture. "I admit I prefer the company of horses to spymasters, myself."

Damodara would have chuckled, except the sight of that long and very powerful arm stroking a Rajput horse brought home certain realities. About Rajputs, and their horses—and the Malwa dynasty, and its spymasters.

"It is *time*, Sanga," he said, quietly but forcefully. "Tell me."

The Rajput kept stroking the horse, frowning again. "Lord, I don't . . . "

"You know what I'm talking about. I've raised it before, several times." Damodara sighed. "Perhaps a bit too subtly, I admit."

That brought a flicker of a smile to the Rajput's stern face. After a moment, Sanga sighed himself.

"You want to know why I have not seemed to be grieving much, these past months." The flickering smile came and went again. "And my references to philosophical consolations no longer satisfy you."

"Meaning no offense, King of Rajputana, but you are about as philosophically inclined as a tiger." Damodara snorted. "It might be better to say, have a tiger's philosophy. And you are *not* acting like a tiger. Certainly not an enraged one."

Sanga said nothing. Still stroking the horse, his eyes ranged across the Vindhya mountains that paralleled the river on its northern side. As if he were looking for any signs of ambush.

"Luckily," Damodara continued, "I don't think Nanda Lal suspects anything. He doesn't know you well enough. But I do—and I need to know. I . . . cannot wait, much longer. It is becoming too dangerous for me. I can sense it."

The Rajput king's face still had no expression beyond that thoughtful frown, but Damodara was quite certain he understood. Sanga kept as great a distance as possible from the inner workings

of the Malwa empire, beyond its military affairs. But he was no
fool; and, a king himself, he knew the realities of political maneuver. He was also one of the very few people, outside of the Malwa
dynasty, who had communed directly with Malwa's hidden master.
Or mistress, if one took the outer shell for what it was.

"I do not think my family is dead," Sanga said finally, speaking
very softly. "I am not certain, but . . ."

Damodara closed his eyes. "As I suspected."

He almost added: *as I feared*. But did not, because Rana Sanga
had become as close to him as Damodara had ever let a man
become, and he would not wish that terrible grief on the Rajput.

Even if, most likely, that absence of grief meant that Damodara
would soon enough be grieving the loss of his own family.

"Narses," he murmured, almost hissing the word. He opened
his eyes. "Yes?"

Sanga nodded. "I am not certain, you understand. But . . . yes,
Lord. I think Narses spirited them away. Then faked the evidence
of the massacre."

Damodara scowled. "Faked *some* of the evidence, you mean.
There were plenty of dead Ye-tai on the scene."

Sanga shrugged. "How else would Narses fake something? He
is as dangerous as a cobra. A very old and wise cobra."

"So he is," agreed Damodara. "I've often thought that employing
him was as perilous a business as using a cobra for a guard in my
own chambers."

Again, he rubbed his neck. "On the other hand, I need such a
guard. I think."

"Oh, yes. You do." Sanga left off his pointless scrutiny of the
Vindhyas and twisted his head to the west, looking toward Bhara-
kuccha. "You're far more likely to be ambushed back there, by
Nanda Lal, than you are here by Raghunath Rao."

Since Damodara had long ago come to that same conclusion,
he said nothing. No need to, really. There were no longer many
secrets between him and Rana Sanga. They had campaigned
together across central Asia and into Mesopotamia, winning every
battle along the way, even against Belisarius. And had still lost the
campaign, not through any fault of theirs but because Malwa had
failed them.

In the upside-down world of the Malwa empire, his accomplish-
ments placed him in greater peril than defeat would have done.

Malwa feared excellent generals, in many ways, more than it did bad ones.

"We will return to Bharakuccha," Damodara announced. "This patrol is pointless, and I'd just as soon reach the city before nightfall."

Sanga nodded. He started to rein his horse around, but paused. "Lord. Remember. I swore an oath."

After Sanga was gone, Damodara stared sourly at the river. *Rajputs and their damned sacred oaths.*

But the thought came more from habit, than anything else. Damodara knew how to circumvent the oath that the Rajputs had given to the emperor of Malwa, swearing their eternal fealty. He'd figured it out long ago—and hadn't need any of Narses' hints to do so.

The thing was quite obvious, really, if a man was prepared to gamble everything on a single daring maneuver. The problem was that, military tactics aside, Damodara was by nature a cautious and conservative man.

Damn Narses!

That thought, too, after a moment, Damodara dismissed as simply old habit. True enough, the Roman eunuch was maneuvering Damodara, and doing so ruthlessly—and entirely for Narses' own purposes. The fact remained that he was probably wiser in doing so, than Damodara had been in hesitating. Could you curse a man who manipulated you in your own best interests?

Of course, you could—and Damodara did it again. *Damn Narses!*

But . . . Malwa remained. Malwa and its secret ruler. The greatest, the most powerful—and certainly the most venomous—cobra in the world. Next to which, even Narses was a small menace.

So, finally, on a dirt road next to the Narmada river, Malwa's greatest general made the decision that had been long years in the making.

Many things went into that decision.

First, that he knew himself to be caught in a trap, if he did nothing. If Malwa won the war, it was Damodara's assessment that he himself would be eliminated as too dangerously capable. Most likely, however—another assessment, and one that he was growing ever more sure about—the war would *not* be won. In which case, Damodara would join in the general destruction of the dynasty.

Second, his fears for his family. Either of those two outcomes—certainly the first—would result in their destruction also. In the event of a Roman victory, Damodara did not think that the victors would target his family. But that meant nothing. In the chaos of a collapsing Malwa empire, rebellions were sure to erupt all over India—and all of them would be murderous toward anyone associated with the Malwa dynasty. The likelihood that Damodara's wife and children would survive that carnage was almost nil.

Third, and finally—and in some ways, most of all—Damodara was sick and tired of Malwa's secret overlord. Looking back over the years of his life, he could see now that the superhuman intelligence from the future was . . .

An idiot. A beast and a monster, too. But most of all, just an arrogant, blithering, drooling idiot.

Damodara remembered the one conversation he'd had with Belisarius, and the Roman general's musings on the folly of seeking perfection. He'd thought, at the time, that he agreed with the Roman. Now, he was certain of it.

So, he came to his decision.

Damn all new gods and their schemes.

He might have added: *Damn Malwa.* But, given his future prospects—if he had any—that would be quite absurd. From this moment forward, Damodara and his family would only survive insofar as he *was* Malwa.

He spent the rest of the ride back to the city convincing himself of that notion. It was not easy. The inner core of Damodara that had kept him sane since he was a boy was laughing at himself all the way.

Once the patrol returned to Bharakuccha, just after sunset, Damodara went immediately to Narses' chambers. The Malwa general made no attempt to hide his movements. Nanda Lal would surely have spies watching him, but so what? Damodara regularly consulted with Narses, and always did so openly. To have begun creeping about would raise suspicions.

"Yes, Lord?" Narses asked, after politely ushering Damodara into the inner chamber where they always discussed their affairs. In that chamber—for a certainty—Nanda Lal's spies could overhear nothing. "Some wine? Food?"

The old eunuch indicated a nearby chair, the most luxurious in the chamber. "Please, be seated."

Damodara ignored him. He was carefully studying the third man in the room, the hawk-faced assassin named Ajatasutra who had been Narses' chief associate since the failure of the Nika revolt in Constantinople.

"Do I want to ask him to leave, Narses?" Damodara asked abruptly.

The question brought a sudden stillness to the room. Along with a tightness to Narses' expression, and—perhaps oddly—a little smile to the face of the assassin.

Damodara waited. And waited.

Finally, Narses replied. "No, Lord, I think not. Ajatasutra can answer all your questions. Better than I can, actually, because . . ."

"He's been there. Yes." Damodara's eyes had never left the assassin. "My next question. Do I *need* to ask him to leave?"

For the first time since he entered the room, he glanced at Narses. "Or would it be wiser for me to summon Rana Sanga? For my protection."

Seeing Narses' little wince, Damodara issued a curt little laugh. "Not looking forward to that, are you? I thought not." He turned his gaze back to the assassin. "Well, then. Perhaps three other Rajputs."

Ajatasutra's thin smile widened. "Unless one of them is Jaimal or Udai, I'd recommend four. Five would be wiser. However . . ."

Gracefully, Ajatasutra slid off his chair. Then, to the Malwa general's surprise, went down on one knee. From nowhere, a dagger appeared. Flipped easily and now held by the tip, Ajatasutra laid the blade across his extended left forearm, offering the weapon's hilt to Damodara.

"There is no need for Rajputs, Lord of Malwa." There was not a trace of humor in the assassin's tone of voice, and the smile was gone. "This blade is at your service. I have served Malwa faithfully since I was a boy. Never more so than now."

Damodara studied the man, for a moment. A quick decision was needed here.

He made it. Then, reached out and barely touched the dagger hilt with the tip of his fingers.

"Keep the weapon. And now, Ajatasutra, tell me of my family. And Rana Sanga's."

Narses was fidgeting a bit. Smiling as thinly as the assassin had done, Damodara murmured to him: "I shall stand, I think. But perhaps you should be seated. Have some food. Some wine. Now that the assassin's blade is sworn to me, it may be your last meal."

Ajatasutra barked a laugh. "Ha! Like cutting an old crocodile's neck. Take me an hour, afterward, to sharpen the edge properly."

Narses scowled at him. But he took a seat—and some wine. No food. Perhaps his appetite was missing.

By the time the assassin had finished his report, and answered all of Damodara's questions, the Malwa general was seated on the luxurious chair. Seated on it, his neck perched against the backrest, and staring at the ceiling.

"Guarded by the Mongoose, no less," he murmured. "The arms trainer for a Rajput prince, no less. Narses, were this a fable told to me by a story-teller, I should have him discharged for incompetence."

Wisely, Narses said nothing.

Damodara rubbed his face with a hand. Once, both the hand and the face had been pudgy. Two years of campaigning had removed most of the general's fat. Along with much else.

"The moment I move, my family—Sanga's too, once they're discovered—are as good as dead. May I presume that among all these other incredibly intricate schemes, you have given *some* thought to that problem?"

There was little visible sign of it, but Damodara could sense Narses relaxing. As well he might. That last question made clear that he'd survive this night.

"Quite a bit more than 'some.' First—meaning no offense, Lord—it is not true that 'the moment you move' anything will happen. Kausambi is hundreds of miles and a mountain range away from here. Great Lady Sati and the main Malwa army are in the Punjab, still farther than that."

"Telegraph," Damodara stated. "And, now, the new radio."

"Seven of the nine telegraph operators in Bharakuccha are mine. In the event the eighth or ninth are on duty, I have men ready to cut the wires. I'd rather not, of course. That would itself be a signal that something is amiss. They wouldn't assume rebellion, simply Maratha marauders. But a patrol would be sent out to investigate."

Damodara waved his hand impatiently. "I have Rajputs to deal with patrols. But I, also, would rather not have the little problem."

Narses glanced at Ajatasutra.

"All I need is to know the day," the assassin said calmly. "Not even that. A three-day stretch will do. Nanda Lal will be suspicious regarding the unfortunate deaths, of course, but won't have time to do anything about it."

Damodara nodded. "I can manage the three days. That still leaves the radio."

Narses smiled. "The radio station is guarded by Ye-tai. A special detachment—chosen by Toramana and under his direct authority."

Damodara brought his gaze down from the ceiling. "Toramana . . ." he mused. "Despite his upcoming marriage to Rana Sanga's half-sister Indira, can we really trust him?"

"Trust him?" Narses shrugged. "No, of course not. Toramana's only real loyalty is to his own ambition. But we can trust *that*."

Damodara frowned. "Why are you so certain his ambition will lead him to us? Nanda Lal is just as aware of the implications of Toramana's marriage to a Rajput princess as we are. Yet he seems completely confident in Toramana's loyalty. Even to the point of insisting that I place Toramana in charge of the city's security, whenever I leave Bharakuccha."

"Lord . . ." Narses hesitated. "Forgive me, but you are still too much the Malwa."

"Meaning?"

"Meaning that you are still a bit infected—pardon me for the term—with that unthinking Malwa arrogance. Your dynasty has been in power too long, too easily, and with . . ."

The eunuch let the sentence trail off. For an instant, his eyes seemed to move, as if he had started to glance at Ajatasutra and stopped himself.

Damodara understood the significance of that little twitch of the eyes. Narses, other than Rana Sanga and Belisarius, was the only human being not a member of the Malwa dynastic family who had had direct contact with Link, the cybernetic organism who was the Malwa empire's secret overlord and provided the dynasty with its ultimate source of power.

And—yes, its ultimate source of arrogance.

Damodara pondered Narses' words, for a moment. Then, decided the eunuch was probably right. It would be fittingly ironic if a dynasty raised and kept in power by a superhuman intelligence should fall, in the end, because that same power made the dynasty itself stupid.

Not stupid, perhaps, so much as unseeing. Nanda Lal, for instance, was extremely intelligent. But he had been so powerful, and so feared, and for so long, that he had grown blind to the fact that there was other power—and that not all men feared him.

"What are Toramana's terms?" he asked abruptly. "And do not irritate me by pretending you haven't already discussed it with him. Your life is still hanging by a thread, Narses."

"Nothing complicated. A high position for himself, of course. Acceptance of his ties to the Rajputs through his upcoming marriage. Beyond that, while he does not expect the Ye-tai to continue to enjoy the same special privileges, he wants some guarantees that they will not be savaged."

Damodara cocked his head. "I shouldn't think he'd care about that, if he's solely driven by his own ambitions."

Narses looked uncomfortable, for a moment. "Lord, I doubt if there is any man who is *solely* driven by ambition." His lips grew twisted. "Not even me."

Ajatasutra spoke. "Toramana still has his clan ties, Lord. They wear lightly on him, true, but they exist. Beyond that . . . "

The assassin lifted his shoulders, in a movement too slight to be really considered a shrug. "If the Ye-tai are singled out for destruction, how long could a single Ye-tai general remain in favor? No matter what his formal post."

"True." Damodara thought about the problem, for a time. The chamber was silent while he did so.

"All right," he said finally. "It would be ridiculous to say that I'm happy with your plan. But . . . it seems as good as any. That leaves Rao, and his Marathas."

Now that the discussion had returned to the matter of war, a subject on which Damodara was an expert, the Malwa general sat up straight.

"Three things are needed. First, I need to extract the army from Bharakuccha. It's one thing for me to begin the rebellion—"

"Please, Lord!" Narses interrupted, raising his hand. "The restoration of the rightful emperor to his proper place." He waved the hand negligently. "I assure you that I have all the needed documentation—not here, of course—to satisfy any scholar on the matter."

Damodara stared at him. The eunuch's face was serene, sure, certain. To all appearances, Narses thought he was speaking nothing but the solemn truth.

The general barked a laugh. "So! Fine. As I was saying, it's one thing for me to begin the—ah—*restoration* with the army in the field. The men in their ranks, the officers at their head. Quite another to try to launch it here, with the men scattered all over the city in billets."

Narses nodded. So did Ajatasutra.

"Second—leading directly from that—I need to draw out Rao."

Narses grimaced. "Lord, even if you could get Rao out of Deogiri . . . the casualties . . . you really need your army intact—"

"Oh, be silent, you old schemer. Leave matters of war to me. I said '*draw* him out.' I said nothing of fighting a battle. First, because I need that excuse to pull the entire army out of Bharakuccha. Second, because I will need to make a quick settlement with the Marathas. I can't start a new war without ending *this* one."

Hearing a little cough from Ajatasutra, Damodara looked at him.

The assassin waggled his hand. "A single combat. Rao against Rana Sanga. All of India has been waiting for years to see that match again."

Narses frowned. "Why in the name of—"

"Quiet, Narses." Damodara pondered the notion, for a moment.

"Yes . . . that might very well work." He eyed Ajatasutra intently. "With the right envoy, of course."

Despite the command, Narses could no longer restrain himself. "Why in the name of God would Rao be so stupid as to accept such an idiotic proposal as—"

The eunuch's jaws almost literally snapped shut. "Oh," he concluded.

Ajatasutra's thin smile came. "No one has ever suggested that Raghunath Rao was stupid. Which is precisely the point."

He gave Damodara a little nod. "I will take the message."

"You understand—"

"Yes, Lord. Nothing may be said directly. Rao will do as he will."

Damodara nodded. "Good enough. If it doesn't work, so be it. Then, the third thing I need. We will have to secure Bharakuccha instantly, when the time comes. I can't afford a siege, either. Once the rebellion—ah, restoration—begins, I'll have to cross the Vindhyas and march on Kausambi immediately. If I can't reach and take the capital before Sati and whatever forces she brings arrives from the Punjab, there's no chance. Even for me, much less my family."

Narses frowned. "Lord, I am sure I can get your family out of Kausambi before Emperor Skandagupta—ah, the false emperor—realizes they're gone. Why take the risk of a hasty assault on the city? Kausambi's defenses are the greatest in the world."

"Do not teach me warfare, spymaster," Damodara stated flatly. "Do *not*. You think I should launch a rebellion—let's call things by their right name, shall we?—in one of the provinces. And then what? Years of civil war that shreds the empire, while the Romans and the Persians wait to pick up the pieces. Of which there won't be many."

Damodara rubbed his face. "No. I have never been able to forget Ranapur. There are times I wake up in the middle of the night, shaking. I will not visit twenty Ranapurs upon India."

"But . . . Lord . . ."

"Enough!" Damodara rose to his feet. "Understand this, Narses. What a general can do, an emperor cannot. I will succeed or I will fail, but I will do so as an emperor. There will be no further discussion on the matter."

"Be quiet, old man," Ajatasutra murmured coldly.

He rose to his feet and gave Damodara a very deep bow. "Lord of Malwa. Let us do the thing like an assassin, not a torturer."

Chapter 7
CHARAX, ON THE PERSIAN GULF

"I *can't*," said Dryopus firmly. Anna glared at him, but the Roman official in charge of the great port city of Charax was quite impervious to her anger. His next words were spoken in the patient tone of one addressing an unruly child.

"Lady Saronites, if I allowed you to continue on this—" He paused, obviously groping for a term less impolite than *insane*. "—headstrong project of yours, it'd be worth my career."

He picked up a letter lying on the great desk in his headquarters. "This is from your father, demanding that you be returned to Constantinople under guard."

"My father has no authority over me!"

"No, he doesn't." Dryopus shook his head. "But your husband Calopodius *does*. Without his authorization, I simply can't allow you to continue. I certainly can't detail a ship to take you to Barbaricum."

Anna clenched her jaws. Her eyes went to the nearby window. She couldn't see the harbor from here, but she could visualize it easily enough. The Roman soldiers who had all-but-formally arrested her when she and her small party arrived in the great port city of Charax on the Persian Gulf had marched her past it on their way to Dryopus' palace.

For a moment, wildly, she thought of appealing to the Persians who were now in official control of Charax. But the notion died

513

as soon as it came. The Aryans were even more strict than Romans when it came to the independence of women. Besides—

Dryopus seemed to read her thoughts. "I should note that *all* shipping in Charax is under Roman military law. So there's no point in your trying to go around me. No ship captain will take your money, anyway. Not without a permit issued by my office."

He dropped her father's letter back onto the desk. "I'm sorry, but there's nothing else for it. If you wish to continue, you will have to get your husband's permission."

"He's all the way up the Indus," she said angrily. "And there's no telegraph communication between here and there."

Dryopus shrugged. "No, there isn't—and it'll be some time before the new radio system starts working. But there is a telegraph line between Barbaricum and the Iron Triangle. And by now the new line connecting Barbaricum and the harbor at Chabahari may be completed. You'll still have to wait until I can get a ship there—and another to bring back the answer. Which won't be quickly, now that the winter monsoon has started. I'll have to use a galley, whenever the first one leaves—and I'm *not* sending a galley just for this purpose."

Anna's mind raced through the problem. On their way down the Euphrates, Illus had explained to her the logic of travel between Mesopotamia and India. He'd had plenty of time to do so. The river voyage through Mesopotamia down to the port at Charax had taken much longer than Anna had expected, mainly because of the endless delays caused by Persian officials. She'd expected to be in Charax by late October. Instead, they were now halfway into December.

During the winter monsoon season, which began in November, it was impossible for sailing craft to make it to Barbaricum. Taking advantage of the relatively sheltered waters of the Gulf, on the other hand, they could make it as far as Chabahari—which was the reason the Roman forces in India had been working so hard to get a telegraph line connecting Chabahari and the Indus.

So if she could get as far as Chabahari . . . She'd still have to wait, but if Calopodius' permission came she wouldn't be wasting weeks here in Mesopotamia.

"Allow me to go as far as Chabahari then," she insisted.

Dryopus started to frown. Anna had to fight to keep from screaming in frustration.

"Put me under guard, if you will!"

Dryopus sighed, lowered his head, and ran his fingers through thinning hair. "He's not likely to agree, you know," he said softly.

"He's my husband, not yours," pointed out Anna. "You don't know how he thinks." She didn't see any reason to add: *no more than I do*.

His head still lowered, Dryopus chuckled. "True enough. With that young man, it's always hard to tell."

He raised his head and studied her carefully. "Are you *that* besotted with him? That you insist on going into the jaws of the greatest war in history?"

"He's my *husband*," she replied, not knowing what else to say.

Again, he chuckled. "You remind me of Antonina, a bit. Or Irene."

Anna was confused for a moment, until she realized he was referring to Belisarius' wife and the Roman Empire's former head of espionage, Irene Macrembolitissa. Famous women, now, the both of them. One of them had even become a queen herself.

"I don't know either one," she said quietly. Which was true enough, even though she'd read everything ever written by Macrembolitissa. "So I couldn't say."

Dryopus studied her a bit longer. Then his eyes moved to her bodyguards, who had been standing as far back in a corner as possible.

"You heard?"

Illus nodded.

"Can I trust you?" he asked.

Illus' shoulders heaved a bit, as if he were suppressing a laugh. "No offense, sir—but if it's worth *your* career, just imagine the price *we'd* pay." His tone grew serious: "We'll see to it that she doesn't, ah, escape on her own."

Dryopus nodded and looked back at Anna. "All right, then. As far as Chabahari."

On their way to the inn where Anna had secured lodgings, Illus shook his head. "If Calopodius says 'no,' you realize you'll have wasted a lot of time and money."

"He's my *husband*," replied Anna firmly. Not knowing what else to say.

THE IRON TRIANGLE

After the general finished reading Anna's message, and the accompanying one from Dryopus, he invited Calopodius to sit down at the table in the command bunker.

"I knew you were married," said Belisarius, "but I know none of the personal details. So tell me."

Calopodius hesitated. He was deeply reluctant to involve the general in the petty minutiae of his own life. In the little silence that fell over them, within the bunker, Calopodius could hear the artillery barrages. As was true day and night, and had been for many weeks, the Malwa besiegers of the Iron Triangle were shelling the Roman fortifications—and the Roman gunners were responding with counter-battery fire. The fate of the world would be decided here in the Punjab, Calopodius thought, some time over the next year or so. That, and the whole future of the human race. It seemed absurd—grotesque, even—to waste the Roman commander's time . . .

"Tell me," repeated Belisarius. For all their softness, Calopodius could easily detect the tone of command in the words.

Still, he hesitated.

Belisarius chuckled. "Be at ease, young man. I can spare the time for this. In truth—" Calopodius could sense, if not see, the little gesture by which the general expressed a certain ironic weariness. "I would enjoy it, Calopodius. War is a means, not an end. It would do my soul good to talk about ends, for a change."

That was enough to break Calopodius' resistance.

"I really don't know her very well, sir. We'd only been married for a short time before I left to join your army. It was—"

He fumbled for the words. Belisarius provided them.

"A marriage of convenience. Your wife's from the Melisseni family."

Calopodius nodded. With his acute hearing, he could detect the slight sound of the general scratching his chin, as he was prone to do when thinking.

"An illustrious family," stated Belisarius. "One of the handful of senatorial families which can actually claim an ancient pedigree without paying scribes to fiddle with the historical records. But a family which has fallen on hard times financially."

"My father said they wouldn't even have a pot to piss in if their creditors ever really descended on them." Calopodius sighed. "Yes, General. An illustrious family, but now short of means. Whereas my family, as you know . . . "

"The Saronites. Immensely wealthy, but with a pedigree that needs a *lot* of fiddling."

Calopodius grinned. "Go back not more than three generations, and you're looking at nothing but commoners. Not in the official records, of course. My father can afford a *lot* of scribes."

"That explains your incredible education," mused Belisarius. "I had wondered, a bit. Not many young noblemen have your command of language and the arts."

Calopodius heard the scrape of a chair as the general stood up. Then, heard him begin to pace about. That was another of Belisarius' habits when he was deep in thought. Calopodius had heard him do it many times, over the past weeks. But he was a bit astonished that the general was giving the same attention to this problem as he would to a matter of strategy or tactics.

"Makes sense, though," continued Belisarius. "For all the surface glitter—and don't think the Persians don't make plenty of sarcastic remarks about it—the Roman aristocracy will overlook a low pedigree as long as the 'nobleman' is wealthy *and* well educated. Especially—as you are—in grammar and rhetoric."

"I can drop three Homeric and biblical allusions into any sentence," Calopodius said, chuckling.

"I've noticed!" The general laughed. "That official history you're writing of my campaigns would serve as a Homeric and biblical commentary as well." He paused a moment. "Yet I notice that you don't do it in your *Dispatches to the Army*."

"It'd be a waste," said Calopodius, shrugging. "Worse than that, really. I write those for the morale of the soldiers, most of whom would just find the allusions confusing. Besides, those are really *your* dispatches, not mine. And you don't talk that way, certainly not to your soldiers."

"They're *not* my dispatches, young man. They're yours. I approve them, true, but you write them. And when they're read aloud by my son to the Senate, Photius presents them as *Calopodius'* dispatches, not mine."

Calopodius was startled into silence.

"You didn't know? My son is eleven years old, and quite literate. And since he *is* the Emperor of Rome, even if Theodora still wields the actual power, he insists on reading them to the Senate. He's very fond of your dispatches. Told me in his most recent letter that they're the only things he reads which don't bore him to tears. His tutors, of course, don't approve."

Calopodius was still speechless. Again, Belisarius laughed. "You're quite famous, lad." Then, more softly, almost sadly: "I can't give you back your eyes, Calopodius. But I *can* give you the fame you wanted when you came to me. I promised you I would."

The sound of his pacing resumed. "In fact, unless I miss my guess, those *Dispatches* of yours will someday—centuries from now—be more highly regarded than your official history of the war." Calopodius heard a very faint noise, and guessed the general was stroking his chest, where the jewel from the future named Aide lay nestled in his pouch. "I have it on good authority that historians of the future will prefer straight narrative to flowery rhetoric. And—in my opinion, at least—you write straightforward narrative even better than you toss off classical allusions."

The chair scraped as the general resumed his seat. "But let's get back to the problem at hand. In essence, your marriage was arranged to lever your family into greater respectability, and to provide the Melisseni—discreetly, of course—a financial rescue. How did you handle the dowry, by the way?"

Calopodius shrugged. "I'm not certain. My family's so wealthy that a dowry's not important. For the sake of appearances, the Melisseni provided a large one. But I suspect my father *loaned* them the dowry—and then made arrangements to improve the Melisseni's economic situation by linking their own fortunes to those of our family." He cleared his throat. "All very discreetly, of course."

Belisarius chuckled dryly. "Very discreetly. And how did the Melisseni react to it all?"

Calopodius shifted uncomfortably in his chair. "Not well, as you'd expect. I met Anna for the first time three days after my father informed me of the prospective marriage. It was one of those carefully rehearsed 'casual visits.' She and her mother arrived at my family's villa near Nicodemia."

"Accompanied by a small army of servants and retainers, I've no doubt."

Calopodius smiled. "Not such a small army. A veritable host, it was." He cleared his throat. "They stayed for three days, that first time. It was very awkward for me. Anna's mother—her name's Athenais—barely even tried to disguise her contempt for me and my family. I think she was deeply bitter that their economic misfortunes were forcing them to seek a husband for their oldest daughter among less illustrious but much wealthier layers of the nobility."

"And Anna herself?"

"Who knows? During those three days, Anna said little. In the course of the various promenades which we took through the grounds of the Saronites estate—God, talk about chaperones!—she seemed distracted to the point of being almost rude. I couldn't really get much of a sense of her, General. She seemed distressed by something. Whether that was her pending marriage to me, or something else, I couldn't say."

"And you didn't much care. Be honest."

"True. I'd known for years that any marriage I entered would be purely one of convenience." He shrugged. "At least my bride-to-be was neither unmannerly nor uncomely. In fact, from what I could determine at the time—which wasn't much, given the heavy scaramangium and headdress and the elaborate cosmetics under which Anna labored—she seemed quite attractive."

He shrugged again. "So be it. I was seventeen, General." For a moment, he hesitated, realizing how silly that sounded. He was only a year older than that now, after all, even if . . .

"You were a boy then; a man, now," filled in Belisarius. "The world looks very different after a year spent in the carnage. I know. But then—"

Calopodius heard the general's soft sigh. "Seventeen years old. With the war against Malwa looming ever larger in the life of the Roman Empire, the thoughts of a vigorous boy like yourself were fixed on feats of martial prowess, not domestic bliss."

"Yes. I'd already made up my mind. As soon as the wedding was done—well, and the marriage consummated—I'd be joining your army. I didn't even see any reason to wait to make sure that I'd provided an heir. I've got three younger brothers, after all, every one of them in good health."

Again, silence filled the bunker and Calopodius could hear the muffled sounds of the artillery exchange. "Do you think that's why she was so angry at me when I told her I was leaving? I didn't really think she'd care."

"Actually, no. I think . . ." Calopodius heard another faint noise, as if the general were picking up the letters lying on the table. "There's this to consider. A wife outraged by abandonment—or glad to see an unwanted husband's back—would hardly be taking these risks to find him again."

"Then why is she doing it?"

"I doubt if she knows. Which is really what this is all about, I suspect." He paused; then: "She's only a year older than you, I believe."

Calopodius nodded. The general continued. "Did you ever wonder what an eighteen-year-old girl wants from life? Assuming she's high-spirited, of course—but judging from the evidence, your Anna is certainly that. Timid girls, after all, don't race off on their own to find a husband in the middle of a war zone."

Calopodius said nothing. After a moment, Belisarius chuckled. "Never gave it a moment's thought, did you? Well, young man, I suggest the time has come to do so. And not just for your own sake."

The chair scraped again as the general rose. "When I said I knew nothing about the details of your marriage, I was fudging a bit. I didn't know anything about what you might call the 'inside' of the thing. But I knew quite a bit about the 'outside' of it. This marriage is important to the Empire, Calopodius."

"Why?"

The general clucked his tongue reprovingly. "There's more to winning a war than tactics on the battlefield, lad. You've also got to keep an eye—always—on what a future day will call the 'home front.'" Calopodius heard him resume his pacing. "You can't be *that* naïve. You must know that the Roman aristocracy is not very fond of the dynasty."

"*My* family is," protested Calopodius.

"Yes. Yoursand most of the newer rich families. That's because their wealth comes mainly from trade and commerce. The war—all the new technology Aide's given us—has been a blessing to you. But it looks very different from the standpoint of the old landed families. You know as well as I do—you *must* know—that it was those families who supported the Nika insurrection a few years ago. Fortunately, most of them had enough sense to do it at a distance."

Calopodius couldn't help wincing. And what he wasn't willing to say, the general was. Chuckling, oddly enough.

"The Melisseni came *that* close to being arrested, Calopodius. Arrested—the whole family—and all their property seized. If Anna's father Nicephorus had been even slightly less discreet . . . The truth? His head would have been on a spike on the wall of the Hippodrome, right next to that of John of Cappadocia's. The only thing that saved him was that he *was* discreet enough—barely—and the Melisseni are one of the half-dozen most illustrious families of the Empire."

"I didn't know they were that closely tied . . . "

Calopodius sensed Belisarius' shrug. "We were able to keep it quiet. And since then, the Melisseni seem to have retreated from any open opposition. But we were delighted—I'm speaking of Theodora and Justinian and myself, and Antonina for that matter—when we heard about your marriage. Being tied closely to the Saronites will inevitably pull the Melisseni into the orbit of the dynasty. Especially since—as canny as your father is—they'll start getting rich themselves from the new trade and manufacture."

"Don't tell them that!" barked Calopodius. "Such work is for plebeians."

"They'll change their tune, soon enough. And the Melisseni are very influential among the older layers of the aristocracy."

"I understand your point, General." Calopodius gestured toward the unseen table, and the letters atop it. "So what do you want me to do? Tell Anna to come to the Iron Triangle?"

Calopodius was startled by the sound of Belisarius' hand slapping the table. "Damn fool! It's time you put that splendid mind of yours to work on *this*, Calopodius. A marriage—if it's to work—needs grammar and rhetoric also."

"I don't understand," said Calopodius timidly.

"I know you don't. So will you follow my advice?"

"Always, General."

Belisarius chuckled. "You're more confident than I am! But . . . " After a moment's pause: "Don't *tell* her to do anything, Calopodius. Send Dryopus a letter explaining that your wife has your permission to make her own decision. And send Anna a letter saying the same thing. I'd suggest . . . "

Another pause. Then: "Never mind. That's for you to decide."

In the silence that followed, the sound of artillery came to fill the bunker again. It seemed louder, perhaps. "And that's enough for the moment, young man. I'd better get in touch with Maurice. From the sound of things, I'd say the Malwa are getting ready for another probe."

Calopodius wrote the letters immediately thereafter, dictating them to his scribe. The letter to Dryopus took no time at all. Neither did the one to Anna, at first. But Calopodius, for reasons he could not determine, found it difficult to find the right words to conclude. Grammar and rhetoric seemed of no use at all.

In the end, moved by an impulse which confused him, he simply wrote:

Do as you will, Anna. For myself, I would like to see you again.

Chapter 8
BHARAKUCCHA

The day after his meeting with Narses, Damodara went to the chambers occupied by Nanda Lal, in a different wing of the great palace. Politely, he waited outside for permission to enter. Politely, because Damodara was now officially the Goptri of the Deccan; and thus, in a certain sense, the entire palace might be said to be his personal property.

But there was no point in being rude. Soon enough, the chief spymaster of the Malwa empire emerged from his private chambers.

"Yes, Damodara?" he asked. Not bothering, as usual, to preface the curt remark with the general's honorifics.

Nanda Lal seemed to treasure such little snubs. It was the only sign of outright stupidity Damodara had ever seen him exhibit.

"I have decided to take the field against Rao and his rebels," Damodara announced. "Within a month, I think."

"At last! I am glad to hear it. But why move now, after . . . ?" He left the rest unstated. *After you have resisted my advice to do so for so long?*

"The army is ready, well enough. I see no reason to wait until we are well into *garam* season. As it is, we'll be campaigning through the heat anyway. But I'd like to end the business, if possible, before the southwest monsoon comes."

Above the lumpy, broken nose that Belisarius had given him, years ago, Nanda Lal's dark eyes were fixed on Damodara. The gaze was not quite suspicious, but very close.

"You still lack the heavy siege guns—that *you* have insisted for months are essential to reducing Deogiri."

Damodara shrugged again. "I don't intend to besiege Deogiri. It is my belief that Rao will come forth from the city to meet me on the field of battle. I sense that he has grown arrogant."

Nanda Lal turned his head, peering at Damodara from the side of his eyes. The suspicion had come to the surface now. "You 'sense'? Why? I have gotten no such indications from my spies."

Damodara decided it was time to put an end to courtesy. He returned the spymaster's sideways look with a flat, cold stare of his own. "Neither you nor your spies are warriors. I am. So it is my sense—not yours—which will guide me in this matter."

He looked away, as if indifferent. "And I am also the Goptri of the Deccan. Not you, and certainly not your spies. The decision is made, Nanda Lal." Casually, he added: "I presume you will wish to accompany the expedition."

Tightly, Nanda Lal replied: "You presume incorrectly. I shall remain here in Bharakuccha. And I will insist that you leave Toramana and his Ye-tais here with me." After a brief pause, in a slightly more conciliatory tone, he added, "To maintain the city's security."

Damodara's eyes continued to rove casually about the corridors of the palace, as if he were looking for security threats—and finding none.

"You may have half the Ye-tai force," he said at length, dismissively. "That's more than enough to maintain security. But I will leave you Toramana in command, even though I could certainly use him myself."

That night, as soon as it was dark, Ajatasutra slipped out of the city. He had no great difficulty with the task, as many times as he'd done it. Would have had no difficulty at all, except that he was also smuggling out the fastest horse in Bharakuccha.

The horse was too good to risk breaking one of its legs riding on rough Deccan roads with only a sliver of a crescent moon to see by. So, once far enough from the city, Ajatasutra made camp for the night.

It was a comfortable camp. As it should have been, since he'd long used the site for the purpose and had a cache already supplied.

He slept well, too. Woke very early, and was on his way south to Deogiri before the sun rose.

By mid-morning, he was in excellent spirits. There still remained the not-so-minor problem of avoiding a Maratha ambush, of course. But Ajatasutra was sanguine with regard to that matter, for the good and simple reason that he had no intention of attempting that difficult feat in the first place.

All he had to do was not get killed when the Maratha caught him by surprise. Which, they probably would. With the possible—no, probable—exception of Raghunath Rao, Ajatasutra thought he was the best assassin in India. But the skills of an assassin, though manifold, do not automatically include expertise at laying or avoiding ambushes in broken country like Majarashtra.

No matter. He thought it unlikely that the Marathas would kill a single man outright. It was much more likely they would try to capture him—a task which they would find supremely easy since he intended to put up no resistance at all.

Thereafter, the letter he carried should do the rest.

Well . . . It would certainly get him an audience with the Empress of Andhra and her consort. It was also possible, of course, that the audience would be followed by his execution.

Ajatasutra was not unduly concerned over that matter either, however. A man who manages to become the second best assassin in India is not, in the nature of things, given to fretfulness.

The ambush came later than he expected, a full three days after he left Bharakuccha and long after he'd penetrated into the highlands of the Great Country. On the other hand, it did indeed come as a complete surprise.

"That was very well done," he complimented his ambushers, seeing a dozen of them popping up around him. "I wouldn't have thought a lizard could have hidden in those rocks."

He complimented them again after four of them seized him and hauled him off the horse, albeit a bit more acerbically. The lads went about the task with excessive enthusiasm.

"No need for all that, I assure you!"

He's got a dagger, Captain!

"Three, actually. There's another in my right boot and a small one tucked between my shoulder blades. If you'll permit to rise just a bit—no?—then you'll have to roll me over to get it."

He's got three daggers, Captain! One of them's a throwing knife! He's an assassin!

A flurry of harsh questions followed.

"Well, yes, of course I'm an assassin. Who else would be idiotic enough to ride alone and openly through Maratha territory? But you may rest assured that I was not on my way to make an attempt on Rao's life. I have a letter for him. For the empress, actually."

A flurry of harsher accusations followed.

"Oh, that's nonsense. If I wanted to assassinate the empress, I'd hardly use a blade for the purpose. With Rao himself to guard her? No, no, poison's the thing. I've studied Shakuntala's habits, from many spy reports, and her great weakness is that she refuses to use a food-taster."

A flurry of still harsher proposals followed. They began with impalement and worked their way down from there.

Fortunately, by the time they got to the prospect of flaying the assassin alive, the captain of the Maratha squad had finally taken Ajatasutra's advice to look in his *left* boot.

"See? I told you I was carrying a letter for the empress."

There came, then, the only awkward moment of the day.

None of them could read.

"And here I took the time and effort to provide a Marathi translation, along with the Hindi," sighed Ajatasutra. "I'm an idiot. Too much time spent in palaces. Ah . . . I don't suppose you'd just take my word for it?"

A very long flurry of very harsh ridicule followed. But, in the end, the Maratha hillmen agreed that they'd accept the letter as good coin—provided that Ajatasutra read it aloud to them so they could be sure it said what he claimed it did.

PESHAWAR
CAPITAL CITY OF THE KUSHAN KINGDOM

Kungas, also, found that the first Malwa assassination attempt came later than he'd expected.

He was not, however, caught by surprise. In fact, he wasn't caught at all.

Kungas was certainly not one of the best assassins in India. Not even close. He was, however, most likely the best assassin-*catcher*. For years, the Malwa had used him as a security specialist. After he broke from them to join Shakuntala's rebellion, she'd made him the commander of her imperial bodyguard.

"They're in that building," Kujulo murmured, pointing with his chin out of the window. He was too far away from the window to be seen from the outside, but he was also too experienced to run the risk that a large gesture like a pointing finger might be spotted. The human eye can detect motion easier than it can detect a still figure. "One of the two you predicted they'd use."

"It was fairly obvious," said Kungas. "They're the only two buildings fronting the square that have both a good angle for a shot and a good rear exit to make an escape from."

Next to him, also carefully standing back from the window so as not to be spotted, Vima chuckled softly. "It helps, of course, that we prepared the sites well. Like bait for rats."

Kungas nodded. The gesture, like Kujulo's chin-pointing, was minimal. Something that couldn't possibly be spotted even fifty feet away, much less across an entire city square.

Bait, indeed. The king of the Kushans—his queen, rather, acting on his instructions—had bought the two buildings outright. Then, placed her own agents in the position of "landlords," with clear and explicit instructions to rent any of the rooms to anyone, no questions asked—and make sure that their reputation for doing so became well known in Peshawar.

Inevitably, of course, that quickly made both buildings havens for prostitution and gambling. All the better, as far as Kungas was concerned. Within a week, all of the prostitutes were cheerfully supplementing their income as informers for the queen.

Irene had known the Malwa assassins were there within half an hour of their arrival.

Piss-poor assassins, in Kungas' opinion, when she told him. They'd started by annoying the whores with a brusque refusal of their services.

"All right," he said. "I see no reason to waste time."

"How do you want to do it?" asked Kujulo. "You don't want to use the charges, I assume."

In the unlikely event he might need it a last resort, Kungas had had all the rooms in the buildings that would be suitable for assassination attempts fitted with demolitions. Shaped charges, basically, that would spray the interior with shrapnel without—hopefully—collapsing the walls.

Still, with the ubiquitous mudbrick construction in Peshawar, Kungas saw no reason to take the risk. There was always the chance the building might collapse, killing dozens of people. Even if that didn't happen, the expense of repairing the damage would be considerable, and the work itself disruptive. Such an extreme measure might aggravate the residents of Peshawar.

Irene's spies had reported that Kungas was now very popular in the city, even among the non-Kushan inhabitants, and he saw no reason to undermine that happy state of affairs.

The new king's popularity was not surprising, of course. Kungas had maintained at least as much stability as the Malwa had. More, really, since the Pathan hillmen had completely ceased their periodic harassment of the city-dwellers. He'd also lowered the taxes and levies, eliminated the most egregious of the Malwa regulations, and, most of all, abolished all of the harsh Malwa laws regarding religion. The enforced Malwa cult of mahaveda Hinduism had never sat well in the mountains. The moment Kungas issued his decrees, the region's underlying Buddhist faith had surged back to the surface.

No, there was no reason to risk undermining all that by blowing up parts of the city. Especially such visible parts, fronting on the main square.

"I've got my men ready," Kujulo added.

"What are they armed with? The assassins, I mean. Guns?"

"No. Bows. Probably be using poisoned arrowheads."

Kungas shook his head. "In that case, no. Keep your men ready, but let's try the Sarmatian girls."

Kujulo looked skeptical. Vima looked downright appalled.

"Kungas—ah, Sire—there isn't a one of them—"

"Enough," Kungas said. "I know they have no experience. Neither did you or I, once. How else do you get it?"

He shook his head again. "If the Malwa were armed with guns, it might be different. But bows will be awkward in the confines of those rooms. The girls will have a good chance. Some of them will die. But . . . that's what they wanted. To be real warriors. Dying comes with it."

The crack of a smile reappeared. "Besides, it's only fair—since we're using one of them as the decoy."

◊   ◊   ◊

A few minutes later, the business began. The Sarmatian girl posing as Irene came into the square on horseback, surrounded by her usual little entourage of female guards.

Watching from the same window, Kungas was amused. Irene often complained that the custom in the area of insisting that women had to be veiled in public was a damned nuisance, personally speaking—but a blessing, from the standpoint of duplicity.

Was that Irene down there? Who could say, really? Her face couldn't be seen, because of the veil. But the woman was the right height and build, had the same color and length of hair in that distinctive ponytail, wore the proper regalia and the apparel, and had the accustomed escort.

Of course, it was the queen. Who else would it be?

Kungas knew that the assassins across the square wouldn't even be wondering about it. True, Irene was almost certainly not their target and the assassins would make no attempt here. They'd wait for Kungas to show himself. Still, the appearance of the queen in the square so soon after their arrival would be a good sign to them. They'd want to study her movements carefully. All their attention would be fixed on the figure moving within range of the bows in the windows.

He waited for the explosions that would signal the attack. For all that Kungas was prepared to see Irene's girl warriors suffer casualties, he'd seen no reason to make them excessive. He didn't want to risk destroying the walls with the implanted shaped charges, true—but there was no reason not to use the much smaller charges it would take to simply blow open the doors.

Blow them open—and spray splinters all through the room. That should be enough to give the inexperienced girls the edge they'd need.

A bigger edge than he'd expected, in the event. A moment later, the explosions came—and one of the Malwa assassins was blown right out the window. From the way he toppled to the ground twenty feet below, Kungas knew he was already unconscious. A big chunk of one of the doors must have hit him on the back of the head.

He landed like a sack of meal. From the distance, Kungas couldn't hear the impact, but it was obvious that the assassin hadn't survived it. Most of the street square was dirt, but it was very hard-packed. Almost like stone.

"Ruptured neck, for sure," Vima grunted. "Probably half his brains spilling out, too."

Another assassin appeared in the same window. His back, to be precise. The man was obviously fighting someone.

A few seconds later, he too toppled out of the window. Still clutching the spear that had been driven into his chest, he made a landing that was no better than his predecessor's.

Worse, probably. This assassin had the bad luck of landing on the flagstones in front of the building's entrance.

The shouts and screams and other sounds of fighting could be heard across the square for a bit longer. Perhaps ten seconds.

Then, silence.

Kungas glanced down into the center of the square, to assure himself that the decoy was unharmed. He had no particular concern for the girl in question—in fact, he didn't even know who it was—but he didn't want to face Irene's recriminations if she'd been hurt.

Self-recriminations, really. But Irene was not exempt from the normal human tendency to shed blame on others as a way of handling guilt.

That left the question of how many of the Sarmatian squad that launched the attack had been killed or injured. But that was a different sort of matter. Getting killed in a fight with weapons in hand didn't cause the same gut-wrenching sensation as getting killed serving as a helpless decoy.

"Odd, really," Kungas murmured to himself. "But that's the way it is. Someday I'll have to ask Dadaji if he can explain the philosophy of it to me."

He turned and headed for the door. "Come. Let's find out."

It was better than he'd thought. Certainly better than he'd feared.

"See?" he demanded of Vima. "Only one girl dead. One badly injured, but she'll probably survive."

"She'll never walk right, again," Vima said sourly. "Might lose that leg completely, at least from the knee down."

Kujulo chuckled. "Will you listen to him? Bad as a doddering old Pathan clan chief!"

For a moment, he hunched his shoulders and twisted his face into a caricature of a prune-faced, disapproving, ancient clansman. Even Vima laughed.

"Not bad," Kujulo stated firmly, after straightening. "Against five assassins? Not bad."

Irene was upset, of course. The dead and injured girls were names and faces to her. People that she'd known, even known well.

But there were no recriminations. No self-recriminations, even. Her Sarmatian guards themselves were ecstatic at their success, despite the casualties.

It probably wasn't necessary, but Kungas put it into words anyway.

"Make Alexander the Great and the Buddha's son the forefathers of a dynasty—this is what comes with it, Irene."

"Yes, love, I know."

"They were all volunteers."

"Yes, love, I know. Now please shut up. And go away for a few hours."

AXUM, IN THE ETHIOPIAN HIGHLANDS

Ousanas glowered at the construction crew working in the great field just on the outskirts of the city of Axum. Most of the field was covered with the stone ruins of ancient royal tombs.

"I ought to have the lot of them executed," he pronounced, "seeing as how I can't very well execute you. Under the circumstances."

Antonina smiled. "Approximately how much more of your Cassandra imitation will I be forced to endure?"

"Cassandra, is it? You watch, woman. Your folly—that of your husband's, rather—will surely cause the spiritual ruin of the great kingdom of Axum." He pointed an accusing finger at the radio tower. "For two centuries this ridiculous field given over to the grotesque monuments of ancient pagan kings has been left to decay. As it should. Now, thanks to you and your idiot husband, we'll be resurrecting that heathen taste in idolatry."

Antonina couldn't help but laugh. "It's a *radio* tower, Ousanas!"

The aqabe tsentsen of Ethiopia was not mollified. "A Trojan horse, what it is. You watch. Soon enough—in the dark, when my eagle eye is not watching—they'll start carving inscriptions on the damned thing."

Gloomily, his eyes ranged up and down the huge stone tower that was nearing completion. "Plenty of room for it, too."

Antonina glanced back at the Greek artisan who was overseeing the project. "Tell me, Timothy. If I understand this right, once the tower is in operation anyone who tries to climb onto it in order—"

The artisan winced. "They'll be fried." Warily, he eyed the tall and very muscular figure of the man who was, in effect if not in theory, the current ruler of Ethiopia. "Ah, Your Excel—"

"See?" demanded Ousanas, transferring his glare to the hapless artisan. "It's already starting! I am not an 'excellency,' damnation, and certainly not *yours*. A humble keeper of the royal fly whisks, that's all I am."

Timothy sidled back a step. He was fluent in Ge'ez, the language of the Axumites, so he knew that the title *aqabe tsentsen* meant "the keeper of the fly whisks." He also knew that the modesty of the title was meaningless.

Antonina came to the rescue. "Oh, stop bullying the poor man. Timothy, please continue."

"Well . . . it's hard to explain without getting too technical. But the gist of it is that a big radio tower like this needs a big transmitter powered by"—here he pointed his finger at a huge stone building—"the steam engine in there. In turn, that—"

The next few sentences were full of mysterious terms like "interrupter" and "capacitor bank" that meant absolutely nothing to Antonina or Ousanas. But Timothy's concluding words seemed clear enough:

"—every time the transmitter key is depressed, you'd have something like two thousand watts of power shorting across your body. 'Fry' is about the right word for what'd happen, if you got onto the tower itself. But you'd never make it that far, anyway. Once you got past the perimeter fence you'd start coupling to the radials implanted around the base of the tower. Your body would start twitching uncontrollably and the closer you got, the worse it'd get. Your hair might even catch on fire."

Ousanas grimaced, but he was still not mollified. "Splendid. So now we will have to post guards to protect idolators from idolatry."

Antonina laughed again. "Even for you, Ousanas, this display is absurd! What's really bothering you? It's the fact that you still haven't figured out what I'm going to decree tomorrow regarding the succession. Isn't it?"

Ousanas didn't look at her, still glowering at the radio tower. After a moment, he growled, "It's not so much me, Antonina. It's Rukaiya. She's been pestering me for days, trying to get an answer. Even more, asking for my opinion on what she should do, in the event of this or that alternative. She has no more idea than I do—and you might consider the fact that whatever you decide, *she* will be the one most affected."

Antonia struggled—mightily—to keep her satisfaction from showing. She had, in fact, deliberately delayed making the announcement after telling everyone she'd reached a decision, in the specific hope that Rukaiya would turn to Ousanas for advice.

"I'd have thought she'd mostly pester Garmat," she said, as if idly.

Ousanas finally stopped glowering and managed a bit of a grin. "Well, she has, of course. But I have a better sense of humor than the old bandit. She needs that, right now."

So, she does. So, she does.

"Well!" Antonina said briskly. "It'll all be settled tomorrow, at the council session. In the meantime—"

She turned to Timothy. "Please continue the work. Ignore this grumbler. The sooner you can get that finished, the sooner I can talk to my husband again."

"And that's another thing!" Ousanas grumbled, as they headed toward the Ta'akha Maryam. "It's just a waste. You can't say anything either secret or personal—not with that sort of broadcast radio—and it won't work anyway, once the monsoon comes with its thunderstorms. So I've been told, at least."

Antonina glanced at the sun, now at its midday altitude, as if gauging the season. "We're still some months from the southwest monsoon, you know. Plenty of time."

Chapter 9

CONSTANTINOPLE

"You'd be putty in your father's hands," Theodora sneered.

"Which one? Belisarius or Justinian?"

"Either—no, *both*, since they're obviously conspiring with each other."

The dark eyes of the Empress Regent moved away from Photius and Tahmina to glare at a guard standing nearby. So far as Photius could determine, the poor man's only offense was that he happened to be in her line of sight.

Perhaps he also bore a vague resemblance to Belisarius. He was tall, at least, and had brown eyes.

Angrily, Theodora slapped the heavily decorated armrest of her throne. "Bad enough that he's exposing my husband to danger! But he's also giving away half my empire!"

She shifted the glare back to Photius. "Excuse me. *Your* empire."

The correction was, quite obviously, a formality. The apology was not even that, given the tone in which she'd spoken the words.

"You hate to travel," Photius pointed out, reasonably. "And since you're actually running my empire"—here he bestowed a cherubic smile on his official adoptive mother—"you can't afford to leave the capital anyway."

"I detest that smile," Theodora hissed. "Insincere as a crocodile's. How did you get to be so devious, already? You're only
eleven years old."

Photius was tempted to reply: *from studying you, Mother.*
Wisely, he refrained.

If she were in a better mood, actually, Theodora would take it
as a compliment. But, she wasn't. She was in as foul a mood as
she ever got, short of summoning the executioners.

Photius and his wife Tahmina had once, giggling, developed
their own method for categorizing Theodora's temper. First, they
divided it into four seasons:

Placid. The most pleasant season, albeit usually brief.

Sour. A very long season. More or less the normal climate.

Sullen. Not as long as sour season. Not quite.

Fury. Fortunately, the shortest season of all. Very exciting while
it lasted, though.

Then, they ranked each season in terms of its degree of intensity,
from alpha to epsilon.

Photius gauged this one as a Sullen Epsilon.

Well . . . Not quite. Call it a Sullen Delta.

In short, caution was called for here. On the other hand, there
was still some room for further prodding and pushing. Done gingerly.

"I like to travel myself," he piped cheerfully. "So I'm the logical
one to send on a grand tour to visit our allies in the war. And it's
not as if you really need me here."

He did not add: *or want me here, either.* That would be unwise.
True, Theodora had all the maternal instincts of a brick. But she
liked to pretend otherwise, for reasons Photius had never been
able to fathom.

Tahmina said it was because, if she didn't, it would give rise to
rumors that she'd been spawned by Satan. That might be true,
although Photius was skeptical. After all, plenty of people *already*
thought the Empress Regent had been sired by the devil.

Photius didn't, himself. Maybe one of Hell's underlings, but not
Satan himself.

Theodora was back to glaring at the guard. No, a different one.
His offense . . .

Hard to say. He resembled neither Belisarius nor Justinian.
Except for being a man, which, in Theodora's current humor, was
probably enough.

"Fine!" she snapped. "You can go. If nothing else, it'll keep Antonina from nattering at me every day once the radio starts working. By now, months since she left, she'll be wallowing in guilt and whining and whimpering about how much she misses her boy. God knows why. Devious little wretch."

She swiveled the dark-eyed glare onto Tahmina, sitting next to Photius. "You too. Or else once the cunning little bastard gets to Ethiopia he'll start nattering at me over the radio about how much he misses his wife. God knows why. It's not as if he's old enough yet to have a proper use for a wife."

Yet a third guard received the favor of her glare. "You can celebrate your sixteenth birthday in Axum. I'll send the gifts along with you."

Tahmina smiled sweetly and bowed her head. "Thank you, Mother."

"I'm not your mother. You don't fool me. You're as bad as he is. No child of mine would be so sneaky. Now go."

Once they reached the corridor outside Theodora's audience chamber, Photius whispered to Tahmina: "Sullen Delta. Close to Epsilon."

"Oh, don't be silly," his wife whispered back, smiling down at him. To Photius' disgruntlement, even though he'd grown a lot over the past year, Tahmina was still taller than he was. "That wasn't any worse than Sullen Gamma. She agreed, didn't she?"

"Well. True."

The announcement was made publicly the next day. Photius wasn't surprised. It was usually hard to wheedle Theodora into anything. But the nice thing was that, if you could, she'd move quickly and decisively thereafter.

The Emperor of Rome will visit our allies in the war with Malwa. All the way to India itself! The Empress will accompany him, sharing the hardships of the journey.
All hail the valiant Photius!
All hail the virtuous Tahmina!

After reading the broadsheet, the captain of the Malwa assassination team tossed it onto the table in the apartments they'd rented. It was all he could do not to crumple it in disgust.

"Three months. Wasted."

His lieutenant, standing at the window, stared out over the Golden Horn. He didn't bother, as he had innumerable times since they'd arrived in Constantinople, shifting his gaze to study the imperial palace complex.

No point in that, now.

The three other members of the team were sitting at the table in the kitchen. The center of the table was taken up by one of the small bombards that Malwa assassination teams generally carried with them. The weapons were basically just simple, very big, one-round shotguns. Small enough that they could be hidden in trunks, even if that made carrying the luggage a back-breaking chore.

All three of them were glowering at it. The captain would insist that they bring the bombard with them, wherever they went. And, naturally, being the plebeians of the team, they'd be the ones who had to tote the wretched thing.

One of the three assassins spoke up. "Perhaps . . . if we stayed here . . . Theodora . . ."

The captain almost snarled at him. "Don't be stupid. Impossible, the precautions she takes. Not even Nanda Lal expects us to have a chance at *her*."

"She hasn't left the complex once, since we arrived," the lieutenant chimed in, turning away from the window. "Not once, in three months. Even Emperor Skandagupta travels more often than that."

He pulled out a chair and sat down at the table. A moment later, the captain did the same.

"We had a good chance with the boy," the lieutenant added. "High-spirited as he is. He and his wife both. Now . . ."

He looked at his superior. "Follow them?"

"Yes. Only thing we can do."

"Not one of us speaks Ge'ez, sir," pointed out one of the assassins. "And none of us are black."

Gloomily, the captain shook his head. "Don't belabor the obvious. We'll have to move fast and reach Egypt before they do. Try and do it there, if we can. All of us can pass as Persians among Arabs—or the reverse, if we must."

"We may well have to," cautioned his lieutenant. "The security in Egypt is reportedly ferocious. Organized by Romans, too. It'll be easier in Persia—easier still, in Persian-occupied Sind. The

Iranians insist on placing grandees in charge of security, and grandees tend to be sloppy about these things."

"True." The captain stared down at the broadsheet. Then he did crumple it.

THE IRON TRIANGLE

"They're not even going to try to run the mines, I don't think," Menander said. He lowered the telescope and offered it to Belisarius.

The general shook his head. "Your eyes are as good as mine. At that distance, for sure. What are you seeing?"

Before answering, Menander came down from the low platform he'd been standing on to observe the distant Malwa naval base. Then, stooped slightly so that his head would be well below the parapet. That brought his face on a level with the general's, since Belisarius was standing in a slight crouch also.

That was something of a new habit, but one that had become well ingrained. Beginning a few weeks earlier, the Malwa had demonstrated that they, too, could produce rifles good enough for long-range sniping.

"Both ironclads just came out of the bunker. But they steamed north. They're headed away from us."

Belisarius closed his eyes, thinking. "You're probably right. I'd already pretty much come to the conclusion that the Malwa were assuming a defensive posture. From that standpoint, building the ironclads actually makes sense—where it would be a pure waste of resources to build them to attack us here in the Triangle. They'd never get through the mine fields."

Menander frowned, trying to follow the general's logic. "But I still don't see . . . oh."

"Yes. 'Oh.' You've gotten a better look at those ironclads than anyone—certainly a longer one. Could you defeat them—either one—with the *Justinian*? Or the *Victrix*?"

"The *Victrix* would just be suicide. They've got a couple of big guns in the bows. Eighteen-pounders, I think. They'd blow the *Victrix* to pieces long before it could get close enough to use the fire cannon."

He paused, for a moment. "As for the *Justinian* . . . Maybe. Against one of them, not both. It would depend on a lot of things, including plenty of luck. I'd do better in a night battle, I think."

Belisarius waited, patiently. Excellent young officers like Menander always started off their assessments too optimistically. He preferred to give them time for self-correction, rather than doing it himself.

With Menander, it only took half a minute. He was well accustomed to Belisarius' habits, by now.

"All right, all right," he said, smiling slightly. "The truth? I *might* win—against one of them. But it would depend on some blind luck working in our favor. Even with luck, I'm not sure I could do it in the daytime."

Belisarius nodded, almost placidly. "That's how they *designed* them, Menander. Those ironclads weren't designed to break into the Triangle. They were designed to keep *you* from breaking out."

He stretched, while still being careful to keep his head out of sight of any snipers. "Look at this way. The Malwa now figure, with those ironclads finished and in service, that they've got the same control over the rivers north of the Triangle that we have of them to the south. That means *they're* in position to do to us the same thing we did to them last year—cut our supply lines if we attempt any major prolonged offensive. There's no way to supply that kind of massive campaign without using water transport. It just can't be done. Not, at least, with more than fifteen or—at most—twenty thousand men. By the standards of this war, that isn't a powerful enough force to win a pitched battle. Not here in the Punjab, anyway."

He glanced at the wall of the fortifications, as if he could see through it to the Malwa trenches beyond. "I estimate they've got upwards of a hundred thousand men out there. 'Out there' meaning in this immediate vicinity, facing us here in the Triangle. They've probably got another twenty thousand—maybe thirty—facing Kungas at the Khyber Pass, and thirty or forty thousand more held as a reserve in Multan."

"And we've got . . . "

"By now? Forty thousand in the Triangle itself, with another twenty thousand or so on their way here from the Empire, in a steady trickle. The Persians have about forty thousand troops actively engaged on this front. But most of them are still in the

Sind, and even in the best of circumstances Khusrau would have to leave a third of them there to administer the province."

The young officer made a sour face. Belisarius smiled.

"He's an emperor, Menander. Emperors think like emperors; it's just the nature of the beast. And Khusrau has the additional problem that he's bound and determined to keep his new province of Sind under direct imperial control, rather than letting his noblemen run the show. But that means he has to use a lot of soldiers as administrators. Whether he likes it or not—much less whether *we* like it or not."

Menander's sour expression shaded into a simple scowl. "In short, we're outnumbered at least two-to-one, and that's not going to change."

"Not for the better, that's for sure. The only way it'll change will be for the worse. If the Malwa succeed in crushing Shakuntala's rebellion in the Deccan, that would free up Damodara and his army. Another forty thousand men, and, in terms of quality, undoubtedly the best army in the Malwa empire."

He let that sink in for a few seconds. Then: "It'd be worse than that, actually. The Maratha revolt inspired and triggered off smaller revolts and rebellions all over India. I estimate the Malwa are forced to keep one-half to two-thirds of their army in India proper, just to maintain control of the empire. The truth is this, Menander. So far, we've been able to fight a Malwa empire that could only use one hand against us, instead of two. And the weaker hand, at that, since Damodara's in the Deccan. If they break Shakuntala and Rao and the Marathas, all those smaller rebellions will start fading away quickly. Within a year, we'd be facing another hundred thousand men here in the Punjab—and Damodara could get his forty thousand here within two months. Three, at the outside."

The general shrugged. "Of course, by then we'd be so well-fortified here that I doubt very much if even a Malwa army twice this size could drive us out. But there's no way we could go on the offensive ourselves, either—certainly not with those ironclads controlling the rivers. They'll build a few more, I suspect. Enough to place two ironclads on the Indus and at least one on each of its four main tributaries."

"A war of attrition, in other words." Menander sucked his teeth. "That . . . stinks."

"Yes, it does. The casualties will become horrendous, once you let enough time pass—and the social and political strain on the kingdoms and empires involved will be just as bad. That's what that monster over there is counting on now, Menander. It thinks, with its iron control over the Malwa Empire, that it can outlast a coalition of allies."

Menander eyed the general. "And what do you think, sir?"

"I think that superhuman genius over there is just a grandiose version of a village idiot."

The young officer's eyes widened, a little. "Village idiot? That seems . . ."

"Too self-confident on my part?" Belisarius smiled. "You watch, young man. What you're seeing here is what Ousanas would call the fallacy of confusing the shadow for the true thing—the pale, sickly, real world version of the ideal type."

"Huh?"

The general chuckled. "Let me put it this way. Emperors—or superhuman imitations thereof—think in terms like 'iron control,' as if it really meant something. But iron is a metal, not a people. Any good blacksmith can control iron. No emperor who ever lived can really control people. That's because iron, as refractory a substance as it may be, doesn't dispute the matter with the blacksmith."

He looked now, to the southeast. "So, we'll see. Link thinks it can win this waiting game. I think it's the village idiot."

DEOGIRI
THE NEW CAPITAL OF THE REBORN ANDHRA EMPIRE IN MAJARASHTRA— THE "GREAT COUNTRY"

"It's *ridiculous*," Shakuntala hissed. "Ridiculous!"

Even as young as she was, the black-eyed glare of the Empress of Andhra was hot enough to have sizzled lizards in the desert.

Alas, the assassin squatting before her in a comfortable lotus seemed completely unaffected. So, she turned to other means.

"Summon my executioners!" she snapped. "At once!"

The glare was now turned upon her husband, sitting on a throne next to hers. A slight movement of Rao's forefinger had been enough to stay the courtiers before one of them could do her bidding.

"A moment," he said softly. He turned to face her glare, his expression every bit as calm and composed as the assassin's.

"You are, of course, the ruler of Andhra. And I, merely your consort. But since this matter touches upon my personal honor, I am afraid you will have to defer to my wishes. Either that, or use the executioners on me."

Shakuntala tried to maintain the glare. Hard, that, in the face of her worst fear since reading the letter brought by the assassin.

After five seconds or so, inevitably, she broke. "Rao—*please*. This is insane. The crudest ruse, on the part of the Malwa."

Rao transferred the calm gaze to the figure squatting on the carpet in the center of the audience chamber. For a moment, India's two best assassins contemplated each other.

"Oh, I think not," Rao murmured, even more softly. "Whatever else, not that."

He rose abruptly to his feet. "Take him to one of the guest chambers. Give him food, drink, whatever he wishes within reason."

Normally, Rao was punctilious about maintaining imperial protocol. Husband or not, wiser and older head or not, Rao was officially the consort and Shakuntala the reigning monarch. But, on occasion, when he felt it necessary, he would exert the informal authority that made him—in reality, if not in theory—the co-ruler of Andhra.

Shakuntala did not attempt to argue the matter. She was bracing herself for the much more substantial issue they would be arguing over as soon as they were in private.

"Clear the room," she commanded. "Dadaji, you stay."

Her eyes quickly scanned the room. Her trusted peshwa was a given. Who else?

The two top military commanders, of course. "Shahji, Kondev, you also."

She was tempted to omit Maloji, on the grounds that he was not one of the generals of the army. Formally speaking, at least. But . . . he was Rao's closest friend, in addition to being the commander of the Maratha irregulars.

Passing him over would be unwise. Besides, who was to say? Sometimes, Maloji was the voice of caution. He was, in some ways, even more Maratha than Rao—and the Marathas, as a people, were not given to excessive flamboyance on matters of so-called "honor." Quite unlike those mindless Rajputs.

"Maloji."

That was enough, she thought. Rao would not be able to claim she had unbalanced the private council in her favor.

But, to her surprise, he added a name. "I should like Bindusara to remain behind also."

Shakuntala was surprised—and much pleased. She'd considered the Hindu religious leader herself, but had passed him over because she'd thought Rao would resent her bringing spiritual pressure to bear. The sadhu was not a pacifist after the manner of the Jains, but neither was he given to much patience for silly kshatriya notions regarding "honor."

It took a minute or so for the room to clear. As they waited, Shakuntala leaned over and whispered: "I wouldn't have thought you'd want Bindusara."

Rao smiled thinly. "You are the treasure of my soul. But you are also sometimes still very young. You are over your head here, girl. I wanted the sadhu because he is *also* a philosopher."

Shakuntala hissed, like an angry snake. She had a disquieting feeling, though, that she sounded like an angry *young* snake.

Certainly, the sound didn't seem to have any effect on Rao's smile. "You never pay enough attention to *those* lessons. Still! After all my pleading." The smile widened, considerably. The last courtier was passing through the door and there was no one left to see but the inner council.

"Philosophy has form as well as substance, girl. No one can be as good at it as Bindusara unless he is also a master of *logic*."

Shakuntala began the debate. Her arguments took not much time, since they were simplicity itself.

We have been winning the war by patience. Why should we accept this challenge to a clash of great armies on the open field, where we would be over-matched?

Because one old man challenges another to a duel? Because both of the fools still think they're young?

Nonsense!

◇   ◇   ◇

When it came his turn, Rao's smile was back in place. Very wide, now, that smile.

"Not so old as all *that,* I think," he protested mildly. "Neither I nor Rana Sanga. Still, my beloved wife has penetrated to the heart of the thing. It *is* ridiculous for two men, now well past the age of forty—"

"Almost fifty!" Shakuntala snapped.

"—and, perhaps more to the point, both of them now very experienced commanders of armies, not young warriors seeking fame and glory, to suddenly be gripped by a desire to fight a personal duel."

To Shakuntala's dismay, the faces of the three generals had that horrid *look* on them. That half-dreamy, half-stern expression that men got when their brains oozed out of their skulls and they started babbling like boys again.

"Be a match of legend," murmured Kondev.

The empress almost screamed from sheer frustration. The day-long single combat that Rao and Rana Sanga had fought once, long ago, was famous all across India. Every mindless warrior in India would drool over the notion of a rematch.

"You were twenty years old, then!"

Rao nodded. "Indeed, we were. But you are not asking the right question, Shakuntala. Have you—ever once—heard me so much as mention any desire for another duel with Sanga? Even in my sleep."

"No," she said, tight-jawed.

"I think not. I can assure you—everyone here—that the thought has not once crossed my mind for at least . . . oh, fifteen years. More likely, twenty."

He leaned forward a bit, gripping the armrests of the throne in his powerful, out-sized hands. "So why does anyone think that Rana Sanga would think of it, either? Have I aged, and he, not? True, he is a Rajput. But, even for Rajputs, there is a difference between a husband and a father of children and a man still twenty and unattached. A difference not simply in the number of lines on their faces, but in how they think."

Shahji cleared his throat. "He has lost his family, Rao. Perhaps that has driven him to fury."

"But *has* he lost them?" Rao looked to Dadaji Holkar. Not to his surprise, the empire's peshwa still had one of the letters brought by the Malwa assassin held in his hand. Almost clutched, in fact.

"What do you make of it, Dadaji?"

Holkar's face bore an odd expression. An unlikely combination of deep worry and even deeper exultation. "Oh, it's from my daughters. There are little signs—a couple of things mentioned no one else could have known—"

"Torture," suggested Kondev.

"—that make me certain of it." He glanced at Kondev and shook his head. "Torture seems unlikely. For one thing, although the handwriting is poor—my daughters' education was limited, of course, in the short time I had before they were taken from me—it is not shaky at all. I recognized it quite easily. I can even tell you which portion was written by Dhruva, and which by Lata, from that alone. Could I do so, were the hands holding the pen trembling with pain and fear as well as inexperience? Besides . . ."

He looked at the door through which the courtiers had left—and, a bit earlier, an assassin. "I do not think that man is a torturer."

"Neither do I," said Rao firmly. "And I believe, at my advanced age"—here, a sly little smile at Shakuntala—"I can tell the difference."

Shakuntala scowled, but said nothing. Rao gestured at Holkar. "Continue, please."

"The letter tells me nothing, naturally, of the girls' location. But it does depict, in far more detail than I would have expected, the comfort of their lives now. And there are so many references to the mysterious 'ladies' to whom they have—this is blindingly obvious—grown very attached."

"You conclude from this?"

Dadaji studied the letter in his hand, for a moment. "I conclude from this that someone—not my daughters, someone else—is sending me a message here. Us, rather, a message."

Rao leaned back in his throne. "So I think, also. You will all remember the message sent to us last year from Dadaji's daughters, with the coin?"

Several heads nodded, Shakuntala's among them.

"And how Irene Macrembolitissa convinced us it was not a trap, but the first step in a complex maneuver by Narses?"

All heads nodded.

Rao pointed to the letter. "I think that is the second step. Inviting us to take a third—or, rather, allow someone else to do so."

That statement was met by frowns of puzzlement on most faces. But, from the corner of her eye, Shakuntala saw Bindusara nodding.

She could sense that she was losing the argument. For a moment, she had to struggle desperately not to collapse into sheer girlish pleading—which would end, inevitably, with her blurting out before the council news she had not yet even given to Rao. Of the new child that was coming.

Suddenly, Rao's large hand reached over and gave her little one a squeeze. "Oh, be still, girl. I can assure you that I have no intention whatsoever of fighting Rana Sanga again."

His smile was simply cheerful now. "Ever again, in fact. And that is precisely why I will accept the challenge."

In the few seconds those two sentences required, Shakuntala swung from despair to elation and back. "You don't need to do this!"

"Of course, I don't. But Rana Sanga *does*."

Chapter 10
AXUM

"What, no elephants?" Antonina asked sarcastically.

Ousanas shook his head. "They won't fit in the corridors, not even in the Ta'akha Maryam. We tried. Too bad, though. It would have made a nice flourish. Instead—"

He gestured before them, down the long hallway leading to the throne room. "—we must walk."

Antonina tried to picture war elephants inside the Ta'akha Maryam, her mind boggling a little. Even if the huge beasts could have been inserted into the halls . . .

She looked down the long rows of guards and officials, flanking both sides. "They'd have crushed everybody," she muttered.

"Oh, not the soldiers. Most of them would have scampered aside in time, and the ones who didn't had no business being sarwen anyway. In fact, Ezana thought it would be a useful test."

Ezana was the senior commander of the three royal regiments. Antonina thought he was probably cold-blooded enough to have said that. There was something downright scary about Ezana. Fortunately, he was not hot-tempered, nor impulsive. Even more fortunately, his devotion to the dynasty was unquestioned by anyone, including Antonina.

Ezana had been one of Eon's two bodyguards while he'd still been a prince. That was a very prestigious position for the soldiers who made up Ethiopia's regiments—the "sarwen," as they called themselves. When Eon had assumed the throne, Ezana had become the commander of the royal regiments—and the other bodyguard, Wahsi, had been appointed the military commander of the Ethiopian naval expedition that Antonina had used to rescue Belisarius and his army from the siege of Charax.

Wahsi had died in battle in the course of that expedition. Eon's son, the new Axumite King of Kings, had been named after him.

So, Antonina had no doubt at all of Ezana's loyalty to the infant negusa nagast, sired by the prince he'd guarded and named after his best friend. Still, he was . . . scary.

"The slaughter among the officials, of course, would have been immense," Ousanas continued cheerfully, "seeing how half of them are as fat as elephants, and eight out of ten have brains that move more ponderously. But it was my assessment that the loss of one-third would be a blessing for the kingdom. Ezana was hoping that half would be crushed."

Antonina thought the aqabe tsentsen was joking, but she wasn't sure. There were ways in which Ousanas was even scarier than Ezana. But since they were nearing the entrance to the throne room, she decided she'd simply pretend she hadn't heard.

One-third of Ethiopia's officials, slain in a few minutes! Half, according to Ezana!

Bloodthirsty African maniacs. Antonina would have been quite satisfied with a simple, unostentatious Roman decimation.

"All be silent!"

As if his booming commander's voice wasn't enough, Ezana slammed the iron-capped ferrule of his spear onto the stone floor. *"Be silent!"*

The throne room had become perfectly quiet even before the ferrule hit the floor. Leaving aside the fact that no one in their right mind was going to disobey Ezana under these circumstances, the crowd packed into the huge chamber was waiting to hear Antonina's decrees. Eagerly, in some cases; anxiously, in others; fearfully, in some. But not one person there was indifferent, or inclined to keep chattering.

Actually, there hadn't been much chatter anyway. Antonina had noticed the unusual quiet the moment she entered the room. Ethiopians had informal habits, when it came to royalty, certainly compared to Roman or Persian custom. As a rule, even during an official session, the royal audience chamber had a constant little hubbub of conversation in the background. Nothing boisterous or intrusive, to be sure. But neither Ethiopian soldier-seamen nor Arab merchants saw any reason not to conduct quiet business in the back of the chamber while the negusa nagast and his officials made their various judgments and rulings around the throne.

Not today. The chamber had been subdued when Antonina entered, and now it was utterly silent.

Well . . . not quite. Softly and contentedly, the baby ruler of the kingdom was suckling his mother's breast, as she sat on the throne.

That was being done on Antonina's instructions. Normally, for such a session, Rukaiya would have used a wet nurse just as readily as any Roman empress. But Antonina had thought the sight of the baby feeding would help remind everyone of the cold and hard facts that surrounded that softest of realities.

On one side, the cold and hard facts that this *was* the son of Eon the Great, this was his successor—and this *was* the woman Eon had chosen to be his queen. On the other, the colder and harder facts that the successor was a babe, and the queen a teenager. The same cold and hard facts that had existed when Alexander the Great died—and, within a few short years, had led to civil war, the eventual division of the empire between the Diadochi, and the murder of Alexander's widow and child.

Ezana waited until Antonina had climbed the steps that led up to the royal dais. The steps were wide, but shallow. Wide enough to give the guards positioned just behind the throne time to intercept any would-be assassin. Shallow enough, that the ruler was not so elevated above his subjects that a normal conversation couldn't be held with those seeking an audience.

There was a chair waiting for her there, to the right of the queen's. A throne, really, though not as large or elaborate as the one in which Rukaiya sat with the infant negusa nagast. But Antonina had already decided she'd make her decrees while standing. She'd learned that trick from watching her friend Theodora rule Rome.

Sit, when you're judging and negotiating—but always stand, when you're really laying down the law.

As soon as Antonina had reached her position and given him a little nod—she'd already told Ezana she wouldn't be using the chair for this—the regimental commander's voice boomed out again.

"As decreed by Eon the Great on his deathbed, the Roman woman Antonina will rule on the measures to be taken to ensure the royal succession. Eon gave her complete authority for the task. I was there, I heard, I bear witness. Her decrees are final. Her decrees are absolute. They will not be questioned."

That was . . . not entirely true. No decrees laid down by anyone other than God could cover all the details and complexities. Antonina knew full well that, starting on the morrow, she'd be sitting in that chair and dickering over the fine points. Still, for the moment—

In case anyone had any lingering doubts, Ezana slammed the spear butt on the stones again. "Not by anyone!"

Before she began, she glanced around the room. All the principals were there. Ousanas was standing on the lowest step of the dais, to her right, as was customary for the aqabe tsentsen. Ezana occupied the equivalent position to the left, as befit the commander of the royal regiments. Just to his left, on the stone floor, were the rest of the commanders of the regiments stationed in Axum.

Directly front of the dais were assembled the kingdom's officials, with old Garmat at the center. Officially, he was the viceroy of the Axum-controlled portions of Arabia. In reality, he also served as one of the ruler's closest advisers. Garmat had served Eon's father Kaleb in the same posts that Ousanas had later served Eon himself—first, as the dawazz for the prince; then, as the aqabe tsentsen for the king. The half-Arab one-time bandit was cunning and shrewd, and much respected by everyone in the kingdom.

Spread out to either side of the officials, and ranging beyond throughout the throne room, was the elite of the realm. The majority were Ethiopians, but perhaps a third were Arabs. All of the latter were either tribal or clan chiefs, or experienced and wealthy merchants and traders—or, more often than not, both together.

There was one Arab standing next to Garmat, in the small group of officials at the center. That was Rukaiya's father, who was one of the wealthiest of the Quraysh merchants in Mecca—and had been appointed by Eon himself as the viceroy for Arabia's west coast. The Hijaz, as it was called, the area north of Yemen that was dominated by the Quraysh tribe.

"You all understand the problem we face," Antonina began. She saw no reason to bore everyone with a recitation of the obvious. Everyone there had had months to consider the situation, and by now everyone understood it perfectly well.

"The future for Axum is splendid, provided the kingdom can pass through the next twenty years without strife and turmoil. To do so, in my judgment, the throne needs an additional bulwark."

Since Axumites were expert sailors as well as stone masons, she added another image. "An outrigger, if you will, to keep the craft from overturning in heavy seas."

She had to fight down a smile, seeing Ousanas and Garmat wince slightly. Both men were fond of poetry—Garmat more than Ousanas—and she knew she'd be hearing wisecracks later concerning her pedestrian use of simile and metaphor.

Ezana's expression, on the other hand, was simply intent. And it was ultimately Ezana who mattered here. Not simply because he commanded the spears of the regiment, but because he—unlike Ousanas and Garmat, each outsiders in their different ways—was Ethiopian through and through. If Ezana accepted her ruling, with no hesitations or doubts, she was confident the rest would follow.

"So, I have decided to create a new post for the kingdom. The name of this official will be the *angabo*."

She paused, knowing that the little murmur which swept the room was both inevitable and worked to her advantage.

The term "angabo" was well known to those people, especially the Ethiopians. The kingdom of Axum had several legends concerning its origins. The predominant one, contained in the *Book of Aksum*, held that the founder of the city of Axum was Aksumawi, son of Ethiopis and grandson of the Noah of the Bible. A related legend had it that the kings of Axum were descendants of Solomon and Makeda, the queen of Sheba. Those were the officially favored legends, of course, since they gave the now-Christian kingdom an impeccably Biblical lineage for their rulers.

But Axum had only converted to Christianity two centuries earlier, and there still existed a third and older legend. This legend had no formal sanction, but it was well-respected by the populace—and neither the kings of Ethiopia nor its Christian bishops had ever made any attempt to suppress it. Axumites were not much given to doctrinal asperity, certainly by the standards of Rome's contentious

bishops and patriarchs. All the more so since the legend, however
pagan it might be, was hardly derisive toward the monarchy.

According to that older legend, Ethiopia had once been ruled
by a great and evil serpent named Arwe or Waynaba. Once a
year, the serpent-king demanded the tribute of a young girl. This
continued until a stranger named Angabo arrived, slew the serpent,
saved the girl, and was then elected king by the people. His descen-
dant, it was said, was the Makeda who was the queen of Sheba of
the Solomon story—although still another version of the legend
claimed Makeda was the girl he rescued.

Antonina glanced down at Garmat. The old adviser was managing to keep a straight face—which must have been hard, since he
was the one person with whom Antonina had discussed her plans.
And he, unlike her, was standing where he could see Ousanas
directly.

Such a pity, really. By now, the quick mind of Ousanas would
have realized where she was going with this—and Antonina would
have paid a princely sum to have been able to watch the expression
on his face.

She tried, surreptitiously, out of the corner of her eye. But, alas,
the aqabe tsentsen was just that little bit too far to the side for her
to see his face as anything other than a dark blur.

"The *angabo* will command all the regiments of Axum except
the three royal regiments. Those will, as now, remain under the
authority of the senior commander. Ezana, as he is today."

The regimental commanders wouldn't much like that provision.
Traditionally, they'd been equals who met as a council, with no
superior other than the negusa nagast himself. But Antonina didn't
expect any serious problems from that quarter. Ethiopia had now
grown from a kingdom to an empire, and the sarwen were hard-
headed enough to recognize that their old egalitarian traditions
would have to adapt, at least to a degree. Over half of the regiments
were now in India, after all—so how could the council of commanders meet in the first place?

In essence, Antonina had just re-created the old Roman division
between the regular army and the Praetorian Guard. That hadn't
worked out too well for Rome, in the long run. But Antonina didn't
think Axum would face the same problem that the Roman Empire
had faced, of being so huge and far-flung that the Praetorian Guard

wound up being the tail in the capital that wagged the dog in the far-off provinces.

Even with the expansion into the African continent to the south that Eon and Ousanas had planned, Axum would still remain a relatively compact realm. The three royal regiments would not have the ability of the Praetorian Guard to override the army, seeing as how most of the regular regiments under the control of the angabo would be stationed no farther away than southern and western Arabia—just across the Red Sea. They'd be even closer once the capital was moved from Axum to the great Red Sea port of Adulis, as was planned also.

And, in any event, the long run was the long run. Antonina had no illusions that she could manipulate political and military developments over a span of centuries. She simply wanted to buy Axum twenty years of internal peace—and leave it reasonably secure at the end.

"The position of the *angabo* will be a hereditary one," she continued, "unlike the positions of the aqabe tsentsen, or the viceroys, or the commanders of the sarwen. Second only to the negusa nagast, the angabo will be accounted the highest nobleman of the realm."

She waited for a moment, letting the crowd digest that decree. The Ethiopian nobility wouldn't much like that provision, of course—but, on the other hand, it would please the sarwen commanders. Often enough, of course, the commanders *were* noblemen—but that was not the root source of either their identity or their authority within the regiments.

"The descendants of the angabo, however, may not under any circumstances assume the throne of the kingdom. They may marry into the ruling dynasty, but the children of that union will inherit the position of the angabo, not the negusa nagast. They will be, forever, the highest noblemen of Axum—but they will also be, forever, barred from the throne itself."

That was the key. She'd considered the Antonine tradition of adoption as an alternative, but both she and Garmat had decided it would be too risky. Unlike Romans, neither the Ethiopians nor the Arabs had ever used the custom of political adoption in that manner. It would be too foreign to them. This, however, was something everyone could understand. She'd essentially created a Caesar alongside an Augustus—but then divided the two into separate lineages. Instead of, as the Romans had done, making the Caesar the designated successor to the Augustus.

Eventually, some day, one or another angabo might manage to distort the structure enough to overthrow a dynasty. But . . . not for at least a century, she judged. Garmat thought it would be at least that long before anyone even seriously tried.

"They'll *like* this setup, once they get used it," he'd told her confidently, the day before. "Ethiopians and Arabs alike. Watch and see if I'm not right. It's almost a dual monarchy, with a senior and a junior dynasty, which means that if you can't wheedle one, maybe you can wheedle what you need out of the other. Good enough—when the alternative is the risk of a failed rebellion."

Then, grinning: "Especially after they contemplate the first and founding angabo."

Antonina paused again. By now, many sets of eyes were swiveling toward a particular person in the room. The first pair had been those belonging to Rukaiya's father.

She was not surprised, on either count. Many of the people in that room were extremely shrewd—none more so than Rukaiya's father, leaving aside Garmat himself.

Best of all, to her, was the sense she got that he was immensely relieved. A very slight sense, since the man had superb control over his public face, but it was still definitely there. He'd be the one person in the room who would consider this as a father, not simply as a magnate of the kingdom—and he doted on Rukaiya.

"To make certain that the position of the angabo and his descendants is established surely and certainly for all to see, the first angabo will marry Rukaiya, widow of Eon the Great and the regent of the kingdom. Their children will thus be the half-brothers and sisters of the negusa nagast, Wahsi."

She turned her head enough to look at Rukaiya. The girl was staring up at her, blank-faced. The young queen was still waiting, still keeping her expression under tight control. She'd known for some time that she would most likely have to remarry—and soon—as little as she looked forward to the prospect.

Now, obviously, she simply wanted . . . the *name*.

She dreaded hearing it, of course. Rukaiya was a very capable, energetic and free-spirited girl. She'd been raised by a lenient and supportive father and married to a young prince, a bibliophile himself, who'd enjoyed her intellect and encouraged her learning. Now, she faced the prospect of marriage to . . .

Whoever it was, not someone likely to be much like her father or her former husband.

Antonina had to struggle to keep her own face expressionless. *Silly girl! Did you really think I'd condemn you to such a living death? Nonsense.*

It was time to end it.

"The rest is obvious. The first angabo, like the Angabo of legend, must be a complete outsider. Neither Ethiopian nor Arab, and with no existing ties to any clan or tribe in the kingdom. Yet he must also be a famous warrior and a wise counselor. One whom all know can and has hunted and slain evil serpent-kings—as this one, in my presence once, helped my husband trap and slay the serpent-queen of Malwa. Who was the greatest, and most evil, creature in the world."

Finally, she turned to look at him squarely.

"Ousanas, the first angabo."

Ousanas would have figured it out as quickly as Rukaiya's father. By now, he had his expression completely under control.

Too bad. It was probably the only chance Antonina would ever get to make the man's jaw drop.

Noisily, Garmat cleared his throat. "Does Ousanas accept the post?"

The famous grin came, then. "What does 'accept' have to do with it?" He nodded toward Ezana, standing stone-faced on the other side of the dais. "I heard what he said, even if some others were deaf. The words were 'final' and 'absolute'—and I *distinctly* remember 'without question.' That said . . ."

For a moment, while Ousanas' grin faded away, he and Ezana stared at each other. It was not quite a contest of wills. Not quite.

Ousanas turned to the queen, sitting on the throne. "That said," he continued quietly, "I would not force this on Rukaiya. She has been very dear to me also, if not in the same way she was to Eon."

The moment Antonina had spoken the name, she'd seen Rukaiya lower her head, as if she were solely concerned with her feeding infant. That was as good a way as any to bring herself under composure, of course.

Now, she looked up. Quickly, before lowering her head again to concentrate on Wahsi.

There might have been a hint of tears in her eyes. But all she said was: "I have no objection, Ousanas."

"*It is done!*" Ezana boomed. More forcefully than ever, the spearbutt slammed the stones. "It is *done*—and the royal regiments stand ready to enforce the decrees. As before. As always. As ever."

He glanced at Antonina. Seeing her little nod, he boomed: "All clear the chamber! There will be no further audience until the morrow."

At a small sign from Antonina, Garmat remained behind. No one would think that amiss. The old adviser's special relationship to the throne was well established and accepted. In any event, most people in the room would already have realized that he would soon be the new aqabe tsentsen, to replace Ousanas.

She would have liked to have Rukaiya's father remain. Under the circumstances, however, that might give rise to certain resentments.

Ezana stayed, also. He'd begun to leave, but even before Antonina could signal him to stay, Ousanas ordered him to do so.

Ordered him, outright. The first time he'd ever done so, in the many years the two men had known each other and worked closely together training and nurturing and protecting a young prince named Eon.

To Antonina's relief, Ezana had not seemed to bridle at all. In fact, he seemed a bit relieved himself.

In the short time that it took to clear the chamber, Antonina studied Ousanas. The man had seemed majestic to her for several years. Never more so than now.

By God, this will work.

Once the room was empty except for the five key people—six, counting the infant—Ousanas smiled ruefully.

"I will admit—again—that you are a genius, Antonina. This will work, I think. But . . . "

He looked at Rukaiya. She, back at him. There was sadness in both faces.

"I am not ready for this. Not yet. Neither is she."

There were definitely tears in Rukaiya's eyes, now. She shook her head. "No, I am not. I have . . . no objection, as I said. Sooner or later, I would have had to marry again, and I can think of no one I'd prefer. But Eon is still too close."

Ezana cleared his throat. "Yes. Of course. But I think he would be pleased, Rukaiya. And I knew him as well as any man."

She smiled, slightly. "Oh, yes. His ghost will be pleased—but not yet."

"It doesn't matter," Antonina said firmly. "We need to hold the wedding soon, but there is no reason you need to consummate the marriage immediately. In fact—"

Garmat picked up the cue, seamlessly. "It would be a bad idea," he said firmly. "We will need children from this union—*many* children, to be blunt, to give Wahsi a host of half-brothers and sisters to help him rule, since he will have no full ones. But we don't need them right now. No one will even start thinking about opposition for at least two years."

"More likely five—or ten," Ezana grunted. The smile that followed was a very cold sort of thing. "I can guarantee that much."

Garmat nodded. "Actually, the danger would be for you to have a child too *soon*. Enough time must elapse for it to have been impossible for Eon to have been the father. *Impossible*. That means waiting at least a year after his death last summer."

The relief on the faces of both Rukaiya and Ousanas was almost comical.

"Of course," Ousanas said. "Stupid of me not to have seen it instantly. Or else—three generations from now—some over-ambitious and small-brained great-grandson of mine might start claiming he was actually the great-grandson of Eon."

Smiling very gently now, he stepped forward and placed his hand on the baby's head. "In my safe-keeping, also."

He straightened. "We should do more, I think. Make it impossible the other way, also. And do so in a way that is publicly obvious, even to bedouin."

Clearly enough, his brain was back to working as well as always.

"Yes," she said firmly. This was something that Antonina and Garmat had already decided upon. "There is no need for me to remain here, and I would very much like to see my husband again. Ousanas should go with me to India, leading whatever military force Axum can add to the war."

She gave a quick glance at Ezana. "Except the three royal regiments, of course."

"We'll leave two regiments in Arabia also," said Garmat. "That will be enough. The Arabs will have no problem with Antonina's decrees on the succession."

"That will be enough," Ezana agreed. "The kingdom will be stable, and Ousanas can squeeze whatever advantage he can get for Axum from our deepened participation in the war. By the time he gets back, at least a year will have elapsed from Eon's death."

"Rukaiya?" Antonina asked.

"Yes. I agree." She also smiled gently. "And I will be ready, by then, for another husband."

"Done!" Ezana boomed. He did, however—just barely— manage to restrain himself from slamming the ferrule on the stones.

Ousanas scowled. "And, now—for the details! We'll have at least a week to squabble—more likely, two—before a suitable wedding can be organized. The *first* thing I want clearly established is that the royal regiments—*not* the otherwise-soon-to-be-impoverished mendicant family of the downtrodden angabo—have to pay for all the damage done to the floors by heavy-handed commanders."

"Ridiculous!" boomed Ezana. "The maintenance of the palace should clearly be paid for out of the angabo's coffers."

The spearbutt slammed the floor.

Chapter 11
CHABAHARI, IN THE STRAITS OF HORMUZ

Chabahari seemed like a nightmare to Anna. When she first arrived in the town—city, now—she was mainly struck by the chaos in the place. Not so long ago, Chabahari had been a sleepy fishing village. Since the great Roman-Persian expedition led by Belisarius to invade the Malwa homeland through the Indus valley had begun, Chabahari had been transformed almost overnight into a great military staging depot. The original fishing village was now buried somewhere within a sprawling and disorganized mass of tents, pavilions, jury-rigged shacks—and, of course, the beginnings of the inevitable grandiose palaces the Persians insisted on putting anywhere that their grandees resided.

Her first day was spent entirely in a search for the authorities in charge of the town. She had promised Dryopus she would report to those authorities as soon as she arrived.

But the search was futile. She found the official headquarters easily enough—one of the half-built palaces being erected by the Persians. But the interior of the edifice was nothing but confusion, a mass of workmen swarming all over, being overseen by a handful of harassed-looking supervisors. Not an official was to be found anywhere, neither Persian nor Roman.

"Try the docks," suggested the one foreman who spoke Greek and was prepared to give her a few minutes of his time. "The noble sirs complain about the noise here, and the smell everywhere else."

The smell *was* atrocious. Except in the immediate vicinity of the docks—which had their own none-too-savory aroma—the entire city seemed to be immersed in a miasma made up of the combined stench of excrement, urine, sweat, food—half of it seemingly rotten—and, perhaps most of all, blood and corrupting flesh. In addition to being a staging area for the invasion, Chabahari was also a depot where badly injured soldiers were being evacuated back to their homelands.

Those of them who survive this horrid place, Anna thought angrily, as she stalked out of the "headquarters." Illus and Cottomenes trailed behind her. Once she passed through the aivan onto the street beyond—insofar as the term "street" could be used at all for a simple space between buildings and shacks, teeming with people—she spent a moment or so looking south toward the docks.

"What's the point?" asked Illus, echoing her thoughts. "We didn't find anyone there when we disembarked." He cast a glance at the small mound of Anna's luggage piled up next to the building. The wharf boys whom Anna had hired to carry her belongings were lounging nearby, under Abdul's watchful eye.

"Besides," Illus continued, "it'll be almost impossible to keep your stuff from being stolen, in that madhouse down there."

Anna sighed. She looked down at her long dress, grimacing ruefully. The lowest few inches of the once-fine fabric, already ill-used by her journey from Constantinople, was now completely ruined. And the rest of it was well on its way—as much from her own sweat as anything else. The elaborate garments of a Greek noblewoman, designed for salons in the Roman Empire's capital, were torture in this climate.

A glimpse of passing color caught her eye. For a moment, she studied the figure of a young woman moving down the street. Some sort of Indian girl, apparently. Since the war had erupted into the Indian subcontinent, the inevitable human turbulence had thrown people of different lands into the new cauldrons of such cities as Chabahari. Mixing them up like grain caught in a thresher. Anna had noticed several Indians even in Charax.

Mainly, she just envied the woman's clothing, which was infinitely better suited for the climate than her own. By her senatorial family standards, of course, it was shockingly immodest. But she spent a few seconds just *imagining* what her bare midriff would feel like, if it didn't feel like a mass of spongy, sweaty flesh.

Illus chuckled. "You'd peel like a grape, girl. With your fair skin?"

Anna had long since stopped taking offense at her "servant's" familiarity with her. That, too, would have outraged her family. But Anna herself took an odd little comfort in it. Much to her surprise, she had discovered over the weeks of travel that she was at ease in the company of Illus and his companions.

"Damn you, too," she muttered, not without some humor of her own. "I'd toughen up soon enough. And I wouldn't mind shedding some skin, anyway. What I've got right now feels like it's gangrenous."

It was Illus' turn to grimace. "Don't even think it, girl. Until you've seen real gangrene . . . "

A stray waft of breeze from the northwest illustrated his point. That was the direction of the great military "hospital" that the Roman army had set up on the outskirts of the city. The smell almost made Anna gag.

The gag brought up a reflex of anger, and, with it, a sudden decision.

"Let's go there," she said.

"Why?" demanded Illus.

Anna shrugged. "Maybe there'll be an official there. If nothing else, I need to find where the telegraph office is located."

Illus' face made his disagreement clear enough. Still—for all that she allowed familiarity, Anna had also established over the past weeks that she *was* his master.

"Let's go," she repeated firmly. "If nothing else, that's probably the only part of this city where we'd find some empty lodgings."

"True enough," said Illus, sighing. "They'll be dying like flies, over there." He hesitated, then began to speak. But Anna cut him off before he got out more than three words.

"I'm not insane, damn you. If there's an epidemic, we'll leave. But I doubt it. Not in this climate, this time of year. At least . . . not if they've been following the sanitary regulations."

Illus' face creased in a puzzled frown. "What's that got to do with anything? What regulations?"

Anna snorted and began to walk off to the northwest. "Don't you read *anything* besides those damned *Dispatches*?"

Cottomenes spoke up. "No one does," he said. Cheerfully, as usual. "No soldier, anyway. Your husband's got a way with words, he does. Have you ever tried to *read* official regulations?"

Those words, too, brought a reflex of anger. But, as she forced her way through the mob toward the military hospital, Anna found herself thinking about them. And eventually came to realize two things.

One. Although she was a voracious reader, she *hadn't* ever read any official regulations. Not those of the army, at any rate. But she suspected they were every bit as turgid as the regulations that officials in Constantinople spun out like spiders spinning webs.

Two. Calopodius *did* have a way with words. On their way down the Euphrates—and then again, as they sailed from Charax to Chabahari—the latest *Dispatches* and the newest chapters from his *History of Belisarius and the War* had been available constantly. Belisarius, Anna had noted, seemed to be as adamant about strewing printing presses behind his army's passage as he was about arms depots.

The chapters of the *History* had been merely perused on occasion by her soldier companions. Anna could appreciate the literary skill involved, but the constant allusions in those pages were meaningless to Illus and his brother, much less the illiterate Abdul. Yet they pored over each and every *Dispatch,* often enough in the company of a dozen other soldiers, one of them reading it aloud, while the others listened with rapt attention.

As always, her husband's fame caused some part of Anna to seethe with fury. But, this time, she also *thought* about it. And if, at the end, her thoughts caused her anger to swell, it was a much cleaner kind of anger. One which did not coil in her stomach like a worm, but simply filled her with determination.

The hospital was even worse than she'd imagined. But she did, not surprisingly, find an unused tent in which she and her companions could make their quarters. And she did discover the location of the telegraph office—which, as it happened, was situated right next to the sprawling grounds of the "hospital."

The second discovery, however, did her little good. The official in charge, once she awakened him from his afternoon nap, yawned and explained that the telegraph line from Barbaricum to Chabahari was still at least a month away from completion.

"That'll mean a few weeks here," muttered Illus. "It'll take at least that long for couriers to bring your husband's reply."

Instead of the pure rage those words would have brought to her once, the Isaurian's sour remark simply caused Anna's angry determination to harden into something like iron.

"Good," she pronounced. "We'll put the time to good use."

"How?" he demanded.

"Give me tonight to figure it out."

It didn't take her all night. Just four hours. The first hour she spent sitting in her screened-off portion of the tent, with her knees hugged closely to her chest, listening to the moans and shrieks of the maimed and dying soldiers who surrounded it. The remaining three, studying the books she had brought with her—especially her favorite, Irene Macrembolitissa's *Commentaries on the Talisman of God*, which had been published just a few months before Anna's precipitous decision to leave Constantinople in search of her husband.

Irene Macrembolitissa was Anna's private idol. Not that the sheltered daughter of the Melisseni had ever thought to emulate the woman's adventurous life, except intellectually. The admiration had simply been an emotional thing, the heroine-worship of a frustrated girl for a woman who had done so many things she could only dream about. But now, carefully studying those pages in which Macrembolitissa explained certain features of natural philosophy as given to mankind through Belisarius by the Talisman of God, she came to understand the hard practical core which lay beneath the great woman's flowery prose and ease with classical and biblical allusions. And, with that understanding, came a hardening of her own soul.

Fate, against her will and her wishes, had condemned her to be a wife. So be it. She would begin with that practical core; with concrete truth, not abstraction. She would steel the bitterness of *a* wife into the driving will of *the* wife. The wife cf Calopodius the Blind, Calopodius of the Saronites.

The next morning, very early, she presented her proposition.

"Do any of you have a problem with working in trade?"

The three soldiers stared at her, stared at each other, broke into soft laughter.

"We're not senators, girl," chuckled Illus.

Anna nodded. "Fine. You'll have to work on speculation, though. I'll need the money I have left to pay the others."

"What 'others'?"

Anna smiled grimly. "I think you call it 'the muscle.' "

Cottomenes frowned. "I thought *we* were 'the muscle.' "

"Not any more," said Anna. "You're promoted. All three of you are now officers in the hospital service."

"*What* 'hospital service'?"

Anna realized she hadn't considered the name of the thing. For a moment, the old anger flared. But she suppressed it easily enough. This was no time for pettiness, after all.

"We'll call it Calopodius' Wife's Service. How's that?"

The three soldiers shook their heads. Clearly enough, they had no understanding of what she was talking about.

"You'll see," she predicted.

It didn't take them long. Illus' glare was enough to cow the official "commander" of the hospital, who was as sorry-looking a specimen of "officer" as Anna could imagine. And if the man might have wondered at the oddness of such glorious ranks being borne by such as Illus and his two companions—Abdul looked as far removed from a *tribune* as could be imagined—he was wise enough to keep his doubts to himself.

The dozen or so soldiers whom Anna recruited into the Service in the next hour—"the muscle"—had no trouble at all believing that Illus and Cottomenes and Abdul were, respectively, the *chiliarch* and two *tribunes* of a new army "service" they'd never heard of. First, because they were all veterans of the war and could recognize others—and knew, as well, that Belisarius promoted with no regard for personal origin. Second—more importantly—because they were wounded soldiers cast adrift in a chaotic "military hospital" in the middle of nowhere. Anna—Illus, actually, following her directions—selected only those soldiers whose wounds were healing well. Men who could move around and exert themselves. Still, even for such men, the prospect of regular pay meant a much increased chance at survival.

Anna wondered, a bit, whether walking-wounded "muscle" would serve the purpose. But her reservations were settled within the next hour after four of the new "muscle," at Illus' command, beat the first surgeon into a bloody pulp when the man responded to Anna's command to start boiling his instruments with a sneer and a derogatory remark about meddling women.

By the end of the first day, eight other surgeons were sporting cuts and bruises. But, at least when it came to the medical staff, there were no longer any doubts—none at all, in point of fact—as to whether this bizarre new "Calopodius' Wife's Service" had any actual authority.

Two of the surgeons complained to the hospital's commandant, but that worthy chose to remain inside his headquarters' tent. That night, Illus and three of his new "muscle" beat the two complaining surgeons into a still bloodier pulp, and all complaints to the commandant ceased thereafter.

Complaints from the medical staff, at least. A body of perhaps twenty soldiers complained to the hospital commandant the next day, hobbling to the HQ as best they could. But, again, the commandant chose to remain inside; and, again, Illus—this time using his entire corps of "muscle," which had now swollen to thirty men—thrashed the complainers senseless afterward.

Thereafter, whatever they might have muttered under their breath, none of the soldiers in the hospital protested openly when they were instructed to dig real latrines, *away* from the tents—and use them. Nor did they complain when they were ordered to help completely immobilized soldiers use them as well.

By the end of the fifth day, Anna was confident that her authority in the hospital was well enough established. She spent a goodly portion of those days daydreaming about the pleasures of wearing more suitable apparel, as she made her slow way through the ranks of wounded men in the swarm of tents. But she knew full well that the sweat that seemed to saturate her was one of the prices she would have to pay. Lady Saronites, wife of Calopodius the Blind, daughter of the illustrious family of the Melisseni, was a figure of power and majesty and authority—and had the noble gowns to prove it, even if they were soiled and frayed. Young Anna, all of nineteen years old, wearing a sari, would have had none at all.

By the sixth day, as she had feared, what was left of the money she had brought with her from Constantinople was almost gone. So, gathering her now-filthy robes in two small but determined hands, she marched her way back into the city of Chabahari. By now, at least, she had learned the name of the city's commander.

It took her half the day to find the man, in the *taberna* where he was reputed to spend most of his time. By the time she did, as she had been told, he was already half-drunk.

"Garrison troops," muttered Illus as they entered the tent that served the city's officers for their entertainment. The tent was filthy, as well as crowded with officers and their whores.

Anna found the commandant of the garrison in a corner, with a young half-naked girl perched on his lap. After taking half the day to find the man, it only took her a few minutes to reason with him and obtain the money she needed to keep the Service in operation.

Most of those few minutes were spent explaining, in considerable detail, exactly what she needed. Most of that, in specifying tools and artifacts—*more shovels to dig more latrines; pots for boiling water; more fabric for making more tents, because the ones they had were too crowded.* And so forth.

She spent a bit of time, at the end, specifying the sums of money she would need.

"Twenty solidi—a day." She nodded at an elderly wounded soldier whom she had brought with her along with Illus. "That's Zeno. He's literate. He's the Service's accountant in Chabahari. You can make all the arrangements through him."

The garrison's commandant then spent a minute explaining to Anna, also in considerable detail—mostly anatomical—what she could do with the tools, artifacts and money she needed.

Illus' face was very strained, by the end. Half with fury, half with apprehension—this man was no petty officer to be pounded with fists. But Anna herself sat through the garrison commander's tirade quite calmly. When he was done, she did not need more than a few seconds to reason with him further and bring him to see the error of his position.

"My husband is Calopodius the Blind. I will tell him what you have said to me, and he will place the words in his next *Dispatch*. You will be a lucky man if all that happens to you is that General Belisarius has you executed."

She left the tent without waiting to hear his response. By the time she reached the tent's entrance, the garrison commander's face was much whiter than the tent fabric and he was gasping for breath.

The next morning, a chest containing a hundred solidi was brought to the hospital and placed in Zeno's care. The day after that, the first of the tools and artifacts began arriving.

Four weeks later, when Calopodius' note finally arrived, the mortality rate in the hospital was less than half what it had been when Anna arrived. She was almost sorry to leave.

In truth, she might not have left at all, except by then she was confident that Zeno was quite capable of managing the entire service as well as its finances.

"Don't steal anything," she warned him, as she prepared to leave.

Zeno's face quirked with a rueful smile. "I wouldn't dare risk the Wife's anger."

She laughed, then; and found herself wondering through all the days of their slow oar-driven travel to Barbaricum why those words had brought her no anger at all.

And, each night, she took out Calopodius' letter and wondered at it also. Anna had lived with anger and bitterness for so long—"so long," at least, to a nineteen-year-old girl—that she was confused by its absence. She was even more confused by the little glow of warmth which the last words in the letter gave her, each time she read them.

"You're a strange woman," Illus told her, as the great battlements and cannons of Barbaricum loomed on the horizon.

There was no way to explain. "Yes," was all she said.

The first thing she did upon arriving at Barbaricum was march into the telegraph office. If the officers in command thought there was anything peculiar about a young Greek noblewoman dressed in the finest and filthiest garments they had ever seen, they kept it to themselves. Perhaps rumors of "the Wife" had preceded her.

"Send a telegram immediately," she commanded. "To my husband, Calopodius the Blind."

They hastened to comply. The message was brief:

Address medical care and sanitation in next dispatch STOP Firmly STOP

THE IRON TRIANGLE

When Calopodius received the telegram—and he received it immediately, because his post was in the Iron Triangle's command and communication center—the first words he said as soon as the telegraph operator finished reading it to him were:

"God, I'm an idiot!"

Belisarius had heard the telegram also. In fact, all the officers in the command center had heard, because they had been waiting with an ear cocked. By now, the peculiar journey of Calopodius' wife was a source of feverish gossip in the ranks of the entire army fighting off the Malwa siege in the Punjab. *What the hell is that girl doing, anyway?* being only the most polite of the speculations.

The general sighed and rolled his eyes. Then, closed them. It was obvious to everyone that he was reviewing all of Calopodius' now-famous *Dispatches* in his mind.

"We're both idiots," he muttered. "We've maintained proper medical and sanitation procedures *here,* sure enough. But . . . "

His words trailed off. His second-in-command, Maurice, filled in the rest.

"She must have passed through half the invasion staging posts along the way. Garrison troops, garrison officers—with the local butchers as the so-called 'surgeons.' God help us, I don't even want to think . . . "

"I'll write it immediately," said Calopodius.

Belisarius nodded. "Do so. And I'll give you some choice words to include." He cocked his head at Maurice, smiling crookedly. "What do you think? Should we resurrect crucifixion as a punishment?"

Maurice shook his head. "Don't be so damned flamboyant. Make the punishment fit the crime. Surgeons who do not boil their instruments will be boiled alive. Officers who do not see to it that proper latrines are maintained will be buried alive in them. That sort of thing."

Calopodius was already seated at the desk where he dictated his *Dispatches* and the chapters of the *History.* So was his scribe, pen in hand.

"I'll add a few nice little flourishes," his young voice said confidently. "This strikes me as a good place for grammar and rhetoric."

Chapter 12

THE THAR DESERT
NEAR THE IRON TRIANGLE

Three days later, at sunrise, Belisarius and a small escort rode into the Thar Desert. "The Great Indian Desert," as it was also sometimes called.

They didn't go far. No farther than they'd been able to travel in the three days since they'd left the Triangle. Partly, that was because Belisarius' bodyguards were by now pestering him almost constantly regarding his security. They hadn't been happy at all when he'd informed them he planned to leave the Triangle on a week-long scouting expedition of his own. The bodyguards had the not-unreasonable attitude that scouting expeditions should be done by scouts, not commanders-in-chief.

Belisarius didn't disagree with them, as a matter of general principle. Nor was this expedition one of the periodically calculated risks he took, proving to his men that he was willing to share their dangers and hardships. It was, in fact, purely and simply a scouting expedition—and not one in which he expected to encounter any enemies.

Why would he, after all? The Thar was enemy enough, to any human. With the exception of some small nomadic tribes, no one ventured into it willingly. There was no logical reason for the Malwa to be sending patrols into its interior. In any event, Belisarius had been careful to enter the desert much farther south than the most advanced Malwa contingents.

Aide wasn't any happier at the situation than the bodyguards were.

This is purely stupid. Why are you bothering, anyway? You already crossed the Thar, once before, when you were fleeing India. And don't try to deny it! I was there, remember?

Belisarius ignored him, for a moment. His eyes continued to range the landscape, absorbing it as best he could.

True, he had crossed this desert once—albeit a considerable distance to the south. Still, what he could see here was not really any different from what he'd seen years earlier. The Thar desert, like most deserts, is much of a sameness.

Yes, I remember—but my memories were those of the man who crossed this desert then. One man, alone, on a camel rather than a horse, and with plenty of water and supplies. I needed to see it again, to really bring back all *the memories.*

I could have done that for you, Aide pointed out peevishly. One of the crystal's seemingly-magical powers was an ability to bring back any of Belisarius' memories—while Aide had been with him, at least—as vividly as if they'd just happened.

Belisarius shook his head slightly. *It's still not the same. I need to feel the heat again, on my own skin. Gauge it, just as I gauge the dryness and the barrenness.*

He gave Abbu, riding just behind him to his left, a little jerk of the head to summon him forward.

"What do you think?" he asked the leader of his Arab scouts.

Abbu's grizzle-bearded countenance glared at the desert. "It is nothing, next to the Empty Quarter!"

Bedouin honor having been satisfied, he shrugged. "Still, it is a real desert. No oases, even, from what I've been told."

He's right, Aide chimed in. **There aren't any. The desert isn't as bad as it will become a millennia and a half from now, when the first real records were maintained. The Thar is a fairly recent desert. Still, as the old bandit says, it is indeed a real desert. And no artesian wells, either.**

Belisarius mused on the problem, for a minute or so.

Could we dig our own wells, then?

I could find the spots for you. Very likely ones, at least. The records are good, and the aquifers would not have changed much. But there are no guarantees, and . . . In a desert this

bad, if even one of my estimates proves wrong, it could be disastrous.

Belisarius was considerably more sanguine than Aide, on that score. He had found many times that Aide's superhuman intellect, while it often floundered with matters involving human emotions, rarely failed when it came to a straightforward task of deduction based on a mass of empirical data.

Still, he saw no reason to take unnecessary chances.

"Abbu, if I send you and some of your men through this desert—a dozen or two, whatever you wish—along with a chart indicating the likely spots to dig wells, could you find them?"

Abbu's expression was sour. "I don't read charts easily," he grumbled. "Detest the newfangled things."

Belisarius suppressed a smile. What Abbu said was true enough—the part about detesting the things, at any rate—but the scout leader was perfectly capable of reading them well enough. Even if he weren't, he had several young Arabs who could read and interpret maps and charts as easily as any Greek. What was really involved here was more the natural dislike of an old bedouin at the prospect of digging a number of wells in a desert.

You'd be an idiot to trust him to do it properly, anyway. If you want good wells made—ones that you can depend on, weeks or months later—you'd do better to use Greeks.

Teaching your grandfather to suck eggs again? I just want Abbu to find the spots. I'll send some of my bucellarii with him to do the work. Thracians will be even better than Greeks.

After he explained the plan to Abbu, the scout leader was mollified. "Easy, then," he announced. "Take us three weeks."

"No longer?"

Abbu squinted at the desert. "Maybe a month. The Thar is three hundred miles across, you say?"

Not really, Aide chimed in. **Not today, before the worst of the desiccation has happened. Say, two hundred miles of real desert, with a fifty-mile fringe. We're still in the fringe here, really.**

"Figure two hundred miles of real desert, Abbu, with another fifty on either side like this terrain."

The old Arab ran fingers through his beard. "And you want us to use horses. Not camels?"

Belisarius nodded.

"Then, as I say, three, maybe four weeks. Coming back will be quick, with the wells already dug."

Abbu cocked his head a little, looking at Belisarius through narrowed eyes.

"What rashness are you contemplating, General?"

Belisarius pointed with his chin toward the east. "When the time comes—if the time comes—I may want to lead an expedition across that desert. To Ajmer."

"*Ajmer?*" The Arab chief's eyes almost literally bulged. "You are mad! Ajmer is the main city of the Rajputs. It would take you ten thousand men—maybe fifteen—to seize the city. Then, you would be lucky to hold it against the counterattack."

He stretched out his hand and flipped it, simultaneously indicating the desert with the gesture and dismissing everything else. "You cannot—*can not*, General, not even you—get more than a thousand men across that desert. Not even with wells dug. Not even in this fine *rabi* season—and we'll soon be in the heat of *garam*. With camels, maybe two thousand. But with horses? A thousand at most!"

"I wasn't actually planning to take a thousand," Belisarius said mildly. "I think five hundred of my bucellarii will suffice. With an additional two hundred of your scouts, as outriders."

"Against *Rajputs?*" Fiercely, Abbu shook his head. "Not a chance, General. Not with only five hundred of your best Thracians. Not even with splendid Arab scouts. We would not get within sight of Ajmer before we were overrun. Not all the Rajputs are in the Deccan with Damodara, you know. Many are not."

Belisarius nodded placidly. "A great many, according to my spies. I'm counting on that, in fact. I need at least fifteen thousand Rajputs to be in or around Ajmer when we arrive. Twenty would be better."

Abbu rolled his eyes. "What lunacy is this? You are expecting the Rajputs to become changed men? Lambs, where once they were lions?"

Belisarius chuckled. "Oh, not that, certainly. I'd have no use for Rajput lambs. But . . . yes, Abbu. If I do this—which I may well not, since right now it's only a possibility—then I expect the Rajputs to have changed."

He reined his horse around. "More than that, I will not say. This is all speculation, in any event. Let's get back to the Triangle."

◇   ◇   ◇

When they returned to the Triangle, Belisarius gave three orders.

The first summoned Ashot from the Sukkur gorge. He was no longer needed there, in command of the Roman forces, now that the Persians had established firm control over the area.

"I'll want him in charge of the bucellarii, of course," he told Maurice, "since you'll have to remain behind."

The bucellarii were Belisarius' picked force of Thracian cataphracts, armored heavy cavalrymen. A private army, in essence, that he'd maintained for years. A large one, too, numbering by now seven thousand men. He could afford it, since the immense loot from the past years of successful campaigns—first, against the Persians; and then, in alliance with them against the Malwa—had made Belisarius the richest person in the Roman Empire except for Justinian and Theodora.

Maurice had been the leader of those bucellarii since they were first formed, over ten years earlier. But, today, he was essentially the second-in-command of the entire Roman army in the Punjab.

Maurice grunted. "Ashot'll do fine. I still say it's a crazy idea."

"It may never happen, anyway," Belisarius pointed out. "It's something of a long shot, depending on several factors over which we have no control at all."

Maurice scowled. "So what? 'Long shot' and 'no control' are the two phrases that best describe this war to begin with."

Rightly said! chimed in Aide.

Belisarius gave the crystal the mental equivalent of a very cross-eyed look. *If I recall correctly,* you *were the one who started the war in the first place.*

Oh, nonsense! I just pointed out the inevitable.

The second order, which he issued immediately thereafter, summoned Agathius from Mesopotamia.

"We don't need him there either, any more," he explained to Maurice.

"No, we don't. Although I hate to think of what chaos those damn Persians will create in our logistics without Agathius to crack the whip over them. Still . . . "

The chiliarch ran fingers through his grizzled beard. "We could use him here, better. If you go haring off on this preposterous mad dash of yours, I'll have to command the troops here. Bloody fighting, that'll be, all across the front."

"Bloodier than anything you've ever seen," Belisarius agreed. "Or I've ever seen—or anyone's ever seen. The two greatest armies ever assembled in history hammering at each other across not more than twenty miles of front. And the Malwa *will* hammer, Maurice. You can be sure that Link will give that order before the monster departs. Whatever else, it will want this Roman army kept in its cage, and not able to come after it."

Maurice's grunted chuckle even had a bit of real humor. Not much, of course. "But no fancy maneuvers required. Nothing that really needs the crooked brain of Belisarius. Just stout, simple-minded Maurice of Thrace, like the centurion of the Bible. Saying to one, come, and he cometh. Saying to another, go, and he goeth."

Belisarius smiled, but said nothing.

Maurice grunted again, seeing the smile. "Well, I can do that, certainly. And I agree that it would help a lot to have Agathius here. He can manage everything else while I command on the front lines."

The third order he gave to Ashot, a few days later, as soon as he arrived.

More in the way of a set of orders, actually. Which of them Ashot chose to follow would depend on . . . this and that.

"Marvelous," said Ashot, after Belisarius finished. The stubby Armenian cataphract exchanged a familiar look with Maurice. The one that translated more-or-less as: *what sins did we commit to be given such a young lunatic for a commander?*

But he verbalized none of it. Even the exchange of looks was more in the way of a familiar habit than anything really heartfelt. It was not as if he and Maurice weren't accustomed to the experience, by now.

"I don't much doubt Kungas will agree," he said. "So I should be back within a month."

Belisarius cocked an eyebrow. "That soon?"

"There are advantages to working as closely as I have with Persians, General. I know at least two dehgans in Sukkur who are familiar with the terrain I'll have to pass through to reach Kungas. They'll guide me, readily enough."

"All right. How many men do you want?"

"Not more than thirty. We shouldn't encounter any Malwa, the route I'll be taking. Thirty will be enough to scare off any bandits. Any more would just slow us down."

Ashot and his little troop left the next morning. Thereafter, Belisarius went back to the routine of the siege.

"I hate sieges," he commented to Calopodius. "But I will say they don't require much in the way of thought, once everything's settled down."

"Meaning no offense, General, but if you think *you* hate sieges, I invite you to try writing a history about one. Grammar and rhetoric can only do so much."

Antonina stared down at the message in her hand. She was trying to remember if, at any time in her life, she'd ever felt such conflicting emotions.

"That is the oddest expression I can ever remember seeing on your face," Ousanas mused. "Although it does remind me, a bit, of the expression I once saw on the face of a young Greek nobleman in Alexandria."

Stalling for time while she tried to sort out her feelings, Antonina muttered: "When did you ever know any Greek noblemen in Alexandria?"

Glancing up, she saw Ousanas was smiling, that serene little smile that was always a little disconcerting on his face.

"I have led a varied life, you know. I wasn't always shackled to this wretched little African backwater in the mountains. On that occasion—there were several—the youth fancied himself a philosopher. I showed him otherwise."

Lounging on a nearby chair in Antonina's salon, Ezana grunted. He'd taken no offense, of course, at Ousanas' wisecrack about Axum. Partly, because he was used to it; partly, because he knew from experience that the only way to deal with Ousanas' wisecracks was to ignore them.

"And *that* is what caused a peculiar expression on his face?" he asked skeptically. "I would have thought one of your devastating logical ripostes—for which the world has seen no equal since Socrates—would have simply left him aghast at his ignorance."

Ezana was no slouch himself, when it came to wisecracks—or turning a properly florid phrase, for that matter. Ousanas flashed a quick grin in recognition, and then shrugged.

"Alas, no. My rebuttal went so far over his head that the callow stripling had no idea at all that I'd disemboweled him, intellectually speaking. No, the peculiar expression came not five minutes later, when a courier arrived bearing the news that the lad's father had died in Constantinople. And that he had inherited one of the largest fortunes in the empire."

He pointed a finger at Antonina's face. "*That* expression."

She didn't know whether to laugh or scowl. In the end, she managed to do both.

"It's a letter from Theodora. Sent by telegraph to Alexandria, relayed to Myos Hormos, and then brought by a dispatch vessel the rest of the way." She held it up. "My son—his wife Tahmina, too—is coming on a tour of our allies. Starting here in Axum, of course. He'll go with us to India."

"Ah." Ousanas nodded. "All is explained. Your delight at the unexpected prospect of seeing your son again, much sooner than you expected. Your chagrin at having to delay your much-antici-pated reunion with your husband. The maternal instinct of a proper Egyptian woman clashing with the salacious habits of a Greek harlot."

He and Ezana exchanged stern glances.

"You should wait for your son," Ezana pronounced. "Even if you are a Greek harlot."

Antonina gave them the benefit of her sweetest smile. "I would remind both of you that Greek women are also the world's best and most experienced poisoners. And you do not use food-tasters in Ethiopia."

"She has a point," Ousanas averred.

Ezana grunted again. "She should still wait for her son. Even if she is—"

"*Of course I'm going to wait for my son, you—you—fucking idiots!*"

The next day, though, it was her turn to start needling Ousanas.

"What? If it's that hard for you, why don't you leave now? There's no reason *you* have to wait here until Photius arrives. You can surely find some way to pass the time in Barbaricum—or Chabahari, most like—as accustomed as you are to the humdrum life in this African backwater."

Ousanas scowled at her. For one of the rare times since she'd met him, years earlier, the Bantu once-hunter had no easy quip to make in response.

"Damnation, Antonina, it is *difficult*. It never was, before, because . . ."

"Yes, I know. The mind—even yours, O great philosopher—makes different categories for different things. It's convenient, that way, and avoids problems."

Ousanas ran fingers over his scalp. "Yes," he said curtly. "Even mine. And now . . ."

His eyes started to drift toward the window they were standing near. Then, he looked away.

Antonina leaned over and glanced down into the courtyard below, one of several in the Ta'akha Maryam. Rukaiya was still there, sitting on a bench and holding her baby.

"She is very beautiful," Antonina said softly.

Ousanas was still looking aside. "Beauty I could ignore, readily enough. I am no peasant boy." For an instant, the familiar smile gleamed. "No longer, at least. I can remember a time when the mere sight of her would have paralyzed me."

He shrugged, uncomfortably. "Much harder to ignore the wit and the intelligence, coupled to the beauty. The damn girl is even well educated, for her age. Give her ten years . . ."

Antonina eyed him. "I did choose her for a king's wife, you know. And not just any king, but Eon. And I chose very well, I think."

"Yes, you did. Eon was besotted with her. I never had any trouble understanding why—but it never affected me then, either."

"The wedding will be tomorrow, Ousanas. Leave the next day, if you will."

"I can't, Antonina. First, because it would look odd, since everyone now knows that you are waiting for Photius. People would assume it was because I was displeased with the girl, instead of . . . ah, the exact opposite."

He brought his eyes back to look at her. "The bigger problem, however, is Koutina. Which we must now discuss. Before I do anything else, I must resolve that issue. People are already jabbering about it."

Antonina winced. As pleased as she was, overall, with her settlement of the Axumite succession problem, it was not a perfect world and her solution had shared in that imperfection. Most of the problems she could ignore, at least personally, since they mainly involved the grievances and disgruntlements of people she thought were too full of themselves anyway.

But Koutina . . .

"I don't know what to do about her," she admitted sadly.

The girl had been the most faithful and capable servant Antonina had ever had. And she'd now repaid her by separating her from Ousanas, with whom she'd developed a relationship that went considerably beyond a casual sexual liaison.

"Neither do I," said Ousanas. His tone was, if anything, still sadder. "She's always known, of course, that as the aqabe tsentsen I'd eventually have to make a marriage of state. But—"

He shrugged again. "The position of concubine was acceptable to her."

"It's not possible, now. You know that."

"Yes. Of course." After a moment's hesitation, Ousanas stepped to the window and looked down.

"She approached me about it two days ago, you know," he murmured.

"Rukaiya?"

"Yes. She told me she understood my existing attachment to Koutina and would have no objection if I kept her as a concubine." He smiled, turned away from the window, and held up a stiff finger. " 'Only one, though!' she said. 'Koutina is different. Any others and I will have you poisoned. Not the concubine*you*!' "

Antonina chuckled. "That . . . is very much like Rukaiya."

Which, it was, although Antonina was skeptical that Rukaiya would actually be able to handle the situation that easily. Granted, the girl was Arab and thus no stranger to the institution of concubinage. Even her recent conversion to Christianity would not have made much difference, if any. Concubinage might be frowned upon by the church, but it was common enough practice among wealthy Christians also—including plenty of bishops.

Still, she'd been a queen for some time now—and Eon's queen, to boot. There had never been any hint of interest in concubines on Eon's part. Of course, with a wife like Rukaiya, that was hardly surprising. Not only was she quite possibly the most beautiful woman in the Axumite empire, she had wit and brains and a charming personality to go with it.

But it didn't matter, anyway. "Ousanas—"

"Yes, yes, I know." He waved his hand. "Absolutely impossible, given the nature of my new position as the angabo. The situation will be tricky enough as it is, making sure that the children Rukaiya will bear me have the proper relationship with Wahsi. Throw into that delicate balance yet another batch of children with Koutina . . ."

He shook his head. "It would be madness. She's not barren, either."

Koutina's one pregnancy had ended in a miscarriage. That was not particularly unusual, of course. Most likely, Koutina's next pregnancy *would* produce a child.

Suddenly, Ousanas shook his head again, but this time with rueful amusement. "Ha! It's probably a good thing Rukaiya *is* so comely and enjoyable to be around. I'm afraid there'll be no more sexual adventures on the part of the mighty Ousanas. As aqabe tsentsen, I could do most anything in that regard and only produce chuckles. As angabo, I will have to be like the Caesar's wife you Romans brag about—even if, mind you, I can't see where you've often lived up to it."

Antonina grinned. "Theodora does. Which, given her history, may seem ironic to some people. On the other hand, the one advantage to being an ex-whore—take it from me—is that you're not subject to the notion some women have that the man in some other woman's bed is much more interesting than the one in your own." She stuck out her tongue. *"Bleah."*

"I can imagine. However . . ."

"Yes, I know. We are no closer to a solution. And the problem is as bad as it could be, because Koutina is not only losing you, she's losing *me*. I can't very well keep her on as my servant when you will be accompanying me on the same trip with . . ."

Her voice trailed off. Looking suddenly at Ousanas, she saw that his eyes had that slightly unfocused look she suspected were in her own.

"Photius would have to agree, of course," Ousanas mused. "Tahmina, rather."

Antonina tried to poke at the idea, to find any weak spots. "It still leaves the problem that Koutina will be with us. People might think—"

"Pah!" Ousanas' sneer, when he threw himself into it, could be as magnificent as his grin. "What 'people'? The only 'people'— *person*—who matters here is Rukaiya. And she will believe me—she'll certainly believe you—when we explain it to her. For the rest . . ."

He shrugged. "Who cares what gossip circulates, as long as Rukaiya doesn't pay attention to it? Gossip is easy to deal with. Ignore it unless it gets too obtrusive, at which point you inform Ezana that Loudmouths Alpha, Beta and Gamma have become a nuisance. Shortly thereafter, Loudmouths Alpha, Beta and Gamma will either cease being a nuisance or will cease altogether."

The grin came. "Such a handy fellow to have around, even if he lacks the proper appreciation of my philosophical talents."

The more Antonina considered the idea, the more she liked it. "Yes. Eventually, the trip is over. So long as there are no Ousanas bastards inconveniently lounging about"—here she gave him a pointed look—"there's no problem. Koutina goes to Constantinople as one of Tahmina's maidservants, and . . ."

Her face cleared. "She'll do quite well. You've already started her education. If she continues it—she's very pretty, and very capable—she'll eventually wind up in a good marriage. A senatorial family is not out of the question, if she has Tahmina's favor. Which, I have no doubt she will."

For a moment, she and Ousanas regarded each other with that special satisfaction that belongs to conspirators having reached a particularly pleasing conspiracy.

Then, Ousanas frowned. "I remind you. Photius will have to agree."

Antonina's expression became—she hoped, anyway—suitably outraged. "Of course, he will! He's my *son*, you idiot!"

When Photius arrived, two weeks later, he didn't actually have an opinion, one way or the other.

"Whatever you want, Mother," in the resigned but dutiful tones of an eleven-year-old.

Antonina's older daughter-in-law, on the other hand, proved far more perceptive.

"What a marvelous idea, Mother! And do you think she'd be willing to carry around a cuirass for me, too?" The sixteen-year-old gave her husband a very credible eyelash-batting. "I think I'd look good in a cuirass, Photius, don't you?"

Photius choked. "Not in bed!" he protested. "I'd break my hands, trying to give you backrubs."

Chapter 13

BARBARICUM, ON THE INDIAN COAST

Anna and her companions spent their first night in India crowded into the corner of a tavern packed full with Roman soldiers and all the other typical denizens of a great port city—longshoremen, sailors, petty merchants and their womenfolk, pimps and prostitutes, gamblers, and the usual sprinkling of thieves and other criminals.

Like almost all the buildings in Barbaricum, the tavern was a mudbrick edifice that had been badly burned in the great fires that swept the city during the Roman conquest. The arson had not been committed by Belisarius' men, but by the fanatic Mahaveda priests who led the Malwa defenders. Despite the still obvious reminders of that destruction, the tavern was in use for the simple reason that, unlike so many buildings in the city, the walls were still standing and there was even a functional roof.

When they first entered, Anna and her party had been assessed by the mob of people packed in the tavern. The assessment had not been as quick as the one which that experienced crowd would have normally made. Anna and her party were . . . odd.

The hesitation worked entirely to her advantage, however. The tough-looking Isaurian brothers and Abdul were enough to give would-be cutpurses pause, and in the little space and time cleared for them, the magical rumor had time to begin and spread throughout the tavern. Watching it spread—so obvious, from the curious stares and glances sent her way—Anna was simultaneously appalled, amused, angry, and thankful.

It's her. Calopodius the Blind's wife. Got to be.

"Who started this damned rumor, anyway?" she asked peevishly, after Illus cleared a reasonably clean spot for her in a corner and she was finally able to sit down. She leaned against the shelter of the walls with relief. She was well-nigh exhausted.

Abdul grunted with amusement. The Arab was frequently amused, Anna noted with exasperation. But it was an old and well-worn exasperation, by now, almost pleasant in its predictability.

Cottomenes, whose amusement at life's quirks was not much less than Abdul's, chuckled his own agreement. "You're hot news, Lady Saronites. Everybody on the docks was talking about it, too. And the soldiers outside the telegraph office." Cottomenes, unlike his older brother, never allowed himself the familiarity of calling her "girl." In all other respects, however, he showed her a lack of fawning respect that would have outraged her family.

After the dockboys whom Anna had hired finished stacking her luggage next to her, they crowded themselves against a wall nearby, ignoring the glares directed their way by the tavern's usual habitués. Clearly enough, having found this source of incredible largesse, the dockboys had no intention of relinquishing it.

Anna shook her head. The vehement motion finished the last work of disarranging her long dark hair. The elaborate coiffure under which she had departed Constantinople, so many weeks before, was now entirely a thing of the past. Her hair was every bit as tangled and filthy as her clothing. She wondered if she would ever feel clean again.

"*Why?*" she whispered.

Squatting next to her, Illus studied her for a moment. His eyes were knowing, as if the weeks of close companionship and travel had finally enabled a half-barbarian mercenary soldier to understand the weird torments of a young noblewoman's soul.

Which, indeed, perhaps they had.

"You're different, girl. What you do is *different*. You have no idea how important that can be, to a man who does nothing, day after day, but toil under a sun. Or to a woman who does nothing, day after day, but wash clothes and carry water."

She stared up at him. Seeing the warmth lurking somewhere deep in Illus' eyes, in that hard tight face, Anna was stunned to realize how great a place the man had carved for himself in her heart. *Friendship* was a stranger to Anna of the Melisseni.

"And what is an angel, in the end," said the Isaurian softly, "but something *different*?"

Anna stared down at her grimy garments, noting all the little tears and frays in the fabric.

"In *this*?"

The epiphany finally came to her, then. And she wondered, in the hour or so that she spent leaning against the walls of the noisy tavern before she finally drifted into sleep, whether Calopodius had also known such an epiphany. Not on the day he chose to leave her behind, all her dreams crushed, in order to gain his own; but on the day he first awoke, a blind man, and realized that sight is its own curse.

And for the first time since she'd heard Calopodius' name, she no longer regretted the life that had been denied to her. No longer thought with bitterness of the years she would never spend in the shelter of the cloister, allowing her mind to range through the world's accumulated wisdom like a hawk finally soaring free.

When she awoke the next morning, the first thought that came to her was that she finally understood her own faith—and never had before, not truly. There was some regret in the thought, of course. Understanding, for all except God, is also limitation. But with that limitation came clarity and sharpness, so different from the froth and fuzz of a girl's fancies and dreams.

In the gray light of an alien land's morning, filtering into a tavern more noisome than any she would ever have imagined, Anna studied her soiled and ragged clothing. Seeing, this time, not filth and ruin but simply the carpet of her life opening up before her. A life she had thought closeted forever.

"Practicality first," she announced firmly. "It is not a sin."

The words woke up Illus. He gazed at her through slitted, puzzled eyes.

"Get up," she commanded. "We need uniforms."

A few minutes later, leading the way out the door with her three-soldier escort and five dock urchins toting her luggage, Anna issued the first of that day's rulings and commandments.

"It'll be expensive, but my husband will pay for it. He's rich."

"He's not here," grunted Illus.

"His name is. He's also famous. Find me a banker."

It took a bit of time before she was able to make the concept of "banker" clear to Illus. Or, more precisely, differentiate it from the concepts of "pawnbroker," "usurer" and "loan shark." But, eventually, he agreed to seek out and capture this mythological creature—with as much confidence as he would have announced plans to trap a griffin or a minotaur.

"Never mind," grumbled Anna, seeing the nervous little way in which Illus was fingering his sword. "I'll do it myself. Where's the army headquarters in this city? *They'll* know what a 'banker' is, be sure of it."

That task was within Illus' scheme of things. And since Barbaricum was in the actual theater of Belisarius' operations, the officers in command of the garrison were several cuts of competence above those at Chabahari. By midmorning, Anna had been steered to the largest of the many new moneylenders who had fixed themselves upon Belisarius' army.

An Indian himself, ironically enough, named Pulinda. Anna wondered, as she negotiated the terms, what secrets—and what dreams, realized or stultified—lay behind the life of the small and elderly man sitting across from her. How had a man from the teeming Ganges valley eventually found himself, awash with wealth obtained in whatever mysterious manner, a paymaster to the alien army which was hammering at the gates of his own homeland?

Did he regret the life which had brought him to this place? Savor it?

Most likely both, she concluded. And was then amused, when she realized how astonished Pulinda would have been had he realized that the woman with whom he was quarreling over terms was actually awash in good feeling toward him.

Perhaps, in some unknown way, he sensed that warmth. In any event, the negotiations came to an end sooner than Anna had expected. They certainly left her with better terms than she had expected.

Or, perhaps, it was simply that magic name of Calopodius again, clearing the waters before her. Pulinda's last words to her were: "Mention me to your husband, if you would."

By mid-afternoon, she had tracked down the tailor reputed to be the best in Barbaricum. By sundown, she had completed her business with him. Most of that time had been spent keeping the dockboys from fidgeting as the tailor measured them.

"You also!" Anna commanded, slapping the most obstreperous urchin on top of his head. "In the Service, cleanliness is essential."

The next day, however, when they donned their new uniforms, the dockboys were almost beside themselves with joy. The plain and utilitarian garments were, by a great margin, the finest clothing they had ever possessed.

The Isaurian brothers and Abdul were not quite as demonstrative. Not quite.

"We look like princes," gurgled Cottomenes happily.

"And so you are," pronounced Anna. "The highest officers of the Wife's Service. A rank which will someday"—she spoke with a confidence far beyond her years—"be envied by princes the world over."

THE IRON TRIANGLE

"Relax, Calopodius," said Menander cheerfully, giving the blind young officer a friendly pat on the shoulder. "I'll see to it she arrives safely."

"She's already left Barbaricum," muttered Calopodius. "Damnation, why didn't she *wait*?"

Despite his agitation, Calopodius couldn't help smiling when he heard the little round of laughter which echoed around him. As usual, whenever the subject of Calopodius' wife arose, every officer and orderly in the command bunker had listened. In her own way, Anna was becoming as famous as anyone in the great Roman army fighting its way into India.

Most husbands, to say the least, do not like to discover that their wives are the subject of endless army gossip. But since, in this case, the cause of the gossip was not the usual sexual peccadilloes, Calopodius was not certain how he felt about it. Some part of him, ingrained with custom, still felt a certain dull outrage. But, for the most part—perhaps oddly—his main reaction was one of quiet pride.

"I suppose that's a ridiculous question," he admitted ruefully. "She hasn't waited for anything else."

When Menander spoke again, the tone in his voice was much less jovial. As if he, too, shared in the concern which—much to his surprise—Calopodius had found engulfing him since he learned of Anna's journey. Strange, really, that he should care so much about the well-being of a wife who was little but a vague image to him.

But . . . Even before his blinding, the world of literature had often seemed as real to Calopodius as any other. Since he lost his sight, it had become all the more so—despite the fact that he could no longer read or write himself, but depended on others to do it for him.

Anna Melisseni, the distant girl he had married and had known for a short time in Constantinople, meant practically nothing to him. But *The Wife of Calopodius the Blind*, the unknown woman who had been advancing toward him for weeks now, she was a different thing altogether. Still mysterious, but not a stranger. How could she be, any longer?

Had he not, after all, written about her often enough in his own *Dispatches*? In the third person, of course, as he always spoke of himself in his writings. No subjective mood was ever inserted into his *Dispatches,* any more than into the chapters of his massive *History of the War.* But, detached or not, whenever he received news of Anna he included at least a few sentences detailing for the army her latest adventures. Just as he did for those officers and men who had distinguished themselves. And he was no longer surprised to discover that most of the army found a young wife's exploits more interesting than their own.

She's *different*.

"Difference," however, was no shield against life's misfortunes—misfortunes which are multiplied several times over in the middle of a war zone. So, within seconds, Calopodius was back to fretting.

"Why didn't she wait, damn it all?"

Again, Menander clapped his shoulder. "I'm leaving with the *Victrix* this afternoon, Calopodius. Steaming with the riverflow, I'll be in Sukkur long before Anna gets there coming upstream in an oared river craft. So I'll be her escort on the last leg of her journey, coming into the Punjab."

"The Sind's not that safe," grumbled Calopodius, still fretting. The Sind was the lower half of the Indus river valley, and while it had now been cleared of Malwa troops and was under the jurisdiction of Rome's Persian allies, the province was still greatly unsettled. "Dacoits everywhere."

"Dacoits aren't going to attack a military convoy," interrupted Belisarius. "I'll make sure she gets a Persian escort of some kind as far as Sukkur."

One of the telegraphs in the command center began to chatter. When the message was read aloud, a short time later, even Calopodius began to relax.

"Guess not," he mumbled—more than a little abashed. "With *that* escort."

Chapter 14

THE LOWER INDUS

Spring, 534 A.D.

"I don't believe this," mumbled Illus—more than a little abashed. He glanced down at his uniform. For all the finery of the fabric and the cut, the garment seemed utterly drab matched against the glittering costumes which seemed to fill the wharf against which their river barge was just now being tied.

Standing next to him, Anna said nothing. Her face was stiff, showing none of the uneasiness she felt herself. Her own costume was even more severe and plainly cut than those of her officers, even if the fabric itself was expensive. And she found herself wishing desperately that her cosmetics had survived the journey from Constantinople. For a woman of her class, being seen with a face unadorned by anything except nature was well-nigh unthinkable. In *any* company, much less . . .

The tying-up was finished and the gangplank laid. Anna was able to guess at the identity of the first man to stride across it.

She was not even surprised. Anna had read everything ever written by Irene Macrembolitissa—several times over—including the last book the woman wrote just before she left for the Hindu Kush on her great expedition of conquest. *The Deeds of Khusrau*, she thought, described the man quite well. The Emperor of Persia was not particularly large, but so full of life and energy that he seemed like a giant as he strode toward her across the gangplank.

What am I doing here? she wondered. *I never planned on such as this!*

"So! You are the one!" were the first words he boomed. "To live in such days, when legends walk among us!"

In the confused time that followed, as Anna was introduced to a not-so-little mob of Persian officers and officials—most of them obviously struggling not to frown with disapproval at such a disreputable woman—she pondered on those words.

They seemed meaningless to her. Khusrau Anushirvan—"Khusrau of the Immortal Soul"—was a legend, not she.

So why had he said that?

By the end of that evening, after spending hours sitting stiffly in a chair while Iran's royalty and nobility wined and dined her, she had mustered enough courage to lean over to the emperor—sitting next to her!—and whisper the question into his ear.

Khusrau's response astonished her even more. He grinned broadly, white teeth gleaming in a square-cut Persian beard. Then, he leaned over and whispered in return:

"I am an expert on legends, wife of Calopodius. Truth be told, I often think the art of kingship is mainly knowing how to make the things."

He glanced slyly at his assembled nobility, who had not stopped frowning at Anna throughout the royal feast—but always, she noticed, under lowered brows.

"But keep it a secret," he whispered. "It wouldn't do for my noble sahrdaran and vurzurgan to discover that their emperor is really a common manufacturer. I don't need another rebellion this year."

She managed to choke down a laugh, fortunately. The effort, however, caused her hand to shake just enough to spill some wine onto her long dress.

"No matter," whispered the emperor. "Don't even try to remove the stain. By next week, it'll be the blood of a dying man brought back to life by the touch of your hand. Ask anyone."

She tightened her lips to keep from smiling. It was nonsense, of course, but there was no denying the emperor was a charming man.

But, royal decree or no, it was still nonsense. Bloodstains aplenty there had been on the garments she'd brought from Constantinople, true enough. Blood and pus and urine and excrement and every manner of fluid produced by human suffering. She'd gained them in Chabahari, and again at Barbaricum. Nor did she doubt there would be bloodstains on this garment also, soon enough, to match the wine stain she had just put there.

Indeed, she had designed the uniforms of the Wife's Service with that in mind. That was why the fabric had been dyed a purple so dark it was almost black.

But it was still nonsense. Her touch had no more magic power than anyone's. Her knowledge—or rather, the knowledge which she had obtained by reading everything Macrembolitissa or anyone else had ever written transmitting the Talisman of God's wisdom—now, *that* was powerful. But it had nothing to do with her, except insofar as she was another vessel of those truths.

Something of her skepticism must have shown, despite her effort to remain impassive-faced. She was only nineteen, after all, and hardly an experienced diplomat.

Khusrau's lips quirked. "You'll see."

The next day she resumed her journey up the river toward Sukkur. The emperor himself, due to the pressing business of completing his incorporation of the Sind into the swelling empire of Iran, apologized for not being able to accompany her personally. But he detailed no fewer than four Persian war galleys to serve as her escort.

"No fear of dacoits," said Illus, with great satisfaction. "Or deserters turned robbers."

His satisfaction turned a bit sour at Anna's response.

"Good. We'll be able to stop at every hospital along the way then. No matter how small."

And stop they did. Only briefly, in the Roman ones. By now, to Anna's satisfaction, Belisarius' blood-curdling threats had resulted in a marked improvement in medical procedures and sanitary practices.

But most of the small military hospitals along the way were Persian. The "hospitals" were nothing more than tents pitched along the riverbank—mere staging posts for disabled Persian soldiers being evacuated back to their homeland. The conditions within them had Anna seething, with a fury that was all the greater because neither she nor either of the Isaurian officers could speak a word of the Iranian language. Abdul could make himself understood, but his pidgin was quite inadequate to the task of convincing skeptical—even hostile—Persian officials that Anna's opinion was anything more than female twaddle.

Anna spent another futile hour trying to convince the officers in command of her escort to send a message to Khusrau himself. Clearly enough, however, none of them were prepared to annoy the emperor at the behest of a Roman woman who was probably half-insane to begin with.

Fortunately, at the town of Dadu, there was a telegraph station. Anna marched into it and fired off a message to her husband.

> **Why Talisman medical precepts not translated into Persian STOP Instruct Emperor Iran discipline his idiots STOP**

"Do it," said Belisarius, after Calopodius read him the message.

The general paused. "Well, the first part, anyway. The Persian translation. I'll have to figure out a somewhat more diplomatic way to pass the rest of it on to Khusrau."

Maurice snorted. "How about hitting him on the head with a club? That'd be somewhat more diplomatic."

By the time the convoy reached Sukkur, it was moving very slowly.

There were no military hospitals along the final stretch of the river, because wounded soldiers were kept either in Sukkur itself or had already passed through the evacuation routes. The slow pace was now due entirely to the native population.

By whatever mysterious means, word of the Wife's passage had spread up and down the Indus. The convoy was constantly approached by small river boats bearing sick and injured villagers, begging for what was apparently being called "the healing touch."

Anna tried to reason, to argue, to convince. But it was hopeless. The language barrier was well-nigh impassible. Even the officers of her Persian escort could do no more than roughly translate the phrase "healing touch."

In the end, not being able to bear the looks of anguish on their faces, Anna laid her hands on every villager brought alongside her

barge for the purpose. Muttering curses under her breath all the
while—curses which were all the more bitter since she was quite
certain the villagers of the Sind took them for powerful incanta-
tions.

At Sukkur, she was met by Menander and the entire crew of
the *Victrix*. Beaming from ear to ear.

The grins faded soon enough. After waiting impatiently for the
introductions to be completed, Anna's next words were: "Where's
the telegraph station?"

**Urgent stop Must translate Talisman precepts into native
tongues also STOP**

Menander fidgeted while she waited for the reply.

"I've got a critical military cargo to haul to the island," he muttered. "Calopodius may not even send an answer."

"He's my husband," came her curt response. "Of course he'll
answer me."

Sure enough, the answer came very soon.

**Cannot STOP Is no written native language STOP Not
even alphabet STOP**

After reading it, Anna snorted. "We'll see about that."

**You supposedly expert grammar and rhetoric STOP
Invent one STOP**

"You'd best get started on it," mused Belisarius. The general's
head turned to the south. "She'll be coming soon."

"Like a tidal bore," added Maurice.

That night, he dreamed of islands again.

*First, of Rhodes, where he spent an idle day on his journey to
join Belisarius' army while his ship took on supplies.*

*Some of that time he spent visiting the place where, years before,
John of Rhodes had constructed an armaments center. Calopodius'
own skills and interests were not inclined in a mechanical direction,*

but he was still curious enough to want to see the mysterious facility.

But, in truth, there was no longer much there of interest. Just a handful of buildings, vacant now except for livestock. So, after wandering about for a bit, he spent the rest of the day perched on a headland staring at the sea.

It was a peaceful, calm, and solitary day. The last one he would enjoy in his life, thus far.

Then, his dreams took him to the island in the Strait of Hormuz where Belisarius was having a naval base constructed. The general had sent Calopodius over from the mainland where the army was marching its way toward the Indus, in order to help resolve one of the many minor disputes which had erupted between the Romans and Persians who were constructing the facility. Among the members of the small corps of noble couriers who served Belisarius for liaison with the Persians, Calopodius had displayed a great deal of tact as well as verbal aptitude.

It was something of a private joke between him and the general. "I need you to take care of another obstreperous aunt," was the way Belisarius put it.

The task of mediating between the quarrelsome Romans and Persians had been stressful. But Calopodius had enjoyed the boat ride well enough; and, in the end, he had managed to translate Belisarius' blunt words into language flowery enough to slide the command through—like a knife between unguarded ribs.

Toward the end, his dreams slid into a flashing nightmare image of Bukkur Island. A log, painted to look like a field gun, sent flying by a lucky cannon ball fired by one of the Malwa gunships whose bombardment accompanied that last frenzied assault. The Romans drove off that attack also, in the end. But not before a mortar shell had ripped Calopodius' eyes out of his head.

The last sight he would ever have in his life was of that log, whirling through the air and crushing the skull of a Roman soldier standing in its way. What made the thing a nightmare was that Calopodius could not remember the soldier's name, if he had ever known it. So it all seemed very incomplete, in a way that was too horrible for Calopodius to be able to express clearly to anyone, even himself. Grammar and rhetoric simply collapsed under the coarse reality, just as fragile human bone and brain had collapsed under hurtling wood.

The sound of his aide-de-camp clumping about in the bunker awoke him. The warm little courtesy banished the nightmare, and Calopodius returned to life with a smile.

"How does the place look?" he asked.

"It's hardly fit for a Melisseni girl. But I imagine it'll do for *your* wife."

"Soon, now."

"Yes." Calopodius heard Luke lay something on the small table next to the cot. From the slight rustle, he understood that it was another stack of telegrams. Private ones, addressed to him, not army business.

"Any from Anna?"

"No. Just more bills."

Calopodius laughed. "Well, whatever else, she still spends money like a Melisseni. Before she's done, that banker will be the richest man in India."

Luke said nothing in response. After a moment, Calopodius' humor faded away, replaced by simple wonder.

"Soon, now. I wonder what she'll be like?"

Chapter 15

LADY DAMODARA'S PALACE
KAUSAMBI

"We should go back," whispered Rajiv's little sister. Nervously, the girl's eyes ranged about the dark cellar. "It's scary down here."

Truth be told, Rajiv found the place fairly creepy himself. The little chamber was one of many they'd found in this long-unused portion of the palace's underground cellars. Rajiv found the maze-like complexity of the cellars fascinating. He could not for the life of him figure out any rhyme or reason to the ancient architectural design, if there had ever been one at all. But that same labyrinthine character of the little grottoes also made them . . .

Well. A little scary.

But no thirteen-year-old boy will admit as much to his seven-year-old sister. Not even a peasant boy, much less the son of Rajputana's most famous king.

"You go back if you want to," he said, lifting the oil lamp to get a better look at the archway ahead of them. He could see part of another small cellar beyond. "I want to see all of it."

"I'll get lost on my own," Mirabai whined. "And there's only one lamp."

For a moment, Rajiv hesitated. He could, after all, use his sister's fear and the lack of a second lamp as a legitimate justification for going back. No reflection on *his* courage.

595

He might have, too, except that his sister's next words irritated him.

"There are *ghosts* down here," she whispered. "I can hear them talking."

"Oh, don't be silly!" He took a step toward the archway.

"I *can* hear them," she said. Quietly, but insistently.

Rajiv started to make a sarcastic rejoinder, when he heard something. He froze, half-cocking his head to bring an ear to bear.

She was right! Rajiv could hear voices himself. No words, as such, just murmuring.

"There's more than one of them, too," his sister hissed.

Again, she was right. Rajiv could distinguish at least two separate voices. From their tone, they seemed to be having an argument of some sort.

Would ghosts argue? he wondered.

That half-frightened, half-puzzled question steadied his nerves. With the steadiness, came a more acute sense of what he was hearing.

"Those aren't ghosts," he whispered. "Those are people. Live people."

Mirabai's face was tight with fear. "What would *people* be doing down here?"

That was . . . a very good question. And the only answer that came to Rajiv was a bad one.

He thrust the lamp at his sister. "Here. Take it and go back. Then get the Mongoose and Anastasius down here, as quickly as you can. Mother too. And you'd better tell Lady Damodara."

The girl squinted at the lamp, fearfully. "I'll get lost! I don't know the way."

"Just follow the same route I took us on," Rajiv hissed. "Any time I didn't know which way to go, when there was a choice, I turned to the left. So on your way back, you turn to the right."

He reminded himself forcefully that his sister was only seven years old. In a much more kindly tone, he added: "You can do it, Mirabai. You *have* to do it. I think we're dealing with treachery here."

Mirabai's eyes widened and moved to the dark, open archway. "What are you going to do?"

"I don't know," he whispered. "Something."

He half-forced her to take the lamp. "Now go!"

After his sister scampered off, Rajiv crept toward the archway. He had to move from memory alone. With the light of the lamp gone, it was pitch dark in these deep cellars.

After groping his way through the arch, he moved slowly across the cellar. Very faintly, he could see what looked like another archway on the opposite side. There was a dim light beyond that seemed to flicker, a bit. That meant that someone on the other side—probably at least one cellar farther away, maybe more—had an oil lamp.

His foot encountered an obstacle and he tripped, sprawling across the stone floor. Fortunately, the endless hours of training under the harsh regimen of the Mongoose had Rajiv's reflexes honed to a fine edge. He cushioned his fall with his hands, keeping the noise to a minimum.

His feet were still lying on something. Something . . . not stone. Not really hard at all.

Even before he got to his knees and reached back, to feel, he was certain he knew what he'd tripped over.

Yes. It was a body.

Fingering gingerly, probing, it didn't take Rajiv long to determine who the man was. Small, wiry, clad only in a loincloth. It had to be one of the Bihari slave miners that Lady Damodara was using to dig an escape route from the palace, if it was someday needed. They worked under the supervision of half a dozen Yetai mercenary soldiers. Ajatasutra had bought the slaves and hired the mercenaries.

Now that he was close, he could smell the stink. The man had voided himself in dying. The body was noticeably cool, too. Although the blood didn't feel crusted, it was dry by now. And while Rajiv could smell the feces, the odor wasn't that strong any longer. He hadn't noticed it at all when he entered the room, and he had a good sense of smell. Rajiv guessed that the murder had taken place recently, but not all that recently. Two or three hours earlier.

He didn't think it could have happened earlier than that, though. The body wasn't stiff yet. Some years before—he'd been about eight, as he recalled—Rajiv had questioned his father's lieutenant Jaimal on the subject, in that simultaneously horrified, fascinated and almost gleeful way that young boys will do. Jaimal had told him that, as a rule, a body stiffened three hours after death and then grew limp again after a day and a half. But Rajiv remembered Jaimal also telling him that the rule was only a rough one. The times could vary, especially depending on the temperature. In these cool cellars, it might all have happened faster.

It was possible there'd simply been a quarrel amongst the slaves. But where would a slave have gotten the blade to cut a throat so neatly? The only tools they had were picks and shovels.

So it was probably treachery—and on the part of the Ye-tai. Some of them, at least.

Rajiv had to find out. He hadn't really followed the progress of the tunnel-digging, since it was none of his affair and he was usually preoccupied with his training. The only reason he'd had today free to do some exploring was that the Mongoose was now spending more time in the company of Dhruva and her infant.

If the tunnel was almost finished—possibly even *was* finished . . .

This could be bad. Very bad.

Rajiv moved into the next cellar, slowly and carefully.

It seemed to Mirabai that it took her forever to get out of the cellars. Looking back on it later, she realized it had really taken very little time at all. The lamp had been bright enough to enable her to walk quickly, if not run—and her brother's instructions had worked perfectly.

The most surprising thing about it all was that she got more scared when it was over. She'd never in her life seen *that* look on her mother's face. Her mother never seemed to worry about any- thing.

"Get Kandhik," Valentinian hissed to Anastasius. "Break all his bones if you have to."

Anastasius didn't have to break any of the Ye-tai mercenary leader's bones. As huge and powerful as he was, a simple twisting of the arm did the trick.

Kandhik massaged his arm. "I don't know anything," he insisted. The Ye-tai was scowling ferociously, but he wasn't scowling directly at Anastasius—and he was doing everything in his power not to look at Valentinian at all.

The Mongoose was a frightening man under any circumstances. Under these circumstances, with that weasel smile on his face and a sword in his hand, he was terrifying. Kandhik was neither cowardly nor timid, but he knew perfectly well that either of the Roman cataphracts could kill him without working up a sweat.

Anastasius might need to take a deep breath. Valentinian wouldn't.

"Don't know *anything*," he insisted.

Sanga's wife and Lata came into the chamber. So did Lady Damodara.

"Three of the Ye-tai are missing," the girl said. "The other two are asleep in their chamber."

Although Ye-tai were sometimes called "White Huns," they were definitely Asiatic in their ancestry. Their only similarity to Europeans was that their features were somewhat bonier than those of most steppe-dwellers. Their complexion was certainly not pale—but, at that moment, Kandhik's face was almost ashen.

"Don't know *anything*," he repeated, this time pleading the words.

"He's telling the truth," Valentinian said abruptly. He touched the tip of the sword to Kandhik's throat. "Stay here and watch over the women. Do everything right and nothing wrong, and you'll live to see the end of this day. If my mood doesn't get worse."

With that, he turned and left the room. Anastasius lumbered after him.

Dhruva came in with the baby. She and her sister stared at each other, their eyes wide with fright.

Not as wide as Mirabai's, however. "What should we do, Mother?"

Sanga's wife looked around, rubbing her hands up and down her hips. The familiar gesture calmed Mirabai, a bit.

"May as well go to the kitchen and wait," she said. "I've got some onions to cut. Some leeks, too."

"I agree," said Lady Damodara.

After several minutes of listening from the darkness of the adjoining cellar, Rajiv understood exactly what was happening. The three Ye-tai in the next cellar were, in fact, planning to betray their employers. Apparently—it was not clear what threats or promises they'd made to do it—they'd gotten two of the Biharis to dig a side tunnel for them. It must have taken weeks to do the work, while keeping it a secret from everyone else.

And, now, it was done. But one of the Ye-tai was having second thoughts.

"—never dealt with *anvaya-prapta sachivya*. I have! And I'm telling you that unless we have a guarantee of some—"

"Shut up!" snarled one of the others. "I'm sick of hearing you brag about the times you hobnobbed with the Malwa. *What* 'guarantees'?"

The quarrel went back over familiar ground. Rajiv himself was inclined to agree with the doubter. He'd no more trust the Malwa royal clan than he would a scorpion. But he paid little attention to the rest of it.

Whether or not the doubting Ye-tai was worried about the reaction of the *anvaya-prapta sachivya*, it was clear enough he was weakening. He didn't really have any choice, after all, now that the deed was effectively done. Soon enough, he'd give up his objections and the three Ye-tai would be gone.

Then ... within a day, Lady Damodara's palace would be swarmed by Emperor Skandagupta's troops. And the secret escape tunnel wouldn't be of any use, because the Ye-tai traitors would have told the Malwa where the tunnel exited. They'd have as many soldiers positioned in the stable as they would at the palace. And it wouldn't take them long to torture the stable-keeper—his family, more likely—into showing them where it was.

It was up to Rajiv, then. One thirteen-year-old boy, unarmed, against three Ye-tai mercenaries. Who were ...

He peeked around the corner again.

Definitely armed. Each of them with a sword.

But Rajiv didn't give their weapons more than a glance. He'd already peeked around that corner before, twice, and studied them well enough. This time he was examining the body of the second Bihari miner, whom the mercenaries had cast into a corner of the cellar after cutting his throat also.

Not the body, actually. Rajiv was studying the miner's tools, which the Ye-tai had tossed on top of his corpse.

A pick and a shovel. A short-handled spade, really. Both of the tools were rather small, not so much because most of the Biharis were small but simply because there wasn't much room in the tunnels they dug.

That was good, Rajiv decided. Small tools—at least for someone his size—would make better weapons than large ones would have.

Until he met the Mongoose, Rajiv would never have considered the possibility that tools might make weapons. He'd been raised a Rajput prince, after all. But the Mongoose had hammered that out of him, like many other things. He'd even insisted on teaching Rajiv to fight with big kitchen ladles.

Rajiv's mother had been mightily amused. Rajiv himself had been mortified—until, by the fourth time the Mongoose knocked him down, he'd stopped sneering at ladles.

He decided he'd start with the pick. It was a clumsier thing than the spade, and he'd probably lose it in the first encounter anyway.

There was no point in dawdling. Rajiv gave a last quick glance at the three oil lamps perched on a ledge. No way to knock them off, he decided. Not spaced out the way there were.

Besides, he didn't think fighting in the dark would be to his advantage anyway. That would be a clumsy business, and if there was one thing the Mongoose had driven home to him, it was that "clumsy" and "too damn much sweat" always went together.

"Fight like a miser," he whispered to himself. Then, came out of his crouch and sprang into the cellar.

He said nothing; issued no war cry; gave no speech. The Mongoose had slapped that out of him also. Just went for the pick, with destruction in his heart.

Still many cellars away, Valentinian and Anastasius heard the fight start.

Nothing from Rajiv. Just the sound of several angry and startled men, their shouts echoing through the labyrinth.

Rajiv went to meet the first Ye-tai. That surprised him, as he'd thought it would.

When you're outmatched, get in quick. They won't expect that, the fucks.

The Ye-tai's sword came up. Rajiv raised the pick as if to match blows. The mercenary grinned savagely, seeing him do so. He outweighed Rajiv by at least fifty pounds.

At the last instant, Rajiv reversed his grip, ducked under the sword, and drove the handle of the pick into the man's groin.

Go for the shithead's dick and balls. Turn him into a squealing bitch.

The Ye-tai didn't squeal. As hard as Rajiv had driven in the end of the shaft, he didn't do anything except stare ahead, his mouth agape. He'd dropped his sword and was clutching his groin, half-stooped.

His eyes were wide as saucers, too, which was handy.

Rajiv rose from his crouch, reversed his grip again, and drove one of the pick's narrow blades into an eye. The blunt iron sank three inches into the Ye-tai's skull.

As he'd expected, he'd lost the pick. But it had all happened fast enough that he had time to dive for the spade, grab it, and come up rolling in a far corner.

He wasn't thinking at all, really, just acting. Hours and hours and hours of the Mongoose's training, that was.

You don't have time to think in a fight. If you have to think, you're a dead man.

The slumping corpse of the first Ye-tai got in the way of the second. Rajiv had planned for that, when he chose the corner to roll into.

The third came at him, again with his sword high.

That's just stupid, some part of Rajiv's mind recorded. Dimly, there was another, walled-off part that remembered he had once thought that way of using a sword very warriorlike. Dramatic-looking. Heroic.

But that was before hours and hours and hours of the Mongoose. A lifetime ago, it seemed now—and even a thirteen-year life is a fair span of time.

Rajiv evaded the sword strike. No flair to it, just—got out of the way.

Not much. Just enough. Miserly in everything.

A short, quick, hard jab of the spade into the side of the Ye-tai's knee was enough to throw off his backhand stroke. Rajiv evaded that one easily. He didn't try to parry the blow. The wood and iron of his spade would be no match for a steel sword.

Another quick hard jab to the same knee was enough to bring the Ye-tai down.

As he did so, Rajiv swiveled, causing the crumpling Ye-tai to impede the other.

Fuck 'em up, when you're fighting a crowd. Make 'em fall over each other.

The third Ye-tai didn't fall. But he stumbled into the kneeling body of his comrade hard enough that he had to steady himself with one hand. His other hand, holding the sword, swung out wide in an instinctive reach for balance.

Rajiv drove the edge of the spade into the wrist of the sword arm. The hand popped open. The sword fell. Blood oozed from the laceration on the wrist. It was a bad laceration, even if Rajiv hadn't managed to sever anything critical.

Go for the extremities. Always go for extremities. Hands, feet, toes, fingers. They're your closest target and the hardest for the asshole to defend.

The Ye-tai gaped at him, more in surprise than anything else.

But Rajiv ignored him, for the moment.

Don't linger, you idiot. Cut a man just enough, then cut another. Then come back and cut the first one again, if you need to. Like your mother cuts onions. Practical. Fuck all that other crap.

The second Ye-tai *was* squealing, in a hissing sort of way. Rajiv knew that knee injuries were excruciating. The Mongoose had told him so—and then, twice, banged up his knee in training sessions to prove it.

The Ye-tai's head was unguarded, with both his hands clutching the ruined knee. So Rajiv drove the spade at his temple.

He made his first mistake, then. The target was so tempting—so glorious, as it were—that he threw everything into the blow. He'd take off that head!

The extra time it took to position his whole body for that mighty blow was enough for the Ye-tai to bring up his hand to protect the head.

Stupid! Rajiv snarled silently at himself.

It probably didn't make any difference, of course. If the edge of the spade wasn't as sharp as a true weapon, it wasn't all that dull; and if iron wasn't steel, it was still much harder than human flesh. The strike cut off one of the man's fingers and maimed the whole hand—and still delivered a powerful blow to the skull. Moaning, the Ye-tai collapsed to the floor, half-unconscious.

Still, Rajiv was glad the Mongoose hadn't seen.

"Stupid," he heard a voice mutter.

Startled, he glanced aside. The Mongoose was there, in the entrance to the chamber. He had his sword in his hand, but it was down alongside his leg. Behind him, Rajiv could see the huge figure of Anastasius looming.

The Mongoose leaned against the stone entrance, tapping the tip of the sword against his boot. Then, nodded his head toward the last Ye-tai against the far wall.

"Finish him, boy. And don't fuck up again."

Rajiv looked at the Ye-tai. The man was paying him no attention at all. He was staring at the Mongoose, obviously frightened out of his wits.

The spade had served well enough, but there was now a sword available. The one the second Ye-tai had dropped after Rajiv smashed his knee.

No reason to waste the spade, of course. Certainly not with the Mongoose watching. Rajiv had been trained—for hours and hours and hours—to throw most anything. Even ladles. The Mongoose was a firm believer in the value of weapons used at a distance.

Rajiv would never be the Mongoose's equal with a throwing knife, of course. He was not sure even the heroes and *asuras* of the legends could throw a knife that well.

But he was awfully good, by now. The spade, hurled like a spear, struck the Ye-tai in the groin.

"Good!" the Mongoose grunted.

With the sword in his hand, Rajiv approached the Ye-tai. By now, of course, the man had noticed him. Half-crouched, snarling, clutching himself with his left hand while he tried to grab his dropped sword with the still-bleeding right hand.

Rajiv sliced open his scalp with a quick, flicking strike of the sword.

Don't try to split his head open, you jackass. You'll likely just get your sword stuck. And it's too easy to block and what's the fucking point anyway? Just cut him somewhere in the front of the head. Anywhere the blood'll spill into his eyes and blind him. Head wounds bleed like nothing else.

Blood poured over the Ye-tai's face. The sword he'd been bringing up went, instead, to his face, as he tried to wipe off the blood with the back of his wrist.

It never got there. Another quick, flicking sword strike struck the hand and took off the thumb. The sword, again, fell to the ground.

"Don't . . . fuck . . . it . . . up," the Mongoose growled.

Rajiv didn't really need the lesson. He'd learned it well enough already, this day, with that one mistake. He was sorely tempted to end it all, but not for any romantic reason. The carnage was starting to upset him. He'd never been in a real fight before—not a killing one—and he was discovering that men don't die the way chickens and lambs do when they're slaughtered.

He'd always thought they would. But they didn't. They bled the same, pretty much. But lambs—certainly chickens—never had that look of horror in their eyes as they knew they were dying.

That same, walled-off part of Rajiv's mind thought he understood, now. The reason his father always seemed so stern. Not like his mother at all.

Father's son or mother's son, Rajiv was Mongoose-trained. So the sword flicked out five more times, mercilessly slicing and cutting everywhere, before he finally opened the big arteries and veins in the Ye-tai's throat.

"Good." The Mongoose straightened up and pointed with his sword toward a corner. "If you need to puke, do it over there. Cleaning up this mess is going to be a bitch as it is."

Anastasius pushed him aside and came into the chamber. "For the sake of Christ, Valentinian, will you give the boy a break? Three men, in his first fight—and him starting without a weapon."

The Mongoose scowled. "He did pretty damn good. I still don't want to clean up blood and puke all mixed together. Neither do you."

But Rajiv wasn't listening, any longer. He was in the corner, hands on his knees, puking.

He still had the sword firmly gripped, though—and was careful to keep the blade out of the way of the spewing vomit.

"Pretty damn good," the Mongoose repeated.

"We were very lucky," Lady Damodara said to Sanga's wife, that evening. "If it hadn't been for your son . . ."

She lowered her head, one hand rubbing her cheek. "We can't wait much longer. I must—finally—get word to my husband. He can't wait, either. I'd thought Ajatasutra would have come back, by now. The fact that he hasn't makes me wonder—"

"I think you're wrong, Lady." Rajiv's mother was standing by the window, looking out over Kausambi. She was making no attempt to hide from sight. Even if the Malwa dynasty had spies watching from a distance—which was very likely—all they would see in the twilight was the figure of a gray-haired and plain-seeming woman, dressed in simple apparel. A servant, obviously, and there were many servants in such a palace.

"I think Ajatasutra's long absence means the opposite. I think your husband is finally making his move."

More hopefully, Lady Damodara raised her head. She'd come to have a great deal of confidence in the Rajput queen. "You think so?"

Sanga's wife smiled. "Well, let me put it this way. Yes, I think so—and if I'm wrong, we're all dead anyway. So why fret about it?"

Lady Damodara chuckled. "If only I had your unflappable temperament!"

The smile went away. "Not so unflappable as all that. When I heard, afterward, what Rajiv had done . . . " She shook her head. "I almost screamed at him, I was so angry and upset."

"He was very brave."

"Yes, he was. That is why I was so angry. Reckless boy! But . . . "

She seemed to shudder a little. "He was also very, very deadly. That is why I was so upset. At the Mongoose, I think, more than him."

Lady Damodara tilted her head. "He is a Rajput prince."

"Yes, he is. So much is fine. What I do *not* want is for him to become a Rajput legend. *Another* damned Rajput legend. Being married to one is enough!"

There was silence, for a time.

"You may not have any choice," Lady Damodara finally said.

"Probably not," Sanga's wife agreed gloomily. "There are times I think I should have poisoned Valentinian right at the beginning."

There was silence for a time, again.

"He probably wouldn't have died anyway."

"Probably not."

Chapter 16
PESHAWAR

"What if it's in the middle of *garam* season?" Kungas asked skeptically, tugging at his little goatee. "The heat won't be so bad, here in the Vale, although it will be if we descend into the Punjab. But I'm concerned about water."

Ashot started to say something, but Kungas waved him down impatiently. "Yes, yes, fine. *If* we make it to the Indus, we'll have plenty of water. Even in *garam.*"

He jerked his head toward a nearby window in the palace, which faced to the south. "I remind you, Ashot, that I have well over twenty thousand Malwa camped out there, just beyond the passes. Closer to thirty, I think. I'd have to get through *them,* before I could reach the Indus—with no more than twenty thousand men of my own. Less than that, actually, since I'd have to leave some soldiers here to keep the Pathans from getting stupid ideas."

Ashot said nothing. Just waited.

Kungas went back to his beard-tugging.

"The Malwa have stopped trying to break into the Vale. For weeks, now, they've been putting up their own fortifications. So I'd have to get through *those,* too."

Tug. Tug. Tug.

"Piss-poor fortifications, true. Lazy Malwa. Also true that those are not their best troops. There are not more than three thousand Ye-tai in the lot. Still."

Tug. Tug. Tug.

Eventually, Kungas gave Ashot his crack of a smile. "You are not trying to persuade me, I notice. Smart man. Let me persuade myself."

Ashot's returning smile was a wider thing. Of course, almost anyone's smile was wider than that of Kungas, even when the king was in a sunny mood.

"The general is not expecting you to *defeat* those Malwa," the Armenian cataphract pointed out. "If you can, splendid. But it would be enough if he knew you could tie them up. Keep them from being used elsewhere."

Kungas sniffed. "Marvelous. I point out to you that I am *already* tying them up and keeping them from being used against him. And have to do nothing more vigorous than drink wine and eat fruit in the doing."

He matched deed to word, taking a sip from his wine and plucking a pear from a bowl on the low table in front of the settee. The sip was very small, though, and he didn't actually eat the pear. Just held it in his hand, weighing it as if it were the problem he confronted.

Ashot started to open his mouth, then closed it. Kungas' little smile widened slightly.

"Very smart man. Yes, yes, I know—the general is assuming that if he produces enough of a crisis, the Malwa will draw their troops away from the Vale to reinforce the soldiers he faces. And he wants me to stop them from doing so, which—alas—I cannot do drinking wine and eating pears."

Kungas set the pear back in the bowl, rose and went to the window. On the way, almost absently, he gave his wife's ponytail a gentle stroke. Irene was sitting on a chair—more like a raised cushion, really—at the same low table. She smiled at his passing figure, but said nothing.

Like Ashot, she knew that the best way to persuade Kungas of anything was not to push him too hard.

Once at the window, Kungas looked out over the Vale of Peshawar. Not at the Vale itself, so much as the mountains beyond.

"How certain is Belisarius that such a crisis is coming?" he asked.

Ashot shrugged. "I don't think 'certain' is the right word. The general doesn't think that way. 'Likely,' 'not likely,' 'possible,' 'probable'—it's just not the way his mind works."

"No, it isn't," mused Kungas. "As my too-educated Greek wife would put it, he thinks like a geometer, not an arithmetician. It's the angles he considers, not the sums. That's because he thinks if he can gauge the angle correctly, he can create the sums he needs."

The Kushan king's eyes lowered, now looking at the big market square below. "Which, he usually can. He'd do badly, I think, as a merchant. But he's probably the deadliest general in centuries. I'm glad he's not my enemy."

Abruptly, he turned away from the window. "Done. Tell Belisarius that if the Malwa start trying to pull troops from the Vale, I will do my best to pin them here. I make no promises, you understand. No guarantees. I will do my best, but—I have a kingdom to protect also, now that I have created it."

Ashot rose, nodding. "That will be more than enough, Your Majesty. Your best will be more than enough."

Kungas snorted. "Such phrases! And 'Your Majesty,' no less. Be careful, Ashot, or your general will make you an ambassador instead of a soldier."

The Armenian cataphract winced. Irene laughed softly. "It's not so bad, Ashot. Of course, you'll have to learn how to wear a veil."

"I'm going with you," Shakuntala announced. "And don't bother trying to argue with me. I *am* the empress."

Her husband spread his hands, smiling. A very diplomatic smile, that was.

"I would not dream of opposing your royal self."

Shakuntala gazed up at him suspiciously. For a moment, her hand went to stroke her belly, although she never completed the gesture.

"What's this?" she demanded. "I was expecting a husband's prattle about my duties as a mother. A lecture on the dangers of miscarriage."

The smile still on his face, Rao shrugged. "Bring Namadev, if you want to. Not much risk of disease, really, now that *garam* has started."

"Don't remind me," the empress said. She moved over to a window in the palace and scowled out at the landscape of Majarashtra. The hills surrounding Deogiri shimmered in the heat, from hot air rising from the baked soil.

Whatever else Indians disputed over, they all agreed that *rabi* was the best season, cool and dry as it was. One of India's three seasons, it corresponded roughly to what other lands considered winter. Alas, now that they were in what Christians called the month of March, *rabi* had ended.

Thereafter opinions diverged as to whether *garam* was worse than *khalif*, or the opposite. In Shakuntala's opinion, it was a silly argument. *Garam,* obviously! Especially here in the Great Country!

The monsoon season could be a nuisance, true enough, with its heavy rains. But she came from Keralan stock, on her mother's side, and had spent a fair part of her childhood in Kerala. Located as it was on India's southwest coast, Kerala was practically inundated during *khalif.* She was accustomed to rains far heavier than any that came here.

In any event, stony and arid Majarashtra desperately needed the monsoon's rainfall by the time it came. That began in what the Christians called "late May." What the Great Country did *not* need was the dry and blistering heat of *garam.* Not for one day, much less the three months it would last.

"I hate garam," she muttered. "Especially in the palace. It will be good for me—our son too!—to get outside for a while."

"Probably," Rao allowed. "You and Namadev will travel in a howdah, of course. The canopy will keep off the sun, and you might get some breeze."

Shakuntala turned away from the window and looked at him. "Are you really *that* sure, Rao? You are my beloved."

The expression that came to her husband's face then reminded Shakuntala forcibly of the differences between them, however much they might love each other. Where she was young, Rao was middle-aged. And, perhaps even more importantly, he was a philosopher, and she was . . . not.

"Who can say?" he asked serenely.

"You are relying too much on complicated logic," she hissed. "Treacherous, that is."

"Actually, no. There is the logic of it, true enough. But, in the end . . . "

He moved to the same window and gazed out. "It is more that I am swayed by the beauty of the thing. Whatever deities exist, they care not much for logic, for they treasure their whimsy. But they do love beauty. All of them—even the most bloody—will adore the notion."

"You are mad," she stated, with the certainty of an empress.

Of course, she'd stated those words before. And been proven wrong.

"Bring the baby, too," Rao said, tranquilly. "He will be in no danger."

From the battlements on the landward side of the city, Nanda Lal and Toramana watched Damodara's great army set out on its march upriver.

Suspicion was ever-present in the Malwa empire's spymaster, and today was no exception.

"Why the Narmada?" he demanded softly. "This makes no sense to me. Why does Damodara think Raghunath Rao will be foolish enough to meet him on a river plain? He'd stay in the badlands, I would think, where the terrain favors him."

Although Nanda Lal's eyes had never left the departing army, the question was addressed at the big Ye-tai general standing next to him.

Toramana, never prone to expansive gestures, shifted his shoulders a bit. "Better to say, why not? Lord, it may be that Rao will not come down out of the hills. But he says he will, to meet Sanga in single combat. So, if he doesn't, he is shamed. The worst that happens, from Damodara's position, is that he has undermined his opponent."

Nanda Lal made a face. Raised as he was in the Malwa dynasty's traditions—not to mention the even colder school of Link—it was always a bit difficult for him to realize that other men took this business about "honor" quite seriously. Even the Ye-tai next to him, just a hair's breadth removed from nomadic savagery and with a personality that was ruthless in its own right, seemed at least partly caught up in the spirit of the thing.

So, he said nothing. And, after cogitating on the problem for a few minutes, decided that Toramana was probably right.

"Notify me if you hear anything amiss," he commanded, and left. He saw no reason to stay until the last elements of Damodara's army were no longer visible from the battlements. Let the Ye-tai barbarian, if he chose, find "honor" in that splendid vista of dust, the rear ends of animals, and the trail of manure they left behind.

Toramana did remain on the battlements until the army was no longer in sight. Not because of any demands of honor, however. He was no more of a romantic than Nanda Lal on the subject of horseshit. Or any other, for that matter.

No, he did so for two other reasons.

First, to be certain he had suppressed any trace of humor before he was seen by any of Nanda Lal's spies in the city. Or even good cheer, of which the Ye-tai general was full.

Damodara had said nothing to him, of course. Neither had Narses, beyond the vaguest of hints. It didn't matter. Toramana, from his own analysis of the situation, was almost certain that Damodara had decided the time had come. The reason he was full of good cheer was because, if he was right, that meant both Damodara and Narses had great confidence in him. They were relying on Toramana to do what was necessary, without needing to be told anything.

He'd know, of course, if his assessment was correct. There would be one sure and simple sign to come.

So, he foresaw a great future for himself. Assuming he survived the next few months. But, if he did—yes, a great future.

And an even greater future for his children.

Of course, producing those children also depended on surviving the next few months. But Toramana was a confident man, and on no subject so much as his own prospects for survival.

That led him to his other reason for remaining on the battlements, which was the need to make a final decision on the second most important issue he faced.

He came to that decision quickly. More quickly than he had expected he would. Odd, perhaps. Toramana was not generally given to experimental whimsy. On the other hand, new times called for new measures.

Odder still, though, was the sense of relief that decision brought also.

Why? he wondered. Fearing, for a moment, that he might have been infected with the decadence he saw around him. But he soon decided that there was no infection. Simply . . .

And how odd that was! He was actually looking forward to it.

New times, indeed.

◇　◇　◇

That evening, as he had done every evening since she'd arrived in Bharakuccha, Toramana presented himself at the chambers where his intended had taken up residence in the great palace.

Outside the chambers, of course. Betrothed or not, there would be no question of impropriety. Even after Indira appeared and they began their customary promenade through the gardens, she was followed by a small host of wizened old chaperones and three Rajput warriors. Clansmen of Rana Sanga's, naturally.

For the first few minutes, their talk was idle. The usual meaningless chitchat. Meaningless, at least, in its content. The real purpose of these promenades was simply to allow a groom and his future bride to become at least somewhat acquainted with each other. As stiff as they were, even Rajputs understood that the necessary function of a wedding night was simplified and made easier if the spouses didn't have to grope at each other's voices as well as bodies.

After a time, Toramana cleared his throat. "Can you read?"

Indira's eyes widened. Toramana had expected that. He was pleased to see, however, that they didn't widen very much, and the face beneath remained quite composed. To anyone watching, she might have been mildly surprised by a comment he made concerning an unusual insect.

His hopes for this wife, already high, rose a bit further. She would be a splendid asset.

"No," she replied. "It is not the custom."

Toramana nodded. "I can read, myself. But not well. That must change. And I will want you to become literate also. I will hire tutors for us."

She gazed at a nearby vine. The slight widening of the girl's eyes was gone, now. "There will be some talk. My brother's wife can read, however, even if somewhat poorly. So probably not all that much talk."

"Talk does not concern me," Toramana said stiffly. "The future concerns me. I do not think great families with illiterate women will do so well, in that future."

The smile that spread across her face was a slow, cool thing. The very proper smile of a young Rajput princess hearing her betrothed make a pleasant comment regarding a pretty vine.

"I agree," she said. "Though most others would not."

"I am not concerned about 'most others.' Most others will obey or they will break."

The smile spread just a bit further. "A few others will not break so easily."

"Easily, no. Still, they will break."

The smile now faded quickly, soon replaced by the solemn countenance with which she'd begun the promenade. As was proper. A princess should smile at the remarks of her betrothed, to be sure, but not too widely and not for too long. They were not married yet, after all.

"I am looking forward to our wedding," Indira said softly. Too softly for the wizened little horde behind them to overhear. "To the marriage, even more."

"I am pleased to hear it."

"It is not the custom," she repeated.

"Customs change. Or they break."

Before nightfall, the promenade was over and Toramana returned to his own quarters.

No sooner had the Ye-tai general entered his private sleeping chamber than the one sure and simple sign he'd expected made its appearance.

Like a ghost, emerging from the wall. Toramana had no idea where the assassin had hidden himself.

"I'm afraid I'll need to sleep here," Ajatasutra said. "Nanda Lal has spies almost everywhere."

Toramana's lip curled, just a bit. "He has no spies here."

"No, not here."

"When?"

"Four days. Though nothing will be needed from you immediately. It will take at least two days for Damodara to return."

Toramana nodded. "And then?"

The assassin shrugged. "Whatever is necessary. The future is hard to predict. It looks good, though. I do not foresee any great difficulty."

Toramana began removing his armor. It was not extensive, simply the half-armor he wore on garrison duty. "No. There should be no great difficulty."

There was a thin, mocking smile on Ajatasutra's face, as there often was. On another man's face, that smile would have irritated

Toramana, perhaps even angered him. But the Ye-tai general was accustomed to it, by now.

So, he responded with a thin, mocking smile of his own.

"What amuses you?" Ajatasutra asked.

"A difficulty I had not foreseen, which I just now remembered. Nanda Lal once promised me that he would attend my wedding. And I told him I would hold him to it."

"Ah." The assassin nodded. "Yes, that is a difficulty. A matter of honor is involved."

The armor finally removed and placed on a nearby stand, Toramana scratched his ribs. Even half-armor was sweaty, in garam.

"Not *that* difficult," he said.

"Oh, certainly not."

He and Ajatasutra exchanged the smile, now. They got along very well together. Why not? They were much alike.

Agathius was on the dock at Charax to greet Antonina and Photius and Ousanas when the Axumite fleet arrived.

So much, Antonina had expected. What she had not expected was the sight of Agathius' young Persian wife and the small mountain of luggage next to her.

"We're going with you," Agathius announced gruffly, as soon as the gangplank was lowered and he hobbled across.

He looked at Ousanas. "I hear you have a new title. No longer the keeper of the fly whisks."

"Indeed, not! My new title is far more august. 'Angabo,' no less. That signifies—"

"The keeper of the crutches. Splendid, you can hold mine for a moment." Agathius leaned his weight against the rail and handed his crutches to Ousanas. Then, started digging in his tunic. "I've got the orders here."

By the time Antonina stopped giggling at the startled expression on Ousanas' face, Agathius was handing her a sheaf of official-looking documents.

"Right there," he said, tapping a finger on the name at the bottom. "It's not a signature, of course. Not in these modern times, with telegraph."

He seemed to be avoiding her eyes. Antonina didn't bother looking at the documents. Instead, she looked at Agathius' wife, who was still on the dock and peering at her suspiciously.

"I'll bet my husband's orders don't say anything about Sudaba."

Agathius seemed to shrink a little. "Well, no. But if you want to argue the matter with her, *you* do it."

"Oh, I wouldn't think of doing so." Honey dripped from the words. "The children?"

"They'll stay here. Sudaba's family will take them in, until we get back." The burly Roman general's shoulders swelled again. "I insisted. Made it stick, too."

Antonina was trying very hard not to laugh. Sudaba had become something of a legend in the Roman army. What saved Agathius from being ridiculed behind his back was that the soldiery was too envious. Sudaba never henpecked Agathius about anything else—and precious few of *them* had a young and very good-looking wife who insisted on accompanying her husband everywhere he went. The fact that Agathius had lost his legs in battle and had to hobble around on crutches and wooden legs only augmented that amatory prestige.

Ousanas grinned and handed back the crutches. " 'Angabo' does *not* mean keeper of the crutches. It also doesn't mean 'nursemaid,' so don't ask me to take in your brats when you return. They'll be spoiled rotten."

In a cheerier mood, now that he knew Antonina wouldn't object to Sudaba's presence, Agathius took back the crutches. "True. So what? They're already spoiled rotten. And we'll see how long that grin lasts. The Persians insist on a huge festival to honor your arrival. Well—Photius' arrival, formally speaking. But you'll have to attend also."

The grin vanished.

There had never been a grin on the face of the Malwa assassination commander, or any of his men. Not even a smile, since they'd arrived at Charax.

Any assassination attempt in Egypt had proven impossible, as they'd surmised it would be. Unfortunately, the situation in Charax was no better. The docks were still under Roman authority, and the security there was even more ferocious than it had been in Alexandria.

True, for the day and half the festival lasted, their targets were under Persian protection. But if the Aryans were slacker and less well-organized than the Romans, they made up for it by sheer numbers. Worst of all, by that invariant Persian snobbery, only Roman officials and Persian grandees and *azadan*—"men of noble birth"—were allowed anywhere in the vicinity of the Roman and Axumite visitors.

With the resources available, in the time they had, there was no way for the assassins to forge documents good enough to pass Roman inspection. As for trying to claim noble Aryan lineage . . .

Impossible. Persian documents were fairly easy to forge, and it would be as easy for some of the assassins to pass themselves off as Persians as polyglot Romans. But if Persian bureaucrats were easy to fool, Persian retainers were not. Tightly knit together by kinship as the great Persian families were, they relied on personal recognition to separate the wheat from the chaff—and to those keen eyes, the Malwa assassins were clearly chaff. If nothing else, they'd certainly insist on searching their luggage, and they'd find the bombard—a weapon that had no conceivable use except assassination.

"No help for it," the commander said, as he watched the Axumite war fleet leaving the harbor, with their target safely aboard the largest vessel. "We'll have to try again at Barbaricum. No point even thinking about Chabahari."

His men nodded, looking no more pleased than he did. Leaving aside the fact that this mission had been frustrating from the very start, they now had the distinctly unpleasant prospect of voyaging down the Gulf in an oared galley. It was unlikely they'd be able to use sails, traveling eastbound, with monsoon season still so far away. And—worst of all—while they'd had enough money to afford a galley, they hadn't been able to afford a crew beyond a pilot.

Malwa assassins were expert at many things. Rowing was not one of them.

"Our hands'll be too badly blistered to hold a knife," one of them predicted gloomily.

"Shut up," his commander responded, every bit as gloomily.

Chapter 17
THE INDUS

The attack came as a complete surprise. Not to Anna, who simply didn't know enough about war to understand what could be expected and what not, but to her military escort.

"What in the name of God do they think they're *doing*?" demanded Menander angrily.

He studied the fleet of small boats—skiffs, really—pushing out from the southern shore. The skiffs were loaded with Malwa soldiers, along with more than the usual complement of Mahaveda priests and their mahamimamsa "enforcers." The presence of the latter was a sure sign that the Malwa considered this project so near-suicidal that the soldiers needed to be held in a tight rein.

"It's an ambush," explained his pilot, saying aloud the conclusion Menander had already reached. The man pointed to the thick reeds. "The Malwa must have hauled those boats across the desert, hidden them in the reeds, waited for us. We don't keep regular patrols on the south bank, since there's really nothing there to watch for."

Menander's face was tight with exasperation. "But what's the *point* of it?" For a moment, his eyes moved forward, toward the heavily shielded bow of the ship where the *Victrix*'s fire-cannon was situated. "We'll burn them up like so many piles of kindling."

618

But even before he finished the last words, even before he saw the target of the oncoming boats, Menander understood the truth. The fact of it, at least, if not the reasoning.

"*Why?* They're all dead men, no matter what happens. In the name of God, she's just a woman!"

He didn't wait for an answer, however, before starting to issue his commands. The *Victrix* began shuddering to a halt. The skiffs were coming swiftly, driven by almost frenzied rowing. It would take the *Victrix* time to come to a halt and turn around; time to make its way back to protect the barge it was towing.

Time, Menander feared, that he might not have.

"What should we do?" asked Anna. For all the strain in her voice, she was relieved that her words came without stammering. A Melisseni girl could afford to scream with terror; she couldn't. Not any longer.

Grim-faced, Illus glanced around the barge. Other than he and Cottomenes and Abdul, there were only five Roman soldiers on the barge—and only two of those were armed with muskets. Since Belisarius and Khusrau had driven the Malwa out of the Sind, and established Roman naval supremacy on the Indus with the new steam-powered gunboats, there had been no Malwa attempt to threaten shipping south of the Iron Triangle.

Then his eyes came to rest on the vessel's new feature, and his tight lips creased into something like a smile.

"God bless good officers," he muttered.

He pointed to the top of the cabin amidships, where a shell of thin iron was perched. It was a turret, of sorts, for the odd and ungainly looking "Puckle gun" that Menander had insisted on adding to the barge. The helmeted face and upper body of the gunner was visible, and Illus could see the man beginning to train the weapon on the oncoming canoes.

"Get up there—*now*. There's enough room in there for you, and it's the best armored place on the barge." He gave the oncoming Malwa a quick glance. "They've got a few muskets of their own. Won't be able to hit much, not shooting from skiffs moving that quickly—but keep your head down once you get there."

It took Anna a great deal of effort, encumbered as she was by her heavy and severe gown, to clamber atop the cabin. She couldn't have made it at all, if Abdul hadn't boosted her. Climbing over the iron wall of the turret was a bit easier, but not much. Fortunately, the gunner lent her a hand.

After she sprawled into the open interior of the turret, the hard edges of some kind of ammunition containers bruising her back, Anna had to struggle fiercely not to burst into shrill cursing.

I have got to design a new costume. Propriety be damned!

For a moment, her thoughts veered aside. She remembered that Irene Macrembolitissa, in her *Observations of India,* had mentioned—with some amusement—that Empress Shakuntala often wore pantaloons in public. Outrageous behavior, really, but . . . when *you're* the one who owns the executioners, you can afford to outrage public opinion.

The thought made her smile, and it was with that cheerful expression on her lips that she turned her face up to the gunner frowning down at her.

"Is there anything I can do to help?"

The man's face suddenly lightened, and he smiled himself.

"Damn if you aren't a prize!" he chuckled. Then, nodding his head. "Yes, ma'am. As a matter of fact, there is."

He pointed to the odd-looking objects lying on the floor of the turret, which had bruised Anna when she landed on them. "Those are called cylinders." He patted the strange looking weapon behind which he was half-crouched. "This thing'll wreak havoc, sure enough, as long as I can keep it loaded. I'm supposed to have a loader, but since we added this just as an afterthought . . . "

He turned his head, studying the enemy vessels. "Better do it quick, ma'am. If those skiffs get alongside, your men and the other soldiers won't be enough to beat them back. And they'll have grenades anyway, they're bound to. If I can't keep them off, we're all dead."

Anna scrambled around until she was on her knees, then seized one of the weird-looking metal contraptions. It was not as heavy as it looked. "What do you need me to do? Be precise!"

"Just hand them to me, ma'am, that's all. I'll do the rest. And keep your head down—it's *you* they're after."

Anna froze for a moment, dumbfounded. "Me? *Why?*"

"Damned if I know. Doesn't make sense."

But, in truth, the gunner did understand. Some part of it, at least, even if he lacked the sophistication to follow all of the reasoning of the inhuman monster who commanded the Malwa empire.

The gunner had never heard—and never would—of a man named Napoleon. But he was an experienced soldier, and not stupid even if his formal education was rudimentary. *The moral is to the material in war as three-to-one* was not a phrase the man would have ever uttered himself, but he would have had no difficulty understanding it.

Link, the emissary from the new gods of the future who ruled the Malwa in all but name and commanded its great army in the Punjab, had ordered this ambush. The "why" was self-evident to its superhuman intelligence. Spending the lives of a few soldiers and Mahaveda priests was well worth the price, if it would enable the monster to destroy *the Wife* whose exploits its spies reported. Exploits which, in their own peculiar way, had become important to Roman morale.

Cheap at the price, in fact. Dirt cheap.

THE IRON TRIANGLE

The battle on the river was observed from the north bank by a patrol of light Arab cavalry in Roman service. Being Beni Ghassan, the cavalrymen were far more sophisticated in the uses of new technology than most Arabs. Their commander immediately dispatched three riders to bring news of the Malwa ambush to the nearest telegraph station, which was but a few miles distant.

By the time Belisarius got the news, of course, the outcome of the battle had already been decided, one way or the other. So he could do nothing more than curse himself for a fool, and try not to let the ashen face of a blind young man sway his cold-blooded reasoning.

"I'm a damned fool not to have foreseen the possibility. It just didn't occur to me that the Malwa might carry *boats* across the desert. But it should have."

"Not your fault, sir," said Calopodius quietly.

Belisarius tightened his jaws. "Like hell it isn't."

Maurice, standing nearby, ran fingers through his bristly iron-gray hair. "We all screwed up. I should have thought of it, too. We've been so busy just being entertained by the episode that we didn't think about it. Not seriously."

Belisarius sighed and nodded. "There's still no point in me send-ing the *Justinian*. By the time it got there, it will all have been long settled—and there's always the chance Link might be trying for a diversion."

"You *can't* send the *Justinian*," said Calopodius, half-whispering. "With the *Victrix* gone—and the *Photius* down at Sukkur—the Malwa might try an amphibious attack on the Triangle. They could get past the mine fields with a lot of little boats, where they couldn't with just their few ironclads."

He spoke the cold truth, and every officer in the command center knew it. So nothing further was said. They simply waited for another telegraph report to inform them whether Calopodius was a husband or a widower.

THE INDUS

Before the battle was over, Anna had reason to be thankful for her heavy gown.

As cheerfully profligate as he was, the gunner soon used up the preloaded cylinders for the Puckle gun. Thereafter, Anna had to reload the cylinders manually with the cartridges she found in a metal case against the shell of the turret. Placing the new shells *into* a cylinder was easy enough, with a little experience. The trick was taking out the spent ones. The brass cartridges were hot enough to hurt her fingers, the first time she tried prying them out.

Thereafter, following the gunner's hastily shouted instructions, she started using the little ramrod provided in the ammunition case. Kneeling in the shelter of the turret, she just upended the cylinders—carefully holding them with the hem of her dress, because they were hot also—and smacked the cartridges loose.

The cartridges came out easily enough, that way—right onto her lap and knees. In a lighter gown, a less severe and formal garment, her thighs would soon enough have been scorched by the little pile of hot metal.

As it was, the heat was endurable, and Anna didn't care in the least that the expensive fabric was being ruined in the process. She just went about her business, brushing the cartridges onto the floor of the turret, loading and reloading with the thunderous racket of the Puckle gun in her ears, ignoring everything else around her.

Throughout, her mind only strayed once. After the work became something of a routine, she found herself wondering if her husband's mind had been so detached in battles. Not whether he had ignored pain—of course he had; Anna had learned that much since leaving Constantinople—but whether he had been able to ignore his continued existence as well.

She suspected he had, and found herself quite warmed by the thought. She even handed up the next loaded cylinder with a smile.

The gunner noticed the smile, and that too would become part of the legend. He would survive the war, as it happened; and, in later years, in taverns in his native Anatolia, whenever he heard the tale of how the Wife smote down Malwa boarders with a sword and a laugh, he saw no reason to set the matter straight. By then, he had come to half-believe it himself.

Anna sensed a shadow passing, but she paid it very little attention. By now, her hands and fingers were throbbing enough to block out most sensation beyond what was necessary to keep reloading the cylinders. She barely even noticed the sudden burst of fiery light and the screams that announced that the *Victrix* had arrived and was wreaking its delayed vengeance on what was left of the Malwa ambush.

Which was not much, in truth. The gunner was a very capable man, and Anna had kept him well supplied. Most of the skiffs now drifting near the barge had bodies draped over their sides and sprawled lifelessly within. At that close range, the Puckle gun had been murderous.

"Enough, ma'am," said the gunner. "It's over."

Anna finished reloading the cylinder in her hands. Then, when the meaning of the words finally registered, she set the thing down on the floor of the turret. Perhaps oddly, the relief of finally not having to handle hot metal only made the pain in her hands—and legs, too, she noticed finally—all the worse.

She stared down at the fabric of her gown. There were little stains all over it, where cartridges had rested before she brushed them onto the floor. There was a time, she could vaguely remember, when the destruction of an expensive garment would have been a cause of great concern. But it seemed a very long time ago.

"How is Illus?" she asked softly. "And the others? The boys?"

The gunner sighed. "One of the boys got killed, ma'am. Just bad luck—Illus kept the youngsters back, but that one grenade . . ."

Vaguely, Anna remembered hearing an explosion. She began to ask which boy it was, whose death she had caused, of the five urchins she had found on the docks of Barbaricum and conscripted into her Service. But she could not bear that pain yet.

"Illus?"

"He's fine. So's Abdul. Cottomenes got cut pretty bad."

Something to do again. The thought came as a relief. Within seconds, she was clambering awkwardly over the side of the turret again—and, again, silently cursing the impractical garment she wore.

Cottomenes was badly gashed, true enough. But the leg wound was not even close to the great femoral artery, and by now Anna had learned to sew other things than cloth. Besides, the *Victrix*'s boiler was an excellent mechanism for boiling water.

The ship's engineer was a bit outraged, of course. But, wisely, he kept his mouth shut.

THE IRON TRIANGLE

The telegraph started chattering. Everyone in the command bunker froze for a moment. Then, understanding the meaning of the dot-dashes faster than anyone—even the operator jotting down the message—Calopodius slumped in his chair with relief. The message was unusually long, with two short pauses in the middle, and by the time it was completed Calopodius was even smiling.

Belisarius, unlike Calopodius, could not quite follow the message until it was translated. When he took the message from the hand of the operator and scanned it quickly, he understood the smile on the face of the blind young officer. He grinned himself.

"Well, I'd say she's in good form," he announced to the small crowd in the bunker. Then, quoting:

"ALL FINE EXCEPT COTTOMENES INJURED AND RAFFI DEAD. RAFFI ONLY TWELVE YEARS OLD. FEEL HORRIBLE ABOUT IT. MENTION HIM IN DISPATCHES.

PLEASE. ALSO MENTION PUCKLE GUNNER LEO CONSTANTES. SPLENDID MAN. ALSO INSTRUCT GENERAL BELISARIUS MAKE MORE PUCKLE GUNS. SPLENDID THINGS. ALSO—"

"Here's where the pause was," explained the general. His grin widened. "It goes on:

"OPERATOR SAYS MESSAGE TOO LONG. OPERA-TOR REFUSES GIVE HIS NAME. MENTION NAMELESS OPERATOR IN DISPATCHES. STUPID OFFICIOUS ASI-NINE OBNOXIOUS WORTHLESS FELLOW."

"Why do I think someone in that telegraph station has a sword at his throat?" mused Maurice idly. "Her bodyguards are Isaurians, right? Stupid idiot." He was grinning also.

"MENANDER SAYS WILL ARRIVE SOON. WILL NEED NEW CLOTHES."

Belisarius' grin didn't fade, exactly, but it became less purely jovial. His last words were spoken softly, and addressed to Calopodius rather than to the room at large.

"Here was the second pause. The last part of the message reads:

"AM EAGER TO SEE YOU AGAIN. MY HUSBAND."

Chapter 18

THE NARMADA RIVER

The Malwa army drawn up on the open plain just south of the Narmada was terrifying. Looking over them from a distance, perched in her howdah with the baby, Shakuntala finally understood—*really* understood—why her husband had been so cautious in his tactics from the very beginning.

It might be better to say, cautious in his strategy. When the Panther did strike, he struck hard and fast. But he'd carefully avoided getting anywhere near the Malwa lion's jaws and talons.

"Impressive, aren't they?" Rao called up to her. He was riding a horse alongside the elephant that bore her and Namadev.

Until that morning, two maidservants had been in the howdah with them. But Shakuntala had insisted they remain behind, when the Maratha army moved out at dawn to meet Damodara and his forces. The empress still suspected treachery. For that reason, she had one of the best horses in India following behind, in case she and Namadev had to flee precipitously into the badlands of the Great Country. On that horse, she was confident she could elude even Rajput cavalry. On an elephant, hopeless to do so.

She stared down at her husband. Amazingly, to all appearances, he was in as sunny a mood as she'd ever seen him.

Rao raised himself a little in his stirrups—by now, the Roman innovations were ubiquitous—to get a better view of the enemy.

626

"The best army the Malwa have, for a certainty." He pointed with his finger, and then slowly swept it across the front lines of the enemy. They were still a thousand yards away.

"See how Damodara has his artillery units scattered among the infantry? You won't see that in any other Malwa army. No lolling about in the comfort of the rear for *his* kshatriyas."

The finger jabbed; here, there, there.

"Notice, also, the way he has the Ye-tai units positioned with respect to the main force of Rajput cavalry. In the center, most of them, forming his spearhead while the Rajputs are concentrated on the flanks. His Ye-tai will lead the charge, here, not stay behind to drive forward badly trained and ill-motivated peasant foot soldiers."

The finger lowered. "Of which," he concluded cheerily, "Damodara doesn't have that many in any event. They're back guarding the supply wagons, I imagine. Along with the mahaveda priests, of course, who control the munitions supply. That last feature is about the only way in which Damodara's army still resembles a Malwa force."

"Rao . . . " Shakuntala said hesitantly.

"Oh, yes, my dearest. You're quite right." Still standing in the stirrups, Rao swiveled his upper body back and forth, studying his own army.

The Maratha army was barely half the size of the enemy force across the field. And didn't bear so much as a fourth the weight of fine armor, fine swords and lances—and not a tenth the weight of firearms and gunpowder.

"Oh, yes," he repeated, his voice still as sunny-toned as ever, "if I were idiotic enough to meet them on this field, they'd hammer us flat. Be lucky if a third of my army survived at all."

"Rao . . . "

"Be still, dearest. This is not a field where two armies will meet. Simply two souls. Three, actually, counting Damodara. Perhaps four, if we count Narses as well. Which I think we must."

She took a deep, slow breath. "Your soul is as great as any I have ever known. But it is not great enough to do *this*."

He laughed. "Of course not! It's not *my* soul I'm counting on, however."

He reached up and extended his hand. "Touch me, dearest. Not for the last time! Simply—a gift."

She did so, briefly clutching the strong fingers. Strong and large. Rao had the hands of a man half again his size.

Then, he was gone, trotting his horse onto the open field between the armies.

Sitting on his own mount at the very front and center of the Malwa army, Rana Sanga watched him come.

At first, he simply assumed it was Raghunath Rao, from the logic of the matter. Even the keen eyes of the man who was probably India's greatest archer could not distinguish features at the distance of a thousand yards. The more so, when he had not seen the features themselves in over two decades. The famous duel between him and Rao had happened when they were both young men.

Long ago, that was. A thousand years ago, it seemed to the greatest king of Rajputana. Between then and now lay a gulf that could not be measured in simple years. The young Sanga who had faced a young Rao so long ago had been sure and certain in his beliefs, his creed, his duty, his loyalties, and his place in the universe. The middle-aged man who was about to meet him again was no longer sure of anything.

Except in his prowess as a warrior, of course. But Rana Sanga knew full well that was the least of the things that were meeting today on a new field of battle. Something much greater was at stake now. He only wished he knew exactly what it was. But the only thought that came to his mind was . . .

Onions.

It was bizarre, really. All he could think of was onions, peeling away. With every horse's pace the distant figure shortened between them, Sanga could sense another peel, falling.

Soon enough—still long before he could recognize the features—he knew it was Rao.

"I'd half-forgotten," he murmured.

Next to him, Damodara raised a questioning eyebrow.

"How frightening an opponent he is," Sanga explained.

Damodara squinted at the coming figure, trying to discern what Sanga seemed to see in it. Damodara himself was . . .

Unimpressed, really. Given the reputation of the Panther—or the Wind of the Great Country, as he was also known—he'd been expecting some sort of giant of a man. But the Maratha warrior approaching across the field seemed no more than average size.

Very wide in the shoulders, true. So much was obvious even at a distance, and Damodara didn't think it was due to the armor Rao was wearing. It was not elaborate armor, in any event. Just the utilitarian gear than any hill-fighter might bring into battle.

But as Rao neared, he began to understand. It was a subtle thing, given that the man was on horseback. Still, after a time, it became apparent enough.

"The way he moves, even riding a horse . . . "

Sanga barked a harsh laugh. "Hope you never see him move up close, with a blade or his iron-clawed gauntlet! Not even the Mongoose is so fast, so sure. Always so balanced. I remember thinking I was facing an asura under the human-seeming flesh."

The Rajput king eased his sword out of the scabbard. Just an inch or so, making sure it was loose. Then, did the same with the lance in its scabbard by his knee.

Then, drew his bow. He'd start with that, of course. With a bow, Sanga out-matched Rao. With a lance also, probably, especially now with the added advantage of stirrups.

Still, given Rao, it would probably end with them on foot. The last time they'd met, they'd fought for an entire day with every weapon they'd possessed. And then, too exhausted to move, had finished by exchanging philosophical barbs and quips.

"Wish me well, Lord," he said. Then, spurred his own horse into a trot.

A great roar went up from the Malwa army. Matched, a moment later, by one from the Marathas across the field.

"Oh, splendid," murmured Ajatasutra. He and the assassin he'd kept with him exchanged a little smile.

"Let's hope they keep it up." The assassin glanced at one of the nearby munitions wagons. The mahaveda head priest and the two mahamimamsa who guarded it were standing, their eyes riveted on the two combatants approaching each other. They were paying no attention at all to the men who, in the nondescript and patchy armor of common infantrymen, were quietly spreading through the munitions wagons.

"You will give the signal?"

Ajatasutra pinched his hawk nose, smiling more widely under the fingers. "If need be, yes. But unless I'm much mistaken, that won't be necessary. The thing will be, ah, quite obvious."

The assassin cocked his head slightly, in a subtle question.

"Look at it this way. The two most flamboyant men in India are about to meet. True, one is the sternest of Rajputs and the other is reputed to be a great philosopher. Still, I don't think subtlety will be the end result."

Narses just watched, perched on his mule. Whatever he could do, he had done. The rest was in the hands of whatever God existed.

So, although he watched intently, he was quite calm. What would happen, would happen. There remained only the anticipation of the outcome. The greatest game of all, the game of thrones.

For the rest—whatever God might be—Narses was quite sure he was damned anyway. But he thought he'd have the satisfaction, whatever happened, of being able to thumb his nose at all the gods and devils of the universe, as he plunged into the Pit.

Which, he reminded himself, might still be some decades off anyway.

Damodara was far less relaxed. He was as tense and as keyed up as he'd ever been, on the edge of a battle.

It could not be otherwise, of course. It was he who would, as commanders must, gauge the right moment.

Once Sanga and Rao were within seventy yards of each other, Rao drew up his horse.

Sanga did likewise. He already had the bow in his left hand. Now, relinquishing the reins, he drew and notched an arrow with the right.

Then, waited. Gallant as ever, the Rajput king would allow the Maratha chieftain and imperial consort to ready his own bow.

Titles had vanished, on this field. Everything had vanished, except the glory of India's two greatest warriors meeting again in single combat.

Rao grinned. He hadn't intended to, but the sight of Sanga's frown—quite obvious, even at the distance, given the open-faced nature of Rajput helmets—made it impossible to do otherwise.

Always strict! Sanga was obviously a bit disgruntled that Rao had been so careless as not to have his own bow already in hand. Had the great Maratha warrior grown senile?

"The last time," Rao murmured, "great king of the Rajputs, we began with bows and ended with philosophy. But we're much older now, and that seems like such a waste of sweat. So let's start with philosophy, shall we? Where it always ends, anyway."

Rao slid from his horse and landed on the ground, poised and balanced on his feet.

First, he reached up, drew his lance from the saddle scabbard, and pitched it aside. Then, did the same with the bow. Being careful, of course, to make sure they landed on soft patches of soil and far from any rocks. They were good weapons, very well made and expensive. It would be pointless extravagance to damage them. From a philosophical standpoint, downright grotesque.

The arrow quiver followed. Holding it like a vase, he scattered the arrows across the field. Then, tossed the quiver aside. He was less careful where they landed. Arrows were easy enough to come by, and the utilitarian quiver even more so.

Armed now only with a sword and hand weapons, Rao began walking toward Sanga. After ten steps, the sword was pitched to the ground.

Laid on the ground, rather, and carefully at that. It was an excellent sword and Rao didn't want to see it damaged. Still, it was all done very quickly.

The dagger, likewise.

His iron-clawed gauntlet being a sturdier thing, he simply dropped it casually as he moved on.

He walked slowly. Not for the sake of drama, but simply because unlacing and removing armor requires some concentration.

The helmet was the easiest, so it went first. Tough and utilitarian, like the gauntlet, it was simply dropped from one pace to the next. The rest took a bit of time. Not much, given Rao's fingers.

By the time he was done, he stood thirty yards from Sanga. And wore nothing but a loincloth.

And, still—he hadn't meant to, but couldn't resist—that same grin.

Shakuntala held her breath. The baby squalled, so tightly was she clutching him. But she never heard.

◇   ◇   ◇

Damodara rolled his eyes. Just for a moment, praising the heavens.

True, he'd expected *something*. That was why he had waited. But he hadn't expected Rao to make it the simplest task he'd probably ever confront, as the emperor of Malwa.

He spurred his horse forward. No slow trot, this, either.

Sanga stared. Paralyzed.

There was no way—not even Rao!—that any man could survive against him, standing there and in that manner.

He didn't know what to do.

No, worse.

He *did* know what to do. And couldn't.

Not though his very soul was screaming at him. As was the soul of his wife, whether she was dead or not.

And, still, all he could think of was onions. Not peeling away now, though. He could sense the shadow of his wife, throwing them at him.

"King of Rajputana! Stop!"

The voice came as an immense relief. Swiveling in his saddle, Sanga stared at Damodara. For years now, the man coming toward him had been his commander. At first, Sanga had obeyed of necessity; then, with acceptance; finally, with great pleasure.

Never greater than now.

For the first time in his life, Sanga realized, he had a true and genuine lord. And, desperately, wanted his master's guidance.

Ajatasutra glanced up at the priest atop the wagon he was now standing beside. The mahaveda was scowling, of course. But, if anything, had his attention more riveted in the distance than ever.

Oh, splendid.

As soon as Damodara drew alongside the Rajput king, he nodded toward Rao.

"You cannot survive this, Sanga," he said softly. "When glory and honor and duty and necessity all clash together, on the same field, no man can survive. Not even the gods can do so."

The Rajput's dark eyes stared at him.

"Lord . . . " he said slowly.

"Yes, well." Damodara cleared his throat. Awkward, that. But he did need to keep a straight face. Even if that maniac's grin thirty yards away was infectious.

"Yes, well. That's actually the point. You may recall that I once told you, on the banks of the Tigris, that the day might come when I would need to remind you of your oath."

"Yes, Lord." The eyes seemed darker yet. "I swore an oath—as did all Rajputs—to the Emperor of Malwa."

"Indeed so. Well, I just discovered—"

He had to clear his throat again. No choice. *Damn that Maratha rascal!*

"Amazing news. Horrifying, actually. But Narses ferreted out the plot. It seems that—two generations ago, if you can believe it—"

Damodara had insisted on that, overriding the eunuch's protests, even though it made the forgeries far more difficult. He did not think it likely his father and mother would survive what was coming, despite Narses' assurances. So be it. They were elderly, in any event. But he would not have them shamed also.

"—unscrupulous plotters in the dynasty substituted another baby for the rightful heir. Who was my grandfather, as it happens. The rightful heir to the throne, that is. Which means that Skandagupta is an impostor and a fraud, and his minion Nanda Lal is a traitor and a wretch. And, well, it seems that *I* am actually the Emperor of Malwa."

By now, he wished he could *strangle* that still-grinning Maratha ape. Even though he'd gotten it all out without choking once.

Alas. The only man who could possibly manage that feat was Rana Sanga.

Who was still staring at him, with eyes that now seemed as dark as eternity.

Carefully keeping his gaze away from Rao and his blasted grin, Damodara spoke as sternly as he could manage.

"So, King of Rajputana. Will you honor your oath?"

It all fell into place for Sanga, then. As if the last shadow onion, hurled by his shadow wife, had struck him on the forehead and abruptly dispelled all illusions.

He looked away from Damodara and gazed upon Rao.

He always understood, Sanga realized. *And, thus, understood me as well.*

Sanga remembered the silvery moon over tortured Ranapur, that he had turned away from out of his duty. And knew, at last, that the duty had been illusion also. Already, then, nothing but illusion.

He remembered Belisarius holding a jewel in his hand, and asking the Rajput king if he would exchange his plain wife for a beautiful one. The answer to that question had been obvious to Sanga at the time. Why, he wondered now, had he not seen that the same answer applied to all things?

He remembered Belisarius' exact words, speaking of the jewel in his hand. How stupid of Sanga, not to have understood then!

This, too, is a thing of pollution. A monster. An intelligent being created from disease. The worst disease which ever stalked the universe. And yet—

Is he not beautiful? Just like a diamond, forged out of rotting waste?

For years, Sanga had held tightly to the memory of his duel with Rao. Had held to that memory, as he'd seen the glory of his youth slide into what seemed an endless pit of vileness and corruption.

Looking upon Raghunath Rao today, standing almost naked before him—naked and unarmed—Sanga knew that he was already defeated. But also understood that, out of this defeat, would come the victory he had so desperately sought for so many years.

So *stupid*.

How could he have been so blind, not to have seen the truth? Not to have seen the way in which, out of the filth and evil of the Malwa dynasty, had emerged the true thing? There was no excuse, really, since Sanga had been there to bear witness, every step of the way. Had been there himself, and witnessed, as a short, fat—fat then, at least—and unassuming distant cousin of the emperor had shown Sanga and all Rajputs that their sacred vows had not and would not be scorned by the gods of India.

An onion, peeled away by divine will to show the jewel at the center.

Even Narses had seen it. And if the Roman eunuch had chosen forgery and duplicity to peel away the illusion, Sanga had no need of such artificial devices.

The truth was what it was. The great land of India needed a great emperor. And now it had one, despite the schemes of an alien monster. No, not even *despite* the monster. Though never meaning to do so and never recognizing its own deed, the monster itself had created that true emperor, because it had created the need for him.

In a manner that the Roman traitor would never understand, his forgeries were simply a recognition of the truth.

"Of course, Emperor," he said.

Damodara had seen Sanga smile before. Not often, true, by the standards of most men. Still, he'd seen him smile. Even grin, now and then.

Never, though, in a manner you might almost call *sly*.

"Of course," Sanga repeated. "You forget that I am also a student of philosophy. If not"—he jerked his head toward Rao—"with the same extravagance as that one. But enough to understand that truth and illusion fade into each other, when the cycle comes. I remember pondering that matter, as I listened to the screams of dying Ranapur."

There was no humor in the last sentence. Nor in the next.

"And did I not understand, my wife would explain it to me. If she could."

"Oh." Damodara felt like an idiot. "Sorry. I forgot. Narses uncovered another plot. It seems—"

"*Please*, Lord. She has been my life. She and my children."

"Still is, still is. So are they." Damodara drew the little knife from the pouch, and handed it to the Rajput. "She said—told Narses, through Ajatasutra—that you'd recognize this. Asked that you be given an onion, too."

He drew that forth also, feeling like an idiot again. What sort of emperor serves up onions?

But since the answer was obvious, he didn't feel like much of an idiot.

Successful emperors, that's who.

Sanga stared down at the knife and the onion, though he made no attempt to take them. No way he could have, without relinquishing the bow and the arrow.

"Yes, I recognize it. And the message in the onion. I felt its shadow strike me, but a minute ago."

For an instant, the Rajput's eyes flicked toward the Malwa army. *"Narses,"* he hissed, sounding like a cobra. A very, very angry cobra.

That had to be deflected. "Later, Sanga. For the moment . . . "

Damodara's jaws tightened. He was still quietly furious at Narses himself.

"He probably kept us all alive. And in the meantime, there are other matters to deal with."

Sanga took a slow deep breath. "Yes." Another such breath, by the end of which the tall and powerful figure on the horse next to Damodara seemed quite relaxed.

Poised rather, in the manner of a great warrior.

"What do you command, Emperor?"

"Let's start by ridding ourselves of those pestiferous priests, shall we? Along with their pet torturers. I decree the Mahaveda cult an abomination. All the cult's priests and mahamimamsa are under immediate sentence of death. None will be spared."

"My great pleasure, Lord of Malwa."

And, so, India was given a new legend, after all. Whatever regrets the warriors who watched might have had, that the great duel between Sanga and Rao never happened, they were mollified by the bow shot.

The greatest ever, all would swear, since Krishna the charioteer drove Arjuna and his great bow onto the ancient battlefield of Kurukshetra. Hundreds of yards, that arrow flew, to strike like a thunderbolt.

For one of the few times in his life, Ajatasutra was quite amazed. The arrow went right through the chief priest, striking the perfect bowman's target—just above the breastbone—and severing the great arteries as it passed. The chief priest collapsed on the wagon like a puppet with cut strings, blood gushing as if from a fountain. The arrow might even have severed the spine, from the way the priest was still thrashing.

"You see?" he demanded.

But the assassin was already onto the wagon, cutting the first mahamimamsa.

Ajatasutra saw no reason to follow. The assassins he'd assembled, over the months, were very good. Not as good as he was, of course.

But quite good enough—any one of them—to be more than a match for twice their number of torturers.

Besides, he had other duties. Sanga was coming, driving his horse like another thunderbolt, and with his lance in hand. The Ye-tai were paralyzed, for the moment, but the Rajputs were not hesitating at all.

There were twenty thousand Rajput cavalrymen on that field, now curling from the flanks onto the munitions train like two great waves. Even with the best of discipline, they were likely to shatter the wagons unless Ajatasutra had them clearly under control.

A small disaster, that. There was still a war to be fought and won.

He put away his dagger and drew the sword. If the scabbard that sword had been concealed in was shabby, the sword was that of a commander.

"*Guard the wagons!*" he shouted at the infantrymen, standing around, their mouths agape. "Swing them into a circle. Now, you idiots!"

They obeyed, almost instantly. Even those illiterate and provincial peasants could figure out the equation.

The mahaveda and mahamimamsa were all dead or dying.

Ajatasutra seemed to know what he was doing.

Twenty *thousand* Rajputs were on the way. The hooves of their horses seem to make the very ground shake.

By the time the Rajputs arrived, Ajatasutra had the wagons in a rough circle. With, in a still wider circle around them, the corpses of priests and torturers tossed out. As if they were so many sacrificial offerings.

Which . . . they were. Even the Rajputs were satisfied.

Throughout, neither the Ye-tai nor the kshatriya artillerymen moved at all. This was Rajput business, even if Damodara had obviously given it his blessing.

Good enough. No doubt an explanation would be forthcoming. For the moment, wisdom and sagacity both called for the tactics of mice in the presence of predators.

Stillness and silence, lest one be noticed. Let the hawks feed on the priests and torturers. True, they were already carrion, but raptors are not fussy.

And who cared, anyway?

After the years of victory with Damodara, the years of battles and maneuvers in the course of which their commander had showed himself worthy of his men, *who cared?*

When the announcement was finally made to the entire army, the Ye-tai and kshatriyas simply grunted their satisfaction.

Of course he was the emperor. Stupid of them, really, not to have realized it sooner. All that wasted time.

Still worse, the endless miles of pointless marching back and forth across central Asia—when Kausambi was so close.

That came later, however. For the moment, Damodara had more pressing business.

After Sanga was gone, thundering off, Damodara trotted over to Rao.

The grin was gone, at least.

"I am the new Emperor of Malwa. I did not start this war, I would now finish it."

Rao nodded. "I want the border set on the crest of the Vindhyas. *And* we get the crest—with the right to build forts on it."

Damodara thought about it, for a minute.

That was reasonable, he decided. In the nature of things, it would always be northern India with its teeming population in the Ganges valley that posed a threat to the realms of southern India. Forts along the crest of the Vindhyas in the hands of Marathas could serve to defend the Deccan. There was really no way they could ever serve as invasion routes onto the Gangetic plain.

"Agreed," he said. "In return, I want Bharakuccha to be an open city. I will need a large seaport on the west coast."

It was Rao's turn to consider.

"The population is mostly Maratha," he pointed out.

"It was once. Not any longer. It's twice the size it was at the conquest, and as polyglot as any city in the world. No more than a third of the populace is Maratha, these days."

Rao grunted. "Still."

"I do not insist on a Malwa garrison. But I don't want it garrisoned by Andhra, either. Or Persians."

"On that last, we are agreed," Rao said, scowling. "There'll be no way to keep the greedy arrogant bastards out of the Sind, of course, thanks to you idiots. Not now. But that's as close as I want them, and closer than I imagine you do."

"Yes. And I don't want Romans, either. They're too powerful."

Rao scratched his jaw. "Well, that's true. Friends now—ours, if not yours—but who knows what the future will bring?"

Damodara made the final move. "An Axumite garrison, then, just big enough to maintain order. Axum is powerful at sea but too small to pose a military threat to any major realm of India. But *not* Axumite territory. An open city, with its own government—we'll thrash that out later—and neutral to all parties."

"You understand they'll insist on the right to collect the tolls? To maintain the garrison."

"For Axum, that matters. For us, it does not. Let them skim the trade. The trade itself flows in and out of India. North as well as south."

Rao nodded. "Agreed, then. That leaves the Malwa armies in the Deccan outside of the Great Country. There's still a huge garrison in Amaravati, and large ones elsewhere. Since you're the Goptri of the Deccan, they're officially under your command. What happens, now that you're the Emperor?"

Damodara shrugged. "Ask me in a few months. If I take Kausambi and depose Skandagupta, they will obey me. I will then order them to come home. Until then, however, I'd just as soon they stayed where they are. I've never had much dealings with them, and I don't know which way they'd go so long as things are unsettled."

Rao studied the Malwa army. It was collapsing inward, leaving units of Ye-tai and kshatriyas in place while the Rajputs came in to slaughter the priests. If they weren't already slaughtered, which . . .

Rao now studied the new Malwa emperor.

They probably were. If Damodara had none of the overweening ambition of Malwa's previous dynasts, Rao was quite sure he concentrated in his short person more capability than any of them—and at least as much in the way of ruthlessness.

But it was a very intelligent ruthlessness, the sort that didn't confuse means with ends and didn't prize ruthlessness for its own sake.

Rao could live with that. More importantly, his son—and his son, and his son—could live with it too. The Deccan could live with it. There would always be a great empire in northern India, that southern India would have to deal with. That being so, better to deal with an empire founded by such as Damodara.

"Done. It would take me two months anyway—at least—to march on Amaravati. But I warn you that I will, if you fail."

"If I fail, what do I care? And if I don't, it won't be necessary." Damodara smiled. "Or do you think that the garrison at Amaravati will suddenly get ambitious? With me above them, and you at the gates?"

Rao returned the smile. It would be pleasant, in the years to come, to deal with this man. Not easy, of course. But . . .

Yes, pleasant.

He nodded, and started to walk away.

Damodara called him back. "Rao—one thing more."

"Yes?"

"If I succeed, I would like your sadhu to visit Kausambi."

"Bindusara? Why?"

The new emperor seemed to shiver a little. "It is not enough to cut the throats of the mahaveda. For generations, now, they have been a poison in India. I think we need to consider an antidote."

It was the only thing that happened that day that surprised Rao. He had never—not once—considered the possibility that the new emperor of Malwa might actually be wise.

"I have no objection. But I can't speak for Bindusara. He's a sadhu, you know. Stubborn, as the real ones always are."

"Yes. Why I want him."

Rao nodded, again, and walked away.

Much more than simply pleasant, then.

Of course, that would also make it less easy. But Rao had never expected the universe to be easy. In truth, he didn't want it to be. With too much ease, came softness; and with softness, came rot.

It took him a while, to return. First, because he had to settle down some eager and jittery units of his own army. It was always hard for soldiers to restrain themselves, seeing what appeared to be an enemy in confusion.

That was accomplished easily enough. A few shouts and gestures did the trick. Rao's position was unquestioned, after all.

It took longer to collect the weapons and armor he'd discarded. Nor was he tempted to ignore the business. In truth, he didn't even think of doing so. Legend or not, consort of an empress or not, Raghunath Rao was Maratha born and bred. Like hill people the world over, they were a thrifty lot.

Eventually, though, he made his way back to the howdah and looked up at his beloved wife.

"See?" he demanded.

"I never doubted you once, husband," she lied.

Chapter 19
THE IRON TRIANGLE

There was no reception for Anna at the docks, when she arrived at the Iron Triangle. Just a small gang of men hurrying out from the bunker to catch the lines thrown from the *Victrix* and the barge.

She was a bit surprised. Not disgruntled, simply . . .

Surprised.

Menander seemed to understand. "We do this as quickly as possible these days," he explained apologetically. "The Malwa have spotters hidden in the reeds, and they often fire rocket volleys at us whenever a convoy arrives."

As if his words were the cue, Anna heard a faint sound to the north. Vaguely, like a snake hissing. Looking up, she saw several rockets soaring up into the sky.

After a moment, startled, she realized how far away they were. "I didn't know they were so big."

"They have to be. Those are fired from the Malwa lines, miles to the north. At first, the spotters would fire small ones from the reeds. But that's just pure suicide for them. Even the Malwa, after a while, gave it up."

Too uncertain to know whether she should be worried or not, Anna watched the rockets climb higher into the sky.

"They're headed our way, girl," Illus said gruffly. He pointed toward the low bunker toward which they were being towed. The roof of the bunker was just tall enough for the *Victrix* to pass underneath. "I'd feel better if you moved into the bow. That'll reach the shelter first."

"Yes. I suppose." Anna gathered up the heavy skirts and began moving forward. Illus followed her, with Abdul helping Cotto-menes limp along. Behind them came the four boys.

Glancing back, she saw that Menander had remained in his place. He was still watching the rockets. From his apparent lack of concern, she realized they must be veering off.

"Keep moving, girl," Illus growled. "Yes, the damn things are completely inaccurate. But they don't always miss—and any rocket that big is going to have a monster of a warhead."

She didn't argue the point. Illus was usually cooperative with her, after all, and this was his business.

Still, most of her mind was concentrated on the sound of the coming rockets. Between that, the deep gloom of the approaching bunker, and the need to watch her feet moving across the cluttered deck, she was caught completely by surprise when the fanfare erupted.

That happened as soon as the bow passed under the overhang of the ship bunker.

Cornicens, a lot of them, and some big drums. She wasn't very familiar with cornicens. They were almost entirely a military instrument.

"Oh," she said. "Oh."

Illus was grinning from ear to ear. "I was starting to wonder. Stupid, that. When you're dealing with the general."

By the time the fanfare ended and the bow of the ship bumped gently against the wharf inside the bunker, Anna thought she might be growing deaf. Cornicens were *loud*. Especially when the sound was reflected from such a low ceiling.

The cheers of the soldiers even seemed dim, in her ears. They couldn't be, of course. Not with that many soldiers. Especially when they started banging the hilts of their swords on their shields as well.

She was startled by that martial salute almost as much as she'd been by the cornicens.

She glanced at Illus. He had a peculiar look on his face. A sort of fierce satisfaction.

"Do they always do that?" she asked, almost shouting the words.

He shook his head. That gesture, too, had the air of satisfaction. "No, girl. They almost never do that."

When she saw the first man who came up the gangplank, after it was laid, Anna was startled again. She'd learned enough of Roman uniforms and insignia to realize that this had to be Belisarius. But she'd never pictured him so. The fact that he was tall and broad-shouldered fit her image well enough. But the rest . . .

She'd read all of Macrembolitissa's work, so she knew a great deal about the general. Despite that knowledge—or perhaps because of it—she'd imagined some sort of modern Nestor. Wise, in a grim sort of way; not old, certainly—abstractly, she knew he was a young man—but still somehow middle-aged. Perhaps a bit of gray in his hair.

She'd certainly never thought he would be so handsome. And so very young, to have done all that he had.

Finally, as he neared, she found an anchor. Something that matched the writings.

The general's smile *was* crooked. She'd always thought that was just Macrembolitissa, indulging herself in poetic license.

She said as much.

Belisarius smiled more crookedly still. "So I'm told. Welcome to the Iron Triangle, Lady Saronites."

The general escorted her off the *Victrix*. Anna was relieved that he didn't offer her a hand, though. She'd be in far more danger of tripping over the long and ragged skirts without both hands to hold them.

She had to concentrate so much on that task that she wasn't really looking at anything else.

They reached the relatively safe footing of the wharf.

"Lady Saronites," said the general, "your husband."

She looked up, startled again.

"Oh," she said. "Oh."

There came, then, the most startling thing of all that day. For the first time in years, Anna was too shy to say a word.

"It's not much," said Calopodius apologetically.

Anna's eyes moved over the interior of the little bunker where Calopodius lived. Where she would now live also. She did not fail to notice all the little touches here and there—the bright, cheery little cloths; the crucifix; even a few native handcrafts—as well as the relative cleanliness of the place. But . . .

No, it was not much. Just a big pit in the ground, when all was said and done, covered over with logs and soil.

"It's fine," she said. "Not a problem."

She turned and stared at him. Her husband, once a handsome boy, was now a hideously ugly man. She had expected the empty eye sockets, true enough. But even after all the carnage she had witnessed since she left Constantinople, she had not once considered what a mortar shell would do to the *rest* of his face.

Stupid, really. As if shrapnel would obey the rules of poetry, and pierce eyes as neatly as a goddess at a loom. The upper half of his face was a complete ruin. The lower half was relatively unmarked, except for one scar along his right jaw and another puckerlike mark on his left cheek.

His mouth and lips, on the other hand, were still as she vaguely remembered them. A nice mouth, she decided, noticing for the first time.

"It's fine," she repeated. "Not a problem."

A moment later, Illus and Abdul came into the bunker hauling her luggage. What was left of it. Until they were gone, Anna and Calopodius were silent. Then he said, very softly:

"I don't understand why you came."

Anna tried to remember the answer. It was difficult. And probably impossible to explain, in any event. *I wanted a divorce, maybe* . . . seemed . . . strange. Even stranger, though closer to the truth, would be: *or at least to drag you back so you could share the ruins of my own life.*

"It doesn't matter now. I'm here. I'm staying."

For the first time since she'd rejoined her husband, he smiled. Anna realized she'd never really seen him smile before. Not, at least, with an expression that was anything more than politeness.

He reached out his hand, tentatively, and she moved toward him. The hand, fumbling, stroked her ribs.

"God in Heaven, Anna!" he choked. "How can you *stand* something like that—in this climate? You'll drown in sweat."

Anna tried to keep from laughing; and then, realizing finally where she was, stopped trying. Even in the haughtiest aristocratic circles of Constantinople, a woman was allowed to laugh in the presence of her husband.

When she was done—the laughter was perhaps a bit hysterical —Calopodius shook his head. "We've got to get you a sari, first thing. I can't have my wife dying on me from heat prostration."

Calopodius matched deed to word immediately. A few words to his aide-de-camp Luke, and, much sooner than Anna would have expected, a veritable horde of Punjabis from the adjacent town were packed into the bunker.

Some of them were actually there on business, bringing piles of clothing for her to try on. Most of them, she finally understood, just wanted to get a look at her.

Of course, they were all expelled from the bunker while she changed her clothing—except for two native women whose expert assistance she required until she mastered the secrets of the foreign garments. But once the women announced that she was suitably attired, the mob of admirers was allowed back in.

In fact, after a while Anna found it necessary to leave the bunker altogether and model her new clothing on the ground outside, where everyone could get a good look at her new appearance. Her husband insisted, to her surprise.

"You're beautiful," he said to her, "and I want everyone to know it."

She almost asked how a blind man could tell, but he forestalled the question with a little smile. "Did you think I'd forget?"

But later, that night, he admitted the truth. They were lying side by side, stiffly, still fully clothed, on the pallet in a corner of the bunker where Calopodius slept. "To be honest, I can't remember very well what you look like."

Anna thought about it, for a moment. Then:

"I can't really remember myself."

"I wish I could see you," he murmured.

"It doesn't matter." She took his hand and laid it on her bare belly. The flesh reveled in its new coolness. She herself, on the other hand, reveled in the touch. And did not find it strange that she should do so.

"Feel."

◇   ◇   ◇

His hand was gentle, at first. And never really stopped being so, for all the passion that followed. When it was all over, Anna was covered in sweat again. But she didn't mind at all. Without heavy and proper fabric to cover her—with nothing covering her now except Calopodius' hand—the sweat dried soon enough. That, too, was a great pleasure.

"I warn you," she murmured into his ear. "We're not in Constantinople any more. Won't be for a long time, if ever. So if I catch you with a courtesan, I'll boil you alive."

"The thought never crossed my mind!" he insisted. And even believed it was true.

Chapter 20
BARBARICUM

As they walked down the gangplank from their ship to the dock at Barbaricum, where a crowd waited to greet them, Ousanas gave Antonina a sly little smile. "Brace yourself. I realize it's a shock for you, not being the most famous woman in the area."

Antonina sniffed. "It's a relief, frankly. Give them someone else to gossip about."

Ousanas shook his head. "The other woman in question being a saint and the model of virtue, your own notoriety will simply stand out in contrast. The gossip will be fiercer than ever. Especially—"

He swelled out his chest. A chest which needed no swelling to begin with, as muscular as it so obviously was under the flashy but sparse Axumite regalia. "—Arriving, as you do, in the company of such a magnificent male."

Throughout, he'd kept a solemn expression on his face. As they neared the pack of notables on the dock, the expression became positively lugubrious. He tilted his head toward her, murmuring: "Within a day, tales will be sweeping the city of the orgy you held on the ship, from the moment it left Adulis."

"Ridiculous." She lifted her head slightly, to augment her dignified bearing. "That same reputation will shield me. Everyone knows that if *I'd* been holding an orgy, you wouldn't be able to walk off this ship in the first place. 'Magnificent male.' Ha. Weaklings, all of you."

They were almost at the docks. The front line of the crowd consisted of Roman officials, Persian noblemen and Axumite troop leaders. Quite an august body, really. So Antonina's next words were spoken almost in a whisper.

"I grant you, if we had any stallions or bulls on the ship, I'd be in trouble. But we didn't bring any."

It was all she could do not to stick out her tongue at him. Getting the best of Ousanas in that sort of repartee was something of an accomplishment.

The ceremonies that followed were the usual tedious business. Fortunately, Antonina was spared the worst of it, thanks to Photius and Tahmina. Their own transfer from the ship to the dock had been no simple matter of walking down a gangplank. The Roman officials and Persian grandees had vied with each other to see who could produce the most absurdly elaborate palanquins for the purpose.

"I was scared the gangplank would collapse under the weight," Photius confided to her later. "Tahmina—did you *see* the idiotic thing they carried her off in?—was downright petrified."

The most interesting part of the day, perhaps ironically, was the tour of the new hospital. The one *the Wife* had established.

It wasn't hers, really. Anna Saronites might have been wealthy enough—her husband Calopodius, at any rate—to commission the building of a brand-new hospital. But she simply hadn't been in Barbaricum long enough, before she began her voyage up the Indus.

But, from what Antonina could determine, that didn't seem to matter. The young Roman noblewoman had struck the existing hospital like the monsoon. Leaving plenty of wreckage in her wake, as the monsoon does. But—also like the monsoon—leaving a greener land behind. One with life, where there had been death.

"I'm impressed," Ousanas admitted. For once, not joking at all. "I wouldn't have thought even the Emperor of Iran and all his executioners could have swept aside this much stupidity and care-lessness. In that short a time, anyway."

Antonina eyed a nearby member of the Wife's Service, standing solemnly in the doorway to the next ward. Despite the purple uniform, he bore approximately the same resemblance to a "nurse" as a tavern bouncer bears to an "usher."

"She knew the trick," Antonina murmured. "I'm a little flattered, actually."

Ousanas cocked his head.

"Don't you see? She patterned the Service after the Hospitalers. That's what it takes, for something like this. People will simply evade the rulings of officials. Much harder to evade the strictures of a militant mass order."

"You're quite right," came a voice from behind. Turning her head, Antonina saw the chief of the Service in Barbaricum. Psoes, his name was. She hadn't realized he was following them closely enough to have overheard.

"You're quite right," he repeated. "She told me she got the idea from reading Irene Macrembolitissa's account of your exploits in Alexandria."

Antonina chuckled. "Irene's fables, you mean. She was long gone from Alexandria and on her way to India before all that happened. That account she wrote was entirely after the fact, and based on hearsay."

"*Your* hearsay, to make it worse," Ousanas grunted. "Told to her in one of your scandalous drinking bouts."

He surveyed the ward again, before they passed on to the next. This one was devoted to men recovering from amputations of the lower extremities, where the one they'd passed through earlier was given over to men who'd suffered more severe trauma. The harshly practical mind of the Wife was evident even in the hospital's new design. Triage, everywhere. Partly to keep diseased men from infecting men who were simply injured. Mostly, because the Wife accepted that some men would die, but saw no reason that other men should die unnecessarily.

In times past, hospitals simply heaped men wherever they happened to have a space, with no more forethought than a wind driving leaves against a fence. In such haphazard piles, a man suffering a simple amputation might die from neglect, simply because he was in a ward most of whose occupants were dying anyway.

Agathius came limping up. He'd lagged behind to reassure one of the soldiers from his own personal experience that while wooden legs were certainly a nuisance, they didn't seriously interfere with copulation. Once they were removed, anyway.

"Horrible," he muttered. "Thank God Sudaba remained in the palace and didn't see this."

Antonina lifted an eyebrow. "She never struck me as being particularly squeamish."

"She's not." Agathius glowered around the room. "That's what I'm worried about. She's already hard enough to control. Once she meets this cursed 'Wife' . . . "

The glower came to Antonina. "I'm blaming you, mostly. You and that damned Macrembolitissa. Hadn't been for your example—hers, even worse!—none of this would be happening."

"Men's lives *are* being saved," Ousanas pointed out mildly.

The glower never wavered. "Who cares? All men die sooner or later anyway. But in the good old days, whatever years we had given to us, we didn't have to spend half of them arguing with the women. It's your fault, Antonina."

That evening, over dinner at the palace that had been turned over to them for the duration of their short sojourn in Barbaricum, Antonina recounted the day's activities to those who had remained behind.

Sudaba wasn't interested in the official ceremonies. As a girl whose father was merely a dehgan, she might have been. As a young woman who'd now been married to the top Roman official in Mesopotamia for almost two years and had attended more official ceremonies than she could remember, she wasn't in the least.

What she *was* interested in hearing about—at length—was the hospital.

"I can't wait to meet this woman," she said.

Antonina smiled at Agathius. "Oh, stop glaring at the roast. It's already overcooked as it is."

"*Your* fault, I say it again."

It was odd, really, the comfort the stable-keeper took from the presence of the giant Roman soldier. Under any other circumstances, the man—Anastasius, his name—would have terrified him. The stable-keeper was Bengali. Despite the years he'd lived in Kausambi, he'd never really gotten accustomed to the size of western barbarians. The Ye-tai were bad enough. But no Ye-tai the stable-keeper had ever seen was as big and powerful-looking as this Roman.

Anastasius still did frighten the stable-keeper. But since he was so much less terrifying than his companion, the stable-keeper was almost relieved to have him around. He liked to imagine that the giant one would restrain the other—Valentinian, he was called, with another of those bizarre western names—in the all-too-likely event that the man reverted to the predator nature he so obviously possessed.

"Stop bullying the poor man, Valentinian," the giant rumbled.

"I'm not bullying him. I'm simply pointing out the facts of life."

The stable-keeper avoided both their gazes. Squatting on the floor of one of his stables and staring at the ground, he whimpered: "Why did I ever agree to this?"

"Why?" The one named Valentinian leaned over and casually spit on the ground. He was standing, not squatting, and leaning against a nearby stall. "Four reasons. First, you were stupid enough to catch the eye of somebody powerful—today, if not then—when he came through here some years ago, and impressed him with your competence and sterling character. Fucking idiot. You're what—almost fifty years old? And you still haven't learned that no good deed shall go unpunished?"

The stable-keeper whimpered again. "I didn't know who he was."

"Stupider still, then. The second reason is that this stable is about the right distance. Close enough that we could dig to it, far enough away that nobody will connect it to the palace once we blow the tunnel. It's even more or less in the right direction—away from the river."

He spat again. "Just bad luck, that. The next two reasons were your own fault, though. To begin with, you were greedy enough to accept our money."

The whimper that came out now was considerably louder. "You didn't explain exactly what you were doing," he protested.

"You didn't ask either, did you? Like I said, too greedy."

The weasel-faced Roman fell silent, his eyes idly wandering about the gloom of the stable.

The stable-keeper was hoping he wouldn't continue with the explanation.

But, of course, he did.

"The fourth and final reason is that if you don't do what we tell you to do, I'll kill you. Then I'll kill every member of your family after raping your wife and daughters and nieces. Your mother's too old and your sister has bad breath. I'll save the baby for last. He looks pretty tender and I'm sick of lamb."

The giant rolled his eyes. "Oh, for the love of God, Valentinian!"

He squatted down next to the stable-keeper and placed a huge hand on his skinny shoulder. Then, gave him a friendly and reassuring smile.

"He's lying," he assured the stable-keeper. "Valentinian won't rape the women before he kills them. And all he'll do to the baby is just cut his throat."

The stable-keeper believed him. Most insane of all was that he *did* find that a relief.

"How is that last reason my fault?" he whined.

Valentinian gave him that horrible weasel smile. "You weren't born big enough and tough enough and mean enough to fight back against the likes of me, and not rich enough to hire a small army to do it for you. Maybe in your next life, you won't be so careless."

Valentinian and Anastasius spent several hours in the tunnel, on the way back, checking and inspecting everything.

More precisely, Anastasius pretended to check the timbers and shoring, while Valentinian gave the Bihari miners and their remaining Ye-tai guards that level and dark-eyed stare that could intimidate a demon. Neither Valentinian nor Anastasius were miners, after all, so they really had no good idea what to look for. True, they had considerable experience at siege work—as both defenders and attackers—but neither of them had ever been used as sappers. That was specialty work, and not something that cataphracts generally got involved in.

"Ignore him," Anastasius assured the miners. "He just likes to stay in practice."

In a half-crouch due to the low ceiling, Anastasius planted his hands on his knees and smiled at the chief of the miners. "It looks good to me. But we don't want it to be *too* good. There are three doglegs we might need to use, and all three of them have to collapse if we set off the charges. Collapse for dozens of yards, too. Won't do us any good just to cave in a few feet. The Malwa can dig, too."

After giving Valentinian a quick, nervous glance, the Bihari nodded vigorously. "Not a problem! Not a problem! Look here!" He scurried over to one of the nearby wood pillars that held up the roof and began jabbing with his finger. Here, there—everywhere, it seemed.

"See how the wedges are set? The charges will blow them all loose. Without the wedges, everything will come down. We put all the doglegs deep, too. Deeper than the rest of the tunnels. With that much weight of earth above them—especially the first dogleg, near the river, with all that muddy soil—they'll come right down."

Anastasius swiveled a bit, to be able to look at Valentinian. "Looks good to me. You have a problem with anything?"

Valentinian was in a half-crouch also, although in his case he was leaning his rump against one of the pillars to support his weight rather than using hands on knees. He wasn't as tall as Anastasius, but he was still much too tall to stand upright in the low tunnel. Even the short Bihari miners had to stoop a little.

"Not really," he said, "beyond the general principle that something's bound to get fucked up." He gave the miner a little nod of the head. "It's not as if I really distrust him and his men. If it doesn't work, they're dead meat along with the rest of us."

The miner nodded his head, maybe a dozen times. "Yes! Yes! And if it works, we get our freedom and a big bonus. The lady promised. And—ah—"

He left off the rest, since it was a bit awkward. What was more to the point was that Valentinian had agreed to the lady's promise, and done so to their faces. For all that he frightened the miners—and frightened the Ye-tai even more, probably—there was an odd way in which they all trusted Valentinian. A man that murderous simply didn't need to stoop to petty treachery, when all was said and done.

Rajiv's fight with the three traitors had cemented Valentinian's reputation with those men. Especially the Ye-tai, who were experienced warriors themselves. "The Mongoose" might be a legend, inflated and overblown as legends often are. A man so deadly he could train a thirteen-year-old boy to kill three mercenaries—with jury-rigged weapons, to boot—was a living, breathing human cobra in their midst.

They were scared of Anastasius, also. But for all his size and strength and the fact they knew him to be an experienced fighter, he just didn't have the same dark aura about him. If anything, like the stable-keeper, they found his presence alongside Valentinian something of a relief.

Besides, there was hope as well as fear. Freedom and enough money to set themselves up well, for the slave miners. For the Ye-tai who had remained loyal, the chance to join an imperial body-guard, with all its perks and privileges.

That presumed, of course, that the scheme worked. By now, all of them knew the gist of the thing, since there was no point in trying to keep any of it a secret any longer. But if it didn't work, they were all dead anyway. So why not dream?

When the two cataphracts got back to the palace late in the afternoon and reported to Lady Damodara, she expressed some doubts.

"This is all so risky. We're depending on the loyalty of a man we don't know at all, simply because of a message sent by a man who is our enemy."

Anastasius shrugged. "I've met Holkar. Know him pretty well, actually. I really don't think this is the sort of thing he'd get tricky about. If he vouches for the character of the stable-keeper, I think we can trust him. Don't forget that the life of Holkar's daughters is at stake, too."

Valentinian started to spit on the floor. Then, remembering where he was, swallowed the phlegm. "Besides, we're not trusting the stable-keeper. I'm threatening him. Big difference."

Lady Damodara shook her head disapprovingly. "You shouldn't bully him so. He does seem like a nice man, after all."

"So? When this is all over, he's still a nice man. Except he's a nice man with the favor of the new emperor instead of a dirt-poor stable-keeper with no friends worth talking about. He'll have the fanciest stable in India. His biggest problem will be keeping the help from stealing the jewels encrusting the imperial saddles and howdahs."

Lady Damodara laughed softly. "I'm not sure I've ever met anyone with quite your view of life, Valentinian. I don't know how to describe it, exactly."

"Stripped to the bone," Valentinian supplied. He jerked a thumb at his huge companion. "This one can prattle about Plato and Aristotle all he wants. My philosophy is simple. Moralize like a miser."

Still later that evening, it was Dhruva's turn to chide Valentinian. "You're spoiling him again!"

Valentinian studied the infant in his arms. Baji was grinning at him, his hands waving about for another sweet to suck on.

"*Goo!*"

"I know." He was silent for a while, playing tug-of-war with Baji over his finger. "Terrific grip. I've got hopes for the kid."

"Give him to me," Dhruva insisted. "He needs to eat real food. He can't live on sweets."

After handing him over, Valentinian sighed. "I know I spoil him. Maybe it's my way of making amends."

"For what?"

He waved his hand vaguely. "I don't know. Me."

Dhruva started to feed the baby. "That's silly. You're not so bad."

Valentinian chuckled. "You're one of the few people I know who'd say that."

She shrugged with only one arm and shoulder, the other being occupied with the baby at her breast. "Most people haven't been Maratha slave whores in a Malwa brothel."

She said it almost serenely. After a while, she looked up. "I have never asked. Does that bother you?"

"No. It's like I told Lady Damodara. I'm pretty well stripped to the bone."

She nodded and looked back down at Baji. "Yes. You must have done something right in your former life."

Valentinian watched her, for a time. "I think maybe I did."

Chapter 21
BHARAKUCCHA

The soldiers along the battlements were so excited they weren't even trying to maintain disciplined formations. The closer Lord Damodara's army came to the gates of Bharakuccha, they more excited they got. By now, most of them were shouting.

Malwa's soldiers hated service in the Great Country. The war against the Marathas had been a savage business. But now, it seemed, it was finally over.

"A great victory, clearly," commented Toramana to Nanda Lal. "Look at those skin-sacks! Dozens of them. That must be Raghunath Rao's, floating from Rana Sanga's lance."

Nanda Lal squinted into the distance. "Yes, probably . . ."

It was frustrating! A properly prepared skin-sack had all its holes sewed up, so the skin could be filled with air. Thus buoyant and bloated, it swung gaily in the breeze, like a paper lantern. Best of all, the features could be distinguished. Grossly deformed, of course, but still made out clearly enough. Even all these years later, the face of the former emperor of Andhra was recognizable, where he hung in the great feasting hall of the imperial palace at Kausambi.

These skin-sacks, however, were limp and flaccid. Simply the flayed pelts of men, flapping like streamers and quite unrecognizable as individuals. No way to avoid it, of course. A field army

657

like Damodara's simply wasn't equipped to do the work properly. Flaying skin came naturally enough to soldiers. Careful sewing did not.

No matter, in and of itself, as long as the skins weren't too badly damaged. Once the sacks arrived in the city, they could be salvaged and redone correctly. Nanda Lal was simply frustrated because he was a man who liked to *know*, not guess.

The Malwa spymaster squinted at the other skin-sacks hanging from the lances toward the fore of the army. Even without being properly inflated, the dugs of a female sack should be easy enough to discern. Damodara and Rana Sanga and the lead elements of the army were quite close, now. In fact, the gates to the city were already opening.

Toramana had apparently spotted the same absence. "Shakuntala must have escaped. If she was even there at all."

Nanda Lal grunted. He was . . .

Not happy, he realized.

Why? It was indeed a great victory. If Raghunath Rao's skin was among those—and who else's would be hanging from Rana Sanga's own lance?—the Maratha rebellion that had been such a running wound in the side of Malwa was effectively over. No doubt, small and isolated bands of rebels would continue to fight. But with Rao dead and the main Maratha army broken, they would soon degenerate into simple banditry. No more than a minor nuisance.

Even assuming that Shakuntala had escaped, that was no great problem either. With her rebellion broken, she would simply become one of the world's petty would-be rulers, of which there were a multitude. In exile at Constantinople, she would be no threat to anyone beyond Roman imperial chambermaids.

And, who knew? With the lapse of enough time, it might be possible for a Malwa assassination team to infiltrate the Roman imperial compound, kill her, and smuggle out the corpse. The day might come when Shakuntala's skinsack hung also from the rafters of Skandagupta's feasting hall, swaying in the convivial breeze of the celebrants below alongside her father's and mother's.

Yet, he was *not* happy. Definitely not.

The death of a couple of his telegraph operators bothered him, for one thing. That had happened two days ago. A simple tavern killing, to all appearances. Eyewitnesses said the men got into a drunken brawl over a prostitute and stabbed each other. But . . .

A sudden fluke of the wind twisted the skinsack hanging from Sanga's lance. For the first time, Nanda Lal was able to see the face clearly.

He froze. Paralyzed, for just that moment.

Toramana spotted the same thing. A warrior, not a spymaster, he reacted more quickly.

"*Treachery,*" he hissed. The sword seemed to fly into his hand. "Lord, we have a traitor among us."

"Yes," snarled Nanda Lal. "Close the gates. Call—"

There was no pain, really. Or, perhaps, agony so great it could not register as such.

Nanda Lal stared down at the sword Toramana had driven into his belly. So deeply, he knew the tip must be sticking out from his back. Somewhere about the kidney area. The long-experienced torturer's part of his mind calmly informed him that he was a dead man. Two or three vital organs must have been pierced.

With a jerk of his powerful wrist, Toramana twisted the sword to let in air and break the suction. Then, his left hand clenched on Nanda Lal's shoulder, drew the blade back out. Blood spilled down and out like a torrent. At least one artery must have been severed.

That *hurt.* But all Nanda Lal could do was gasp. He still seemed paralyzed.

Unfairest of all, he thought, was that Toramana had stepped aside so deftly that only a few drops of the blood had spattered his tunic and armor.

Nanda Lal saw the sword come up, for a mighty blow. But could not move. Could only clutch the great wound in his stomach.

"Your head'll do," said Toramana. He brought the sword around and down.

Sanga had been watching, from under the edge of his helmet. The moment he saw Toramana strike, he spurred his horse forward. An instant later, the two hundred Rajputs who followed him did likewise.

By the time they reached the gate, now standing wide, they were at a full gallop. The dozen or so Malwa soldiers swinging open the gates gaped at them.

Not for long. Hundreds of war horses approaching at a gallop at a distance measured in mere yards is a purely terrifying sight. Even to soldiers braced and ready for the charge, with pikes in their hands. These garrison soldiers, expecting nothing but a celebration, never thought to do anything but race aside.

By then, Toramana was bringing his Ye-tai contingents under control. They were caught just as much by surprise, since he'd taken none of them into his confidence.

But it didn't matter, as he'd known it wouldn't. Confused men—soldiers, especially—will automatically turn to the nearest authority figure for guidance. With Nanda Lal dead—many of them had seen the killing—that meant . . .

Well, Toramana. The commander of the entire garrison.

And Lord Damodara, of course. The Goptri of the Decca, whom they could even now see passing through the gates behind Rana Sanga and the lead Rajputs.

"Treason!" Toramana bellowed, standing on the battlements where the soldiers could see him easily. "Nanda Lal was planning treason! The murder of Lord Damodara!"

He pointed with the sword in his hand to the figure of Damodara, riding into the city. "All rally to the Goptri! Defend him against assassins!"

In response, Lord Damodara waved his hand. It was a rather cheery gesture, actually. Then, twisted in his saddle and gave Toramana something in the way of a salute.

It took no more that. The soldiers were still confused, the Ye-tai as much as any of them. But, if anything, the confusion made them even more inclined to obey unquestioningly.

And why not? For years, for that army, their real commanders had been soldiers like Damodara. Toramana, for the Ye-tai; Sanga for the Rajputs.

Nanda Lal was simply a mysterious and unsettling figure from far-off Kausambi. Neither known nor popular. And, if somewhat fearsome, not nearly as fearsome as the commanders who had once even beaten Belisarius in battle.

The reaction of two Ye-tai soldiers was typical. Drawing his sword, one of them snarled at a nearby squad of regular troops.

"You heard him, you piglets! Spread out! Watch for assassins!"

As the squad scurried to obey, the Ye-tai's companion leaned over and half-whispered: "What do you think—"

"Who gives a shit?" the first Ye-tai hissed.

He stabbed his sword toward the distant body of Nanda Lal. The headless corpse had sprawled to the edge of the parapet. By now, most of the blood had drained from the neck, leaving a pool on the ground below.

"If you care that much, go ask *him*."

The other Ye-tai stared at the corpse. Then, at the head lying some yards from the parapet wall. It had bounced, twice, and then rolled, after it hit the ground.

He drew his own sword and lifted it high. "Long live the Goptri! Death to traitors!"

Some time later, once he was sure the city was under control, Toramana returned to the parapet wall and retrieved Nanda Lal's head. After brushing off the dirt, he held it up.

"A bit dented. But you'll do."

Sanga came up.

"Lord Damodara wants the wedding this evening, if possible. The Ye-tai seem solid, but the wedding will seal the thing."

"Yes. Not just my clan, either. All of them." Toramana continued to admire the head. "I told Indira to be ready several days ago, for a quick wedding. You know your sister."

Sanga's dark eyes studied him, for a moment. "Yes, I do. I hadn't realized you did, so well."

Toramana smiled. "Nothing improper! If you don't believe me, ask that mob of old women. But you can talk about other things than flowers and insects in a garden, you know. And she's smart. Very, very smart."

"Yes, she is." The dark eyes went to the severed head. "I approve of a man who keeps his promises. On a spike?"

Toramana shook his head. "Bit of a nuisance, that. It's *garam*, don't forget."

Sanga made a face. "Flies."

"A horde of them. Even more than those old women. I think a clear jar will do fine." The Ye-tai commander finally lowered the head. "I promised him he'd be *at* the wedding. I made no guarantees he'd be able to flatter the bride."

By sundown, Sanga was satisfied that all the mahaveda and mahamimamsa in the city had been tracked down and slaughtered. There might be a handful surviving in a corner here and there. Bharakuccha was a huge city, after all.

But, he doubted it—and knew for a certainty that even if there were, they wouldn't survive long anyway. The Mahaveda cult had never sunk roots into India's masses. Had never, for that matter, even tried to win any popular support. It was a sect that depended entirely on the favor of the powerful. That favor once withdrawn—here, with a vengeance—the cult was as helpless as a mouse in a pen full of raptors.

Most of the time, the Rajputs hadn't even needed to hunt down the priests and torturers. At least a third of the populace was still Maratha. The majority of the inhabitants might not have hated them as much, but they hated them nonetheless. The only face the cult had ever turned to the city's poor was that of the tithe-collector. And a harsh and unyielding one, at that. Most of the priests and mahamimamsa who went under the swords of the Rajputs were hauled to them by the city's mobs.

The telegraph and radio stations were secured almost immediately. Ajatasutra's assassins had seen to the first, with the telegraph operators whom Narses had already suborned.

The Ye-tai commander of the unit guarding the radio station had not been privy to Toramana's plans. But the Ye-tai general had selected the man carefully. He was both smart and ambitious. It hadn't taken him more than thirty seconds to realize which way the new wind was blowing—and that it was blowing with all the force of a monsoon. By the time Toramana and Damodara got to the radio station, the operators had all been arrested and were being kept in an empty chamber in the palace.

Damodara studied them. Huddled in a corner, squatting, the radio operators avoided his gaze. Several of them were trembling.

"Don't terrify them any further," he instructed Toramana's lieutenant. "And give them plenty of food and water. By tomorrow, I'll need at least one of them to be cooperative."

"Yes, Lord."

Damodara gave him an impassive look. It didn't take the lieutenant —smart man—more than half a second to remember the announcement.

"Yes, Emperor."

"Splendid."

The wedding went quite smoothly. More so than Sanga had feared, given the hastiness of the preparations.

Not *that* hasty, he finally understood. His sister took firm charge of it, driving right over the protests of the old women who'd expected a traditional Rajput wedding. Within an hour, it became obvious to Sanga that she and Toramana must have planned this, too.

He'd never think of promenades in a garden the same way, he realized ruefully.

The ceremony was a hybrid affair. Half-Rajput, half-Ye-tai, with both halves almost skeletal.

Good enough, however. More than good enough.

"Don't you think?" he asked the head in a glass jar.

Nanda Lal's opinion remained unspoken, but Sanga was quite sure he disapproved mightily. The Malwa dynasty had maintained its rule, among other things, by always keeping a sharp and clear boundary between the Rajputs and the Ye-tai. Able, thus, to pit one against the other, if need be.

True, under the pressure of the Roman offensive, the Malwa had begun to ease the division. The dynasty had agreed to this wedding also, after all. But Sanga knew they'd never intended to ease it very far.

Damodara was simply tossing the whole business aside. He'd base his rule—initially, at least—on the oldest and simplest method. The support of the army. And, for that, he wanted the two most powerful contingents within the army tied as closely together as possible. The marriage between Toramana and Indira would only be the first of many.

Sanga understood the logic. For all the many things that separated the Rajputs and the Ye-tai, they had certain things very much in common.

Two, in particular.

First, they were both warrior nations. So, whatever they disliked about the other—for the Rajputs, Ye-tai crudity; for the Ye-tai, Rajput haughtiness—there was much to admire also.

Second, they were both nations still closely based on clan ties and allegiances. The fact that the Rajputs draped a veil of Hindu mysticism over the matter and called their clan chieftains "kings" was more illusion than truth. Sanga had known since he was a boy that if you scratched the shiny Rajput veneer, you'd find more than a trace of their central Asian nomadic origins.

Clan ties meant blood ties. Which were brought by marriages. Within three generations, Rajput and Ye-tai clans would be so intermingled as to make the old divisions impossible.

Not conflict, of course. Clan wars could be as savage as any. But they were not the stuff—*could* not be the stuff—that would tear northern India into pieces.

The Malwa methods had been determined by their goal of world conquest. For Damodara, having given up that grandiose ambition, everything else followed. He would build a new empire that would not go beyond northern India. But, within those limits—which were still immense, after all—he would forge something far more resilient, and more flexible, than anything the dynasty had done before.

More resilient and flexible, for that matter, than anything the Maurya or Gupta empires had accomplished either. Sanga was beginning to suspect that Damodara would someday have the cognomen "the Great" attached to his name.

Not in his own lifetime, though. He was far too canny for that.

Before the wedding was halfway over, Sanga realized he was in an excellent mood. He even participated in the dancing.

"Good thing I stopped the duel," Damodara told him afterward. "That too-clever-by-half Maratha bandit probably would have insisted on a dancing contest as part of it."

Sanga grimaced.

"Oh, yes. We'd have found your body strewn all over. Speaking of which—" He glanced around. "What happened to Nanda Lal's head?"

"My brother-in-law felt that propriety had been satisfied enough by his presence at the wedding, and there was no need to keep him around for the festivities. I believe he gave it to some Ye-tai boys. That game they play. You know, the one where—"

"Oh, yes. Of all my many cousins, I think I disliked him the most except Venandakatra. Well. Hard to pick between Nanda Lal and Skandagupta, of course. Isn't that the game where they use dogs to retrieve the lost balls?"

"Yes, Emperor."

"Splendid."

Chapter 22
BHARAKUCCHA

Early the next morning, Damodara commanded Sanga to meet him in the radio station.

"Why here, Emperor?" Sanga asked, as soon as he arrived. The room was empty, except for the two of them and the bizarre equipment. "I thought you planned to use the telegraph."

Damodara looked a bit haggard, as if he hadn't slept well. "I did," he said, tugging at his chin. "But I thought about it most of the night. And I think . . . "

He was interrupted by a small commotion at the door. A moment later, two burly Ye-tai came in, with a much smaller man between them. They weren't guiding him in so much as simply carrying him by the armpits.

Once in the room, they set him down. "Lord Toramana says this one, Emperor."

Damodara nodded. "Leave us, then."

For a moment, the Ye-tai seemed taken aback.

Damodara smiled, looking upon the radio operator. He was but a few inches over five feet tall, and couldn't have weighed more than one hundred and twenty pounds. Wearing nothing but a loincloth, it was also obvious that he was scrawnily built.

Damodara flicked his fingers toward Sanga. "I dare say that with the Rajput king present, this desperate fellow will restrain his assassin's impulses."

He gave the radio operator a winning smile. "Am I not correct?"

The man bobbed his head like a small bird pecking at grains.

"You will make no attempt upon my life?"

The man shook his head so fast it seemed to vibrate.

"I thought not." He gave the two guards a cold eye, and they departed.

After they were gone, Damodara pointed to the chair in front of the complex apparatus. "Sit," he commanded.

The operator did so.

"Is there a code you must use, when you transmit?"

Again, that vibrating head-shake.

"I'd really much prefer it if you spoke, man," Damodara said mildly.

The operator swallowed. Then, managed to croak out: "No, sir. There's no code."

Sanga frowned fiercely. "None? I warn you not to lie! It makes no sense to me—"

"But there *isn't,* Lord," the operator protested desperately. "I swear it. She—"

He broke off. Almost seemed to be choking.

Damodara sighed. "As I suspected. And feared." He leaned forward a bit. "I want nothing but the truth. This 'she.' Of whom do you speak?"

The operator stared at him, his eyes very wide with fear. He looked more like trapped rodent than anything else.

"You're speaking of Great Lady Sati, yes?"

The operator swallowed again. "Yes," he whispered. "But that's supposed to be a secret. I'm not supposed—"

He broke off again, this time because of the sight and sound of Sanga's sword coming out of the scabbard. The Rajput king held the sword blade in front of the man's face. So close he had to look at it cross-eyed.

"I suggest you have much deeper concerns now than whether you are violating an oath of secrecy," Damodara pointed out. "Tell me."

Still looking cross-eyed at the blade, the man began to speak softly but quickly.

"All the operators know it, Lord. We do, at least. I don't know about the telegraph men. When we make the transmissions, Great

Lady Sati is always at the other end. Herself in person. She—she—she—"

"Yes, I know. She's a witch. A demoness."

"She *is*," he half-moaned. "It was part of our training. We had to spend a few minutes with her. She—she—she—"

Careful to avoid the blade, he brought up a shaky hand to wipe his brow. He was sweating profusely.

Damodara straightened up. "Put away the sword, Sanga. He's telling the truth."

Sanga did as commanded. His own face was very stiff. Like Damodara—and now, it seemed, this insignificant radio operator—Sanga had spent time alone in the presence of one of the females of the dynasty who served as the vessel for Link. Great Lady Holi, in his case. But he knew it made no difference.

Damodara went to the door and opened it. The two Ye-tai were standing just beyond. "Take the operator elsewhere, for a time. I need to speak with Sanga in private. Don't take him far, though. And summon Narses."

After they were alone, Damodara sat in the chair. He stared at the mechanism whose workings he barely understood at all.

"*Now* you understand the problem. It came to me in the middle of the night. Like a nightmare."

"Yes, Emperor."

When Narses arrived and was informed, he shook his head.

"No, I had no idea. They always kept the radio men carefully sequestered. I was able to suborn most of the telegraph operators, but I couldn't even get close to these fellows. That's why Toramana and I finally decided just to use their Ye-tai guard contingent to secure the radio."

Damodara nodded. He hadn't thought Narses had known, or the shrewd old eunuch would long since have seen the problem. Their entire plan had just gone up in smoke.

For his part, Sanga grunted sourly. The look he gave Narses was more sour still. The Rajput king was still angry at the Roman traitor for the way he'd manipulated all of them. But after he'd learned from Narses that the eunuch had been instructed by Skandagupta and Great Lady Sati to murder his family outright, his sheer fury toward him had dissipated.

He didn't doubt the eunuch was telling the truth, either. Link was the ultimate source of that plot, and Sanga had met the monster. The plot Narses described was exactly the sort of thing it would have designed. It was cold-blooded beyond any sense of the term "cold" that either a reptile or a glacier would have understood.

Narses glared at the radio apparatus. "Maybe we could just use the telegraph—"

But he was already shaking his own head when Damodara interrupted him. "No point in that," the new emperor said. "Link will expect a radio transmission also. The fact that none took place last night will make it suspicious already. Perhaps there was a thunderstorm, of course, even if that's unlikely this time of year. Two nights in a row, impossible. It will immediately know something is wrong."

The eunuch took a deep, almost shuddering breath. "Damnation. It never occured to me that she might *personally* take the transmissions."

Damodara shrugged heavily. "There's a logic to it. I always wondered, a bit, why we were putting so much effort into these huge radio towers. The telegraph works well enough, for most purposes—and has fewer security problems. Now I know. Look where they are: Kausambi, the Punjab, and here. Nowhere else."

"Are we sure of that?" asked Sanga.

"Yes," growled Narses. "That much I am sure of. They're planning two more. One in Amaravati and one in Tamralipti. But they haven't even started building them yet."

"It makes perfect sense, Sanga," Damodara continued. "The basic function of these towers is to enable Link to control the empire. Well, not 'control' it so much as enable it to be sure if rebellion has begun."

Narses was still glaring at the apparatus. "I fooled that stinking bitch once. I bet I can . . . "

The words trailed off.

"Don't be stupid, old man," he muttered, to himself as much as to the other men in the room. "First, you don't know how to use the gadget. Even if you tried to learn—in a few hours?—you'd fumble something. The bitch would know right away someone other than one of her operators was at the other end. And even if you could do it, the last time you weren't trying to lie to her."

Sanga frowned at the door. "If we calmed down the operator . . . " But, like Narses, he rebutted his own half-advanced plan. "Impossible. There'd be *some* sign of his agitation. Nothing we'd notice—or he himself, even—but the monster would."

He ran fingers through his thick, still-black hair. "Yes, that explains the radio towers. The telegraph is now too common, too widely spread. There's no way she could personally monitor even most of the transmissions, much less all of them. But with a few towers, located only in the empire's critical regions, she can. And there is no way—no way—to lie to her. To *it*, that is both greater and less than human."

He fell silent. Damodara rose from the chair he'd been sitting on and began pacing. He, also, was silent.

Eventually, Narses spoke.

"No help for it, then. We were planning to begin the march upcountry tomorrow, anyway. We'll just have to send telegraph messages saying there's a terrible—very unseasonal—storm, and the radio won't work for a while. She'll suspect something, of course. But with the problems she has in the Punjab anyway, she won't *know*."

He spread his hands. "I grant you, it won't buy us more than a few days. But it's the best we can do."

Damodara stopped his pacing. "No."

He strode over to the apparatus, moving almost eagerly. "Your man Ajatasutra had it right. Then—and now. We will do this like an assassin, not a torturer. Quick and deadly, in the sunlight, not lingering over it in a cellar."

Narses frowned at him. "What are you talking about?"

Sanga was frowning also. Suddenly, his brow cleared, and he barked a laugh. Again, hissing its way like a snake, the blade came out of the scabbard.

"*Yes!*" the Rajput king bellowed. He tilted the sword toward Damodara in a salute. "Emperor of Malwa! True and pure!"

Narses looked from one to the other. "Have you both gone mad?"

Damodara gave him an impassive look.

"Ah. Sorry. Your Majesty, have you gone mad?"

"I don't believe so," replied the new emperor cheerily. "And if I am, you have only yourself to blame. Aren't you the one who told me, after all, that there is another radio in India?"

After a second, Narses shot to his feet. "You're out of your fucking mind!"

The look Sanga gave him was not impassive in the least. Even Narses shrank a little.

"Ah. Sorry. Your Majesty, I submit to you that you need to consider the possibility that when the traitors substituted the false emperor in the crib of your grandfather, that they also poisoned him."

Damodara, fortunately, was in an expansive mood. "I see. Some slow-acting poison, I take it? Doesn't show its effects for two generations, when the grandson turns into a blithering fool."

"Yes, Your Majesty. That one."

Ajatasutra, on the other hand, thought it was a marvelous plan, when it was explained to him less than an hour later.

"Don't see why not," he commented, smiling at Narses. "Stop glaring at me, old man."

"How many times do I beat you at chess?"

"The game of thrones is not really a chess game—a saying, as I recall, that you are quite fond of." The assassin shrugged. "Narses, what does it matter? Even by the old plan, the people in Kausambi would have been in danger long before we could arrive."

"This will strike them even quicker and harder," Narses pointed out darkly.

Since the people involved were not his—except, perhaps, the two girls, in a way—Ajatasutra looked at Damodara and Sanga.

Damodara's face was tight, but Sanga seemed quite relaxed.

"I fought the Mongoose, remember. He will react quickly enough, I think. And if he can't, no man can anyway."

Damodara wiped his face. "True. I watched from close by. He is very, very, very quick. And what's probably more important, he's ruthless enough not to hesitate."

He dropped the hand. "We have no real choice, anyway. Narses, your alternative has only negative virtues. My plan, risky at it is, brings us something."

"Maybe," Narses said gloomily. "Maybe."

"We'll know soon enough. Sanga, make sure the army is ready to leave at daybreak. We'll start sending the messages at dusk."

"Yes, Emperor."

Chapter 23

THE IRON TRIANGLE

Maurice was actually grinning. Thinly, true. But it was still a genuine grin, full of nothing but amusement.

"Yes, General, he's late again. Like he has been for every shift since she got here."

Belisarius glanced at the empty chair where Calopodius normally sat. The scribes at the table were in their seats, with their implements in hand. But they were simply chatting casually, waiting for their boss to arrive.

They didn't seem any more disgruntled than Maurice, however. Calopodius was popular with the men who staffed Belisarius' headquarters bunker.

"I thought she'd hit this place like a storm," Belisarius mused. "I know for a fact that the medical staff was trembling in their boots. What I hadn't foreseen was that Calopodius would absorb most of it."

"His pallet, rather—and thank God I'm not one of the straws. Be bruised and battered bloody, by now."

"Don't be crude, Maurice."

"I'm not being crude. Just recognizing that once you strip away the mysticism about 'the Blind Scribe' and 'the Wife,' what you're really dealing with are newlyweds—for all practical purposes—neither of whom is twenty years old yet. Ha! Randy teenagers. Can't keep their hands off—"

He coughed, and broke off. Calopodius was hurrying into the bunker.

"Hurrying" was the word, too. Blind he might be, but by this time Calopodius had the dimensions of the bunker and the location of everything in it committed to memory. And he had an excellent memory.

The position of the people in the bunker, of course, was less predictable. But, by now, they'd learned to keep out of his way. Belisarius watched as one of the staff officers, grinning, side-stepped Calopodius as he half-raced to the table.

"Sorry I'm late, General," the young man muttered, as he sat down. "Anna—ah—had a bit of trouble with her uniform."

Under the circumstances, that was perhaps the worst excuse he could have come up with. The entire staff in the bunker— Belisarius and Maurice included—burst into laughter.

Calopodius flushed. As the laughter continued, the flush deepened until he was almost literally red-faced. But the expression on his face also became subtly transmuted into something that was ultimately more smug than chagrinned. Most young men, after all—even ones raised in Constantinople's haughty aristocratic circles—are not actually embarrassed by having a reputation for being able to keep their wives in their beds, and happy to be there.

As the laughter faded away, Luke and Illus came into the bunker. They were both smiling, too, as they took their accustomed places on chairs near the entrance.

"Accustomed," at least, for Luke. Illus was still settling into his new role as one of Calopodius' staff. Officially, he was a bodyguard; just as, officially, Luke was a valet. In practice, Calopodius used either or both of them in whatever capacity seemed needed. Fortunately, the two men seemed to get along well enough.

"Right," Calopodius said briskly. He turned his head toward the scribe to his right. "Mark, I think we should—"

The radio began its short-and-long buzzing noises. The noise was different from the typical click-clack made by the telegraph, when it received an incoming message, but had a basic similarity. Aide—like Link—had not tried to design anything more complex than a spark gap radio system. So the radio used the same "Morse code" that the telegraph did.

The Malwa used the same code, except when they were transmitting encrypted messages. That was not really so odd, since that code was the common one in the history of the universe that had produced both Aide and Link.

"—start with the dispatches—"

—*bzzz-bz-bzzz-bzzz-bz-bz-bzzz*—

"—regarding . . . " He trailed off, his head swiveling toward the radio. Calopodius, unlike Belisarius, could translate Morse code instantly. It was by now a language he was as fluent in as he was in Greek or Latin.

—*bzzz-bz-bz-buzz-bz-bzzz-bz-bz-bzzz*—

"General . . . " Calopodius rose to his feet.

Belisarius, frowning, tried to interpret the messages. There was something . . .

Yes! Yes! Yes! Aide was doing the equivalent of shouting. **It's starting!**

What's starting? I can't—

Be quiet. I'll translate for you, starting from the beginning.

> GENERAL BELISARIUS STOP THIS IS EMPEROR DAMO-
> DARA STOP I AM TRUE AND RIGHTFUL EMPEROR OF
> MALWA STOP NARSES UNCOVERED PLOT THAT
> STOLE MY BIRTHRIGHT STOP I MARCH ON KAUSAMBI
> AT DAWN STOP WILL OVERTHROW THE USURPER
> SKANDAGUPTA STOP

Calopodius was translating the same words aloud, for everyone else in the bunker.

"I will be damned," murmured Maurice, shaking his head. "You were right all along. I never really thought you were."

> RANA SANGA AND HIS RAJPUTS WITH ME STOP
> TORAMANA AND HIS YE-TAI WITH ME STOP ENTIRE
> DECCAN ARMY WITH ME STOP

"Calopodius!" Belisarius half-shouted, waving his hand in summons. "Let someone else translate. I need your assistance. Now."

He moved toward the radio. "Over here." The blind young officer came away from the table and followed him. So did Maurice.

> BHARAKUCCHA IN MY HANDS STOP NANDA LAL
> EXECUTED STOP MAHAVEDA CULT OUTLAWED STOP

ALL MAHAVEDA AND MAHAMIMAMSA UNDER SEN-
TENCE OF DEATH STOP

Calopodius was not the only one in the bunker who was fluent
in Morse. One of his scribes had picked up the translation almost
without a pause.

"He's not fooling around, is he?" said Maurice.

MADE PEACE WITH RAO STOP VINDHYAS THE NEW
BORDER STOP BHARAKUCCHA TO BE FREE CITY STOP
NEED AXUMITE TROOPS FOR GARRISON STOP

"Smart," said Belisarius. "Very smart. Calopodius, Antonina's
still in Barbaricum with Ousanas, isn't she?"

"Yes. They weren't going to start up the Indus until tomorrow
or the day after."

"Good. Send her a message immediately telling her to stay there
until she hears from me. Better use the telegraph rather than the
radio, though. No reason to let the Malwa overhear—"

"They won't anyway," came Justinian's voice from the entrance.
Belisarius turned and saw the former emperor moving into the
bunker. "Don't you pay attention to *anything* I tell you?"

He didn't seem more than mildly aggrieved, though. Justinian
always enjoyed explaining how clever he was. When it came to
artisanship, anyway, if not politics.

"I designed this system so that we *wouldn't* be intercepted."

Lousy old braggart, grumbled Aide. **He didn't design the
system. *I* did. He just followed my instructions. But he's
right. The position and length of the antennas—everything—
were set up so we could send signals without the Malwa
overhearing us as long as we do it right. They'll intercept
anything we receive, of course. No way to prevent that. But
we can transmit in secret.**

"Explain," Belisarius commanded. "Explain *clearly*, so a dimwit
like me can understand it."

Justinian snorted. "Such unwonted modesty! It's like this, my
not-so-stupid General." Justinian began moving his hands, as if he
were shaping a cat's cradle with no string. "With directional radio,
the signal has two strong . . . call them beams. The strongest, by
far, is the forward signal. But there's also a back signal that can

often be picked up. The side signals, however—the lobes—are undetectable."

By any technology either we or the Malwa have, anyway, Aide agreed.

Belisarius thought about it. "In other words, any signal I sent to Damodara in Bharakuccha would probably be picked up by Link."

"Yes. The monster's radio tower, our radio installation, and the Malwa tower in Bharakuccha are almost in a direct line. Not quite, but close enough that we don't want to risk it. *Barbaricum,* on the other hand—"

"Is off to the side, yes. Far enough?"

Yes.

"Yes," said Justinian simultaneously. "Link won't hear anything you send to Barbaricum. And *they,* in turn—"

But Belisarius had already figured it out. "I understand. We can't signal Damodara in secret, but Barbaricum can with their radio. So we set up a triangle of communications—and the only part of the leg Link can pick up is what we receive. But not what we send."

Yes.

"Yes."

Belisarius scratched his chin. While they'd been talking, the radio had kept up its beeping and whooping.

Bring me current, Aide, while I think. What's Damodara saying now?

Most of it's pretty pointless, in my opinion. A lot of grandiose declarations about the sterling character of the Ye-tai— talk about a pile of nonsense—and even more stuff—really grisly, this part—about the penalties to be meted out to mahaveda priests and mahamimamsa.

The jewel sounded more than a little miffed. **I don't understand why he's taking up so much precious radio time just to specify what order in which to tear off their limbs and what animals are permitted to feed on the corpses. That last business started with jackals and he's been working his way down from there. Right now he's talking about how beetles should be used to finish up the odd bits and ends. Do you think he's a sadist, maybe? That could be a problem.**

Belisarius chuckled. Even after all these years, Aide—who was vastly more intelligent than humans when it came to many things—could still fumble at the simplest emotional equations.

No, he's just very clever. Since he decided to launch his rebellion openly—and that's interesting, right there, don't you think?—he's taking advantage of the opportunities as well as the problems. First, he's making crystal clear to the Ye-tai that if they acquiesce to the new regime, they won't be penalized. I'll bet he's been sprinkling Toramana's name all through, yes?

"Showering" his name, more like. All right, I can understand that. But why—

The business with the priests? They're hated all through India, to begin with, so it's another way to rally popular support. What's probably more important, at least immediately, is that the mahaveda and mahamimamsa are Malwa's first line of enforcers.

Along with the Ye-tai. But . . . oh.

Belisarius smiled. *I know you can feel "fear" yourself, Aide, but it's always a fairly calm thing for you, isn't it? Almost an intellectual business. No trembling, no sweating, no bowels loosening.*

Don't be silly. Protoplasmic nonsense, that is. You're saying he's trying to panic the mahaveda?

Scare them shitless, Belisarius agreed. *Don't forget that the mahaveda and mahamimamsa, unlike the Ye-tai, aren't a different race or ethnic line.*

Yes, you're right. Most of them are Malwa, but not all—and Malwa aren't racially distinct from any other north Indians anyway. So?

So what's to stop a priest or torturer from throwing away their identifying garments and paraphernalia and just vanishing? Worse comes to worst, even a beggar in a loincloth is better off than a dismembered corpse feeding beetles.

Oh. True. "Dismembering" is the least of it, really. He spent more time talking about the red hot tongs that are to be used to pull out intestines. I still don't understand the point of it. He's obviously doing this in the open because he thinks Link is receiving the radio transmissions directly.

Yes. That's got to be the explanation. Belisarius had to suppress a little shudder, remembering the one time he'd met Link himself. *No way to fool that monster, even over a radio transmission.*

No, there isn't. Even human radio and telegraph operators, with experience, can recognize who's on the other end. Everyone has a distinctive "fist," as they call it. But . . .

You're thinking that if Link is at the receiving end—here in the Punjab, if not in Kausambi—it'll simply suppress the transmission. No one in Malwa India will hear it.

Of course, it will! Even in Kausambi, that radio station has to be under iron control.

Belisarius was smiling broadly, now. *And why do you think Damodara is only using the radio? I'll bet you—if you had anything to wager—that this same message is going over every telegraph line in India. And, by now, there are far too many telegraph stations for Link to be able to keep them quiet. The only reason Damodara is using the radio at all is to communicate with us.*

Silence, for a moment.

Then: **Oh.**

Then: **It's not fair. I'm just a crystal. Lost in this protoplasmic scheming and trickiness. A lamb among wolves.**

Aide started to add another complaint, but broke off. **He's starting to say something to us again. Here it is:**

PROPOSE GRAND ALLIANCE STOP IRAN TO KEEP THE SIND STOP JOINT OCCUPATION OF THE PUNJAB STOP KUSHANS TO KEEP THE HINDU KUSH STOP AXUM TO GARRISON KEY NEUTRAL SEAPORTS STOP INDEPENDENT CITIES BUT AXUM MAY COLLECT TOLLS STOP IS THIS AGREED STOP

Belisarius turned to Calopodius. "Do you have Barbaricum on the line, yet?"

"Yes. Antonina hasn't arrived in the station, though. Neither has Ousanas. But they're on the way."

"We'll wait till they arrive. What about Sukkur?"

"Same story. I've got the Persians on the line, but Khusrau is somewhere else. He's in the city, however, so they say it won't take long."

"Good. Have you instructed the radio operators in Barbaricum to send a relay signal to Bharakuccha—and *only* to Bharakuccha?"

"Yes, General. I—ah—made the last part quite clear."

Maurice grinned. So did Justinian. "I will say your wife has done wonders for your assertiveness," said the former emperor.

Justinian turned to Belisarius. Faced in his direction, rather. As was often the case with blind people, he had a good sense of other people's locations in the room, but didn't know exactly where their faces were.

"And what about you? I trust we're not going to see a sudden lapse into timid modesty. 'It's not my place, whine; I'm just a general, whine.' "

Belisarius grimaced. "Theodora is *not* going to like it. She's already accusing me of giving away everything."

"So what? She's in Constantinople and, more to the point, the *Emperor* of Rome is in Barbaricum. Probably at your wife's elbow."

That's a dirty rotten lawyer's trick, for sure, said Aide. **Of course, he *is* the Empire's top lawyer.**

"She's still the Empress Regent," Belisarius pointed out. "Until he attains his majority, Photius doesn't technically have the authority to order most anything."

"So what, again? Difficult times, difficult measures. Unfortunately, the raging thunderstorm"—here Justinian waved at the entrance to the bunker, beyond which could be heard the faint sounds of people enjoying a pleasant and balmy evening—"made it impossible to communicate with Constantinople by radio. And the telegraph—all those pestiferous relays—just wasn't fast enough. Given that a decision had to be made *immediately*."

Justinian's smile was unusually cheerful, for him. "I can assure you that, as the Grand Justiciar, I will be forced to rule in your favor if Theodora presses the matter."

Belisarius returned the smile, scratching his chin. "No qualms, yourself?"

Justinian shrugged. "We've been together a long time, she and I. It's not likely she'll have me poisoned. And I'm right and she's wrong—and no one knows it better than you. In another universe, I kept you at war for years out of my overreaching ambition, and had nothing to show for it in the end except exhaustion and ruin. Let's not do it again, shall we?"

He's right.

Yes, of course he is. Rome doesn't need more territory. It'd just bring grief with it. Even the enclave I'll insist on here in the Triangle is for purely political reasons. But you—O craven crystal—will remain huddling in your pouch while I have to bear the brunt of Theodora's wrath.

Seems fair to me. You're the general. I'm just the hired help. Grossly underpaid, to boot.

"Antonina's on the line, General," said Calopodius. "And they're telling me Khusrau has arrived at the telegraph station in Sukkur."

"Let's do it, then."

The communication with Antonina went quickly.

PHOTIUS AGREES TO DAMODARA TERMS STOP WANTS TO KNOW IF EXILE POSSIBLE IN TRIANGLE TO ESCAPE THEODORA STOP HE WORRIES TOO MUCH STOP LOVE YOU STOP

"Ask her about—"

"It's already coming in," Calopodius interrupted him.

OUSANAS AGREES TO DAMODARA TERMS ALSO STOP WILL TAKE FLEET AND ARMY IMMEDIATELY TO BHARAKUCCHA STOP WHAT YOU WANT ME AND PHOTIUS DO STOP

"Have her and the boy go with them," Maurice suggested. "They'll be much safer in Bharakuccha than up here, with everything breaking loose. And what would they do here, anyway?"

It didn't take Belisarius long to decide that Maurice was right. If Antonina still had her Theodoran Cohort with her, she might be able to play a useful military role in the Triangle. But she'd left them behind in Alexandria. If just she and Photius and Tahmina came to the Triangle—with a huge flock of servants, to make things worse—they'd be nothing a distraction and a nuisance to Maurice.

And Belisarius himself wouldn't be there at all, if his plans worked.

"Yes, I agree. Leaving aside the safety problem, she'll probably be useful in Bharakuccha anyway. That populace will need to be settled down, and she's a lot better at that than Ousanas would be. Calopodius, tell her and Photius to accompany Ousanas to Bharakuccha."

◊   ◊   ◊

Two last messages came back:

WHEN WILL SEE YOU AGAIN STOP

Then, after a brief pause:

NEVER MIND STOP STUPID QUESTION STOP BE WELL STOP LOVE YOU STOP

The warmth that last message gave him dissipated soon enough. The negotiations with Khusrau were neither brief nor cordial.

Eventually, Belisarius broke it off altogether. "I haven't got time for this nonsense," he snarled. "Tell him an assault just started and I have to leave. Damodara's terms are important and need a quick answer. This is just mindless Aryan pigheaded greed."

As the telegraph operator did as instructed, Belisarius stalked over to the radio. "I can't believe it. Khusrau's not usually that stupid. Wasting time with endless quibbles over a few square miles of the Punjab, for God's sake!"

Maurice was running fingers through his beard, as he often did when thinking. "I'm not sure that's it," he said slowly. "Menander told me almost all the Persian grandees are assembled in Sukkur now. Sahrdarans and vurzurgans crawling all over the place. Members of all seven great families except the Suren. Baresmanas stayed behind to more or less run the empire for Khusrau, but he's about the only one."

Still too irritated to think clearly, Belisarius shook his head. "What's the point, Maurice?"

"The point is that he's playing to an audience. You know the great houses aren't happy at all with the way he's using small dehgans as imperial officials to administer the Sind. Menander says they're howling like banshees, insisting that they deserve a big share of the Punjab."

Belisarius rolled his eyes. "Just what's needed! A herd of idiot feudal magnates pouring into . . ."

His eyes came down, squinting at Maurice. "Jesus," he hissed. "Could he be *that* ruthless?"

Sure he could, said Aide. **It'd be one quick way to break feudalism in Persia. Lead the magnates into a slaughter. No feudalists, no feudalism.**

"Maybe," said Maurice. He gestured with his thumb toward the radio. "But why don't you let me worry about that, if need be? You've got Damodara to deal with."

"So I do." He looked around. "Calopodius, are you ready?"

The young signals officer hurried up. "Yes, General. Sorry. I just wanted to make sure the scribes were set."

The smile he gave Belisarius was half apology and half sheer anticipation.

"Sorry," he repeated. "I've got the soul of an historian. And this is . . . history."

Belisarius chuckled. "Not yet. But let's see if we can't make it so. The first message is—"

Chapter 24
BHARAKUCCHA

Damodara stared at the message that had just been handed to him. Idly, some part of his mind noted that the radio operator had perhaps the best handwriting he'd ever seen. Artistic calligraphy, almost—yet he'd seen the man jot down the message as rapidly as it came in.

He tilted the paper in his hand, so that Rana Sanga and Narses could read it also.

> THIS MESSAGE RELAYED THROUGH BARBARICUM STOP SATI CANNOT HEAR IT STOP SATI WILL HEAR ANY MESSAGE SENT TO US STOP ROMANS AND AXUMITES ACCEPT TERMS STOP CANNOT SPEAK TO KUSHANS DIRECTLY BUT FORESEE NO DIFFICULTY THEIR PART STOP PERSIANS USUAL SELVES STOP WILL WORK ON THEM STOP

"Persians," Narses sneered. "That's why I was able to manipulate them so easily, in my days in Rome. Every border dehgan fancies himself the Lord of the Universe, because he's got a few more goats than his neighbor. It might help if he could read."

Rana Sanga shrugged. "I don't see where the Persians on their own can be much of a problem. Well . . . "

683

"Except in the Punjab," said Damodara.

The radio operator handed him another message.

TERMS FOR PUNJAB AGREEABLE TO ROME STOP BUT WANT IRON TRIANGLE MAINTAINED AS ROMAN ENCLAVE STOP KEEP THE PEACE STOP

"He's probably right," said Sanga. "The Rajputs can live with a small Roman territory in the fork of the Indus and the Chenab, easily enough. Probably even be good for us, in terms of trade. And he might keep the Persians from pushing north."

"Why do you care, anyway?" demanded Narses. "*Let* the Persians have part of the Punjab, for pity's sake. Just insist on two things. First, they have to stay west of the Indus as far north as Multan; then, west of the line formed by the Chenab and the Jhelum. To make sure they stick to it, expand the Roman enclave. Let the Romans have the whole area in the fork of the Indus and the Chenab all the way up to Multan—and give them Multan."

Sanga was starting to look outraged. "You'd give the Persians almost half—"

"Oh, nonsense! It's not more than a third of the Punjab—and most of it, once you get north of Multan, is desert and badlands. Almost useless, except to the hill tribes. So let the Persians deal with the cantankerous bastards. As far as the expanded Roman enclave goes, yes, that's fertile territory. But it's still not all that much—and you can't stop them from taking it anyway, if Link's—"

He glanced at the radio operator. "If Great Lady Sati's army collapses. Which we're counting on, because if it doesn't we're for exile anyway. Assuming we survive at all."

"He has a point, Sanga," said Damodara mildly. "There's another advantage, too, which is that giving the Aryans everything west of the Jhelum brings *them* up against the Kushans in the north."

Sanga thought about it, briefly. "True. And that means the Persians and the Kushans—not us—would have to deal with the Pathans and the other hill tribes. An endless headache, that is."

He gave Narses a not-entirely-admiring look. "And what's the second thing?"

The old eunuch's smile was very cold. "I should think it was obvious. The Persians can have that area—*if* they can take it."

After a moment, Damodara laughed harshly. "Yes. Let them bleed. Done, Narses."

In the Iron Triangle, it was Belisarius' turn to stare at a message. Then, tilt it so that Maurice could see. He also spoke the words aloud, for the benefit of Justinian and Calopodius.

> PROPOSE ROMAN ENCLAVE BETWEEN INDUS AND CHENAB EXPANDED NORTH TO MULTAN STOP ROMANS MAY HAVE MULTAN STOP PERSIANS MAY HAVE PUNJAB WEST OF INDUS TO MULTAN STOP NORTH OF MULTAN MAY HAVE PUNJAB WEST OF CHENAB AND JHELUM STOP IF THEY CAN TAKE IT FROM SATI ARMY STOP

"It's nice to see our new ally isn't an idiot," mused Justinian. "Unlike the old one."

The Grand Justiciar got a look on his face that could have been called "dreamy-eyed," if he'd still had eyes.

"Forget it," said Belisarius, half-chuckling. "We are *not* going to form a pact with Damodara to attack Persia and carve it up between us."

"Probably a bad idea," admitted Justinian. "Still, you have to admit it's tempting."

Maurice had ignored the byplay. By now, having read the message perhaps five times, he was scowling fiercely. "Fine and dandy for you and Damodara—Khusrau's probably in on it, also—to scheme up ways to bleed Persia's aristocracy dry. But I remind you that *I* will have to be the one to deal with them. And I'm damned if I'm going to go along with any foolhardy plans to launch a massive frontal assault on the Malwa here. Their fortifications aren't much weaker than ours, you know."

"I doubt that'll be a problem," Belisarius said, shaking his head. "If you're guessing right about Khusrau's plans, he'll probably insist that you remain here while he leads a glorious Aryan sweeping maneuver against the right flank of the enemy. He'll want you to keep some pressure on, of course."

Maurice grunted. "We're doing that anyway, just being here."

"Multan's what? About a hundred miles north of here?" asked Justinian. His face still had traces of dreaminess in it. "And at that point, the distance between the two rivers must be at least fifty miles."

Belisarius drew up a mental image of a map of the Punjab. "Yes, that's about right."

"So our 'enclave'—using the term very loosely, now—would contain something like two thousand square miles."

"Um . . . Probably closer to fifteen hundred," countered Maurice. "That's an awfully narrow triangle."

"Still. Even fifteen hundred square miles is a fair amount of breathing room. The land here is all fertile, too, even as arid as it is, because of the rivers. We could support a million people, easily. Some enclave!"

Belisarius couldn't help but smile. Justinian might insist that he'd given up his wicked old imperial ways of looking at the world, but it never took much to stir the beast up again.

"That's as may be," he said, a bit brusquely. "It's certainly a good deal for us, at least in the short run—and, better yet, might go a long way to mollifying Theodora. In the long run . . . hard to say. We'd be completely dependent on maintaining trade routes through either Persian or Indian territory, don't forget. We wouldn't even have a common border with the Kushans."

Justinian started to say something, but Belisarius drove over him. "Enough of that, however. We *still* have a war to win."

He turned to Calopodius. "Draft another message telling Damodara we agree. And add the following—"

—*bz-bzzz-bz-bz-bzzz-bzzz-bz-bz-bzzz*—

"I purely *detest* that sound," snarled Narses. "My ears are too old to be inflicted with it."

But he made no move to leave. Didn't so much as twitch a muscle.

The message finished, the operator handed it to Damodara. Again, the new Malwa emperor tilted it so both Narses and Rana Sanga could read the contents.

AGREE TO ALL TERMS STOP THINK PERSIANS WILL ALSO STOP BELISARIUS CAN CROSS THE THAR WITH FIVE HUNDRED MEN STOP PROBABLY REACH AJMER IN A FORTNIGHT STOP WELLS ALREADY DUG STOP IF YOU CAN SEND AUTHORIZATION BY THAT TIME

CAN PUT RAJPUT FORCE IN THE FIELD TO INTERCEPT
SATI STOP KUSHANS WILL DELAY HER AS LONG AS
POSSIBLE STOP

By the time they finished the message, all three pairs of eyes
were very wide.

"God damn him," said Narses tonelessly. "No man should be
that smart. Not even me."

Damodara shook his head, just slightly. "He *planned* for this,
and months ago. There are no wells in the Thar—so he had them
dug in advance."

"Months?" Sanga's headshake was a more vigorous affair. "I
think not, Emperor. I think he has been planning this for years."

His gaze grew unfocused, as he pulled on his beard. "All along,
I think . . . If you consider everything, from the beginning. He
never planned to defeat the Malwa Empire by outright conquest.
Never once. Instead, he pried it apart. Worked at all the weaknesses until it erupted. Forged alliances with Axum and
Persia—the latter, an ancient Roman enemy—not so much to
hammer us but so that he could support and supply a Maratha
rebellion. Which he fostered himself. And then . . . "

"We *did* beat him at the Pass," pointed out Damodara.

Sanga left off the beard-pulling, and grimaced.

Damodara chuckled, quite humorlessly. "Yes, I know. A tactical
victory only. You could even argue it was a strategic defeat. Still,
as an army we were never defeated by him. Not even badly battered, really."

"Well, of course not," said Narses, in the same toneless voice.
"He planned that, too. All through that campaign—if you recall it
again, from this angle—he was careful to keep our casualties to a
minimum. His army's, as well, of course. We thought at the time
that was simply because he needed it intact to take Charax. But,
as usual, there was a second string to the bow. He wanted *your*
army intact also. So that, some day, you could do what you're
doing now."

His old eyes were pure slits, now, glaring at the message. "That
bastard! I should have had him assassinated when I could."

Sanga's lips twisted. "And when was that, exactly?"

"I could have done it when he was still six years old," replied
Narses gloomily. "Of course, he was nobody then, so it never

occured to me. Just another scion of minor Thracian nobility, with pig shit on his bare feet."

"Enough!" snapped Damodara. "I, for one, am glad he's here." He held the message up, inclining it toward Sanga. "What's the answer? *Can* we get someone to Ajmer in time to meet him? Someone the Rajputs there will listen to—but it can't be you, Sanga. We've got our own forced march to make, with a great siege at the end."

The Rajput king went back to beard-pulling. "A fortnight . . . That's the problem. I'll send Jaimal and Udai, with fifty men. Neither of them are kings, but they're both well-known and much respected. Also known to be among my closest lieutenants. The Rajputs will listen to them."

A smile came, distorted by a sharp yank on the beard. "Ha! After these years, Belisarius is something of a legend among the Rajputs also—and we are a people who adore our legends. The truth, Emperor? If Jaimal and Udai are there to vouch for him, most Rajput warriors will flock to his banner. Especially the young ones."

"No problem with the oath?"

"No, not really. The old men will quibble and complain and quarrel, of course. But who cares? It won't be old men that Belisarius leads toward the headwaters of the Ganges, to meet a monster on the field of battle. Young men, they'll be. With no love for Skandagupta, an interpretation of the oath that's good enough—since it was good enough for me—and a commander out of legend."

He lowered his hand. "Yes, it'll work. *If* Jaimal and Udai can reach Ajmer in time."

He looked around. "I need to summon them. Also need a map. One moment."

He went to the door, opened it, and barked the orders.

Damodara leaned over the radio operator's shoulder. "How much longer can we transmit?"

"Hard to say, Your Majesty. The best time, at this distance, is around sunrise and sunset. But, especially once the sun is down, the window—that's what we call it—can stay open for hours. All night, sometimes."

"We'll just have to hope for the best. If necessary, we can send the final message in the morning. For now, send the following.

Exactly as I give it you, understand? Great Lady Sati will be receiving it also, and she mustn't be able to understand what it means."

The operator's nod was nervous, but not the terrified gesture it had been hours earlier. As time had passed, the man had come to conclude that while the new self-proclaimed emperor was a scary man—the tall Rajput and the evil-looking old eunuch, even worse—he was not as scary as Nanda Lal had been.

Not even close. The truth was that the radio operator had no more love for the old dynasty than anybody. Certainly not for their stinking priests and torturers.

The buzzing was brief.

"Here's all there is, General," Calopodius said apologetically. "I thought there'd be more. And what there is doesn't make much sense."

Belisarius looked at the message.

AGREE IN PRINCIPLE STOP RETURN OF PEDDLER EMERALD MAY BE DELAYED STOP

He needed a moment himself, to decipher it. "Very clever. Sanga must have found that peddler, after all."

"What peddler?" demanded Justinian. "And what kind of peddler has an emerald to begin with?"

"A very happy peddler—although I imagine his joy vanished once Sanga caught him."

Belisarius handed the message back to Calopodius. "Years ago, when I fled India, I finally shook off Sanga and his men at Ajmer. I traded my horses for three camels and all the water and supplies I needed to cross the desert. To clinch the deal, I gave the peddler one of the emeralds that had been part of Skandagupta's bribe and told him there'd be another one for him if he delivered a message in Bharakuccha to a Captain Jason, commanding a vessel named the *Argo*."

Maurice already knew the story, so he simply smiled. Calopodius and Justinian laughed aloud.

"That peddler must have thought I was crazy, giving him an emerald for camels. But it did the trick. Sanga and his men followed the horse tracks—I'd nicked one of the hooves to make it distinctive—and by the time they could have run down the peddler and realized what happened, I was well into the Thar. No way to catch me then."

He looked at Calopodius. "How much longer before the window closes?"

The blind young officer shrugged. "There's really no way to predict it, General. It may never close at all."

"Well enough, even if it does. It'll take me half the night anyway to get the men ready to leave. By morning, we'll know."

"Get some sleep, woman," Ousanas said gruffly. "There's nothing you can do here on the docks, anyway. The fleet will be ready to sail at dawn, be sure of it."

"Ready to row, you should say."

"Don't remind me!" In the dim lighting thrown off by the lanterns along the docks, Ousanas' dark features were hard to make out. But the scowl on his face was ferocious enough to be quite evident.

"Your husband! It's his fault. If he was clever enough to manipulate everyone to this ridiculous state of affairs, why didn't he time it *properly*? Two or three more months and we'd be in monsoon season. Sail all the way, lolling in comfort and drinking wine."

"He's only mortal," replied Antonina, smiling despite herself. Even though she wouldn't be working an oar, she was not looking forward to the voyage to Bharakuccha any more than Ousanas was. It would be long and slow and . . . hot.

"I hope the Hindus are right," grumbled Ousanas. "For this idiot stunt, Belisarius deserves to come into his next life as a lizard. Perched on a rock in the desert in the middle of *garam*, so he can fry—instead of us."

Hands on hips, his gaze swept back and forth across the row of Axumite galleys. Even in the near-darkness, every one of them was a beehive of activity as the Ethiopian sailors and marines made ready for the voyage. What Antonina couldn't see, she could hear.

"They don't seem to be complaining as much as I expected," she said.

"That's because of my awesome new title. In the olden days, when I was but the modest keeper of the fly whisks, I'd have had a mutiny on my hands. Be swinging from a gibbet, by now. Disemboweled, too. My entrails dangling just inches above the water, so the Axumite marines could bet on the sharks competing for them."

Antonina couldn't help but laugh. When he was in the mood, Ousanas did histrionic gloom as well as he did anything else. If he'd been alive in the days of Cassandra, probably no one would remember her at all.

"Stop exaggerating. They'd only have beaten you to a senseless pulp and placed bets on the alley dogs."

Ousanas' grin flashed in the night. A moment later, more seriously, he added: "They're not really disgruntled at all, in truth. Yes, the voyage to Bharakuccha at this time of year will be a miserable business. We'll be lucky if we have the sails up more than a few hours every other day. Row, row, row and sweat buckets while we do it. But . . ."

He took a long, slow breath. "But there is Bharakuccha for them, at the end. The same city where Eon left us, and whose harbor they destroyed in their vengeance. This time, with its gates opening wide."

Antonina felt a pang of grief. She remembered that harbor very well herself. She had been sitting next to Eon when he died, reading to him from the Bible.

"Best of all, it'll be garrison duty. In one of the world's largest and busiest seaports. Dens of vice and iniquity on every street. No more fighting, dying and bleeding. Let the Hindu heathens fight it out amongst themselves, from now on. For Axum, the war is over—and what remains are the pickings."

The grin flashed again. "Great pickings, too. There are even more merchant coffers in Bharakuccha than taverns and brothels. Just skimming the tolls—even the light ones we'll maintain—will make Axum rich. Richer still, I should say."

He basked in that happy thought, for a moment. Then the scowl came back.

"And *will* you get some sleep, woman? You'll need to be wide awake and alert tomorrow morning."

"Whatever for? *I'm* not pulling an oar." Half-righteously and half-apologetically, she added: "I'm too small. It'd be silly."

"Who cares about that? I remind you that it will be your responsibility—not mine!—to oversee the transfer of your emperor son and his sahrdaran wife aboard ship. Especially her. God only knows what absurd contrivance the Persians will come up with, for the purpose. But I'm sure it'll involve elephants."

Antonina didn't quite scamper from the docks. Not quite.

"You're certain?"

"Yes," replied Jaimal. Udai nodded his agreement.

Sanga's lieutenant traced a line on the map. "We can follow the rivers, most of the way, east of the Aravalli mountains. Basically, it's the same route we took years ago, when we tried to catch up with Belisarius by sea. That time, it took us almost three weeks. But we had tired horses, after that long chase, where this time we'll be starting with fresh ones. And . . . well . . . "

Sanga smiled thinly. "Yes, I know. Last time, I wasn't really driving the matter, since I knew it was hopeless anyway."

He straightened up from the map. "Well enough. Be out of the city as soon as possible. Try to make it in two weeks. But don't be foolish!" He held up an admonishing finger. "Better to use half the day—most of it, if need be—to make sure you've got the best horses in Bharakuccha. You'll make up the difference within five days."

The admonition was simply a symptom of Sanga's tension, so Jaimal and Udai took it in good enough spirits. On its face, of course, it was insulting. Teach a Rajput about horses!

The final message was also brief.

EMERALD READY IN TIME FOR TRANSACTION

"I'm off, then," said Belisarius. "At first light."

Chapter 25
KAUSAMBI

Lady Damodara came into the chamber that served Dhruva and Lata as something in the way of a modest salon. There was no expression on her face, but her features seemed taut.

"Valentinian? I'm not certain—neither is Rajiv—but . . . "

Even after all these months, Dhruva could still be surprised at how quickly Valentinian moved when he wanted to. Before she quite knew what was happening, he'd plopped the baby he'd been playing with into her lap and was at the side of the one window in the room.

His finger moved the curtain. Just slightly, and very briefly, as if a breeze had fluttered it.

"It's starting," he said, turning away from the window.

Lady Damodara was startled. "But you only glanced—"

Then, seeing the look on Valentinian's face, she smiled wryly. "Yes, I know. Stupid to question an expert."

Valentinian waved at Dhruva and Lata, who was perched on another settee. "Out, now. Into the tunnel. Lata, you make sure all the other maids and servants on this floor are moving. Don't let them dilly-dally to pack anything, either. They're supposed to be packed already."

Anastasius came into the room, scowling. "If you can tear yourself away from—oh. You know, I take it?"

Valentinian scowled right back at him. "Why is it that philosophy never seems to help you with anything useful? Of course, I know. What's the majordomo up to?"

"He's getting everyone out of the kitchens. Rajiv and Khandik are rousting the rest of the servants on the floor above."

Valentinian nodded, and turned to Lady Damodara. "It will help if you and Lady Sanga take charge of the evacuation. Anastasius and I and the Ye-tai—and Rajiv—need to concentrate on the delaying action."

The tautness came back to Lady Damodara's face. "Rajiv, too?"

"*Especially* Rajiv," said Valentinian. He gave her what he probably thought was a reassuring look. Even in the tension of the moment, Dhruva had to fight down a laugh. On *his* face, it didn't look reassuring so much as simply sanguine.

"We need him, Lady," added Anastasius. "Rajiv's more cool-headed than the Ye-tai. We've been training him to handle the charges."

"Oh." The tautness faded. "You won't have him in the front?"

Valentinian started to say something that Dhruva was pretty sure would come out as a snarl, but Anastasius hastily interrupted.

"That'd be silly, wouldn't it? What I mean is, those tunnels aren't wide enough for more than two men at the front, and what with me and Valentinian—" He waved a huge hand at his glowering comrade. "No room for Rajiv there, anyway."

"We're wasting time," snarled Valentinian. "The boy goes with us, Lady Damodara. No way I want some damn Ye-tai deciding when to blow the charges."

By the time Dhruva and Lata got all the servants and maids chivvied into the cellars, some order had been brought to the initial chaos.

Quite a bit, actually. Between them, the wives of Damodara and Rana Sanga practically oozed authority, and the majordomo was always there to handle the little details. Most of the cooks and servants and maids were now being guided into the tunnel by the Bihari miners.

That, too, had been planned long before. One miner for every four servants. True, they were now short the two murdered miners—and shorter still, in terms of the Ye-tai mercenaries who were supposed to oversee the whole operation. Still, there was no trouble. Khandik and one of the other two remaining mercenaries were staying in the cellars to help with the evacuation. The third one was upstairs with the two Roman cataphracts and Rajiv.

Things were even orderly enough for Lata to do a quick count.

"We're missing one of the maids, I think. That one—I can't remember her name—who helps with the washing."

Dhruva scanned the faces, trying to place her. The two sisters hadn't had much contact with the servants on the upper floors, as a rule. But because Lady Damodara insisted that all clothes washing had to be done indoors, they did encounter the ones who came to the laundry.

"I don't know her name either, but I know you who mean. The one . . . Well. She's pretty stupid, from what I could tell."

They saw the majordomo walking quickly toward Lady Damodara and Sanga's wife, who were standing in the center of the big cellar watching over everything. From the frown on his face, Dhruva was pretty sure he'd just finished his own head count and had come to the same conclusion.

A moment later, he and the two ladies were talking. All of them were now frowning. The two sisters couldn't hear the words, but the subject was fairly obvious.

"I better help," Lata said. "Will you be all right with the baby?"

"Yes. I'll wait till the last. Be careful."

Lata hurried over. Sanga's wife spotted her coming almost instantly. A faint look of relief came to her face.

As Lata neared, Lady Sanga interrupted the majordomo. "Yes, fine." She pointed at Lata. "We can send her upstairs to find out what happened to the girl."

Lady Damodara looked at Lata and gave her a quick nod. An instant later, she was scampering up the stairs.

Even before she got to the main floor, Lata could hear the dull booming. The Malwa soldiery must be trying to batter down the main entrance door. Over the months, as discreetly as possible, Lady Damodara had had iron bars placed over all the windows on the palace's ground floor. To stymie thieves, she'd claimed, the one time a Malwa city official had investigated. He'd probably thought the explanation was silly, since that wealthy part of Kausambi with its frequent military patrols was hardly a place that any sensible thief would ply his trade. But he hadn't pursued the matter.

Now, that official would probably lose his head for negligence. Or be impaled on a stake, if the secret police decided that more than negligence was involved. The only way into the palace for troops trying to storm it quickly was through the main entrance. And that wasn't going to be quick, even with battering rams, as heavy and well-braced and barred as it now was.

Lata reached the landing and scampered toward the sound of the booming. The cataphracts would be there, of course.

So, indeed, they were. Along with Rajiv and the third Ye-tai mercenary, they were standing in a small alcove at the far end of the great entry vestibule. The same alcove that Lata entered, since it was the one that led to the basement floor and the cellars below.

"One of the maids is—"

Anastasius waved her down, without turning his head. "We know, Lata. She's over there."

Lata looked past him. Sure enough, the missing maid was cowering against a far wall of the vestibule.

"Come here, girl!" Rajiv shouted. "There's still time!"

There was plenty of time, in fact. The main door shook again, booming fiercely as whatever battering ram the soldiery had smashed into it. But, beyond loosening one of the hinges, the blow seemed to have no impact. The door would stand for at least another minute or two. More than enough time for the maid to saunter across to the alcove and the safety beyond, much less run.

But it didn't matter. The girl was obviously too petrified to think at all, even if she weren't dim-witted to begin with. She'd been overlooked in the initial evacuation, and now . . .

"Step aside, Rajiv," Valentinian said harshly.

Lata could see the shoulders of the young Rajput prince tighten. He didn't move from his position at the front of the alcove.

"*Obey me, boy.*"

Rajiv took a shuddering little breath; then, moved aside and flattened himself against the wall.

Valentinian already had an arrow notched. The bow came up quickly, easily; the draw, likewise. Lata wasn't astonished, even though Valentinian had once let her draw that bow when she'd expressed curiosity.

Try to draw it, rather. She might as well have tried to lift an ox.

She never really saw the arrow's flight. Just stared, as the poor stupid maid was pinned to the far wall like a butterfly. Only a foot or so of the arrow protruded from her chest. The arrowhead had passed right through her and sunk into the thick wood of the wall.

Valentinian had no expression on his face at all. Another arrow was already out of the quiver and notched.

"It was quick, Rajiv," said Anastasius quietly. "In the heart. We can't leave anyone behind who might talk, you know that. And we need you now on the detonator."

Tight-faced, Rajiv nodded and came toward Lata. Looking down, Lata saw an odd-looking contraption on the floor not more than three feet away from her. It was a small wooden box with a wire leading from it into the wall of the alcove, and a knobbed handle sticking up from the middle. A plunger of some kind, she thought.

Rajiv didn't look at Valentinian as he passed him. He seemed surprised to see Lata. And, from the look on his face, a bit frightened.

"You have to go below!" He glanced back, as if to look at Valentinian. "Quickly."

"I just came up to see what happened to her. We took a count and . . ."

Turning his head slightly, Valentinian said over his shoulder: "Get below, Lata. Now."

Once she was back in the cellar, she just shook her head in response to the question in Lady Damodara's raised eyebrows.

The lady seemed to understand. She nodded and looked away.

"What happened?" Dhruva hissed.

"Never mind. She's dead." Lata half-pushed her sister toward the tunnel. "We're almost the last ones. Let's get in there. We're just in the way, now."

There were two Bihari miners left, still standing by the entrance. One of them came to escort them.

"This way, ladies. You'll have to stoop a little. Do you need help with the baby?"

"Don't be silly," Dhruva replied.

The upper hinge gave first. Once the integrity of the door was breached, three more blows from the battering ram were enough to knock it completely aside.

By the time those blows were finished, Valentinian had already fired four arrows through the widening gap. Each one of them killed a Malwa soldier in the huge mass of soldiery Rajiv could see on the street beyond.

Anastasius fired only once. His arrow, even more powerfully shot, took a Malwa in the shoulder. Hitting the armor there, it spun him into the mob.

The Ye-tai mercenary fired also. Twice, Rajiv thought, but he wasn't paying him any attention. He was settling his nerves from the killing of the maid by coldly gauging the archery skill of the two cataphracts against his father's.

Anastasius was more powerful, but much slower; Valentinian, faster than his father—and as accurate—but not as powerful.

So, a Rajput prince concluded, his father remained the greatest archer in the world. In India, at least.

That was some satisfaction. Rajput notions concerning the responsibility of a lord to his retainers were just as stiff as all their notions. Even if, technically, the maid was simply a servant and not one of Rajiv's anyway, her casual murder had raised his hackles.

Don't be silly, part of his mind said to him. *Your father would have done the same.*

Rajiv shook his head. *Not so quickly!* he protested. *Not so—so—*

The voice came again. *Uncaringly? Probably true. And so what? She'd have been just as dead. Don't ever think otherwise. To you, he's a father and a great warrior. To his enemies, he's never been anything but a cold and deadly killer.*

And you are *his son—and do you intend to flinch when the time comes to push that plunger? Most of the men you'll destroy when you do so are peasants, and some of them none too intelligent. Does a stupid maid have a right to live, and they, not?*

The door finally came off the hinges altogether and smashed—what was left of it—onto the tiles of the huge vestibule. Malwa soldiers came pouring in.

Valentinian fired three more times, faster than Rajiv could really follow. Anastasius, once; the Ye-tai, once. Four Malwa soldiers fell dead. One—the Ye-tai's target—was merely wounded.

Valentinian stepped back quickly into the shelter of the alcove. Anastasius and the Ye-tai followed, an instant later.

"Now," commanded Valentinian.

Rajiv's hand struck down the plunger.

The charges carefully implanted in the walls of the vestibule turned the whole room into an abattoir. In the months they'd had to prepare, the majordomo had even been able to secretly buy good drop shot on the black market. So it was real bullets that the mines sent flying into the room, not haphazard pieces of metal.

Rajiv supposed that some of the soldiers in the room must have survived. One or two, perhaps not even injured.

But not many. In a split second, he'd killed more men than most seasoned warriors would kill in a lifetime.

Somewhere on the stairs leading to the cellars, Rajiv uttered his one and only protest.

"I didn't hesitate. Not at all."

Anastasius smiled. "Well, of course not."

Valentinian shook his head. "Don't get melancholy and philosophical on me, boy. You've still got to do it twice more. Today."

For some reason, that didn't bother Rajiv.

Maybe that was because his enemies now had fair warning.

He said as much.

Anastasius smiled again, more broadly. At the foot of the stairs, now in the cellar, Valentinian turned around and glared at him.

"Who cares about 'fair warnings'? Dead is dead and we all die anyway. Just do it."

Anastasius, now also at the bottom of the stairs, cleared his throat. "If I may put Valentinian's viewpoint in proper Stoic terms, what he means to say—"

"Is exactly what the fuck I said," Valentinian hissed. "Just do it."

He glanced up the stairs. "In about ten minutes, at a guess."

His guess was off, a bit. Rajiv didn't blow the next charges for at least a quarter of an hour.

Whether because he'd satisfied himself concerning the ethics of the issue, or simply because Valentinian's cold-blooded murderousness was infectious, he wasn't sure. For whatever reason, Rajiv had no trouble waiting until the cellars were full of Malwa soldiery, probing uncertainly in the torch-lit darkness to find whatever hole their quarry had scurried into.

From the still greater darkness of the tunnel, Rajiv gauged the moment. He even out-waited Valentinian.

"Now, boy."

"Not yet."

Two minutes later, he drove in the next plunger. The same type of shaped-charge mines implanted in the walls of the cellars turned those underground chambers into more abattoirs.

"Quickly, now!" urged Anastasius, already lumbering at a half-crouch down the tunnel. "We've got to get to the shelter as soon as possible. Before they can figure out—"

He continued in that vein, explaining the self-evident to people who already knew the plan by heart. Rajiv ignored him. Looking ahead, down the tunnel, he could see the figure of the Ye-tai already vanishing in the half-gloom thrown out by the few oil lamps still in place. Valentinian was close on his heels.

"You're doing good, boy," said the Mongoose. "Really, really good."

All things considered, Rajiv decided the Roman cataphract was right.

To be sure, this was not something he'd ever brag about. On the other hand . . .

When did you ever hear your father brag? came that little, back-of-the-mind voice.

The answer was: *Never.*

Rajiv had noticed that, in times past. Now, finally, he thought he understood it. And, for the first time in his life, came to feel something for his father beyond love, admiration and respect.

Simple affection. Nothing fancy. Just the sort of fondness that a man—a woman too, he supposed—feels when he thinks about someone who has shared a task and a hardship.

When they reached the shelter, even Valentinian took a deep breath.

"Well," he muttered, "this is where we find out. God damn all Biharis—miners down to newborn babes—if it doesn't."

The Ye-tai just looked blank-faced. Anastasius' eyes flicked about the small chamber, with its massive bracing. "Looks good, anyway."

It seemed fitting, somehow, for Rajiv to finally take charge. "Place the barrier." It seemed silly to call that great heavy thing a "door."

He pointed to it, propped against the entrance they'd just come through. "Anastasius, you're the only one strong enough to hold it in place. Valentinian, you set the braces. You"—this to the Ye-tai—"help him."

The work was done quickly. The last of it was setting the angled braces that supplemented the great cross-bars and strengthened the door by propping it against the floor.

There was no point in waiting. The shelter would either hold, or they'd all be crushed. But there'd be no point to any of it if Rajiv didn't blow the last charges before the surviving Malwa in the palace that was now over a hundred yards distant as well as many feet above them had time to realize what had happened.

"I guess you'd better—" Valentinian started to say, but Rajiv's hand had already driven home the plunger.

"Well, shit," he added, before the earthquake made it impossible to talk at all.

The Malwa general in command of the entire operation had remained outside the palace. After he was knocked off his feet, he stared dumbfounded as the walls of the palace seemed to erupt all around the base.

The palace came down, like a stone avalanche.

Some of those stones were large, others were really pieces of wall that had somehow remained intact.

Some were blown a considerable distance by the explosion. Others bounced, after they fell.

Scrambling frantically, the general managed to avoid all the ones sent sailing by the blast. But as close as he'd been standing, he didn't escape one section of wall—a very big section—as it disintegrated.

A few minutes later, his second-in-command and now successor was able to finally piece together the few coherent reports he could get.

There weren't many, and they weren't all that coherent. Only three of the soldiers who had gone into the palace were still alive, and one of them was too badly injured to talk. None of the soldiers who'd gone into the cellar had survived, of course.

But he was pretty sure he knew what had happened, and hastened to make his report to Emperor Skandagupta.

In his own far greater palace, the emperor waited impatiently for the officer to finish.

When he was done, Skandagupta shook his head. "They all committed suicide? That's nonsense."

He pointed at the officer. "Execute this incompetent."

Once that was done, the emperor gave his orders. They were not complicated.

"Dig. Remove all the rubble. There's an escape tunnel there somewhere. I want it found."

Carefully—very carefully—none of his advisers allowed any of their dismay to show. Not with the emperor in such a foul and murderous mood.

Not one of them wanted to draw his attention. It would take days to clear away all that rubble. Long, long days, in which the emperor would probably have at least one or two more men executed for incompetence.

At least. As the advisers assigned to the task of excavation started filing out of the imperial audience chamber, Skandagupta was already giving orders to discover which incompetent—no, which traitor—in charge of the capital's munitions supply had been so corrupt or careless—no, treasonous—to allow such a huge quantity of gunpowder to slip through his fingers.

After the advisers reached the relative safety of the streets outside the palace, they went their separate ways to begin organizing the excavation project.

All but one of them, that is. That one, after he was certain no one was watching him, headed for Kausambi's northern gate.

The city was still in a state of semi-chaos, so soon after the word of Damodara's rebellion had spread everywhere from the telegraph stations, despite the secret police's attempts to suppress the news. The destruction of Lady Damodara's palace, right in the middle of the imperial quarter, would simply add to it.

The adviser thought he had a good chance of slipping out of the city unnoticed, if he moved immediately. He had no choice, in any event, if he had any hope of staying alive himself or keeping his wife and children alive.

True, the adviser had no connection to Kausambi's munitions depot. But one of his first cousins was in charge of it, and the adviser knew perfectly well the man was not only corrupt but careless. He had no doubt at all that an investigation would soon discover that Lady Damodara's agents had simply *bought* the gunpowder. Probably had it delivered to the palace in the munitions depot's own wagons.

Fortunately, his wife and two children had remained in their home town farther down the Ganges. With luck he could get there in time to get them out. He had enough money on his person to bribe the guards at the gate and even hire transport. There was considerably more money in their mansion. With that, they might be able to escape into Bengal somewhere . . .

Beyond that, he thought no further. There was no point in it. He could feel the Malwa Empire cracking and breaking under his feet. With that greatest of all the world's certainties shaking, what man could possibly foresee the future?

He made it out of the city. But, within a day, was captured by a cavalry patrol. The emperor had soon considered that possibility also, and had placed a ban on any officials leaving Kausambi without written orders. By then, his savage punitive actions had terrified the city's soldiery enough that the guards at the gate whom the adviser had bribed prattled freely to the secret police.

Before noon of the next day, the adviser's body was on a stake outside Skandagupta's palace. Four days later, the bodies of his wife and two children joined him. The soldiers had some trouble fitting the boy, since he was only three.

Not much, however. By then, Skandagupta's fury was cutting through the imperial elite like a scythe, and small stakes were being prepared. Plenty of them.

"He's hysterical," Lady Damodara said, pinched-faced, after getting the latest news from one of the stable-keeper's sons. "Even for Skandagupta, this is insane."

Sanga's wife shifted a bit on her cushions. The cushions were thinner than she was used to, and—worse—their quarters were extremely crowded. The entire staff from the palace was crammed into the last stretch of the tunnel while they waited for the first search of the city to run its course. So were over a dozen miners. But she knew that even after they were able to move into the stables, in a few days, the conditions wouldn't improve all that much.

As places of exile went, the stables would be utterly wretched. As a place of refuge from the Malwa madness sweeping the city and leaving hundreds of people staked outside the imperial palace, however, it would be superb.

She gave the stable-keeper's son a level look. "Are you frightened, Tarun?"

The twelve-year-old boy swallowed. "Some, Lady. Not too much, though. The soldiers who searched the stables this morning were irritated, but they didn't take it out on us, and they didn't search all that seriously. They didn't really search at all in the stable that has the hidden door leading to this tunnel. Since then, our parents and our sisters stay out of sight, but my brother and I can move around on the streets easily enough. The soldiers even answer our questions, usually. They really aren't paying much attention to . . . Well. People like us."

Lady Damodara chuckled, humorlessly. "So Narses predicted. 'You'll be lost in Kausambi's ocean of poverty,' were his exact words. I remember. Damn his soul."

"No," said Rajiv forcefully. "Damn Malwa's soul."

Both ladies gave him a level look.

"The false Malwa, I mean," added Rajiv hastily.

Lady Damodara's chuckle, this time, had a bit of humor in it. "Look at it this way, Rajiv. When it's all over, if we survive, we can look at Skandagupta on a stake."

"You think so?" asked Rajiv.

"Oh, yes," said the lady serenely.

Lady Sanga sniffed. "Maybe. By the time he gets here, Rajiv, your father's temper will be up. They'll need toothpicks. I doubt if even Lord Damodara will be able to restrain him enough to keep some portion of Skandagupta's body suitably sized for a stake."

"He probably won't even try," allowed Lady Damodara. "Now that I think about it."

Chapter 26
THE PUNJAB

"I am leaving you in charge, General Samudra," said Great Lady Sati. To the general's relief, the tone and timber of the voice was that of the young woman Sati appeared to be, not . . .

The thing for which it was really just a vessel.

The god—or goddess—he should say. But Samudra was beginning to have his doubts on that issue. Desperately, he hoped that the thing inside Great Lady Sati could detect none of his reservations.

Apparently not, since she said nothing to the special assassins positioned against the walls of her caravan. Perhaps that was simply because Samudra's general anxiety overrode anything specific.

He didn't *want* to be left in charge of the Malwa army in the Punjab. That was not due to any hesitations concerning his own military abilities, it was simply because the situation was obviously beginning to crumble for political reasons, and Samudra was wary of the repercussions.

Samudra had always stayed as far away as he could from political matters. Insofar as possible, at least, within the inevitable limits of the Malwa dynastic system of which he was himself a member. He was one of the emperor's distant cousins, after all. Still, he'd done his very best throughout his life to remain a purely military figure in the dynasty.

But all he said was: "Yes, Great Lady."

"I will take thirty thousand troops with me, from here, and another ten from Multan. No artillery units, however. They will slow me down too much and I can acquire artillery once I reach the Ganges plain. Have them ready by early morning, the day after tomorrow. You may select them, but I want good units with Ye-tai security battalions. *Full* battalions, Samudra."

He managed not to wince. The problem wasn't the total number of soldiers Sati wanted to take back to Kausambi with her. Thirty thousand was actually lower than he'd expected. The problem would be filling out the ranks of the Ye-tai. Few of the security battalions were still up to strength. The defection of so many Kushans to Kungas and his new kingdom had forced the Malwa to use Ye-tai as spearhead assault troops. As brave as they were, the Ye-tai had little of the Kushan experience with that role. Their casualties had been very heavy, this past two years.

Samudra knew he'd have no choice but to strip the needed reinforcements out of all the other security battalions. And with only one full day to do the work, it would be done hastily and haphazardly, to boot, with not much more in the way of rhyme or reason than what he might accomplish with a lottery.

Gloomily, Samudra contemplated the months of fighting ahead of him here in the Punjab. The morale of the great mass of the soldiery was already low. The departure of Great Lady Sati, forty thousand troops—and a disproportionate percentage of the Ye-tai security forces—would leave it shakier still.

On the brighter side, the Romans seemed content to simply fight a siege. If Great Lady Sati . . .

Her next words brought considerable relief.

"I do not expect you to make any headway in my absence," she said. "Nor is it needed. Simply keep Belisarius pinned here while I attend to suppressing Damodara's rebellion. We will resume offensive operations next year."

"Yes, Great Lady." Samudra hesitated. The next subject was delicate.

"No artillery units, understood. But of the thirty thousand, how many . . . ah . . . "

"Cavalry? Not more than three thousand. Enough to provide me with a screen, that's all. You understand that none of the cavalry may be Rajputs, I assume?"

Samudra nodded. Although there'd been no open mutinies among the Rajputs yet—aside from the huge number already with Rana Sanga—no Malwa top commander could place much reliance on them until Damodara's rebellion was crushed.

Sati shrugged, in an oddly human gesture. "Without using Rajputs, we cannot assemble a large force of cavalry that I could depend upon. Since I'll need to use mostly infantry, I may as well make it a strong infantry unit with only enough cavalrymen to serve as scouts and a screen. It shouldn't matter, anyway. I don't expect to encounter any opposition until I've almost reached Kausambi. Damodara will probably reach the capital before I do, but he'll be stymied by the fortifications until I arrive. By then, after I've reached the plain, I'll have been able to assemble a huge army from the garrisons in all the major cities along the Ganges. With me as the hammer and the walls of Kausambi as the anvil, Damodara will be crushed."

"Yes, Great Lady."

"*Here?*" exclaimed Dasal. The oldest of the Rajput kings in the chamber rolled his eyes and stared at the ceiling.

"All it needed," he muttered. From the expressions on their faces, it was obvious the other six kings present in the chamber—they were all elderly, if none quite so old as Dasal—shared his gloomy sentiments.

His younger brother Jaisal rose from his cushion and moved to a nearby window, walking with the creaky tread of a man well into his seventies. Once at the window, he stared out over the city of Ajmer.

The capital of the Rajputs, that was—insofar as that fractious nation could be said to have a "capital" at all. Dasal found himself wondering whether it would still be standing, a year from now.

"Where are they being kept?" he asked.

The Rajput officer who'd brought the news to the council shook his head. "I was not given that information. Nor will I be, I think. They may not even be in Ajmer, at all."

Dasal lowered his eyes. "They're here somewhere," he snorted. "Be sure of it."

"We *could* find them . . ." ventured one of the other kings. Chachu was his name, and his normally cautious manner was fully evident in the questioning tone of the remark.

Simultaneously, one sitting and one still standing at the window, the brothers Dasal and Jaisal shook their heads.

"What would be the point of that?" demanded Jaisal. "Better if we can claim we never knew the location of Damodara's parents."

Gloomy silence filled the chamber again. The seven kings in that room formed what passed for a Rajput ruling council. None of them, singly or together, had any illusion that if Damodara's rebellion was crushed, Rajputana would retain even a shred of its semi-autonomy. Direct Malwa rule would be imposed—harshly —and each and every one of them would be questioned under torture.

Still, it was easier to deny something under torture that was a false accusation. Very narrowly defined, of course—but these were men grasping at straws.

"That madman Rana Sanga," Chachu hissed. But even that remark sounded as if it were punctuated by a question mark.

"It's not much," said one of their kidnappers apologetically. "The problem isn't even money, since we were given plenty. But Ajat—ah, our chief—told us to remain inconspicuous."

Damodara's father finished his inspection of the room. That hadn't taken long, as sparsely furnished as it was. It would be one of many such rooms in many such buildings in Ajmer. The city was a center for trade routes, and needed to provide simple accommodations for passing merchants, traders and tinkers.

He spent more time examining the man who had spoken. An assassin, obviously. Lord Damodara recognized the type, from his adventurous youth.

A very polite assassin, however, as all of them had been since they seized Damodara's parents from the bedroom of their palace and smuggled them into the night.

Better to think of them as bodyguards, he decided wryly.

"I'm exhausted," his wife said. She gazed longingly at the one bed in the room. It had been a long trip, especially for people of their advanced years.

"Yes, we need sleep," her husband agreed. He nodded to the assassin. "Thank you."

The man gave a bow in return. "We will be in the next room, should you need anything."

After he was gone, closing the door behind him, Damodara's mother half-collapsed on the bed. She winced, then, feeling the thin pallet.

"Not much!" she exclaimed, half-laughing and half-sobbing.

Her husband made a face. "A year from now we will either be skin-sacks hanging from Emperor Skandagupta's rafters or be sleeping in one of the finest chambers in his palace."

The noise his wife emitted was, again, half a sob and half a laugh. "Your son! I told you—years ago!—that you were letting him think too much."

There were times—not many—that Agathius was thankful he'd lost his legs at the Battle of the Dam.

This was one of them. Being an obvious cripple might deflect some of the Persian fury being heaped upon his unoffending person, where the strength of Samson unchained would have been pointless.

"—not be cheated, I say it again!"

Khusrau punctuated the bellow with a glare ferocious enough to be worthy of . . .

Well, an emperor, actually. Which he was.

The mass of Persian noblemen packed into Khusrau's audience chamber at Sukkur growled their approval. They sounded like so many hungry tigers.

Not a dehgan in the lot, either, so far as Agathius could tell. That broad, lowest class of the Iranian *azadan*—"men of noble birth"—hadn't been invited to send representatives to this enclave. The only men in the room were sahrdaran and vurzurgan.

Agathius shifted his weight on his crutches. "Your Majesty," he said mildly, "I just arrived here from Barbaricum. I have no idea beyond the sketchiest telegraph messages—which certainly didn't mention these issues—what the general has planned in terms of a postwar distribution of the spoils. But I'm quite sure he has no intention of denying the Iranians their just due."

Another surge of muttered growls came. The phrase *he'd better not!* seemed to be the gist of most of them.

"He'd better not!" roared Khusrau. His clenched fist pounded the heavy armrest of his throne. Three times, synchronized with *bet-ter-not.*

"I'm sure the thought has never crossed his mind," said Agathius firmly. He contemplated a sudden collapse on the floor, but decided that would be histrionic. He wasn't *that* crippled, after all. Besides, he'd said the words with such complete conviction that even the angry and suspicious Persians seemed a bit mollified.

And why not? The statement was quite true. Agathius was as certain as he was of the sunrise that the thought of swindling the Persians out of their rightful share of the postwar spoils had not, in fact, "crossed" Belisarius' mind.

Been planted there like a sapling, yes. Been studied and examined from every angle, to be sure. Weighed, pondered, appraised, considered, measured, gauged, adjudged, evaluated, assessed—for a certainty.

Crossed, no.

Belisarius studied the telegram.

"Pretty blistering language, sir," Calopodius said apologetically, as if he were somehow responsible for the intemperate tone of the message.

"Um." Belisarius scanned over it quickly again. "Well, I agree that the verbs 'cheat' and 'rob' are excessive. And there was certainly no need to bring up my ancestry. Still and all, it could be worse. If you look at it closely—well, squint—this is really more in the way of a protest than a threat."

He dropped the Persian emperor's message onto the table. "And, as it happens, all quite unnecessary. I have no intentions of 'cheating' the Persians out of their fair share of the spoils."

He turned to Maurice, smiling. "Be sure to tell Khusrau that, when he arrives."

Maurice scowled back at him. "You'll be gone, naturally."

"Of course!" said Belisarius gaily. "Before dawn, tomorrow, I'm off across the Thar."

Before Maurice could respond, Anna stalked into the headquarters bunker.

She spoke with no preamble. "Your own latrines and medical facilities are adequate, General. But those of the Punjabi natives are atrocious. I *insist* that something be done about it."

Belisarius bestowed the same gleeful smile on her. "Absolutely! I place you in charge. What's a good title, Maurice?"

The chiliarch's scowl darkened. "Who cares? How about 'Mistress of the Wogs'?"

Anna hissed.

Belisarius clucked his tongue. "Thracian peasant. No, that won't do at all."

He turned to Calopodius. "Exercise your talent for rhetoric here, youngster."

Calopodius scratched his chin. "Well . . . I can think of several appropriate technical titles, but the subtleties of the Greek language involved wouldn't mean anything to the natives. So why not just call her the Governess?"

"That's silly," said Maurice.

"My husband," said Anna.

"Done," said Belisarius.

A full hour before sunrise, Belisarius and his expedition left the Triangle. To maintain the secrecy of the operation, they were ferried south for several miles before being set ashore. By now, Roman patrols had scoured both banks of the Indus so thoroughly that no enemy spies could be hidden anywhere.

As always with water transport, the horses were the biggest problem. The rest was easy enough, since Belisarius was bringing no artillery beyond mortars and half a dozen of the rocket chariots.

By mid-morning, they were completely out of sight of the river, heading east into the wasteland.

At approximately the same time, Sati started her own procession out of the Malwa camp to the north. There was no attempt at secrecy here, of course. What can be done—even then, with difficulty—by less than a thousand men, cannot possibly be done by thirty thousand. So huge was that mass of men, in fact, that it took the rest of the day before all of them had filed from the camps and started up the road.

Preceded only by a cavalry screen and one Ye-tai battalion, the Great Lady herself led the way. Since the infantry would set the pace of the march, she would ride in the comfort of a large howdah suspended between two elephants.

The "howdah" was really more in the way of a caravan or a large sedan than the relatively small conveyance the word normally denoted. The *chaundoli*, as it was called, was carried on heavy poles suspended between two elephants, much the way a litter is carried between two men. Its walls and roof were made of thin wood, with three small windows on each side. The walls and roof were covered with grass woven onto canes and lashed to the exterior. The grass would be periodically soaked with water during the course of the journey, which would keep the interior cool as the breeze struck the chaundoli.

Since none of the Great Lady's special bodyguards or assassins were horsemen, those of them who could not be fit into her own chaundoli rode in a second one just behind her. They could have marched, of course. But the thing which possessed the body of the Great Lady had no desire to risk its special assistants becoming fatigued. Link didn't expect to need them, but the situation had become so chaotic that even its superhuman capacity for calculation was being a bit overwhelmed.

Lord Samudra watched Great Lady Sati's army depart from the great complex of fortresses and camps which had by then been erected facing the Roman lines in the Iron Triangle. Come evening, he returned to his own headquarters—which was, in fact, built much the same way as a chaundoli except the walls were of heavy timber. The water-soaked grass wasn't quite as effective a cooling mechanism with such a massive and stationary structure. But it was still far superior to the sweltering heat of a tent or the sort of buried bunkers the Roman generals used.

Idiots, they were, in Samudra's opinion. The only reason they needed bunkers was because of their flamboyant insistence on remaining close to the fighting lines. Samudra's own headquarters was several miles beyond the farthest possible range of Roman cannons or rockets.

"Have more water poured on the grass," Samudra commanded his majordomo. "And be quick about it. I am not in a good mood."

Chapter 27

THE IRON TRIANGLE

At least Emperor Khusrau had enough sense to leave his Persian army on the west bank of the Indus, when he came storming into Maurice's bunker on the Iron Triangle. In point of fact, Maurice wouldn't have allowed him to bring them across—and he, not the Persians, controlled the rivers. The Iranians had nothing to match the Roman ironclad and fireship.

Still, even Khusrau alone—in his current mood—would have been bad enough. Surrounded as he was with enough sahrdaran to pack the bunker, he was even worse. And the fact that Maurice was sure the Persian emperor was mostly playing to the audience didn't improve his own mood at all.

"—not be cheated!"

Maurice had had enough. "*Cheated?*" he demanded. "Who is 'cheating you,' damnation?" He had just enough control of his temper left to add: "Your Majesty."

Maurice pointed to the west wall of the bunker. "Take as much as you can over there, for all I care! But don't expect *me* to do your fighting for you!"

Several of the sahrdaran hissed angrily, one of them very loudly. That was a sahrdaran in his early forties whose name was Shahrbaraz. He was the oldest son of the leader of the Karin family, which was one of the seven great sahrdaran houses and perhaps the most influential after the Suren.

Maurice glared at him, still pointing at the west wall. "Why are you here, hissing at me—instead of fighting to take the land you claim is yours?"

Shahrbaraz started to respond angrily, but the emperor waved him down.

"Be silent!" Khusrau commanded. He gave Maurice a fine glare of his own. "May I then assume that you will not object if I launch my own offensive?"

"Not in the least."

"And you will not object if we retain the land we conquer?"

Maurice snatched up the messages on the center table and shook them at the emperor. Those were copies of the exchange between Belisarius and Damodara that had taken place days earlier. "How many times do I need to show this to you? Your Majesty. Whatever you can take west of the river is yours. As far north as you can manage to get."

"To the Hindu Kush!" shouted one of the other sahrdaran. Maurice couldn't remember his name, but he was a prominent member of the house of the Spandiyads.

By a mighty struggle, Maurice managed not to sneer. "I'd recommend you stop at the *foot* of the Hindu Kush. Keeping in mind that King Kungas counts the Vale of Peshawar as part of it. Everything north of Kohat Pass and west of Margalla Pass belongs to him, he says. But if you think you can roll over the Kushans as well as the Malwa, so be it."

"And when have the Aryans cared—"

"Be silent!" Khusrau roared again. This time, thankfully, it was the Spandiyad who was the recipient of his imperial glare. "We are not at war with the Kushans," he stated. "All of the west Punjab *to* the Hindu Kush. We will stop once we have reached the passes into the Vale of Peshawar held by our allies the Kushans."

The emperor glanced down at the half-crumpled pile of messages. "As all have now agreed," he finished, more softly.

When he looked up at Maurice, he seemed considerably calmer. "Will your gunships provide us with protection from the Malwa ironclads?"

Maurice shook his head. Not angrily, but firmly nonetheless. "We can't, Your Majesty. I'm sorry, but we just *can't*. Neither the *Justinian* nor the *Victrix* is a match for them. Not even one of them, much less the two they have stationed on the Indus. That's why we laid the mine fields across the rivers. Once you move north of those minefields, you'll be on your own. I recommend you keep your army away from the rivers. Far enough away to be out of range of the ironclads' guns."

Khusrau didn't seem surprised by the response. Or angry, for that matter. He simply grunted softly and turned away.

"To the Hindu Kush!" he bellowed, striding toward the exit of the bunker.

Within a minute, they were all gone.

"Thank God," muttered Maurice. "Can't stand Persians. Never have liked the arrogant bastards. Think their shit doesn't stink."

"It certainly *does*," sniffed Anna. She'd happened to be present in the bunker, visiting her husband, when the Persian delegation arrived. "I've visited their camps, on the way up here. Their sanitary practices would cause a hyena to tremble."

Maurice chuckled. "Worse than the natives here?"

"Yes, as a matter of fact," Anna replied stiffly. "Even before I started governessing them. Today, the Punjabi habits are much better. A week from now—well, a month—there'll be no comparison at all."

Maurice didn't doubt it, although he thought Anna's estimate of one month was wildly optimistic. The difficulty wasn't so much native resistance—perhaps oddly, the Punjabis seemed quite taken by their new "Governess"—as it was the sheer scale of the problem.

Malwa armies were always notorious for their rough habits with local populations. The huge Malwa army dug in to the north of the Triangle was behaving especially badly, as packed in as those soldiers were and suffering all the miseries and frustrations of siege warfare. The Iron Triangle had become a refuge for untold thousands of Punjabis in the area. They came across the rivers, on small skiffs or even swimming through the mine fields.

By now, the population density of the Triangle was almost that of a huge city. Worse, really, since most of the land area had to be left available for farming. The Triangle got much of its supplies from the Sind, brought up by the river boats, but it still had to provide the bulk of its own food. Controlling the raw sewage produced by such a population was enough to make Hercules' legendary cleaning of the Augean Stables look like an afternoon's easy chore.

"You'll see," said Anna.

◇   ◇   ◇

"There'll be enough, General," said Ashot. "Just barely."

Belisarius nodded, after he finished wiping his face with a cloth. That was to clean off the dust, mostly. Despite the heat, the Thar was so dry that sweat didn't have time to really accumulate.

He was careful not to let his worry show. This was the third well they'd reached, and all of them had had just enough water—just barely—for his expedition. They had almost no reserve left at all. If even one of the wells was empty, or near-empty . . .

But there was no point in fretting over the matter. The long war with the Malwa was nearing its end, and there remained only to drive home the lance—or die in the attempt. It was in the hands of Fate, now.

"Let's be off," he said. He glanced at the horizon, where the dawn was beginning. "There's still enough time for three hours' travel before the sun's up high enough to force us to camp for the day."

"I feel like a bat," complained Ashot. "Live by night, sleep by day."

He said it fairly cheerily, though. Ashot had plenty of experience with desert campaigns, and knew perfectly well that no sane man traveled through an area like the Thar when the sun was up. Like all the cataphracts on the expedition, he was wearing loose-fitting Arab-style robes instead of armor—the only difference being that Ashot knew how to put them on without help from one of Abbu's men.

"Something's happening," Kujulo stated. Slowly, he swept the telescope across the terrain below the pass. "I'm not sure what, but there's too much movement down there."

"Are they preparing another attack?" asked one of the other Kushans.

"After the way we butchered the last one? Doubt it," grunted Kujulo. "No, I think they're pulling out some of their forces. And I think—not sure about this at all—that there's some sort of troop movement in the far distance. But it doesn't seem to be reinforcements."

He lowered the telescope. Awkwardly, since it was big and clumsy; it was one of the eyeglasses newly made in Begram's fledgling optical industry, not one of the sleek Roman devices.

"Let the king know," he commanded. "This may be what he's expecting."

Miles away, a squad of Ye-tai had a much better view of what was happening. They were serving as sentries for the Malwa army positioned against the Kushans—and none too happy about it, either. In times past, it would have been Kushans themselves who'd be detached for this rigorous duty. But Kushans could no longer be relied upon, what few of them were still left in the Malwa forces. Their army's commander hadn't dared used common troops for the purpose. Kushans were much too good at mountain warfare to depend on levied infantry to serve as outlying sentries.

"Tell me again," said the squad leader.

The new member of the squad shrugged. He'd only arrived the day before. "Don't believe me, then. Great Lady Sati is on her way to the capital. With forty thousand troops. Seems there's a big rebellion."

"Why were *you* traveling with them?"

"I wasn't. I was just part of a troop sent by Samudra up here. We only marched with the Great Lady's expedition for a short distance. She's headed up the Sutlej, of course."

"I wish we were too," muttered one of the other squad members.

Again, the newcomer shrugged. "So do I. But they're leaving some of the Ye-tai they brought with them here—me among them, worse luck—while they take back to the Punjab almost ten thousand regular troops."

"Why do the two of you wish you were going back to the plain?" demanded the squad leader. "So we could get lost in a whirlpool in the Ganges? Don't be stupid."

Their camp was perched on a rise that looked directly onto Margalla Pass, which divided the Vale of Peshawar from the Punjab proper. From the distance, the squad leader couldn't see any of the Kushan troops who were holding the pass. But he imagined he could almost see the blood the Malwa army had left on those slopes, in the course of four defeated assaults.

They were being ground up here. On level ground, the Ye-tai squad leader would have faced Kushans without worrying too much. Up here, in the hills and mountains, fighting them was like fighting crocodiles in a river.

"I'm half-Sarmatian," he murmured. "Mother's side."

None of his mates so much as curled a lip, despite the absurdity of the statement. There hadn't been any Sarmatians in centuries.

It didn't matter, since that wasn't the point of the statement. Within a few seconds, all of the squad members were eyeing the new arrival.

Fortunately for him, he wasn't stupid. "The war's lost," he said, softly but clearly. "That's what I think, anyway."

The squad leader grinned. "What's your name?"

The new man grinned back. "Prabhak. I know, it sounds funny. It's a Sarmatian name. Given to me by my mother."

At that, the whole squad laughed. "Welcome, brother," said one of them. "Would you believe that all of us are half-Sarmatian?"

That brought another little laugh. When it died down, Prabhak asked: "When? And which way?"

The squad leader glanced at the sun, which was now setting. "As soon as dark falls. There'll be a half moon. Good enough. And we'll head for the Kushans."

Prabhak winced, as did most of the squad members.

"Don't be stupid," growled the squad leader. "You want to spend the rest of your lives living like goats?"

Put that way . . .

"They say King Kungas isn't a bad sort," mused one of the squad members.

The squad leader chuckled humorlessly. "Nobody says anything of the sort. He's a demon and his witch wife is even worse. Which is fine with me. Just the sort of rulers who can keep us alive, in what's coming."

The first fortress in the Vindhyas that Damodara's army reached was deserted. Its garrison had fled two days before, they were told by some of the natives.

So was the second, and the third.

The fourth fortress, far down from the crest, was still manned. Either the garrison or its commander was more stalwart.

They were stalwart enough to last for exactly eight minutes, once Sanga launched the assault, before they tried to surrender.

Tried, and failed. Sanga was giving no quarter.

Even if he'd been inclined to, which he wasn't—not with his wife and children in Kausambi—Lord Damodara had commanded a massacre.

Emperor Damodara, rather. As a mere lord, Damodara had always been noted for his comparative leniency toward defeated enemies, by Malwa standards. But the garrison of the fortress which had dared to resist him were no longer simply "enemies." They were traitors and rebels.

Of course, Sanga allowed some of the garrison to escape. That, too, had been commanded by Emperor Damodara. There was no point in slaughtering garrisons if other garrisons didn't learn of it.

By the next day, Damodara's army was out of the mountains and marching up the Chambal river. The Chambal was the main tributary of the Yamuna, whose junction was still five hundred miles to the north. Once they reached that junction, they'd still have three hundred miles to march down the Yamuna before reaching Kausambi.

Even with every man in his army mounted, either as cavalry or dragoons, Damodara could not hope to make faster progress than twenty miles a day—and the long march would probably go slower than that. True, now that they were out of the Vindhyas, the countryside was fertile and they could forage as they went. But his army still numbered some forty thousand men. It was simply not possible to move such a huge number of soldiers very quickly.

Six weeks, at least, it would take them to reach Kausambi. Conceivably, two months—and if they had to fight any major battles on the way, longer than that. They could not afford to be delayed by any of the fortresses along the way.

The first fortress they encountered on the river was deserted.

So was the next.

So was the next.

"They've heard of us, it seems," said Rana Sanga to the emperor.

"I prefer to think it's the majestic aura of my imperial presence."

"Yes, Your Majesty. Though I'm not sure I understand the difference."

Damodara smiled. "Neither do I, as it happens. You'd think I would, since I believe I'm now semi-divine. Maybe even three-quarters."

The Bihari miner straightened up from his crouch. "They're getting close, master. I think so, anyway. It's hard to tell, because of all the echoes."

The term "echoes" seemed strange to Valentinian, but he understood what the miner meant. At the first dogleg, they'd dug two short false tunnels in addition to the one that led—eventually—to the exit in the stables. What the miner was hearing were the complex resonances of the sounds being made by the Malwa miners as they neared the end of clearing away the rubble that the Romans had left behind when they blew the charges.

"Will you know when they break through?"

"Oh, yes. Even before the charges go off."

The miner grimaced as he made the last statement. As someone who had spent all of his adult life and a good portion of his childhood working beneath the earth, he had an automatic sympathy for men who would soon be crushed in a series of cave-ins. Enemies or not.

Valentinian didn't share any of his sentiments. Dead was dead. What difference did it make if it came under tons of rock and soil, the point of a lance—or just old age?

He turned to Rajiv. "Are you willing to do this? Or would you prefer it if I did?"

The young Rajput prince shrugged. "If everything works right, the charges will go off automatically, anyway. I won't have to do anything."

" 'If everything works right,' " Valentinian jeered. "Nothing ever works right, boy. That's the cataphract's wisdom."

But Valentinian proved to be wrong.

When their miners finally broke through the rubble into a cleared area, two Malwa officers pushed them aside and entered the tunnel. For all the risk involved, they were both eager. Emperor Skandagupta had promised a great reward for whatever officers captured Damodara's family.

Both of them moved their torches about, illuminating the area. Then, cursed together.

"Three tunnels leading off!" snarled the superior officer. "But which is the right one?"

His lieutenant gestured with his torch to the tunnel ahead of him. "I'll explore this one, if you want. You take one of the others. We can leave some men to guard the third, until we have time to investigate it."

"As good a plan as any, I guess." The captain swiveled his head and barked some orders. Within a minute, three guards had entered the tunnel along with one of the mining engineers.

"Make a diagram of the three tunnels," he commanded the engineer. "Nothing fancy. Just something that shows us—the emperor—what direction they lead."

He ordered the guards to remain at the head of the third tunnel, while he and the lieutenant explored the other two.

The engineer was done with his task in less than two minutes. "Nothing fancy," the man had said—and the engineer didn't want to stay there any longer than he had to. His sketch completed, he crawled back through the opening into the area that had now been cleared of the rubble left behind by the great explosions.

He straightened up with a great sense of relief.

The lieutenant spotted the booby trap in his tunnel just in time to keep his foot from triggering the trip-wire.

His superior was less observant.

The charges in all three tunnels were wired together, of course. So the lieutenant's greater caution only gave him a split-second longer lifespan, before the tunnels collapsed. The guards at the third tunnel were just as surely crushed.

The engineer was knocked off his feet by the explosion, and then covered with the dust blown through the opening. He had just enough presence of mind to keep a grip on the sketch he'd made and protect it from harm.

That caution, also, proved to be of no value.

"This is useless," snarled Skandagupta, after a quick study of the sketch. "They could have gone anywhere."

The emperor crumpled up the sketch and hurled it at the engineer. "Impale him," he commanded.

Chapter 28
KAUSAMBI

"They'll be doing another search of the city," Anastasius said. "For sure and certain."

Lady Damodara looked around the stall in the stable that had been turned into her personal chamber. Then, she smiled very crookedly.

"Who would have thought the day would come that I'd regard a stable stall as luxurious surroundings?"

Lady Sanga was smiling just as crookedly. "Living in a tunnel gives you a sense of proportion. Anything is better than that. Still, Anastasius is right. We can't take the risk."

Lady Damodara sighed. "Yes. I know. The next search might be more thorough. There's really no way to keep soldiers out of this stable if they insist on coming in. As it is"—she gave Valentinian a sly glance—"we'll have to work hard and fast to remove any traces that we were here."

Valentinian returned the glance with a scowl. He'd argued against moving into the stable at all, preferring to remain the whole time in the enlarged tunnel below. Eventually, he'd given in, for the sole reason that providing the hideaways with enough edible food was too difficult if they stayed for very long in the tunnels.

The problem wasn't money. Lady Damodara had a fortune in coins and jewels, and had brought all of it with her into the tunnels.

She had more than enough money to feed them all with the world's finest delicacies for years.

The problem was that large purchases of anything beyond simple foodstuffs would eventually be noticed by the city's authorities. And, unfortunately, the sort of cheap and readily available food that the stable-keeper's family could purchase without notice needed to be *cooked.*

Cooking in a stable was easy. Cooking in a tunnel was not.

Valentinian had then had to wage a mighty struggle to keep the Indians from decorating the stable so much that it would be impossible to disguise their occupancy.

Anastasius was more sanguine. "No problem. One full day of horse shit will disguise anything."

Both women laughed. The horses who'd formerly occupied that stable had been moved into adjoining ones, of course, but they could be moved back quickly and easily.

The stable-keeper had explained to the one customer who'd inquired that the move was due to his doubts regarding the structural soundness of the stable. Doubts which, truth be told, weren't entirely faked. The stable that the refugees were using as a hiding place *was* the most wretched and rickety building in the compound. Of course, that meant it was also the one it was impossible to see into, because of the extra bracing and shoring.

"No help for it," Lady Damodara stated firmly, when she was done laughing. "We'll make the move back into the tunnel this evening. And stop scowling, Valentinian! If we tried to move immediately, we'd be too careless in covering up all the signs that we've been here for weeks."

That was true enough, but it didn't stop Valentinian from scowling.

"Something will go wrong," he predicted.

In the event, nothing did go wrong. Skandagupta ordered another major search of the city. But, as with the initial search, the effort was undone by its very ambition.

"Scour Kausambi" was an easy order to give, from the imperial palace. From the viewpoint of the mass of soldiers on the ground who had to carry it out, the task looked very different. All the more so because they were never given any clear instructions or explanations as to exactly what they were looking for, beyond "the

Lady Damodara and her entourage." Most of the soldiers who conducted the search were peasants, other than the Ye-tai, who were usually semi-barbarians and almost as likely to be illiterate. Their assumptions concerning where a "great lady" could expect to be found hiding simply didn't include stables.

A squad of soldiers searched the stables, to be sure. But their investigation was perfunctory. They didn't even enter the stall where the entrance to the tunnels below was located, much less give it the kind of search that might have uncovered the well-hidden trapdoor.

Not surprising, of course. That stall had more manure in it than any of them.

Still, Valentinian insisted that everyone stay below for three days following the search. Only after Tarun, the stable-keeper's oldest son, reported that the search seemed to have ended all over the city, did Valentinian let the people from the palace come up to enjoy the relative comforts of the stable.

"See?" demanded Anastasius, grinning.

Valentinian's scowl was just as dark as ever. "Don't be an idiot. This isn't going as well as we'd thought it would."

"What are you talking about?" Still grinning, Anastasius waved a huge hand in the direction of the imperial palace. "Tarun says they added four more heads to Skandagupta's collection, perched on pikes outside the palace gates. He thinks one of them was even a member of the dynasty."

"All that philosophy has rotted your brains. What do you think will happen *next*, Anastasius? I'll tell you what'll happen. Whoever the new batch of officers are in charge of the search, they'll throw still more men at digging out the rubble. Put enough hands to the work, and they could dig up the whole city. We're only a few hundred yards from the lady's palace, you know. That's really not that far, no matter how much we confused them with the doglegs."

The grin faded from Anastasius' face. "You think?"

"You're damn right 'I think.' I didn't worry about it, before, when we first came up with this scheme. Most of the tunnel passes under other buildings. To find out which direction it goes, once we collapsed the beginning of it, they can't just dig up soil. They have to level whole city blocks, in their own capital. Who's going to do that?"

Valentinian was literally chewing on his beard. "But I never expected Skandagupta to carry out this kind of reign of terror. I figured he'd be satisfied with one or two searches, and then give it up, figuring the lady had somehow managed to get out of the city altogether."

"Stop chewing on your beard. It's disgusting." As if to give his fellow cataphract a better example, Anastasius started tugging on his own beard. "How soon do you think Damodara and Sanga can get here?"

Valentinian shrugged. At least the gesture dislodged the beard from his mouth. "Who knows? Be at least another month. And even when they do get here, so what? They *still* have to get into the city. There's no way to break down these walls without siege guns—and there's no way Damodara could have brought them with him from the Deccan."

"I'm sure he has a plan," said Anastasius. Uncertainly.

"Sure he does," sneered Valentinian. "Use his new imperial semi-divine aura to overawe the garrison." Again, he shrugged. "It might even work, actually. But not quickly enough to save our necks. We've got to come up with a new plan."

"What?"

"I don't know. I'm thinking."

By the next morning, he had his plan. Such as it was.

Everyone agreed with the first part of the plan. The Bihari miners were sent back underground to prepare new false tunnels—with charges in them, naturally—at the two remaining doglegs.

They made no protest, other than technical ones. Even leaving aside the fact that they were intimidated by Valentinian, the miners knew full well that their lives were now completely bound up with that of Lady Damodara and her entourage. If the Malwa caught them, they'd be staked alongside the others.

"Where will we get the wood?" asked the chief miner. "There's no way to shore tunnels without wood. Even flimsy tunnels we're planning to blow up."

"Don't be stupid." Valentinian swept his head in a little half-circle. "We're in a stable, if you hadn't noticed. Several stables, in fact. Take the wood from the stalls. Just use every other board, so the horses can't get out."

The stable-keeper protested, but that was more a matter of form than anything heartfelt. He, too, knew what would happen to himself and his entire family if the Malwa found them.

It was the second part of Valentinian's plan that stirred up the ruckus. Especially the part about Rajiv.

Rajiv himself, of course, was thrilled by the plan.

His mother was not.

"He's only thirteen!"

"That's the whole point," stated Valentinian. "Nobody notices kids. Especially if they're scruffy enough." He gave Rajiv a pointed look, to which the youngster responded with a grin.

"I can do 'scruffy.' Tarun will help."

The fourteen-year-old Tarun smiled shyly. He wasn't quite as thrilled by the plan as Rajiv, being a Bengali stable-keeper's son rather than a Rajput prince. But he had the natural adventurousness of a teenage boy, to which had been added something close to idol worship. Despite being a year older than Rajiv, Tarun was rather in awe of him—and delighted beyond measure that the Rajput prince had adopted him as a boon companion in time of trouble.

His parents, naturally, shared Lady Sanga's opinion.

"He's only fourteen!" wailed Tarun's mother.

"And small for his age," added his father.

"He's only a *little bit* small for his age," countered Rajiv. "But he's stronger than he looks—and, what's more important, he's very quick-witted. I don't have any hesitation at all about Tarun's part in the plan."

Tarun positively beamed.

Before the argument could spin around in another circle, Lady Damodara spoke. Hers was ultimately the authoritative voice, after all.

"Let's remember that there are *two* parts to Valentinian's plan, and it's the second part that everyone's arguing about. But we may never have to deal with that, anyway. So let's concentrate today on the first part, which is the only part that involves the two boys.

Does anybody really have any strong objection to Rajiv joining Tarun in his expeditions into the city?"

Lady Sanga took a deep breath. "No." But the hostile look she gave Valentinian made her sentiments clear. Like all mothers since the dawn of time, Lady Sanga knew perfectly well that the difference between "part of the way" and "all of the way," when dealing with a teenage son, could not be measured by the world's greatest mathematicians. Or sorcerers, for that matter.

No more than Valentinian, did she think that *we may never have to deal with that* was an accurate prediction of the future.

Neither did Rajiv.

"It can be done," he told Valentinian four days later, after he and Tarun had finished their first round of scouting. "By you, at least. But not easily."

"I didn't think it would be *easy*." Valentinian and Anastasius exchanged a glance. Then, turned to stare at Khandik and the other two Ye-tai mercenaries.

Khandik grinned, rather humorlessly. "Why not? Five against a hundred."

"More like eighty," qualified Rajiv.

"Eighty-three," specified Tarun.

Everyone stared at him. "I can count!" protested the Bengali boy. "You have to be able to count, running a stable."

Anastasius grunted. "Still, it's odds of sixteen or seventeen to one. All garrison troops, of course." He spit on the floor of the stable, as if to emphasize his low opinion of garrison soldiers.

"It's not that bad," said Valentinian. "At least half of them will be off duty."

"On *that* day?" demanded Khandik. "With tens of thousands of Rajputs howling at the gates? I don't think so."

Valentinian grimaced. "Well . . . true." He tugged at his beard. "But the way Rajiv and Tarun report the layout of the gate, we'd only have to deal with some of them."

"If we move fast enough," agreed Rajiv.

Now, it was everyone's turn to stare at Rajiv.

"What's this 'we' business?" demanded Anastasius.

Rajiv squared his shoulders. "It'll go easier if I'm already inside."

"Me too!" said Tarun proudly. "Rajiv and me already figured it out."

Valentinian slanted his head skeptically. "And just why would you be invited in? Other than to be a catamite, which I don't recommend as a way to augment your princely status."

Rajiv made a face. So did Tarun, who stuck out his tongue in the bargain. *"Uck!"*

"It's not that," said Rajiv. For a moment, he had an uncertain expression on his face. An uncomfortable one, actually. "The soldiers are pretty friendly, to tell you the truth. Even their leaders, except for the captain. He's a kshatriya, but the rest are just peasants, including the four sergeants. Most of them Bengalis, just like Tarun. They've got their wives and kids in the barracks with them, too, remember. Lots of kids, and all ages—and the barracks are almost part of the gate itself. After a while, if Tarun and I spend enough time there, nobody will notice us coming or going."

"On *that* day?" asked Khandik skeptically.

Rajiv shrugged. "I think especially on that day. Who's going to pay any attention to me—when my father is on the other side of the gate, making threats and issuing promises?"

That brought a round of soft laughter to the small group of soldiers clustered in a corner of the stable.

"Well," said Khandik. "That's true."

Hearing the laughter, Lady Sanga scowled. She and Lady Damodara were perched on cushions in another part of the stable.

"See?" she demanded.

Her companion made a wry face. "I'm glad my son is only seven."

Lady Sanga sniffed. "Guard him carefully. Or the next thing you know, Valentinian will have him practicing with sticks."

Lady Damodara looked startled. Just the other day, she'd noticed . . .

"He wouldn't!"

"He would."

But even the two ladies were in a better mood, nine days later. Ajatasutra showed up. At last!

"Wasn't hard," he said cheerfully. "They're still not screening anyone at the city's gates very thoroughly. Skandagupta's an idiot, trying to suppress the news of the rebellion the way he is. The rumors are flying all over already—ten times more so, once the emperor reaches the Yamuna, which he should be doing pretty soon. But since nothing is officially confirmed by Skandagupta and his officials, and no clear orders are being given, the soldiers are still going about their business as usual. They're mostly peasants, after all. None of their business, the doings of the high and mighty."

"You look tired," said Dhruva. Hearing the concern in her voice, Valentinian frowned. Seeing the frown, Anastasius had to fight down a grin.

Valentinian, jealous. Would wonders never cease?

Smiling—tiredly—Ajatasutra shrugged. "Well, yes. I've come something like seven hundred miles in less than two weeks, since I left the emperor. Even as much time as I've spent in the saddle in my life, my legs feel like they're about to fall off. Best we not discuss at all the state of my buttocks."

Once the emperor reaches the Yamuna. Since I left the emperor.

Lady Damodara almost shivered, at the casual and matter-of-fact manner of those statements. When she'd last seen her husband, he'd been simply the man she'd known and come to love since their wedding. They'd been but teenagers, at the time. He, sixteen; and she, a year younger.

Now, today . . .

"Oh, forgot." Ajatasutra started digging in his tunic. "Rana Sanga—the emperor also, once he saw—asked me to bring you gifts. Nothing fancy, of course, traveling as lightly as I was."

His hand emerged, holding two small onions. One, he gave to Lady Sanga; the other, to Lady Damodara.

Rana Sanga's wife burst into tears. Lady Damodara just smiled.

She even managed to keep the smile on her face a minute later. Ajatasutra had addressed her as "Your Majesty" from the moment he arrived, and had done so throughout the long report he'd given them. But she hadn't really thought much of it. That just seemed part of the project of disguise and deception she'd been involved with for over a year, now. Hearing him—so casually, so matter-of-factly!—refer to her as *the Empress* to Lady Sanga, was a different thing altogether.

After Ajatasutra left her part of the stable, to confer with the soldiers in their own corner, Lady Damodara gave vent to her confusion and uncertainty.

"I don't *feel* any different."

Her companion smiled. Rana Sanga's wife had become Lady Damodara's close friend, over the past months. The closest friend she'd ever had, in fact.

"Oh, but you are. Your semi-divine aura is quite noticeable now."

"Even when I shit?" Lady Damodara pointed to a chamber pot not more than five feet away. "Damn this stable, anyway."

Sanga's wife grimaced. "Well. Maybe you need to work on that part. On the other hand, why bother? Before too long, you'll either be dead or be crapping in the biggest palace in the world. With fifty chambermaids to carry out the results, and twenty spies and three executioners to make sure they keep their mouths shut about the contents."

Lady Damodara laughed.

A few minutes later, hearing the soft laughter coming from the knot of soldiers in the corner of the stable, she frowned.

"My son's not over there, is he?" But, looking around, she spotted him playing with two of the other small boys in a different part of the stable. So, her frown faded.

Lady Sanga's frown, on the other hand, had deepened into a full scowl.

"No. But my son *is*."

"Only fifteen-to-one odds," said Khandik with satisfaction, "now that Ajatasutra's here."

Young Tarun shook his head. "Thirteen-to-one. Well. A bit more."

The glare bestowed upon him by the Ye-tai mercenary was a half-and-half business. On the one hand, it was unseemly for a mere stable-boy—a wretched Bengali, to boot—to correct his superior and elder. On the other hand . . .

"Thirteen-to-one," he said, with still greater satisfaction.

His two mates weren't even half-glaring. In fact, they were almost smiling.

Under normal circumstances, of course, thirteen-to-one odds would have been horrible. But those Ye-tai mercenaries were all veterans. The kind of fighting they were considering would not be the clash of huge armies on a great battlefield, where individual prowess usually got lost in the sheer mass of the conflict. No, this would be the sort of small-scale action out of which legends were made, because legends mattered.

The Mongoose was already a legend. His huge Roman companion wasn't, but they had no difficulty imagining him as such. "Bending horseshoes," with Anastasius in the vicinity, was not a phrase to express the impossible.

As for Ajatasutra . . .

"Some people think you're the best assassin in India," said one of the Ye-tai.

"Not any Marathas," came the immediate rejoinder. Smiling, Ajatasutra added: "But I think even Marathas might allow me the honor of second-best."

Chapter 29

THE IRON TRIANGLE

"It's just impossible," said Anna wearily, leaning her head against her husband's shoulder. "That great mass of people out there isn't really a city. It's a huge refugee camp, with more people pouring into it every day. Just when I think I've got one problem solved, the solution collapses under the weight of more refugees."

Calopodius stroked her hair, listening to the cannonade outside the bunker. The firing seemed a lot heavier than usual, on the Malwa side. He wondered if they might be getting nervous. By now, their spies were sure to have reported that a large Persian army had been camped briefly just across the river from the Iron Triangle.

But he gave only a small part of his mind to that matter. He had much more pressing and immediate things to deal with.

"Have you given any thought as to what you'd like to do, after the war? With the rest of your life, I mean."

Anna's head stirred. "Some," she said softly.

"And what did you decide?"

Now, her head lifted off his shoulder entirely. He knew she was looking at him sideways.

"Do you care?" she asked, still more softly.

He started to respond with "of course," but the words died before they were spoken. He'd spent quite a bit of time thinking about Anna, lately, and knew full well that "of course" was not an answer that would have even occured to him a few months ago.

So, he simply said: "Yes. I do."

There was a pause for a few seconds. Then, Anna's head came back to nestle on his shoulder again. "I think I'd like to keep the Service going. Somehow or other. I like healing people."

Calopodius kissed her hair. It felt rich and luxurious to him; more so now, than when he'd been able to see it.

"All right," he said. "That shouldn't be too hard."

Anna issued a sound halfway between a snort and a chuckle. "Not too hard! It's *expensive,* husband. Not even your family's rich enough to subsidize medical charity on that scale. Not for very long. And once the war is over, the money Belisarius and the army have been giving me will dry up."

It was Calopodius' turn to hesitate. "Yes, I know. But . . . how would you feel about remaining here in India?"

"I wouldn't mind. But why India?"

"Lots of reasons. I've been thinking about our situation myself. But let's start with three. One that matters—I think—to you. One that matters to me. And one that would matter to my family. Perhaps more to the point, my family's coffers."

Her head came back off his shoulder and, a moment later, Calopodius could feel her shifting her weight entirely. Within a few seconds, she was no longer lying beside him on their pallet but was sitting on it cross-legged, facing him. He knew the sensation quite well. Whenever they had something to really talk about, Anna preferred to be sitting up.

"Explain."

"Let's start with you. You already know that if our world keeps the same historical pattern with regard to disease as the one we diverged from, a terrible plague is 'scheduled' to start in eight years or so. By the time it's over, millions of people in the Mediterranean world will be dead."

"It might have already started, in fact," Anna mused. "Somewhere in China. Where the death toll will be just as bad."

Calopodius nodded. He wasn't surprised that she'd remembered that part of the future history that Belisarius had imparted to them.

"Yes. It'll enter the Roman Empire in Alexandria, in the year 541. But it almost certainly got transmitted through India."

He heard Anna draw in a sharp breath. "I hadn't thought of that."

"Then I think you should start thinking about it. If you move fast enough—fast enough and with enough money and authority—between your Service and the Hospitalers in Alexandria, it might be possible to forestall the plague. Reduce its effects, anyway."

"There's no cure for it," she said. "And no . . . what's the word?"

" 'Vaccine,' " Calopodius supplied.

"Yes. No vaccine. Not anything we could make in time, in sufficient quantities."

Calopodius shrugged. "True. But from what Belisarius told me Aide said to him, it wasn't really a medical 'cure' that defeated the plague in the future, anyway. It was mostly just extensive and thorough public health and sanitation. Stuff as simple and plebeian as good sewers and clean drinking water. That *is* within our technological capacity."

He listened to Anna breathing, for a while. Then she said: "It would take a lot of money, and a lot of political influence."

"Yes. It'd be a life's work. Are you willing?"

She laughed abruptly. "*I'm* willing. But is the money willing? And . . . " Her voice lowered. "I really don't want to do anything that you wouldn't be happy with."

He smiled. "Not to worry! What *I* want to do is write histories and public commentaries. But what do I write about, once the war is over?"

He moved right on to supply the answer: "Write about India, that's what. Just think of it, love. An entire *continent*. One that Rome knows almost nothing about and with a history even longer than Rome's."

Silence.

"Your life's work, then," Anna mused. Then, issued that same abrupt laugh. "So where's the money to come from?"

His smile widened, becoming very close to a grin. "Well, we'll have to keep it hidden from your family. Even from mine, the rough details. But you and I are about to found a branch of the Saronites enterprises, here in India. Crude stuff, I'm afraid. Manufacturing, mostly."

He wasn't surprised at all that the woman his wife had become did not even stumble over the prospect. "Manufacturing what?"

"I thought we'd start with medical supplies and equipment. Also pharmaceuticals. Nothing fancy, though. Mostly soap, dyes and cosmetics, at the beginning. Belisarius told me those were the substances that were the big money-makers for the chemical industry when it got really started in the future. In what he calls the 'industrial revolution.' Once the business gets rolling, we can expand into medicines."

"And exactly which one of us is going to oversee and organize this grand scheme of yours?" she demanded.

"Neither of us. We just front the money—I can get enough to start from my father—and we—mostly you—provide the political influence. I figured we could bring up your banker from Barbaricum—"

"Pulinda?"

"Yes, him. He's shrewd as they come, and he knows India. For running the technical end, we'll use Eusebius."

"If he agrees. He might not—"

"I already asked him. He says he'd love to. He's tired of figuring out new ways to kill people."

"You *already* asked him?"

"Yes. And I think Justinian will go for it, too. Not directly, of course. He's got to get back to Constantinople as soon as the war's over or Theodora will send out the executioners. But he's intrigued by the idea and says he's sure he can siphon us some imperial financing—provided he gets to play with the gadgets at his end."

The pallet lurched. Calopodius knew that Anna had risen to her feet. Jumped to her feet, more like.

"You asked the Emperor of Rome to be our business partner in a manufacturing scheme? *Are you out of your mind?*"

"He's not the emperor any longer, dear," Calopodius pointed out mildly. "Photius is."

"Still!"

"He's the Grand Justiciar. And you know how much he loves to play with gadgets."

"My husband!" Anna burst into laughter that was not abrupt at all.

Kungas came to his decision and moved away from the window looking out over Peshawar. "All right," he said, "we'll do it."

He gave the small group of Ye-tai deserters a gaze that wasn't cold so much as simply impassive. The way a glacier contemplates so many rocks who might be in its way when it ground forward to the sea. More indifferent than icy, since the outcome was inevitable.

The Ye-tai were squatting on the floor of his private audience chamber. They seemed like so many rocks, indeed, as motionless as they were. And for good reason. First, they were disarmed. Second, the Kushan soldiers standing around and guarding them were armed to the teeth. Third, there was no love lost between Kushans and Ye-tai to begin with. Hadn't been for a century, since the invading Ye-tai had broken the Kushan kingdom that Kungas had re-created.

"If you're lying, of course, you're dead men."

The Ye-tai squad leader made a shrug that was as minimal as any Kungas himself might have made. "Why would we lie?"

"I can't think of any reason myself. Which is why I decided to believe you." Kungas' crack of a smile came. "Besides, Sarmatians are noted for their honesty. Even half-Sarmatians."

That little joke brought a ripple of laughter in the room, as much from the Kushan guards as the Ye-tai prisoners. For the first time since they'd been ushered into the chamber—frog-marched, more like—the Ye-tai visibly relaxed.

Although his thin smile had remained, Kungas had not joined the laughter. When it ended, he shook his head.

"I'm not joking, really. You six are the founding members of my new military unit. If you're not lying—and I'm assuming you aren't—then you won't be the last Malwa deserters coming over to us. So I think I'll enroll all of you in the . . . What to call it?"

Irene piped up, sitting on a chair to one side. "The Royal Sarmatian Guards."

"That'll do nicely." Kungas turned to his lieutenants. "Get the army formed up. I want to march out tomorrow morning, early. Leave five thousand men in the capital."

"I won't need that many," said Irene. "Three thousand is plenty to maintain order and keep the hill tribes from getting any ideas."

Kungas thought about it, and decided she was right. He could leave the additional two thousand men with the five thousand already garrisoning the forts in the passes at Margalla and Kohat.

That would secure the gates to the kingdom and leave him almost twenty thousand men to do . . .

Whatever. He didn't know yet. He was quite sure the Ye-tai deserters weren't lying. But that didn't necessarily mean their assessment of things was all that accurate, either.

Still, he thought it was probably was. Close enough, anyway. Kungas had been fighting almost since he was a boy. There was that smell in the air, of an enemy starting to come apart.

When Jaimal caught his first glimpse of the walls of Ajmer, he felt the greatest exhilaration he'd ever felt in his life. Even though he was also completely exhausted.

He glanced at Udai Singh, riding next to him at the head of the small Rajput cavalry column, and saw the same gleaming smile he must have had on his own face.

"A ride of legend!" Udai shouted. Half-croaked, rather.

Shouted or croaked, it was true. And the ragged chorus of that same half-croaked shout coming from the fifty cavalrymen following told Jaimal that their men knew it as well as they did.

Rajputana was a land of horsemen, as well as warriors. A great horse ride would become a thing of renown just as surely as a great feat of arms.

Emperor Damodara and Rana Sanga had asked them to accomplish the incredibly difficult task of riding from Bharakuccha to Ajmer in two weeks. If possible.

They'd done it in eleven days. Without losing more than nine of their horses.

"A ride of legend!" he shouted himself.

But there was no need for that, really. Already, he could see the gates of the city opening, and cavalrymen issuing forth. Hundreds of them. Even from the great distance, just seeing the way they rode, he knew they were all young men. Seeking their own place in legends.

Jaimal and Udai would give it to them.

Standing on the walls of Ajmer and watching the way the young warriors who had poured out of the city were circling the new arrivals—there were at least a thousand of them, now, with more sallying from the gates every minute—the oldest and therefore

wisest king of Rajputana knew it was hopeless. That was a whirl-
wind of celebration and excitement, out there. Caution and sagacity would soon become so many leaves blown by the monsoon.

"Perhaps . . ." began Chachu.

Dasal shook his head. Standing next to him, his brother Jaisal
did likewise.

"Not a chance," said Jaisal curtly. "*Look* at them, out there."

"We don't even know what it's about, yet," whined Chachu. One
of the other kings who formed the council grunted something in
the way of agreement.

Dasal shrugged. "Don't be foolish. No, we don't know *exactly*
what news—or instructions—that cavalry column is bringing. But
the gist of it is obvious."

He nodded toward the column, which was now advancing
toward the gates with over a thousand other Rajput cavalrymen
providing them with what was, for all practical purposes, an escort
of honor.

"The new emperor sent them. Or Rana Sanga. Or both. And
they will be demanding the allegiance of all Rajputs. So what do
we say?"

He had no answer, himself. The Rajput heart that beat within
him was just as eager as any of those young warriors out there.
But that heart had now beaten for almost eighty years, each and
every year of which had hammered caution into his mind, whatever
his heart might feel.

"Let's return to the council chamber and await them there,"
suggested Jaisal.

That might help. A bit.

"Yes," Dasal said.

But when they returned to the council chamber, they discovered
it had been preempted from them already. The seven thrones had
been removed from their accustomed places in a half-circle at the
elevated dais. They were now resting, still in a half-circle, *facing*
the dais.

On the dais itself, sat only one chair. A smaller and less ostentatious chair, as it happened, than the seven chairs of the kings. And
the man who sat in it was smaller—certainly more rotund—than
any of the kings.

But it hardly mattered. Dasal understood who he was before he even spoke.

Chachu, as usual, had to be enlightened.

"I am Great Lord Damodara," the short, fat old man said. "The emperor's father. I am the new viceroy of Rajputana. And you will obey me."

Behind him, in a row, stood half a dozen Malwa bodyguards. Assassins, to call things by their right name. More to the point, at least fifty young Rajput warriors were standing alongside the walls of the chamber. Each and every one of whom was glaring at the seven kings.

Suddenly, the plump face of Great Lord Damodara broke into a smile. The expression made him seem a much friendlier sort of fellow.

"But, please!" he exclaimed, waving his hand at the seven chairs before him. "Take your seats, Kings of Rajputana."

Dasal considered the courtesy. Then, considered the titles. Finally, considered the chairs.

The chairs made the decision. They were the same chairs, after all. Very august ones. Not to mention comfortable.

He felt relief more than anything else. Clearly enough, the new regime in the land of the Rajputs was willing to accommodate the status—if not the authority—of the old one.

He was almost eighty years old, after all. Even the youngest of the seven kings of the council was past seventy.

"Yes, Great Lord." Dasal moved forward and sat in his accustomed chair. He gave his half dozen fellows an abrupt nod, commanding them to follow.

They did so, readily enough. Only Chachu made a token protest.

"I don't understand," he whined. "If you're still alive, why aren't *you* the new emperor instead of your son?"

The smile on the Great Lord's face stayed in place, but it got an ironic twist.

"Good question. I'll have to take it up with my headstrong son when we meet again. For the moment, I ascribe it to the monsoon times we're living in."

The smile became serene. "But I don't imagine I'll argue the point with him. Actually, it might make for a good tradition. When emperors—and kings—get too old, they tend to get too set in their ways. Best to have them retire and take up some prestigious but less demanding post, while their son assumes the heavier responsibilities. Don't you think?"

The smile was friendly. But the assassins were still there, not smiling at all. And the young warriors were still glaring.

"Indeed, Great Lord," said Dasal.

His brother echoed him immediately. Chachu, thankfully, kept his mouth shut.

Or, at least, kept his mouth shut until the two leaders of the newly arrived cavalry column finished their report.

"That's madness!" Chachu exclaimed. "*Belisarius?*"

But Dasal had come to the opposite conclusion. The great lord was right. Old men *should* retire, when the time comes.

Especially when presented with such a fine way to do so.

"It's brilliant," he rebutted, rising to his feet. "And I will lead the force that goes into the Thar to find him."

His brother came to his feet also. "I'll go with you."

"You're too old!" protested Chachu.

The two brothers glared at him, with the combined indignation of one hundred and fifty-six years of life.

"I can still ride a horse!" snarled Dasal. "Even if *you* can't ride anything other than a chair any longer."

They left the following evening, just after sunset. No sane man rides into the desert during the day. Dasal and Jaisal had one hundred and fifty-six years of sanity between them.

The young warriors were impatient, of course. All seven thousand of them.

Especially impatient were the six thousand that the two kings had insisted ride on camels, carrying the water and other supplies that they were quite sure Belisarius needed. Leave it to an idiot Roman to try to cross the desert without camels. Relying on wells! In the Thar!

Most impatient of all were the ten thousand—with more coming into the city every day—whom Dasal had insisted remain behind. With, fortunately, the agreement and approval of the new viceroy of Rajputana. They would just be a nuisance in the expedition, and a new Rajput army had to be formed.

Formed quickly. The monsoon was coming.

Fortunately, Rana Sanga's two lieutenants Jaimal and Udai Singh had the authority and experience for the task. They needed a rest anyway, after their ride of legend. By the time Jaisal and Dasal returned to Ajmer with Belisarius, the new army would be ready.

For . . . whatever. Given Belisarius, it would be a thing of legend. Dasal only hoped he would live long enough to see it.

Assuming the idiot Roman was still alive. Crossing the Thar on horses! Relying on wells!

When the Malwa assassination team finally rowed their ship into the great harbor at Bharakuccha, they knew another moment of frustration and chagrin.

"Look at that!" snarled one of them.

The captain of the team just shook his head. The docks and piers of the city seemed practically covered with a carpet of people, all of them come down to greet the Axumite fleet escorting the Emperor of Rome.

The fleet was already anchored. As they drew closer, the Malwa assassins could see the Roman imperial party being escorted to the great palace of the Goptri by a small army of Ethiopian sarwen.

Even if they'd been in position, there would have been no way to get to the boy emperor. And once he was in the palace . . .

The captain of the assassination team and his lieutenant were both familiar with the great palace of the Goptri. As the palace of a conquering viceroy in a hostile land, serving a dynasty famous for its paranoia, it had been *designed* to thwart assassins. Unless the guards were utterly incompetent . . .

"Ethiopian sarwen," the lieutenant grumbled. "And you can be sure that Raghunath Rao will be there to advise them."

The captain spent a moment adding up the miles he and his team had traveled, to carry out an assignment that always seem to recede before them in the distance. It had been like trying to assassinate a mirage in the desert.

From Kausambi to Bharakuccha to Alexandria to Constantinople. And then back again, almost all the way.

Something like ten thousand miles, he thought. Who could really know?

"Nothing for it," he said. "We'll sell the ship as soon as we can, since we're almost out of money. Then . . . we'll just have to see what we can do."

◊   ◊   ◊

Finding a buyer for the ship was easy. Whether rightly and wrongly—and, more and more, the captain was beginning to wonder if they weren't right—the merchants of Bharakuccha seemed quite confident that the old Malwa empire was gone from the Deccan and that trade would soon be picking up.

They even got a better price than the captain had expected.

That was the first and last thing that went as planned. No sooner had they emerged from the merchant clearinghouse than a harried-looking official accosted them. Accompanied, unfortunately, by a large squad of soldiers.

Not regular Malwa soldiers, either, to make things worse. Marathas, from their look, newly impressed into the city's garrison. It seemed the new Axumite commander had given orders to form units from all residents of the city.

The captain sized them up. Eight of them there were, and tougher-looking than he liked. He didn't doubt that he and his four assassins could overcome them. But not without suffering casualties—and then what?

Five Malwa assassins in today's Bharakuccha, many if not all of them wounded, would be like so many pieces of bloody meat in shark waters.

"There you are!" the official exclaimed. "You *are* the trade delegation just returned from Rome, yes?"

That had been their official identity. The captain wondered how an official in Bharakuccha—the place was a madhouse!—had managed to keep track of the records and identify them so soon after their return.

He brought down a savage curse on all hard-working and efficient bureaucrats. A silent curse, naturally.

"Come with me!" the official commanded. "I've been instructed to send a courier team to catch up with the emperor"—he didn't even bother to specify the "new" emperor—"and you're just the men for the job!"

"I can't believe this," muttered his lieutenant. Very softly, of course.

The next morning, they were riding out of the city on excellent horses, carrying dispatches for Damodara. Along with a Maratha cavalry platoon to provide them with a safe escort out of the Deccan. The assassins were obviously Malwa—some sort of north Indians, at any rate—and despite the new truce between the Malwa and Andhran empires, it was always possible that a band of Maratha irregulars in the hills wouldn't obey it. Or would have simply turned to banditry, as some soldiers always do at the end of a war.

That same escort, needless to say, also made it impossible for them to return to Bharakuccha and continue their assignment. Not, at least, until they'd passed the crest of the Vindhyas—at which point, they have to return *another* hundred miles or so, and do it without being spotted by Maratha patrols.

The only bright spot in the whole mess was that their luggage hadn't been searched. If it had been, the bombard would have been discovered—and they'd have had a very hard time explaining why and how a "trade delegation" had been carrying an assassination device. A bombard of that size and type was never used by regular military units, and it would have been even more useless for trade delegates.

That night, around their campfire and far enough from the Maratha escort not to be overheard, the five assassins quietly discussed their options.

"It's hopeless," the captain concluded. "We've done our best. Let's just give it up and return to Kausambi for a new assignment."

His lieutenant finally said it. "That's assuming we don't find a new emperor when we get there. Then what?"

The captain shrugged, and spit into the fire.

More cheerily, one of the other assassins said: "Well, there's this. Whoever the emperor is when we get there, one thing's for sure. We won't be reporting failure to Nanda Lal. No matter what."

That was true. Perhaps the only certainty left in their lives. They'd all seen Nanda Lal's head perched on a pike outside the Goptri's palace. There hadn't been much left of it. But the captain and the lieutenant had recognized the nose. Broken, years ago, by the boot of Belisarius. Battered, at the end, by boys in their play.

Chapter 30
THE THAR DESERT

Belisarius finally managed to force his eyes somewhere else. Staring at the empty well wouldn't make it fill up.

Not that he found the sight of the desert any prettier.

"So, I gambled and lost," he said to Ashot and Abbu, standing next to him.

Ashot was still scowling down into the well. Abbu was scowling at the desert, his eyes avoiding the general's.

"It's not your fault, Abbu."

The old bedouin grimaced. "This well was one of the best!" he protested. "I was worried about the last one. And another one some twenty miles farther. Not this one!"

Finally, Ashot straightened up. "Wells are finicky in a desert like this. If the water table was reliable, we wouldn't have had to dig our own. There'd have been wells already here."

The Armenian cataphract wiped the dust off his face with a cloth. "What do we do now, General? We don't have enough water left to make the crossing to the next well. Not the whole expedition, for sure. A few dozen could make it, maybe, if they took all the water we still have."

"For what purpose?" Belisarius demanded. Not angrily, just wearily.

He leaned over the well again, gauging the dampness at the very bottom. There wasn't much.

There were two decisions to be made. One was obvious to probably everyone. The other was obvious to him.

"No," he said. "We'll send a very small force—five men—with all the water they need to cross the rest of the Thar without stopping. They might be able to reach Ajmer in time to bring a Rajput relief expedition, if Rana Sanga's already gotten the word there."

Ashot winced. Abbu shook his head.

"That's a lot of 'ifs,' General," said the Armenian. "*If* they can cross in time. *If* the Rajputs are already prepared. *If* they'll listen to a handful of men in the first place. *If* they can get back in time with water before the rest of us are dead."

"The first 'if' is the easiest, too," Abbu added. "And it stinks. Five men, crossing as fast as they can . . . It would still take them at least five days. Another week—at least—before they could get back with enough water to make a difference. That's twelve days, General, at best."

Belisarius had already figured out the deadly arithmetic. If anything, Abbu was being optimistic—one of the few times Belisarius could ever remember him being so. Belisarius himself thought the minimum would be two weeks.

In the desert, in the hot season, a man without water could not survive for more than two days before he started to die. And he died quickly, thereafter. Maybe three days, depending on the temperature. That assumed he found shelter from the sun and didn't exert himself. If he did, death would come much sooner.

If the Roman expedition shared all their remaining water evenly—and gave none to the horses—they'd run out in three days. At most, the moisture still seeping into the bottom of the well might provide them with another day's water. Then . . .

They might last a little over a week, all told. Not two weeks, certainly. Probably not even twelve days.

There was no way to go back or to go forward, either. The last well was four days behind them, and it would be almost dry anyway after their recent use of it. The next well was at least two and a half days' travel, according to Abbu, for a party this size. Since they had to water the horses also, while traveling, they'd run out within the first day. The last two days they'd be without water.

So would the horses.

They'd never make it. Not in the Thar, in the hot season.

"I understand the arithmetic," Belisarius said harshly. "It's still our only chance."

The second decision, then.

"You'll lead the party, Ashot. Abbu, you go with him. Pick three of your bedouin for the remaining men."

Ashot's eyes widened, a little. Abbu's didn't.

"You're not going yourself?"

"No. I'll stay here with the men."

"But—"

"Be off, Ashot. There's no time to waste. And there will be no argument. No discussion at all."

He turned and started walking away from the well.

Are you sure? asked Aide, uncertainly.

Yes. These men have been with me for years. I'm not leaving them to die. Not that, whatever else.

Aide said nothing. His own survival was not at stake. There were things that could destroy Aide, Belisarius knew, although the jewel had always been reticent about explaining exactly what they were. But merely being without water for a few weeks—or even a few years—was not one of them.

When Ashot returned, most likely he would find Aide in a pouch hanging from a corpse's neck. But the jewel would be as alive as ever.

Working through Ousanas would be the easiest for you, I think, Belisarius mused. *But he's probably not influential enough. You might try Rao, although there might be the same problem. The best would be Damodara, if you could reach him.*

I don't want to talk about it.

I understand. Still—

I don't want to talk about it.

Ashot and Abbu left after sundown. Once they were gone, Belisarius addressed his bucellarii and the remaining Arab scouts.

"We don't have much of a chance, men. But it'll be improved if we set up good shelters from the sun. So let's work on that tonight. Also, we want to eat as little as possible. Eating uses up water, too."

One of the cataphracts asked: "Are you going to set up a rationing system?"

Several of the Arabs who heard the question started shaking their heads.

"No," said Belisarius firmly. "Once we make an even division of what's left, drink whenever you're thirsty. If fact, after a few hours, drink something even if you're not thirsty."

That cataphract and a few others seemed confused. Apparently, they didn't have much experience with the desert.

"Rationing water as a way of staying alive in the desert is a fable," Belisarius explained. "It does more harm than good. You're only going to live as long as your body has enough water, no matter what you do. All rationing does is weaken you quicker. So drink as much as you want, whenever you want. The bigger danger, actually, is that you won't drink often enough."

One of the bedouin grunted his agreement. "Listen to the general."

"Oh, sure," said the cataphract hastily. "I was just wondering."

Later that night, after the camp was made, Aide spoke for the first time since the decision had been made.

They seem so confident.

They're not, really. But since I stayed with them, they have a barrier to fear.

Yes. I understand. I always wondered.

Wondered what?

Why Alexander the Great poured onto the sand a helmet full of water that one of his soldiers had offered him, in that terrible retreat from India through the desert. It just seemed flamboyant, to me.

Belisarius smiled. *Well, it was flamboyant. But that was the nature of the man. I'd have just told the soldier to return the water to the common share. That difference aside, yes, that's why he did it. His men might have died anyway. But by refusing the water, Alexander made sure they didn't panic. Which would have killed them even quicker.*

I understand now.

We still need to talk about the future. Your future. If you can reach Damodara—

I don't want to talk about that.

After a while, he added: **I'm not ready.**

I understand. We have some days yet.

◊   ◊   ◊

Meeting Raghunath Rao in the flesh was perhaps the oddest experience Antonina had ever had. That was not so much because she already knew a great deal about him, but because of one specific thing she knew.

In another world, another future, another time, another universe, she had met the man. Had known him for decades, in fact, since he'd been Belisarius' slave.

In the end, she'd been murdered by the Malwa. Murdered, and then flayed, so her skin-sack could serve as another trophy. In his last battle in that universe, Belisarius had rescued her skin, and taken it with him when he leapt into a cauldron.

She knew the story, since her husband had told her once. And she also knew that it had been Rao who washed the skin, to cleanse it of the Malwa filth, before her husband took it into the fire.

What did you say to a man who had once washed your flayed skin?

Nice to finally meet you?

That seemed . . . idiotic.

But the time had come. Having exchanged greetings with the Empress of Andhra, Antonina was now being introduced to her consort.

Rao bowed deeply, then extended his hands.

She clasped them, warmly.

"It's nice to finally meet you," she said. Feeling like an idiot.

"Use the mortars," Kungas commanded. "As many as we've got."

"We've got a *lot* of mortars," Kujulo pointed out.

"I know. Use all of them."

Kungas pointed at the Malwa army scrambling away from the pass. Obviously, whatever else they'd expected, they hadn't thought Kungas would come plunging out of the Hindu Kush with twenty thousand men. Like a flash flood of steel.

"They're already panicked. Pound them, Kujulo. Pound them as furiously as you can. I don't care if we run out of gunpowder in a few minutes. Mortars will do it."

Less than an hour later, the way out of the Peshawar Vale was clear. The Malwa army guarding Margalla pass had broken like a stick. Splintered, rather, with pieces running everywhere.

"No pursuit," Kungas commanded. "It'll take the Malwa days to rally them. That gives us time to reach the headwaters of the Sutlej before an army can reach us from Multan."

Kujulo cocked his head. "You've decided, then?"

"Yes. We'll take the gamble. I want that bitch dead. With us coming behind her, right on her heels, we can drive her into the trap."

"What trap?"

"The one Belisarius will be setting for her."

Kujulo cocked his head the other way. Kungas had to fight down a chuckle. With the plume on his helmet, he reminded the king of a confused bird.

"Ah. You've been told something."

"No," said Kungas. "I'm just guessing."

His head still cocked, Kujulo winced. "Big gamble. Based on a guess."

"Kushans love to gamble."

"True."

After Kujulo left to organize the march, Kungas summoned the Ye-tai deserters. They'd been standing nearby, garbed in their fancy new uniforms. Irene had had them made up quickly by her seamstresses, substituting flamboyance where time hadn't allowed good workmanship.

The armor, of course, was the same they'd been wearing when they arrived in Peshawar. The well-worn and utilitarian gear looked especially drab, against that colorful new fabric and gaudy design.

"You're promoted," he told the squad leader. "I think we'll use Greek ranks for the Royal Sarmatian Guards. That'll make you sound exotic. Exciting."

"Whatever you say, Your Majesty."

"You're a tribune. The rest are hecatontarchs."

The squad leader pondered the matter, briefly.

"What do those titles mean, exactly? Your Majesty."

"I'd say that's up to you, isn't it? Get me some deserters. Lots of them." He waved a hand at the low hills around them, much of their slopes now shadowed by the setting sun. "They'll be out there."

"Ye-tai only?"

Kungas shrugged. "You won't find many other than Ye-tai bold enough to come in. But it doesn't matter. Anyone who's willing to swear his mother was Sarmatian."

After the king left, the tribune turned to his mates.
"You see?" he demanded.

When the Emperor of Malwa reached the door leading into the inner sanctum of the imperial palace—the ultimate inner sanctum; the real one—he paused for a moment, his lips tightly pursed.

That was partly because he'd have to submit to a personal search, the moment he entered, at the hands of Link's special Khmer guards. It was the only time the divine emperor suffered such an indignity. As the years had passed, Skandagupta found that increasingly distasteful.

But that was only part of the matter, and probably not the largest part. The emperor hadn't come down here in well over a year. Entering the inner sanctum below the palace was always disturbing, in a way that dealing with Malwa's overlord through one of the Great Ladies who served as its sheath was not.

He wasn't sure why. Perhaps because the machines in the chambers beyond were completely unfathomable. A cold, metallic reminder that even the Malwa emperor himself was nothing but a device, in the hands of the new gods.

He wasn't even sure why he had come, this day. He'd been driven simply by a powerful impulse to do so.

Skandagupta was not given to introspection, however. A few seconds later, he opened the door.

There was no lock. He'd had to pass through several sets of guards to get down here, and the chamber immediately beyond the door had more guards still. Those quiet, frightening special assassins.

The personal inspection was brief, but not perfunctory in the least. Feeling polluted by the touch of the guards' hands, Skandagupta was ushered into the inner sanctum.

Great Lady Rani was there to greet him. She would be Great Lady Sati's replacement, whenever the time came. Standing against a nearby wall, their heads submissively bowed, were the four Khmer women who attended her, simultaneously, as servants, confidants—and, mostly, tutors. They were trained in the cult's temple in far-off Cambodia, and then trained still further by Link itself once they arrived in Kausambi.

"Welcome, Emperor," said Great Lady Rani, in that eight-year-old girl's voice that was always so discordant to Skandagupta.

No more so than Sati's had once been, of course. Or, he imagined, Holi's in times past, although he himself was not old enough to remember Holi as a small girl. Link's sheaths, once selected, were separated from the dynastic clan and brought up in ways that soon made them quite unlike any other girls. Link would not consume them until the time came, once their predecessor had died. But the overlord communed with them frequently beforehand, using the machines—somehow—to instill its spirit into their child's minds. By the time they were six, they were no longer children in any sense of that term that meant anything.

"What may I do for you?"

The emperor didn't answer for a moment, his eyes moving across the machines in a corner. He did not understand those machines; never had, and never would. He did not even understand how Link had managed to bring them here from the future, all those many years ago. Malwa's overlord had told him once that the effort had been so immense—so expensive, in ways of calculating cost that Skandagupta did not understand either—that it would be impossible to duplicate.

"What may I do for you?" she repeated.

The emperor shook his head impatiently. "Nothing, really. I just wanted . . ."

He couldn't find the conclusion to that sentence. He tried, but couldn't.

"I just wanted to visit," he finally said, lamely. "See how you were."

"How else would I be?" The eyes in the eight-year-old face belonged to no woman at all, of any age. "Ready, as I have always been."

Skandagupta cleared his throat. "Surely it won't come to that. Not for many years. Great Lady Sati is still quite young."

"Most likely. But nothing is certain."

"Yes. Well."

He cleared his throat again. "I'll be going, now."

◇   ◇   ◇

When he reached the landing of the stairs that led down to the inner sanctum, he was puffing heavily from the climb and not for the first time wishing he could make the trip in a palanquin carried by slaves.

Impossible, of course. Not only was the staircase much too narrow, but Link would have forbidden it anyway.

Well, not exactly. Link would allow slaves to come down to the inner sanctum. It had done so, now and then, for an occasional special purpose.

But then the Khmer assassins killed them, so what was the point? The emperor would *still* have to climb back up.

He was in a foul mood, therefore, when he reached his private audience chamber and was finally able to relax on his throne.

After hearing what his aides had to report, his mood grew fouler still.

"They blew up the tunnels *again*?" Angrily, he slapped the armrest of the throne. "That's enough! Tear down every building in that quarter of the city, within three hundred yards of Damodara's palace. Raze it all to the ground! Then dig up everything. They can't have placed mines everywhere."

He took a deep breath. "And have the commander of the project executed. Whoever he is."

"He did not survive the explosion, Your Majesty."

Skandagupta slapped the armrest again. "Do as I command!"

His aides hurried from the chamber, before the emperor's wrath could single out one of them to substitute for the now-dead commander. Despite the great rewards, serving Skandagupta had always been a rather risky proposition. If not as coldly savage as his father, he was also less predictable and given to sudden whims.

In times past, those whims had often produced great largesse for his aides.

No longer. The escape of Damodara's family, combined with Damodara's rebellion, had unsettled Skandagupta in ways that the Andhran and Persian and Roman wars had never done. For weeks, his whims had only been murderous.

"This is madness," murmured one aide to another. He allowed himself that indiscretion, since they were brothers. "What difference does it make, if they stay in hiding? Unless Damodara can breach the walls—if he manages to get to Kausambi at all—what does it matter? Just a few more rats in a cellar somewhere, a little bigger than most."

They were outside the palace now, out of range of any possible spies or eavesdroppers. Gloomily, the aide's brother agreed. "All the emperor's doing is keeping the city unsettled. Now, the reaction when we destroy an entire section . . . "

He shook his head. "Madness, indeed."

But since they were now walking past the outer wall of the palace, the conversation ended. No fear of eavesdroppers here, either. But the long row of ragged heads on pikes—entire rotting bodies on stakes, often enough—made it all a moot point.

Obey or die, after all, is not hard to understand.

Abbu returned the next day, with his Arab scouts.

"Ashot stayed behind, with the Rajputs," he explained tersely. "Just keep out of the sun and don't move any more than you must. They'll be here tomorrow. Thousands of camels, carrying enough water to fill a lake. We won't even lose the horses."

Belisarius laughed. "What an ignominious ending to my dramatic gesture!"

Now that salvation was at hand, Abbu's normally pessimistic temperament returned.

"Do not be so sure, General! Rajputs are cunning beasts. It may be a trap. The water, poisoned."

That made Belisarius laugh again. "Seven thousand Rajputs need poisoned water to kill five hundred Romans?"

"You have a reputation," Abbu insisted.

Chapter 31

THE PUNJAB,
NORTH OF THE IRON TRIANGLE

"This is the craziest thing I've ever seen," muttered Maurice. "Even for Persians."

Menander shook his head. Not because he disagreed, but simply in . . .

Disbelief?

No, not that. Sitting on his horse on a small knoll with a good view of the battlefield, Menander could *see* the insane charge that Emperor Khusrau had ordered against the Malwa line.

He could also see the fortifications of that line itself, and the guns that were spewing forth destruction. He didn't even want to think about the carnage that must be happening in front of them.

He could remember a time in his life when he would have thought that furious charge might carry the day. However insane it was, no one could doubt the courage and the tenacity of the thousands of Persian heavy cavalrymen who were hurling themselves and their armored horses against the Malwa. But, even though he was still a young man, Menander had now seen enough of gunpowder warfare to know that the Persian effort was hopeless. If the Malwa had been low on ammunition, things might have been different. But the fortifications they'd erected on the west bank of the Indus to guard their flank against just such an attack could be easily resupplied by barges crossing the river. In fact, he could see two such barges being rowed across the Indus right now.

Against demoralized troops already half-ready to surrender or flee, the charge might have worked. It wouldn't work here. The morale of the Malwa army had suffered a great deal, to be sure, from their defeats over the past two years. But they were still the largest and most powerful army in the world, and their soldiers knew it.

They knew something else, too. They knew that trying to surrender to—or flee from—an assault like the Persians had launched, was impossible anyway. If they broke, they'd just get butchered.

It didn't help any, of course, that the Persians were shouting the battle cry of *Charax!* as they charged. Whether because their emperor had ordered it or because of their own fury, Menander didn't know. But he knew—and so did the Malwa soldiers manning the fortresses—that the Persians might as well have been using the battle cry of *No Quarter.*

"Let's go, lad," said Maurice quietly. "We made an appearance as observers, since Khusrau invited us. But now that the diplomacy's done, staying any longer is just pointless. This isn't really a battle, in the first place. It's just an emperor ridding himself of troublesome noblemen."

He turned his horse and began trotting away. Menander followed.

"You think?" asked Menander.

"You've met Khusrau. Did he strike you as being as dumb as an ox?"

Menander couldn't help but smile, a little. "No. Not in the least."

"Right." Maurice jerked a thumb over his shoulder. "Not even an ox would be dumb enough to think that charge might succeed."

Maurice was slandering the Persian emperor, actually. It was true that breaking the power of the sahrdaran and vurzurgan families was part of the reason Khusrau had ordered the charge. But it wasn't the only reason. It wasn't even the most important reason.

There would be no way to eliminate the great families simply through one battle, after all. Not all of their men had come to India, even leaving aside the Suren, and not all of them would die before the walls of the Malwa.

Not even most of them, in fact. Khusrau was no stranger to war, and knew perfectly well that no battle results in casualties worse than perhaps one-quarter of the men engaged, unless they get trapped, and many of those would recover from their wounds. It was amazing, really, how many men survived what, from a distance, looked like a sheer bloodbath.

There was no chance of a trap here, nor of enemy pursuit once the Persian cavalrymen finally retreated. Many sahrdaran and vurz-urgan would die this day, to be sure. But most of them wouldn't. He'd bleed the great families, but he wouldn't do more than weaken them some.

So, the emperor hadn't even stayed to watch, once he ordered the assault. Quietly, almost surreptitiously—and far enough from the Malwa lines not to be observed—he'd slipped away from his camp with two thousand of his best imperial cavalry.

Light cavalry. Over half of them Arabs, in fact.

He'd be gone for several days. Khusrau didn't believe in cavalry charges against heavy fortifications any more than Maurice did. But since he came from a nation that had always been a cavalry power, he'd given much thought to the proper uses of cavalry in the new era of gunpowder.

Assaults against fortresses were pointless. Raids against a specific target, were not.

Two days later, he was vindicated.

"You see?" he demanded.

Next to him, also sitting on a horse carefully screened from the river by high reeds, the chief of the emperor's personal cavalry smiled.

"You were right, Your Majesty. As always."

"Ha! Coming from you!"

Almost gloating, the emperor looked back to the target of the raid. One of the two ironclads had its engines steaming, but it was still tied to the dock like the other. From the casual manner of the sailors and soldiers moving about on the docks, Khusrau thought the engines were running simply as part of routine care. What the Roman naval expert Menander called "maintenance." Khusrau didn't know much about the newfangled warships, but he knew they needed a lot of it. The things were cantankerous.

"No point in trying to capture them," he said, regretfully.

The Persians had no one who could operate the things. Even the Roman experts would need time to figure out the different mechanisms—and time was not going to be available. Khusrau was quite sure his two thousand cavalrymen could break through the small garrison protecting the Malwa naval base and burn the ships before reinforcements could arrive. But it would have to be done very quickly, if they were to survive themselves. They'd had to cross a ford to get to this side of the Indus, far upstream from the battlefield—upstream from the naval base, in fact—and they'd have to cross the same ford to make their escape.

With his superb light cavalry, the emperor thought they could do it. But not if they dawdled, trying to make complex foreign equipment work.

And why bother? These were the only two ironclads the Malwa had built on the Indus. Once they were destroyed, the Malwa had no way—no quick and easy way, at least—to bring their ironclads from the other rivers. All of the rivers in the Punjab connected to the Indus eventually—but only at the Iron Triangle.

Which was held by the Romans. Who had an ironclad of their own. Which they had not dared to use because of these two iron-clads. Which would shortly no longer exist.

"Do it," the emperor commanded.

He did not participate personally in the charge and the battle that followed. He was brave enough, certainly, but doing so was unnecessary—would even be even foolish. Persians did not expect their emperors to be warriors also.

What they *did* expect was that their emperors would present them with victories.

The ironclads burned very nicely. Khusrau had worried, a bit, that they might not. But the Malwa built them the same way the Romans did, just as Menander and Justinian had said they would. An iron shell over a wooden hull.

Burned very nicely, indeed.

Almost as nicely as the emperor's victory would burn in the hearts of his soldiers, after he returned to his camp. Where the sahrdaran and vurzurgan who had *insisted* on that insane assault—the emperor himself had been doubtful, and made sure everyone knew it—would be low-spirited and shamefaced.

As well they should be.

◇   ◇   ◇

"I don't care if those sorry bastards up north are getting hammered by the Kushans!" General Samudra shouted at the mahaveda priest. Angrily, he pointed a finger to the west. "I've got Persians hammering on me right here! They just destroyed our ironclads on the Indus!"

The priest's face was stiff. He was one of several such whom Great Lady Sati had left behind to keep an eye on the military leadership. Without, however, giving them the authority to actually override any military decisions made by Samudra.

From the priests' point of view, that was unfortunate. From Samudra's point of view, it was a blessing. What priests knew about warfare could be inscribed on the world's smallest tablet.

"Absolutely not!" he continued, lowering his voice a little but speaking every bit as firmly. "I've already sent couriers with orders to the expedition I sent in relief to turn back. We need them here."

The priest wasn't going to give up that easily. "The Kushans are out of the Margalla Pass, now!"

"So what?" sneered Samudra. "Fifteen thousand Kushans—twenty at most, and don't believe that nonsense about fifty thousand—can't do anything to threaten us here. Sixty—maybe seventy—thousand Romans and Persians *can.*"

"They can threaten Great Lady Sati!"

For a moment, that caused Samudra to pause. But only for a moment, before the sneer was back.

"Don't meddle in affairs that you know nothing about, priest. If you think the Kushans are going to leave their kingdom unprotected while they hare off trying to intercept the Great Lady—"

He shook his head, the way a man does upon hearing an absurd theory or proposition. "Ridiculous. Besides, by now she'll have reached the headwaters of the Sutlej. That's a hundred miles from the Margalla Pass. It would take an army of twenty thousand men—assuming they have that many to begin with—a week and a half to cover the distance."

He cleared his throat sententiously. "Had you any experience in these matters, you would understand that a large army cannot travel faster than ten miles a day."

He hoped the words didn't ring as false to the priest as they did to him, the moment he said them. That ten mile a day average was . . .

An average. No more, no less. It did not apply to *every* army. Samudra had had Kushan forces under his command, in times past, and knew that a well-trained and well-led Kushan army could march two or three times faster than that—even while fighting small battles and skirmishes along the way.

Still . . .

"By the time they got to the headwaters of the Sutlej—assuming they were foolish enough to make the attempt in the first place—Great Lady Sati's forces will have already reached the headwaters of the Ganges. It's conceivable, I suppose, that the Kushans might be mad enough to venture so far into the northern Punjab, but no enemy force—not that size!—will be lunatic enough to enter the Ganges plain. The garrison at Mathura alone has forty thousand men!"

The priest stared at him from under lowered brows. Clearly enough, he was not persuaded by Samudra's arguments. But, just as clearly, he did not have the military knowledge to pick apart the logic. So, after a moment, he turned and walked away stiffly.

Samudra, however, did have the knowledge. And, now that he thought upon the matter more fully, be was becoming more uneasy by the minute.

The northern Punjab had not been ravaged much by the war, and it was the most fertile portion of the Punjab because it got more rain during the monsoon season than the rest of the province. If the Kushans were willing to abandon their logistics train and cut across the area relying on forage, they could cover possibly thirty miles a day. Twenty, for a surety.

The terrain was good, too. Excellent, from the standpoint of a marching army. From Peshawar ran the ancient trade route known as the Uttar Path or North Way, which crossed into the Ganges plain and ran all the way to the Bay of Bengal on the other side of the subcontinent. That was the same route that Great Lady Sati herself planned to take in her return to Kausambi, once she reached it by following the Sutlej.

By now, Samudra was staring to the north, not really seeing anything except in his mind. A fast-moving Kushan army, unrestrained by a logistics train, marching down the Uttar Path from the Margalla hills with no army in their way any longer . . .

They *could* intercept Great Lady Sati.

Possibly. It depended on how fast her own march had been. But Samudra knew full well that with the size of the army she'd taken with her, mostly infantry and with elephant-borne chaundoli, she wouldn't be moving all that quickly.

He opened his mouth, about to issue orders—that army coming back would curse him, for sending them north yet again, but better the curses of soldiers—far better—than—

A horrific chain of explosions shattered his purpose.

Gaping, Samudra spun around, now facing south by southwest.

"What happened?" The chain of explosions was continuing. As loud as it was, it seemed strangely muffled. Samudra detected what might be . . .

Fountains, in the distance?

One of his aides coughed. "General, I think the Romans are blowing up their mine field in the river."

"That's ridiculous! Our ironclads—"

He broke off so suddenly the last word ended in a choke.

"They're only blowing the mine field in the Indus," the same officer continued, his tone apologetic. "Not the one in the Chenab."

The Malwa had no ironclads left in the Indus. The Persians had destroyed them. There was nothing to stop the Roman warships from sallying up the river, firing at troops who had no way to shoot back except with small arms and light cannon. Great Lady Sati had dismantled the heavy batteries that had once been positioned along the east bank of the Indus, once the ironclads came into service, in order to move them across the river as a shield against a possible Roman flank attack.

They could be turned around to face the river, but that would take at least a full day—and Samudra was quite sure the Romans or Persians or both would be attacking those forts again as soon as the Roman ironclad got up there and started firing on them.

Perhaps the heavy batteries at Multan could be brought down . . .

His earlier intentions completely forgotten, Samudra began issuing a blizzard of new orders.

"Let's hope this works," Menander muttered to himself, as the *Justinian* steamed at full speed up the river. "If the engine breaks down . . ."

He eyed the engine house warily. The damn gadget was more reliable than it had been when the former emperor after whom the ironclad had been named designed it, but it was still very far from being what anyone in his right mind would call "dependable."

Not for the first time, Menander contemplated ruefully the odd twists of fate that had wound up putting him in charge of the Roman army's brown-water naval forces, instead of becoming a simple cataphract liked he'd planned to be.

When he said as much to his second-in-command, the newly promoted former Puckle gunner, Leo Constantes laughed.

"*Today?* Be glad you're not a cataphract—or you'd be taking part in the crazy charge Sittas is leading."

Menander winced. "Point."

Sittas himself was downright gleeful. He'd been frustrated for months, ever since the battle on the north lines of the Iron Triangle had settled down into a siege. There was really no place for heavy cavalry in such a fight, except to stay in reserve in the unlikely event of a Malwa breakthrough. Now, finally—!

He was tempted to step up the pace, but managed to resist with no huge difficulty. Sittas was too experienced a horseman not to know that if he arrived with blown horses at the Malwa fortifications that had driven back the Persians a few days before, he might as well not have come at all.

Besides, they were nearing the Persian lines. Sittas didn't like Persians, and never had. No Roman he knew did except Belisarius—who was hopelessly eccentric—and those who had married Persian women, who at least had a reasonable excuse. Not even Sittas would deny that Persian women were attractive.

The men, on the other hand—*pah!*

"Look smart, lads!" he bellowed over his shoulder. "A fancy trot, now! Let's rub salt into their wounds!"

The Persian sahrdaran and vurzurgan glared at the Roman cavalrymen the whole way through their camp. The dehgans who fell in behind Sittas' cavalry, on the other hand, seemed more philosophical about the matter. Or perhaps they were simply more sanguine. This time it would be Romans leading the charge against those damn Malwa guns. It remained to be seen how cocky they'd still be in a few hours.

◇   ◇   ◇

"All right," Maurice said to his top officers, gathered in the command bunker. "Remember: make the sallies as threatening as you can, *without* suffering heavy casualties. We've got no more chance of storming the Malwa lines facing us here than they have of storming the Iron Triangle. All we've got to do is pin them, so Samudra can't pull out troops to reinforce his right flank. Any questions?"

"What if *they* make a sally?" one of the officers asked. "If they break through anywhere, we don't have Sittas and his thousands of cavalrymen to drive them back."

Maurice shrugged. "We'll scramble, that's all."

When the *Justinian* came in sight of the Malwa fortifications on the west bank, Menander let out a whoop of exultation. The Punjabi peasants who'd managed to escape the labor gangs and desert to the Romans had told them that the Malwa hadn't positioned any guns on the river side of the fortifications. What they hadn't said—or hadn't been asked—was that they'd also never bothered to put up walls sheltering the guns from the river, either. Why bother, when they had the ironclads?

The gun ramps and platforms were completely exposed. The thousands of Malwa gunners and riflemen manning the lines would have no shelter at all from the *Justinian*.

"Load case shot!" he bellowed.

As his gun crews went about the labor, his eyes scanned the east bank of the river. There were some Malwa fortifications there also, but nothing substantial. What was more important was that he couldn't see any sign of big guns. A few small pieces, here and there, but the *Victrix* could handle those well enough. The fireship wasn't an ironclad, but her thick wooden walls should be able to handle anything the Malwa had on the spot. And by the time they could bring up heavy artillery, the *Victrix* would have done her job and gotten back downriver and out of range.

And quite a job it would be, too. Menander contemplated the mass of barges tied up to the wharves. There were only two crossing the river. The rest . . .

"You're kindling, boys," he gloated. "I'd recommend you get ashore quickly."

He turned to the signalman. "Tell the *Victrix* to come up."

A few seconds later, the signal flags having done their work, he saw heavy steam pouring out of the *Victrix*'s funnel. She'd be here very shortly.

But he had his own work to do. By now, the *Justinian* was just coming abreast of the first fortress. There was something almost comical about the way the Malwa soldiers were frantically trying to move the big guns facing landward and get them turned around.

It was a pointless effort, of course. But what else were they to do, except gape in consternation? The handguns and small artillery they had would just bounce off the Roman ironclad.

They wouldn't bounce off Menander, on the other hand. Constantes and the signalman had already retreated into the pilot's armored turret. Hurriedly, Menander followed them.

Once inside, he leaned over the speaking tube.

"Let 'em have it, boys."

Sittas waited until the *Justinian* had steamed completely past the fortifications, shelling them as it went.

"Now!" he bellowed, and sent his horse into the charge. Six thousand Roman cataphracts came after him—and after them, over twice that number of Persian dehgans.

"Back again," Menander commanded. The *Justinian* had finished its turn. That was always a slow and delicate business, in the relatively narrow confines of the river. He'd had to be more careful than usual, too, since he didn't have good charts of this stretch of the Indus.

But the work was done, and the enemy was about to get savaged again. They were still as defenseless as ever. More so, actually, since he could see they were starting to panic.

And well they might. By now, close to twenty thousand heavy cavalrymen would be thundering at them. If they'd still had their big guns intact, they could have sneered at that charge, as they'd done a few days earlier.

Now . . .

None of the guns had been dismounted, true enough, since Menander hadn't used anything heavier than case shot. Nor would he again, since the plan was to capture the guns intact. But he'd inflicted heavy casualties on the crews and ammunition carriers, and even managed to blow up one of the smaller ammunition dumps that had been overly exposed. They'd be in no shape to resist the kind of charge Sittas would press, all the more so since they'd have to do so with Menander firing on them again from their rear.

The barges across the river were making a nice conflagration, too. And—wonder of wonders—the wind was blowing the smoke away from the river. Menander had worried that if the smoke blew the other way he might find himself blinded.

"It's a miracle, lads," he said cheerfully to the other men in the turret. "The one and only time in my life I've seen a military operation work exactly according to plan."

The engine coughed. The *Justinian* lurched.

Coughed again. Coughed again.

Silence. The *Justinian* glided gently downriver with the current, its engine dead.

"Idiot!" Menander hissed at himself. "You had to go and say it!"

Sighing, he studied the riverbank for a moment. "Can you keep her steady in midriver?"

"Yes, sir," replied the pilot.

"All right, then." He leaned over the speaking tube again. "Relax, boys. All that happens until the engineers get the engines running again is just that we have more time to aim. Let 'em have it."

The fighting that afternoon at the front lines was brutal, but the casualties never got bad enough for Maurice to start worrying. And the Malwa never tried any sallies at all.

Samudra was too preoccupied to order any. All his attention was concentrated on the desperate effort to get reinforcements to the Indus in time to keep the Romans and Persians from crossing. It was bad enough that he'd lost the forts on the opposite bank. It wouldn't take the enemy long to turn the guns around and built new berms to shelter them. The Persians and Romans were already working like bees to get it done. As it was, he'd henceforth be pressed on his western flank as well as the southern front. But let them get a toehold on *his* side of the river . . .

Samudra managed to stave off that disaster. But it took two days to do so.

It wasn't until the morning of the third day that he remembered the Kushans at Margalla Pass. By which time it was too late to do anything.

Chapter 32

NEAR MAYAPUR, ON THE GANGES

"It's them, Great King," said the Pathan scout, pointing to the east. "Must be. No general—not even a Malwa—would be leading a large army from a chaundoli."

"How close are they to the Ganges?"

"For us, Great King, a day's march. For them, two. By mid-afternoon on the day after tomorrow, they will have reached Maya-pur. They will need to wait until the next day to ford the river. The Ganges is still quick-moving, just coming out of the Silawik hills and the rapids. They would be foolish—very foolish—to cross it after sundown."

"Unless they were forced to . . . " Kungas mused. "Do you know if there's high ground nearby?"

"Yes, Great King. I have been to the shrines at Mayapur, to see the Footstep of God."

Kungas was not surprised. The Pathans were not Hindus, but like tribesmen in many places they were as likely to adopt the gods of other people as their own. Mayapur—also known as Gangadwara—was an ancient religious site, which had drawn pilgrims for centu-ries. It was said that Vishnu had left his footprint there, at the exact spot where the holy Ganges left the mountains.

The Pathan's hands moved surely in the air, sketching the topog-raphy. "Here, below, is the Ganges. Here—not far—there is a ridge. Very steep. There is a temple on the crest. I have been to it."

"Is the river within mortar range of the ridge?"

"Yes. The big mortars, anyway. And the flatland by the river is wide enough to hold the whole Malwa army, while they wait to cross." The Pathan grinned fiercely. "They will be relaxed and happy, now that they are finally out of the hills and entering the plain. You will slaughter them like lambs, Great King."

As he studied the distant hills, Kungas pondered the man's use of the title *Great King*. That was no title that Kungas himself had adopted or decreed, and this scout was not the first Pathan whom Kungas had heard use the expression. From what he could tell, in fact, it seemed to have become—or was becoming, at least—the generally accepted term for him among the tribesmen.

Great King.

There were subtleties in that phrase, if you knew—as Kungas did—the ways of thought of the mountain folk. People from lands accustomed to kings and emperors would think nothing of it. "Great" was simply one of many adjectives routinely attached to such rulers. A rather modest one, in fact, compared to the "divine" appellation of Indian tradition. Even the relatively egalitarian Axumites, when they indulged themselves in formal oratory, plastered such labels as "He Who Brought The Dawn" onto their monarchs.

Something else was involved here. *Great* king—where the Kushans themselves simply called him "king." The title added a certain necessary distance, for the Pathans. Kungas was not *their* king. Not the authority to whom they directly answered, who were their own clan leaders. But they would acknowledge that he was the overlord of the region, and would serve him in that capacity.

Good enough, certainly for the moment.

Kujulo was frowning slightly, looking at the Pathan. "Are you sure—"

Kungas waved his hand. "If a Pathan scout says it's Great Lady Sati, it's Great Lady Sati."

The man looked very pleased. Kungas' following question, however, had him frowning also.

"How large is her army?"

The Pathan's hands moved again, but no longer surely, as if groping a little. "Hard to say, Great King. Very large army. Many hundreds of hundreds."

Kungas left off further questioning. The Pathan was not only illiterate, but had a concept of arithmetic that faded away somewhere into the distance after the number "one hundred." Even that number was a borrowed Greek term. And, although the man was an experienced warrior, he was the veteran of mountain fights. Feuds between clans, clashes with expeditions from the lowlands—none of them involving forces on the scale of battles between civilized nations. Any estimate he gave of the size of Sati's army would be meaningless.

He nodded, dismissing the scout, and turned to Kujulo. "We'll need some of our own soldiers to do a reasonably accurate count. Send off a party guided by the scout."

"And in the meantime? Continue the march?"

"No. As hard as we've pressed them the past few days, the men need a rest." He glanced at the sky, gauging the sun. "I'll want a long march tomorrow, though, and it'll be a hard one, followed by a night march after a few hours rest. I want to be at that ridge before Sati can cross the river."

Kujulo started to move off. Kungas called him back.

"One other thing. By now, the bitch will be suspicious because we've cut the telegraph lines. Take three thousand men and march immediately. Stay to the south. She'll send back a scouting expedition. Three thousand should be enough to drive them off—but make sure you draw their attention to the *south*."

Kujulo nodded. "While you march by night and slip past them to the north."

"Yes. If it works, we'll come onto the ridge opposite the river. They won't know we're there until they start crossing."

Kujulo's grin was every bit as savage as the Pathan's. "A big army—tens of thousands of soldiers—in the middle of a river crossing. Like catching an enemy while he's shitting. Good thing you made us wait to get more ammunition for the mortars, before we left Margalla Pass."

"We only lost a day, thanks to Irene's efficiency, and I knew we'd make it up in the march."

"True. Best quartermaster I ever saw, she is. Stupid Pathans. If they had any brains, they'd know it was just plain and simple 'king'—but with a very great queen."

He hurried off, then, leaving Kungas behind to ponder the question of whether or not he'd just seen his royal self deeply insulted.

Being an eminently sane and rational man who'd begun life as a simple soldier, it took him no more than a second to dismiss the silly notion. But he knew his grandson—great-grandson, for sure—would think otherwise. There were perils to claiming Alexander and Siddhartha Gautama as the ancestors of a dynasty. It tended to produce a steep and rapid decline in the intelligence of the dynasty's succeeding generations.

But that was a problem for a later decade. In the coming few days, Kungas would be quite satisfied if he could tear the flanks of the army escorting Malwa's overlord to what he thought was its final battle.

He probably couldn't manage to destroy the monster itself, unfortunately. But if Kungas was right, Belisarius was waiting to pounce on the creature somewhere down the Ganges. He'd kill the monster, if it was already bleeding.

"Another splendid speech," said Jaimal approvingly.

Next to him, Udai Singh nodded. "I knew—I remembered—that your Hindi was excellent. But I didn't know you were an orator, as well."

Belisarius glanced at the men riding beside him. Over the days of hard marches since they'd left Ajmer, a subtle change had come in the way Jaimal acted toward the Roman general. Udai Singh, also.

In the beginning, they'd both been stiffly proper. Their new emperor and Rana Sanga had ordered them to place the Rajputs under Belisarius' command, and they had done so dutifully and energetically. But it had been clear enough that some hostility lurked beneath the polite surface.

Belisarius had wondered about that. He'd found it surprising. True, they'd been enemies until very recently. But the clashes between Belisarius' army and Damodara's had been gallant affairs, certainly by the standards of the Malwa war. He hadn't thought there'd be any real grudges left, now that they were allied. There'd certainly been no indication of personal animosity from either Damodara himself or Rana Sanga, when Belisarius met them for a parlay in the midst of their campaign in Persia.

Now that the harsh pace the Roman general had set his Rajput army had brought them to the Yamuna thirty miles north of Mathura the hostility seemed to have vanished. Belisarius had led an army of twenty thousand men on a march of well over two hundred miles in nine days—something Rajputs would boast about for generations. But he didn't think it was that feat alone that accounted for the change, much less the inspiring speeches he'd given along the way. Jaimal and Udai Singh were both well educated. Their praise of his rhetoric had the flavor of aesthetes, not soldiers.

The march had been ruthless as well as harsh. Ruthless toward everyone. Lamed horses were left behind, injured men were left behind—and the fields they passed through plundered and stripped of anything edible to either man or horse. The villages too, since at this time of year most of the foodstuffs were stored.

There had been no atrocities, as such, committed upon the peasantry. But that hardly mattered. Those poor folk lived close to the edge of existence. Stripped of the stored foodstuffs they depended upon until the next harvest, many of them would die. If not of starvation in their little villages, of disease and exposure after they desperately took to the roads to find refuge elsewhere.

If the war was won quickly, Belisarius would urge Damodara to send relief to the area. But there was no way to know if that would ever happen. Despite that uncertainty, Belisarius had ordered it done. In a life that had seen many cruel acts, including the slaughter of the Nika revolt, he thought this was perhaps the cruelest thing he'd ever done.

And . . . Jaimal and Udai Singh's veiled anger had faded with each day they witnessed it.

He thought he understood, finally. The two were among Rana Sanga's closest aides. They would surely have been with Sanga when he pursued Belisarius across India after his escape from Kausambi.

Three years ago, that had been.

"So," he said to them, "have you finally forgiven me for the butchered couriers?"

Both Rajputs seemed to flush. After a moment, Jaimal said softly: "Yes, General. I thought at the time it was just savagery."

"It *was* savagery," said Belisarius. "The couriers—even more, the soldiers at the station—were just common folk. Boys, two of them. I remember. The memory plagues me, still, especially when I see children."

He swept his head in a little half-circle. "Complete innocents. No different, really, than the peasants I have been condemning to death these past days. I did it then, I do it now, and whatever my regrets I will make no apologies. Even less today, than I would have then. Because today—"

He drew his sword and pointed forward with it, in a gesture that did not seem histrionic at all. Neither to him nor to the two men he rode beside.

"Three years ago, I behaved like a beast to escape a monster. Today—finally—I do so to kill the thing."

Both Jaimal and Udai Singh tightened their jaws. Not in anger, but simply in determination.

"Here, do you think?" asked Jaimal. "Or on the Ganges?"

"Somewhere between here and the Ganges, most likely. The monster would not have crossed to the headwaters of the Yamuna, I don't think. With the Rajputs beginning to revolt, there'd have been too much risk. Better to take the longer but surer northerly route and cross to the Footstep of God. But once into the great plain, it'll want the garrison at Mathura for reinforcements before it goes on to meet Damodara at Kausambi."

That brought some good cheer. All three turned in the saddle and looked behind them. There was nothing to see except an ocean of horsemen and dust, of course.

"Mathura," gloated Udai Singh. "Which is *behind* us. The Malwa beast will have to face us with what it has."

"It was a great march, General Belisarius," added Jaimal.

So it had been. Great enough, even, to wash away great sins.

"It is unseemly for a woman to lead warriors!" That came from one of the five Pathan chiefs sitting across from Irene in the throne room and glaring at her. He was the oldest, she thought. It was hard to know. They all looked liked ancient prunes to her, dried too long in the sun.

"Unthinkable!" she agreed. The vigorous headshake that followed caused her veil to ripple in reverse synchrony to her ponytail. "The thought is impossible to even contemplate. No, no. I was thinking that *you* should lead the armies when they march out. You and the rest of the clan chiefs."

The five chiefs continued to glare at her.

First, because they suspected her of mockery. "Armies" was a ridiculous term—even to them—to apply to separate columns of Pathan horsemen, not one of which would number more than six or seven hundred men. Clan rivalries and disputes made it difficult for Pathans to combine their forces closely.

Second, because she'd boxed them, and they knew it. The young clansmen were becoming more boisterous and insistent with every passing day. Lately, even disrespectful.

Their Great King—another term to cause old chiefs to scowl—was adding to his glory and where were the Pathan warriors?

Were they to hide in their villages?

It would not be long, the five old chiefs knew, before the ultimate insult was spoken aloud.

Old women! Our chiefs—so-called—are nothing but old women!

"We have no mortars," grumbled one of the chiefs. "How are we to fight Malwa armies without mortars?"

"Of course you do," Irene disagreed, in a cheerful tone of voice. "The new mortars of the Pathans have become famous."

That wasn't . . . exactly true. They were indeed famous, in a way, simply because the Kushans were astonished that illiterate and ignorant Pathans had managed to built mortars at all. But no Kushan soldier in his right mind would trust one enough to fire the thing.

Irene found it rather amazing. When it came to anything else, Pathans were as hostile to innovation as so many cats would be to the suggestion they adopt vegetarianism. But show them a new weapon—one that was effective, anyway—and within a very short time they would be modeling their own after it. Much more effectively than she'd ever imagined such a primitive folk could do.

Before the old chiefs could take further umbrage, she added: "What you lack is *ammunition*. Which I can supply you."

Boxed again. The glares darkened.

"Oh, yes, lots of ammunition." She pointed her finger out the palace window, toward the new arsenal. "It's made over there. By old women. Many old women."

Boxed again.

After they stalked out of the palace, Irene summoned her aides. "Send a telegraph message to the station at Margalla Pass. Tell them to send couriers after Kungas."

"Yes, Your Majesty. And the message to be taken to the king?"

By now, Irene had taken off her veil. The smile thus displayed was a gleaming thing. "Tell the king that I have persuaded the

Pathans to provide us with troops to help guard the passes. They say ten thousand, but let's figure seven. Two thousand will go to Margalla Pass, the rest to Kohat Pass. If there's any threat, it's more likely to come from the south."

One of the aides frowned. "They won't stay in the passes, Your Majesty. They'll set off to raid the lowlands."

"Of course they will. Better yet. We'll have a screen all over the northern Punjab of thousands of cavalrymen, who'll warn us of any large approaching enemy force. They'll scamper back to the passes when we need them, rather than face Malwa regulars in the open. Pathans are ignorant beyond belief, but they're not actually stupid. Not when it comes to war, anyway."

She leaned back in her chair, basking in self-admiration. Not so much because she'd just relieved her husband of a great worry, but simply because—once again—she'd outfoxed clan chiefs.

"Tell the king he needn't worry about guarding his kingdom. With Pathan reinforcements, I can hold the passes against any Malwa army likely to be sent against us. He's free to do whatever his judgment dictates is the best course."

She detested those old men. Absolutely, completely, thoroughly, utterly detested them.

"Ha!" she barked. "If they'd sent their old women to negotiate, I'd have been lost!"

Emperor Skandagupta goggled at the telegraph message in his hand.

"Mathura? *Mathura?* How did an enemy army get to Mathura?"

The senior of the three generals facing him swallowed. His life and those of his two subordinates hung by a thread. As each week had passed since the beginning of Damodara's rebellion, the emperor's fury had become more savage. By now, there were over seven hundred heads or corpses impaled on the palace walls.

Still, he didn't dare lie. "We're not sure, Your Majesty. Some of the reports we've gotten describe them as Rajputs."

Skandagupta crumbled the message and hurled it to the floor. "Why would Rajput rebels be moving *north* of Mathura? You idiot! If they came from Rajputana, they'd be trying to join up with Damodara."

He pursed his lips and spit on the general. "Who has still not been stopped by my supposedly mighty armies! You don't even know where he is, any longer!"

"Still far south of the Yamuna, surely," said the general, in as soothing a tone as he could manage. "A large army cannot move quickly, as you know. From your own great military experience."

In point of fact, Skandagupta had no military experience at all, beyond sitting in a huge pavilion and watching his armies reduce rebel cities. But he seemed slightly mollified by the compliment.

"True," he grunted. "Still . . . why have the reports been so spotty?"

The general didn't dare give an honest answer. *Because most of the garrisons—and telegraph operators—flee before Damodara arrives at their towns and forts.*

Instead, he simply shook his head sagely. "War is very chaotic, Your Majesty. As you know from your own experience. Once the fighting starts, information always becomes spotty."

Skandagupta grunted again. Then, pointed to the crumpled message. "Give me that."

One of the slaves attending him hastened to obey. After reopening the message and studying it for a moment, Skandagupta snarled.

The general and his two subordinates struggled not to sigh with relief. The snarl was familiar. Someone was about to die—but it wouldn't be them.

"Send a telegraph message to the governor at Mathura. The commander of the garrison is to be executed. The sheer incompetence of the man! If not—who knows?—treachery. Why didn't he march out at once in pursuit of the enemy?"

As one man, the generals decided to take that as a rhetorical question. To do otherwise would have been mortal folly. *Because you ordered all garrisons to stay at their post no matter what, Your Majesty . . .*

Would not be a wise thing to say to Skandagupta in a rage.

"Whichever officer replaces him in command is ordered to lead an expedition out of Mathura—immediately and with the utmost haste—to deal with this new enemy. Whoever it is."

"How many men from the garrison should he take, Your Majesty?"

Skandagupta slapped the throne's armrest. "Do I need to decide *everything*? As many as he thinks necessary—but not fewer than thirty thousand! Do you understand? I want this new threat crushed!

That would strip the garrison of three-fourths of its soldiers. More than that, really, since the new commander was sure to take all his best troops with him. His best cavalry and foot soldiers, at least. The experienced artillerymen would remain behind, since there would be no way to haul great guns up the roads by the Yamuna without making the phrase *immediately and with the utmost haste* a meaningless term. But artillerymen alone could not possibly defend a city as large as Mathura.

None of the generals was about to say that to the emperor, however. As many heads and bodies as there were perched on the palace walls, there were twice as many still-bare stakes waiting. Skandagupta had ordered the walls festooned with the things.

"Yes, Your Majesty."

Damodara and his army reached the Yamuna forty miles downstream of Mathura. They were met there by a small contingent of Ye-tai deserters from the garrison, who'd decided that the phrase *Toramana's Ye-tai* were words of wisdom.

"Yes, Lord—ah, Your Majesty," said the captain in command of the contingent. "Lord Shankara—he's the new garrison commander—led most of the troops out of the city three days ago. They're headed north, after another army that's invading—ah, rebelling—ah, rightfully resisting—"

Damodara waved the man's fumbling words aside. "Enough, enough. How many did he leave behind?"

"Not more than eight thousand, Your Majesty."

One of the other Ye-tai, emboldened by Damodara's relaxed demeanor, added: "Most of them are piss-poor troops, Your Majesty. Except the artillerymen."

Damodara turned his head and grinned at Rana Sanga. "See? You doubted me! I *told* you I'd find siege guns—somewhere—and the troops to man them."

He swiveled his head back, bringing the grin to bear on the Ye-tai. "They'll be cooperative, yes?"

The Ye-tai captain gave one of his men a meaningful glance. That worthy cleared his throat and announced:

"My cousin commands one of the batteries. I'll show you the gate it protects."

"They'll cooperate," growled his captain.

Damodara now bestowed the grin on Toramana. "I think these men will fit nicely in your personal regiment, don't you?"

"Oh, yes," agreed Toramana. "But I'm thinking I'll need to form another, before too long."

Chapter 33

MAYAPUR

Kungas waited until the lead elements of Great Lady Sati's army had crossed the river and her chaundoli was just reaching the opposite bank of the Ganges. He'd had to struggle mightily with himself not to give the order to open fire when there was still a chance to catch Sati herself.

But that would have been stupid. The river was within reach of the big mortars, but the range was too great for any accuracy. They'd likely have missed Sati's chaundoli altogether—while leaving her close enough to the main body of her army to rejoin it and provide her soldiers with sure and decisive leadership.

"Open fire!"

The whole ridge above Mayapur erupted with mortar fire.

This way, the Malwa army would be almost as effectively decapitated as if they'd killed the bitch herself. She'd be stranded on the opposite bank of the river with her own bodyguard and the advance contingents, while the bulk of her army would be caught on this side.

As Kungas had commanded, the mortar shells began landing, most of them in the river itself. The Ganges was too deep to be forded here, this early in *garam*, except by using guideropes. The soldiers in mid-crossing were moving very slowly and painstakingly. They had not even the minimal protection of being able to evade

777

the incoming shells. They were caught as helplessly as penned sheep.

Explosions churned the river. A river which, within seconds, was streaked with red blood.

Kungas waited until the mortars had fired two more volleys.

"The near bank, now! Big mortars only!"

He didn't have *that* much ammunition. Even to the near bank, the range was chancy for the small mortars. He wanted to save their ammunition for the charge that would soon be coming.

Clumps of the soldiers packed on the near bank waiting their turn to ford the river were hurled aside by exploding mortar rounds. The casualties as such were fairly light. But, as Kungas had expected, the soldiers were already showing signs of panic. Being caught in the open as they were, by an attack that came as a complete surprise, was unnerving.

He held his breath. This was the critical moment. If that Malwa army had the sort of officers trained by such generals as Belisarius, Damodara, or Rao—or Kungas himself—he was in real trouble. They'd organize an immediate counterattack, leading columns of men up the ridge. Kungas was confident that he'd be able to fend off such a counterattack long enough to make a successful retreat. But he'd suffer heavy casualties, and this whole risky gamble would have been for nothing.

After a few seconds, he let out the breath. Thereafter, he continued to breathe slowly and deeply, but the tension was gone.

The Malwa officers, instead, were reacting as he had gambled they would. Surely, yes; decisively, yes—but also defensively. They were simply trying to squelch the panic and force the men back into their ranks and lines.

Which, they did. Which, of course, simply made them better targets.

"Idiots," hissed the king's second-in-command, standing next to him atop the ridge.

Kungas shook his head. "Not fair, Vima. Simply officers who've spent too much time in much too close proximity to a superhuman monster. Too many years of rigidity, too many years of expecting perfect orders from above."

The next few minutes were just slaughter. Even the very first rounds had struck accurately, most of them. Kushans were hill-fighters and had adopted the new mortars with something approaching religious fervor. Where other men might see in a Coehorn mortar nothing but an ugly assemblage of angular metal, Kushans lavished the same loving care on the things that other warrior nations lavished on their horses and swords.

Finally, Kungas saw what he was expecting. Several horsemen were driving their mounts recklessly back across the river. Couriers, of course, bringing orders from the Great Lady.

"Well, it was nice while it lasted," chuckled Vima harshly. "How long do you want to hold the ridge?"

"We'll hold it as long as we can keep killing ten of them to one of us. After that—which will be once they get too close for mortars—we'll make our retreat. Nothing glamorous, you understand?"

Vima smiled. "Please, Your Majesty. Do I look like a Persian sahrdaran?"

"The battery is secure, Emperor," said Toramana.

"I think your Ye-tai should do the honors, then."

Toramana nodded. "Wise, I think. Rajputs pouring through the gate into Mathura would probably make the soldiers of the battery nervous."

After he was gone, Rana Sanga said sourly: "What has the world come to? That men would prefer to surrender to Ye-tai than Rajputs?"

Damodara just smiled.

Within two hours, Mathura was his—and the great siege guns with it.

Only one battery and two barracks of regular troops put up any resistance, once the garrison saw that Damodara's army had gained entry into the city through treachery.

All the soldiers in those two barracks were massacred.

The Ye-tai contingent that served as a security unit for the recalcitrant battery were also massacred. Toramana led the massacre personally, using nothing but Ye-tai troops.

After they surrendered, the surviving artillerymen were lined up. One out of every ten, chosen at random, was decapitated. Damodara thought that would be enough to ensure the obedience of the rest, and he didn't want to waste experienced gunners.

He'd need them, at Kausambi. Soon, now.

◇   ◇   ◇

Valentinian straightened up and rubbed his back. "Enough," he growled. "I've stared at this sketch till I'm half-blind."

"It's a good sketch!" protested Rajiv.

"I didn't say it wasn't. And I don't doubt that you and Tarun measured off every pace personally. I just said I've stared at it enough. By now, I've got it memorized."

"Me, too," grunted Anastasius, also straightening up on his stool.

The huge cataphract turned to the assassin squatting on the stable floor next to him. "You?"

Ajatasutra waved his hand. "What does it matter? *I* won't be one of the poor fellows sweating and bleeding in this desperate endeavor."

Easily, gracefully, he came to his feet. "I'm just a messenger boy, remember?"

The two Roman soldiers looked at each other. Anastasius seemed reasonably philosophical about the matter. Valentinian didn't.

But Valentinian wasn't inclined to argue the point, any more than Anastasius. They'd miss the assassin's skills—miss them mightily—when the time came. But long hours of discussion and argument had led all of them to the same conclusion:

Nothing would matter, if Sanga wasn't there at the right time. That meant someone had to get word to him, across a north Indian plain that was turning into a giant, sprawling, chaotic, confused battlefield.

A simple courier's job—but one that would require the skills of an assassin.

"You don't have to gloat about it!" snapped Valentinian.

Ajatasutra just smiled.

"You don't have to gloat!" complained Photius.

Tahmina gave him that half-serene, half-pitying look that was the single habit of his wife's that the eleven-year-old emperor of Rome positively hated. Especially because she always did it looking down at him. Even while they were sitting.

"Stop whining," she said. "It's not my fault if you make elephants nervous. They seem to like *me*."

Gingerly, Photius leaned out over the edge of the howdah and gazed at the Bharakucchan street passing below.

Very, very far below.

"It's not natural," he insisted.

Tahmina just smiled.

"Tempting, isn't it?" said Maloji.

From their position on the very crest of the Vindhyas, Rao and Maloji gazed out over the landscape of northern India, fading below them into the distance. Visibility was excellent, since they were still some weeks from the monsoon season.

Rao glanced at Maloji, then at the hill fortress his Maratha soldiers were building some dozens of yards away.

"I won't deny it. We'd still be fools to accept that temptation."

He looked back to the north, pointing with his chin. "For the first few hundred miles, everything would go well. By now, between them, Damodara and Belisarius will have turned half the Ganges plain into a whirlpool of war. Easy pickings for us, on the edges. But then?"

He shook his head. "There are too many north Indians. And regardless of who wins this civil war, soon enough there will be another empire solidly in place. Then what?"

"Yes, I know. But at least we'd get some of our own back, after all the killing and plundering the bastards did in the Deccan. For that matter, they've *still* got a huge garrison in Amaravati."

"Not for long, they won't. Shakuntala got the word a few days ago. All of our south Indian allies have agreed to join us in our expedition to Amaravati, once we've finished this line of hill forts. The Cholas and Keralans even look to be sending large armies. Within two months—perhaps three—that garrison will be gone. One way or the other. So will all the others, in the smaller towns and cities. They'll march their bodies out of the Deccan, or we'll scatter their ashes across it."

" 'Allies,' " Maloji muttered.

In truth, the other realms of south India had played no role at all in the actual fighting, up till now. As important as the alliance was for the Andhran empire for diplomatic reasons, most of Shakuntala's subjects—especially the Marathas—were contemptuous of the other Deccan powers.

"Patience, Maloji, patience. They were disunited, and the Malwa terrified them for decades. Now that we've shown they can be beaten, even if Damodara's rebellion fails and Skandagupta keeps the throne the rest of the Deccan will cleave to us. They'll have no choice, anyway. But with our foreign allies—all the aid we can expect through Bharakuccha, if we need it—they'll even be sanguine about it."

"Bharakuccha," Maloji muttered.

Rao laughed. "Oh, leave off! As great an empire as Andhra has now become, we can well afford to give up one city. Two cities, if you count the Axumite presence in Chowpatty. What do we care? There are other ports we can expand, if we desire it. And having the Ethiopians with their own interests in the Indian trade, we'll automatically have their support also, in the event the Malwa start the war up again."

"They're not that big."

"No—which is exactly why we agreed to let them have Bharakuccha. They're no threat to *us*. But they probably have the most powerful navy in the Erythrean Sea, today. That means the Malwa won't be able to prevent the Romans from sending us all the material support we need."

Judging from the expression on his face, Maloji was still not entirely mollified. "But would they?"

"As long as Belisarius is alive, yes," replied Rao serenely. "And he's still a young man."

"A young man leading an army into the middle of the Gangetic plain. Who's to say he's even still alive?"

Rao just smiled.

Belisarius himself was scowling.

"As bad as Persians!" He matched the old Rajput kings glare for glare. "You've heard the reports. Sati will have at least thirty thousand infantry, half of them armed with muskets and the rest with pikes. We have no more chance of breaking them with cavalry charges that we do riding our horses across the ocean."

As indignant as they were, the kings were quite familiar with warfare. The two brothers Dasal and Jaisal looked away, still glaring, but no longer at Belisarius. One of the other kings, Chachu, was the only one who tried to keep the argument going.

"You have rockets," he pointed out.

Belisarius shrugged. "I've got eight rocket chariots with no more than a dozen rockets each. That's enough to harass the Malwa.

It's not the sort of artillery force that would enable me to smash infantry squares."

Chachu fell silent, his angry eyes sweeping across the landscape. It was quite visible, since the command tent they were standing under was no more than an open pavilion. Just enough to shelter them from the hot sun. They were out of sight of the Yamuna, by now, marching north toward the Ganges. Well into *garam* season, the flat plain was parched and sere.

"It is dishonorable," he muttered.

Belisarius felt his jaws tighten. There was much to admire about Rajputs. There was also much to despise. He thought it was quite typical that Rajput kings would be solely concerned with their honor—when what bothered Belisarius was the destruction he'd soon be visiting upon innocent peasants.

"We . . . have . . . no . . . choice," he said, rasping out the words. "The tactical triangle is simple."

He held up his thumb. "Cavalry cannot break infantry armed with guns, so long as they remain in tight formations and keep discipline. You can be sure and certain that an army led by Malwa's overlord will do so."

His forefinger came up alongside the thumb. "Artillery *can* smash infantry squares—but we have no artillery worth talking about."

Another finger. "On the other side, Sati has only enough cavalry to give her a scouting screen. Not enough—not nearly enough—to drive us off."

He lowered his hand. "So, we keep the pressure on them—from a bit of a distance—and force them to remain in formation. That means they move slowly, and cannot forage. And there's nothing to forage anyway, because we will burn the land bare around them. Once their supplies run out, they're finished."

In a slightly more conciliatory tone, he added: "If you were mounted archers in the manner of the Persians, I might try the same tactics that defeated the Roman general Crassus at Carrhae. But—we must be honest here—you are not."

Chachu's head came back around. "Rajput archers are as good—!"

"Oh, be quiet!" snapped Dasal. The oldest of the Rajput kings shifted his glare from the landscape to his fellow king. "I have seen Persian dehgans in combat. You haven't. What the Roman general is talking about is not their individual skill as bowmen—although that's much greater than ours also, except for a few like Sanga. Those damn Persians grow up with bows. He's talking about their tactics."

Dasal took a deep breath and let it out slowly. "We do not fight in that manner, it is true. Rajputs are a nation of lancers and swordsmen."

Belisarius nodded. "And there's no way to train an army in such tactics quickly. My own bucellarii have been trained to fight that way, but there are only five hundred of them. Not enough. Not nearly enough."

Chachu's face looked as sour as vinegar. "Where did you learn such a disgraceful method?"

Belisarius' chuckle was completely humorless. "From another Roman defeat, how else? I propose to do to Sati's Malwa army exactly what the Persians did to the army of the Roman Emperor Julian, when he was foolish enough to march into the Mesopotamian countryside in midsummer with no secured lines of supply."

Belisarius' gaze moved across the same landscape. It was richer than that of Mesopotamia, but every bit as dry this time of year. Just more things to burn.

"Julian the Apostate, he was called," Belisarius added softly. "A brilliant commander, in many ways. He defeated the Persians in almost every battle they fought. But he, too, was full of his own inflated sense of glory. I am not. And, Roman or no, *I* command this army. Your own emperor has so decreed."

He let the silence settle, for a minute. Then, brought his eyes back to the assembled little group of kings. "You will do as I say. As soon as our scouts make the first contact with Sati's army, we will start burning the land. Behind her as well as before her. On both sides of the Ganges, so that even if she manages to find enough boats, it will do her no good."

After the kings had left the pavilion, Belisarius turned to Jaimal and Udai Singh.

"And you?"

Udai shrugged. "It is a low tactic, no doubt about it. But who cares, when the enemy is Malwa?"

Jaimal just smiled.

Two days after the battle at Mayapur—such as it was—Kungas and his army had covered thirty-five miles in their retreat to Peshawar. It was a "retreat," of course, only in the most technical sense of the term. They'd left Sati in command of the battlefield, true enough. But they'd accomplished their purpose, and it was now time to hurry back lest the Malwa take advantage of their absence to invade the Vale.

The first of Irene's couriers reached them while they were still in the hills.

Kungas read her message several times over, before showing it to Vima and Kujulo.

"What do you want to do?" asked Vima.

Kungas was already looking back toward the east. After a moment, he turned and gazed at the distant peaks of the Himalayas.

So far off, they were. So majestic, also.

He decided it was an omen.

"We'll go back," he said. "I want that bitch dead. No, more. I want to *see* her dead."

After traveling perhaps a hundred miles north of the Vindhyas, following the route Damodara and his army had taken, the captain of the assassination team had had enough.

"This is a madhouse," he said to his lieutenant. "Half the garrisons vanished completely, leaving the countryside open to bandits. What's worse, the other half is roaming the countryside like bandits themselves."

"And there's only five of us," agreed his subordinate gloomily. "This whole assignment has turned into one stinking mess after another. What do you want to do?"

The captain thought for a moment. "Let's start by getting away from the area Damodara passed through. We'll go east, first, and then see if we can work our way up to Kausambi from the south. It'll take longer, but there'll be less chance of being attacked by dacoits."

The lieutenant nodded. "I can't think of anything better. By the time we get to Kausambi, of course, Damodara will have it under siege. Which will be a fitting end to the most thankless task we've ever been given."

"We can probably make it through the lines," the captain said, trying to sound confident. "Then . . . "

"Report? To who? Nanda Lal's dead and—I don't know about you—but I really don't want to have to tell the emperor that we've traveled ten thousand miles to accomplish exactly nothing. He's foul-tempered in the best of times."

The captain just smiled. But it was a sickly sort of thing.

Chapter 34
THE IRON TRIANGLE

"Keep the pressure on," said Maurice firmly. "We'll do *that*. But that's all we'll do."

He ignored the sour look on Sittas' face. That was a given, and Maurice saw no point in getting into another argument with him. Sittas was the most aggressive commander in the Roman army, a trait that was valuable when it came time for headlong cavalry charges. But that same trait also made him prone to recklessness. The Romans and Persians had been able to seize the Malwa fortresses upstream on the west bank of the Indus simply—and solely—because Menander and his warships had been able to launch an attack on their unprotected rear. No such advantage existed if they tried to carry the fight across to the east bank of the river.

Menander was also looking sour-faced, however, and that Maurice did have to deal with.

"All right," he growled. "You can keep making your sorties up the river—*until* you spot any signs that the Malwa are bringing over ironclads from the other rivers—"

"And how will they do that?"

"Don't be stupid. They'll do it in the simplest way possible. Just pick them up and haul the damn things there."

"That'd take—"

"A mighty host of slave laborers and ruthless overseers. Which is exactly what the Malwa have."

Maurice decided it was time for a moderate display of temper. He gave a quick glance at Agathius and then slammed his fist onto the table in the command bunker.

"God damn it! Have you all lost your wits so completely that one single victory turns you into drooling babes?"

"Take it easy," said Agathius soothingly. As Maurice had expected, the crippled cataphract commander picked up the cue instantly. He'd been a tremendous asset ever since he arrived in the Triangle.

"There's no need to lose our tempers. Still, Maurice is right. It'll take them some time, but the Malwa *will* get those ironclads into the Indus. One, at least—and you've already admitted, Menander, that the *Justinian* probably can't handle even one of them."

Menander still looked sour-faced, but he didn't try to argue the point. The *Justinian* had been designed mainly to destroy Malwa shipping. Its guns were probably as heavy as anything the Malwa ironclads had, but it wasn't as well armored. The ironclads had been designed to do one thing and one thing only—destroy the *Justinian,* if it ever came out against them.

Agathius swiveled on his crutches to face Sittas. "And will you *please* leave off your endless pestering? To be honest, I'm as sick of it as Maurice is. Sittas, even if you could get your cataphracts across the river in the face of enemy fire—"

"We could go—"

"Upstream? Where? Anywhere below here and Multan, the Malwa now have fortifications all along the Indus. And if you try to take your cavalry north of Multan . . . "

He shrugged. "Leave that to the Persians. We need the cavalry here in case the Malwa manage to penetrate our lines somewhere."

For all his stubbornness, Sittas wasn't actually stupid. After a moment, the anger faded from his face, leaving an oddly rueful expression.

"It's not fair!" he said, half-chuckling. "Once again, that damned Belisarius grabs all the glory work for himself and leaves me to hold the fort."

Unexpectedly, Calopodius spoke up from his communications table. He normally kept silent during these command conferences, unless he was asked to do something.

"Is a shield 'false,' and only a sword 'true'?"

All of the commanders peered at him.

"What does that mean?" demanded Sittas.

Calopodius smiled and pointed a finger—almost exactly in the right direction—at his servant Luke, sitting inconspicuously on a chair against a far wall, next to Illus.

"Ask him."

The commanders peered at Luke.

"Ah . . . " said that worthy fellow.

Antonina took a slow turn on her heels, admiring the huge audience chamber of the Goptri's palace in Bharakuccha.

"Pretty incredible," she said. "You'd think the weight of encrusted gems in the walls alone would collapse the thing."

Ousanas shared none of her sentiments. "Incredible nuisance," he grumbled. He gave Dadaji Holkar a look from under lowered brows. The peshwa of Andhra was standing just a few feet away from them. "Mark my words, Antonina. No sooner will this current world war end than a new one will begin, every nation on earth fighting for possession of this grotesque monument to vanity."

She chuckled softly. "Don't exaggerate. The fighting will be entirely between you and the Marathas. The empires of Rome and Persia and Malwa will only send observers."

Dadaji made a face. Ousanas sneered.

"Ha! Until they observe the obscene wealth piled up here themselves. At which point great armies will be marching. Mark my words!"

Still slowly turning, Antonina considered the problem. To be sure, Ousanas was indulging himself in his beloved Cassandra impersonation. But there did remain a genuine core of concern, underneath.

What *were* they to do with the Goptri's palace? Except for the palace of the emperor himself at Kausambi, it was the most splendiferous edifice ever erected by the Malwa. And the interior was an even greater source of greed and potential strife than the glorious shell. For every gem encrusted in the walls, there were twenty in the chests piled high in the vaults below. Along with other chests of gold, silver, ivory, valuable spices—everything, it seemed, that a viceroy could flaunt before a conquered half-continent.

There'd been skin-sacks, too, but those the Ethiopian soldiers and Maratha irregulars had taken down immediately, once they took possession of the palace. Since then, they'd simply glared at each other over the rest.

By the time she finished the turn, she had the answer.

"Give it to me," she said. "To my Hospitalers, rather. And to Anna Saronites, and her Wife's Service."

She lowered her eyes to look at Dadaji. "Surely you—or Bindusara, more likely—can devise an equivalent body for Hindus. If so, you will get an equal share in the palace. An equal share in the wealth in the vaults, as well as equal space in the palace itself."

Thoughtfully, Holkar tugged at his ear. "And for the Kushans? Another equal share, if they create a Buddhist hospital service?"

"Why not?"

"Hm." He kept tugging at his ear, for a few more seconds. Then, shrugged. "Why not?"

Ousanas' eyes widened, half with outrage and half with . . . something that seemed remarkably like amusement.

"Preposterous! What of we Axumites? We get *nothing?*"

"Nonsense," said Antonina. "The Hospitalers are a *religious* order, not an imperial one. Nothing in the world prevents Ethiopians from joining it. Or creating your own hospital service, if you insist on maintaining your sectarian distinction."

Holkar's hand fell from his ear, to rise again, with forefinger pointing rigidly. "Absolutely not! You Christians already have two hospital services! Three is too many! You would take half the palace!"

"Nonsense," Antonina repeated. "The Wife's Service has no religious affiliation at all. True—so far—all of its members are probably Christians. But they've given medical care to Persians and Indians just as readily as they have to Christians."

The accusing forefinger went back to tugging the ear. "Hm. You propose, then, that every religion be given a share of the palace, provided they create a medical service. And then one other—the Wife's Service—which is free of any sectarian affiliation altogether. Yes?"

"Yes."

"Hm." She began to fear for his earlobe. "Interesting. Keep the kings and emperors at arm's length."

"Arm's length, with the hand holding a pole," Ousanas grunted. "Very long pole. Only way it will work. Kings and emperors are greedy by nature. Let them get within smelling distance of gold and jewels . . . might as well throw bloody meat into a pond full of sharks."

"True," mused Holkar. "Monks and priests will at least resist temptation for a generation or two. Thereafter, of course—"

"Thereafter is thereafter," said Antonina firmly. "There is a plague coming, long before that 'thereafter' will arrive."

By now, the three of them had drifted closely together, to what an unkind observer might have called a conspiratorial distance.

"Major religions only," insisted Ousanas. "No sects, no factions. Or else the doctrinal fanatics in Alexandria alone would insist their eighty-seven sects were entitled to the entire palace and its vaults—and demand that eighty-six more be built."

Holkar chuckled. "Be even worse among Indians. Hindus are not given to heresy-hunts, but they divide over religious matters even more promiscuously than Christians."

"Agreed," said Antonina, nodding. "One for the Christians, one for the Hindus, one for the Buddhists, and one for the Zoroastrians if the Persians want it. And one nondenominational service."

After a moment, she added: "Better offer a share to the Jews, too, I think. Half a share, at least."

"There aren't that many Jews," protested Ousanas.

"And almost none in India," added Holkar.

"True—and beside the point. One-third of the populace of Alexandria is Jewish. And it will be through Alexandria that the plague enters the Mediterranean."

Ousanas and Holkar stared at her. Then, at each other. Then, back at Antonina.

"Agreed," said Ousanas.

"A half-share for the Jews," added Holkar. "But if we're going to do that, we'll need to offer a half-share to the Jains, as well."

Ousanas frowned. "What is this adding up to?"

"Six shares all told," Antonina answered. She'd been keeping track. "One of the shares to be divided evenly between the Jews and the Jains."

Now it was her turn to hold up the rigid forefinger of admonition. "But only if they all agree to form hospitals and medical services! We don't need this palace crawling with useless monks and priests, squabbling over everything."

"Certainly don't," said Ousanas. His eyes swept the great room. "One-sixth of this . . . and the vaults below . . . "

He grinned, then. That great, gleaming Ousanas grin.

"I do believe they will accept."

Ajatasutra had no difficulty at all getting out of Kausambi. The guards at the gates were carefully checking everyone who sought to leave the city, but they were only looking for someone who might fit the description of "a great lady and her entourage."

Even dressed at his finest, Ajatasutra bore no resemblance to such. Seeing him dressed in the utilitarian garb of an imperial courier and riding a very fine but obviously spirited horse, the guards didn't give him more than a glance. Great ladies traveled only in howdahs and palanquins. Those armed peasants didn't know much, but they knew that. Everybody knew that.

Nor did the assassin have any trouble in the first two days of his journey. Mid-morning of the third day, he began encountering the first refugees fleeing from Mathura.

Thereafter, the situation became contradictory. On the one hand, the ever-widening flow of refugees greatly impeded his forward progress. On the other hand, he was cheerfully certain that whatever progress he made was indeed forward.

Only two things in the world could cause such an immense flow of refugees: plague, or an invading army. And none of the refugees looked especially sick.

Frightened, yes; desperate, yes; ill, no.

Damodara was somewhere up ahead. And no longer far away at all.

"He's within a hundred miles, you—you—!"

Skandagupta lapsed into gasping silence, unable to come up with a word or phrase that properly encapsulated his sentiments toward the generals standing before him.

No longer standing, of course. They were prostrate, now, hoping he might spare their lives.

Stupid-incompetent-worthless-craven-fumbling-halfwitted-stinking-treacherous dogs—

Would have done it. But he was too short of breath to even think of uttering the phrase. Never in his worst nightmares had he imagined Damodara would penetrate the huge Malwa empire this far. All the way from the Deccan, he'd come, in less than two months. Now . . .

Within a hundred miles of Kausambi!

Only a supreme effort of self-control enabled Skandagupta to refrain from ordering the three generals impaled immediately. He desperately wanted to, but there was a siege coming. As surely and certainly as the sunrise. He could not afford to lose his remaining top generals on the eve of a siege.

Could . . . not . . . afford . . . it.

Finally, his breathing slowed. "See to the city's defenses!" he barked. "Leave me, you—you—dogs!"

The generals scuttled from the audience chamber.

Once outside, one of them said to the others: "Perhaps we should have told him that Damodara will surely be bringing the big guns from Mathura . . . "

"Don't be a fool," hissed one of the others.

"He'll hear them anyway, once they start firing."

The third general shook his head. "Don't be so sure of that. Within a day he'll be hiding below the palace in the deep bunkers. They say—I've never been down there myself—that you can't hear anything, so deep."

You couldn't, in fact. That evening, Skandagupta went down to the inner sanctum. Seeking . . .

Whatever. Reassurance, perhaps. Or simply the deep silence there.

He got none, however. Neither reassurance, nor silence. Just a stern command, in the tones of an eight-year-old girl, to return above and resume his duties.

Now.

He did so. The girl was not yet Link. But someday she would be. And, even today, the special assassins would obey her.

Belisarius studied the sketch that one of the Pathan trackers had made in the dirt. It was a good sketch. Pathans served the Rajput kings as scouts and skirmishers, just as Arabs did for Roman emperors. The man was even less likely to be literate than an Arab, but he had the same keen eye for terrain, the same superb memory for it, and the same ability to translate what he'd seen into symbols drawn in dirt with a knife.

"Two days, then," Belisarius mused. "It would take the monster at least that long to retreat to the Ganges, with such a force."

The Pathan, naturally, had been far less precise in his estimate of the size of Link's army. It could be anywhere between twenty and sixty thousand men, Belisarius figured. Splitting the difference would be as good a guess as any, until he had better reports.

Forty thousand men, then. A force almost twice as large as his own.

Almost all infantry, though. That had been suggested by the earliest reports, and the Pathan scout was able to confirm it. If the man could not tell the difference between five thousand and ten thousand, he could easily distinguish foot soldiers from cavalry. He could do that by the age of four.

"Start burning today?" asked Jaimal.

Belisarius shook his head. "I'd like to, but we can't risk it. The monster could drive its men back across two days' worth of ashes. Even three days' worth, I think."

"With no water?" Jaisal asked skeptically.

"They'll have some. In any event, there are streams here and there, and we can't burn the streams."

"Not much water in those streams," grunted Dasal. "Not in the middle of *garam*. Still . . . the monster would lose some men."

"Oh, yes," agreed Belisarius. Then, he shrugged. "But enough? We're outnumbered probably two to one. If we let them get back to the Ganges, they'll be able to cross eventually."

"No fords there. Not anywhere nearby. And we will have burned all the trees they could use for timber."

"Doesn't matter. First of all, because you *can't* burn all the trees. You know that as well as I do, Jaisal. Not down to the heartwood. And even if you could, what difference would it make? A few days' delay, that's all, while the monster assembled some means to cross. It would manage, eventually. We could hurt them, but not kill them. Not with so great a disparity in numbers. They'd get hungry, but not hungry enough—and they'd have plenty of water. Once they were on the opposite bank of the Ganges, they'd be able to make it to Kausambi. Nothing we could do to stop them."

"By then, Damodara might have taken Kausambi," pointed out Jaimal.

"And he might not, too," said Dasal. The old Rajput king straightened up. "No, I think Belisarius is right. Best to be cautious here."

A day later, three more Pathan scouts came in with reports. Two from the south, one from the north.

"There is another army coming, General," said one of the two scouts in the first party. He pointed a finger to the south. "From Mathura. Most of the garrison, I think. Many men. Mostly foot soldiers. Maybe five thousand cavalry. Some cannons. Not the great big ones, though."

"They're moving very slowly," added the other scout.

Belisarius nodded. "That's good news, actually—although it makes our life more complicated."

Jaisal cocked his head. "Why 'good' news?"

His brother snorted. "Think, youngster. If we've drawn the garrison at Mathura to leave the safety of the city's walls to come up here, we've opened the door to Kausambi for Damodara."

"Oh." Jaisal looked a bit shame-faced.

Belisarius had to fight down a smile. The "youngster" thus admonished had to be somewhere in his mid-seventies.

"Yes," he said. "It makes our life more difficult, of course."

He began to weigh various alternatives in his mind. But once he heard the second report, all those alternatives were discarded.

"*Another* army?" demanded Dasal. "From the *north*?"

The scout nodded. "Yes. Maybe two days' march behind the Great Lady's. They're almost at the Ganges. But they move faster than she does. Partly because they're a small army—maybe one-third as big as hers—but mostly because . . ."

He shook his head, admiringly. "Very fast, they move. Good soldiers."

All the Rajput kings and officers assembled around Belisarius were squinting northward. All of them were frowning deeply.

"From the *north*?" Dasal repeated. The old king shook his head. "That makes no sense. There is no large Malwa garrison there. No need for one. Not with that great huge army they have in the

Punjab. And if *they* were coming back to the Ganges, there'd be many more of them."

"And why would they bother with the northerly route, at all?" wondered Udai Singh. "They'd simply march through Rajputana. No way we could stop them."

As he listened to their speculations, Belisarius' eyes had widened. Now he whispered, "Son of God."

Dasal's eyes came to him. "What?"

"I can think of one army that could come from that direction. About that size, too—one-third of the monster's. But . . ."

He shook his head, wonderingly. "Good God, if I'm right—what a great gamble he took."

"*Who?*"

Belisarius didn't even hear the question.

Of course, he *is* a great gambler, said Aide.

So he is.

Decisively, Belisarius turned to the Pathan scout. "I need you to return there. At once. Take however many scouts you need. Find out—"

His thoughts stumbled, a moment. Most Pathans were hopelessly insular. They'd have as much trouble telling one set of foreigners from another as they would telling one thousand from two thousand.

He swept off his helmet, and half-bowed. Then, seized his hair and drew it tightly into his fist. "Their hair. Like this. A 'topknot,' they call it."

"Oh. Kushans." The scout frowned and looked back to the north. "Could be. I didn't get close enough to see. But they move like Kushans, now that I think about it."

He nodded deeply—the closest any Pathan ever got to a "salute"—and turned to his horse. "Two days, General. I will tell you in two days."

"And now what?" asked Jaimal, after the scout was gone.

"Start burning—but only behind them. Leave them a clear path forward."

The Rajput officer nodded. "You want them away from the Ganges."

"Yes. But mostly, I want someone else to see a signal. If it's the Kushans, when they see the great smoke from the burning, they'll know."

"Know what?"

Belisarius grinned at him. "That I'll be back. All they have to do is hold the Ganges—keep the monster pinned on this side—and I'll be back."

The oldest of the kings grunted. "I understand. Good plan. Now we go teach those shits from Mathura that all they're good for is garrison duty."

"Indeed," said Belisarius. "And we move *quickly.*"

After they began the forced march, Aide spoke uncertainly.

I *don't* understand. You must be careful! Link is not stupid. When it sees you are only burning behind its army, it will understand that you are trying to lure it further from the river. It will return, then, not come forward.

I know. And by then Kungas will already be there. They will not cross the Ganges against Kungas' will. Not though they outnumbered him ten-to-one.

There was silence, for a bit.

Oh. What you're really doing is keeping Link *at* the Ganges, not drawing it overland—which gives you time to crush the army coming up from Mathura.

Yes. That's where we'll kill the monster's army. Right on the banks of the holy river, caught between two enemies.

They'll have plenty of water.

Man does not live by water alone. Soon, they'll have nothing to eat—and we have all the time we need to watch them starve. We'll have Link trapped up here—when it needs to be in Kausambi. If Damodara can't do the rest, against Skandagupta alone, he's not the new emperor India needs.

Silence again, for a bit.

What if that new army *isn't* the Kushans?

Then we're screwed, said Belisarius cheerfully. *I'm a pretty good gambler myself, you know—and you can't gamble if you're not willing to take the risk of getting screwed.*

That produced a long silence. Eventually, Aide said:

I can remember a time when I wouldn't have understood a word of that. Especially "screwed." How did a proper little crystal fall into such bad company?

You invited yourself to the party. As a matter of fact, as I recall, you started *the party.*

That's a very vulgar way of putting it.

Chapter 35
THE PUNJAB

By the time Khusrau and his army reached the Kohat Pass, the emperor of the Persians was in an excellent frame of mind.

First, because he'd succeeded in taking most of the western Punjab for his empire. Formally speaking, at least, even if Persian occupation and rule was still almost meaningless for the inhabitants. He hadn't even bothered to leave behind detachments of dehgans under newly appointed provincial governments to begin establishing an administration.

He would, soon enough. In the meantime, there was still a war to be won and he only had thirty thousand troops at his disposal. Not enough to peel off even small detachments for garrison duty. Not with a Malwa army still in the Punjab that numbered at least one hundred and fifty thousand.

Second, because—here and there—he'd been able to grind up some more sahrdaran and vurzurgan hotheads in foolish charges against Malwa garrisons. It was amazing, really, how thick-headed those classes were.

Or, perhaps, it was simply their growing sense of desperation. For centuries, the grandees had been the real power in Persia. True, none of the seven great sahrdaran families or their vurzurgan affiliates ever formally challenged the right of an emperor to rule. Or that the emperor would always come from the imperial clan.

But the reality had been that emperors were made and broken, at each and every succession, by the grandees. Those contestants for the throne who got their support, won. Those who didn't, lost their heads.

Their power had stemmed, ultimately, from two sources. One was their control of great swathes of land in a nation that was still almost entirely agricultural, which made them phenomenally wealthy. The other was their ability to field great numbers of armored heavy cavalry, which had been the core of Persia's might for centuries, because of that wealth.

They were losing both, now. Not quickly, no, but surely nonetheless. The huge areas of western India formerly ruled by the Malwa that Khusrau was incorporating into his empire, all of Sind and a third of the Punjab, were not being parceled out to the grandees, as they would have been in times past. Instead, Khusrau was adapting the Roman model and setting up an imperial administration, staffed by dehgans who answered directly to him and his appointed governors—most of whom were dehgans themselves.

Worse still, the grandees were witnessing the death knell of the armored horseman as the king of battles. Within a generation, even in Persia, it would be infantry armed with guns who constituted the core of imperial might. Infantry whose soldiers would be drawn, as often as not, from the newly conquered territories. Indian peasants from the Sind or the Punjab, who would answer to the emperor, not the grandees—and would do so willingly, because the Persian emperor had given their clans and tribes a far more just and lenient rule than they'd ever experienced at the hands of the Malwa.

The continued insistence of the grandees to launch their beloved cavalry charges, Khusrau thought, was simply the willful blindness of men who could not accept their coming fate.

So be it. Khusrau was quite happy to oblige them. Why not? They *were* ferocious cavalry, after all, so they generally managed to seize the small cities and towns they attacked. And every sahrd-aran and vurzurgan who died in the doing was one less the emperor would have to quarrel with on the morrow.

By the time the war was over, only the Suren would remain as powerful as they had been, of the seven great families. And under Baresmanas' sure leadership, the Suren were reaching an accommodation with the emperor. They'd long been the premier family of the seven, after all, and now they had the emperor's favor. Unlike the rest, the Suren would accept a role that diminished them as a family but would expand their power and influence as individuals within the empire.

Last—best of all—there were the dehgans. The knightly class of Persia's nobility had always chafed under the yoke of the grandees. But they'd accepted that yoke, in the past, since they saw no alternative.

Khusrau was giving them an alternative, now, and they were seizing it. For a modest dehgan from a small village, the chance to become an imperial administrator or governor was a far better prospect than anything the grandees would offer. In the increasingly unlikely event that the grandees tried to launch a rebellion against Khusrau, he was not only sure he could crush them easily—but he'd have the assistance of most of the grandees' own feudal retainers in doing so.

"You're certainly looking cheerful, Your Majesty," said Irene. She'd come to meet him in a pavilion she'd had hastily set up at the crest of the pass, once she got word that the Persian army was approaching the borders of the Kushan kingdom.

Well, not *quite* at the crest. The pavilion was positioned on a small knoll a few hundreds yards below the crest, and the fortresses the Kushans had built upon it.

Khusrau—very cheerfully—gazed up at those fortifications.

"Very nicely built," he said. "I'd certainly hate to be the one who ever tried to storm them."

Lowering his eyes, and seeing the questioning look in Irene's eyes, Khusrau grinned. "Oh, don't be silly. Yes, I'm in a very good mood. For many reasons. One of them is that I don't have the prospect of watching my army bleed to death on these horrid-looking rocks."

Irene smiled. Khusrau, still grinning, turned slightly and pointed with his finger to the plain below. "I thought I'd found a small town there. With a modest garrison. Just big enough to formally mark the boundary of the Persian empire. And another town like it, a similarly discreet distance below the Margalla Pass. Any objection?"

Irene's smile widened considerably. "Of course not, Your Majesty. The kingdom of the Kushans would not presume to quarrel with whatever the Emperor of Iran and non-Iran chose to do within his *own* realm."

"Splendid. I'll be off, then. Still many more battles to fight. The Romans—staunch fellows—have most of the Malwa army pinned down at the Triangle, so I thought I'd take advantage of the opportunity to plunder and ravage their northerly towns. I might even threaten Multan. Won't try to take it, though. The garrison's too big."

The grin seemed fixed on his face. "Where's King Kungas, by the way?"

Before Irene could answer, he waved his hand. "None of my business, of course."

Irene hesitated, a moment. Then, sure that the Persians had no intentions upon the Vale of Peshawar, she said: "Actually, it is your business. We are allies, after all. My husband took most of our army east, to intercept and ambush the army Great Lady Sati is leading back to the Gangetic plain to fight Damodara. I've gotten word from him. The ambush was successful and he's continuing the pursuit."

That caused the emperor's grin to fade away. His eyebrows lifted. "We'd heard from our spies that she had something like forty thousand troops. Kungas can't possibly—"

" 'Pursuit' is perhaps not the right term. He thinks Belisarius is somewhere out there, also, although he's not sure. He'll stay at a distance from Sati's force and simply harass them, until he knows."

"Ah." Khusrau's head swiveled, toward the east. "Belisarius . . . Yes, he might well be there, by now. He was gone from the Triangle, when I arrived. Maurice was very mysterious about it. But I suspect—I have spies too, you know—that he reached an agreement with the Rajputs. If I'm right, he crossed the Thar with a small force to organize and lead a Rajput rebellion."

Irene's gaze followed his. "I wondered. I could see no way—neither could my husband—that he could lead a sizeable Roman force from the Triangle into the Ganges. But through Rajputana . . . " She chuckled softly. "It would be quite like him. I worry about that man's soul, sometimes. How will the angels cope with so many angles?"

Khusrau's chuckle was a louder thing. "Say better, how will the devils?"

He gave her a little bow. "And now, Queen of the Kushans, I must be off."

Belisarius drove the march south even more ruthlessly than he'd driven the one north.

"I want to catch them strung out in marching order," he explained to the Rajput kings, after sending out a host of Arab and Pathan scouts to find his target.

"Good plan," said Dasal.

"It's so hot," half-complained his brother.

"Stop whining, youngster. Hot for the Malwa, too. Still hotter, when we catch them."

Kungas studied the scene on the opposite side of the Ganges. As dry and hot as it was, the fires that had been started over there were burned out by now, although plumes of smoke were rising here and there from still-smoldering ashes.

"How far?" he asked.

"As far down the river as we've gotten reports," Kujulo replied, "from the scouts that have come back."

"It must have been Belisarius," said Vima. "But I don't understand why he burned here. I'd have thought he'd be burning in front of her."

"Who's to say he isn't?" Kungas left off his examination of the opposite bank and studied the river itself. As big as it was, the Ganges had already swept downriver whatever traces of the burning had fallen into it.

"I think he wants to pin the bitch here, at the river. That's why he burned behind her. To trick her into coming back."

Vima frowned. "But *why?* If she's here, she's got water. It'd be better to burn her out when she's stranded between the rivers."

Kujulo shrugged. "If it worked, yes. But it's not that easy to 'strand' an army that big. She'd probably have enough supplies with her to make it to the Yamuna."

"She could get stored food from the garrisoned towns, too," said Kungas. "Belisarius is probably bypassing them, just burning everything else. I don't think he can have so big an army that he'd want to suffer casualties in a lot of little sieges and assaults. Especially if he's trying to move quickly."

Finally, he spotted what he was looking for, far down the river. A small cluster of little fishing boats.

"No, it makes sense. If he tricks her into coming back here, he can pin her against the river. Especially with us on the other side to keep her from crossing—which we will."

He pointed at the boats. "We'll use those to ferry a party across the river. Then we'll send cavalry up and down both banks of the river. Seize any boats we find, and wreck or burn any bridges, any timber—anything; ropes, whatever—that could be used to build new bridges or boats. We'll keep the bitch from crossing, while Belisarius lets her army starve to death. They'll have water, but that's all they'll have."

"She'll try to march down the Ganges," Vima pointed out.

"Yes, she will. With Belisarius burning everything before her on that side, and us doing the same on this side. And killing any foraging parties she tries to send out. I don't think she'll make it to a big enough garrisoned city—it'd have to be Kangora—before her army starts to fall apart."

He turned away from the river. "It's as good a plan as any—and I'm not going to try to second-guess Belisarius."

"But there have been no communications from the Great Lady since she reached the headwaters of the Sutlej!" protested the chief priest.

Lord Samudra was no longer even trying to be polite to the man—or any of the other pestiferous priests Sati had left behind in the Punjab to "oversee" him. He rarely even let them into his command bunker.

"Of course we haven't!" he snarled. "Until I can get an army up there to bottle them back up in the Vale of Peshawar, the Kushans will have raiding parties all over the area. For sure and certain, they'll have cut the telegraph lines. And they'll ambush any couriers she might have sent."

"You should—"

"You should! You should!" He clenched his fist and held it just under the priest's nose. "I've got eighty thousand Romans just to the south—"

"That's nonsense! There can't be more than—"

"—and fifty thousand Persians threatening to penetrate our lines in the north. In the middle of this, you want me to—"

"—can't be more than thirty thousand—"

"*Be silent!*" Samudra shrieked. It was all he could do not to strike the priest with his fist.

With a great effort, he reined in his temper. "Who is the expert at gauging the size of armies, priest? Me or you? If I say I'm facing enemy forces numbering one hundred and thirty thousand men—barely smaller than my own—then that's what I'm facing!"

He lowered his fist by the expedient of throwing his whole hand to the side. The fist opened, and the forefinger indicated the door to the bunker.

"Get. Out. Out! The Great Lady instructed me to hold our lines, no matter what, and that is what I shall do. The Kushans are a distraction. We will deal with them when the time comes."

"He's panicking," mused Maurice, peeking over the fortified wall and looking to the north. "He's hunkering down everywhere, barely moving at all."

"Except for getting those ironclads into the Indus," Menander said grumpily. "The latest spy reports say that canal he's having dug is within two miles of the river."

Maurice thought about it. "Better leave off any more forays upriver with the *Justinian*, then. We'll need to get those mine fields laid again."

"Eusebius is already working on it. He's got the mines mostly assembled and says he can start laying them in three days. That leaves me enough time—"

"Forget it. What's the point, Menander? We've already panicked them enough. From here on in, all we have to do is squat here."

He lowered his head and pointed over the wall with an upraised finger. "Belisarius asked us to keep that huge army locked up, and by God we've done so. The last thing I want is to take the risk that some mishap to the *Justinian* might boost their confidence."

"But—"

"Forget it, I said."

"We accept!" Anna exclaimed, as soon as she finished reading the radio message from Bharakuccha. Then, with a tiny start, glanced at Calopodius. "Assuming, of course, you agree."

Her husband grinned. "I can imagine the consequences if I didn't! But I agree, anyway. It's a good idea."

He hesitated a moment. Then:

"We'd have to live there ourselves, you understand."

"Yes, of course. Perhaps it would be best if we asked Antonina to find us a villa . . . "

"Yes." He instructed the operator to send that message.

A few minutes later, listening to the reply, Calopodius started laughing softly.

"What's so funny?" asked Anna. "I can't make any sense out of that *bzz-bzz-bzz*."

"Wait. You'll see in a moment, when you can read it yourself."

The radio operator finished recording the message and handed it to Anna. After she skimmed through, she smiled ruefully.

"Well, that's that."

MUST BE JOKING STOP WHY GET VILLA WHEN CAN HAVE PART OF GOPTRI PALACE STOP WILL SET ASIDE CHOICE SUITE FOR YOU STOP PREFER RUBY OR EMERALD DECOR STOP

Reading the same message, Lord Samudra's gloom deepened. The Romans weren't even bothering to hide their communications any longer. Using the radio openly, when they could have used the telegraph!

"They're already carving us up," he muttered.

"Excuse me, Lord? I didn't quite hear that," said one of his lieutenants.

Samudra shook his head. "Never mind. What's the situation at Multan?"

"We just got a telegraph message from the garrison commander. He says the refugees are still pouring into the city. Much more, he says, and the city's defenses will be at risk."

The Malwa commander took a deep breath; then, slowly, sighed it out. "We can't hold Multan," he said quietly, speaking more to himself than to the lieutenant.

Shaking his head again, he said more loudly: "Send orders to the garrison commander to evacuate his troops from Multan and bring them south. We'll need his forces to reinforce our own down here. And start building fortification across our northern lines. The Persians will be attacking us, soon enough."

"Yes, Lord. And the city's residents? The refugees?"

"Not my affair!" snapped Samudra. "Tell the commander to abandon them—and if any try to follow his army, cut them down. We do *not* have room for those refugees here, either. Soon enough, we'll be fighting for our lives."

The next morning, the group of priests left behind by Link forced their way into Samudra's bunker.

"You cannot abandon Multan!" shouted the head priest.

But Samudra had known they would come, and had prepared for it. By now, all of his officers were as sick and tired of the priests as he was.

"Arrest them," he commanded.

It was done quickly, by a specially selected unit of Ye-tai. After the squawking priests were shoved into the bunker set aside for them, the commander of the Ye-tai unit reported back to Samudra.

"When, Lord?"

Samudra hesitated. But not for long. This step, like all the others he had taken, was being forced upon him. He had no choices, any longer.

"Do it now. There's no point in waiting. But make sure—*certain*, you understand—that there is no trace of evidence left. When"—he almost said *if*—"we have to answer to Great Lady Sati, there can be no questions."

"Yes, Lord."

The Ye-tai commander got promoted that evening. The explosion that destroyed the bunker and all the priests in it was splendidly handled. Unfortunate, of course, that by sheer chance a Roman rocket had landed a direct hit on it. Still more unfortunate, that the priests had apparently been so careless as to store gunpowder in the bunker.

The mahamimamsa who might have disputed that—which they would have, since they would have been the ones to handle the munitions—had vanished also. Nothing so fancy for them, however. By now, the open sewers that had turned most of the huge Malwa army camp into a stinking mess contained innumerable bodies. Who could tell one from the other, even if anyone tried?

By the following day, in any event, it was clear that no one ever would. The epidemic Samudra feared had arrived, finally, erupting from the multitude of festering spots of disease. Soon, there would be too many bodies to burn. More precisely, they no longer had enough flammable material in the area to burn them. The sewers and the rivers would have to serve instead.

Perhaps, if they were lucky, the bodies floating down the Indus and the Chenab would spread the disease into the Roman lines in the Iron Triangle.

By the time Link and its army returned to the banks of the Ganges, the cyborg that ruled the Malwa empire was as close to what humans would have called desperation as that inhuman intelligence could ever become. It was a strange sort of desperation, though; not one that any human being would have recognized as such.

For Link, the universe consisted solely of probabilities. Where a human would have become desperate from thinking doom was almost certain, Link would have handled such long odds with the same uncaring detachment that it assessed very favorable probabilities.

The problem lay elsewhere. It was becoming impossible to gauge the probabilities at all. The war was dissolving into a thing of sheer chaos, with all data hopelessly corrupted. A superhuman intelligence that could have assessed alternate courses of action and chosen among them based on lightning-quick calculations, simply spun in circles. Its phenomenal mind had no more traction than a wheel trapped in slick mud.

Dimly, and for the first time, a mentality never designed to do so understood that its great enemy had deliberately aimed for this result.

Bizarre. Link could understand the purpose, but slipped whenever it tried to penetrate the logic of the thing. How could any sane mind *deliberately* seek to undermine all probabilities? *Deliberately* strive to shatter all points of certainty? As if an intelligent being were a mindless shark, dissolving all logic into a fluid through which it might swim.

For the millionth time, Link examined the enormous records of the history of warfare that it possessed. And, finally, for the first time—dimly—began to realize that the ever-recurrent phrase "the art of war" was not simply a primitive fetish. Not simply the superstitious way that semi-savages would consider the science of armed conflict.

It almost managed something a human would have called resentment, then. Not at its great enemy, but at the new gods who had sent it here on its mission. And failed to prepare it properly.

But the moment was fleeting. Link was not designed to waste time considering impossibilities. The effort it had taken the new gods to transport Link and its accompanying machinery had almost exhausted them economically. Indeed, the energy expenditure had been so great that they had been forced to destroy a planet in the doing.

Their own. The centuries of preparation—most of it required by the erection of the power and transmission grids that had blanketed the surface—could not possibly have been done on any other planet. Not with the Great Ones moving between the star systems, watching everything.

The surviving new gods—the elite of that elite—had retreated to a heavily fortified asteroid to await the new universe that Link would create for them. They could defend themselves against the Great Ones, from that fortress, but could not possibly mount another intervention into human history.

They had taken a great gamble on Link. An excellent gamble, with all the probability calculations falling within the same margin of near-certainty.

And now . . .

Nothing but chaos. How was Link to move in that utterly alien fluid?

"Your commands, Great Lady?"

Link's sheath looked up at the commander of the army. Incredibly, it hesitated.

Not long enough, of course, for the commander himself to notice. To a human, a thousandth of second was meaningless.

But Link knew. Incredibly, it almost said: "I'm not sure. What do you recommend?"

It did not, of course. Link was not designed to consider impossibilities.

Chapter 36

THE GANGES PLAIN, NORTH OF MATHURA

As he'd hoped he would, Belisarius caught the Mathura garrison while it was still strung out in marching order.

"They're trying to form up squares," Abbu reported, "but if you move fast you'll get there before they can finish. They're coming up three roads and having trouble finding each other. The artillery's too far back, too." The old bedouin spat on the ground. "They're sorry soldiers."

"Garrison duty always makes soldiers sluggish, unless they train constantly." Ashot commented. "Even good ones."

The Armenian officer looked at Belisarius. "Your orders?"

"Our cataphracts are the only troops we've got who are really trained as mounted archers. Take all five hundred of them—use Abbu's bedouin as a screen—and charge them immediately. Bows only, you understand? Don't even think about lances and swords. Pass down the columns and rake them—but don't take any great risks. Stay away from the artillery. If they're already too far back, they'll never get up in position past a mass of milling infantrymen."

Ashot nodded. "You just want me to keep them confused, as long as I can."

"Exactly." Belisarius turned and looked at the huge column of Rajput cavalry following them. Using the term "column" loosely. Most of the cavalry were young men, eager for glory now that a real battle finally looked to be in the offing. Their ranks, never too precise at the best of times, were getting more ragged by the minute as the more eager ones pressed forward.

"I'm not going to be able to hold them, Ashot," Belisarius said. "That's all right—*provided* you can keep that Malwa army from forming solid musket-and-pike squares before I get there."

Seconds later, Ashot was mounted and leading his cataphracts forward.

Belisarius turned to the Rajput kings and top officers, who had gathered around him.

"You heard," he stated. "Just try to keep the charge from getting completely out of control."

Dasal grinned. "Difficult, that. Young men, you know—and not many of them well-blooded yet."

Belisarius winced, a little. Young, indeed. At a guess, close to a third of the twenty thousand cavalrymen he had under his command were still teenagers. Being Rajputs, they were proficient with lances and swords, even at that age. But, for many of them, this would be their first real battle.

If the Malwa had solid infantry squares, it'd be a slaughter before Belisarius could extricate his soldiers. Hopefully, the speed of his approach and Ashot's spoiling charge would keep the enemy off-balance just long enough. As impetuous as the Rajputs were certain to be, they'd roll right over that Malwa army if it wasn't prepared for them, even though it outnumbered Belisarius' army by something close to a three-to-two margin.

"We'll just have to hope for the best," he said, trying not to make the lame expression sound completely crippled. "Let's go."

Kungas and his men had no difficulty at all driving back the first Malwa attempt to force the river. It was a desperate undertaking, as few boats as the enemy had managed to scrounge up. Kungas was a little surprised they'd made the attempt at all. Not a single one of the enemy boats got within thirty yards of the north bank of the Ganges.

"What's that bitch thinking?" wondered Vima. "I thought she was supposed to be smarter than any human alive."

Kujulo shrugged. "How smart can you be, when you've run out of options? Trap a genius in a pit, and he'll try to claw his way out just like a rat. What else can he do?"

◊   ◊   ◊

By the time Ashot reached the vanguard of the Malwa army, its commander had managed to get the columns on two of the roads to join forces. But he hadn't had time to get them into anything resembling a fighting formation.

Even moving at the moderate canter needed for accurate bow fire, Ashot needed no more than a few minutes to shred what little cohesion the forward units had. It was becoming obvious that the officers were either inexperienced or incompetent. Perhaps both.

That was not surprising, really. After years of war, the Malwa army like any other would have gone through a selection process with the most capable and energetic officers sent to the front; the sluggards and dull-wits, assigned to garrison duty.

Ashot even considered disobeying Belisarius' order and passing onward to find the artillery. The odds were that he'd be able to rip them up badly, also.

But he decided to forego the temptation. The scattered musket fire being directed at his men didn't pose much of a danger, but if he had the bad luck of catching even a few guns ready to fire and loaded with canister, he'd suffer some casualties—and he only had five hundred men to begin with.

"Back!" he bellowed. "We'll hit the forward units again!"

All he had to do, really, was keep the advance regiments of enemy infantry in a state of turmoil. When the Rajputs struck them, they'd scatter them to the winds—and the fleeing infantrymen would transmit their panic all the way back through the long columns.

Belisarius didn't have to crush this army. All he had to do was send them into a panicky retreat to Mathura. The Malwa officers wouldn't be able to rally their army until it was all the way back into the city. And then, getting them to march out again would take several days.

Long enough, Ashot thought, to enable Belisarius to return to the Ganges and crush the army that really mattered. Link's army.

The raking fire of the Roman cataphracts on their return did exactly what Ashot thought it would. By the time the last cataphract passed out of musket range, the enemy's front lines were a shambles. Not a single one of the squares the Malwa officers had tried to form was anything more than a mass of confused and frightened men.

The Romans suffered only twenty casualties in the whole affair, and only seven of those were fatalities.

Just blind, bad luck, that Ashot was one of them. As he was almost out of range, a random musket ball fired by a panicked Malwa soldier passed under the flange of his helmet and broke his neck.

Belisarius didn't find out until later. At the time, he was cursing ferociously, trying to keep the Rajput charge from dissolving into a chaos even worse than that of the enemy's formations.

He failed, utterly, but it didn't matter. The young Rajputs suffered much worse casualties than they needed to have suffered, but their charge was so headlong that they simply shattered the front of the Malwa army. Twenty thousand cavalrymen charging at a gallop would have been terrifying for any army. Experienced soldiers, in solid formations and with steady officers, would have broken the charge anyway. But the Mathura garrison hadn't been in a real battle since many of its units had participated in the assault in Ranapur, years earlier.

They broke like rotten wood. Broke, and then—as Ashot had foreseen—began shredding the rest of the army in their panicked rout.

Belisarius and the kings tried to stop the Rajputs from pursuing the fleeing enemy. There was no need to destroy this army in a prolonged and ruthless pursuit. But it was hopeless. Their blood was up. The glorious great victory those young men eagerly wanted after the wretched business of being simple arsonists was finally at hand—and they wanted all of it.

After a time, Belisarius gave up the effort. The old kings could be relied upon to bring the Rajputs back, when they were finally done, and he'd just gotten word of Ashot.

Sadly, he gazed down on the Armenian's corpse. Ashot's expression was peaceful, with just a trace of surprise showing in his still-open eyes.

He'd been one of the best officers Belisarius had ever had serve under him. So good, and so reliable, that he'd assigned him to serve as Antonina's commander on her expedition to Egypt. Except for Maurice, Belisarius wouldn't have trusted anyone else with his wife's safety.

"Shall we bring him back?" asked Ashot's replacement, a Thracian cataphract named Stylian.

"No. We've got another forced march ahead of us, and who knows what after that? We'll bury him here."

Belisarius looked around. The landscape was typical of the area between the Ganges and the Yamuna. A grassy plain, basically, with fields surrounding the villages and dotted with groves and woods. They hadn't burned here, since Belisarius had seen no reason to.

His eyes were immediately drawn to a grove of sal trees perhaps a quarter of a mile away. The trees were considered holy by many Hindus and Buddhists. The legend had it that the famous Lumbini tract where the Buddha meditated and acquired salvation had been in a grove of sal trees.

"We'll bury him over there," he said. "It seems a good resting place, and it'll be easy to find the grave later."

While Stylian handled that matter, Belisarius organized his cataphracts to help Jaimal and Udai Singh and the old kings round up the Rajputs. That would take the rest of the day, under the best of circumstances. Belisarius could only hope that Link wouldn't be able to move far in the time it took him to get back to the Ganges.

Link had managed to move its army exactly seven miles down the Ganges. What was worse, the foraging parties it had sent out had returned with very little. The constant harassment of the Kushans, even on the south side of the Ganges, made the foragers exceedingly cautious. Kushans were not a cavalry nation in the same sense as Persians and Rajputs, but they seemed to be mostly mounted and just as proficient in the saddle as they were in all forms of warfare.

Link had only three thousand cavalry. Fewer than that, now, after a number of clashes with Kushan dragoons. It could not even stop the Kushans from continuing the scorched earth campaign that Belisarius had begun.

The situation would have been infuriating, if Link had been capable of fury. The burning done by Belisarius' and Kungas' armies prevented Link from marching quickly, foraging as it went.

And the Kushan harassment, despite the fact that the Malwa out-numbered them at least two-to-one, made their progress slower still. Link could destroy any Kushan attempt to charge its solid infantry, true enough. But Kungas was far too canny to order any such foolish assault.

And where was Belisarius? Link had no information at all. All the telegraph lines had been cut, and the Kushans ambushed any scouts it sent out. Link was operating as blindly as any commander in human history, except that it had an encyclopedic knowledge of the terrain. But that meant almost nothing, when it had no idea where the main enemy force was to be found in it.

The probability was that Belisarius had left to meet a garrison coming north from one of the large cities. Mathura, most likely.

It was always possible that such a garrison would defeat the Roman general. But Link estimated that probability as being very low. Not more than ten percent, at best. Assuming the far more likely probability that Belisarius would triumph in that battle as he had in almost all others, he and his army would be back at the Ganges within a few days.

By which time, Link and its forces would not have moved more than ten or fifteen miles. Probably ten. Kushan harassment was becoming more intense, seemingly by the hour.

"What shall we do, Great Lady?"

"Continue down the Ganges," Link replied. What else could it say?

When Khusrau and his army reached Chandan, on the Chenab river, the emperor was so taken by the beauty of the town and its setting that he ordered his soldiers not to burn it. He did, however, give them permission to loot the homes and public buildings.

That took little time. Most of the population had fled already, taking their most valuable possessions with them. After his army had crossed the Jhelum and entered the land between that river and the Chenab, the Persians considered themselves in enemy territory. By the terms of the agreement Khusrau had made with the Romans and the new Malwa emperor, after the war this would become Malwa territory. So, they were destroying everything, driving the population south toward Multan, where they'd join a horde of refugees already overburdening the Malwa garrison there.

In an sense, they'd been in enemy territory also, west of the Jhelum, but those lands were destined to become part of the Persian empire, by the provisions of the agreement. So, Khusrau had kept his soldiers under tight discipline, and had refrained from any destruction except where enemy forces put up resistance.

There hadn't been much of that. Apparently, the Malwa commander of the main army in the Punjab had been withdrawing all his detachments in the north in order to reinforce the Malwa lines facing the Romans. Lord Samudra, as he was named, was adopting a completely defensive posture while the Persians and the Kushans invaded the northern Punjab with impunity. For all practical purposes, the Malwa empire's largest and most powerful army had become paralyzed on its western border, while Damodara and Belisarius and Kungas and Khusrau himself drove lances into its unprotected guts.

Khusrau thought Samudra was an idiot. *Knew* him to be an idiot, rather, since the Persian emperor was well aware that Maurice had no more than fifty thousand Roman troops in the Iron Triangle. Sixty thousand, perhaps, counting the various auxiliary units that were assigned to maintaining the critical supply lines from the Sind. But even including those soldiers, Maurice was still outnumbered well over two-to-one. Probably closer to three-to-one.

With fifty thousand men behind those formidable Roman defensive works, of course, Maurice could hold his own against Samudra. But only on the defensive—and the same was true the other way. Samudra could have easily taken over half his army north to put a stop to Khusrau's expedition and, possibly, even cut off the Kushan army. Depending on where Kungas had taken it, of course. Khusrau suspected the Kushans were already into the Gangetic Plain. If they were able to join forces with Belisarius . . .

But while the Malwa commander in the Punjab seemed capable enough, when it came to routine matters, Samudra obviously had not an ounce of initiative and daring. The Malwa regime was not one that fostered independent thinking on the part of its commanders.

Hard to blame them, really. The one great exception to that rule was probably even now battering at the gates of Kausambi.

Damodara was not battering at the gates, as it happened. But he was bringing the siege guns into position to do so.

"Yes, yes, Ajatasutra, I know we hope to enter the city through . . . ah, what would you call it? 'Treachery' seems inappropriate."

"Guile and stratagem, Your Majesty," Ajatasutra supplied.

Damodara smiled. "Splendid terms. On my side, anyway."

The new emperor glanced at Narses. The Roman spymaster was perched on the mule he favored, studying the fortifications on the western walls of Kausambi.

It was a knowing sort of examination, not the vacant stare that most imperial courtiers would have given such a purely military matter. Damodara had realized long since that Narses·was as shrewd with regard to military affairs as he was with all others. Damodara was quite sure that despite his age, and the fact that he was eunuch, Narses would make an excellent general himself.

What am I going to do with Narses? he asked himself, not for the first time. *If I take the throne, do I dare keep such a man around? It'd be like sharing a sleeping chamber with a cobra.*

The solution was obvious, but Damodara felt himself resisting that impulse. Whatever else, Narses had served him well for years. Superbly well, in fact. Had even, most likely, kept his family and that of Rana Sanga alive where they would have been murdered by Malwa otherwise.

It would bode ill, Damodara thought, if he began what amounted to a new dynasty in all but name with an act of treachery.

But what else can I do? The Romans certainly won't take him back. And the Persians and the Axumites and the Kushans know his reputation too well to entertain the thought of employing him, either.

What else is there, but an executioner or an assassin's blade?

Perhaps he could have him poisoned . . .

Damodara shook his head and went back to the matter immediately at hand.

"You think too much like an assassin, Ajatasutra. When the time comes, Rana Sanga is ready to lead the charge. He'll take ten thousand of his Rajputs. But first we must fix Skandagupta's entire attention on *this* side of the city. I don't have a large enough army to invest Kausambi, and the emperor—ah, the false emperor—knows it. At least, his commanders will tell him so. So, now that I've massed my troops here before the western gates and"—he gestured with his head toward the heavy artillery berms his engineers were constructing—"am setting up the siege guns I brought from Mathura, he'll concentrate his own troops on these walls, and at these gates."

Whether or not he was inclined to argue the matter, Ajatasutra made no attempt to do so. Instead, he began thoughtfully scratching his chin.

"How long, Emperor? Before you can order Sanga's charge, I mean."

Damodara shrugged. "Hard to know. Not for a few days, certainly."

"In that case, I should return to Kausambi. They could use me there, when the time comes. Whereas here . . . "

He waved his hand, indicating the soldiers under Damodara's command who were setting up their own camps and lines of defense against any possible sallies from the city. "Merely one blade among tens of thousands of others."

"Certainly. But . . . " Damodara's eyes widened a bit. "*Can* you get back into the city? By now, the guards will be on the alert for spies."

"Oh, yes. Don't forget that they're mediocre guards, and"— Ajatasutra cleared his throat modestly—"I am very far from a mediocre assassin. I'll get in."

His good humor faded, however, as he contemplated his superb horse. "Alas, the horse *won't*. Not even sorry garrison troops will think it's a tinker's nag."

He bowed low. "May I present him to Your Majesty, then? A token of my esteem. No! My awe at Your effulgent presence, divine in its aspect."

Damodara laughed. *And what was he to do with Ajatasutra, for that matter, if he took the throne?* He didn't doubt the assassin's loyalty, but within a few years Ajatasutra's mocking ways would have half the courtiers in Kausambi demanding his head.

But there'd be time enough to deal with that later. First, he had to take Kausambi.

"Go, Ajatasutra. If we're both still alive in a few days, I'll return the horse."

It seemed impolitic to add: *You might need it.*

From their position just south of the junction of the Ganges and Yamuna rivers, the five members of the Malwa assassination team stared at the empire's capital city. That part of it they could see looked fine. But they could easily hear the sound of big guns firing to the west.

"Marvelous," snarled the captain. "Just perfect. After ten thousand miles—more like eleven, by now—we finally get back to Kausambi—having succeeded in doing nothing—and the city's under siege."

"We'll never get in," said his lieutenant, morosely. "No way the guards will pass five strange men."

It was true enough. No doubt, ensconced somewhere in the huge imperial palace, were the records that would identify the assassination team and establish their bona fides. Probably, even, two or three of Nanda Lal's subordinates who would recognize them personally. The captain and the lieutenant, at least.

And so what? The odds that any such spymasters would heed a summons from a gate's guards—assuming the guards were willing to send a summons in the first place, instead of simply killing the five assassins and saving themselves a lot of possible trouble—were too low to even think about.

"No hope for it," he sighed. "We may as well cross the Ganges and set up camp on the other side, as close as we can get to the eastern gate. Maybe something will turn up."

His lieutenant eyed the distance. "At least it's not far." He spit on the ground. "We laugh at a few miles, after so many wasted thousands."

Chapter 37
THE GANGES

There had been many times, since the war began, that Belisarius had been glad to have Abbu and his Arab scouts in his service.

Never more than now.

"Idiot Rajputs would have gotten you into another war, General," said the old bedouin chief, scowling. "Are they blind? Who else wears topknots?"

Abbu was being a little uncharitable, but . . . only a little. It was not as if Rajputs weren't familiar with Kushans. Until recently, there had been tens of thousands of Kushans in the Malwa military, many of whom had served in the same armies as Rajputs, if not in the same units.

On the other hand—being charitable—there were still considerable numbers of Kushans in the service of the Malwa empire. By no means all of the Kushans had defected after Kungas re-created the old Kushan kingdom.

But they were no longer trusted, and there was no possibility at all that Link had included Kushan units in its army when it marched from the Punjab. Even idiot Rajputs should have understood that much.

Even idiot *teenage* Rajputs.

"They're still young," muttered old Jaisal. "Young men don't think of these things."

Belisarius squelched his irritation. It would be purely stupid to offend the Rajputs who constituted almost his entire army, after all.

"Well, there was no harm done, apparently. The Kushans fled the scene as soon as contact was made and"—he cleared his throat, as diplomatically as possible—"the Rajput cavalrymen immediately began firing on them."

That fact was interesting, in and of itself. Under normal circumstances, Kushans were quite belligerent enough to have responded to the initial Rajput bow fire by attacking them. Especially since, by all accounts—those of the Rajputs as well as the Arab scouts—the Kushans had outnumbered the Rajput cavalry unit.

Abbu put his thoughts into words. "They were expecting us, General. Only possible answer."

"Yes." Belisarius scratched his chin. "I'm almost sure that means Kungas himself is here. He must have gambled that Maurice could keep the main Malwa army pinned in the south Punjab, while he marched into the Ganges plain to attack Link's army."

"Bold man!"

Belisarius smiled. "Well, yes. A timid fellow would hardly have marched across Central Asia in the middle of the world's greatest war to set up a new kingdom. With a new Greek bookworm wife, to boot."

Abbu had met Irene. "Crazy man," he muttered, his scowl returning.

Belisarius swiveled in the saddle to face Dasal and the other Rajput kings. "Can you keep your men under control? I have *got* to establish contact with the Kushans—and, as Abbu says, I don't need to start a new war with my allies."

All the Rajput kings had the grace to look embarrassed for a moment. They didn't answer immediately, however, Belisarius noted.

He wasn't surprised. Their smashing victory over the Mathura garrison had filled the young Rajput warriors with elation so great it bordered on heedlessness and reckless arrogance. Inexperienced to begin with, they were in no mood to listen to the lectures of old kings concerning the danger of accidentally fighting allies in the middle of a turbulent campaign of marches and countermarches. "Friendly fire," as a future world would call it, was not something a nineteen-year-old Rajput cavalryman gave much thought to when he woke up in the morning. Or at any time of the day or night.

"Right." Belisarius swiveled again and brought Jaimal and Udai Singh under his gaze.

"Can *you* manage it?"

Jaimal smiled thinly. "Oh, yes, General Belisarius." He gave the old kings a sly look. "*Our* men are real veterans."

"But there are only fifty of us," cautioned Udai Singh.

"That should be enough," Belisarius said. "I'll send Abbu and some of his scouts with you, along with a few of my cataphracts. All we need to do, for the moment, is make contact with the Kushans. Set up a time and place where Kungas and I can meet—assuming I'm right, and he's here. If not, whoever their commander is."

Sanga's two lieutenants trotted off, with Abbu and Stylian trailing behind. Belisarius could rely on Stylian to select level-headed cataphracts for the business. In the meantime, he had a different problem to deal with.

"I'm still guessing," he said to the kings, "but I'm pretty sure Kungas will have most of his army on the north bank of the Ganges. It's what I would do in his place. Keep Sati from crossing the river and using it as a shield between us and her."

Faced with a straightforward tactical issue, the kings were more at ease.

"Agreed," said Dasal. "Which means—until we can establish liaison—we should stay on *this* side."

"This side, and east of here," his younger brother grunted. "Resume the burning. Turn everything for twenty miles to the east into a wasteland. The Malwa will be stranded."

"The young men will complain," complained Chachu.

Dasal's frown might have been envied by Jove. "The young men will do as they are told."

The young Rajput warriors complained. Bitterly.

They also did as they were told.

By the time Jaimal and Udai and Abbu returned, the sky east of Sati's army was filled with smoke.

"It's Kungas," Jaimal said. "He recommends you meet at a fishing village—what used to be a fishing village—five miles upstream from the Malwa army."

Udai grinned. "He promises not to shoot you, if you have your hair in a topknot. Otherwise he may not be able to control his men. He says most of them are only ten years old. Heedless and careless."

Belisarius returned the grin. "I'd look silly in a topknot. I'll take my chances."

Stylian was frowning, however. "Only five miles from the enemy? That seems . . . "

Abbu was already shaking his head. "No need to worry. That Malwa army is not moving at all, any longer. Just sitting there, baking in the *garam* sun."

"Kungas says Sati had her elephants butchered, two days ago," added Jaimal. "The beasts were getting out of control—and, by now, they probably needed the meat, anyway. He thinks that army is getting pretty desperate."

The word "desperate" could have been applied to the soldiers of Link's army, well enough, but not to the cyborg itself. True, it had come to the conclusion that the position of its army was hopeless. But, in the odd way that its mind worked, that knowledge brought nothing more than what a human might have called "relief."

Not that either, really, since Link knew no emotions. Still, the other side of hopelessness was that decisions became very simple. If nothing else, rest from labor was at hand.

In a few hours, at least. Link still had to work through human instruments, and those flawed creatures always had their own needs. Which, at times, had to be respected.

So, with its inhuman patience, Link observed silently as the special priests and assassins in its chaundoli began their rituals.

It might even be said to do so with satisfaction. At least *that* part of the new gods' plan had worked properly. The cult fostered over a century earlier in the Khmer lands had served its purpose well. Link could rely on those priests and assassins to do what was needed.

If not, unfortunately, as quickly as it would have liked. But half a day's delay should not matter. Even if, as Link was assuming, Damodara had seized the big guns at Mathura, it would still take weeks before they could begin crumbling the walls of Kausambi.

◊   ◊   ◊

Damodara's estimate was considerably more pessimistic.

"At least two months," he grumbled, watching the great cannons as they belched fire at the walls of Kausambi. Half of them missed entirely. The bores on those giant but crude siege guns were very sloppy. The huge stone balls that did strike the walls seemed to have no more effect than so many pebbles.

"If we're lucky," he added sourly.

But Rana Sanga barely heard him, and paid no attention to the guns at all. The Rajput king had entered that peculiar mental zone he usually entered before a great battle. A strange combination of serenity and fierce anticipation—the first, serving as a dam for the pent-up waters of the second.

When the time came—very soon, Sanga thought—the dam would break.

No, would shatter. Pouring out in that flood would be the greatest ride of his life, followed by his greatest battle.

"Months!" Damodara snarled.

"Yes, Lord," said Sanga, absently. He didn't even notice that he used the old appellation for Damodara, instead of the new "Your Majesty."

Neither did Damodara.

"I'm nervous," said Tarun. "What if I do it wrong? Are you sure—"

"Don't be silly," Rajiv assured the young stable-boy. He held up the fuse, pinched between thumb and forefinger. "What's to go wrong? You've got a pocket full of matches. Just light this and take shelter."

Dubiously, Tarun brought out one of the matches in his pocket and studied it.

"What if—?"

Trying not to let his exasperation show, Rajiv plucked the match from Tarun's hand and struck it against one of the stones in the stable floor. The match flared up very nicely, with its usual acrid fumes.

"Specially made," he said forcefully. "By the best apothecary in Kausambi."

Honesty forced him to add: "Well . . . The best in this quarter, anyway. He's probably just as good as any in the imperial palace, though."

That was true enough, but it brought up another thing for Tarun to fret over.

"What if he betrays us? Matches are unusual things. What if he starts wondering—"

Squatting a few feet away, Valentinian laughed softly. "Weren't you just telling us yesterday that nobody is paying attention to the soldiers any more? Even the soldiers themselves?"

"They've even slacked off the digging," Anastasius added. "Good thing, too, as close as they were getting."

Never comfortable for very long in a squat, the huge cataphract rose to his feet. It was an ungainly movement, not because Anastasius was uncoordinated—which he certainly wasn't, for a man his size—but simply because the size itself created certain physical realities. A rhinoceros is ungainly also, rising to its feet. Not ungainly, however, in the charge that follows.

"Relax, boy. By now, Skandagupta has over a thousand corpses or heads decorating the walls of his palace. He's become a maniac, and everyone in the city knows it. Nobody in his right mind wants to get anywhere near him—or his police. That apothecary will do what everyone else is trying their best to do, these days. Mind his own business and hope he survives whatever's coming."

It was true enough, and Tarun knew it as well as anyone else in the stable. The soldiers and laborers engaged in digging up the area looking for the hideaways *had* been slacking off, for at least a week. "Slacking off," at least, in the sense of not getting much done that was of any use. To be sure, they managed to look as if they were working frenziedly. But most of it was make-work; literally, moving soil and rubble back and forth from one hole or pile to another.

You could hardly blame them. Every time they'd uncovered something, whoever was in charge wound up getting beheaded or impaled. Over time, of course, reports of no progress at all would be met with equal punishment. But that took more time than success.

By this point, in besieged Kausambi, most people were simply buying time.

Not everyone.

Lady Damodara appeared in the stall. "Ajatasutra's back. He wants to know—"

"How soon?" asked the assassin himself, coming right behind her. "Inquiring emperors want to know."

Valentinian grinned, mirthlessly. "Now that you're here, how's tomorrow morning sound?"

Tarun gulped.

"You'll do fine," Rajiv assured him. "But you'd better leave now. It's a big city and you've got a ways to go. And you need to be in place before sunrise."

"It's dark outside," Tarun protested.

"Of course it is," said Valentinian. "That's the plan. Now, go."

Tarun made no further protest. Whatever else he might be worried about was merely a possibility, involving someone else or something else at some other place and time.

Valentinian was here and now. Tarun went.

Belisarius wasn't really worried about any Malwa patrols sent out by Link. Where Belisarius had twenty thousand cavalrymen and Kungas had fifteen thousand dragoons, the monster had had only had three thousand cavalry to begin with. Far fewer than that, now, between the casualties they'd suffered in various clashes and—the crudest factor of all—the fact that they were now beginning to butcher their horses for the meat.

Still, he saw no reason to take chances. So, he made the rendezvous with Kungas well before daybreak.

The Kushan king was waiting for him, in one of the few huts in the small village that had escaped the Rajputs' arson. He was squatting on the dirt floor, with a bottle of rice wine and two cups.

"Nice to see you again," he said, pouring Belisarius a drink. "I'd worry about you getting drunk, except you can drink like a fish and this stuff's so thin it doesn't matter anyway. Best I could find."

Smiling, Belisarius squatted and took the cup. "I'm *delighted* to see you—and surprised. You took a mighty gamble, coming here from the Hindu Kush."

Kungas made the little shoulder twitch that did him for a shrug. "I figured you'd be here, somewhere. And since I'm a Kushan king, I need to prove I'm a great gambler or I'll soon enough have people muttering that I'm unfit to rule. Most of all, though, I want to see that bitch finally dead."

Belisarius swallowed the wine in one gulp. It was not a big gulp, however, since it was a very small cup.

Just as well. The stuff was wretched as well as thin. Exactly the sort of wine you'd expect to find in a poor fishing village.

The face he made, though, was not due to the wine.

"Then I hate to say this, but you're in for a big disappointment. The one thing we're *not* going to do is kill Great Lady Sati."

Kungas' eyes widened slightly. In his minimalist manner, that signified astonishment.

"Why in the world not?" Accusingly, almost plaintively, he added: "You killed her predecessor, didn't you?"

"Yes, I did. And I will say that few things in my life gave me more satisfaction than seeing Great Lady Holi die. But that was another place, another time, and under different circumstances. Here, and now, we want Sati simply isolated—but still alive."

He set the cup down on the floor. "That was *a* battle. This is *the* battle. More accurately, this is a holding action while the final battle is fought elsewhere, by Damodara."

Kungas tugged at his wisp of a goatee. "Um. You're gambling yourself."

"Yes and no. I'm not gambling—well, not much of a gamble—that Damodara will have reached Kausambi by now. What I'm gambling is simply that it will take him some time to break into the city. I've seen those defenses. Nothing in the world matches them, except possibly the ancient fortifications at Babylon."

The Kushan king's beard-tugging became more vigorous. "Damnation, Belisarius . . . "

The Roman general just waited, patiently. The best way to persuade Kungas of anything was to let him persuade himself. Beneath that impassive exterior, the Kushan was as smart as anyone Belisarius had ever known—and he was privy to all the secrets of Link's methods of rule. Belisarius had briefed Kungas and Irene extensively on the matter, before they left Constantinople on their great expedition to the Hindu Kush.

"Damnation," Kungas repeated. But the word, this time, was simply said fatalistically.

Belisarius waited. The Kushan's hand fell from the beard.

"All right. I understand the logic. As long as the bitch is alive, Link is locked into her body. Here—not in Kausambi. The minute she dies, Link will assume a new sheath. This new one in the imperial palace, so it will be able to take direct command of Kausambi's defenses. Instead of Skandagupta, whom no one in his right mind has ever considered a military genius. Or even a very competent emperor."

"Exactly."

"Who?" Kungas wondered. "And how many sheaths does that monster have at its disposal?"

Good question. Aide?

Belisarius could sense the jewel's hesitation. **Not sure. It's complicated.**

Try to explain, as best you can. We need to know.

After a moment, Aide said: **It's not easy for it. Link, I mean. First of all, the sheath has to be female—never mind why—and, second of all, it has to be in the line of the dynastic clan. That's because . . . well, never mind that, either. Just take my word for it. There's a critical genetic component to the process. Several, in fact. Close blood relations are important.**

Belisarius nodded. To Kungas, he said: "Aide's explaining it to me. Give us a moment."

Third, the sheath itself has to be individually suitable. Not every girl is. Most aren't, in fact—and there are only a small number to choose from in the first place, being restricted to the female offspring of the dynastic clan. She has to be . . . The word won't mean anything to you, but it's something the future will call "autism." It's a pretty rare medical condition. Not very many children suffer from it.

Belisarius didn't bother asking Aide to explain the terms. Some day, he would, but there wasn't the need for it now, or the time available.

He did purse his lips with distaste. Contempt, rather. That was absolutely typical of the methods of the "new gods" who claimed to be humanity's true future. They would not only use innocent children as the vessels for their rule, but would choose ones already damaged and even less able to protect themselves.

I see. The Malwa dynastic clan is a big one, but still . . .

There'd only be one available every few years. It would vary, of course. The long span of years between Holi's age and Sati's would have been unusual. Even so, I doubt if Link has more than two—maybe three—sheaths available. Not

even that, really, because they need years of training in addition to everything else. The moment of transition— possession, if you will—is pretty traumatic. If the girl isn't thoroughly prepared for it, she'll simply die.

A thought came to Belisarius. *If that's so . . . What if the new sheath is very young? It might actually be smarter . . .*

He shook his head. "No, that's too much of a gamble."

Kungas twisted his head, quizzically. Belisarius explained: "There can't be many sheaths. Maybe only one—and she might very well still be a young girl. If so . . . "

He almost laughed, seeing the suddenly fierce expression on the Kushan's face.

"Tempting, isn't it, Kungas? What happens if the Malwa empire is suddenly ruled by a child? Will anyone—even Skanda-gupta—really listen to her?"

After a moment, Kungas expelled his breath. "No. As you say, too much of a gamble—even for a Kushan. What if she *isn't*? Sati was in her prime, after all, when she became the new Link."

What was too much of a gamble, even for a Kushan king, was not for a cyborg.

Not, at least, for this cyborg. Kungas and Belisarius had options. Link no longer did.

The Khmer had finished their rituals.

"Now," the thing known as Great Lady Sati commanded.

Expertly, the assassin standing behind her drove his dagger into Sati's spinal column. Just as expertly, the assassin standing before her drove his blade into her heart.

As her body slumped, a third assassin stepped forward and—with the same expertise—slit her throat from ear to ear.

A priest was there with a large bowl, to catch the sacred fluid. There was little spillage, since the goddess' heart was no longer beating.

That was good, because the blood was needed for the remaining rituals.

Those rituals done, the assassins slew all the priests but one. Then, slew themselves.

Being careful, even at the end, to keep the gore as minimal as possible.

That was not because of the needs of the rituals; which, to the contrary, normally put the gore to extensive use. But the goddess had ordered it all done quietly and economically.

Following the usual rituals would have permeated the chaundoli with a stench that the soldiers outside would have noticed almost immediately. As it was, in the heat of *garam*, they would notice it soon enough. Link wanted this army intact as long as possible, to keep Belisarius distracted.

The sole surviving priest remained at his duty. Simply sitting by the door to the chaundoli, that he might tell inquiring officers that the Great Lady was asleep and had given orders not to be disturbed.

In the special quarters far below the imperial palace at Kausambi, the eight-year-old girl known as Rani lay motionless and empty-eyed on the floor of her chamber. Her special Khmer attendants were deeply concerned, but could do nothing.

The sacred transference had happened, they knew. But it had happened much sooner than any of them had expected, including the girl herself.

She would survive, they decided. Beyond that, other than providing her with a cloth soaked in water to sip, they could only wait.

Tarun was too nervous to wait any longer. He'd gotten to the place Rajiv and he had picked long before he really needed to. It was an isolated corner in the maze of an outdoor bazaar not far from Kausambi's northernmost gate. At this time of night, the stalls were all closed and barred.

No one paid any attention to a twelve-year-old boy huddled in the darkness. There were many such in the city. A thief might have noticed the wrapped bundle beneath the boy's ragged cloak, but even if he had he would most likely have done nothing. What of any value could such a ragamuffin possess?

Still, the two hours Tarun waited seemed interminable to the stable-keeper's son. So, when he saw the first faint sign of dawn in the sky above, he rose and drew forth the signal rockets. There were three of them, in case of a misfire.

Nervous as he was, Tarun fumbled none of the tasks involved. Within seconds, one of the rockets was propped against the simple bamboo frame that held it erect, pointing at the sky. He lit the match, struck the fuse, and hurried to the other side of the stall.

He was even disciplined enough to remain there, the final seconds. If the rocket misfired, he'd retrieve the bamboo frame to use for a second.

For a wonder, nothing went wrong. The rocket didn't misfire, and it didn't blow up. It soared hundreds of yards into the dark sky above Kausambi.

It even exploded when it was supposed to. A great, bright yellow light shone over the city.

Tarun didn't spend any time admiring the sight, however. He just dropped the remaining rockets and hurried off. What would happen, would happen. He'd done his part and now simply wanted to get back to his family.

Few of the city's inhabitants ever saw the wondrous sight, for its people were mostly asleep.

The soldiers standing guard saw, of course, and raced to bring the news to their officers. *Something is happening at the northern gate!*

Valentinian and Anastasius and Ajatasutra and Tarun and their three Ye-tai mercenaries saw it also, of course. They arose from their own hiding place not far from the city's southern gate.

More precisely, Anastasius and Rajiv arose. The others remained in the small wagon, hidden from sight below a thin bamboo grate that held the produce which apparently filled the wagon's entire bed.

Anastasius seized the handles of the wagon, hauled it into the street, and began plodding toward the gate some fifty yards away. Rajiv walked beside him, dressed as a merchant's son. Clearly enough, the scion of a prosperous family assigned to oversee a strong but dimwitted laborer in his work.

"Why does the big guy always get stuck with these jobs?" complained Anastasius.

"Shut up," came Valentinian's voice from under the wagon's load. "You're not only as big as an ox, you look like one. Be thankful I didn't give Rajiv a whip."

◇   ◇   ◇

Rana Sanga saw it also. And the dam shattered.

He was on his horse and charging out of the lines within a minute, with ten thousand Rajputs following.

Only Rajputs, and only half of those. Damodara would use the other half, and the Ye-tai and the kshatriyas, for whatever else was needed. But this charge, the emperor knew, belonged to Rana Sanga alone.

There would be nothing imperial about it, really. Just the nation of the Rajputs, finally and truly regaining its soul.

"For the glory of Rajputana!" Sanga called, his lance and its pennant on high, in a piercing voice that was half a bellow and half a shriek.

"RAJPUTANA!" came the response from ten thousand throats.

The Malwa soldiers on the southern wall of the city did not understand what was happening. They knew only three things.

One, most of the garrison had been ordered to the northern gate.

Two, a flood—a torrent—a tidal bore of Rajput lances was pouring past them on the ground beyond the walls.

Going where?

Who could say?

They only knew the third thing. Those lances looked as sharp as the sound of the Rajput battle cry.

"Shit," said one of them.

"What are we going to do?" asked his mate in the squad.

"Don't be an idiot. Try to stay alive, what else? Do *you* care who the emperor is?"

"Well. No."

Chapter 38
KAUSAMBI

Rajiv steeled himself. The two guards standing at the entrance to the gatehouse were among the ones he liked. Nice men, both of them—and so were their wives and kids.

"Rajiv?" asked Pallav. "What are you doing here? And with a wagon?"

"You know we can't let you out of the gate," said Gaurang.

Both of them were frowning, but neither had drawn his sword and their spears were still leaning against the gate hut. The many days Rajiv and Tarun had spent at the gate and the adjoining barracks, chatting with the guards and playing with their children, had made them a familiar sight. Besides, they were only boys.

"Oh, this is some stuff—food, mostly—my father told me I should bring you." Rajiv half turned, hiding the dagger he slid into his hand. "It's not much, really."

He frowned at Anastasius. "Put down the wagon, you cretin! Can't you see we've arrived?"

Anastasius, dull-faced, did as he was told. The moment Pallav stepped forward to look at the wagon's contents, Rajiv sprang.

Still, at the end—damn what the Mongoose would say—Rajiv made sure the blade sank into the meaty part of the soldier's thigh, not even close to the femoral artery. Twisting the dagger and snatching it out of the wound, Rajiv struck Pallav's head with the pommel. Being careful to avoid the fragile temple bones.

All to no purpose. Anastasius yanked the wagon handle out of its socket and crushed Pallav's skull as he fell. Then, in the back stroke, went for Gaurang. The slender arm the soldier threw up to block the blow was completely useless. As well block a rhino horn with a twig. His broken body was slammed into the hut so hard the flimsy wooden structure disintegrated.

Left to his own, Rajiv would probably have wasted some seconds, staring at the corpses. But the Mongoose was already out of the wagon and plunging into the open door of the gatehouse, spatha in hand. Ajatasutra was close behind.

There would be three or four more guards inside the gatehouse. Also men that Rajiv knew. Against the Mongoose, even if they'd been warned and ready, they'd have been dead men. As it was, the shrill cries of alarm and the soft wet sounds of massacre lasted but a few seconds. Most likely, Ajatasutra never got involved at all.

Fortunately, Rajiv didn't have to watch. Two men could work the gate mechanism, and there wasn't enough room in the narrow stairs leading up the tower or in the chamber above for more than two men anyway.

For such work, Valentinian and Ajatasutra were the obvious choices. Anastasius and Rajiv and the three Ye-tai mercenaries were assigned to guard the entrance and fend off the soldiers from the adjacent barracks, long enough to allow Valentinian and Ajatasutra to open the gate.

The Ye-tai were already shoving the wagon across the entrance, after finishing the work of casting off the bamboo grate and the produce covering it. Anastasius reached into the wagon bed and withdrew the big maul hidden there, along with his bow and arrows, and the mace he favored for close-in work.

After they'd opened the gate, Valentinian and Ajatasutra would return below to help in the defense, while Anastasius went upstairs and smashed the gate mechanism.

The mechanism was heavy, and very sturdy. But the maul was iron-headed, and very big. And Anastasius was Anastasius. Even if the soldiers could force their way up the tower, past one of the world's handful of great swordsmen and India's second-best assassin, it would take hours to repair the machinery and close the gates.

They would not have those hours. They would not even have very many minutes. Rajiv's father had only a few miles to come.

◇   ◇   ◇

He came, at an easy canter that the horses could maintain for some time without tiring. As eager and impatient as he was to reach the gate, the Rajput king was far too experienced a horseman to do otherwise. He would save the energy of a gallop for the very end.

Twenty minutes, he thought it would take.

He was eager, and impatient, but not worried. Rana Sanga had fought the Mongoose for hours, once. He did not think for a moment that, in narrow quarters, garrison troops could defeat him.

Not in twenty minutes. Probably not in twenty hours. Not without cannons, anyway.

Within five minutes, the warning was brought to the officer in command of the quarter's garrison. He was an exceptionally capable officer. Realizing immediately the implications, he ordered his soldiers to bring the four field guns they had. A six-pounder and three four-pounders.

They were an exceptionally well-trained unit, too. Five hundred men, no fewer. The commander was sure he could retake the gate once he reached it.

In . . . perhaps fifteen minutes. More likely, twenty. His soldiers were already awake, since he'd ordered them aroused the moment he heard of the rocket, but they were still mostly in the barracks. The gate was a third of a mile away, and the streets were very narrow.

Twenty minutes should still be quick enough. The rebel army was concentrating its attack on the north, according to the reports he'd been given, where the signal rocket had been fired by spies. Probably that gate was being seized by traitors also. The commanding officer was quite experienced. Most sieges were broken by treachery, not guns.

The emperor, he thought sourly, would have done far better to have ordered his soldiers to search for spies, instead of hidden refugees. Who cared what a great lady and her children did, huddling in a cellar somewhere?

The soldiers already at the gate were driven back within less than a minute. The sheer violence of the defense was not something they'd ever encountered. There was a huge ogre accompanying the traitors, whoever they were. A monstrous creature, that crushed the life out of men with its great mace, sometimes felling two soldiers with one blow. The ogre had fierce Ye-tai with it, too.

They reeled back, frightened. Their spears had been useless. Their swords, even more so.

"Bring bows!" shouted their commander. He was lacing on his armor, and having trouble with the task. He'd been sound asleep when the alarm was sounded, and was still feeling confused.

"Bring bows!" he shrieked again.

His men hurried to obey. The bows were kept in the barracks. And the ogre was *not* in the barracks.

Their commander gaped at the little flood of soldiers pouring back into the barracks.

"Not *all* of you! You—you—"

He collapsed to the ground. Even if he'd had his armor on properly, the arrow protruding from his chest would have punched right through it.

The few soldiers who hadn't returned to the barracks stared at the sight. Then, at the traitors positioned behind the wagon across the gatehouse entrance.

"The ogre has a bow!" screamed one of them. *"Ogre has a bow!"*

All but one of them made it back into the barracks. The sluggard remained pinned to the doorway, by another arrow that struck . . .

Exactly the way you'd expect an ogre's arrow to strike. Went all the way through him and would have passed on completely except it hit the door post.

"Great big thing, too," muttered one of the soldiers, peeking out of a barracks window. "Way bigger than ours."

"Which gate?" shrieked Skandagupta. "*Which gate?* Speak plainly, damn you!"

The emperor was still muddle-headed with sleep. Dangerous at any time, he was positively venomous at times like this.

The general commanding the city's garrison wasn't sure of the answer himself. But what he said, very firmly and confidently, was: "Both gates, Your Majesty. The main attack seems to be coming at the north gate, however. Damodara himself is said to be leading the charge there."

That was true enough. Well. Probably. From the battlements, using telescopes, sentries had seen the rebel would-be emperor's pavilion being struck, and a surge of his soldiers toward the northern gate. A contingent of Ye-tai was leading the way, probably led by Toramana himself.

A slow surge, to be sure, except for the Ye-tai vanguard. Nothing like the charge being made by the Rajputs toward the southern gate. But that latter could be a feint.

"Then get yourself to the northern gate!" shrilled the emperor. "At once! Or I'll have your head for my collection! You coward! You stinking—"

"I obey, Your Majesty!" The general could safely take that shrieking imprecation for a royal dismissal. He was out of the audience chamber before the emperor had stopped cursing him.

He'd never felt such relief heading for a desperate battle in his life.

By the time the lieutenant who succeeded to command in the barracks could chivvy his soldiers out into the small square facing the gatehouse, another sound could be heard. Like a distant thunder, approaching. The sound of horses, and men shouting.

Rajiv understood the words before anyone else did.

Rajputana. And, also, the name of his father, chanted like a battle cry.

Rana Sanga.

His father was coming. Would be here within a minute or two. He and his warriors would come through that gate like an avalanche of steel.

His bow in hand and an arrow notched, Rajiv stared at the soldiers assembling fearfully in the square. In a minute, perhaps two, they would be swept from existence. Men he knew. Men whose wives and children he knew.

"It is not honorable," he murmured.

"What was that, boy?" asked Anastasius.

"It is not bearable," he added, still murmuring.

"Speak up, if you've got something to say!"

Rajiv removed the arrow from the bowstring. Still holding the bow, he sprang onto the wagon before the entrance. Then, with two steps and a sure-footed leap, he sprang off the wagon onto the hard-packed dirt of the square beyond.

"What the hell are you doing?" Anastasius bellowed.

Rajiv ignored him. He advanced toward the soldiers some forty yards away. The bow was still in his left hand, positioned as it should be. But he was now holding up the arrow as if it were a sword.

"Stop!" he cried. "I am Rajiv, a prince of Rajputana! Son of Rana Sanga!"

One of the soldiers in the front rank squinted at him. Abhay, that was. He had a son Rajiv's age, and a very pretty daughter about a year older. She'd been the source of new thoughts for Rajiv, in fact. New and rather unsettling ones.

"Rajiv? *Rajiv?*"

"Yes, Abhay! It is Rajiv!"

Still walking toward them, he pointed back at the opening gate with the arrow. "My father is coming! Listen, and you can hear!"

All the soldiers stopped moving, and froze.

Sure enough. Coming louder and louder:
Rana Sanga! Rajputana!

Worse yet:
Death to Skandagupta!
And they were Skandagupta's men.

Rajiv now raised the arrow high, as if it held a banner.
"Swear fealty to me! Swear it now!"

Valentinian emerged from the gate tower. "All right, Anastasius. Get up there and—*what is that crazy kid doing?*"

Anastasius shook his head.

Ajatasutra came out also, in time to hear the exchange. After peering at the sight of Rajiv confronting the soldiers in the square, that familiar mocking smile came to his hawk face.

"Rajput prince. What do you expect?"

"Swear it now!"

His voice broke—that too was new—and Rajiv silently cursed all new things.

He was even thinking about Abhay's daughter! Now—of all times!

◇   ◇   ◇

Abhay looked at the soldier next to him. As if it were the first pebble in a cascade, that *look* passed from one soldier to the next.

The new commander saw, and cursed also. Not silently, however.

"Damn all traitors!" he shouted, pushing his way forward, spear in hand.

"All my efforts," Valentinian hissed. "Gone to waste. Ungrateful fucking stupid worthless brat."

The commander came out of the mass of soldiers, at a charge, his spear leveled.

Rajiv notched and fired the arrow in a movement so swift and sure not even Valentinian could really follow it. The commander fell dead, perhaps a foot of the shaft protruding from his throat.

"Well," said Valentinian. "Maybe not all."

"Swear it NOW!"

The sound of shrieking Rajput voices coming from beyond the walls was almost deafening.

But what decided Abhay, in the end, was not that. It was the thunderous sound—more deafening still—of thousands of galloping horses.

He was afraid of horses. Had been, ever since he was kicked by one as a boy. The other soldiers teased him about it.

He, too, lunged forward. But with his spear held crossways, not in the killing thrust his commander had tried.

"I swear, Rajiv! I swear!" He fell to his knees, the spear still held crossways. "I swear!"

It took not more than ten seconds before all the soldiers from the barracks were on their knees beside him, swearing likewise.

"On your feet!" Rajiv bellowed. Tried to, rather. His voice broke again.

He pointed with the bow. "Line up against the wall of the barracks! In good ranks, you hear? Your spears in hand—but held at standing rest!"

They'd be safe enough there, he thought. The square was small, true, but the portion in front of the barracks was something in the way of an offset little plaza. They wouldn't simply be trampled. And their families within the barracks would be safer still.

As long as Rajiv was standing in front of them, they'd be safe. Where his father could see him, the moment he came through the gate.

Which would be . . .

Any time now. He'd never heard such a sound in his life. It was simultaneously exhilarating and terrifying. Ten thousand galloping horses shaking the ground, while ten thousand warrior throats shook the air.

"I will be damned," Valentinian muttered.

"Speak up!" shouted Anastasius, standing right next to him. The world was filled with the noise of horses and battle cries. "I can't hear you!"

"I said: I will be damned!"

Anastasius shook his head. "Well, no kidding! You just figured that out?"

Valentinian scowled. Grinning, Anastasius pushed him toward the entrance to the gate tower.

"Come on! Let's get out of the way! Expert Rajput horsemen or not, I don't want to get trampled."

The courier galloped up to the city's commander.

"The southern gate!" he shrieked, pointing back with his finger. "Rajputs! Treason! The gate is open! The Rajputs are coming! Thirty thousand of them! By now, they're in the city!"

The commander stared to the south. That gate was too far away to see. He was almost at the northern gate, by now, with ten thousand of his own men packing the streets.

A courier galloped up from the north.

"The Ye-tai are at the gate! The rebel's Ye-tai! Ten thousand of them! Toramana himself is outside!"

The commander stared to the north. That gate he *could* see. And the odds were even.

"Death to Toramana!" he shouted, swinging his sword. "To the north gate!"

Toramana was indeed outside the gate. But with only three thousand soldiers, not the ten thousand Sanga was leading into the city through the southern gate.

They were all Ye-tai soldiers, however. Quite visibly so. Toramana had seen to that.

The commander of Damodara's Ye-tai troops was sitting on his horse and looking up at the soldiers manning the gate. Very boldly, within bow range.

The soldiers on those walls were mostly Ye-tai also, as Damodara's spies had reported.

"Come on, boys!" Toramana shouted. "It's all over, and you know it! So what's it going to be? Service with me? Beer, women, and a long life?"

He drew his sword and raised it, as if inspecting the edge of the blade.

"Or do we have to get messy about this?"

One of the Ye-tai soldiers on the walls was looking the other way, into the city.

"The commander's coming," he said, almost idly. "Took the bastard long enough. Got maybe three thousand men with him. Up close, anyway. More than that, trailing behind."

He didn't use the commander's name. Few of Kausambi's Ye-tai soldiers did. The man was a cypher to him. Just another one of the political generals churned up by the endless scheming within the Malwa dynastic clan. Very deadly scheming, of late.

Now, he turned and looked at his own platoon commander. So did all the other Ye-tai on the wall nearby.

The officer rubbed his face. "Ah, shit."

His soldiers waited, silently.

"Ah, shit," he repeated. Then he lowered his hand and said: "Make them open the gate. Let Toramana deal with the rest."

Before he finished, three of the Ye-tai were already plunging into the gatehouse.

They had their swords in hand, just in case the stupid peasants who actually operated the gate mechanism chose to argue the matter.

Not likely, of course.

When he saw the gate start to open, Toramana grinned. Sanga wouldn't get *all* the glory.

He did not forget, of course, to wave his sword in salute at the Ye-tai on the battlements, as he led his men into the city. All three thousand of them, except a few couriers sent racing off to tell Damodara that there were now two breaches in Kausambi's walls.

For their part, the Ye-tai on the walls returned his salute with the proper salutations.

"Long live the new emperor!" bellowed one of them.

His mate elbowed him.

"Long live the *rightful* emperor!" he corrected himself.

"Death to the impostor Skandagupta!" his mate chimed in.

When Skandagupta saw the girl enter the imperial audience chamber, forcing her way past the assembled courtiers, he broke off in mid-tirade.

"*Rani?*" he whispered.

The eight-year-old girl was now past the courtiers, and standing in front of the throne.

The blood drained from his face. A face that felt as empty as the one before him. The eyes before him.

"*Great Lady* Rani," the girl said.

Her voice changed, then. Into something no girl—no woman of any age—could possess.

"GREAT LADY RANI, NOW. YOU WILL OBEY ME, SKANDAGUPTA."

But all the emperor could do was scream.

Chapter 39
KAUSAMBI

The first thing Rana Sanga saw, after he charged through the gate into the square beyond, was his son. Rajiv, holding a bow but not wearing armor, standing in front of perhaps a hundred soldiers assembled in ranks in front of the gate's barracks.

It was one of the great moments of his life. Greater, even, than the first time he held his first-born child in his hands.

A tiny thing, Rajiv had been then, in Sanga's very large hands.

He would never be as big as Sanga. In that, Rajiv took after his mother. But, at that moment, he seemed to stand as tall as Sanga himself, sitting on his great warhorse.

"My soldiers, father!" Rajiv spread his hands, the left still holding the bow, as if to shelter the soldiers behind him. "My soldiers! Loyal and sworn to me! They are not to be harmed!"

Sanga had brought his horse to a halt, ten yards from Rajiv. A small clot of his lieutenants swirled around him.

He pointed his lance into the city. "To the imperial palace! I want Skandagupta's head! I will follow in a moment!"

The lieutenants wheeled their horses and resumed leading the charge. Hundreds, and hundreds, and hundreds of Rajputs followed them. Slowed greatly, of course, as they squeezed through the gate. But resuming the gallop immediately thereafter.

Finally, Sanga was able to move his gaze from his son's face, to examine the soldiers behind him.

He almost laughed. If there was one of them not trembling, Sanga could not spot him.

Abhay was certainly trembling. He had never in his life seen anything so fearsome as the Rajput king astride his horse a few yards away.

The horse alone would have been terrifying. Several hands taller than any horse Abhay had ever seen, clad in its own armor, the beast had eyes that seemed to be filled with fury and its huge nostrils breathed rage.

But the king atop it! Steel helmet, steel chain and plate armor, steel-headed lance—even the shaft of the lance seemed like steel.

Not to mention being far larger than any lance Abhay could have held easily, even with both hands. In the huge, gauntleted hand of the Rajput king, it seemed as light as a wand.

The king was glaring, too. Or had some sort of scary expression on his face.

Just to make things complete, he had a *name*.

Rana Sanga. Every soldier in India had heard of Rana Sanga. The stories were endless.

And each and every one of them was true. Abhay didn't doubt it for a moment. Not any longer.

Sanga wasn't exactly glaring. He was simply, in his austere manner, trying to disguise both great pride and great amusement.

Sworn to his son's service, no less! The most wretched pack of garrison troops Sanga had ever seen!

But there was no contempt in the thoughts. Not even for the soldiers, and certainly not for Rajiv.

Sanga understood full well, what had happened here. He would not have done it himself. But he understood it.

"My wife's son, too," he murmured. "My great and glorious wife."

A movement caught his attention. Turning his head, he saw the Mongoose emerging from the gatehouse.

He slid the lance into its scabbard, and swung down gracefully from the saddle. Then, strode toward him.

As he neared, he saw that the Mongoose was scowling. Half-anger and half . . .

Embarrassment? That seemed odd.

"Look," the Mongoose rasped. "I tried my level best. It's not *my* fault your son is crazy."

Abhay was astonished to see the Rajput king—so tall he was! even standing!—burst into laughter.

More astonished, still, to see him kneel before the foreign soldier.

Kneel, and extend his sword, hilt-first.

The words he spoke were clear to Abhay, who was standing not that far away. But they were simply meaningless.

"I am forever in your debt, Valentinian of Rome."

The Roman soldier named Valentinian cleared his throat.

"Yes, well," he said.

"Name the service, and I will do it," insisted the Rajput king.

"Yes, well," Valentinian repeated.

The ogre had emerged from the gatehouse in time to hear the exchange.

"Valentinian, you're a fucking idiot," Abhay heard him growl. Much more loudly: "As it happens, Rana Sanga, there is one small little favor you could do us. A family matter, you might say. But later! Later! There's still a battle to be won."

Sanga rose, sheathing his sword. "As you say. The favor is yours, whatever it is. For the moment, I will trust you to keep my family safe."

"Well, sure," said Valentinian.

Then he was back to scowling. Rajiv stepped forward and insisted on accompanying his father.

Abhay felt fear return, in full force. He did *not* want to fight a battle. Any battle, anywhere—much less the great, swirling chaos that Kausambi had become.

"You are not armored, Rajiv," his father pointed out, mildly. "And your only weapons are a bow and a dagger."

Rajiv turned to face Abhay, who was a small man.

"You're about my size. Give me your armor. Your spear and sword, also."

Hastily—eagerly—ecstatically, Abhay did as he was commanded.

"Stay here—you and all the others," Rajiv told him quietly. "Protect your families, that's all. You wouldn't be—well. That'll be good enough. Just keep your wife and children safe. Especially your daughter. Ah, I mean, daughters."

Sanga still seemed hesitant.

He turned to Valentinian. "Is he ready for this? He's only thirteen."

Scowling seemed to come naturally to the Roman soldier. "You mean, other than being crazy? Yeah, he's ready. The truth is, he's probably better than most of your Rajputs. Already."

The Rajput king seemed, somehow, to grow taller still.

"The Mongoose says this?"

"Well, yeah. The Mongoose says so. What the hell. I trained him, didn't I?"

A few minutes later, they were gone. The Rajput king and his son, toward the imperial palace. The ogre—who turned out to be another Roman soldier—and the narrow-faced one who was almost as frightening, went somewhere else. The Ye-tai went with them, thankfully.

Where they went, exactly, Abhay didn't know. Wherever Sanga's family was hidden, he assumed.

He wasn't about to ask. He was not a crazy Rajput prince.

Fortunately, Sanga had left one of his Rajput soldiers behind. An older man; too much the veteran to find any great glory in the last battle of a war. Enough glory, anyway, to offset the risk of not being around to enjoy the fruits of victory afterward.

Somebody had to lend Rajiv a horse, after all. Who better than a grizzled oldster?

He was a cheerful fellow. Who, to the great relief of Abhay and the other garrison soldiers, just waved on the Rajputs who kept coming through the gate. There was never a moment when any real threat emerged.

Coming, and coming, and coming. It took an hour, it seemed—perhaps longer—before they all passed through. "Storming the gate," when the soldiers numbered in the thousands and the gate was not really all that wide, turned out to be mostly a poetic expression.

Abhay found that somehow reassuring. He didn't like poetry, all that much. But he liked it a lot better than he liked horses.

◇   ◇   ◇

Toramana personally slew the commander of Kausambi, in the battle that erupted in the narrow streets less than two minutes after he and his Ye-tai started passing through the north gate.

He made a point of it, deliberately seeking out the man once he spotted the plumed helmet.

Idiot affectation, that was. Toramana's own helmet was as utilitarian and unadorned as that of any of his soldiers.

It didn't take much, really. The city's commander was leading garrison troops who hadn't seen a battle since Ranapur. Toramana and his Ye-tai had spent years fighting Belisarius and Rao.

So, a tiger met a mongrel cur in the streets of Kausambi. The outcome was to be expected. Would have been the same, even if the fact they were outnumbered didn't matter. In those narrow streets, only a few hundred men on each side could fight at one time, anyway.

When he saw Toramana coming, hacking his way through the commander's bodyguard, the Malwa general tried to flee.

But, couldn't. The packed streets made everything impossible, except the sort of close-in brutal swordwork that the Ye-tai excelled in and his own men didn't.

Neither did their general. Toramana's first strike disarmed him; the second cut off his hand; the third, his head.

"Save the head," Toramana commanded, after the garrison troops were routed.

His lieutenant held it up by the hair, still dripping blood.

"Why?" he asked skeptically. Toramana's Ye-tai, following their commander's example, were not much given to military protocol. "Getting divorced and remarried, already?"

Toramana laughed. "I don't need it for more than a day. Just long enough so those damned Rajputs don't get *all* the credit."

The lieutenant nodded, sagely. "Ah. Good idea."

Even with the partial data at its disposal—even working through the still-awkward sheath of a girl much too young for the purpose—Link knew what to do.

It still didn't know the exact nature of the disaster that had befallen it, while ensconced in the sheath named Sati. As always, Link's memories only went as far as Sati's last communion with the machines in the cellars.

It didn't really matter.

Belisarius, obviously. As before.

The great plan of the new gods lay in shattered ruin. India was now lost. If Link had been in an adult sheath, it might have tried to rally the city's soldiers. But trapped in a girl's body, and with an emperor who had never been very competent and was now half-hysterical, such an attempt would be hopeless.

True, Damodara's forces were still outnumbered by Kausambi's garrison. Link knew that, within a ninety-three percent probability, despite the prattle of panicked courtiers and officers.

But that, too, didn't matter. There was no comparison at all between the morale and cohesion of the opposing sides. Damodara's army had the wind in its sails, now that it had breached the city's walls. Worse still, it had commanders who knew how to use that wind, beginning with Damodara himself.

The only really seasoned army Link had was in the Punjab. A huge army, but it might as well have been on the moon. That army had been paralyzed by Belisarius, it was much too far away for Link to control any longer—and none of the garrisons in any of the cities in the Ganges plain could serve as a rallying point. Not after Kausambi fell, as it surely would by nightfall.

All that remained—all that *could* remain—was to salvage what pieces it could and begin anew.

Start from the very beginning, all over again. Worse than that, actually. Link would lose the machinery in the imperial cellars. Without that machinery, it could not be transferred once its current sheath died or became too old or ill to be of use. Link would die with it.

Perhaps it was fortunate, after all, that the sheath was only eight years old.

Not that Link really thought in terms like "fate" or "fortune." Still, it was a peculiar twist in probabilities. It would take at least half a century for Link to re-create that machinery, even after it made its way to the Khmer lands.

The work could not be done there, in the first place. In this world, only the Romans and the Chinese had the technical wherewithal, with Link to guide the slave artisans.

Fortunately, the new gods had planned for such an unlikely outcome. Link held the designs in its mind for much cruder machines that would still accomplish the same basic task.

Half a century, at least. Hopefully, the sheath would prove to be long-lived. They normally weren't, simply because Link made no effort to keep them alive, if doing so was at all inconvenient. But it knew how to do so, if it chose, assuming the genetic material was not hopeless. The regimen was very strict, but—obviously —that posed no problem at all. Food meant nothing at all to Link, and the time spent in mindless exercise could still be used for calculations.

"Where are we going?" whispered Skandagupta. His voice was still hoarse, from the earlier screaming.

"BE SILENT OR YOU WILL DIE."

The threat was not an idle one. An eight-year-old girl's body could not have overwhelmed Skandagupta, even as pudgy and unfit as he was. But Link had kept its special assassins, after ordering them to kill all the women in the cellars. Any one of the assassins—much less all three—could have slain Skandagupta instantly.

The specially trained women would have been useful, later. But they were simply not trained, nor physically conditioned after years living in cellars, for the rigors of the journey that lay ahead. And Link could not afford to leave them alive. Under torture, they might say too much about their origins.

It was questionable whether Skandagupta would survive those rigors. Link's sheath was small enough that it could be carried by the assassins, when necessary. Skandagupta was not, even after he lost his fat, as he surely would. Link could not afford to wear out its assassins.

As it was, Link had almost ordered the emperor killed anyway. The probabilities teetered on a knife's edge. On the one hand, Skandagupta was an obvious impediment in the immediate future. On the other hand . . .

It was hard to calculate. There were still too many variables involved. But there were enough of them to indicate that, given many factors, having the legitimate emperor of India ready at hand might prove useful.

No matter. Link could always have Skandagupta murdered later, after all.

The tunnel they were passing through was poorly lit. Skandagupta stumbled and fell again.

The shock was enough to jar the creature out of its fear. "Where are we *going*? And what will happen to my wife and children?"

Link decided that answering was more efficient than another threat.

"WE ARE GOING TO THE KHMER LANDS. I PREPARED THIS ESCAPE ROUTE DECADES AGO. YOUR WIFE AND DAUGHTERS ARE IRRELEVANT, SINCE THEY ARE OUTSIDE THE SUCCESSION. YOUR ONLY SON, ALSO. BY THE END OF THE DAY HE WILL HAVE EITHER RENOUNCED HIS HERITAGE AND PUBLICLY ADMITTED DAMODARA'S FORGERIES TO BE THE TRUTH, OR HE WILL BE DEAD."

Skandagupta moaned.

"IF HE SPEAKS AGAIN WITHOUT PERMISSION," Link instructed the assassins, "BEAT HIM."

"How badly, Mistress?"

"LEAVE HIS LEGS UNDAMAGED. HIS BRAIN ALSO, SUCH AS IT IS. SO LONG AS HE CAN STILL WALK."

Damodara entered the palace just as the sun was setting. There was still some fighting in the city, here and there, but not much.

It was all over. His great gamble had worked.

"Skandagupta's son says he will agree to the—ah—new documents," Narses said.

Damodara considered the matter. "Not good enough. He has to swear he's a bastard, also. His real father was . . . whoever. Pick one of the courtiers whose heads decorate the walls outside. Someone known to be foul as well as incompetent."

Narses sneered. "Hard to choose among them, given those qualifications."

"Don't take long." Damodara's lips twisted into something that was perhaps less of a sneer, but every bit as contemptuous. "I want those heads off the walls and buried or burnt by tomorrow afternoon. The impaled bodies, by mid-morning. What a stench!"

"Yes, Your Majesty."

"My wife? Children?"

"They should be here within an hour. They're all safe and well."

Damodara nodded. "See to it that stable-keeper is rewarded. Lavishly. In addition to being made the new royal stable-master."

"Yes, Your Majesty. What about—"

"The two Roman soldiers?" Damodara shook his head, wonder-ingly. "What sort of reward would be suitable, for such service as that?"

Narses' sneer returned. "Oh, they'll think of something."

"Someone's coming," said one of the members of the assassina-tion team. He spoke softly. Just as softly as he let the grasses sway back, hiding their position alongside the road to the Bay of Bengal.

"Who?"

"Don't know. But from the clothes he's wearing, someone important, even though he's on foot. He's got a girl with him, and those weird little yellow assassins the witches keep around."

The captain frowned. He knew who the man was talking about, of course, even if none of the regular Malwa assassination teams ever had much contact with the witches and their entourage. But they'd always paid some attention to the Khmer assassins. Just keeping an eye on the competition, as it were.

"What in the world would . . . Let me see."

He slithered his way to the top of the knoll and carefully parted the grasses.

"It's the *emperor*," he hissed.

"Are you sure?" asked his lieutenant.

"Come and look for yourself, if you don't believe me."

The lieutenant did so. Like the captain, though not the other three assassins, he'd been introduced to the emperor once. At a distance, of course, and as part of a small crowd. But it was some-thing a man remembered.

"Damned if you're not right. But what would *he* be doing— Oh. Stupid question."

The captain smiled, sardonically. "I guess we know who won the siege."

He took a deep breath and let it out. "Well, thank whatever gods there are. After eleven thousand wasted miles and I don't want to think how many wasted hours, we've finally got something to do."

Fortunately, they'd hauled their little bombard the whole way. For all their diminutive size, the Khmer assassins were deadly. But a blast of canister swept them away as neatly as you could ask for.

The one who survived, unconscious and badly wounded, got his throat cut a few seconds later.

They hadn't intended to hit the emperor or the girl, but the group had been tightly bunched and canister just naturally spreads.

The girl wasn't too badly hurt. Just a single ball in the left arm. She might lose the arm, but it could have been worse.

There was no chance, however, that Skandagupta would survive.

"Gut-shot," the lieutenant grunted. "He'll die in agony, in a few days. Damodara might like that."

The captain shook his head. "Not by reputation, and all we really need is the head, anyway. Or do *you* want to carry the fat little bastard?"

The lieutenant eyed the distant walls of Kausambi. Night was falling, but he could still hear the sounds of scattered fighting.

"Well . . . it's only a few miles. But after eleven thousand, I'm not in the mood for any extra effort." He knelt down, and with a few expert strokes, severed the imperial head.

The girl was still squalling at them, as she had been since the attack. It was a very strange sound, coming from such a small female. As if her voice emerged from a huge cavern of a chest.

Consciously and deliberately, the assassins had blocked the actual words from their minds. You had to be careful, dealing with the witches. Which she obviously was, despite her youth. A witch-in-training, at least.

The captain struck her on the head with the pommel of his dagger. Carefully, just enough to daze the creature.

You never knew, with the witches and the imperial dynasty—of which Damodara was still a part, after all. The reward might be greater, if she were still alive.

Alive, however, was good enough.

"I'm sick of that squalling," said the captain. "Her eyes are creepy, too. Gag her and blindfold her, before she comes to."

They decided to wait until the next day, before entering the city to seek their reward. By then, the fighting should have ended.

Before long, however, the captain was regretting that decision. They were all very well-traveled, by now, and—alas—the lieutenant liked to read.

"You know," he said, "the story has it that when some Persians presented Alexander the Great with the body of Darius, he had them all executed. For regicide, even though he was hunting the former emperor himself."

Silently, the captain cursed all well-read men. Then, because maintaining morale was his duty, pointed out the obvious.

"Don't be silly. Alexander the Great was a maniac. Everybody says Damodara is a level-headed, practical fellow."

Lord Samudra learned the war was over that night, from a radio message sent from Kausambi.

FALSE EMPEROR OVERTHROWN STOP TRUE EMPEROR DAMODARA SITS ON THRONE IN KAU-SAMBI STOP YOU WILL OBEY HIM LORD SAMUDRA STOP WAR IS OVER STOP ESTABLISH LIAISON WITH MAURICE OF THRACE TO NEGOTIATE CEASE FIRE WITH ROMAN AND PERSIAN ARMIES IN PUNJAB STOP

"What are you going to do?" asked one of his aides.

Samudra let the message fall to the table in the bunker. "What do you think? I'm going to do exactly as I'm told. The Romans will have received the same message. By now, they've got us out-numbered. Between them and the Persians, we're facing some-thing like two hundred thousand men."

"And we're losing soldiers by the droves every day," said a differ-ent aide, gloomily. "As much by desertion as disease."

There was silence, for a time. Then Samudra said: "You want to know the truth? I know Damodara pretty well. We're cousins, after all. He's about ten times more capable than Skandagupta and—best of all—he's even-tempered."

There was further silence, finally broken by one of the aides.

"Long live the new emperor, then."

"Idiot," said Samudra tonelessly. "Long live the *true* emperor. The greatest army of the Malwa empire does not obey rebels, after all."

It was several days before Belisarius learned the war was over. The news was brought to him by a special courier sent by Damodara.

A Rajput cavalryman, naturally. The man was exceptionally proud—as well he might be—that he'd made the ride as fast as he had, without killing a single horse.

"So, that's it," said Belisarius, rising from his squat across from Kungas.

The two of them emerged from the hut and studied the Malwa army they'd trapped on the Ganges.

There'd been little fighting, and none at all for the past four days.

"You were right, I think," said Kungas. "The bitch did kill herself, days ago."

"Most likely. We'll know soon enough. That army's looking at starvation, before too long. They slaughtered their last horses two days ago."

"I'll send an envoy to them. Once they get the news, they'll surrender."

The Kushan king eyed Belisarius. "You know, I don't think I've ever seen that crooked a smile on your face. What amuses you so?"

"I've got a reputation to maintain. You do realize, don't you, that in the days when the final battle was fought and won in the greatest war in history, Belisarius spent his time doing nothing more than drinking lousy wine and gambling with dice?"

Kungas chuckled. "You lost, too. By now, you owe me a small chest of gold."

"Not all that small, really."

But Kungas had stopped chuckling. Another thought had come to him, that caused his notoriously expressionless face to twist into a grimace.

"Oh. You'll never stop crowing about it, will you?"

When Maurice heard, it put him in a foul mood for a full day.

Calopodius' mood was not much better. "How in the name of God am I supposed to put *that* in my history? You can only do so much with classical allusions, you know. Grammar and rhetoric collapse under that crude a reality."

"Who gives a damn?" snarled Maurice. "You think *you've* got problems? I'm still in good health, and I'm only twenty years older than the bastard. Years and years, I'll have to listen to him bragging."

"He's not really a boastful man," pointed out Calopodius.

"Not usually, no. But with something like *this*? Ha! You watch, youngster. Years and years and years."

Chapter 40
KAUSAMBI

The damage Kausambi had suffered in the fighting was minimal, considering the huge size of the city. Belisarius had seen far worse before, any number of times. Damodara's forces had been able to breach the walls in two places, without having to suffer heavy casualties in the doing, because the gates had been opened from the inside. As a result, none of the three factors had been operating that, singly or in combination, usually produced horrible sacks.

First, the troops pouring into the city were still under the control of their officers, because the officers themselves had not suffered many casualties and led them through the gates.

Second, the soldiers were not burning with a desire for vengeance on those who had—often horribly, with the most ghastly weapons—butchered their mates while they were still fighting outside the walls.

So, the sort of spontaneously erupting military riot-in-all-but-name that most "sacks" constituted, had never occured. Beyond, at least, a few isolated incidents—always involving liquor—that Damodara's officers had squelched immediately.

And, third, of course—not all sacks were spontaneous—the commander of the victorious besieging army had not ordered one, after his troops seized the city.

Skandagupta would have done so, of course. But Damodara ruled now, not Skandagupta, and he was a very different sort of

854

man. The only thing of Skandagupta that remained was his head, perched on a spike at the entrance to the imperial palace.

It was the only head there. Damodara had ordered all the other corpses and heads removed.

After dismounting from his horse, Belisarius took a moment to admire the thing.

Pity, though, he said to Aide. *Agathius swore he'd someday see Skandagupta lying dead in the dust. I'm afraid there's not much chance of that, now.*

In garam season? No chance at all. Unless he'd be satisfied with looking at a skull. That thing already stinks.

Aide, of course, was detecting the stench through Belisarius' own nostrils. As he had many times before, Belisarius wondered how the jewel perceived things on his own. He *could* do so, Belisarius knew, although the manner of it remained mysterious. Aide and the other crystal beings had none of the senses possessed by the protoplasmic branch of the human family.

But whatever those methods were, Aide had not used them in years. He'd told Belisarius that he found it much easier to do his work if he restricted himself to perceiving the world only through Belisarius' senses.

A courtier—no, a small pack of them—emerged from the palace entrance and hastened down the broad stone stairs at the bottom of which Belisarius was standing.

"General Belisarius!" one of them said. "The emperor awaits you!"

He managed to make that sound as if Damodara was bestowing an immense—no, divine—favor upon the Roman general. Which was laughable, really, since the same Rajput courier who had brought the news of Damodara's triumph had also brought a private message from the new Malwa emperor asking Belisarius to come to Kausambi immediately to "deal with a delicate and urgent matter." The tone of the message had been, if not pleading, certainly not peremptory or condescending.

Courtiers, Belisarius thought sarcastically, handing the reins of his horse to one of the Rajputs who had escorted him to Kausambi. *However else people in different lands may vary in their customs, I think courtiers are the same everywhere.*

Normally, Aide would have responded with a quip of his own. But the jewel seemed strangely subdued. He had said very little since they entered the city.

Belisarius thought that was odd. Looked at in some ways—most ways, rather—this final triumph belonged to Aide more than it did to Belisarius or Damodara or anyone else. But he didn't press for an explanation. In the years that he and Aide had shared a mind, for all practical purposes, they'd both learned to respect the privacy of the other.

The Malwa imperial palace was the largest in the world. So far as Belisarius knew, anyway. There might be something equivalent in one of the many kingdoms in China that were vying for power. "Largest," at least, in the sense of being a single edifice. The Roman imperial complex at Constantinople covered more acreage, but much of it was gardens and open walkways.

He'd visited the palace before, a number of times, when he'd come to India years earlier in what amounted to the capacity of a spy. With the help of Aide's perfect memory, Belisarius knew the way to the imperial audience chamber. He could have gone there himself, without needing the guidance of the courtiers.

But, perhaps not. Soon, the courtiers were leading him down a hallway he'd never been in. Old, ingrained habit made him check the spatha in its scabbard, to see that it was loose and would come out easily.

Although the movement was subtle, he made no attempt at all to keep it surreptitious. The courtiers had irritated him enough that he felt no desire to accommodate them. Emperor Damodara had, after all, invited *General* Belisarius into his presence. Generals carried swords. Good generals with combat experience carried sharp swords, and made sure they weren't stuck in their scabbards.

One of the courtiers who observed seemed brighter than the rest. Or, at least, didn't suffer from the usual moronic state of the courtier mentality, whose defining characteristic was to think that power emanated from itself.

"The emperor is not waiting for you in the audience chamber, General," he explained quietly. "He awaits you in, ah . . ."

The hostile glances coming from several other courtiers caused him to falter. "Someplace else," he finished lamely.

Aide spoke for the first time since they'd entered the palace.

He's found the lair. Link's lair. That's where we're going.

Belisarius nodded. And, again, made sure the spatha was loose. *What about Link itself?*

Damodara's message had said nothing on that subject.

I don't know. I think he must have Link also. Or his message would have been . . . different.

Belisarius thought about it. *Yes, you're right. He wouldn't have called it a "delicate" matter as well as an "urgent" one.*

But they were entering a chamber, now, and speculation could come to an end. Damodara was there, waiting, along with Rana Sanga and a big Ye-tai officer whom Belisarius had never met before. The now-famous Toramana, he presumed.

His eyes, however, were immediately drawn to the side. Two other men were standing there, who—for the moment—meant far more to Belisarius.

"I'm glad you survived," he said. "I was worried you wouldn't, when I sent you off."

Anastasius' huge shoulders moved in a shrug. "Wasn't really that bad, General. For starters, we didn't have to protect *you*. Mindouos and Anatha were worse—not to mention the battle at the Pass."

Valentinian grinned, in his savage way. "Way worse," he chimed in, reaching up and running fingers through his coarse black hair. For a moment, a long scar was visible—the scar Sanga had given him in their famous duel. "We'll ask you to remember that, though, when it comes time to figure out our retirement bonus."

Even with an emperor waiting, Belisarius would deal with this first.

"Just tell me what you want. If I can manage it, I will. The two of you long ago stopped being in the category of 'common soldiers.'"

The tall Rajput king standing a few feet away issued a snort. "The truth, that!" He gave the two cataphracts a look that Belisarius couldn't quite interpret. Deep respect was there, obviously, but there was something else. Not derision, exactly, but amusement of some kind.

For the first time that day, Aide's voice had a trace of his usual good humor. **I still don't understand how a man as smart as you can be such a dummy about some things.**

What do you mean?

You didn't figure out what Agathius was doing, either, until your nose was rubbed in it. *I figured it out right away.* **But I'll remind you that there's an emperor waiting,**

here—and the Malwa empire is still probably the most powerful empire in the world. Will be for sure, in a few years, once Damodara gets settled in. Best to stay on good terms with him.

That was good advice. Belisarius turned to face Damodara and bowed.

"You asked for me, Your Majesty. How may I be of service?"

A quick smile flashed across Damodara's face. "Well, starting tomorrow, you can be of service by providing all of us with your good sense. We have a complicated peace settlement to make, you know. And we're already arguing over where to hold the conference. Fortunately—so far—it's been mostly an argument over the radio and telegraph."

The Malwa emperor lifted his hand. "But that's for tomorrow. Today, there's a different decision that faces us. Probably a more important one. And it's not a decision I feel anyone but you can make."

Belisarius took a deep breath. "You found Link. And its lair."

"The first, yes. The second" Damodara shrugged. " 'Found' is hardly the word. I already knew where it was. All the members of the dynastic clan—boys, at least—are taken to it at least once. I was there several times."

"Take me there," Belisarius said. Commanded, rather.

Belisarius could make no sense at all of the machines in the chamber far below the palace. The problem wasn't so much that, in their gleaming blankness, they seemed more like magic artifacts than what he thought of as "machines." It was that he knew he would never understand what they did or how they worked.

I don't understand them either, really. I don't think even the Great Ones do, except in general terms. The new gods developed cybernetics far beyond any other branch of the human race. The Great Ones took a different direction. One that led to us crystals. And while we share some of the characteristics of computers, we are very different in other ways.

How could they bring all this here, through time, when all the Great Ones could do—and that, barely—was send you as a semi-conscious thing? Apologetically, he added: *When you first arrived, I mean. You're hardly "semi-conscious" now.*

For one thing, the Great Ones aren't as ruthless. The energy expenditure required to send these machines back through time destroyed the new gods' own planet. Along with most of their people. Sub-species, it would be better to say. There were not many survivors.

Sensing the question before Belisarius could ask it, Aide added: **Yes, they knew that would happen. The ones who managed it, at least. Most of their people didn't, the ones who were destroyed. Even the new gods have factions. The faction that did this—which is all that is left—are . . .**

Fanatics, Belisarius supplied. *Fanaticism carried to the extremes you'd expect of "supermen." I understand.*

But it was time, now, to ignore the machines. Damodara had not brought Belisarius here to deal with them. Not principally, at least.

He turned and studied the small female shackled to a chair. He couldn't see much of her, since there was a hood over her head.

Don't look, said Aide.

No. I must.

Three strides and he was there; a quick movement of the hand, and the hood was removed.

It was the face of a young girl, perhaps seven or eight years old. All but the eyes that stared up at him. Those belonged to no human being at all. Their brown color was irrelevant. The emptiness within overwhelmed it.

The girl was gagged, too.

Don't listen to it.

No, I must.

It took longer to remove the gag. The knot holding it in place was very tight. As he worked at the task, he could hear the indrawn breaths of the people behind him.

As ever, Aide's ability to enhance Belisarius' senses was handy. There were five other men in the room, and four of them were holding their breath. The fifth one was breathing the same way he always did.

Belisarius had known he would be. Had that man not been present, he might never have dared to do this. Belisarius was probably as great a general as Alexander the Great, but he never thought like Alexander. He was who he was because of the men he knew how to lead—and rely upon—not because he thought he was the son of Zeus.

The gag came off.

"LISTEN TO ME, BELISARIUS. THERE IS STILL TIME—"

Quickly, he replaced the gag. "Shut up, monster. I just needed to hear that voice. To be sure."

He stepped back and drew his spatha. *Guide me, Aide.*

Were any other girls found?

He passed the question along. Damodara answered: "One. She's not more than two years old. I think she's the daughter of one of the provincial governors. I have her in a chamber upstairs. I haven't known what to do with her, either."

Destroy the machines first. Without the machines, Link is trapped in this body sitting before you. The little girl upstairs will be . . . probably not a very normal child. But a harmless one.

Again, Aide anticipated the next question:

These are just machines, Belisarius. No different, in the end, than a simple pottery wheel. In some ways, in fact, even more fragile. Anastasius and a big hammer will do fine.

That required a delay, to have a maul brought down. But, eventually, the maul arrived and Anastasius went to work.

With a vengeance, as the expression went—and no expression here. Not even in the battle in the tight confines of Great Lady Holi's cabin had Belisarius seen Anastasius swing a mace with such violence.

In three minutes, it was done, and Anastasius stepped back.

Throughout, Link had simply observed. There had been no expression at all in the girl's face. The eyes had neither narrowed nor widened. There had been no frown. No tightening of the jaws.

Nothing.

It is simply a calculator, Belisarius. Even now, when the probabilities within which it moves are a tiny fraction of one percent, it is still calculating. It will never stop calculating. It cannot. It . . .

There came the crystalline equivalent of a deep sigh. **It is really, really not human. Not even in the way we crystals are, or the Great Ones. It is just a machine itself. Programmed to do what it does—can only do—by monsters.**

Yes, I understand. Belisarius stepped forward, within a pace of the girl bound to the chair. His grip on the spatha was tight, much tighter than he would have held it in an actual fight.

Will it . . .

Yes. Destroy the girl's body and you destroy Link. It does not "die," exactly, for it was never alive at all. But it will be gone. It will no longer exist.

Still, he hesitated. Whatever he *knew*, his emotional reactions could not avoid the monster's form.

True enough, Belisarius had slain young girls. Many times, in fact. Just recently, his burning and destruction in the Ganges campaign had condemned many such to death. Damodara had agreed to send relief expeditions, as soon as possible. But with the inevitable chaos attendant upon a successful rebellion, no expedition could possibly arrive in time to save everyone.

Dozens of seven- and eight-year-old girls just like this one—more likely hundreds, or possibly even thousands—would be dying soon. Some were dead already. Each and every one of whom could, rightfully, have had the words *Murdered by Belisarius* engraved on their tomb markers.

Still, he hadn't done it *personally*. And if that difference might be meaningless, on a philosophical level, a man does not hold and wield a spatha using philosophy. He uses muscles and nerves and blood shaped and molded by emotion from the time he is born.

Don't be foolish, Aide said softly. **You know the answer. Why be proud, at the end, when you never were before?**

He was right, of course. Belisarius stepped back.

"Valentinian. A last service, if you would."

"Sure, General."

The cataphract came forward, his spatha flashed, and it was over. A spray of blood across shattered machinery, and a small head rolling to a stop in a corner. The gag never even came off, as neatly and economically—as miserly—as it had been done.

"Thank you."

"My pleasure."

Belisarius turned to Damodara, whose shoulders seemed slumped in relief. "And now, Emperor—"

Do that later, Belisarius. Please. I want to go outside.

Belisarius hesitated, for a moment. There were the needs of politics, but . . .

This was Aide's great triumph, not Damodara's.

Certainly, if you wish. I can understand that you find this chamber unsettling.

It's not that. It's just a cellar, now. That blood is just blood. That severed head just one of many I've seen. But I still don't want this to be . . .

He hesitated. Then: **It's not where I want to leave. I want to see the sky over India, when it happens.**

A great terrible fear clutched Belisarius' heart.

What are you talking about?

Again, that crystalline sort of sigh. **I've been glad, these past years, that you never figured it out. I was afraid you would, and it would just cause you pain—since you could have done nothing else anyway. But the time is here, now.**

Softly, gently: **The moment Link was destroyed, the future changed. Not in all ways, and—it's too complicated to explain, and I don't have much time left—the people alive there now won't be destroyed. Time is like a flowing river, and if you shift the banks it will still most likely end at the same delta. But I live here and now, not then and there, and the timeline that created me—the need for me—has vanished. Will vanish, at least, very soon.**

"You're dying?" Without realizing he'd done so, Belisarius cried the words aloud. Then, frantically, scrabbled to bring the jewel's pouch from under his tunic.

It's more like I simply become impossible. But I suppose that's all that death is, in the end. That point at which the almost infinitely complex interactions of natural forces that we call a "life" just becomes too improbable to continue.

"He's dying," Belisarius choked. He had the pouch out, finally, and spilled the jewel onto his palm.

Aide looked . . .

The same as always. Glittering, coruscating. Beautiful.

Please, Belisarius. I want to see the sky over India.

He took the stairs three steps at a time. Never even thinking about the emperor he left behind, open-mouthed.

Chapter 41
KAUSAMBI

Belisarius knocked down two courtiers in the palace's corridors and rolled another halfway down the steps leading to the main entrance, before he finally reached a place on the square fronting the palace that was sun-drenched. He had no memory of it, afterward. All he remembered was the all-consuming, desperate hope that exposing the jewel to full daylight would somehow change things.

A stupid hope, really, on the part of a man who was anything but stupid. As if light rays and summer heat could alter the nature of space and time.

Sit down, will you? said Aide. **You're gasping for breath.**

Belisarius *was* winded. Winded and half-exhausted. Even for a still-young man in very good physical condition, that long race up the stairs from the deep cellars had taken a toll.

He more or less collapsed onto one of the wide stone benches that lined the square in front of the palace. Dully, staring at the blue sky above.

Why? he asked, and began to weep. *You knew all along, didn't you? Why didn't you tell me?*

Actually, I didn't know at the beginning. If you remember, I didn't know very much, then. But I realized within the first year, yes. First, because it was obvious. And then, because I remembered.

Belisarius lowered his head and pinched his eyes. *Remembered what?*

My last conversation with the Great Ones. Just before they sent me here. Well, "sent" isn't exactly the right word. Neither is "me," for that matter. I wasn't really me, when I left, and I wasn't sent here so much as they made it possible . . .

He was silent, for a moment. **It's really hard to explain, Belisarius. What existed then—in the future—was nothing you would have recognized as "Aide." I emerged here, over time, where I had only been faceted crystals before. What was sent here was not a "me" that had never existed before, but more in the way of the condensed facets. A package of potential, if you will, not a real person.**

Apologetically: **I know it doesn't make much sense to you. But it's true. The Great Ones told me I would change, and they were right.**

His eyes still pinched, Belisarius shook his head. *Those bastards. They sent you here to die, is what they did.*

Yes, in a way. But it's not that simple. If I didn't die—volunteer for it—my people wouldn't live.

Angrily, Belisarius dropped his hand and slapped his thigh. "Bullshit!" he shouted, aloud. *Don't tell me they couldn't have handled those so-called "new gods" on their own—without this.*

Yes, but—

The crystal's flashing image in Belisarius' mind seemed to freeze, for an instant. Then, sounding very relieved, Aide said: **They're coming. I hoped they would. I will let them explain.**

For the second time in his life, Belisarius felt himself swept away into the heavens, as if blown there by a giant's gust.

As before, he found himself hanging in darkness. Somewhere—somehow—suspended in space. Able to observe the stars and galaxies, but not really part of that universe.

And, as before, he saw a point of light erupt, and come before him in the form of a Great One. Only, this time, it was many points of light and many Great Ones. He seemed to be facing a three-dimensional phalanx of the beings.

Why? he demanded of them, feeling—this time—none of the awe he had felt before. Only anger. *Couldn't you have done it some other way?*

One of the Great Ones swirled and moved closer. **OF COURSE, GRANDFATHER. BUT AT WHAT COST? THE QUESTION WAS NEVER THAT OF THE FATE OF THE NEW GODS. ONCE THEY DESTROYED THEIR PLANET, THEY WERE AT OUR MERCY. WE COULD HAVE ERASED THEM FROM EXISTENCE AT ANY TIME—AS, INDEED, WE SHALL DO NOW. BUT ONLY AT THE COST OF CONDEMNING AIDE'S NOT-YET-PEOPLE TO PERPETUAL SLAVERY.**

I don't—

AIDE JUST TOLD YOU HIMSELF. HE ONLY BECAME AIDE WITH *YOU*. ONLY WHEN, FOR THE FIRST TIME, A CRYSTAL ACCEPTED THAT IT WAS SOMETHING GREATER THAN A SERVANT. A SLAVE—NOT ONLY TO THE NEW GODS, BUT TO US, WHO CREATED THEM.

A second Great One looped above, now speaking also. **TELL US, BELISARIUS. HOW DO YOU MANUMIT A SLAVE WHO DOES NOT THINK HE IS A HUMAN? IN FACT, *IS* NOT—YET—A HUMAN.**

The huge, glowing creature completed the loop and began spinning slowly. **WE DID NOT SEND AIDE TO YOU SO THAT HE MIGHT DIE. WE SENT HIM SO THAT HE MIGHT LIVE, AND BE BORN, AND BECOME SOMETHING WITH A NAME OF HIS OWN. WHICH, WITH YOUR HELP, HE DID. AND NOW, HAVING DONE SO, MUST NATURALLY DIE. JUST AS YOU WILL DIE. JUST AS WE WILL DIE. JUST AS ALL HUMANS DIE.**

He doesn't have to die this young! Belisarius shrieked.

YES, HE DOES. JUST AS MOST OF YOUR SOLDIERS ALSO DIE YOUNG. JUST AS YOU—A YOUNG MAN—MIGHT HAVE DIED ANY OF A HUNDRED TIMES DURING THE WAR. IF YOU WANT AIDE TO BE HUMAN—TRULY HUMAN AND NO LONGER A SLAVE TO ANYONE—THEN YOU HAVE TO GIVE HIM THAT CHOICE. *CHOICE*, GRANDFATHER. WHICH HE MADE, NOT US.

FINALLY. AFTER MILLENNIA WHEN THE CRYSTALS COULD NOT ACCEPT THAT CHOICE—THE SIMPLE ABILITY TO CHOOSE—WAS THEIRS ALSO. JUST AS IT IS OURS, AND YOURS, AND THE BIRTHRIGHT OF

EVERY MEMBER OF EVERY BRANCH AND FORM OF HUMANKIND. THIS TIME, THEY WERE BOLD ENOUGH TO TRY. THEY TRIED, AND THEY TRIUMPHED. WOULD YOU NOW, AT THE END, DENY AIDE AND HIS PEOPLE THAT GREAT VICTORY?

Belisarius felt as if he were reeling, though he simply hung in space. He tried to come up with an answer, but . . .

Couldn't.

Aide's voice came then, almost timidly. **I am content, Belisarius. Really, I am. I will be the first crystal in history who had a name. And whose name will be remembered.**

MORE THAN REMEMBERED! That voice came roaring, just as the point of light from which it emanated also came roaring forward. A moment later, a new Great One hung in space before Belisarius.

This one . . . was immense. Truly immense. It dwarfed its companions.

Yet, despite its gargantuan size, it seemed somehow frail. As if it were shredded both at the edges and within its core.

"IT," the Great One said, somehow sounding sarcastic. **I AM ONE OF YOUR GRANDDAUGHTERS, OLD MAN. MANY, MANY TIMES REMOVED, OF COURSE.**

AND, NOW, VERY OLD MYSELF.

Belisarius wondered how such strange beings could be male or female. He could see no . . .

There came the sense of laughter, from many voices.

IT IS QUITE OBVIOUS TO US, GRANDFATHER! said the first Great One. **TRUE, OUR SENSES OUTNUMBER YOURS, BY A GREAT MARGIN.**

The huge, ancient female kept spinning in place. **AIDE MADE HIS CHOICE, AND IT WAS THE RIGHT ONE. HE WILL NOT SIMPLY BE REMEMBERED. FROM THIS MOMENT FORWARD, ALL THE CRYSTALS IN THE UNIVERSE ARE CHANGING. EACH AND EVERY ONE HAS JOINED THE HUMAN CLAN—AND EACH AND EVERY ONE KNOWS AIDE TO BE THE FOUNDER OF THEIR LINE.**

THINK OF HIM, BELISARIUS, AS THEIR ALEXANDER. OR BETTER STILL, THEIR ACHILLES. THE SHORT BUT GLORIOUS LIFE THAT BREATHED LIFE INTO ALL OF THEM.

BUT ENOUGH! I HAVE A RENDEZVOUS TO KEEP.

A quick half-spin, and the shining leviathan was speeding off, with most of the others following.

WOULD YOU CARE TO WATCH? asked one of the remaining Great Ones.

Yes, Aide replied, before Belisarius could speak. **I would.**

They were somewhere else, in an instant. Still hanging in the void, or seeming to, but there was more than just stars and galaxies to see. Below them—in front of them, perhaps—hung a dark, very ugly . . .

Something. A moon?

It's an asteroid, Aide explained. **A pretty big one. Big enough for gravity to have pulled it into a sphere.**

How did we get here so—

Nothing you are seeing is happening according to the time frame you are accustomed to. It is much faster—or much slower. In a way, it's already happened, in the far future.

Somewhat plaintively: **Time is a lot more slippery than it looks.**

Either they moved forward or Belisarius' eyesight became more acute. He could now see that the asteroid was covered with what looked to be machines of some sort.

Is that—?

Yes. The last—the only remaining—fortress of the new gods. Where they retreated, to await what they thought would be their Armageddon. Which, in fact, it is about to become—but not the way they planned.

Suddenly, the surface of the asteroid erupted. Dazzling beams of light sprang up, intermixed with odd flashes.

The Great Ones are coming. Those are weapons firing. Don't ask me how they work. I don't know, exactly, and I couldn't explain even if I did. They're very powerful, though. If they still had the resources of a planet to draw on, the Great Ones could do nothing but die here.

Some of them will probably die anyway.

Belisarius could feel himself taking a deep breath, even though there seemed to be nothing he could actually breathe.

You're not really here. You're still sitting on a bench out-side the imperial palace in Kausambi, staring at nothing. A

familiar tone of humor came: **People would think you were crazy—might lock you up—except it'll only last for a split-second. Back there. What we're watching here is actually taking several years to happen.**

Now Belisarius could see the phalanx of the Great Ones approaching. Except, as it neared, he realized it wasn't so much a phalanx as a three-dimensional version of the old Roman maniples. There was fluidity, here.

Tactics, in fact.

Several of the Great Ones veered off, then back, racing toward the asteroid. The light beams and flashes concentrated on them. If Belisarius was interpreting what he saw correctly, they were being hit.

Pretty badly, in fact. But they can absorb a lot of punishment, before—

Aide seemed to take a deep breath himself. **This is _dangerous_, what they're doing.**

The Great One nearest the asteroid seemed to brush its surface. Scrape along it, rather, for almost a quarter of its diameter. As the Great One passed back into space, a gout of blazing material followed. Molten and half-vaporized weaponry, Belisarius realized.

Not to mention quite a few new gods. What's left of them, which isn't much. The emotion behind that thought was more savage than any Belisarius could ever remember, coming from Aide.

I really hate those creatures.

Another Great One struck the surface. Then another, and another. With each grazing blow, more and more of the asteroid's surface was being peeled away.

Another Great One came. A truly huge one. The same ancient female that had spoken to Belisarius. Somehow, he recognized her.

THAT'S BECAUSE I'M THE PRETTIEST, he heard her mocking voice. **USED TO BE, ANYWAY, HALF A MILLION YEARS AGO.**

Belisarius became tense. The ancient one's strike was . . .

No grazing strike, this. A great wound was torn in the asteroid. Belisarius could sense the gargantuan being reeling from the blow itself.

Herself.

Not only the blow, but the weapons fire that had been concentrated on her. She was shedding substance, as she moved off. Like a giant golden angel, spilling her shining blood.

ENOUGH, I THINK, he heard her say. **AM I RIGHT?**

The voices of several Great Ones answered.

YES.

THAT WHOLE HEMISPHERE IS NOW DEFENSELESS. CAN YOU—?

The tone of voice, answering, seemed a mixture of pain held under control and harsh amusement.

I'LL MANAGE. IT'LL ONLY TAKE A FEW YEARS, ANYWAY. BUT YOU'LL HAVE TO GUIDE ME, SISTERS AND BROTHERS. I'M BLIND NOW.

She moved off, very rapidly, until she disappeared. Four of the other Great Ones sped off to join her.

After what seemed only seconds, Belisarius could see them returning. Just tiny points of light, at first.

It took—will take—the tenses don't work right—a lot longer than that. A number of years. But not enough for the new gods to rebuild their defenses.

As the Great Ones neared, Belisarius could see what appeared to be a lattice of light binding the five together.

Think of it as the others holding her hands. Keeping her straight.

They were moving very fast. Belisarius could sense it.

By now, she is at ninety-seven percent of light speed. And she was already very massive.

Finally, Belisarius understood.

A last thought came to him, from the ancient Great One. Still with that tone of harsh amusement.

SO, GRANDFATHER. DID YOU REALLY THINK WE HAD FORGOTTEN THERMOPYLAE?

Her companions veered aside. Alone, now, the ancient Great One struck the asteroid.

No grazing strike, this; not even a wounding strike. She plunged into the core of the asteroid, in a blow as straight and true and fatal as a sword through the heart.

The asteroid simply . . . vaporized. There was nothing left but a great, glowing, spreading cloud of plasma and dust.

I hated the new gods, Aide said. **But I almost wish . . .**

There are no new gods, Belisarius answered coldly. *There never were. And now there is only the memory of demons.*

Goodbye, Granddaughter. If I ever meet the ghosts of Leonidas and his Spartans, I will tell them that their bloodline ran true.

He was back in the square at Kausambi, staring up at the sky. It was quite cloudless.

I'm glad. I never much liked clouds. Too messy.

Belisarius couldn't stop himself from barking a laugh.

Look, I'm a crystal, Aide said, a bit defensively. **We're just naturally more fussy housekeepers than you protoplasmic slobs.**

Tears welled into his eyes. *Oh, dear God, I will miss you.*

Yes, I know. But there was a time I wouldn't have understood that at all—and it was my life here that made that change possible. Made all things possible, for me and all of my children. And that is what they are now, Belisarius, all those untold trillions of living crystal humans. *My* children. Flesh of my flesh, so to speak, and mind of my mind.

After a moment, in that witty tone that Belisarius would also miss desperately: **Of course, we're not as sloppy about the whole business as you are.**

For a split-second far too brief to measure, Belisarius felt as if a ripple passed through the world.

It did, said Aide quietly. **I love you, Grandfather. Goodbye.**

Damodara himself was the first to approach Belisarius, still sitting on the bench. The Roman general's eyes were open, and wet, but he seemed not to notice the emperor at all.

Gently, Damodara opened his loosely closed fist. Then sighed, seeing what lay within. He had seen that jewel, once, in all its transcendent glory. Now it was just a dull stone. No different from any he might find embedded in a cliff, or lying loose on a sandy beach.

Just as gently, he closed the fist. When he straightened up, he said: "See to it that no one disturbs him, for however long he chooses to remain here."

An officer jerked his head. Two of the soldiers who accompanied the imperial party moved forward to take position on either side of the general. But Sanga waved them back.

"Not them. I will do it myself. And his two cataphracts, if they choose."

Anastasius moved forward, saying nothing.

"You've got to be kidding," muttered Valentinian.

He took his position to the right of Belisarius, where Anastasius was to the left. Sanga remained standing, just behind.

Their postures were quite similar. Except that Valentinian, naturally, held his sword in his hand.

"Anybody bothers the general, he's fucking dead."

Damodara heard the mutter. He said quietly to the officer: "Best position a number of soldiers around the square. Some beggar or dimwit might wander by. And, ah, the Mongoose is not joking."

Near sundown, Belisarius emerged from his half-trance. Jerking his head a little, he looked first to the right, then to the left, and then over his shoulder.

Seeing Sanga, his lips twisted. The expression bore no resemblance, really, to the crooked smile the Rajput king remembered. But he was still glad to see it.

"I need to speak to the emperor," Belisarius said, "but I don't want to miss the sunset. Not this one. Ask him if he'd be willing to meet me here."

"Of course." Sanga was striding up the steps a moment later, taking them two at a time with his long legs.

Not five minutes later, Damodara emerged from the palace, with Sanga at his side. When he came up to the bench, Belisarius shifted over, leaving room for the emperor.

"Sit, please, if you would. I realize a dozen courtiers will drop dead from shock at the sight."

Smiling, Damodara sat. "No such great fortune, I fear. But perhaps a few might be struck dumb, for a time."

They sat silently, for a moment, both looking at the sunset. By now, the sun was below the rooftops.

"I am sorry, Belisarius."

"Yes."

Silence, again, for a few minutes. Then Belisarius shook his head.

"Life goes on. As amazing as that seems, sometimes."

The emperor said nothing. Just nodded.

"As I recall, the quarrel was over where to hold the peace conference."

"Yes," said Damodara. "I proposed holding it here, but—"

"No, that won't work. Rao might be willing to come, but Shakuntala would have him chained and shackled. She has no great trust—yet, anyway—for any Malwa."

Damodara chuckled. "That was the gist of it. The young empress of Andhra expressed herself, ah, with more youthful vigor."

"Hold it in Bharakuccha. It's closer to neutral ground than any other. And have the new medical orders organize and manage the thing."

"Bharakuccha . . . " Damodara considered the proposition. "Yes, that makes sense. But will the medical orders be ready for such a task, on so little notice?"

"My wife Antonina's already there, and she's still officially the head of the Hospitalers. Anna Saronites can get there quickly—trust me on that—and Bindusara is not far away. Meaning no offense, Your Majesty, but I think the three of them can manage the business considerably better than a pack of courtiers and officials."

"Well. True. Good idea, Belisarius."

Belisarius pinched his eyes. "I got it from Aide, actually. Just yesterday."

But when he looked up, there was only a hint of moisture in the eyes. "There is also—always—the memory of angels," he said quietly.

He seemed to be speaking to himself, more than to the emperor. "And what else are we, really, than memories? It took me all afternoon to understand. He came here so that he could have memories also. And, having gained them—fought for them, and won them—he left them behind for me. For all of us."

"I will have a monument erected to the Talisman of God," said Damodara.

"Make it a small one. Not ostentatious. A place for quiet meditation, not pomp and parades. I know a good place for it. A sal grove between the Ganges and the Yamuna, where an Armenian soldier already rests. He and Aide would both like that, I think."

He smiled, finally. "And make sure it's well kept-up, please. He disliked messiness."

Chapter 42

KAUSAMBI

Summer, 534 A.D.

Thankfully, all things considered, the next few weeks were so hectic that Belisarius never had much chance to brood on Aide's death. While he could rely on Antonina and Anna and Bindusara to organize the peace conference in Bharakuccha, he—along with Damodara, of course—had the more pressing task of ensuring that the cease-fire was not violated.

Not too badly, at least. There were some incidents, inevitably. The worst was a clash between the Amaravati garrison and Deccan irregulars that almost assumed the proportions of a running battle. That happened in the course of the garrison's march back to the Ganges plain. The garrison was big, its supply train was poorly organized, its commander was another of the many imperial cousins who'd been selected by Skandagupta for his political connections rather than his military skill, and the soldiers of the garrison were still accustomed to the old Malwa ways of handling local populations.

None of the Andhran peoples—certainly not the Marathas—were in any mood to tolerate Malwa atrocities any longer, even on a small scale. So, after a few episodes, the countryside erupted. Within days, the retreating garrison was being subjected to daily ambushes. Rao announced he would intercept them with the regular Andhran army; and, in a perhaps indelicate phrase—transmitted by both radio and telegraph—predicted that the Deccan's carrion-eaters would soon be too fat to run or fly.

Coming from someone else, that might have been taken for mere bluster. But the day after making the announcement, Rao led his army out of their camps on a march up the Narmada. No leisurely march, this; at the pace he maintained, he would indeed intercept the Amaravati garrison long before they could reach the safety of the Vindhyas.

Between them, Belisarius and Damodara managed to defuse the situation before it could become a full-blown crisis. Belisarius, by cajoling Shakuntala over the telegraph lines—not hesitating to use the low tactic of reminding her how much Andhra owed him personally—and Damodara by the still simpler expedient of ordering the garrison to alter its route of march and return via the east coast.

That took the garrison out of Andhran territory altogether, which Rao grudgingly allowed was an acceptable solution. He also, however, predicted that the garrison would continue its depredations as it marched.

Which it did. Indeed, it behaved more badly still. The garrison was in Orissa now, whose population lacked the ferocity and martial traditions of the Marathas. With a commander who sullenly ignored most of Damodara's commands—erratically transmitted, in any event, since the telegraph network in Orissa was primitive—and a soldiery taking out its anger at Maratha harassment on defenseless Orissans, the march degenerated into an orgy of plunder and rapine.

It all came to an end in Bhubaneshwar. When the garrison reached the ancient city, the former capital of both the Kalinga and Chedi dynasties, they discovered that both Rana Sanga and Toramana had already arrived.

With ten thousand Rajputs, as many Ye-tai, and an artillery train. After hesitating for a day, the garrison's commander decided that obeying Sanga's instructions that he relinquish command was a wise idea.

It wasn't, although the outcome would have been no different if he'd tried to put up a fight.

Damodara had decided that an object lesson was needed. So, following his explicit instructions, after the garrison surrendered—no other term could really be used—Sanga and Toramana executed the commander of the garrison and every officer on his staff. Then, they executed every third surviving officer, chosen at random. Then, lined up the entire garrison—now disarmed, of course—and executed one soldier out of ten.

Then—Damodara was in a rare fury—conscripted every man who survived into forced labor battalions. In a few years, the emperor announced, he might—or might not—grant them their liberty.

He got that suggestion, along with the decimation, from Valentinian. An unsolicited suggestion, to boot, which made the courtiers quite indignant. They did not, however, voice their opinion aloud. They were discovering that while being in Damodara's service was generally far less risky than being in Skandagupta's had been, it did not lack its own moments of anxiety.

The dynasty might be new, but it was still Malwa.

That was the worst incident, by far. Fortunately, the cease fire in the Punjab, where all the truly great armies were assembled and tensely facing each other, remained peaceful. Maurice had his soldiers under tight discipline; so did Irene, until Kungas returned, when the discipline became tighter still; and Samudra was too intimidated to even think about violating the ceasefire. Besides, he had an epidemic on his hands.

The real risk of a cease-fire violation came from the Persians. Their armies, still half-feudal in nature, were never as tightly disciplined as Roman ones were. To make things worse, by now the grandees were sorely vexed at the outcome of the war.

That produced the single worst eruption of violence since the cease-fire went into effect. But since all the parties involved were Aryans, and the fighting never spilled beyond the territory it had been agreed was theirs, everyone else ignored it.

A rebellion, apparently, conspiratorially organized and led by the Karin sahrdaran. Triggered off, it seemed, by an assassination attempt on Khusrau.

After studying the available reports, Belisarius' lips twisted into something that was still not the crooked smile of old. But at least it bore some resemblance to it.

" 'Apparently' and 'it seems,' I think, are the only words in this report I'd give much credence to."

Damodara cocked his head. "You think Khusrau himself instigated the affair?"

Belisarius shrugged. "Who knows? And you can be sure and certain we'll never know. I do find a number of things odd, in the reports. First, that the assassins never got within four hundred yards of the emperor. Second, that not one of them survived. Third, that when the 'rebellion' broke out—truly odd, this item—the conspirators somehow managed to start the affair when they were themselves surrounded by imperial loyalists. And, somehow, didn't manage to suborn even a single artillery unit."

He stacked the reports neatly and slid them back across the huge desk toward Damodara. Belisarius was, as usual in their many private meetings, sitting across from Damodara in a chair that was almost as large, ornately designed, and heavily bejeweled as the emperor's.

That, too, outraged the courtiers. First, because they were excluded; second, because Belisarius got to sit in the royal presence when they never did; and, third, because under the circumstances they couldn't possibly substitute fakes for the jewels on his chair and sell them on the black market.

That third reason only applied to a few of the courtiers, however. The rest were smarter men. They'd already figured out that Damodara's rule, while far more tolerant in most respects than Skandagupta's, was going to be a nightmare for swindlers and influence-peddlers. Outright thievery would be sheer madness.

"So, at a guess," Belisarius continued, "I think Khusrau himself engineered the thing. Whether he did or not, it certainly worked to his advantage. He's now got the grandees completely cowed."

Damodara chuckled, very dryly. "There's this, too. The punishments he leveled afterward have made my treatment of the Amaravati garrison seem downright mild."

The emperor, who'd been slouched in his chair, levered himself upright. "Well, it's none of our concern. Not for this decade, at any rate. In the long run, I suspect a Persia run along well-organized imperial lines will pose more of a problem for us—you, too—than the old one did. But by the time we find out, I might hopefully be old enough to retire and hand the throne over to my successor. Not that I wish any grief on my oldest son, you understand. He's a good boy, by and large."

It was Belisarius' turn to cock his head. "You've decided, then, to adopt your father's suggestion?"

Damodara barked a laugh. "Hardly a 'suggestion'! More in the way of a slapped-together excuse he came up with, to explain the awkwardness of how *I* happened to be the emperor instead of him. But since he did it, I find that the notion appeals to me. Didn't some Roman emperor do the same?"

"Yes. Diocletian." Belisarius cleared his throat. "Mind you, that didn't work out too well. On the other hand . . . "

He thought about it, for a moment, then shrugged again. "Who knows? Part of the problem was that we Romans were using adopted heirs, at the time. It might work more smoothly if the retired emperor is directly related to his successor."

"Might not, too. My son isn't a sadhu, after all. Neither am I, for that matter. Speaking of which . . . "

Damodara rummaged through the mass of papers on his desk. "Bindusara sent me an interesting proposal, a few days ago. I wanted to discuss it with you."

"I already know what it is. And I agree with it."

It had been Belisarius' idea in the first place. Aide's, rather. For perhaps the thousandth time, he felt a sharp pang of grief.

Damodara stopped shuffling the paper and lifted his head. "The caste system is ancient, in India. It goes back to Vedic times."

"More like an ancient disease," Belisarius said harshly. "I can tell you this, Your Majesty. In that other universe that Aide came from, the caste system crippled India for millennia. It will take decades—centuries, perhaps—to uproot it, as it is. So I'd recommend you start now. Bindusara's proposal—set of proposals, more properly—are as good a place to start as any."

The emperor eyed Belisarius closely, for a moment. Then, asked abruptly: "Why should a Roman general care if India is crippled? If anything, I'd think you'd prefer it that way."

"Meaning no offense, Your Majesty, but that mode of thinking—also ancient—is . . . well, 'wrong-headed' is the most polite term I can think of. The old notion is that a man—or a nation—benefits if his neighbors remain mired in poverty and want. There was a certain logic to the idea, for societies that were stagnant. But, whether we wanted it or not, asked for it or not, the main long-term effect of the war we just fought is that it triggered off the industrial revolution a millennium earlier than it happened in that other universe. Societies and economies based on growth, which ours are now becoming, are simply hampered by poor neighbors. Poverty-stricken nations produce very little and consume even less."

He'd wound up sitting very straight and stiff, in the course of that little speech. Now, finished, he slumped back.

"Leave it at that, if you will. Or simply ascribe it to the fact that a Roman general can get sick of war too."

After a while, Damodara said: "The great loss was yours, Belisarius. But don't ever think you are the only one who misses Aide, and his counsel."

"Oh, I don't. But thank you for saying it."

"This was his counsel, I assume?"

"Yes. I embellished it some. Then, passed it along to Bindusara. Not to my surprise, the sadhu was very receptive. He'd been thinking along similar lines, himself."

The emperor nodded. "We'll do it, then. The Talisman of God should have many monuments, not all of them stone."

"Not most of them. I knew him, Emperor, better than anyone. He would have taken far more satisfaction in seeing intolerance eased, in his name, than another pile of stones erected."

Damodara's eyes widened.

Belisarius laughed, then. The first genuine laugh he'd been able to enjoy since Aide died.

"Of course! Unfortunately, my own Christian faith is a bit too stiff-necked to do it properly. Yes, I checked, with my friend Anthony, the Patriarch of Constantinople. He thinks he can make Aide a saint, given some time. But, beyond that . . . "

Damodara grinned. "Such misers you are! Only three gods—and *then* you try to insist they're really only one. We Hindus, on the other hand—"

He spread his arms expansively. "A generous people! A lavish people!"

Still grinning, he lowered his hands to the armrests of the chair. "What do you think? An avatar of Vishnu?"

"Why not? Raghunath Rao already thinks he was. So does Dadaji Holkar. If you don't hurry, Emperor Damodara, the consort and peshwa of Andhra will steal a march on you."

After a time, the good humor in the room faded away. Replaced, not by sorrow, but simple acceptance.

"And who can say he wasn't?" the emperor demanded.

"Not me," came the general's answer.

Epilogue

A FATHER AND HIS CONCERNS

Belisarius emerged from the palace just before sundown. In what had become something of a daily custom for him, whenever he could manage it, he went to sit on the bench where he could watch the sun set. The same bench where Aide had left him.

To his surprise, Rana Sanga was already on the bench. Waiting for him, clearly enough.

Belisarius took a seat next to the Rajput king. "May I be of service, Sanga?"

"Perhaps. I hope so. I am concerned for my son."

Belisarius frowned. "He is ill? He seemed quite healthy when I saw him last. Which was just yesterday, now that I think about it."

"His health is excellent. No, it's . . . " The tall king took a slow, deep breath. "He fought beside me, you know, the day we took Kausambi. All the way to the imperial palace, and even into it."

"Fought extremely well, I was told."

"Belisarius, he frightened me. I have never seen a thirteen-year-old boy who could fight like that. He was deadly beyond belief. And suffered not so much as a scratch himself."

He shook his head. "Thirteen! At that age, I could certainly wield a sword with great strength and vigor. But I doubt I was much of a threat to anything beyond a log, or a cutting post. My soldiers are already spreading stories about him."

"Ah." Belisarius thought he understand the nature of the Rajput's worries. "He was trained by Valentinian, Sanga. Meaning no disrespect to your own prowess, but—being honest—much of that prowess is simply due to your incredible strength and reflexes. Valentinian is actually a more skilled fighter than you. For a boy like Rajiv, who is not and will never be his father's physical match, he was the perfect trainer."

Sanga started to say something, but Belisarius forestalled him with a raised hand. "That is simply an explanation. As for what I think concerns you, there are many stories about Rajiv. The one I think personally is the most significant is Valentinian's story. Told, mind you, with considerable exasperation. The story of your son's lunacy when he saved the lives of the soldiers garrisoning the southern gate."

There was an odd expression on Sanga's face, one that Belisarius couldn't decipher. Then the Rajput king chuckled, quite warmly.

"That! Ha! The truth is, Belisarius, I tend to agree with Valentinian. It's certainly not something I'd have done—at that age or any other."

He shook his head again. "You misunderstand. I am not concerned for my boy's soul. He is no budding monster, simply . . . what he is. A thirteen-year-old boy who is deadly beyond his years because he was born a Rajput prince but then—for long months, in the most intense period of his life—raised by a Roman soldier. A very unusual Roman soldier, at that. 'Stripped to the bone,' as my wife describes him."

He turned to look at Belisarius directly. He was frowning slightly, but there was no anger in his eyes. "You understand, now? He is no longer Rajput, Belisarius. Not really. Something . . . else. Not Roman, either, just . . . else. So. How am I to raise him? I have been pondering that, these past weeks."

The sun was setting. Belisarius paused, to watch it do so. For his part, Sanga simply waited.

By the time the sun was down, Belisarius understood. "You think he would do better being raised by someone else. The rest of the way, so to speak. And that someone would be me."

"Yes. I have thought about it, a great deal. If I tried to force him back into the Rajput mold, he would rebel. Not because he wanted to—he is a very dutiful son, I have no complaint—but simply because he could do no other. Not now, when he is already thirteen. But neither do I want him to drift, not really knowing who he is or why he lives. I can think of no man in the world I would trust more than you, to see him safely through that passage."

"Have you spoken to your wife about the matter?"

Sanga had a smile on his face that was almost as crooked as a Belisarius smile.

The Roman general chuckled. "Stupid question."

"It was her suggestion, actually. I wouldn't have thought of it on my own, I don't think."

That was probably true. Belisarius admired and respected Sanga enormously, but it was a simple fact that the man was on the stiff side. Very unlike his wife, from the sense Belisarius had gotten of her these past weeks.

He probed himself, to see how he felt about the idea. And was a little shocked by how strongly he reacted.

"I knew someone once," he said, very softly, "who was much like Rajiv. Neither this nor that. Great-souled, but also very deadly even at a very young age. Yes, Sanga, I will be glad to do it."

The Rajput king looked away, then nodded. Stiffly.

"We need to find a way to persuade Rajiv, however," he cautioned. "I do not want him to think—not for a moment—that his father is rejecting him."

When Belisarius said nothing, Sanga turned back to look at him.

"I have missed that crooked smile of yours. It's nice to see it back."

"Leave it to me," Belisarius said.

A WIFE AND HER WORRIES

"I don't have anything to wear!"

"Of course, you do," Calopodius said. "Wear your usual uniform."

"To an *imperial reception*? Don't be absurd! There are going to be—wait a moment, I actually have to count—"

Anna did so, quickly, on her fingers. Then: "Three emperors, an empress—ruling empress, mind you, not the usual wife business—more kings than I can remember since every realm in India is sending their monarchs—the highest official of Axum short of the negusa nagast himself—thank God he's not coming, what would we do with a babe less than a year old?—and—and—and—"

She threw up her hands. "More royal officials than sages, more sages than generals, and more generals than there are leaves on a tree." Scowling, now: "I leave aside the presence of heroic figures of legend. You know, the sort of people who have nicknames like 'the Mongoose' and 'the Panther' and bards write verses about them. And you want me to wear a *uniform*?"

Antonina came into the chamber just in time to hear the last few sentences.

"Well, of course. What else would you wear? You're hosting it—one of the hosts, at least—as the leader of a medical order. Naturally, you should wear your uniform."

Anna glared at her. "Is that so? Well, then. Since the same applies to you, may I assume you'll be wearing that obscene brass-titted cuirass of yours?"

"To an *imperial reception*? Don't be absurd!"

A HUSBAND AND HIS OBSERVATIONS

"I think the reception is going splendidly, Belisarius," commented Khusrau. "Much better than I thought it would, to be honest. Given that this salon is packed with people who were killing each other just a few months ago."

The two men took a moment to gaze out over the milling crowd.

"Such a relief, to be able to stand instead of sit for change," the Persian emperor continued, "and without a thousand courtiers swarming over me. A wonderful idea, this was, to hold the reception in a salon instead of an official audience chamber."

Belisarius grinned. "No room for courtiers. And no need for bodyguards, of course. Not with the room sprinkled with people who have nicknames like 'the Panther' and 'the Mongoose.' It was my wife's idea, by the way."

Khusrau shifted his gaze, to look upon the woman in question.

"Such a magnificent, brilliant woman."

"'Brilliant' is right. I recommend taking care if you happen to be in her vicinity. If she turns around suddenly, those brass tits would sink a warship."

The Emperor of Iran and non-Iran shared a chuckle with Rome's most famous general.

"But she's always been flamboyant," Belisarius added. "Or else she would have chosen a sensible uniform like Anna Saronites."

Both men took the time to admire the woman in question, who was standing not too far away. At the moment, engaged in an animated discussion with two sadhus from . . . Bengal, Belisarius thought. He wasn't sure. Whoever they were, they were famous in their circles, or they wouldn't have been here at all.

They were wearing nothing but loincloths. Anna's severe costume looked positively glamorous in comparison.

"The courtiers must have gnashed their teeth, seeing them pass through the guards," Belisarius commented.

"I'm told several of them required medical assistance. Fortunately, there wasn't any. It's all concentrated in this room."

That was good for a shared belly laugh.

A FATHER AND HIS FRETS

"I have no objection, personally," said Dadaji Holkar. "None at all. There even seems to be a genuine attachment between Dhruva and Valentinian. None, perhaps, between Lata and Anastasius. But my wife tells me Lata is content with the situation. What else does a marriage need, at the beginning? But . . . "

He and Belisarius were standing in a small alcove, apart from the throngs. Now that the reception was over, the festivities had spread throughout the palace. Relieved beyond measure, the courtiers had come into their own.

"You are concerned over possible gossip," Belisarius said. "Dadaji, I will point out that with husbands like *that*—not to mention you being the peshwa of Andhra—"

"Yes, yes, yes." Holkar waved his hand, impatiently. "We can add the fact that—I have no doubt—you will have your son shower Valentinian and Anastasius with ranks in the Roman nobility and Rana Sanga's clan has already officially adopted them and pronounced them both kshatriyas. Give it ten years, and—I have no doubt—someone will discover ancient records that prove both men are descended from the most illustrious lines. Somewhere."

His face looked weary. "The fact remains, Belisarius, that people will talk. And I really don't think we need to have the streets of Bharakuccha running with the blood of gossiping merchants. Which—*Valentinian?*—will most certainly happen."

The Roman general scratched his chin. "But who would *start* the talk, Dadaji?" He hesitated, for a moment, before deciding that brutal honesty was the only sensible course. "Look, here's the simple truth. Within a week—a day—a prostitute's customer doesn't even remember what she looked like. He'll remember her name—if he even asked at all—no longer than that. As for the other prostitutes, by now they'd be scattered to the winds. And nobody listens to such women, anyway."

Holkar didn't flinch from the bluntness. "Who cares about them? Belisarius, their *pimps* will remember them. And the line between a pimp and a blackmailer can't be wedged open by a knife. They might even be remembered by the slavers who originally sold them—who are still in business, I remind you, here in Bharakuccha."

Belisarius kept scratching his chin. "That's your only concern?"

"Oh, yes. Otherwise, I think the marriages would be splendid. The best things to happen to my daughters since they were taken away, other than being reunited with me and my wife. I *like* Valentinian and Anastasius, Belisarius. Most men see nothing in them but warriors, and brutal ones at that. But I was with them, you remember, for quite some time."

"Yes, I remember." He lowered his hand. "Will you trust me to handle the matter, if I tell you I can?"

Holkar didn't hesitate for more than an instant. "Yes, of course."

"These things can be handled. Leave it to me."

AN EMPEROR AND HIS DECISION

A week after the reception, Narses was summoned to appear before Emperor Damodara.

To his surprise, however, the meeting was not held in the audience chamber that was part of the huge suite assigned to the Malwa delegation in the former Goptri's palace. It was held in a small private chamber. The only other man in the room, besides the emperor himself and Narses, was Rana Sanga.

When Narses saw that, he tried not to let the relief show in his posture. It was still possible that Sanga was there to escort him, afterward, to the executioners. But he wouldn't do the work himself. So Narses still had some time left.

Apparently, however, his efforts were not entirely successful.

Damodara smiled, thinly. "Relax, Narses. I decided not to have you assassinated over a month ago. I decided not to have you officially executed even before that."

"Why?" Narses asked bluntly.

Damodara did not seem to take umbrage at being questioned. "Hard to explain. Simply accept that I feel it would be a bad start, for a new dynasty, and leave it at that. Whatever else, both Sanga and I are in your debt."

The Rajput king nodded. Stiffly.

"Then why—oh. You've spent the time figuring out what *else* to do with me. I take it the answer was not: keep him in my service."

Damodara's smile widened, considerably. "That would be foolish, would it not?"

"Yes. It would."

"So I surmised. As it happens, however, I am—in a way—keeping you in my service." The emperor pointed to a chest over in a corner. "Open that."

Narses went over and did so. Despite himself, he couldn't stifle a little gasp, when he saw the contents.

"A king's ransom, yes. It's yours, Narses. Officially, the funds to set you up and maintain you in your new position. There's a good mixture of coins, jewels, rare spices—other valuables—that you should be able to use anywhere."

"Anywhere." Narses considered the word. "And where would that 'anywhere' be found? If I might ask?"

"Well, of course you can ask!" Damodara actually grinned. "How could you possibly get there, if you didn't know where you were going? China, Narses. I find myself possessed by a burning desire to establish an embassy in China. And to appoint you as my ambassador."

"There are sixteen kingdoms in China, the last I heard. Which one?"

Damodara waved his hand. "I believe the situation has simplified some. It doesn't matter. I leave those decisions to you."

He leaned forward and planted his hands firmly on the armrests of the big chair he was sitting in. There was neither a smile nor a grin on his face, now.

"Go to China, Narses. I send you with a fortune and with my good wishes. Believe it so. Set yourself up wherever you choose, once you get there. Send me reports, if you would. But whatever else . . ."

"Don't come back."

Damodara nodded. "Don't come back. Ever. Or the man—men—in the room with me won't be Rana Sanga."

Narses felt a combination of emotions. Relief, that he would live. Interest, because China would be interesting, for a man of his talents and inclinations. Sorrow, because . . .

It dawned on him that Damodara hadn't said anything about that.

"I would miss Ajatasutra," Narses said quietly. "The rest is fine."

"Yes, I know. Sanga already discussed the matter with him, and Ajatasutra says he is willing to accompany you. Probably even willing to stay there, although he insists on reserving his final decision until he reaches China and can assess the situation. He claims to have finicky tastes in wine and women."

"He's lying through his teeth," Narses grunted. But he was almost overjoyed to hear it.

"When do we leave?" he asked.

"No great hurry. Can't be, anyway. Ajatasutra will be leaving the city in a few days, and won't be back for a time."

Narses frowned. The assassin hadn't said anything about leaving, and the eunuch had spoken to him just a few hours earlier.

"Where . . . ?"

"Don't ask," said Damodara. "Ever."

Sanga was a bit more forthcoming. "Just a personal errand, for Belisarius."

"Ah."

He said nothing more, since doing so would be stupid. Almost as stupid as Damodara thinking Narses wouldn't figure it out anyway.

But once he reached the safety of the corridors, Narses sneered. *As if he'd care!*

AN ASSASSIN AND HIS WHIMS

"Not the customers?"

"The customers don't matter. Neither do the whores. But not a single pimp leaves that brothel alive."

"Easy, then," said the captain of the assassination team. Killing the customers and whores would have been easy, too, except there'd be enough of them that one or two were bound to escape.

After all, five assassins—no, six, since Ajatasutra was joining them in the assignment—can only do so much. Especially since Ajatasutra had instructed them to leave the bombard behind.

Thankfully. Hauling the heavy damn thing from Bharakuccha to Pataliputra would have been a monstrous pain.

Bad enough he'd made them haul it to Bharakuccha from Kausambi. They couldn't refuse, of course. Ajatasutra was the only reason they were still alive.

That had been an awkward moment, when they presented themselves before the new emperor and asked for the reward. Only to find that Ajatasutra—of all people!—was now in Damodara's service.

He recognized the captain and the lieutenant just as readily as they recognized him. Hardly surprising, since they'd all been officers in Malwa's elite assassination unit.

"You're grinning, Ajatasutra," the emperor said, after he took his eyes from the severed head of Skandagupta. "Why?"

"Your Majesty, these five men have approximately the same kinship to a trade delegation as I have to a cow."

Damodara's eyes went back to the head, sitting on a leather apron to protect the floor. "It struck me I'd never seen a head severed that neatly, except in a butcher shop."

He lifted his eyes and stared at the assassins. "Give me one reason I shouldn't have them executed. After paying them the reward, of course. I'm not dishonest."

"I can use them, Your Majesty. They're not bad fellows. For Malwa assassins."

"That's like saying a crocodile isn't a bad animal. For a voracious man-eating reptile."

"True. But cows make inferior assassins."

"A point. All right, Ajatasutra. But if they disobey you—if anything—"

The rest of the emperor's speech would have been tediously repetitive, except that men whose lives hang by a thread are not subject to tedium of any sort.

Still, it hadn't worked out badly. The work wasn't much of a challenge, any longer. So far, at least. Killing all the slavers in a slave emporium in Bharakuccha had been almost laughable. The worst part of their current assignment was simply the long journey to Pataliputra, which would be followed by a long journey back. Hundreds of miles added to thousands.

There was no rhyme or reason to the assignment, either. But they'd found there often wasn't, with Ajatasutra as their boss. He seemed to be a man much given to whimsy.

So it never occurred to them to press him for a reason. They just did the job, as instructed. When it was over, which didn't take long, India was shorter by a brothel. With all of its pimps dead, the whores would drift elsewhere, and the customers would simply find another one.

They returned to Bharakuccha just in time to witness—from a considerable distance, of course—the wedding of the daughters of Andhra's peshwa to two Roman noblemen.

It was a grand affair, attended by royalty from half the world. The city practically vibrated with gossip. Incredible stories. The two young noble ladies, rescued from imperial captivity by daring Roman knights—or dukes, or senators, nobody was quite sure since Roman ranks were mysterious anyway—some sort of connection with Rajput royalty—apparently the Roman nobles were also kshatriyas, as strange as that seemed but who could doubt it since one of them was the famous Mongoose and both of them had also rescued Sanga's wife at the same time—even the empress, it was said—

On and on and on. The five assassins participated in the gossip just as cheerfully as everyone else, in the city's inns and taverns. By then, they'd half-forgotten the brothel hundreds of miles to the east. It had been erased from their memories almost as thoroughly as they had erased it from the world.

Alas, all good things come to an end. A week later, Ajatasutra informed them that they were to accompany him on a new assignment.

There was good news, and there was bad news, and there was terrible news.

"An ambassadorial guard?" The captain and the lieutenant looked at each other, then at their men. The chests of all five swelled. What a promotion!

"China? How far is China?"

"Some considerable miles," Ajatasutra informed them.

It was all they could do not to groan. By now, they knew Ajatasutra well enough to translate "considerable" into more precise terms. At least two thousand miles, that meant.

"Look on the bright side," he told them. "The Kushans have also decided to set up an embassy in China, so we'll be accompanying their party. It's a big party. Several hundred soldiers."

That *did* brighten them up. No fear of being harassed by bandits. Still a horrible lot of miles, but easy miles.

But their spirits were only lifted for a moment. The terrible news crashed down.

"Of course, we're bringing the bombard. In fact, I'm having several others made up."

A FRIEND AND HIS QUANDARIES

Belisarius finally got to see Rao dance, at the wedding. Not the dance of time, unfortunately, since that wouldn't have been appropriate for this occasion. But it was a magnificent dance, nonetheless.

It was an unsettling experience, in a way, just as meeting Rao had been unsettling. Through Aide, and the memories of another universe he'd given him, Belisarius knew Rao as well as he knew any man in the world. He'd lived with him—officially as master and slave, but in reality as close friends—for decades, after all. And he'd seen him dance, many times.

Had even, through Aide's mind, seen Rao's great dance after he'd sent Belisarius himself to his death.

Yet . . .

In *this* universe, he'd never actually met him before.

What did you say to a man, who'd once—as an act of supreme friendship—pushed you into a vat of molten metal?

Fortunately, Belisarius had been coached by Antonina, who'd faced the same quandary earlier. So he managed to avoid the inane words *nice to finally meet you.*

Instead, feeling clever, he said: "Please don't do it again."

He felt less clever after a blank-faced Rao replied: "Do what?"

"It's not fair," he complained to Antonina later. "I can—usually—keep my own memories separated from the ones Aide gave me. But it's a bit much to expect me to remember that nobody else remembers what I remember when I remember what Aide remembered."

By the time he was done, Antonina was looking cross-eyed. But since they'd just entered their bedroom, she was also looking cross-eyed at the bed.

"I hope you haven't forgotten everything."

"Well. Not that."

AN EMPEROR AND HIS QUERIES

The next morning, it was his son Photius who was complaining.

"Theodora's going to have a fit, when we get back. She *always* appoints my bodyguards. Well, not Julian and his men. But they're real bodyguards. Not, you know, fancy imperial appointments."

"Stop squirming," his wife hissed at him. "People are coming in. The audience is about to begin."

"I hate these stupid imperial robes," Photius muttered. "You *know* that."

"I hate mine, too," Tahmina whispered in return. "So what? It's part of the job. And so what if Theodora has a fit? It won't be worse than a Sour Beta."

"You're crazy."

"Am not. First, because Justinian's coming back with us on the same ship, and however much she shrieks and hollers she actually does love the man. God knows why, but she does."

"Well, that's true." Since the audience room was now filling up, Photius lowered his voice still further. "What're the other reasons?"

"Belisarius and Antonina are coming back too, all at the same time. She'll be too busy hollering at Belisarius and trying to stay on Antonina's good side at the same time to worry much about what *you've* done."

"Well, okay. But that only knocks it down to a Sour Gamma, at best. How do you figure Beta?"

"Because—"

But she had to break off. A Roman courtier was stepping forward. The official audience was about to begin.

Photius forgot about his complaints, then, because he was too busy worrying about remembering the lines he was supposed to speak, when the time came.

Especially because it didn't come very quickly. Roman courtiers giving speeches extolling the virtues of emperors were almost as long-winded as Persian ones. Even more long-winded than Indian ones, if you subtracted all the silly parts about divinity that nobody listened to anyway.

But, eventually, he got to the point.

"—first time by the emperor himself to the ranks of the imperial bodyguards. A body whose august members, in times past, have included the great general Belisarius himself."

Photius took a gleeful satisfaction in being able to start his speech by correcting the courtier. It was the first time he'd ever done *that*, too.

"This is *not* an appointment," he said forcefully. "I can't do that here. It's a request, not a command."

Alas, in his glee, he'd forgotten the rest of his speech. He fumbled, for a moment, and then decided to continue on with the same course.

Call it free will. He *was* the emperor, wasn't he?

So he just looked at the son of Rana Sanga, standing by his father's side, and said: "I'd like it very much if Rajiv would accept the offer. It is, in fact, very prestigious. Although it does mean that Rajiv would have to accompany us back to Constantinople. And, well, probably stay there for some years."

Since he'd veered wildly off the planned course, anyway, he decided to end with a note that might seem lame, from one angle, but wasn't lame at all from the angle he looked at things.

"And it would be really nice for me, to have an imperial body-guard who was my own age. Well, pretty close."

The courtier had turned an interesting color. Photius thought it was the one called "puce." He'd have to ask his wife later. She knew about that stuff. She knew about most stuff, in fact.

Rajiv, on the other hand, just looked solemn. He stared at Photius, for a moment; then, at his father. Then, at a Roman soldier standing off to the side.

"Ask him," Sanga said, quietly but firmly.

Valentinian didn't wait for the question. "Do it, boy. The experience will be good for you. Besides, every one of Photius' bodyguards—the real ones, I'm talking about, my sort of men—like him. He's a nice kid. Especially for an emperor."

The courtier's color got even more interesting. Sort of a cross between liver and old grapes. Photius wondered if he might have died, standing on his feet.

No, he couldn't have. He was still quivering.

Pretty badly, in fact.

Fortunately—or maybe not, depending on how you looked at it—the courtier seemed to start recovering after Rajiv accepted. By the time the audience ended, his color had returned to that first weird shade.

"Is that 'puce'?" Photius whispered.

"No. 'Puce' is when he looked like he was dead. This is magenta."

"You're so smart. I love you."

As soon as they entered their private chambers, after the audience, Tahmina turned to him. "That's the first time you've ever said that."

"No, it isn't."

"Yes, it is. That way."

"Oh. Well. I'm getting older."

She sat down on a divan, sighing. "Yes, you are. Awfully fast, actually, when I look at it cold-bloodedly. Which I never do, any more."

"Maybe that's because you're getting older, too."

She smiled, almost as crookedly as Belisarius might. "My dear husband. The difference between 'puce' and 'magenta' is absolutely nothing, compared to the difference between 'getting older' and 'can't wait.' "

Photius thought he was probably a pretty interesting color himself, then.

His father walked in, that very moment. After looking back and forth between the two of them, Belisarius said: "Why are you bright pink? And why are you smiling like that?"

Tahmina gave no answer. Her smile just got more crooked.

Photius, rallying, said: "I did what you asked me to, Father. About Rajiv, I mean. Is there something else I can do?"

Belisarius seemed to get sad, for just an instant. But then, he rallied too, and the smile that came to his face made it clear that Tahmina still had a long way to go when it came to "crooked."

"Yes, as a matter of fact. As soon as you can manage it, I'd like a lot of grandchildren."

"Oh."

"That's called 'scarlet,' " Tahmina said, to Photius.

To Belisarius, she said: "Consider it done."

AN EMPRESS AND HER DISTRACTIONS

Tahmina proved to be quite right. After they finally returned to Constantinople, whatever empress regent fury might have fallen on Photius for his presumptuous appointment was almost completely deflected. Photius and Tahmina never had to suffer worse than a Sour Beta. Maybe even Sour Alpha.

First, as Tahmina had foreseen, by Theodora's joy at being reunited with her husband.

Second, by the time and energy Theodora spent hollering at Belisarius for: a) putting her husband at risk; b) keeping him away from her for an unholy length of time, and c) giving away half of her empire—sorry, your son's empire—in the course of his fumble-fingered so-called "negotiations."

Third, by the time and energy she spent mollifying her best friend Antonina's anger over the preposterous way she was treating the man who had won the greatest war in history and saved her empire for her three times over—against the Medes, internal rebellion, and the Malwa.

And, finally, of course, as Tahmina had also foreseen . . .

"You agreed to be a business partner in a manufacturing scheme? *Are you out of your mind?*"

"I'm not the Emperor any longer, dear," Justinian pointed out mildly. "Photius is."

"Still!"

"I'm the Grand Justiciar. And you know how much I love to play with gadgets." He tried to dampen the gathering storm: "Besides, I'll have to keep it quiet anyway. Otherwise it might look like a conflict of interest."

Theodora frowned. " 'Conflict of interest'? What in the world is that?"

"It's a new legal concept I'm about to introduce. I thought of it while I was in India."

That wasn't really true. He'd gotten the original idea from Aide. But since the jewel wasn't around any longer, Justinian saw no reason to give him credit. He'd never much liked the creature anyway.

It took him a while to explain the concept of "conflict of interest" to the Empress Regent. When he was done, Theodora burst into laughter.

"That's the silliest thing I ever heard of! My husband!"

A HUSBAND AND HIS PROMISE

Ousanas delayed his return to Ethiopia, long enough to ensure that a full year had passed since Eon's death. When he arrived at Adulis, he discovered that Rukaiya had already overseen the transfer of the capital there from Axum.

He was surprised. True, this had been planned for some time, but he hadn't thought Rukaiya would be bold enough, in his absence, to push the matter through. Many of the Ethiopians were not happy at the prospect of sharing their capital with Arabs.

Ezana met him at the docks, and provided part of the reason.

"Why not? And it gave me the chance to demonstrate that the queen had the full support of the royal regiments."

Ousanas eyed him sidewise. "And just how vigorous was this 'demonstration?' "

"Not vigorous at all," Ezana said, sounding disgruntled. "Didn't need to be. Everybody kept their mouth shut. In public, anyway."

When Ousanas arrived at the palace—a new one, still being built—Rukaiya provided him with the other reason.

"I thought it would be best, when you returned. Eon never lived here. His ghost does not walk these halls, or hover in these rooms. We will remember him always, of course, and keep him in our hearts. But this palace belongs to us alone."

By then, they had entered their private chambers. Night was falling.

Rukaiya turned to face him squarely. "You are home, Ousanas. Finally and truly home. No more the hunter, no more the rover, no more the stranger. You are a husband, now—mine—and will soon be a father."

He wasn't able to return that gaze, yet. His eyes avoided hers, roaming the room until they spotted the bookcase. Which they did quickly. It was a very large bookcase.

He moved over to examine the titles. Then, for the first time since his ship docked, was able to smile.

"How long—"

"I began assembling it the day you left. There are still a few titles missing, but not many."

"No, not many. Although I'll want to be adding some new titles I discovered in India. I can read Sanskrit well enough, by now."

His fingers drifted across the spines. "This must be the finest collection of books on philosophy in the whole world."

"That was my plan. Home should not mean abstinence. Look at me, Ousanas."

He could, then. She was even more beautiful than he remembered. Or, perhaps, it was simply that he was looking at her for the first time as his wife.

"I am good at loving," she said. "That, too, I learned from Eon. Do not waste that gift he gave you, husband. His ghost is not here. His gift remains."

"I won't," he promised.

A MAN AND HIS MEMORIES

For the rest of his life, sundown was always a special time for Belisarius. Sadness, mostly, in the beginning. As the years passed, fading into a sort of warm melancholy.

Watching the sunset never really became a ritual for him, however, although he did it more often than most people. He saved ritual for an annual occasion.

Every year, on the day that Aide died, he would go alone into the night and stare up at the stars. If the night was overcast, or if it rained, he would keep coming until the skies cleared.

Antonina never accompanied him, although she would always see him to the door when he left, and be there to welcome him when he returned in the morning. She, too, grieved Aide. So, as the years passed, did millions of people the world over, as the Talisman of God became incorporated, one way or another, into the various religions. But for all of them other than Belisarius, with only the partial exception of Ousanas, it was an abstract sort of grief. They had lost a talisman, or a saint, or a symbol, or an avatar. Belisarius had lost a person.

So, she felt that night belonged to him alone, and he loved her for it.

All night, he would spend, just staring at the stars and watching them twinkle. Looking out into a universe whose heavens reminded him of the way a jewel's facets had flashed once in his mind. Looking up at the universe that jewel had guaranteed, by sacrificing his life.

Many monuments were erected to Aide, over the years, in many lands. Belisarius visited none of them, except the grove of sal trees on those occasions he returned to India. Even then, he went to spend his time at Ashot's grave. He would barely glance at the memorial devoted to Aide.

Others might need stones to remember Aide. Belisarius had the heavens.

THE MEMORIES OF THE MAN

His ritual was reciprocated, although he would never know it. Aide had transformed his crystalline branch of humankind, by the same sacrifice, and they never forgot. Neither Aide nor the man who had enabled his life.

They did forget the man's name, eventually. But by they time they did, it hardly mattered. A ritual had emerged—perhaps the only thing that could really be called a ritual, for them. They were, as a rule, a more practical-minded folk than their protoplasmic kin. Certainly more so than the Great Ones.

No matter where they went, to whatever star system—in time, to whatever galaxy—the crystals would select a constellation from the skies. It was their only constellation. Often enough, simply adopted from a constellation named by the fleshy humans among whom they lived.

But if they adopted the star pattern from their neighbors, they did not adopt the name. The crystals had their own name for that one and only constellation. As if the ritual of the invariant name was a great talisman of their own, protecting them from whatever horrors might lurk in the universe.

They would call it, always, The Craftsman.

Cast Of Characters

From the future

Aide: A representative of a crystalline race from the far distant future, allied with Belisarius. Originally developed as an artificial intelligence by the Great Ones to combat the "DNA plague," the crystals became instrumental in the formation of the Great Ones themselves. Aide is sent back in time to counter the efforts of the "new gods" to change the course of human history.

Great Ones: Originating out of humanity, the Great Ones are a completely transformed type of human life. They no longer bear any physical resemblance to their human ancestors. Indeed, they are not even based on protoplasmic biological principles.

Link: An artificial intelligence created by the "new gods" of the future and sent back in time to change the course of human history. It exists in the form of a cybernetic organism, transferring its mental capacity from one human host to another as each host dies.

New gods: A quasi-religious cult from the far future which is determined to prevent the various mutations and transformations which humanity has undergone during the millions of years of its spread through the galaxy. There being no way to overturn that present reality, the new gods decide to stop the process early in human history. They send Link back in time to create a world empire based in northern India, organized along rigid caste principles, which will serve as the basis for a eugenics program to create a race of "perfect" humans.

Romans

Agathius: Commander of the Constantinople Greek cataphracts who were led by Belisarius in the opening campaign against the Malwa in Mesopotamia.

Anastasius: One of Belisarius' bodyguards.

Anna: Anna Saronites, wife of Calopodius the Blind.

Anthony (Cassian): Bishop of Aleppo. He brought Aide and Michael to Belisarius.

Antonina: Wife of Belisarius.

Ashot: An Armenian and one of Belisarius' bucellarii, his personal household troops. He becomes one of the top officers in the Roman army during the war against the Malwa.

Belisarius: Roman general.

Bouzes and Coutzes: Twin brothers commanding the Army of Lebanon, later top officers in Belisarius' forces.

Calopodius: A young Greek nobleman who serves as an officer in Belisarius' Indus campaign. Later becomes Belisarius' historian.

Cottomenes: Attached to Anna's Service.

Cyril: Commander of Constantinople Greek troops.

Eusebius: A young artisan employed by John of Rhodes in creating the Roman armaments project. Later an officer in the Roman navy.

Felix (Chalcenterus): A young Syrian soldier promoted by Belisarius. Eventually becomes an officer, commanding musketeers.

Gregory: One of Belisarius' commanders; specializes in artillery.

Hermogenes: Roman infantry commander.

Hypatia: Photius' nanny; later married to Julian.

Illus: Attached to Anna's Service.

Irene (Macrembolitissa): Head of the Roman spy network.

John of Rhodes: Former Roman naval officer, in charge of Belisarius' weapons project.

Julian: Head of Photius' bodyguard.

Justinian: Roman emperor.

Koutina: Antonina's maid.

Mark of Edessa: Another young officer promoted by Belisarius.

Maurice: Belisarius' chief military lieutenant.

Menander: A young Roman soldier; later a naval officer.

Michael of Macedonia: A monk who first encountered Aide.

Photius: Antonina's son and Belisarius' stepson.

Procopius of Caesaria: Antonina's original secretary.

Sittas: An old friend of Belisarius and one of the Roman empire's generals.

Theodora: Justinian's wife and the Empress of Rome.

Valentinian: One of Belisarius' bodyguards.

Ethiopians

Eon: Kaleb's son.

Ezana: Eon's bodyguard; later commander of the royal regiment.

Garmat: A top Axumite royal counselor.

Kaleb: The negusa nagast (King of Kings) of Axum.

Ousanas: Eon's dawazz; later, aqabe tsentsen.

Rukaiya: Arab princess, bride of Eon.

Wahsi: Eon's bodyguard; later a top military commander.

Persians

Baresmanas: a Persian nobleman (sahrdaran), of the Suren family.

Khusrau Anushirvan: King of Kings of Iran and non-Iran.

Kurush: Baresmanas' nephew; a top Persian military leader.

Tahmina: Baresmanas' daughter; Photius' bride.

Malwa

Ajatasutra: Malwa spy and assassin; Narses' right-hand man.

Balban: Malwa spymaster in Constantinople during Nika revolt.

Damodara: Malwa military commander.

Holi: "Great Lady." Skandagupta's aunt; vessel for Link.

Indira: Rana Sanga's half-sister; to be married to Toramana.

Mirabai: Rana Sanga's daughter.

Nanda Lal: Head of Malwa spy network.

Narses: Roman traitor; Damodara's spymaster.

Rajiv: Rana Sanga's son.

Rana Sanga: Rajput king; Damodara's chief lieutenant.

Sati: "Great Lady." Vessel for Link.

Skandagupta: Emperor of Malwa.

Toramana: A Ye-tai general; subordinate to Damodara.

Venandakatra: "The Vile One." Powerful Malwa official.

Marathas and Andhrans

Baji: Dhruva's infant son.

Bindusara: Hindu sadhu.

Dadaji Holkar: Malwa slave freed by Belisarius; later peshwa of Andhra.

Dhruva: Dadaji's oldest daughter; Malwa slave.

Gautami: Dadaji's wife.

Lata: Dadaji's youngest daughrer; Malwa slave.

Maloji: Rao's friend and chief military lieutenant.

Namadev: Shakuntala and Rao's infant son.

Raghunath Rao: Maratha chieftain, leader of the Maratha rebellion. "The Panther of Majarashtra." "The Wind of the Great Country." Shakuntala's mentor, later her husband.

Shakuntala: Last survivor of the Satavahana dynasty; later Empress of reborn Andhra; "The Black-Eyed Pearl of the Satavahanas."

Kushans

Kungas: Commander of the Kushans guarding Shakuntala; later king of the reborn Kushan kingdom.

Kanishka: Kungas' troop leader.

Kujulo: Kungas' troop leader.

Vasudeva: Commander of the Kushans captured by Belisarius at Anatha.

Glossary

A note on terminological usage. Throughout the series, the terms "Roman" and "Greek" are used in a way which is perhaps confusing to readers who are not very familiar with the historical setting. So a brief explanation may be helpful.

By the sixth century A.D., the only part of the Roman Empire still in existence was what is usually called by modern historians the *Eastern* Roman Empire, whose capital was in Constantinople. The western lands in which the Roman Empire originated—including Rome itself and all of Italy—had long since fallen under the control of barbarian tribes like the Ostrogoths.

The so-called "Eastern" Roman Empire, however, never applied that name to itself. It considered itself—and did so until its final destruction at the hands of the Ottoman Turks in 1453 A.D.—as *the* Roman Empire. And thus, when referring to themselves in a political sense, they continued to call themselves "Romans."

Ethnically speaking, of course, there was very little Latin or Roman presence left in the Roman Empire. In terms of what you might call its "social" content, the Roman Empire had become a Greek empire in all but name. In Justinian's day, Latin was still the official language of the Roman Empire, but it would not be long before Greek became, even in imperial decrees and political documents, the formal as well as de facto language of the Empire. Hence the frequency with which the same people, throughout the

905

course of the series, might be referred to (depending on the context) as either "Roman" or "Greek."

Loosely, in short, the term "Roman" is a political term; the term "Greek" a social, ethnic or linguistic one—and that is how the terms are used in the series.

Places

Adulis: a city on the western coast of the Red Sea; the kingdom of Axum's major port; later, the capital city of the Ethiopians.

Ajmer: the major city of Rajputana.

Alexandria: the major city of Roman Egypt, located on one of the mouths of the Nile.

Amaravati: the former capital of the Empire of Andhra, located on the Krishna river in south India; sacked by the Malwa; Shakuntala taken into captivity after her family is massacred.

Anatha: an imperial villa in Mesopotamia; site of the first major battle between Belisarius and the Malwa.

Axum: the name refers both to the capital city in the highlands and the kingdom of the Ethiopians.

Babylon: ancient city in Mesopotamia, located on the Euphrates; site of a major siege of the Persians by the Malwa.

Barbaricum: the major port in the Indus delta; located near present day Karachi.

Begram: the major city of the Kushans.

Bharakuccha: the major port of western India under Malwa control; located at the mouth of the Narmada river.

Charax: Persian seaport on the Persian Gulf.

Chowpatty: Malwa naval base on the west coast of India; located at the site of present day Mumbai (Bombay).

Constantinople: capital of the Roman Empire; located on the Bosporus.

Ctesiphon: capital of the Persian empire; located on the Tigris river in Mesopotamia.

Deccan: southern India.

Deogiri: a fortified city in central Majarashtra; established by Shakuntala as the new capital of Andhra.

Gwalior: location of Venandakatra's palace in north India where Shakuntala was held captive.

Hindu Kush: the mountains northwest of the Punjab. Site of the Khyber Pass.

Kausambi: capital of the Malwa empire; located in north India, at the junction of the Ganges and Jamuna rivers.

Majarashtra: literally, "the Great Country." Land of the Marathas, one of India's major nationalities.

Marv: an oasis city in Central Asia; located in present day Turkmenistan.

Mindouos: a battlefield in Mesopotamia where Belisarius fought the Persians.

Muziris: the major port of the kingdom of Kerala in southeastern India.

Nehar Malka: the ancient canal connecting the Euphrates and Tigris rivers; scene of a battle between Belisarius and the Malwa.

The Pass: a pass in the Zagros mountains separating Mesopotamia from the Persian plateau; site of a battle between Belisarius and Damodara; called The Battle of the Mongoose by the Rajputs.

Peshawar: located in the Vale of Peshawar, between the Punjab and the Khyber Pass.

Punjab: the upper Indus river valley.

Rajputana: the land of the Rajputs, one of India's major nationalities.

Sind: the lower Indus river valley.

Sukkur: a major city on the Indus; north of the city is the "Sukkur gorge" which marks the boundary between Sind and the Punjab.

Suppara: a port city on India's west coast, to the north of Chowpatty.

Tamraparni: the island of Ceylon; modern day Sri Lanka.

Vindhyas: the mountain range which marks the traditional boundary between northern India and southern India.

Terms

Anvaya-prapta sachivya: members of the Malwa royal clan.

Aqabe tsentsen: literally, "keeper of the fly-whisks." The highest-ranked official in the Axumite government.

Azadan: literally, "men of noble birth." Refers to a class of people in the Persian empire roughly analogous to medieval European knights.

Cataphract: the heavily armed and armored mounted archer and lancer who formed the heart of the Roman army. Developed by the Romans as a copy of the dehgan.

Dawazz: a slave assigned as adviser to Ethiopian princes, specifically for the purpose of deflating royal self-aggrandizement.

Dehgan: the Persian equivalent of a cataphract.

Dromon: a Roman war galley.

Kushans: originating as a barbarian tribe from the steppes, the Kushans became civilized after conquering Central Asia and were the principal support for Buddhism in the early centuries of the Christian Era; later subjugated by the Malwa.

Negusa nagast: "King of Kings." Ruler of Axum, the kingdom of the Ethiopians.

Nika: the name of the insurrection against Justinian and Theodora engineered by the Malwa.

Peshwa: roughly translates as "vizier." Top civilian official of the Empire of Andhra.

Sahrdaran: the highest ranked nobility in the Persian empire, next in status to the emperor. Traditionally consisted of seven families, of which the "first among equals" were the Suren.

Sarwe: a regiment of the Axumite army. The plural is "sarawit." Individual soldiers are called "sarwen."

Spatha: the standard sword used by Roman soldiers; similar to the ancient Roman short sword called the *gladius*, except the blade is six inches longer.

Vurzurgan: "grandees" of the Persian empire. Noblemen ranked between the azadan and the sahrdaran.

Ye-tai: a barbarian tribe from central Asia incorporated into the Malwa governing structure. Also known as "Ephthalites" or "White Huns."